"One historical mystery series that never gets boring or dull."
—*Midwest Book Review*

WHAT WOULD SCOTLAND YARD DO WITHOUT DEAR MRS. JEFFRIES?

Even Inspector Witherspoon himself doesn't know—because his secret weapon is as ladylike as she is clever. She's Mrs. Jeffries—the charming detective who stars in this unique Victorian mystery series. Enjoy them all . . .

The Inspector and Mrs. Jeffries

A doctor is found dead in his own office—and Mrs. Jeffries must scour the premises to find the prescription for murder . . .

Mrs. Jeffries Dusts for Clues

One case is solved and another is opened when the inspector finds a missing brooch—pinned to a dead woman's gown. But Mrs. Jeffries never cleans a room without dusting under the bed—and never gives up on a case before every loose end is tightly tied . . .

The Ghost and Mrs. Jeffries

Death is unpredictable, but the murder of Mrs. Hodges was foreseen at a spooky séance. The practical-minded housekeeper may not be able to see the future—but she can look into the past and put things in order to solve this haunting crime . . .

Mrs. Jeffries Takes Stock

A businessman has been murdered—and it could be because he cheated his stockholders. The housekeeper's interest is piqued, and when it comes to catching killers, the smart money's on Mrs. Jeffries . . .

continued . . .

Mrs. Jeffries Takes the Cake

The evidence was all there: a dead body, two dessert plates, and a gun. As if Mr. Ashbury had been sharing cake with his own killer. Now Mrs. Jeffries will have to do some snooping around to dish up clues . . .

Mrs. Jeffries Rocks the Boat

Mirabelle had traveled by boat all the way from Australia to visit her sister—only to wind up murdered. Now Mrs. Jeffries must solve the case— and it's sink or swim . . .

Mrs. Jeffries Weeds the Plot

Three attempts have been made on Annabeth Gentry's life. Is it due to her recent inheritance, or was it because her bloodhound dug up the body of a murdered thief? Mrs. Jeffries will have to sniff out some clues before the plot thickens . . .

Mrs. Jeffries Pinches the Post

Harrison Nye may have had some dubious business dealings, but no one expected him to be murdered. Now Mrs. Jeffries and her staff must root through the sins of his past to discover which one caught up with him . . .

Mrs. Jeffries Pleads Her Case

Harlan Westover's death was deemed a suicide by the magistrate. But Inspector Witherspoon is willing to risk his career to prove otherwise. Mrs. Jeffries must ensure the good inspector remains afloat . . .

Mrs. Jeffries Sweeps the Chimney

A dead vicar has been found, propped against a church wall. And Inspector Witherspoon's only prayer is to seek the divinations of Mrs. Jeffries . . .

Mrs. Jeffries Stalks the Hunter

Puppy love turns to obsession, which leads to murder. Who better to get to the heart of the matter than Inspector Witherspoon's indomitable companion, Mrs. Jeffries . . .

continued . . .

Mrs. Jeffries Speaks Her Mind

Someone is trying to kill the eccentric Olive Kettering, but no one believes her—until she's proven right. Without witnesses and with plenty of suspects, Mrs. Jeffries will see justice served . . .

Mrs. Jeffries Forges Ahead

The marriageable daughters of the upper crust are outraged when the rich and handsome Lewis Banfield marries an artist's model. But when someone poisons the new bride's champagne, Mrs. Jeffries must discover if envy led to murder . . .

Mrs. Jeffries and the Mistletoe Mix-Up

When art collector Daniel McCourt is found murdered under the mistletoe, it's up to Mrs. Jeffries to find out who gave him the kiss of death . . .

Mrs. Jeffries Defends Her Own

When the office manager of Sutcliffe Manufacturing is killed, no one is really surprised—the tyrannical bully had lots of enemies. But who hated him enough to shoot him dead? Mrs. Jeffries must find out . . .

Visit Emily Brightwell's website at
www.emilybrightwell.com

Also available from Berkley Prime Crime
The first three Mrs. Jeffries Mysteries in one volume
Mrs. Jeffries Learns the Trade

MRS. JEFFRIES
TAKES A SECOND LOOK

EMILY BRIGHTWELL

BERKLEY PRIME CRIME, NEW YORK

THE BERKLEY PUBLISHING GROUP
Published by the Penguin Group
Penguin Group (USA) Inc.
375 Hudson Street, New York, New York 10014, USA

Penguin Group (Canada), 90 Eglinton Avenue East, Suite 700, Toronto, Ontario M4P 2Y3, Canada (a division of Pearson Penguin Canada Inc.) • Penguin Books Ltd., 80 Strand, London WC2R 0RL, England • Penguin Group Ireland, 25 St. Stephen's Green, Dublin 2, Ireland (a division of Penguin Books Ltd.) • Penguin Group (Australia), 250 Camberwell Road, Camberwell, Victoria 3124, Australia (a division of Pearson Australia Group Pty. Ltd.) • Penguin Books India Pvt. Ltd., 11 Community Centre, Panchsheel Park, New Delhi—110 017, India • Penguin Group (NZ), 67 Apollo Drive, Rosedale, Auckland 0632, New Zealand (a division of Pearson New Zealand Ltd.) • Penguin Books (South Africa) (Pty.) Ltd., 24 Sturdee Avenue, Rosebank, Johannesburg 2196, South Africa

Penguin Books Ltd., Registered Offices: 80 Strand, London WC2R 0RL, England

This book is an original publication of The Berkley Publishing Group.

MRS. JEFFRIES TAKES A SECOND LOOK

PUBLISHING HISTORY
Berkley Prime Crime trade paperback edition / September 2012
Mrs. Jeffries Takes Stock Berkley Prime Crime mass-market edition / June 1994
Mrs. Jeffries on the Ball Berkley Prime Crime mass-market edition / December 1994
Mrs. Jeffries on the Trail Berkley Prime Crime mass-market edition / April 1995

Library of Congress Cataloging-in-Publication Data

Brightwell, Emily.
Mrs. Jeffries takes a second look / Emily Brightwell.—Berkley Prime Crime trade paperback ed.
p. cm.
ISBN 978-0-425-25928-3 (pbk.)
1. Jeffries, Mrs. (Fictitious character)—Fiction. 2. Women household employees—Fiction.
3. Murder—Investigation—Fiction. 4. Police—Great Britain—Fiction. I. Title.
PS3552 R46443M7358 2012
813'.54—dc23   2012016162

PRINTED IN THE UNITED STATES OF AMERICA

10 9 8 7 6 5 4 3 2 1

CONTENTS

MRS. JEFFRIES TAKES STOCK

To Marjory Robinson,
one of those rare people
whose love of books and reading
touched so many lives

CHAPTER 1

Inspector Gerald Witherspoon clasped his handkerchief to his nose and sneezed. He flinched as the undignified noise echoed off the silent walls of St. Thomas Hospital.

"Bless you, sir," Constable Barnes said kindly. He smiled sympathetically at the inspector and edged closer to the sheet-shrouded body lying on the table. "Now I expect you'll be wanting to examine the victim."

"Ah . . . ah . . . choo." Witherspoon sneezed again. "Oh drat. This cold is dreadful," he complained. "I really should be home in bed, not standing about a chilly hospital mortuary. It'll be a wonder if I don't catch my death in here."

"Yes, sir, I'm sure you're right. But unfortunately you've not got much choice in the matter. If you'd have a look at the deceased, sir." Barnes reached for the edge of the sheet.

"Spring colds are the worst," the inspector continued, ignoring the constable's attempts to get him to look at the body one second before he had to. "They hang on for ages. I seem to have spent the last two weeks coughing my head off and fighting off the chills."

"Makes you miserable, colds do," Barnes agreed with a cheerful smile. "Guess I'm one of the lucky ones. I never get them. Now, sir, if you'd just have a quick look at the deceased, we could get you out of here, back to the station and fix you up with a nice cuppa tea."

Witherspoon wiped his watery eyes and noticed Barnes was watching him expectantly. He sighed. "I suppose you're right. I best get this over with. One must do one's duty." He broke off as another sneeze racked him. "Oh drat. Duty or not, I don't see why I had to be called from my sickbed on this one. Why isn't Inspector Nivens here? He was up for the next murder."

"Well, sir, there's a bit of a problem with that." Barnes gave up trying to lift the sheet.

"Problem?" Witherspoon looked puzzled. "I don't see why there's a problem. There's a murdered man lying here and Inspector Nivens was promised the next murder. I heard the chief tell him so myself. It was right after Nivens recovered Lady Spangler's jewels. The Home Office was so grateful that Nivens managed to avert a scandal. I mean, after all, we all knew the jewels hadn't really been stolen." He shook his head. "Women are such strange creatures, Constable. I don't think I'll ever understand them. Imagine giving all those valuables to that young bounder?"

"Yes, sir," Barnes replied dryly, his craggy face set in lines of patience. "Lady Spangler was foolish, but she's not the first to have her head turned by someone half her age. There's plenty of men about who've done the same thing. But grateful as everyone was for Inspector Nivens's discretion, there's still a bit of a wrinkle in giving him this case." The constable gave up waiting for the inspector to make a move towards the corpse. Barnes's feet were cold and he wanted a cup of tea, too. He decided to take matters into his own hands. He lunged at the sheet, tossed it back, and revealed the body before the inspector could witter on about his cold.

Witherspoon moaned and quickly closed his eyes. He really didn't want to look. Bodies weren't very nice. Even the tidy ones that weren't drenched in blood were awful, and this one was a drowning. Or a shooting, or something equally wretched. He couldn't quite remember exactly what Barnes had told him earlier. Gracious, it's a wonder he could even remember his own name, considering how miserable he was.

"This one isn't too bad," Barnes murmured as he stared at the bloated corpse. "Not like that last one we had. Pity Nivens won't get a crack at this case, but it can't be helped. Nivens might be a suspect himself."

"What?" The inspector's eyes flew open.

The constable chuckled. "Only foolin', sir. Of course Inspector Nivens isn't really a suspect. But the reason he isn't getting this one is because he knew the victim. Actually did business with the man, so to speak. The dead man's name is Jake Randall. He's American. He were found this morning floating in the Thames, and he weren't going for a swim, either. He's got a bullet in his chest."

"And you say Inspector Nivens did business with the deceased?" Witherspoon asked curiously. He forced himself to look at the dead man and then wished he hadn't.

The body was puffed, the skin a pale gray and the bullet hole in the man's chest a dark gaping pit. Witherspoon quickly averted his eyes and silently thanked his lucky stars that at least with this cold, his nose was so clogged up he couldn't smell anything.

"Not directly. Inspector Nivens owns stock in Randall's mining company. He's not a major shareholder, mind you. But he owns enough to make it a bit awkward for him to take the case. Name of the company is Randall and Watson."

"That's not exactly doing business with the man," Witherspoon exclaimed. "I own shares in government bonds. That hardly means I'm doing business with Her Majesty."

"True." The constable took his helmet off, shook off the remaining drops of rainwater and then flicked a last few drops off his curly gray hair. "But then, Her Majesty is hardly bein' accused of defrauding her investors."

"Oh dear." Witherspoon sighed. Behind the lenses of his spectacles, his clear blue-gray eyes narrowed in concern. "I take it that means that Mr. Randall was suspected of defrauding his investors?"

Barnes shook his head slowly, his craggy face somber. "That's about the size of it, sir." He popped his helmet back on and adjusted the strap. "I got a bit of background information out of Inspector Nivens. He was called to the scene when they fished this bloke out of the river this morning. 'Course, soon as the inspector saw who he was, he took himself off the case. That's when the chief sent me 'round to get you."

Witherspoon blew his nose so hard his bowler hat slipped forward onto his forehead. He pushed the hat firmly back into place over his thinning brown hair and cleared his throat. "What else did Inspector Nivens tell you?"

"Not all that much, sir," Barnes admitted. "But he did say the victim was supposed to have met with the other stockholders in his company a couple of days ago. They had a meeting scheduled for Monday, March seventh. Randall never showed."

"Where did Mr. Randall live?"

"He had a set of rooms near Hyde Park. I've already sent someone 'round to speak to the landlady," Barnes said. "She said that Jake Randall moved out on the first of this month. Supposedly, he's been living at a hotel since then. The landlady didn't know which one it was, and Inspector Nivens didn't know either."

"Hmmm . . ." Witherspoon muttered. He closed his eyes briefly and tried to think of something to ask. "Er, perhaps we'd better send a few lads 'round the hotels and try and find which one the deceased was staying at."

"Yes, sir." Barnes coughed slightly. "I've already done that. I thought it might help us establish the last time the man was seen alive."

"Good work, Constable," Witherspoon replied. "I don't suppose Dr. Potter's made any estimate as to how long the victim's been dead?"

Barnes raised one shaggy gray eyebrow. "Hardly, sir. You know Dr. Potter, the man won't even tell you it's daytime unless he looks outside first." He paused and glanced over his shoulder toward the door. Except for the body on the table, the small room was empty. "I hope you don't mind, sir," Barnes said, dropping his voice to a whisper, "but I saw that young chap Dr. Bosworth when they brought the body in, and I took the liberty of havin' a quick word with him."

Witherspoon wondered why Constable Barnes was whispering . . . or maybe his cold was so bad he was starting to lose his hearing. "Really. About what?"

"About havin' a look at the body, sir." Barnes raked the door with another furtive glance. "Remember on that case we had last year, sir. It were Dr. Bosworth that found out the victim was pregnant, and that information helped us find out who killed her."

Witherspoon stared at him in admiration. "Very good, Constable." Barnes was referring to a case where Dr. Bosworth's medical knowledge had shed a whole new light on the investigation. "And what did the doctor say?"

"He didn't have much time to look this morning," Barnes acknowledged. "The best he could come up with was an estimate on the time of death. Bosworth thinks Randall was probably shot on the evening of March the seventh. That'd make it two days ago."

"Oh dear." The inspector's long nose wrinkled as he fought to hold back another sneeze. He struggled mightily for a few seconds and actually smiled as he realized he'd won. "Too bad he didn't have time to give the victim a thorough examination."

"He's going to have another go at it tomorrow afternoon," Barnes said quickly. "Dr. Potter won't be here then. He'll have to be testifying at the inquest. He's doing the autopsy in the morning. Dr. Bosworth wanted to wait until after the bloke were sliced open before he started snoopin' about. Claimed it would be easier that way. He'll be able to have a right good look at the innards, said he'd be able to tell us quite a bit then."

Witherspoon hoped he didn't look as green as he felt. But really, Constable Barnes obviously had a strong stomach. "Er, excellent."

The household at Upper Edmonton Gardens, home of Inspector Gerald Witherspoon, was in an uproar. Mrs. Jeffries, the housekeeper, stared at the mutinous faces surrounding the kitchen table and sighed inwardly. "Really," she said calmly, "I don't know what all the fuss is about."

"That's easy for you to say," Mrs. Goodge, the cook, said. "You're not the one that's going to have to try to feed this household on a pittance." She jabbed one plump red finger at the piece of notepaper lying in front of Mrs. Jeffries. "You've got to talk to the inspector. This is daft. I don't mind bein' a bit frugal. But what he wants is ridiculous. And prices are going up all the time. What's he expect me to do? Feed everyone fried bread instead of decent cuts of meat?" Her chin bobbed up and down as she spoke, dislodging a tendril of white hair from under her cook's hat.

"And what about the coal supplies?" Wiggins, the footman, interjected. He stared earnestly at the housekeeper, his round, placid face creased in worry. "This house don't stay warm by itself, you know. We've got to keep the fires going or we'll all freeze. It gets bloomin' cold up in that attic. Even Fred notices it." He glanced down at the shaggy black-and-brown mongrel resting next to his chair. Fred, when he heard his name called, lifted his head and then settled back down to sleep.

"Does this mean we're goin' to get our wages cut?" Betsy, the maid, asked. Young, pretty, and with plenty of natural intelligence, she got right to the heart of what was really worrying all of them.

"Of course it doesn't mean you're going to get your wages reduced," Mrs. Jeffries assured them quickly. "The inspector merely wants us to trim the household expenses a bit, that's all."

"I'm not cuttin' back on the 'orses' feed," Smythe, the coachman, added. He crossed his arms over his broad chest and leaned back in his seat. He was a big man, with dark brown hair and harsh, almost brutal

features, save for a pair of twinkling brown eyes. His eyes weren't twinkling now, though. "Just because the inspector don't use Bow and Arrow
all that much don't mean they ain't deservin' the best."

"Please, calm down," Mrs. Jeffries commanded. "You're all jumping
to conclusions much too quickly. All the inspector is saying is that we've
got to cut back a bit on the household expenses. He's not going to starve
his horses, freeze his servants, or force us to eat bread and water." Her
normally placid face creased in a frown, and her brown eyes narrowed in
irritation. "Furthermore, I should think you'd all be a bit ashamed. Have
you ever known the inspector to be unfair? Has he ever treated any of us
with less than the utmost kindness?"

Smythe cleared his throat. "Uh, we didn't mean no disrespect to the
inspector," he said uneasily, "but you've got to admit it's a bit of a worry.
I mean, 'im all of a sudden comin' up with this grand scheme to save a few
pounds each month. We all knows how much we owes the inspector."

Wiggins shoved a lock of dark brown hair off his forehead. "What's
this all about, then? What's wrong? The inspector ain't losin' his position,
is he?"

"No," Mrs. Jeffries replied firmly. She didn't like making them feel
guilty, but really, she had to do something. This discussion was getting
completely out of hand. Besides, complaining about the inspector's newest
household management scheme wouldn't do them a bit of good. It was far
better to go along with his plan and let the inspector see the results of
"cutting back" himself. Mrs. Jeffries was confident that within a very few
weeks the household would be back to its normal routine. "The inspector
isn't losing his position, Wiggins," she said. "But—and I suppose it's only
fair you should know this—some of his investments aren't doing all that
well."

"Cor blimey." Wiggins shook his head. "That doesn't sound good."

"Here now. I'm sorry about the inspector's investments, but how on
earth am I expected to entertain on this amount of money?" Mrs. Goodge
asked. She jabbed her finger again at the dreaded piece of paper.

Mrs. Jeffries stared at the cook in amazement. "Entertain? I'm afraid
I don't understand what you mean. The inspector never entertains."

"I weren't talkin' about him," Mrs. Goodge replied earnestly. She
waved her arm around the table. "I was talkin' about us. We've got Luty
Belle and Hatchet comin' by for tea tomorrow—" She broke off and
snatched a plate of cherry tarts out from under Wiggins's fingers. "We'd

best save these," she continued, ignoring the footman's yelp of outrage. "These'll do for tomorrow, and I can save the last of them currants for a batch of buns. Though goodness knows what I'll do if we have to start helpin' the inspector on one of his cases. I won't be able to get anyone to tell me a bloomin' thing if I don't have some decent food to put on their stomachs."

Mrs. Jeffries sighed. She knew Mrs. Goodge was referring to the fact that all of the servants at Upper Edmonton Gardens helped Inspector Witherspoon solve his most difficult murder cases. Naturally, the inspector had no idea whatsoever that he was getting any help. She smiled at the others. Despite their complaints, they were a devoted lot. They dashed all over London questioning servants, following suspects, and chasing after clues. And they did it all because they loved and admired their dear Inspector Witherspoon. And, of course, because they were all natural-born snoops. As Betsy once said, following suspects and ferreting out clues was a lot more interesting than changing bed sheets or polishing floors. Even Mrs. Goodge, who rarely left the kitchen, did her fair share.

The cook had a virtual army of delivery boys, chimney sweeps, gas men, and fruit peddlers that she fed and watered. When they were on a case, Mrs. Goodge could ferret out the most minute bits and pieces of gossip and information. No wonder she was in a mood, Mrs. Jeffries thought. Without adequate supplies, she wouldn't be able to contribute anything. And the housekeeper knew how important it was for the elderly woman to contribute as much as the rest of them.

Mrs. Jeffries gave her a reassuring smile. "Don't worry, Mrs. Goodge," she said confidently, "we're not investigating anything at the moment, and perhaps by the time we are, the household will be back to normal."

Mrs. Goodge snorted. "Well, I certainly hope so."

"So do I," Betsy said. She jerked her chin towards the piece of paper. "Maybe if we had a decent murder to investigate, we wouldn't mind puttin' up with this . . ." She stopped speaking and tried to remember the words the housekeeper had used.

"Household management scheme," Smythe said, giving the girl a cheeky grin.

"Cor blimey, Betsy," Wiggins protested. "Haven't we had enough murders? A body could do with a bit of peace and quiet every now and again. Besides, it's not right, wantin' someone dead just so we can 'ave a bit of sport."

"I wasn't sayin' that," Betsy said defensively, her lovely cheeks flaming red. She appealed to Mrs. Jeffries. "You know that's not what I meant at all."

"Of course you didn't," Mrs. Jeffries said soothingly. Actually, she rather agreed with Betsy. Life was so much more interesting when they were digging about in one of the inspector's cases. "Wiggins is merely teasing you. After all, you do go after him rather mercilessly at times."

"Only because the lad asks for it," Smythe put in. He reached over and cuffed the grinning footman on the head. "Always hangin' about moonin' over some girl . . ."

Wiggins's various infatuations with the young females of London were legion.

"Nonetheless," Mrs. Jeffries said briskly, "you can't blame him for wanting to get a bit of his own back."

"Hmmph," Mrs. Goodge snorted again. "We only tease the ones we like," she muttered. "If we didn't care for the boy, we wouldn't say a word about all that silly poetry he writes for them girls."

"Me poems ain't silly," Wiggins yelped. "Elsie Tanner told me that one I wrote her was the prettiest thing she'd ever heard."

"Heard?" Smythe said. "Don't you mean 'read.'"

Wiggins shrugged. "Well, I had to read it to 'er meself."

"That's 'myself,'" Mrs. Jeffries corrected him quickly. She didn't correct the other servants because their speech offended her, she corrected them so they could improve their lot in life. They were all highly intelligent, hardworking people, and the housekeeper was secretly determined that one day they'd have an opportunity to advance themselves. Inspector Witherspoon was the kindest of masters. He treated his servants as human beings rather than objects put on this earth to answer his every whim. Yet kind as he was, Mrs. Jeffries harbored the hope that one day the younger servants would have to call no man master. One day they'd be master of their own fates.

"Right," Wiggins said. "I had to read it to her myself. Elsie can't read. But she said it were wonderful."

"She may have thought it were wonderful," Mrs. Goodge said, "but that didn't stop her from gettin' engaged to Lady Canonberry's gardener."

Smythe glanced at Wiggins. The footman dropped his gaze and stared at the tabletop as a blush crept up his cheeks. The lad was good-natured about their teasin' but he was still raw over the subject of Elsie Tanner. Wiggins hadn't been in love with the lass or anythin' like that, but he'd been smitten enough to get his feelin's hurt bad when she up and got herself engaged to another bloke.

Smythe decided to change the subject. "Do you think we'll be gettin' somethin' interestin' to do soon?" he asked the housekeeper.

Mrs. Jeffries smiled sadly. "Not for a while, I'm afraid. You see, the inspector told me that the next murder that comes along goes to Inspector Nivens."

"Inspector Nivens?" they all chorused at once.

"But that's daft!" Mrs. Goodge exclaimed.

"Nivens couldn't find a singer at a music hall, let alone catch a killer," Smythe charged.

"He's always lookin down his nose at people," Betsy said earnestly. "How can someone like that ever learn anything?"

"Well, I think it's about time that someone other than our inspector had to do it," Wiggins said. "It isn't fair that he always gets stuck with the bad ones."

"Oh dear, sir," Mrs. Jeffries said to Inspector Witherspoon as she ushered him into the drawing room, "you really shouldn't have gone out. Not with that terrible cold."

"I didn't have much choice, Mrs. Jeffries," he replied as he settled himself in his favorite wing chair by the fireplace. He glanced around the normally cozy drawing room. "When one is summoned, one must go. I say, it's a bit chilly in here. Why isn't the fire going?"

"I didn't think you wanted one, sir," she replied calmly. "After you left this afternoon, I assumed that you wouldn't be in here very long. Wiggins has laid a fire in your room, sir. Naturally, as you've instructed us to be more careful about our expenditures, I didn't think you'd want to waste a bucket of coal to heat a room you'd only be sitting in for a few minutes."

Witherspoon frowned slightly, but said nothing.

Mrs. Jeffries firmly clamped down on the surge of hope welling up inside her as she poured the inspector a glass of sherry. She'd known when the inspector was summoned by the chief inspector earlier that afternoon that something important was happening, but she hadn't dared let herself believe it might be another murder investigation. That's why she hadn't said anything to the others. She didn't want to get their hopes up.

"Here, sir." She handed him a glass of pale amber liquid. "This ought to take the chill off."

"Thank you, Mrs. Jeffries," he replied absently as he took the glass from her fingers and raised it to his lips. As the liquid hit his tongue his eyes bulged. "I say, this doesn't taste like our usual sherry?"

"It's not, sir," she said, giving him a placid smile. "You finished the last of your usual kind yesterday. Naturally, in accordance with your instructions to trim our spending, I ordered this brand. It's Spanish, you know. Far less costly than Harvey's. The wine merchant assured me it would do nicely. Now, sir, why don't you tell me why you were summoned out of your sickbed today?"

Witherspoon tentatively took another sip. He grimaced. The wine merchant might say it would do nicely, he thought, but he wasn't the one having to drink the ruddy stuff. Still, he couldn't complain to Mrs. Jeffries. She was only following his instructions.

"Inspector?" Mrs. Jeffries prompted gently.

"Ah, oh yes. Why was I summoned to the Yard." He laid his glass to one side. "Because of a murder, of course."

Mrs. Jeffries sat up straighter. "A murder?"

He nodded weakly and plucked his handkerchief out of his pocket. "I'm afraid so. Fellow by the name of Jake Randall was found floating in the Thames."

"Floating in the Thames," she repeated slowly, her mind working furiously. She knew that murder by drowning was difficult to prove, impossible really, unless there was an eyewitness or unless the body was marked in such a way as to rule out any other conclusion. She'd learned quite a bit living with her late husband, a police constable in Yorkshire for over twenty years. "How extraordinary. What makes the police think it's murder and not an accidental drowning?"

The inspector sneezed so hard he didn't hear the question. He pulled out his handkerchief and blew his nose. "Uh, I say, Mrs. Jeffries, what is Mrs. Goodge cooking up for dinner tonight?"

"Spring stew of veal and brown bread pudding," she answered quickly, knowing the inspector would be far more receptive to her questions once he knew he was going to be fed properly.

Witherspoon brightened considerably. "That's one of my favorite dishes. One of my favorites." He tucked his hankie back in his pocket. "Now, what was that you asked?"

Betsy stuck her head in the drawing room. "Dinner's served," she announced just as there was a knock on the front door.

"Answer the door, Betsy," Mrs. Jeffries said as she rose to her feet.

"Odd time for someone to come calling," the inspector murmured. He was really quite hungry. He hoped he wasn't being called out again. Surely they wouldn't have found another corpse floating in the river. Even *his* luck wasn't that bad.

Betsy returned a moment later. Inspector Nigel Nivens was right behind her. Mrs. Jeffries stiffened. She didn't like Inspector Nivens, and she was fairly certain he didn't like her either.

He was a man of medium height, with dark blond hair slicked straight back from his high forehead. His chin was weak, his gray eyes cold and shifty, and he was forever trying to figure out precisely how Inspector Witherspoon solved all those complicated murder cases.

Nivens flicked the housekeeper a brief, suspicious glance before turning to Inspector Witherspoon. "Good evening, Witherspoon," he said politely. "Mrs. Jeffries." He acknowledged her presence with a slight nod. "I'm terribly sorry to barge in like this, but it's imperative that I speak with you. It's about that man they fished out of the Thames today. Jake Randall."

"You're not barging in, dear fellow," Witherspoon said with a welcoming smile. "It's nice to see you again."

"Should I ask Betsy to hold dinner?" Mrs. Jeffries asked softly. Really, sometimes she felt like shaking her employer. He was so very innocent. He didn't have the slightest notion that Inspector Nivens thought he was a fool. Nivens's sarcasm and innuendo rolled right off Inspector Witherspoon's back.

Witherspoon's brows rose. "I don't think that will be necessary," he replied. "I'm sure that Inspector Nivens will dine with me." He looked hopefully at the other man. "Won't you?"

Nivens smiled. "As long as it's no trouble, I'd be delighted."

"It's not a bit of trouble," the inspector assured him. "Come along, the dining room is through here," He led the way out of the room with Nivens trailing at his heels. Mrs. Jeffries, sure that something was up because she knew good and well that Inspector Nivens hadn't called around to inquire about her employer's health, followed at a more cautious pace. But she was determined to find out why the odious man had come. If he was going to browbeat the inspector into giving up this case . . . well, she'd just have to take matters into her own hands.

She didn't have to wait long. Just as the two men were entering the dining room, Witherspoon said, "I'm jolly sorry you're not getting this case. I know how much you wanted a chance at a murder."

"I'm sorry, too. But circumstances being as they are, we've no choice in the matter." Nivens turned his head and saw her loitering in the hall. She gave him an innocent smile.

"I knew the victim, you see," Nivens said when it was clear that Mrs. Jeffries wasn't going to be cowed. "And I've got some information I think will help with your investigation. Details, that sort of thing."

"Yes, I'm sure you'll be most helpful," Witherspoon murmured. He really didn't want to talk about murder while he ate his dinner. But obviously, Inspector Nivens felt it was important enough to come 'round personally. He was duty bound to listen attentively, even if his stomach was growling and his head was so stuffed he could barely think. He gestured toward the chair on his right and sat down. "Do sit down, Inspector."

Mrs. Jeffries heard Betsy coming up the backstairs with the main course. She turned and fairly flew down the hall.

"Here," she hissed to the surprised maid, "I'll serve. You nip back into the drawing room."

"What for?" Betsy's blue eyes mirrored her confusion. Serving dinner was one of her duties.

"Because I want to know everything that Inspector Nivens says tonight, and I'm fairly certain he'll take care not to say anything important while I'm in the room."

"What are you on about, Mrs. J?"

"Murder," she hissed. "If Nivens doesn't see me hovering about the dining room, he'll assume I'm eavesdropping by the door and he might close up tighter than a bank vault. Even worse, the odious little man might deliberately give the inspector the wrong information just so he can try to trap me. We can't take that risk."

Mrs. Jeffries knew she wasn't being her normal articulate self, but she was in a hurry. She was certain that Nigel Nivens suspected that Inspector Witherspoon's "phenomenal success" at solving murders was due to the fact that he had help. She was equally certain that he'd guessed precisely where that help had come from. But she didn't have time to explain all this to Betsy right now.

"You mean Nivens is onto us?"

"Perhaps," she whispered. "And I want him to see me serving dinner. It might allay his suspicions. So I want you to go into the drawing room. If you huddle down behind that wing chair opposite the fireplace and put your ear to the wall, you can hear every word that's being said in the dining room."

"You mean you want me to eavesdrop?"

"Of course I want you to." The housekeeper took the platter out of the girl's hand. "Murder's been done and our inspector is on the case."

She didn't have to explain further. Betsy nodded and slipped down the hallway into the drawing room. Mrs. Jeffries continued into the dining room.

Secure in the knowledge that Betsy was listening to every word, Mrs. Jeffries calmly served dinner. She was aware that every time she entered the room, Nivens broke off and waited until she'd left before speaking again. She deliberately made as much noise as possible as she went back and forth between the kitchen and dining room. She clicked her heels loudly against the hallway floor, stomped up and down the steps hard enough to cause the banister to vibrate, and banged the plates together every time she served a course. She was sure her plan was working.

She placed a plate of brown bread pudding in front of the two inspectors and turned for the door. She left it open as she tromped down the hall, her footsteps loud enough to wake the dead. She smiled to herself as she reached the staircase leading to the kitchen. From behind her, she could hear the murmur of voices.

Nivens, secure in the knowledge that she couldn't possibly be eavesdropping, was talking his head off. He was annoying, but she wasn't in the least worried. Even if Betsy suddenly went stone-deaf, she'd still find out what was going on.

Inspector Witherspoon told her everything.

CHAPTER 2

Betsy kept one eye on the door and pressed her ear to the wall. The voices of the two men were low, but very clear. From outside the front window, she heard the rattle and clop of a carriage. She frowned and shot a quick glare toward the road as the noise of the horses' hooves and rumble of the wheels drowned out Inspector Nivens's first words. Blast, she thought, pressing her head closer to the wall; if this keeps up, I won't hear a bloomin' thing.

From behind the panelling, she heard Inspector Witherspoon say, "Now precisely what was it you wanted to tell me, Inspector Nivens. Oh, do help yourself to more veal, it's one of cook's best recipes."

There was the scrape of silverware against china. Betsy guessed that Nivens was loading his plate up. He looked like the kind that'd make a pig of himself, she thought. She hoped he wouldn't keep his mouth so full that he couldn't talk. Then relief filled her as she heard Nivens start speaking. Betsy held her breath, hoping he wouldn't take too long to say something interesting.

"As I'm sure you know, Jake Randall was pulled from the Thames this morning," Nivens said. "We know it was murder because he had a bullet in his chest."

"I saw the body this afternoon," Witherspoon replied. Betsy had to strain to catch his words. His voice seemed to have gone a bit faint.

"I assume Constable Barnes told you why I had to give up the case," Nivens continued.

She heard a muffled grunt in reply.

"My business with Mr. Randall wasn't extensive," Nivens said, "nor was it directly with Mr. Randall himself. It's true I own shares in Randall and Watson Mining Company, but I purchased that stock through a Mr. Lester Hinkle. He represents several small investors like myself. That's really all there is to it. I'd never even met the victim, but you know what a stickler for propriety the chief is, and I thought it best to take myself off the case."

"Er, excuse my asking, but if you'd never met Mr. Randall," the inspector said hesitantly, "then how did you know it was him when you saw the body?"

There was a long pause before Nivens answered. "We may not have been acquainted, but I had seen him before. When Mr. Hinkle recommended I purchase the shares, I took it upon myself to inquire into Mr. Randall's background. During the course of that inquiry, I happened to see him coming out of Hinkle's office on Throgmorton Street."

"Hmmm, I see. What kind of mine is it?" Witherspoon asked.

"Silver," Nivens answered. "It's in the United States, in Colorado to be exact."

"Hmmm," the inspector said.

Betsy rolled her eyes. If Inspector Witherspoon didn't get on with it, she'd be here all night.

Inspector Nivens, perhaps coming to the same conclusion that Betsy had, suddenly got to the heart of his story.

"A few days ago," he said, "Mr. Hinkle contacted me. He said he had it on good authority that Jake Randall wasn't using our investment money to buy equipment, hire miners, or dig for silver. It seems that one of Mr. Hinkle's relations happened to be visiting Colorado. He visited the mine site and found it was nothing more than a hole in the side of a mountain." Nivens stopped and Betsy took the chance to rub the crick out of her neck.

She quickly put her ear back against the wall when she heard Nivens start up again.

"Furthermore, Mr. Hinkle's relation had taken the trouble to meet the other owner of the mine, a man called Tib Watson. These Americans have such strange names." He paused. "Watson was nothing more than an old drunk. The only mining equipment he had was a pickax and a half-blind old mule." Nivens snorted in anger.

"Oh dear, that doesn't sound at all right," Witherspoon murmured sympathetically.

"It wasn't right. Naturally, Mr. Hinkle was concerned. Not only had he invested my money and the money of several other people, but he'd also invested a huge amount of his own," Nivens complained bitterly. "He came to me because I'm with the police. He wanted to know if we should have Mr. Randall arrested. I told him that he didn't have enough evidence. I offered to contact the American authorities, but Mr. Hinkle was afraid the press would get wind of it, so he asked me not to do anything yet. He decided to talk with other shareholders about the situation. He did that and they decided their best course of action would be to confront Mr. Randall and ask him for an explanation."

Betsy's foot began to cramp. She eased it out from beneath her, cringing as the sole of her shoe scraped noisily against the floorboards. But she needn't have worried about being overheard. Both men were too intent upon their subject to take any notice of unusual noises.

She shifted slightly into a more comfortable position. Through the wall, she heard the inspector ask the obvious question.

"But surely, if you knew there was no mining going on and you'd all given him money, you could have picked Mr. Randall up for fraud."

"Hardly, Inspector Witherspoon."

Betsy's eyes narrowed at the cool contempt she heard in Nivens's voice. How dare he speak to their inspector in that tone?

"Why ever not?" Witherspoon asked innocently.

"To prove fraud, you must prove intent," Nivens replied. "But that's neither here nor there. We couldn't prove intent, nor did we have enough evidence to arrest Randall. The unsubstantiated word of someone's cousin isn't reason enough to arrest a man with the kind of important connections that Randall had. The other shareholders decided to have a meeting and confront Jake Randall. He was either going to have to give them back their money or come up with a reasonable explanation. The meeting was scheduled for March seventh. Randall agreed to be there. But he wasn't. On March ninth his body was found."

"Er, uh, who else was due at this meeting?"

"All the other shareholders. One of whom is Rushton Benfield, he's the son of Sir Thaddeus Benfield. Mr. Benfield is the main reason Lester Hinkle bought into the company. As you know, the Benfields are one of the most prominent families in England."

Betsy heard the sound of a chair scraping across the floor and decided that Nivens had stuffed himself so full he needed more room.

Nivens continued. "The other stockholders are John Cubberly, a businessman. He lives on Davies Street just off Chester Square. The meeting was going to take place at his home. The other major shareholder is a gentleman named Edward Dillingham. Hinkle, Benfield, Cubberly, and Dillingham essentially represented all the stockholders in Randall and Watson. Between them, they'd put in over fifty thousand pounds."

"Oh dear, dear." Witherspoon clucked his tongue. "That's a frightful amount of money."

"Yes, it is. I'm sure you can appreciate how all the stockholders felt when they were confronted with the rumor that Jake Randall wasn't to be trusted."

"Hmm . . . uh, if Mr. Randall had only recently sold stock in his company," Witherspoon asked, "perhaps he hadn't had time to buy any equipment or hire any workers?"

That's a good point, Betsy thought. She thought it was most clever of the inspector to ask. She heard Nivens laugh harshly.

"He'd had plenty of time," Nivens cried. "Six months, in fact. You see, this was the second time he'd issued stock. Six months ago, these same investors put up the initial development money for the mine. This second issue was merely to raise more capital."

Betsy jumped as she heard a loud crack. It sounded like someone had smacked the top of the table with their fist. Betsy grinned. Ol' Nivens had worked himself up to a real fit! Served him right, too, she thought.

The air in the kitchen crackled with excitement. Mrs. Jeffries had taken a few minutes between serving the dinner courses to tip Mrs. Goodge off to the fact that they now had a murder to investigate. The cook hadn't wasted a moment. By the time Inspector Witherspoon had said good-bye to his guest and retired for the night, she'd managed to get the rest of the servants into the kitchen and around the table.

Mrs. Jeffries sat down and waited until Mrs. Goodge had filled five mugs with hot, steaming tea.

"Is the inspector abed yet?" Betsy asked, glancing uneasily to the door that led to steps.

"He retired half an hour ago," Mrs. Jeffries replied. "And don't worry, he didn't have any idea that you were listening to his discussion with Inspector Nivens."

"Betsy were listenin'?" Wiggins exclaimed. "Whatever for?" He turned and frowned at the maid. "'Ere, that's not very nice, listenin' in on the inspector."

"It's all right, Wiggins," Mrs. Jeffries interjected. "I told her to do it. We've no time to waste on this case. If I'd had to wait until breakfast tomorrow to pry the details out of the inspector, we'd have lost a whole morning. None of us can investigate anything without knowing the facts of the case."

"All right." Mrs. Goodge planted her elbows on the table. "Let's have it, then. Who got done in?"

"The victim was an American named Jake Randall," Mrs. Jeffries began. She didn't stop until she'd told them everything she'd learned. "So you see, we're not precisely sure even where the man lived."

"I think I can help a bit there," Betsy said.

"Did Nivens know, then?" Smythe asked.

"Not exactly, but I did hear Nivens tell the inspector they think they may have found the hotel Randall was stayin' at."

"Why don't you start at the beginning and tell us everything," Mrs. Jeffries suggested. She was quite relieved that Smythe wasn't in a state over Betsy having gotten a start on the investigation. The two of them had been quite competitive on their last couple of cases, and Mrs. Jeffries was glad to see that this particular nonsense had run its course.

"All right, then," Betsy said. Blessed with both good hearing and a remarkable memory for details, she repeated the information Inspector Nivens had given Inspector Witherspoon.

Everyone listened carefully.

When Betsy had finished, Mrs. Goodge shook her head. "Let's see now, I want to make sure I've got it right. This Jake Randall had sold off shares in a mining company that weren't no good. All the people that had bought those stocks and given him their money got wind of what he was up to and demanded a meeting."

"That's right," Betsy said.

"And then, instead of Randall showin' up for that meetin', he's found a couple of days later floating in the river with a bullet through his heart." Mrs. Goodge pursed her lips. "Sounds to me like one of them that lost their money done him in."

"But we don't know that for sure," Smythe said cautiously. He looked at Mrs. Jeffries, his expression puzzled, "There's somethin' I don't understand 'ere."

"What is it?"

"Where's the money? Did he 'ave it on 'im, or was it in the bank? I mean, why would one of the stockholders shoot Randall unless it meant they was goin' to get their money back?"

Mrs. Jeffries looked thoughtful. "You know, you're absolutely right. And I think that's one of the first things we've got to find out. What happened to the money?"

"I wish Inspector Witherspoon had thought to ask that," Betsy said. "It'd save us a bit of time. If that money is sitting in a bank somewhere, then it's a sure bet that none of the shareholders did the man in."

Wiggins frowned. "'Ow do you figure that? Could be one of 'em was angry about what he'd tried to do and decided to teach him a lesson."

"They wouldn't teach him a lesson until after they got their money back, now, would they?" Betsy persisted. "That class of people don't do murder over somethin' like that."

"Meanin' that it's only the lower classes that murder 'cause they're angry," Smythe put in. He raised one eyebrow and stared at the maid. "Come on, girl, you know better than that. You've snooped about in enough of the inspector's cases to know that the rich ain't any different from the poor when it comes to hatin' and madness. But they are better at hidin' it than the rest of us."

"I'm not sayin' they're different. I'm just sayin' that unless one of those investors could have gotten his money back by killin' Randall, they wouldn't have bothered." Betsy shrugged. "Why take the risk of murderin' someone when it'd be a lot easier just to hire a solicitor and take the man to court? That's the way the rich take care of their problems. They go to the law."

"I don't understand if he was drowned or if he was shot," Wiggins interrupted.

"What difference does it make?" Mrs. Goodge asked impatiently. "Drowned or shot, he's still dead."

Mrs. Jeffries did think the cause of death was important, but she didn't wish to embarrass the cook by arguing the point. "We don't know the exact cause of death," she replied. "But that matter should be cleared up by tomorrow. That's when they're having the inquest. Dr. Potter's doing the autopsy."

There was a collective groan.

"I know," Mrs. Jeffries said soothingly, "But it can't be helped. Let's just hope that Dr. Potter surprises us and actually knows something useful."

Betsy, her blue eyes sparkling, eagerly leaned forward. "What do we do first?"

Mrs. Jeffries considered the question. "We've learned enough to get started with our inquiries," she mused, "yet we don't have much in the way of facts."

"We know where the body come up, don't we?" Smythe asked.

"Yes, just under Waterloo Bridge," Mrs. Jeffries replied thoughtfully. She frowned. "But I'm not sure that will do us much good. The body may have been spotted there, but considering the currents and tides in the river, we've no reason to think that Randall was shot anywhere near the bridge."

Wiggins gasped. "You mean he was shot somewhere else and the body just floated down the Thames until someone happened to see it?"

"No, no, Wiggins," Mrs. Jeffries explained hastily. "Dead bodies don't float, they generally sink to the bottom for a few days, bloat up a bit and then pop to the surface. But the point is, we've no idea if the victim died of drowning or the bullet wound. In either case, the body could have gone into the river several miles from where it was actually found." She knew this because her late husband had investigated several deaths by drowning.

"Why don't I take a run down to Waterloo Bridge anyway?" Smythe suggested. "You never know, Mrs. J. We might get lucky."

She looked at the coachman. "All right. But afterwards, I think you'd better take on the task of learning everything you can about Rushton Benfield."

"Do you know where he lives?"

"No," she replied. "But he shouldn't be hard to find. His father is Sir Thaddeus Benfield."

"I can help there," Mrs. Goodge said. "Well, I can tell you where Sir Thaddeus lives. He's got a fancy house near Regent's Park. I expect if Smythe hits the locals 'round there, he can find out where young Mr. Benfield calls home these days."

Mrs. Jeffries nodded. She was no longer amazed by the cook's enormous amount of information on the gentry of London.

"Excellent. Now, Wiggins," she said, ignoring the boy's less-than-enthusiastic expression, "I want you to find out everything you can about Lester Hinkle."

Betsy suddenly interrupted. "Lester Hinkle lives near the Cubberlys'— he lives right on Chester Square. I heard Inspector Nivens tellin' our inspector that before he left. He give Inspector Witherspoon all their addresses exceptin' for Mr. Benfield's."

"Very good, Betsy." Mrs. Jeffries beamed proudly at the girl.

"What do you want me to learn about this 'ere Mr. 'inkle?" the footman asked grudgingly.

"Everything you can, but most especially, I want to find out as much as possible about his movements between March seventh and ninth."

Mrs. Goodge leaned her ample bulk forward. "Why just them dates?"

"Because the meeting was called for March seventh and the body was found on March ninth. As Mr. Randall didn't show up for the meeting, there's a possibility he was already dead."

"Cor blimey," Wiggins groaned. "That's gonna be right 'ard. What if I can't learn nuthin'?"

Mrs. Jeffries sighed. Wiggins was obviously assailed by self-doubt again. She wondered if it had anything to do with Elsie Tanner's defection. Amazing really, how one totally unrelated event in a life could affect everything else. She peered closely at the boy. His mouth was turned down, there were faint circles under his eyes, and his usually round cheeks were pale and sunken.

Oh dear, she thought, he really was in a bad way. Perhaps she'd better put her foot down if there were any more teasing. Wiggins had always been good-natured about it in the past, but he didn't look at all his normal, jolly self. "Of course you'll learn something," Mrs. Jeffries assured him. "You always do. Why, you were instrumental in solving our last two cases."

Wiggins raised his eyes and stared at her hopefully. "Really?"

"You and Fred both," the housekeeper said enthusiastically. "That's why I don't think you'll have any trouble getting all sorts of information about Mr. Hinkle. Just do what you normally do, make contact with a footman or a gardener or perhaps a pretty housemaid and use your charm."

"My charm?" Wiggins grinned. "Well, if you say so, Mrs. Jeffries. By the way, where is Fred?" He ducked his head and looked for the stray dog he'd brought in a few months back. "Fred," he called softly, "here, boy . . ."

"He's not here," Mrs. Jeffries said hastily. "He's in the inspector's room."

"Again!" Wiggins's good mood began to vanish. "What's he doin' in there? 'E's my dog, you know. 'E's supposed to sleep up with us."

"Well . . ." Mrs. Jeffries tried to think of a diplomatic response. "Of course he's your dog and we all know how devoted he is to you. But the inspector's become very fond of him, too."

"But Fred's my dog," the footman complained. "'E ought to be with me, not the inspector. I thought dogs was supposed to be loyal."

"Fred is loyal," Mrs. Jeffries argued. "But like all creatures, he likes his comfort. And I think it is warmer in the inspector's bedroom." She didn't add that Witherspoon was always slipping Fred little treats and that she suspected he let the dog sleep at the foot of the bed and not the floor.

If she'd known how difficult bringing the dog into the house was going to be, she'd have thought differently about allowing it to happen. It wasn't that Fred was any trouble. Except for being overly fond of sausages and occasionally stealing one off the table when no one was looking, he was a fine animal. The problem was that both Wiggins and the inspector felt the dog belonged to them. And they were just a tad jealous of one another.

But Mrs. Jeffries really felt that Inspector Witherspoon should have the animal. Wiggins was one of *them*. They formed an unusual, but very real family circle, even though none of them were related by blood. The inspector, on the other hand, though he had the respect and devotion of his servants, was very much alone.

They had each other. Inspector Witherspoon had no one. Mrs. Jeffries refused to give up on her ambition of acquiring a wife for him, but the man was so ridiculously shy around women, she knew it might be ages before she could complete that task. In the meantime, Fred would just have to do. Witherspoon needed the dog far more than Wiggins did. But she wasn't about to tell Wiggins that. "You don't want Fred to catch cold, do you?"

"'Course not," Wiggins said. "But it in't that cold up in our room, is it, Smythe?"

"I wouldn't call it toasty," the coachman said dryly. "And you do insist on keepin' that ruddy window cracked a few inches. Poor mutt probably feels the chill."

"There, you see, we're all agreed. Fred should just go right on sleeping in the inspector's room." Mrs. Jeffries smiled confidently.

"You've got the dog all day to yourself," Betsy put in. "The inspector only gets to see him of an evening, and he's got right fond of the animal."

Wiggins nodded, but grumbled under his breath.

Thinking the matter settled, Betsy eagerly turned to the housekeeper. "What do you want me to do tomorrow?"

"If you'll pop 'round and see what you can find out about the Cubberly's," Mrs. Jeffries said slowly, "I'll see what I can learn about Edward Dillingham."

"So we'll have all four of 'em that were due at that meeting covered, right?" Smythe said.

"Correct."

"I reckon you want me to suss out what gossip there is about all of them," Mrs. Goodge said. Her broad face was creased in a worried frown. "That's not goin' to be easy, seein' as we're supposed to be cuttin' back and all."

"Come on, Mrs. Goodge," Betsy said cheerfully, "surely you can make do."

"That's easy for you to say, you won't have half a dozen people droppin' 'round and expectin' a decent bite to eat. The more buns and cakes I stuff down their throats, the longer they stay. The longer they stay, the more they talk." The cook cast a quick glance toward the pantries off the hallway. "I expect you're right, though. If I trim back a bit on meals, I ought to be able to make do."

"I still don't understand what learnin' about these four people is goin' to do," Wiggins complained. "We don't know for sure if they 'ad anything to do with Randall's murder. No one even seems to know the last time the bloke was seen alive. He could have been murdered days before he were even due at the meeting at the Cubberly house."

Mrs. Jeffries gave the footman a surprised look. He was right. Suddenly it became imperative to find out when Jake Randall was killed, or failing that, to find out when he was last seen alive.

"Good morning, sir," Mrs. Jeffries said cheerfully as she carried the inspector's breakfast into the dining room. "I hope you slept well."

Witherspoon yawned. "Very well, thank you." He smiled as she put a plate of hot food in front of him. Then he saw what was on it. "Er, no bacon and eggs this morning?"

"Oh no, sir." Mrs. Jeffries turned her head so he wouldn't see the impish twinkle in her eyes. She'd known that Mrs. Goodge was up to something this morning. The cook had been chuckling to herself as she'd cooked the inspector's breakfast. "Mrs. Goodge has found several breakfast dishes that are far less costly than bacon and eggs. She hopes you like this one."

Witherspoon picked up his fork and prodded the square brownish-gray object. "Yes," he murmured, "I'm sure I will. What is it exactly?"

"Marrow toast." She poured herself a cup of tea and took the chair next to the inspector. When she looked up, he'd blanched. "Oh dear, sir, are you feeling ill this morning?"

Witherspoon pushed his plate away. "Just a touch off-colour," he replied. "I expect it's just this wretched cold. Er, I think I'll just have tea this morning."

"Are you sure, sir?" she asked. "I could ask Mrs. Goodge to fix some porridge for you."

"No, no, it's quite all right." Witherspoon held up a hand and gave her a weak smile. "Tea will do nicely. I mustn't complain because everyone's following my instructions so very enthusiastically. I appreciate all Mrs. Goodge's efforts to trim back the food budget. I'm sure her marrow toast is wonderful, but I do have a poor stomach this morning."

"All right, sir." Mrs. Jeffries took a sip of tea. She stifled a pang of conscience. They were laying it on a bit thick. Mrs. Goodge had spent half the morning poring over cookery books. She'd come up with the most appallingly cheap and nasty recipe she could for breakfast. It would be interesting to see what she came up with for dinner. But the inspector had to understand that if one cut back, one had far less comfort and pleasure in life. She knew perfectly well that Inspector Witherspoon wasn't in any real financial difficulty. He'd merely panicked when the price of some of his shares had dropped. "Do you have a full day planned?"

"Indeed I do, Mrs. Jeffries," Witherspoon replied. "Today I've got Jake Randall's inquest. Then I thought I'd pop 'round to Davies Street and begin questioning some of the victim's business associates."

"Do you think your men will have any luck in finding out where Mr. Randall has been staying?" she asked casually. "You did mention that he'd left his lodgings on the first of the month."

"Oh, I'm sure we'll find out soon. Nivens said he was seen going into a hotel near the Strand last week." Witherspoon gave her his worldly smile. "From what I know of the victim, he enjoyed the finer things of life. He was probably staying at one of the larger hotels. You know my methods, Mrs. Jeffries. It's vitally important that we trace the man's movements prior to his death."

Mrs. Jeffries desperately wanted to ask him about the fifty thousand pounds, but she wasn't certain this was the right time. "Do you think Dr. Potter will be able to give you an estimate on the time of death?"

Witherspoon shrugged. "I suppose he'll try, but you know Potter, he's very cautious. Actually, though, we've had a spot of luck there."

"How so, sir?"

"Dr. Bosworth is also going to have a look at the victim," the inspector explained. "He's quite a bright chap, and I'm hoping to get a bit more information out of him."

"Isn't that a bit unusual, sir?" Mrs. Jeffries asked. She was delighted that the inspector had realized that young Bosworth had more brains in his little finger than Dr. Potter had in his entire head.

"A tad," he replied cautiously. "Actually, it's quite unofficial and there's no disrespect intended towards Dr. Potter. He's a fine physician. But Dr. Bosworth is so much more up-to-date on . . . well . . . medicine. Did you know he spent several years studying in the United States? The chap really likes looking at corpses, and from what I gather, the Americans have plenty of them."

"As usual, sir, you've got everything well in hand."

Mrs. Jeffries stood on the Lambeth Palace Road and stared at one of the several doors of St. Thomas's Hospital. The huge building had far too many entrances for her liking. It was only by a tedious process of elimination that she had determined this one was the most likely choice for her to catch her prey.

A blast of sharp March wind gusted off the river. She pulled her cloak tighter and hoped she wasn't on a fool's errand. Perhaps Dr. Bosworth wouldn't be able to tell her anything at all useful. But she felt she must try.

The door opened and several men dressed in heavy overcoats stepped outside. Right behind them, another single figure emerged. Mrs. Jeffries darted across the busy road. She caught up with Dr. Bosworth and fell into step with him. "Hello, Dr. Bosworth," she said cheerfully.

Surprised, he stared at her. "Hello," he replied cautiously.

She laughed gaily. "We have met before, sir. A few months ago, I accompanied a friend to the mortuary. You very kindly assisted us."

He smiled suddenly, his blue eyes lighting up in recognition. "Yes, of course. You were with that American lady. How very nice to see you again, Mrs. . . ."

"Jeffries."

"I'm so sorry," he mumbled, a blush creeping up his cheeks, "but I've an appalling memory for names."

"That's quite all right. Do you mind if I walk with you? One feels so much safer these days in the company of a strong, young man."

Bosworth straightened. "I'd be delighted to accompany you, Mrs. Jeffries. I'm just on my way over the bridge to the station."

"I'm on my way to Great George Street," she replied, "This is most kind of you, Doctor. Sometimes one just doesn't feel safe upon the streets anymore. Not like when I was a girl," she continued chattily, though actually, when she was younger, there was just as much crime and violence as there was now. "But of course, you know all about how unsafe the streets are, what with helping the police and all."

Bosworth's chest swelled. "Really, Mrs. Jeffries, I don't do all that much."

"Why, sir, I know that's not true. Inspector Witherspoon has mentioned several times how very brilliant you are."

"Inspector Witherspoon," he said, clearly puzzled.

"Yes, I'm his housekeeper. Had you forgotten?"

"Yes, yes, of course," He beamed with pleasure. "That's right, you work for the gentleman. I must say, it's very kind of him to mention me. But in all honesty, I haven't done all that much."

"You're much too modest, Doctor," she said, taking his arm as they started across Westminster Bridge. "The inspector tells me you're going to examine his latest victim. He's every confidence you'll be able to tell him far more than Dr. Potter. No disrespect meant for Dr. Potter, of course. But I understand you're rather an expert on bodies. You studied in the United States, I believe."

"Yes," he said enthusiastically. "I was in San Francisco, and I made the acquaintance of the most remarkable doctor. Chap named Spurgeon Smith. Quite a peculiar fellow, really. Spent more time with cadavers than he did with patients. But gracious, he was a fountainhead of knowledge."

Mrs. Jeffries slowed her pace. They were halfway across the bridge and she didn't want the doctor to arrive at the Westminster Bridge Station before he'd told her what he'd learned from examining Jake Randall's body. She listened patiently while he went on about his stay in the American west. Then she steered the conversation toward Randall.

Dr. Bosworth took the bait. His own footsteps slowed as he told her about his findings. "Of course, I realize it isn't admissible evidence in court," he continued, "but according to Dr. Smith, they used to dredge up bodies out of the San Francisco Bay all of the time. One can determine how long the body had been in the water by testing for various gases. Now, Dr. Potter wouldn't even hear of doing such a thing, but as he wasn't there and the test is relatively simple I took a chance and tested the victim anyway."

"How very commendable of you, sir." She smiled encouragingly. "And what were your conclusions?"

"I'd say the body was in the water for at least thirty-six hours. But of course, that's only an estimate. The tests aren't infallible. Dr. Smith says there are so many other factors that can affect decomposition."

Mrs. Jeffries glanced over the side of the bridge at the river. "But wouldn't the body have gone out on the tide?"

Bosworth chuckled. "Generally, yes. But the victim had a long flat bruise on his leg, like he'd been pinned beneath a piling or something. My conclusion is that he was killed very close to where he came up. It's a fairly well-populated stretch of river. The body was spotted literally as it floated to the surface."

"Did Mr. Randall drown, then?"

"Oh no. He was dead before he hit the water," Dr. Bosworth said cheerfully. He looked enormously pleased with himself. "The bullet killed him. A shot directly to the heart from a Colt forty-five will generally finish you straight off."

Stunned, Mrs. Jeffries stopped. She looked at him in amazement. "You mean you know what kind of gun was used?"

Bosworth shrugged modestly. "Oh yes. It's not admissible in one of our courts, of course. But I'd stake my life that Jake Randall was shot by a Colt forty-five. They call it the 'peacemaker' over in America. You know, Mrs. Jeffries, we don't see all that many bullet wounds here, but they do in America," he said wistfully. "There certainly isn't any shortage of murders over there. I'm sure Dr. Potter would tell me it's impossible to know. But believe me, after a year of working with Dr. Smith on the Bar-

bary Coast, I've seen enough entrance wounds to be able to identify half a dozen different kinds of guns."

"Gracious, Dr. Bosworth." Mrs. Jeffries was truly impressed. "Why on earth don't the police use your remarkable abilities?"

Bosworth sighed. "To be perfectly honest, it's my own fault that I haven't advanced further. You see, the only way to advance is to have important people as your patients."

"But surely you're a very good physician," she protested.

"Oh, I'm competent," he admitted, "but I don't much care for live patients. I'm afraid I'm a bit like my friend Dr. Smith. I much prefer the dead ones. They don't complain if you make a mistake, and of course, if you make a really dreadful mistake, you can't hurt them. They're already dead."

CHAPTER 3

Inspector Witherspoon and Constable Barnes waited patiently in the drawing room of the Cubberly home. The large, well-appointed room wasn't quite as nice as one's first impression suggested. The inspector squinted through his spectacles as he gazed at his surroundings. The crimson velvet curtains were badly frayed along the railing, the gold-leaf carpet was thin and worn in spots, and in the corners there was a layer of dust on the dark hardwood floors. "Bit odd, this place," he muttered softly.

"Yes, sir," Barnes agreed. He, too, was taking in the details of the room. "Beneath all the elegance, it's a bit tatty, isn't it? Not what you'd think the place would be like judgin' from the neighborhood. Did you notice the banister, sir? When the maid went up the stairs, it rattled every time she touched it."

Witherspoon hadn't noticed. He'd been too busy staring at the elderly, slovenly dressed woman who'd answered the door to take any notice of the staircase. Naturally, one didn't want to be judgmental, but in a home like this, one would have expected a neatly uniformed housemaid or butler to answer the door.

From behind them, they heard footsteps approaching. Witherspoon and Barnes both turned as a dark-haired man with mutton-chop whiskers entered the room. He stopped by the door and stared at them coldly out of the smallest blue eyes the inspector had ever seen.

"I take it you're the police?" he said.

"I'm Inspector Gerald Witherspoon and this is Constable Barnes." He held out his hand. "We're sorry to disturb you, but we're here to ask you a few questions."

"Yes, expected you would be. I'm John Cubberly." He hesitated for a moment before shaking the inspector's hand. He dropped it quickly. "You're here about Jake Randall?"

Witherspoon nodded. "When was the last time you saw Mr. Randall?"

Cubberly shrugged. "I'm not precisely sure of the date. I think it was a fortnight ago."

"We understand that you were one of the major investors in Mr. Randall's mining company, is that correct?" Witherspoon asked. He had a feeling this interview was going to be tedious. Mr. Cubberly had not asked them to sit down. In all fairness, he's not obliged to, the inspector thought. But really, it would be ever so much more comfortable if they could all have a seat.

"That's correct." Cubberly smiled slightly.

Drat, the inspector thought, this *is* going to be tedious. The man obviously wasn't going to volunteer anything. "You were expecting Mr. Randall here for a meeting on March the seventh, weren't you?"

"Yes. But he didn't come."

"I see." Witherspoon's stomach growled. Embarrassed, he began talking quickly. "What was the purpose of this meeting, Mr. Cubberly?"

"The purpose?" Cubberly repeated hesitantly. "Well, I suppose you could say we—by that I mean myself and the other stockholders—called the meeting because we'd heard some very alarming rumors concerning Mr. Randall."

"What kind of rumors?" Witherspoon desperately wanted a cup of tea. His throat was absolutely parched.

"We'd heard that Randall hadn't invested any of the money he'd raised in the mine." Cubberly turned and began to pace slowly back and forth between the two policemen and the marble fireplace. "Naturally, considering the amount of money we'd all put in, we became concerned. We asked Mr. Randall here to explain his actions, but as I've said, he didn't show up."

"And who are the other gentlemen who were scheduled to come that day?" Witherspoon already knew that information, but he'd just remembered something his housekeeper had once said. "Oh yes, sir," she'd said, "my late husband always made it a point never to tell people anything. He waited for them to tell him what he already knew. He claimed that was one of the ways he could tell if someone was lying."

"There were four of us. Myself, Rushton Benfield, Edward Dillingham, and Lester Hinkle. Together, we constitute the major investors in the company."

Witherspoon nodded. "I see. Could you tell me, sir, what did you and the others decide to do when Mr. Randall failed to keep his appointment?"

"Do?" Cubberly stopped pacing. "We didn't *do* anything. When he didn't show up, the others left as well. There wasn't much point in having a meeting unless Randall was here."

"I'm sorry, sir," the inspector said, "but I really don't understand that. By your own admission, you were concerned that Mr. Randall had stolen your money—"

"Stolen?" Cubberly interrupted. "We never accused him of stealing. We merely wanted him to explain the situation."

"Are you saying, sir, that you don't think he was stealing from you?" Constable Barnes asked quietly.

"We didn't know for sure," Cubberly snapped. "All we wanted was an explanation. You're making it sound like we'd already tried and convicted the man. That's not the case at all."

Witherspoon persisted; he wasn't sure what he was getting at, but he had the feeling it was important. "But surely, when Mr. Randall didn't show up as scheduled, you and the others reached some sort of decision."

"Well, we did think it might be prudent to contact the bank where the funds were being held," Cubberly admitted slowly.

"And what bank would that be, sir?" Witherspoon asked.

Cubberly stared at them for a moment before answering. "It's the London and San Francisco Bank on Old Broad Street. Randall chose it."

Witherspoon nodded. "Which one of you contacted the bank?"

"Rushton Benfield. He'd opened the account with Randall. That was one of our terms and conditions."

"Was the money there?" For once, Witherspoon was certain this was a pertinent question.

"I don't know." Cubberly shrugged as though the matter was of no importance. "Benfield hasn't called 'round to tell me."

"And you didn't think it important enough to contact him to find out?" Barnes asked incredulously.

"As a matter of fact, no." Cubberly resumed his pacing. "The mining venture isn't my only investment. I'm a very busy man. Naturally, I assumed that if Mr. Benfield found something amiss, he'd inform the rest of us. As he has not done so, then I think it's safe to assume that all the money is accounted for."

Witherspoon was confused, but determined not to let it show. He didn't wish to accuse Mr. Cubberly of lying, but really, the man must think the police were absolute fools if he expected them to believe he had so little interest in whether or not his money was safe!

"Now, sir"—Cubberly rubbed his hands together—"if you've no further questions—" He broke off as the door opened and a short, slender red-haired woman stepped inside. She paused in the doorway and stared at the two policemen.

Her eyes were a pale, clear brown and they slanted at the corners over a long, sharp nose and pointy chin. She reminded the inspector of an intelligent fox. She wore an elegant day dress of dark green and her thin hair was pulled back in a tight bun beneath a gray hair net.

Cubberly frowned at her. "What is it, Hilda?"

"I'm sorry, John," she replied. "I didn't realize you had anyone with you."

"Just the police," he said brusquely, "and they'll be gone in a few moments."

"I'm Hilda Cubberly," she announced. "Are you here about Jake Randall's murder?"

"Of course they're here about Randall," Cubberly said impatiently. "Why else would they be here? Now, what was it you wanted?"

Hilda Cubberly didn't seem offended by her husband's manner. "The new girl is here for the housemaid's position. You said you wanted to interview her."

"Tell her to wait," he ordered. "As I said, the police are almost ready to leave."

"I'm afraid we've a few more questions, sir," the inspector said.

"Well then, get on with them, man," Cubberly snapped. "I've already explained I'm very busy. Besides, I don't know what else I could possibly tell you. I haven't seen Jake Randall in two weeks."

"Really, John," Mrs. Cubberly interrupted irritably. "Have you forgotten? You saw him going into St. George's Baths on Buckingham Palace Road just last week. You told me about it when you got home." She turned to the inspector. "Honestly," she complained, "he's getting so absent-minded."

Cubberly hesitated and then smiled weakly. "Why yes, now that you mention it, I did see Randall. I'd forgotten."

Gracious, Witherspoon thought, Mrs. Cubberly has a rather sharp tongue.

Mrs. Cubberly gave a delicate, ladylike snort, as though she expected no better from a male. "If you gentlemen will excuse me, I must get back to the housekeeper's rooms. I'll bring the girl down in ten minutes," she called over her shoulder to her husband as she left the room.

"Did you speak with Mr. Randall when you saw him last week?" the inspector asked.

"No. I was in a hurry."

Witherspoon wondered what else he might have forgotten. But he couldn't see that Cubberly's forgetting to mention a small detail could have any bearing on the murder. "How did you and the others contact Mr. Randall? To get him to the meeting, I mean. Did someone go 'round personally and tell him he must be here?"

"We sent a note to his rooms."

"When?"

Cubberly stared at him suspiciously. "The day before the meeting."

"That would be on March the sixth?"

"Yes," he replied slowly. "I suppose that's right. Wait a moment, I've made a mistake. Benfield didn't take the note to his rooms, he took it to Randall's club. Yes, that's right. Randall had moved into a hotel by then. But we know he got the note. The porter at the club assured us he'd given it to him."

Witherspoon paused on the bottom step, took out his handkerchief and blew his nose.

Barnes clucked his tongue sympathetically. "Still got me cold, I see, sir."

"Yes, I'm afraid I'm going to have it forever. I say, Constable, what did you think of Mr. Cubberly?"

Barnes, who had the highest respect for Inspector Witherspoon, even if he was occasionally confused by his methods, answered honestly. "I think he was hidin' something, sir."

"I had that impression, too, Constable," the inspector replied as they started up Davies Street towards Chester Square. "And I must say, I didn't like the way he side-stepped that question about the note."

"You mean the way he suddenly remembered that the note couldn't have gone to Randall's rooms." Barnes chuckled. "He's a sly one. Almost stepped right into your trap."

Witherspoon wasn't aware he'd been setting a trap, but he didn't want his constable to know that. "Er, yes, well, clever is as clever does."

"Still, I suppose he couldn't have done it, not if he were home like he said he was." Barnes stopped and glanced back at the house. "Do you think I ought to nip back and have a word with the servants? It's no good asking Mrs. Cubberly to confirm he were home the rest of the day. A wife'll say anything her husband wants."

"I think we ought to do that tomorrow," Witherspoon said. "We'll interview the other shareholders before we begin verifying alibis. Have the uniformed lads come up with the name of Randall's hotel yet?"

"Not yet, sir. He wasn't stayin' at the one on the Strand. But we're still workin' on it. What did you think of Dr. Potter's evidence this morning?"

"I'm sure Dr. Potter did his best," Witherspoon replied, forcing himself to be fair. "But frankly, I do wish the man would be more precise in his opinions. The only thing he was certain about was that the man was dead. According to him, Randall could have been shot on the seventh, eighth or even the ninth of March. That's hardly helpful. I do hope young Dr. Bosworth will have more useful information for us."

"He will, sir. I told him we'd pop 'round to St. Thomas's late this afternoon. Is that all right with you, sir?"

"That'll be fine."

"Are we going to the bank now, sir?"

Witherspoon sighed. He had a long day ahead of him. Between spending the morning at the inquest and then dashing all the way over here to begin the interviews, he was exhausted. But he knew his duty. It was imperative that they confirm that the investment money was still in the bank. Then he had to interview the other three investors in the company. After that, there was Dr. Bosworth to see. His stomach growled again, reminding him of how hungry he was. A vision of roast beef and new potatoes popped into his head. Witherspoon licked his lips.

Then he remembered Mrs. Goodge's marrow toast and he shuddered. Surely the cook didn't mean to turn every meal into a pauper's feast? They came out onto Eccleston Street. The inspector spotted a tea shop on the corner next to the bank. His mouth watered and he quickened his steps. Perhaps they could pop into that tea shop for some sticky buns. The inspector dearly loved sticky buns. "We'll go to the bank after we finish the interviews this afternoon. I say, I could do with some tea, Constable," he announced. "I don't know about you, but I'm famished."

"He's a nice little dog," the housemaid said as she patted Fred gently. "Mr. Hinkle's got a dog, too, but he's so old and cranky he growls if you try and touch him. Not like your Fred 'ere."

Wiggins smiled at the lovely brown-eyed girl who was fussing over his dog. He was right proud of himself. He'd only been on the job, so to speak, for half an hour and already he'd met someone from the Hinkle household. And she was so pretty, too. "Uh, what kind of dog is it?"

"An old bulldog. His name's Albert." She straightened and shifted the basket she was carrying back onto her arms. "Well, I expect I'd better get crackin'. I've got to take this 'ere basket over to the church."

"Can I carry it for ya?" he asked. "I'm goin' that way myself."

"That's very nice of you," she replied shyly, "All right, if it's no trouble. It'd be nice to have some company. It's a long walk to St. Bartholomew's." She gave him her burden. "It's a poor basket. Mr. Hinkle sends food over to 'em every Friday."

"Is that who you work for?" Wiggins started slowly up the street.

"Yes, Mr. and Mrs. Lester Hinkle. I've been there three years, ever since I was fourteen." She fell into step next to Wiggins. Fred gave up trying to sniff the contents of the basket and trotted after them.

"Your Mr. Hinkle sounds like he's a good one to work for, then. I mean, 'is 'eart must be in the right place if he gives food to the poor."

"Oh, he's a nice man, he is. By the way, my name's Jane. Jane Malone."

"Pleased to meet you, Miss Malone," Wiggins said politely. He'd much rather spend his time finding out about Miss Malone than Lester Hinkle, but he knew he'd better have something to report when he got back to Upper Edmonton Gardens. Besides, he'd already come up with a right clever way of findin' out what he needed to know.

"Hinkle, Hinkle," he mumbled. "I say, isn't he the bloke that got coshed over the 'ead by that robber?"

"What you talkin' about?" Jane stopped and stared at him. Fred stopped, too, and had another sniff at the basket.

"I read about it in the papers," Wiggins continued. "The story were right on the front page. It said a feller got 'it on the 'ead by some robbers outside Victoria Station this past Monday. That'd be March the seventh. Was it your Mr. Hinkle?"

Jane laughed. "Nah, must be someone else." She looked at him curiously. "You read the papers, do you?"

"Every day," he said proudly. "But are you sure it weren't your Mr. Hinkle?"

Jane absently patted Fred on the head and started walking again. "I'm sure. Last Monday, my Mr. Hinkle was at a meeting over near Chester Square. I 'eard he and the missus talkin' about it when he come home that night."

"Oh." Wiggins tried to think what to ask next. "Well, maybe he got coshed after the meetin'?"

Jane cast him a curious glance. "No. He weren't nowhere near Victoria Station. I 'eard Mr. Hinkle tellin' Mrs. Hinkle that he'd spent the entire day chasin' about lookin' for some feller who never showed up. He didn't get home that night till past ten. I know, 'cause I let him in and he were right as rain. I'da noticed if he'd had his 'ead bashed in." She stopped abruptly and faced Wiggins. "Look 'ere, why are you askin' all these questions?"

Luty Belle Crookshank cocked her snow-white head to one side and regarded Mrs. Jeffries thoughtfully out of her bright black eyes. "You know, Hepzibah, you've been watchin' that door like you're expectin' the Queen herself to come sashayin' through it any minute."

"Have I really?" Mrs. Jeffries said innocently. She forced herself to smile calmly. She'd only made it back to the house herself moments before Luty Belle and Hatchet arrived for tea. Betsy had only just come in, Mrs. Goodge was in a foul mood because she'd found out nothing from any of her sources, and Wiggins and Smythe were nowhere to be seen. She wasn't worried about the footman's safety, but she was concerned he'd come flying in with Fred at his heels and give the game away. Luty Belle and Hatchet were trusted friends. Indeed, they'd helped out on two of the inspector's other cases. But Mrs. Jeffries didn't want to take advantage of the elderly American. And of course, there was her age.

"Yes," Luty said bluntly. "You have. What's wrong?"

"Nothing's really wrong," Mrs. Jeffries said. She helped herself to another tart. "I suppose I'm a bit concerned about Wiggins. He's so very fond of you. I'm surprised he isn't back yet."

"Not like the lad to be late for tea," Mrs. Goodge said darkly.

"He'll be here any minute," Betsy said cheerfully.

"Where is he?" Luty asked.

Unfortunately, they all spoke at once.

"He's gone to the butcher's," Mrs. Jeffries replied.

"He's walkin' the dog," Mrs. Goodge said.

"He's helpin' Smythe to wash down the carriage," Betsy said.

"I knew it." Luty banged her teacup down and glared at the three women. "You're up to something." She turned to her butler. "They's up to something, ain't they, Hatchet?"

Hatchet, a tall, dignified white-haired man, tilted his chin and studied each of them carefully. "Yes, madam, I believe you're correct. Mrs. Jeffries has indeed given the backdoor an unwarranted amount of attention. Mrs. Goodge has been most distracted, and even Miss Betsy has fidgeted about in her chair like a schoolgirl waiting for the teacher to leave the room. My guess, madam," he continued as he turned and stared at his employer, "is that they've embarked upon another murder investigation."

Mrs. Goodge gasped, Betsy flushed guiltily, and even Mrs. Jeffries was embarrassed.

"Now, Luty," the housekeeper began.

The backdoor burst open and Wiggins and Fred flew inside. "You'll never guess what I've found out. On the day of the murder, Lester Hinkle told his missus he's spent the whole day chasin' after—" He broke off and blushed crimson as he caught sight of Luty Belle and Hatchet.

"Aha." Luty jumped to her feet and placed her hands on her hips. "I told ya," she shouted.

"True, madam," Hatchet said. "You did. And I think it's most unsporting of them to not to let us in on it."

"Now, Luty," Mrs. Jeffries began again.

"Don't you 'now, Luty,' me," the elderly American snapped. "You know good and well that Hatchet and I like to help you investigate. I thought we was friends. I thought I could count on you."

"But of course we're friends," Mrs. Jeffries said quickly, "and we were going to tell you about the case. I was merely waiting until everyone was present."

Luty regarded her suspiciously. Then she glanced at Hatchet. One of his white patrician eyebrows was raised in disbelief. "What do ya think, Hatchet? Was they gonna tell us?"

The butler considered the matter. "Madam, I would never deign to consider that Mrs. Jeffries was capable of lying to us."

Luty snorted but sat back down. "I wouldn't like to think you was keepin' this from me 'cause of my age, Hepzibah."

"That was the furthest thing from my mind," Mrs. Jeffries replied. She hated lying, but obviously, she'd severely miscalculated how much being included meant to Luty. She wouldn't make that mistake again. "While we're waiting for Smythe to arrive, why don't I fill you in on all the details."

Smythe arrived fifteen minutes later. He cuffed Wiggins on the back, winked at Betsy, and smiled broadly at Luty. "I see you've let her in on it."

"But of course," Mrs. Jeffries said. "And now that you're here, we can all share what we've learned. Then Luty and Hatchet will be fully informed."

"Git off my foot, Fred." Luty shoved the hound off her feet, patted his head, and slipped him a bite of her cake. Fred gulped down the treat and butted her knees with his head.

"It's your own fault, madam," Hatchet pointed out. "You do keep slipping the animal bites."

"I only give the critter a little seedcake," Luty protested. "Can't stand to see a creature hungry. Afore any of you start, I've got a couple of questions. Exactly where was this silver mine?"

"Didn't I mention that?" Mrs. Jeffries said. "It's in Colorado."

"You told me that," Luty replied. "But does anyone know exactly where in Colorado?"

They all looked at one another. None of them knew.

"Is it important?" Mrs. Goodge asked.

"Well"—Luty drummed her fingers on the top of the table—"it could be. Why don't you see if you can find out exactly where this place is, and when you do, be sure and let me know."

"All right." Mrs. Jeffries didn't see that it mattered all that much. But she'd do as Luty requested. She had great respect for her intelligence. "Now, who would like to go first?"

"I've not got all that much," Betsy said glumly. "I tell ya, that Cubberly household must be the worst place in the world to work. I spent half the day hangin' about waitin' for a servant to come out and the only thing I saw was the inspector and Constable Barnes. They must lock their servants up."

"Don't be discouraged, Betsy," Mrs. Jeffries said kindly. "You tried your best and tomorrow is another day."

"Oh, I didn't let that stop me," the maid said. "When it were clear that I wasn't going to find someone from the household, I made the rounds of the local shops."

Mrs. Jeffries beamed in approval. Betsy was very good at prying information out of tight-lipped merchants and chatty shopgirls. "Excellent."

"Still didn't find out much. But I did learn that Mr. Cubberly is a right old miser, and he and Mrs. Cubberly have only been married two years."

"Hmmm," Mrs. Jeffries said thoughtfully. "I wonder if his miserliness is recent. If so, it could mean he was desperate for money."

Betsy shook her head. "I don't think so. From what I heard, he's always been tightfisted. He makes his servants pay for their tea and sugar every month. I heard that from a shop assistant that used to be sweet on one of the Cubberly maids. He even made the scullery maid repay him when she borrowed his wife's glycerine for her chapped hands. He wouldn't buy soft soap for his floors, he was always haggling with the butcher and the grocer over their bills, and Mrs. Cubberly complained to anyone that would listen that she hadn't had a new dress since she married him."

Luty snorted in disgust. "Sounds just like Jake Turtle."

"Who's he?" Wiggins asked.

"The biggest skinflint that ever lived," Luty said. "He kept the first dollar he ever made. His wife finally got so tired of livin' on beans and wild greens that she locked him out in the snow during a blizzard. Froze to death. He was clutchin' his purse right next to his heart when they found him the next day."

"Was his wife tried for murder?" Betsy asked.

Luty cackled. "Murder? Nah. Martha Tuttle claimed that Jake went outside on his own. Said he'd dropped a penny in the snow and wanted to find it. Her story was she went on to bed and didn't hear him bangin' on the door to git back inside. 'Course ol' Jake was such a miser, we half believed her."

They laughed, and even Hatchet cracked a smile.

"I reckon I'll go next," Mrs. Goodge announced. "Not that I've all that much to tell, and if you don't mind my saying so, it's the inspector's fault."

"Really, Mrs. Goodge—" Mrs. Jeffries began, but the cook cut her off.

"But it is his fault," she said stubbornly. "If he didn't have us cuttin' back every which way so he can save a few pennies, I'da had a much better day. One cup of tea is barely enough to wet someone's whistle. They won't talk if you don't feed them."

"What's she talkin' about?" Luty asked curiously.

"The inspector has asked all of us to decrease our household expenditure a bit, that's all," Mrs. Jeffries said soothingly. "Mrs. Goodge has merely had a less than successful day."

"I didn't find out anything," the cook wailed. She looked like she was going to burst into tears.

Mrs. Jeffries knew that Mrs. Goodge was more upset over her failure to learn anything useful than she was with the inspector's newest household management scheme.

"Don't distress yourself, Mrs. Goodge," she said sympathetically. "You know perfectly well you're absolutely brilliant at prying information out of your network of sources. But even the most brilliant of people occasionally have a bad day." She reached over and patted her friend's work-worn hands. "Tomorrow will be better. I'm sure that by this time tomorrow evening, you'll have learned more than the rest of us put together."

"Sure you will, Mrs. G," the coachman put in.

"Don't feel bad. I didn't learn much today either," Betsy added.

"You're better at findin' out things than you are at cookin'," Wiggins said. "And we all know what a great cook you are. Just give it another day or two. That's all you need do."

Mrs. Goodge sighed and hastily brushed at her eyes. "Got a piece of grit in my eye," she muttered. "All right, I'll try again tomorrow."

Mrs. Jeffries was deeply touched by the others. All of them had realized what was bothering Mrs. Goodge, and all of them had done their best to make her feel included, important and, most of all, needed. "I haven't had all that much success with my inquiries today either," she said. "However, I did have a chat with that nice Dr. Bosworth. You remember him, don't you, Luty? He works at St. Thomas's."

Luty nodded.

Mrs. Jeffries went on to tell them about Dr. Bosworth's contention that the victim had been killed on the evening of the seventh. "But the most interesting thing I learned was that Dr. Bosworth is almost certain that Jake Randall was shot with a Colt forty-five."

"How could he possibly be sure of such a thing?" Hatchet asked.

"That's what I asked him," Mrs. Jeffries said, "but as it turns out, Dr. Bosworth spent a lot of time in San Francisco working with a doctor there named Spurgeon Smith. As he put it, they have an awful lot more bodies with bullets in them than the English do. He's seen dozens of bullet wounds. Bosworth claims he can now identify half a dozen weapons just by the kind of wound they make entering the body. I don't know if what he's saying is correct or not, but it sounded quite possible to me."

"I reckon it's true," Luty muttered. "Stands to reason, don't it? Nell's bells, even I can tell the difference between a shotgun hole in someone's gut and one of them fancy little derringers."

"So that means that Jake Randall was shot with an American gun," Hatchet said.

Betsy, who didn't know all that much about firearms, asked, "Can you only get that gun in America?"

"I expect you kin git it in England," Luty replied. "But it's far more common over there than it is over here."

"Hmmph," Mrs. Goodge muttered. "Sounds to me like you found out a lot of useful information."

"Yes, but not about Edward Dillingham." Mrs. Jeffries sighed. "I drew a complete blank there. The only person who came out of the Dillingham house was an elderly gentleman. Quite well dressed. He was carrying a Bible. The butcher's boy told me he was Phineas Dillingham, Edward's father. As he hasn't anything to do with Jake Randall, I didn't bother following him." She glanced at Wiggins. "As you seem to have actually learned something useful, why don't you go next?"

Wiggins shrugged. "All I heard was that Lester Hinkle didn't come home from the meetin' on the seventh until around ten o'clock that evening. And when he come in, he told his missus that he's spent the day on a wild-goose chase. Said he'd been lookin' for someone."

"Jake Randall probably." Mrs. Jeffries straightened. "I wonder if he found him?"

"Jane didn't know that. All she overheard was him complainin' to Mrs. Hinkle that he'd been all over London and he was bloomin' tired."

"If he used the expression 'wild-goose chase,' then we can surmise that he was unsuccessful," Mrs. Jeffries mused.

"If he was lookin' for Randall," Luty pointed out.

"Really, madam," Hatchet interrupted. "Who else would Hinkle be looking for?"

"Rushton Benfield," Smythe said softly.

They all stared at him.

"Wait a minute," Wiggins protested. "I'm not through yet."

"Sorry," the coachman said. He sat back in his chair. "I'll wait my turn."

"Now, what else did you learn, Wiggins?" Mrs. Jeffries asked patiently.

The footman squirmed in his seat. "Well, not much, really. But Jane did tell me that Mr. Hinkle's been worried lately. And she thinks it's because he's got some money problems. She 'eard Mr. Hinkle tellin' Mrs. Hinkle that if they didn't get their 'ands on some money soon, they'd be ruined."

"Mr. Hinkle must have been frantic when Jake Randall didn't show up at the meeting," Mrs. Jeffries murmured. "Anything else?"

"No." Wiggins sighed, remembering Jane Malone. He'd done some fast talking when she'd demanded to know why he was asking so many questions, and he feared his answers hadn't been clever enough for her. She'd looked at him like she thought he was lying. She probably wouldn't want to see him again.

All of them turned and stared at Smythe. He cleared his throat. "Right then, I've learned a few things. First of all, let's not decide that Lester Hinkle were out lookin' for Jake Randall. He could've been lookin' for Rushton Benfield. According to one of his 'ousemaids—"

"Housemaid," Betsy interrupted. "You talked to a housemaid today?"

They all stared at her in surprise. Mrs. Jeffries sighed inwardly, wondering what was the matter now. She'd so hoped that Betsy and Smythe wouldn't be so very competitive on this murder.

The maid blushed. "I mean, that's a bit odd. Smythe usually talks to hansom drivers or butlers or street arabs to get his information."

The housekeeper fully expected the coachman to come back with some clever comment, but instead Smythe looked oddly pleased.

"This time I talked with a 'ousemaid," he said. "Nice girl she was, very pretty. Her name's Lydia Stivey."

"We don't need to know her bloomin' name," Betsy muttered. "Just get on with it."

Smythe grinned widely. "Accordin' to Lydia, Rushton Benfield left on the afternoon of March seventh for his meeting with the other shareholders. But he never come back. No one's seen 'ide nor 'air of the man."

CHAPTER 4

———— ◆◆◆ ————

"I say, my name's not going to be mentioned in the newspapers, is it?" Edward Dillingham asked anxiously.

"Er, I'm not really sure," Inspector Witherspoon replied. He could hardly assure the gentleman his name wouldn't be in the press. It simply wasn't a guarantee the police could give, not with so many enterprising and aggressive reporters snooping about. "This is a free country, Mr. Dillingham, and as such, we do have a free press."

"Well, it's rather important that I be kept out of it, you see." The tall, blond-haired man drummed his fingers on the top of the inspector's desk. "I mean, I've done my duty. I've come along here of my own free will because I was sure you'd want to speak with me. Not that I was all that familiar with Mr. Randall, of course. He was merely a business acquaintance."

"Yes, sir, we do appreciate your coming 'round," the inspector said.

"Actually, I didn't have to come here at all."

"We're aware of that, sir," Witherspoon said patiently. "Now, if you'll just answer a few simple questions, you can be on your way." His mind went utterly blank. For the life of him, he couldn't think of how to begin. To give himself time to gather his scattered thoughts, he stared at the pale spring sunshine streaming in through the small windowpanes of his office.

After several moments he heard Constable Barnes, who was sitting behind Dillingham in a chair by the door, clear his throat. Witherspoon pushed some papers to one side and straightened his spine. Best to plunge straight in, he thought.

"You are one of the major shareholders in the Randall and Watson Mining Company."

Dillingham nodded. "Yes, but that won't be in the papers, will it? I mean, I shouldn't want anyone to know about my involvement."

"Why not, sir?" the inspector asked curiously. "A silver mine is a perfectly respectable enterprise." Gracious, he thought, the man was acting like he'd been accused of running a white slavery ring.

"Yes, yes, of course it is. It's just that one doesn't like to have one's private business matters made public." Dillingham gave him a weak smile, shifted in his seat, and crossed his legs. "At least, not someone in my position."

"I quite understand, Mr. Dillingham," Witherspoon replied. "But we are investigating a murder."

"I know, Inspector," Dillingham said defensively. "That is why I've come. Please, go on with your questions."

"Do you have any idea where Jake Randall had been staying since he left his lodgings the first of this month?"

"Why would I know that?" Dillingham asked as he drummed his fingers on the top of the desk again. "The man wasn't a friend of mine, he was a business associate."

"Yes, but people frequently know their business associates' addresses."

"I do business with my grocer, Inspector." He uncrossed his legs and leaned back in his chair. "But I hardly know where he lives. Nor do I care. And that was my attitude towards Mr. Randall. I invested in his silver mine. I didn't see him socially."

Witherspoon wished the young man would stop fidgeting. "When was the last time you did see Mr. Randall?"

Dillingham's pale eyebrows drew together in thought. "Let's see, I'm not really sure. . . . I know. It was last week. I saw him walking in Hyde Park."

"Was he alone?"

"He was with a woman."

"Did you speak to him?"

"No," Dillingham stated. "I was in a hurry."

"Do you know who this woman was?" Witherspoon desperately hoped he did. He was tired of investigating a victim that no one seemed to know very well.

"Hardly." He gave a nervous high-pitched laugh, then stopped abruptly as the inspector continued to stare at him. "I mean, I didn't know the lady's name, but she did look awfully familiar."

"Familiar," the inspector repeated hopefully. "You mean you'd seen her before?"

"I shouldn't say that I'd seen her before," Dillingham said slowly. He leaned forward and gave the inspector a knowing smile. "It was more that I'd seen her kind before. Do you know what I mean?"

Witherspoon hadn't the faintest idea what the man was talking about. A person was either familiar because you'd seen them before or they were not. "No," he said honestly. "I'm afraid I don't."

Dillingham blinked and drew back. "Well, Jake was a bit of a ladies' man, if you get my drift. In the six months I've known him, I've seen him with several young women. They're always the same type. Small, blond and—" he coughed delicately—"a tad flashy."

Witherspoon was disappointed. Drat. Why couldn't people just say what they meant? "So you're saying that in your judgement, this woman wasn't well-known to the victim?"

"I'm not sure," he said hesitantly. "I mean, how could one possibly know such a thing?"

"I wouldn't expect you to be certain," the inspector replied, "but one does occasionally hear rumours or gossip. That sort of thing." He had no idea where this line of inquiry would lead, but perhaps it would lead somewhere.

"Actually, now that you mention it," Dillingham said brightly, "I have heard gossip—not that I ever really listen, of course. But still, one can't help what one hears."

"Of course. Now what was it that you'd heard about Mr. Randall?" Witherspoon's hopes soared. Finally, someone was going to tell him something useful about Jake Randall.

"Rumour has it that he's quite smitten with someone."

"Where did you hear this rumour, sir?" Barnes asked softly.

Dillingham jerked at the constable's words. He swiveled in his chair and stared at the man sitting by the door. "Oh, I'd forgotten you were back there. I don't quite remember where I heard about the girl."

"Do you know the woman's name?" the inspector asked.

"I'm afraid not." Dillingham shrugged.

Barnes looked up from his notebook. "Who would have been likely to know about Mr. Randall's personal life?"

"The only person who would really be in a position to know would be Rushton Benfield. But it's no good your asking him. He's gone."

"Maybe Benfield's been murdered, too," Mrs. Goodge said.

"Nah." Smythe shook his head. "Accordin' to Lydia, this in't the first time 'e's taken off. Rushton Benfield may be Sir Thaddeus Benfield's son, but 'e's not known for 'is good character. Seems like this in't the first time 'e's played fast and loose with someone else's money. Not that anyone ever proved anything against 'im, but Lydia claims there's people who cross the road when they see 'im comin'."

"But I thought it was Randall that was the crook," Luty said. "He's the one with a bullet in his heart."

Smythe shrugged his massive shoulders. "I told you, it didn't make much sense. You'd think if a man 'ad a reputation as bad as Benfield's, 'e couldn't raise enough money to buy a drink, let alone 'elp swindle people out of fifty thousand pounds. But that's exactly what 'e did. Benfield is the one that got everyone else to invest in the mine. 'E give these big fancy parties and introduced Jake Randall to the others."

Mrs. Jeffries gazed at Luty speculatively. "I think," she said slowly, "we've just found the perfect task for you and Hatchet."

Luty smiled brightly. "You want us to try and find Benfield?" she asked excitedly.

"That shouldn't be so difficult," Hatchet muttered.

"Partly," Mrs. Jeffries said. "But I don't want you to merely find the man, I also want you to find out why someone like him would form such a close association with a man like Jake Randall in the first place."

"Has anyone found out where Randall was stayin'?" Wiggins asked.

"No." The housekeeper frowned. "And that's also something we need to do. It's imperative not only that we locate his lodgings, but also that we find out as much as we can about him."

"That's not gonna be easy." Betsy shook her head. "It's not like we've got much to go on. We don't know where he was stayin', we don't know who he were with, and we don't know for sure why he was even killed."

"Precisely my point," Mrs. Jeffries said firmly. "I suddenly realized that until we learn more about the victim, we won't get anywhere. So let's not worry about what we don't know and concentrate on what we do know. Jake Randall was a close associate of Rushton Benfield."

"Who is now missin'," Mrs. Goodge pointed out.

"True. But even if he's missing, that shouldn't stop us learning what we can about him." Mrs. Jeffries looked directly at the cook. "Benfield is a member of a very prominent family. It should be easy for you to pick up quite a bit of information about him. Find out what his habits are, which club he belongs to, who his other friends might be."

Wiggins scratched his chin. "But I thought you said we should concentrate on learnin' about this Randall fella?"

"We will." The housekeeper smiled. "I think we'll find out all about Mr. Randall by finding out about Mr. Benfield."

"Birds of a feather flock together," Luty muttered. She gave Mrs. Jeffries an admiring glance. "I've got to hand it to ya, Hepzibah, that's right good thinkin'. Randall and Benfield had to meet somewhere, and they had to get to know each other well enough for Benfield to agree to front fer Randall in this here mining swindle."

"What do you want the rest of us to do?" Betsy asked.

"We need to find out who among the shareholders at that meeting might own a Colt forty-five," she said carefully. "And we also want to independently confirm that the meeting broke up early in the afternoon and that all the shareholders have alibis."

"You don't want much, do ya?" Smythe grinned. "So we've got to find out all we can about Randall and Benfield, locate Randall's hotel and see which stockholder owned a gun, is that it?"

"I know it sounds difficult," Mrs. Jeffries said firmly, "but I've complete faith in you. By the way, did you have any luck when you went to the river? Had anyone seen or heard anything?"

Smythe shook his head. "No. But then again, I weren't askin' the right questions. We weren't even sure what time the bloke was killed. Now that I know Randall was probably murdered close to where he floated up, and since we've narrowed down the time he was shot, I might be able to find somethin' out."

"Listen." Mrs. Goodge crossed her arms over her ample bosom. "Now, we all don't want to be runnin' about gettin' in each other's way, so I'll do as Mrs. Jeffries suggested and find out all I can about Benfield. I think Smythe and Wiggins ought to take on findin' Randall's lodgin's and Betsy would be best for checkin' up on the shareholders on the evenin' of March seventh. But it seems to me that Luty and Hatchet are the best ones for tryin' to find out who owned the gun. Luty's an American, and it's an American gun."

They all stared at her blankly.

The cook sighed loudly. "Don't you get it, Luty can pretend it's an old family heirloom or somethin' that she's tryin' to track down."

"That'd be kinda difficult," Luty said dryly. "The Peacemaker ain't been around long enough to qualify as anyone's heirloom. But I agree with ya about me tryin' to find the gun. I think that'll suit Hatchet and me jus' fine. 'Course, while we're at it, we'll try and find Benfield, too."

Mrs. Jeffries wasn't certain this was a particularly good idea. Luty had an inordinate fondness for firearms. She glanced at the bright peacock-blue muff the elderly American had in her lap. Hatchet caught her eye.

"Don't worry, Mrs. Jeffries," he said calmly. "Madam has left her own weapon at home today."

"I only carry it when I think I'm gonna need it," Luty said tartly.

"True, madam," Hatchet replied. "But your opinion and my opinion about when it is necessary to arm oneself are decidedly different. As I recall, you seemed to think it perfectly reasonable to take a weapon to Lady Fitzwaller's garden party last week."

"'Course I did," Luty agreed. "We had to drive over fifty miles to get there. Nobody back home would ever take off on the trail without takin' a gun of some kind."

"Agreed, madam," he said, "but I hardly think one needs to worry about bear attacks, rattlesnakes, or stagecoach robbers in Essex."

Luty snorted. "You'd be surprised. But that's neither here nor there. The point is, you and I'll have a sniff 'round for the gun."

"By two thirty, we realized that Randall wasn't coming," Lester Hinkle said calmly. He was a gray-haired portly gentleman with a ruddy complexion and anxious brown eyes. "The meeting was called for one o'clock, so it wasn't just a matter of him being a few moments late. When it became apparent he wasn't going to show, we all left."

"I see," the inspector said. He wished he could think of something else to ask. Both of the other shareholders had told him essentially the same thing. "Were you upset?"

"Upset." Hinkle smiled sadly. "Of course. Wouldn't you be if you thought you were losing a great deal of money? And not just your money, but other people's as well."

"Naturally. How did you meet Mr. Randall?" the inspector asked.

"Through Rushton Benfield." Hinkle sighed and turned to stare at the fire burning in the grate. "He introduced us last year."

"Were you one of the original investors in the mining operation?" Witherspoon thought that sounded quite good. "I understand this was the second time investment money was raised."

"That's correct," Hinkle said. He gazed around his study. "We were first approached six months ago. I invested over ten thousand pounds of my money in the venture at that time. Then, a few weeks ago, Benfield contacted me and claimed they needed more capital. Said the original estimates of the cost of equipment were underpriced. I wasn't happy about it, but I didn't want to lose my original investment, you see. So I came up with another ten thousand pounds. I also bought more shares for a group of smaller investors that I represented." He smiled bitterly. "That is what bothers me the most. I'm not a wealthy man, gentlemen," he said to Witherspoon and Barnes, "but I can weather a loss. The people who trusted me to look after their money, well, what can I say? I failed them and I'll never forgive myself."

Witherspoon felt a wave of sympathy wash over him. Poor man. "Was anyone other than the four of you gentlemen present during the meeting?"

"Only Mrs. Cubberly."

"Mrs. Cubberly sat in on the meeting?" Witherspoon was quite surprised.

"Not really, but she was sitting in the drawing room sewing, and we were right next door in the study. I daresay, tempers began to get a bit hot when we realized Jake wasn't coming. I expect we owe Mrs. Cubberly an apology. I must remember to do that. Language was used that shouldn't have been used in the presence of a lady."

"Where did you go after the meeting?" Constable Barnes asked.

Hinkle jerked his gaze away from the fire. "Home," he said quickly. "I went straight home to bed."

"Is there anyone who can confirm that?" the inspector asked.

"No." Hinkle got to his feet. "There isn't. My wife wasn't home that day. She was in the country visiting relatives."

"What about your servants, sir?" Barnes asked.

Hinkle looked confused. "Well, I suppose one of them heard me come in," he mumbled, "but I was so distressed, I went right up to my bedroom and lay down. I fell asleep and didn't wake up till late in the evening."

"So no one saw you come home?" Witherspoon thought that most odd. He glanced around the beautifully furnished study. The mahogany desk was polished to a bright gloss, the late sunlight sparkling through windows revealed not a speck of dust anywhere. The Hinkle home was large, elegant, and exquisitely furnished. When he and Barnes had arrived, a butler had let them inside. As they'd walked past the stairs he'd seen a tweeny polishing the carpet railings, and there'd been a parlor maid in the drawing room as they'd passed. This was obviously a large household. Yet Mr. Hinkle was claiming that no one saw him come home.

"Not that I'm aware of." Hinkle coughed. "I know that sounds odd. But it was past three when I came in. The servants were in the kitchen having their tea, my wife was gone, and as I said, I was most distraught. I went right up to my room and lay down."

Witherspoon stifled a sigh. This wasn't going well at all. So far he'd interviewed three men who knew the victim, yet he didn't think he'd learned anything at all useful. He pulled his watch out and glanced at the time. If he hurried, he and Constable Barnes could probably get over to the London and San Francisco Bank before it closed for the day. Drat, he should have done that right after lunch. But it had started to rain and the bank was some distance away. And there was still Dr. Bosworth to see before he went home for the evening. He rose to his feet and smiled politely at Lester Hinkle. "Thank you for your cooperation, sir."

By the time the inspector arrived home that evening, he was in a much better mood.

"I say, Mrs. Jeffries," he said to his housekeeper as she picked up the decanter of sherry, "I do believe I'd prefer a brandy tonight."

"Oh dear, sir," she said, "is the sherry not to your liking? Is there something wrong with it?"

"Oh no, no," he said quickly, not wanting to admit that he found the vile stuff undrinkable. "Not at all. But with this cold, well, brandy is so much more, more . . ."

"Medicinal," she finished. She turned so he wouldn't see her pleased smile and pulled out a bottle of brandy from beneath the cupboard. "How was your day, sir? Any progress on the case?"

"The day didn't start out particularly well, but I must say, it improved enormously late this afternoon."

Mrs. Jeffries handed him his brandy. "In what way, sir?"

"As you know, I spent the morning at the inquest." He paused and took a sip. "Well, you know how Dr. Potter is, the only thing he'd say for sure was that Jake Randall was dead."

She clucked her tongue in sympathy. "How very trying for you, sir. I suppose Dr. Potter wouldn't speculate as to the time of death?"

"Does he ever?" Witherspoon asked. "But not to worry, we got 'round old Potter. Constable Barnes and I had a word with young Dr. Bosworth. And he told us some very useful information. Very useful indeed."

As Mrs. Jeffries already knew what Dr. Bosworth had found, she kept her expression carefully blank. "Really, sir?"

"Oh indeed. Dr. Bosworth is certain Randall was killed on the evening of the seventh." The inspector frowned. "I'm not exactly sure how he knew this, something to do with the gases in the corpse." He shuddered delicately and took another sip from his glass. "But the most interesting thing was Bosworth is equally certain that Randall's wound was made with an American gun. One of those nasty firearms that are so very popular in the western part of the United States. Now, what is the name of it?"

"The Colt forty-five, sir?" she asked casually.

"Why yes, that's it."

Mrs. Jeffries patiently listened to the inspector as he told her the details of his day. She already knew much of the information, and it wasn't until they'd made their way into the dining room that he said something that made her ears tingle.

"The bank confirmed that Jake Randall had withdrawn the money on the morning of the seventh?" she repeated, staring at the inspector.

Witherspoon barely heard her question. He was too busy staring at his plate. "Er, Mrs. Jeffries, exactly what is this?"

"Hash," she said quickly. "Mrs. Goodge is quite proud of this dish, sir. It's most economical. Now, sir, what were you saying about the money?"

"Is there any potato to go with this uh . . . hash?" he asked hopefully.

Mrs. Jeffries turned to the sideboard and took down a covered bowl. Lifting the lid, she dumped the two tiny new potatoes onto the inspector's plate. "Mrs. Goodge says hash is so filling you don't need many vegetables to go with it," she announced. She knew she'd never get the inspector's mind back on the case until he was fed.

He glanced sadly at his plate, picked up his fork and tentatively took a bite of the ground meat. "Actually, this isn't too bad."

"I do hope you like it, sir," Mrs. Jeffries said.

What he'd like was some nice steak, but he could hardly complain. The cook was merely following his instructions.

"About the money, sir," Mrs. Jeffries prompted.

"Oh yes, the bank manager was most cooperative. It seems there are only two people who had access to the investment money. Jake Randall and Rushton Benfield." The inspector smiled. "And as I said, Randall withdrew it all the morning of the meeting."

"Goodness, sir," Mrs. Jeffries mused. "Do you think that means Randall had found out the other investors were getting suspicious of him?"

"Oh, I expect so, Mrs. Jeffries. And of course, things are so much clearer to me now. The money is gone and Randall is dead. I think, perhaps this case isn't going to be as difficult as I'd first thought."

Alarmed, Mrs. Jeffries stared at him. "What do you mean by that?"

"Randall's dead. Benfield and the money are missing." Witherspoon chewed eagerly. "Now, if one man is dead and the other is missing, there's really only one conclusion one can draw."

"Which is?"

"Benfield killed Randall and stole the money." Witherspoon smiled happily. "It's so very simple. Benfield found out Randall had taken the money, so he tracked him down, took the money for himself, and shot his partner."

"But, sir," Mrs. Jeffries said. "How could Benfield have done it? How did he know that Randall had withdrawn the money from the bank? And how did he find Randall? All the other stockholders claim that no one knew where Randall was staying."

"Perhaps they didn't know. But I bet Mr. Benfield did." The inspector shook his head. "Furthermore, the bank manager also told us that Rushton Benfield had been into the bank on that very same morning. The chief clerk had told him about Randall withdrawing the money. So you see, Benfield knew the money was gone. Oh no, Mrs. Jeffries. This is a very simple case. Benfield is missing and the money is missing. Find one and you find the other. Why, I'll turn this city upside down. I'll have blood-hounds looking for the man. I'll comb the darkest alleys and the most dangerous neighborhoods, but find Benfield, I will."

"I don't think it's fair," Betsy complained. She glanced pointedly at the clock on the mantel. "They promised they'd be back by half eight and they're not here."

"They're only two minutes late," Mrs. Goodge said as she placed a pot of cocoa on the table. "Go easy on the lads."

"Well, it weren't fair that they got to go out again and ask questions," the maid continued petulantly, "I've got to wait until the morning."

Mrs. Jeffries came in just as Betsy was speaking. "Now, you mustn't let that worry you," she said to the girl as she took her seat, "you'll have plenty of time for your own investigations tomorrow." She smiled at Mrs. Goodge. "Tonight's dinner was a success. Where on earth did you find that recipe?"

"The inspector liked it, did he?" the cook said innocently. Then she grinned. "I found the recipe in Mr. Francatelli's book. *A Plain Cookery Book for the Working Classes*. Had that one for years, but I've never used it much. But seein' as how the inspector got us all on this new house-hold management scheme, I'll have to see what else I can cook for him."

Remembering the inspector's expression as he'd doggedly ploughed through his dinner, Mrs. Jeffries nodded. "Oh, I think that's a very good idea."

From behind them they heard the door open. Fred was the first one into the room. Tail swishing madly, he bounded toward the table. "Hello, Fred," the cook muttered. "There's a nice bit of mutton over in your dish."

Smythe and Wiggins hurried toward the table and took their seats. "Sorry we're late," the footman said. "But Smythe's had the best bit of luck." Wiggins pulled a pair of gloves out of his pocket and slapped them on the table.

"What's that, then?" Betsy asked suspiciously.

"Rushton Benfield's gloves," Smythe announced casually. "I found the driver that picked him up on the day of the meetin'. That's why we're late. We were over near Chester Square."

"So you've found out something?" Mrs. Jeffries said. "Good, so have I." She then proceeded to tell them everything the inspector had told her.

"So you see," she finished, "the inspector is convinced that Rushton Benfield shot Randall and stole the money. He's going to be combing the city for the man. He even said he'd use bloodhounds, but I do think he was joking about that."

"What's 'e need bloodhounds for," Wiggins said earnestly, "'E can use Fred here. 'E's as good as any bloodhound." He reached down and patted the dog.

"Don't be daft, Wiggins," Smythe snapped impatiently. "Fred's a right good dog, but he ain't trained for trackin'. Besides, Mrs. Jeffries has already told us that the inspector was only joking. Now, I've got a lot to say—"

"Just a minute, 'ere," Wiggins interrupted. "I don't see that the inspector is so far off the mark. Why couldn't you use dogs to track someone? And just because Fred's no bloodhound, don't mean he couldn't do it."

Mrs. Jeffries was tired of wasting time. "Yes, Wiggins, I'm sure you're right. But why don't we discuss it later?"

"Right," Smythe agreed. "Let's get on with it. We went over to Chester Square, and I started askin' some of the hansom drivers a few questions. Didn't think I was goin' to learn anythin' 'cause no one could remember pickin' up a fare on the afternoon of the seventh."

"Maybe all the shareholders come in their own carriages," Betsy suggested.

"Nah, before I started on the drivers, I asked one of the street arabs that 'angs about that area if he'd seen any private carriages going to the Cubberly 'ouse last Monday. The boy said he seen hansoms going down Davies Street."

"There's a lad with a good memory," Mrs. Goodge muttered. "Did ya part with any money for that bit of information?"

"Don't be so suspicious, Mrs. Goodge," Smythe explained. He grinned. "The lad remembers 'cause he was runnin' an errand for someone on Davies Street 'imself."

"Go on, please," Mrs. Jeffries prompted. Really, she thought, all this competitiveness between them must stop.

"Anyhows, like I said, I decided to start lookin' for the drivers." He paused and poured himself a cup of cocoa. "Well, I didn't have no luck findin' the cabs that brought any of the three there before the meeting, but I did find two drivers that brought two of 'em back late that evening."

"What do you mean, brought them back?" Betsy asked. "No one said anything about them goin' back to the Cubberly house that night."

"They may not have said it," Smythe continued. "But that's what they did. All three of 'em. Everyone but Rushton Benfield returned to Davies Street around nine thirty that night."

"And I talked to the cabbie that picked Benfield up that afternoon," Wiggins interjected proudly. "That's where I got these gloves. Benfield was in such a rush he left them in the cab. Cost me a bit, too, I can tell you." Suddenly his eyes widened. "You know, I bet Fred 'ere could find that Benfield fellow." He grabbed the gloves and knelt down beside the table. "Come on, boy, take a good sniff now."

Fred trotted over and dutifully sniffed the gloves.

"Don't be such a fool, boy," Mrs. Goodge admonished. "That dog's no bloodhound. It takes years to train a dog to track someone."

"'E can do it, I tell you," Wiggins insisted. "That's right, boy, get the scent."

Fred jerked his head away from the gloves and looked at the footman.

"Leave off, Wiggins," Smythe commanded. "We've got a lot to talk about. Put them ruddy gloves down and pay attention."

"You all go on with your talkin', I'm not givin' up." He kept stuffing the gloves under the dog's nose. Poor Fred looked really confused by now. He'd sniff the gloves and then stare at Wiggins as though asking him what in the world he was supposed to do.

"Wiggins," Mrs. Jeffries said gently, "Smythe is right, we really must get on with this."

"I'm listenin'," Wiggins promised, "Just let me 'ave a few more minutes."

Betsy opened her mouth to protest as well, but Mrs. Jeffries raised her hand for silence. "Leave the boy be," she ordered quietly.

Suddenly they heard the knocker on the front door. Before any of them could move, Fred suddenly leapt for the stairs.

"'Ere, where you goin'," Wiggins yelped. But the dog ignored him and kept on going. He barked noisily as he went.

Smythe and Mrs. Jeffries joined in the chase.

They hurried up the stairs and down the hallway to the front door. The knocking was louder now. Fred arrived there first. He began scratching on the door and whining.

Mrs. Jeffries quickened her steps. She reached for the doorknob, but Smythe stopped her.

"Let me answer it," he said. "It's almost nine o'clock and we don't know who is out there."

Fred howled.

"Quiet, boy," Wiggins hissed as he grabbed the dog by the collar and pulled him back. But Fred broke off and rammed into the door again.

"Cor," Smythe whispered. "The animal's goin' mad." He shoved the dog out of his way and Wiggins grabbed him. He yanked the door open.

Constable Barnes and another gentleman were standing there.

"Good evening, Constable," Mrs. Jeffries said loudly. She had to shout. Fred had started barking again.

The man with Barnes took a step back. Even the constable regarded the barking animal uncertainly.

"Sorry to be disturbing you, Mrs. Jeffries," he said, never taking his gaze off Fred. "But I'd like to see the inspector. It's important."

Mrs. Jeffries had no doubt about that. "Certainly, Constable. Do please come in." She smiled at the thin, sandy-haired man standing next to him.

"This gentleman is Mr. Rushton Benfield," Barnes began.

From behind her, she heard a gasp.

"And he'd like to make a statement to the inspector."

"I say, is something wrong?" Witherspoon's voice came from the top of the staircase.

"Nothing's wrong, sir," Mrs. Jeffries called back. "But Constable Barnes is here. He's got Mr. Benfield with him. I believe they'd like to speak with you."

CHAPTER 5

———◦◦◦◦———

"I told you 'e could do it," Wiggins hissed at Smythe. He patted the dog approvingly. Fred bounced up and down a time or two, basking in his master's praise.

"'E didn't do nothing," Smythe whispered back.

Inspector Witherspoon came slowly down the stairs and into the hallway. He wore an old wool dressing gown over his clothes, his hair was mussed, and his feet were clad in slippers. Fred broke away from Wiggins and dashed over to greet him.

"Er, hello, boy," the inspector murmured, reaching down to scratch the animal behind his ears. He straightened and stared in confusion at the group of people standing by the front door. "Er, I say, did I hear correctly? Goodness, indeed I did. Constable Barnes is here and the gentleman with him is Rushton Benfield, I take it."

"Yes, sir." Mrs. Jeffries stepped forward. She decided she'd better take charge of the situation.

"I see," he replied. He glanced at Smythe and Wiggins. "Er, there does seem to be more than just Constable Barnes and Mr. Benfield, though. Is something wrong?"

"Smythe and Wiggins escorted me to the front door," Mrs. Jeffries explained. "We were downstairs having a cup of tea when we heard them knocking."

"We didn't think Mrs. Jeffries ought to be answerin' the door on her own," the coachman said quickly. "Not with it bein' after dark, sir. So Wiggins and I come up, too."

"Ah." The inspector smiled in approval. "Jolly decent of you, and you even had the presence of mind to bring Fred up as well. Good boy." He patted the dog again. "That's right, guard the household."

Constable Barnes cleared his throat. "Excuse me, sir, I didn't mean to intrude on your evenin', but Mr. Benfield here would like to talk to you. He come by the station right before I was leavin'. Knowin' how anxious you was to have a word with him, I took the liberty of bringin' him 'round."

Witherspoon blinked. "Yes, yes. Of course, Constable." He glanced at the man standing behind Barnes. "How do you do, Mr. Benfield."

Benfield nodded and looked nervously behind him at the open door.

"Would you like some tea brought up, sir?" Mrs. Jeffries inquired softly.

"That would be nice," he replied. "And some buns perhaps," he added, "if that wouldn't inconvenience anyone." The inspector realized he was quite hungry.

Mrs. Jeffries, Smythe, and Wiggins went down the hall towards the kitchen stairs. Fred stayed with the inspector.

As soon as they'd reached the kitchen, Wiggins grinned triumphantly. "I told you Fred could do it," he announced to Betsy and Mrs. Goodge.

"Do what?" Betsy asked. "And what's goin' on up there? We heard voices."

"Constable Barnes has brought Rushton Benfield here to talk to Inspector Witherspoon," Mrs. Jeffries explained.

"Benfield! Here?" Mrs. Goodge exclaimed.

"Yes, here. Now. Upstairs and talking his head off to the inspector," Mrs. Jeffries said. "Quick, Betsy, you know what to do."

"Right." The girl shot to her feet and started for the stairs. "Should I try the study?"

"No, they'll be in there. Use the dining room. I'll pick up what I can as I serve the tea, but mostly we'll be relying on you." She turned to the cook. "We'll need a pot of tea and some buns."

"What's she up to?" Wiggins asked, his gaze following Betsy as she disappeared up the stairs. He was depressed that no one else was as delighted with Fred's tracking ability as he was.

"She isn't goin' up to dust the chairs," Smythe snapped. "She's gonna be eavesdroppin' again."

Mrs. Goodge muttered mutinously as she gathered the tea things on the tray. She stalked to the cupboard and pulled out a cloth-covered plate.

"How did he know I had these baked? I was savin' them for tomorrow. Got lots of people droppin' by, and now I'll have to get up extra early and bake another batch."

She glanced up as she poured the boiling water into the pot. "What was you on about, Wiggins?"

"I was talkin' about Fred." The footman grinned from ear to ear. "He tracked that Benfield feller just like I told you he would."

The coachman rolled his eyes heavenward. "Don't be daft. Fred did no such thing. 'E run up the ruddy stairs 'cause 'e 'eard someone at the front door."

"Fred's never done it before," Wiggins insisted. "I tell you, he 'ad the scent. He were trackin'."

"Why don't we discuss this later?" Mrs. Jeffries said as she placed the sugar bowl on the tray. She gazed at Smythe. His brows were drawn together in a worried frown, and his eyes were glued to the stairs. "Don't worry about Betsy," she said. "She's smart enough not to get caught."

"Are you sure, Mrs. J?" Smythe gave her a long, hard stare. "The inspector's a kind man, but if 'e catches the girl, even 'e wouldn't put up with 'er spyin' when 'e was talkin' official police business. I don't want to see 'er lose 'er position."

"She won't lose her position," Mrs. Jeffries promised softly. "I give you my word."

He continued to stare at her for a long moment, then he grinned. "All right. Now, do you want me to 'ang about 'ere or go out and try to see if I can learn anythin' from the pubs near Waterloo Bridge?"

Mrs. Jeffries picked up the loaded tea tray. "Stay here. We don't know what Benfield is going to tell the inspector. Let's see what he has to say before we do anything. His information may lead us up a completely different avenue of inquiry."

"Maybe I should get up to the dinin' room, too," he said. "I might 'ear somethin' that needs action right quick."

Mrs. Jeffries thought about it. She shook her head No, it's too dangerous to have both of you hovering in there. At least if someone spots Betsy, she can always claim she's laying the table for breakfast."

Inspector Witherspoon couldn't help but notice Rushton Benfield's hand shaking as he lifted the teacup to his mouth. The man was slender, below average height, and had a weak chin and long nose. His attire, though of excellent cut and quality, was a mess. His black silk cravat was askew, two buttons were missing from his waistcoat, his shirt was wrinkled, and there was a long, dark stain on the lapel of his coat.

Inspector Witherspoon regarded him with a mixture of curiosity and despair. The man hardly looked the part of a murderer. Perhaps this case wasn't going to be as simple as he'd hoped. Drat. Rushton Benfield had seemed such a likely candidate as the killer. But unless he'd come here tonight to confess, and the inspector suspected that wasn't going to happen, then this case was just as muddled as it had been from the start.

"Mr. Benfield," he began hesitantly. He wasn't sure exactly what to ask the man.

"Inspector." Benfield put his cup down and reached for a bun. "I thank you for seeing me at such an unorthodox hour. But I had to talk to you about Jake Randall."

"Yes, I gathered that was why you came." Witherspoon wondered what was so urgent that it couldn't wait until the morning. But perhaps it would be best simply to let the fellow talk as he would. Obviously, Benfield had something to tell him. Something important. He decided to let the man have his say in his own good time. Besides, Benfield was stuffing that bun in his mouth like he hadn't eaten for days.

"I know I should have waited until tomorrow morning," Benfield mumbled around a mouthful of food. "But I couldn't stand another night of hiding, another night of constantly looking over my shoulder and wondering if they'd found me."

"If who found you?" Witherspoon asked. Fred plopped his head on the inspector's knees and stared at his roll.

"The killer, of course," Benfield exclaimed.

"Someone is trying to kill you?"

"Yes," Benfield said earnestly, his eyes darting to the door. "That's why I came here tonight. Whoever killed Jake Randall is going to kill me, too."

"Why should anyone want to kill you?"

"Why?" Benfield cried shrilly. He threw his hands out and gestured wildly. "Because they think I stole their bloody money, that's why. And I didn't. I didn't have a thing to do with that. That was all Randall's doing. But you can't expect a madman to be reasonable. You've got to give me protection, Inspector. You've got to."

Alarmed, Witherspoon stared at the agitated man. "We'll give you all the protection you need," he promised. And he meant it, too. The inspector knew his duty. Though sometimes, like tonight, he was a bit confused as to how to perform that duty. "Now please, calm yourself and sit down. Why don't you start at the beginning and tell us where you've been and why you're afraid."

Benfield closed his eyes and took a deep breath. "I'm sorry," he murmured. "I'm not myself."

"We understand, sir," Barnes said kindly. "Now, why don't you take a few minutes to pull yourself together? We already know about the meeting last week, and we've heard the rumours about Mr. Randall defrauding the investors out of their money. So why don't you tell us why you're so frightened? Take your time."

"All right, I'll start at the beginning. Last week, Lester Hinkle contacted me and told me that he'd heard from a source in America that none of our investment money had actually been put into the mine operations." He shook his head. "I was shocked, utterly shocked. I couldn't believe it was true."

"Why couldn't you believe it, sir?" Witherspoon asked. He broke his bun in two and gave half of it to the dog.

"Because I trusted Jake Randall. He may be a lot of things," Benfield said earnestly. "He certainly isn't a gentleman, but I didn't think he was an out-and-out thief." He paused and smiled bitterly. "I was wrong. But I didn't know it at the time. I assured the other investors that Randall would have a perfectly reasonable excuse for why the mine wasn't being operated, why there weren't miners being hired and equipment being purchased. Until Monday morning, I believed it myself."

Barnes glanced at the inspector and then asked, "What caused you to change your mind?"

"I went to the bank that morning, for another matter entirely. The chief clerk called me over. He was in a state. He kept asking me if there was something wrong with their service or if we were displeased. I told him no. They handled our business very well, and I asked him why he was so concerned." Benfield stopped and took another deep breath. "He told me that Mr. Randall had been in that very morning and withdrawn every penny from our account. Naturally, I told the clerk he'd made a mistake. Surely, Mr. Randall had merely transferred, via a letter of credit, the funds into the American branch of the bank. That's the way we'd done it before. But the clerk assured me that wasn't the case. Randall had made a flat-out cash withdrawal. Fifty thousand pounds! They'd had to open the vaults to pay him off."

"Excuse me," Witherspoon said, "but are you saying you weren't really concerned until you found out the money was gone? Surely, you must have been upset when you heard the rumours about the mine?"

"But they were only rumours," Benfield insisted. "And there could have been dozens of reasons why Jake hadn't started the mining operation."

"Really," Witherspoon said. "Such as?"

"It could have been the weather. The mine's in Colorado, in the Rocky Mountains. There's been one blizzard after another in that part of the world since last October. So naturally, I didn't panic until after I'd talked to the bank clerk."

"So you knew the money was gone when you arrived at Mr. Cubberly's house for the meeting with the other investors?" Witherspoon said. He found himself believing Benfield. They already knew that Benfield had been to the bank that day and learned the truth about the money being gone.

Benfield nodded. "Yes. I kept praying that Randall would show up. That he'd have a legitimate reason for his actions."

"Were the other investors unduly alarmed at that point?"

Benfield pursed his lips in thought. "Not exactly alarmed," he said, "but they were concerned."

"Only concerned, sir? One of them had already contacted the police," the inspector pointed out. "Mr. Hinkle asked Inspector Nivens to look into the matter for him."

"Hinkle's inquiry was very casual, I'm sure. The only reason he went to Nivens was because he knew the man. If he hadn't known a policeman, he wouldn't have brought the matter up at all."

Witherspoon wasn't sure he believed that. According to Nivens, Hinkle had been most upset. And it had been one of Hinkle's relations that had raised the alarm in the first place. "I see."

"At first the meeting was convivial," Benfield continued. "Everyone assumed that Jake would show up. They kept assuring one another that everything was all right, that it was just a mistake of some sort. John Cubberly insisted we all have a drink while we waited. He got out a bottle of whiskey and we started drinking to pass the time. But the minutes ticked by and Randall didn't come."

Witherspoon poured himself another cup of tea. "Did you tell the others about the money being gone?"

"Not at first. I didn't want them to panic. But by two o'clock, I realized Jake wasn't coming. So I told them about the money being withdrawn from the bank."

"And what was their reaction?"

"They were furious. They accused me of covering up for Jake. Said I'd known since I walked into the house that the money was gone and hadn't told them." Benfield's hands curled into fists. "By this time, they were all drunk. They'd been drinking steadily since half past one. Cubberly started ranting and raving about what he'd do when he got his hands on Randall, Hinkle kept moaning that he was ruined, and Dillingham was almost hysterical."

"And what did you do, sir?" Barnes asked.

"Me? I kept trying to reason with them, but it was no good. At about two-fifteen, I offered to try and find Jake. Dillingham immediately accused me of being in on the swindle with Randall. Said he'd go find him himself. The minute he spoke, everyone jumped on the idea of looking for Jake Randall."

"So all of you knew that Randall had moved out of his lodgings?" The inspector was quite proud of himself for thinking of that question.

"Randall hadn't made a secret of it," Benfield said. "Of course, looking back, I realize he very carefully never told us where he was staying."

"Then how did any of you know where to look for him?" Barnes asked.

"We didn't," Benfield said flatly. "But that didn't stop anyone. We all knew Jake's haunts and habits."

"So all of you decided to go out and look for the man? Is that correct?"

"No," Benfield said fiercely. "They went out looking for Randall. I left when John Cubberly started to get physically violent. He shoved me against a wall and said he'd kill me if I didn't tell him where Randall and the money were. Hinkle and Dillingham pulled him off. By this time, Mrs. Cubberly had come into the room and demanded to know what was going on. I took the opportunity to get out of there. I left so fast I almost knocked a maid down. And I've been in hiding ever since. I tell you, Inspector, one of those three men found Jake that day and killed him. Whoever did it is going to try and get me next."

"But why should they do that, sir?" Witherspoon was genuinely confused. "Presumably, if one of them killed Mr. Randall, they also got their hands on the missing money."

"But that's just it," Benfield moaned. "What if Jake didn't have it with him? You don't understand. They were screaming and yelling that I was in on it. If Jake didn't have that money on him when one of them caught up with him, then I'm a dead man."

"Why would you think Randall didn't have the money with him?" the inspector queried.

Benfield gave a short, harsh bark of laughter. "Because I know the bastard. He was a sly one. Thinking back, I realized he'd planned the whole thing all along. Take my word for it, the first thing he did when he withdrew that money on Monday morning was to hide it. He wasn't stupid enough to carry it around with him, not when he knew the game was up."

"How would Randall have found out the other investors were suspicious of him?" Witherspoon asked. "Did you tell him?"

"No, I haven't seen him since last week." Benfield scratched his chin. "I don't know how he found out. Hinkle was blabbing his suspicions all over town, though. Jake's got a lot of acquaintances. I'm sure he heard about it from one of them."

An hour later Mrs. Jeffries closed the door behind Constable Barnes and Rushton Benfield. She glanced over her shoulder and saw Betsy slipping out of the dining room. Nodding at the maid, she hurried into the study.

She stopped just inside the room. Inspector Witherspoon sat slumped in his chair, his gaze on the carpet and his expression glum. "Why, Inspector," she said, "whatever is wrong?"

He looked up at her. "What isn't wrong?" he said. "This case is getting more and more difficult. I don't think I'm any closer to solving it. I was sure that Rushton Benfield had murdered Randall and stolen the money." He sighed. "But I don't think that's what happened after all. According to Benfield, he's been in hiding since last Monday."

Mrs. Jeffries immediately grasped the implication of the inspector's words. "But sir," she said, "that doesn't sound right? According to Dr. Bosworth, Jake Randall wasn't killed until Monday evening at the earliest. It wasn't reported in the press until Thursday, so why would Mr. Benfield be in hiding? He couldn't have known Randall was dead until Thursday morning."

Witherspoon shook his head. "At that point, he wasn't hiding from the killer, he was hiding from the other investors. It seems they got most upset when he told them about Randall withdrawing their investment money from the bank. Benfield told me he decided to lay low for a day or two, to give their tempers time to cool off, but when he saw the newspapers on Thursday morning, he got genuinely frightened. He thinks one of the three of them did it. He's convinced that one of them found Randall and shot him." Witherspoon moaned. "I tell you, Mrs. Jeffries, it's all a terrible muddle. Now I've got three suspects and no clues. If Benfield's story is correct, any one of them could have murdered Randall. According to him, the other shareholders were so furious about the money, they decided to go and look for Jake Randall when he didn't show up for the meeting. If Benfield's telling the truth, that means all three of them were lying in their statements to me."

"Now, now, sir." She clucked her tongue sympathetically. "You mustn't get discouraged. It's late and you're tired. But come the morning, you'll be refreshed and ready to take on the hunt."

"Hmmm." Witherspoon absently patted Fred on the head. "I hope you're right. Actually, I'm not precisely sure what to do next—"

"Come now, sir." She laughed. "You're teasing me again. I know precisely what you'll do and so do you."

"I do?" He looked at her hopefully.

"Of course you do, and just to prove to you that I'm finally learning your methods, I'll tell you."

"Oh, please do."

"You'll go back to the Cubberlys, of course! If Cubberly, Hinkle, and Dillingham went out to look for Randall, they probably agreed to meet back at the Cubberly home sometime that day to compare notes. Obviously, if one of them found him, the others would want to know about it." She laughed again. "You see, sir. I'm onto you. I know how you like to pretend you're totally in the dark as to what do next, and then you like to surprise us all by coming up with something absolutely brilliant." She paused and beamed at him.

Her words cheered him enormously. Witherspoon sat up straight and lifted his chin. Come to think of it, he told himself, he was jolly good at solving murders. Perhaps it didn't matter that he hadn't quite figured out *how* he solved them. "I wouldn't say I was brilliant," he tried to say modestly. "But as it happens, you're absolutely right. Naturally, it had struck me that if they went out looking for Randall, they'd probably agreed to come back to the Cubberly residence sometime that day." His eyebrows drew together, and he got to his feet. "Now the thing is, I really must find out if indeed they did come back that day. And more importantly, which one of them found Jake Randall."

"And I presume you'll be looking for the gun?"

"Oh, I don't think there's much point in that, Mrs. Jeffries."

"Why ever not?"

Witherspoon smiled confidentially. "Randall was murdered by the river. Obviously, no one would be stupid enough to hang on to the murder weapon, not when they could so easily chuck it into the Thames."

Mrs. Jeffries sighed and glanced at the sleepy figures around the table. All of them were dead tired. Betsy's eyes were half-closed against the bright spring sunshine coming in through the window, Mrs. Goodge's chin was propped on her hand, Wiggins was rubbing the sleep out of his eyes, and Smythe was hunched over a cup of tea.

They'd been up very late. They'd spent a good hour listening to Betsy and Mrs. Jeffries tell what they'd learned. Then they'd spent another hour arguing over what it all meant.

"What do we do next?" Betsy asked halfheartedly. "Seems to me the inspector's doin' all right on this case on his own. We certainly haven't been much help."

"That's not precisely true," Mrs. Jeffries said.

"Oh yes, it is," Mrs. Goodge declared. "So far the only thing we've found out before the inspector was that they all come back to the house late that night."

Mrs. Jeffries thought she really ought to argue the point, but she couldn't. It was true. So far they hadn't learned anything useful. Still, she wasn't going to let them give up. "Nevertheless," she declared stoutly, "you must all buck up. We've a lot to do today." She turned her gaze to the coachman. "Smythe, you must continue talking to the hansom drivers near Chester Square."

"What good will that do? Already I found two of the drivers that brung 'em back that night, and I didn't find out anythin'. Findin' the third one won't help any. We still won't be any closer to figurin' out who shot the bloke."

"We won't know that until you try," Mrs. Jeffries said stoutly. Really, it wasn't like them to be so very down in the mouth. "You can find out where all the men were picked up that evening. See if any of them came from the vicinity of Waterloo Bridge. And after that, try going back to the bridge again. As you said yesterday, now that we've established the place and time of the murder, you may have better luck."

"All right," Smythe said tiredly. "But I don't think it'll do much good."

"You're doing better than I am," Mrs. Goodge grumbled. "I haven't had hardly anyone through this kitchen that's even heard of any of the suspects, let alone known any gossip about them."

"Well, at least I've found out that Fred's a good trackin' dog," Wiggins declared.

"Yoo-hoo, anyone home?" Luty's voice came from the back passage.

"We're right here, Luty," Mrs. Jeffries called out.

A moment later Luty and Hatchet emerged into the kitchen. "Good mornin', everyone. Lovely day, isn't it?" She stopped near the table. "For land's sake, you've all got faces longer than an undertaker's apron. What's wrong?"

"We're not doin' too well with our inquiries," Smythe volunteered.

"We're not findin' out much of anythin'," Mrs. Goodge grumbled.

"Oh, feelin' sorry for yourselves, huh?" Luty flounced into an empty chair. Hatchet bowed formally and took the one next to her. "Well, nell's bells, that's okay," she continued. "We all got a right to feel sorry fer ourselves once in a while."

"It's not really a case of self-pity," Mrs. Jeffries explained. "We're all a bit tired, too. Rushton Benfield was here last night." She went on to bring Luty and Hatchet up to date on everything they knew. "So the point is, we're not really certain what to do next."

"I know what you should do next," Luty declared.

They all stared at her.

"You can figure out a way to get your inspector to have a word with Zita Brown."

"Who's that?" Wiggins asked.

Luty grinned. "John Cubberly's housekeeper. Me and Hatchet had quite a nice chat with her last evenin', didn't we, Hatchet?"

"Yes, madam, we did." He shuddered.

Luty laughed. "Hatchet's got his nose out of joint 'cause we spent the evenin' at a tavern. Zita Brown talks more when ya wet her whistle."

"Hmmph," Hatchet snorted in derision. "I would hardly call that particular establishment a tavern. The place was disgusting. Utterly filthy. It was filled with the most disreputable band of people I've ever seen. For once, I was glad that madam had her gun with her."

"The place wasn't very nice," Luty admitted. "But I've seen worse. Still, you ain't interested in hearing about the gin swillers at the White Rose. Let me tell ya what Zita told us. It'll make your hair curl."

The air of apathy around the table abruptly vanished.

"First of all, I know who owned the gun that killed Randall." Luty paused dramatically.

"Please, madam." Hatchet sighed. "Do get on with it."

Luty shot her butler a disgruntled frown. "Oh, all right. You won't, even give a body a chance to build up to a good story. John Cubberly owns a Colt forty-five."

Mrs. Jeffries gazed at the elderly American with admiration. "Gracious, that's excellent, Luty. How on earth did you find that out?"

"Let me tell ya what else I heard first," she answered. "Otherwise Hatchet here will have a hissy fit."

"I've never had a 'hissy fit,' whatever that is, in my entire life," the butler mumbled. "But do, please, finish your story. We can fill them in on the nefarious details later."

"Not only does Cubberly own the gun," Luty continued. "But he was wavin' it around and threatenin' to kill Randall with it, too."

"Why didn't Benfield tell the inspector that Cubberly had a gun?"

"I ain't sure." Luty shrugged. "But let me finish before you start askin' questions. There's more. Zita said she was standin' in the kitchen washin' out some tea towels when all of a sudden the maid come runnin' in like the hounds of hell was after her. Zita asked the girl what was wrong, and the girl said that Mr. Cubberly was wavin' a gun around and threatenin' to shoot someone. Before Zita could stop her, she'd grabbed her coat and run out the backdoor." She paused and laughed. "Poor girl, she ain't been back since. Accordin' to Zita, though, that ain't the first time someone had run off from that household and not come back. Seems they was always losin' servants."

"Did Zita Brown actually see the gun?" Mrs. Jeffries asked.

"Yup." Luty nodded. "Saw it with her own eyes. She said she stood there fer a few minutes wonderin' what she ought to do when she heard footsteps in the front hall. Zita went up and had a look. Cubberly and the other two were strugglin' into their coats. She watched them stagger out the front door, then she went upstairs and stuck her head into the drawing room. That was when she saw the gun. It were layin' in plain sight."

"Bloomin' Ada," Smythe exclaimed. "If it were still there when those three went out lookin' for Randall, then none of them could 'ave shot the bloke."

"Maybe one of them came back and got it?" Betsy suggested.

"Maybe," Luty replied. "Maybe not. There's no way to know fer sure. Right after that, Mrs. Cubberly started yellin' fer the maid. Zita told her the girl had gone and went back to the kitchen. Said Mrs. Cubberly was right put out about it."

"All right, then." Smythe regarded Luty speculatively. "Tell us 'ow you got the woman to talk."

Hatchet snorted again. Luty ignored him "That were' easy." She withdrew her gun from her muff and laid it on the table. Everyone except Hatchet stared at the weapon. "It's a Colt forty-five," Luty explained. "I took it with me yesterday evening. When I got to the Cubberly house, I went 'round to the kitchen door and told Zita Brown I'd heard there was a gun in their house. Told her it was the mate to this one and that I'd pay a right good price to git it fer myself. Told her I was a collector."

Wiggins frowned. "I don't understand. Why should this Zita Brown have anything to do with Mr. Cubberly's gun?"

"She shouldn't," Smythe replied. He looked at Luty with grudging admiration. "What Luty was doin' was lettin' the woman think she'd be willin' to pay to get the gun for her collection."

Wiggins was truly shocked. His eyes grew round as saucers. "You mean, you wanted her to steal if for you?"

Hatchet snickered. Luty had the grace to look embarrassed. "I wouldn'a really bought the danged thing," she said defensively. "But I had to come up with some story to find out who of 'em owned a Colt. It didn't take more'n two minutes of talkin' to the woman to figure out that she drank like a danged fish and that she'd tell ya anything ya wanted to know as long as you kept pourin' gin down her throat. So we took her to her local waterin' hole and let her talk her head off. And it worked, too."

"Indeed it did, Luty," Mrs. Jeffries said. She wasn't sure she approved of Luty's methods, but then again, she was in no position to be judgmental. She'd bent the truth herself a time or two when she was ferreting information out of someone.

Luty picked her gun up. "Nice, ain't it?" she muttered as she ran her hands over the handle.

"Really, madam," Hatchet said. "I think you ought to put that thing away before someone gets hurt."

"Quit yer fussin'," she said, making no move to put the gun away. "Do ya think I'm a fool? The gun's not loaded."

"I say." Witherspoon's voice floated down from the stairwell. "Hello. Is anyone home?" They froze as they heard his footsteps clambering down the stairs.

Luty hastily tried to stuff the gun back into her muff, but the barrel got caught in the loop of a tassel.

The inspector came into the kitchen. "Oh, I am sorry to disturb your tea break," he began. He stopped, his expression surprised when he saw Luty Belle and Hatchet. "I say, it's so very nice to see you again. Do forgive the intrusion, but I was wondering if there were any of those buns left. Constable Barnes and I were so close I thought I'd pop in and have one with a cup of tea."

"There are plenty of buns left," Mrs. Jeffries said as she leapt to her feet.

But she was too late: Witherspoon had spotted the gun in Luty's lap. "I say, is that a . . . a . . ."

"Gun," Luty finished. She grinned at him. "Yep, it's a Colt forty-five. You know, the strangest thing has happened. Hepzibah tells me you think a gun like this was used to shoot that Randall feller. I read about it in the newspapers—took kinda a special interest, on account of him bein' a countryman of mine." She glanced at Mrs. Jeffries.

The housekeeper nodded slightly and hoped that Luty knew what she was doing.

"Er, yes," the inspector said uncertainly. "We think he may have been shot with a weapon like yours. But that's not the sort of information we want spread around."

"Don't worry, Hatchet and I can keep our traps shut," Luty assured him. "But what I'm tryin' to tell ya is I think I might have run across some information that might help ya. I don't know if you know it, but I'm a gun collector."

"Er, no. I didn't."

"Been collectin' them fer years, but that's neither here nor there."

Mrs. Jeffries held her breath.

Luty smiled confidently. "The point is, Inspector, us collectors are always on the lookout for addin' one or two good pieces to our collection. Now, there ain't that many guns like this in London." She held the weapon up and Witherspoon stepped back a pace. "And this one's got a scratch on the handle. Here, have a look and you'll see what I mean."

"Oh, that's all right." Guns made the inspector very nervous.

"Anyways, I had my sources puttin' feelers out tryin' to find me a Colt for my collection so I could get shut of this one. I want my collection to be as perfect as I can get it. Well, I run across the name of a man who might have one for sale."

"Really?" Witherspoon wished she would get to the point. He was dying for a cup of tea and a bun.

"Really." Luty grinned. "And after talkin' to Hepzibah here, I suddenly realized it was a name you might be interested in."

Witherspoon forgot about his stomach. "Who is it?"

"John Cubberly. I believe he's one of the people involved with that murder you're investigatin'."

CHAPTER 6

Constable Barnes hurried to keep up with the inspector. "You say you heard that Mr. Cubberly had a gun from this American friend of yours?"

"She's really more a friend of Mrs. Jeffries, my housekeeper," Witherspoon replied as they turned the corner onto Davies Street. "Rather eccentric woman. But I like her. I'm not so sure I like her pastime, though. Whoever heard of collecting guns!" He clucked his tongue in disapproval "These Americans do the oddest things. But as I said, she'd heard through one of her sources that John Cubberly bought a Colt forty-five from a dealer last spring. Goodness knows why, but he did. Mrs. Crookshank, who, of course, knew nothing of our investigation, happened to mention Mr. Cubberly's name to my housekeeper, who immediately informed her that she ought to have a word with me."

"Bit of a coincidence," Barnes muttered. They'd reached the gate to the Cubberly house.

"True," Witherspoon agreed. "But then coincidences happen all the time." He pushed the wrought-iron gate open and stepped onto the paving stones. "That's why they're called coincidences."

Barnes shot his inspector a startled look and followed him up to the door. "Do you think Cubberly will admit to ownin' it?"

"I certainly hope so. You know, one does get so tired of people who think they can pull the wool over our eyes. I must say, I think his not mentioning the gun earlier puts a very black mark against him. Leads one to believe Cubberly's got something to hide." Witherspoon banged the knocker against the door. "We'll get the truth this time, Constable. Even if we have to question the servants again."

Barnes smiled cynically. "There aren't any servants, sir. At least none that I've seen, exceptin' that old harridan who calls herself a house-keeper." He clamped his mouth shut as the door cracked open and a pair of suspicious brown eyes stared out at him.

"Oh, it's you again." A fat, gray-haired woman wearing a dirty apron over a black dress grudgingly opened the door.

"Hello, Mrs. Brown," Constable Barnes said politely.

She ignored his greeting. "I suppose you want to see 'im?"

"We'd like to have a word with Mr. Cubberly, please," the inspector replied.

"'E's in the study." She jerked her head down the hall and stepped back to let them pass.

Witherspoon noticed a strong scent of spirits as he passed the woman. He wondered why on earth a respectable businessman like John Cubberly would have such slovenly household staff.

Mrs. Cubberly stepped out of the drawing room as they walked down the hall. She stared at them coolly, her chin tilted to one side. She didn't appear to be surprised to see them.

"Good day, Mrs. Cubberly," Witherspoon said. "We're sorry to disturb you, but we'd like a word with your husband."

"What about?" Her voice was as cool as her expression.

Startled by the blunt question, Witherspoon blinked. "Why, our investigation, of course."

She continued to stare at him as though she were deciding whether or not to comply with his request. Then she raised her hand and waved at the drawing room. "Go in and sit down," she ordered brusquely. "My husband is in the study, I'll get him."

"There's no need for that," a voice said from behind them. "I'm right here." John Cubberly, a frown on his face, came down the hallway and stopped in the door. He glanced uneasily at the police and then turned to his wife. "This doesn't concern you, Hilda. Why don't you go upstairs?"

"Just a moment," the inspector said. "I would like to have a word with Mrs. Cubberly, if you don't mind." He hadn't a clue what he'd ask the woman, but her behavior was so peculiar he decided he really should ask her something.

"I do mind," Cubberly replied. "Presumably you're here about Randall's murder. My wife has nothing to do with my business affairs. She barely knew the man."

"It's all right, John," Mrs. Cubberly said. "I'll answer their questions." Ignoring her husband's frown of displeasure, she turned and walked back into the drawing room.

The three men followed her. Barnes, who apparently didn't think he was going to be invited to sit down, took the initiative and headed for one of the matching armchairs next to the fireplace. As soon as he was seated, he whipped out his notebook and then looked inquiringly at his boss. Witherspoon followed his example and sat down next to him, the leather creaking as he settled himself. The Cubberlys sat rigidly on the faded velvet settee.

The inspector decided to get right to the point. "Mr. Cubberly, we have it on good authority that you own a gun."

Cubberly gaped at them, his small eyes widening in shock. "Rubbish," he replied, recovering quickly. "I've no idea where you heard such nonsense, but I assure you—"

Mrs. Cubberly interrupted. "Many people own guns, Inspector."

"For God's sake, Hilda," Cubberly snapped, glaring at his wife. "Do be quiet and let me handle this."

"I was merely pointing out a fact," she replied tartly.

"Thank you, Mrs. Cubberly," the inspector replied. "We're aware of the fact that many people in London possess firearms. The question is, does your husband?"

"There's no need to be impertinent," Mrs. Cubberly reprimanded.

Cubberly said quickly, "I'll admit that I do own a weapon."

"You don't have to tell them anything, John," she said. "They've no right to come here asking their silly questions. You've told them everything you know."

"Hilda, please," he pleaded. "Let me take care of this."

"Let you take care of this!" She snorted.

Cubberly clamped his lips together in a flat, grim line.

Witherspoon cringed inwardly. He was dreadfully embarrassed. Arresting people for murder was one thing, but watching a domestic disagreement was quite another kettle of fish. He didn't like it at all. But he knew his duty. "Where is your gun now, sir?"

Cubberly closed his eyes briefly and took a long, deep breath of air. "It's locked in the drawer of my desk."

"What kind of weapon is it, sir?" Barnes asked.

"A Colt forty-five." Cubberly's voice was barely audible.

"You realize, sir," Witherspoon said seriously, "that is the same kind of weapon we believe Jake Randall was murdered with."

"How on earth could you possibly know what kind of gun the man was killed with?" Mrs. Cubberly charged.

"How we know is completely irrelevant," the inspector replied. He wasn't about to tell her that they only had Dr. Bosworth's word for the kind of gun that had been used in Randall's murder and that it wasn't admissible as evidence. "Could you please fetch the gun? We do, of course, need to examine it."

Cubberly didn't seem to hear him; he was staring at the carpet.

"This is absurd," Hilda Cubberly snapped. "We don't have to show you anything unless you've a warrant."

Gracious, the inspector thought. Mrs. Cubberly certainly seemed well informed about the law. And she was determined to protect her husband.

"Actually, madam, I believe you do." Witherspoon wished he'd paid a bit more attention to all those lectures and notices about Judge's Rules. He wasn't sure whether she had to show him the weapon or not. After all, they had allowed him into the house without a warrant. For a moment the inspector racked his brain, trying to remember Justice Hawkins's foreword to the Police Code. That had explained everything about those tedious rules. And they were so very complex.

Goodness, how on earth was anybody supposed to remember every little detail? It wasn't as if he hadn't read them—he had. Five years ago. Drat. Judge's Rules. He really must make a point of reading them again. It would be so very helpful in a situation like this.

"No disrespect intended, Mrs. Cubberly," Barnes said, "but the inspector's right. Your husband's already admitted he owns a gun. Now you don't have to show us, but we've a right to station a man here or to detain the both of you at the police station while we do get a warrant."

"Oh, all right," Cubberly said, his tone resigned. He turned and smiled weakly at his wife, his expression unexpectedly tender. "Hilda, dear, stop worrying. I know you think you're protecting me, but I've nothing to hide," he told her softly. "I haven't done anything wrong. The gun's safely locked in my desk."

He got up and left the room. Witherspoon and Barnes followed him into the study.

The inspector stood beside a dusty table and absently took off his spectacles. He watched Cubberly take a small gold key off his watch fob. Sitting his spectacles down, he stepped closer to the desk.

Cubberly inserted the key into a locked drawer. His hands were steady as he pulled it out. He looked inside and gasped. "Oh, my God," he said, his expression stunned.

Barnes edged Cubberly out of the way, glanced inside and looked at the inspector. "There's no gun here, sir," he said.

"But this is impossible," Cubberly muttered. Wild-eyed and pale, he shook his head in disbelief. "It's got to be here, I put it here myself. But it's gone. The bloody thing is gone."

"This is very serious, Mr. Cubberly," Witherspoon stated. "Very serious, indeed."

"When was the last time you saw the weapon, sir?" Barnes asked.

"I . . . I . . . I'm not sure," Cubberly said weakly.

"But you just admitted you locked it in there yourself," the constable continued, his voice hardening in suspicion.

"That's because I had to have put it away," Cubberly cried, "The drawer is always locked, and I'm the only one with the key."

"Was it Monday, the day of the meeting?" Witherspoon asked. "Was that when you locked the gun away? Was that the last time you saw it? We know that you and the other investors were furious when Jake Randall didn't show up for the meeting. We know that you went looking for him. Did you take the gun with you?"

"Of course I didn't take it with me."

"Are you sure, sir?" the inspector pressed.

"I'm bloody certain," Cubberly yelled. "Who told you we went looking for Randall that day?"

"Never mind how we acquired that information," Barnes put in. "Just answer the inspector's questions. And while you're at it, we'd like to know where you went that afternoon."

Witherspoon suddenly remembered his conversation with his housekeeper. "And we'd also like to know when you all came back here, please."

"They left here at half past two and they returned that evening at half past nine," Hilda Cubberly said. She was standing in the doorway. "Furthermore, any of them could have taken that gun. John left it lying here in plain sight."

"Hilda," Cubberly whimpered. "Are you trying to put a noose around my neck?"

"Don't be ridiculous," she said bluntly, "I'm trying to save you. My husband had the gun out that day. Everyone saw it. I did, the housekeeper did, the maid saw it, the other shareholders. Anyone could have taken it."

"It was probably that damned girl," Cubberly cried.

"What girl?" Barnes asked suspiciously.

Cubberly turned to his wife, his expression beseeching. "Tell them, Hilda, tell them how the maid disappeared without a word. In the middle of the day."

"Excuse me, Mr. Cubberly," Witherspoon interjected, "but what has your maid got to do with a missing gun?"

"What's she got to do with it?" he replied, his voice trembling. "It's bloody obvious what happened. She saw the gun, waited till the room was empty and then snatched it up. She probably planned to sell it."

Witherspoon thought that sounded a bit farfetched. He'd noticed that when trouble brewed, people of Mr. Cubberly's station always tried to blame a servant. But really, this was a bit too much. Yet he was duty bound to look into it. "What's the girl's name?"

"Lottie Grainger," Mrs. Cubberly replied.

"That would explain why she left so suddenly," Cubberly added hastily. "It's so obvious. You'd best start looking for her right away. I'm sure she stole the gun."

"What would she want with a weapon, sir?" Barnes asked wearily. From the tone of his voice, the inspector was fairly certain the constable had come to the same conclusion as he himself.

"I've already told you," Cubberly said impatiently, "She wants to sell it. A Colt forty-five is quite valuable, you know. And of course, her sort think nothing of stealing."

The constable's eyebrow's rose. "Her sort, sir?"

"What my husband means is that she was completely untrained," Mrs. Cubberly explained. "She comes from the East End. Her references weren't very good. I only took her on because I felt sorry for her. She'd only worked for us for a few months. She'd previously worked for some actress. But my husband is right—she did disappear that day. Left without a word. You can verify that by talking with our housekeeper."

Witherspoon tried to keep everything straight, but it was getting difficult. And he still had so many more questions he needed to ask. He didn't think for one minute that the maid had stolen the gun. But he didn't know for sure. There was always the possibility that the Cubberlys were telling the truth. What if the maid really had taken the gun? That would probably mean it wasn't the weapon that had killed Jake Randall. But if the gun was left lying out for anyone to see, someone else could have taken it. Drat.

By the time Witherspoon and Barnes left the Cubberly residence a half hour later, the inspector's stomach was growling and his head hurt.

Barnes hailed a hansom cab, gave the driver the address, and they climbed inside. "Do you think he was tellin' the truth, sir?" he asked the inspector.

"I've no idea, Constable, no idea at all. But I do know, if that gun was lying about, any one of them could have nipped back and taken it." He sighed. "Mrs. Cubberly's admitted anyone could have gained entrance to the house. She was upstairs lying down, and her room is at the back. The housekeeper had gone down to the kitchen and the front door was unlocked. Really, you'd think people would have more sense than that, leaving a loaded weapon out where any fool could get his hands on it."

"They were drunk."

"True," Witherspoon mused. "But Mrs. Cubberly wasn't. She should have made sure the gun was put away."

"But she didn't. Silly woman, took to her bed with a headache."

"That's understandable, Constable," the inspector said. "She told us she was dreadfully upset. First her husband acting like a madman and then finding out the maid had run off. We'd better send some lads over to the East End to see if they can find this young woman . . . what was her name again?"

"Lottie Grainger." Barnes sighed deeply. "We can send 'em over there, but the chances of us findin' this girl are pretty slim. Especially if she don't want to be found."

"But why wouldn't she want to be found?"

"It's been my experience, sir," Barnes explained, "that there's lots of people that don't think of the police as friends. Especially them from that part of London. But that doesn't mean she's a thief. When she saw Cubberly wavin' that gun around, she probably got scared and ran."

"Yes, I think I know what you mean. But we've got to try. That's not to say that I believe Cubberly's accusation. From the sound of it, three drunken men and a loaded gun, I've no doubt you're right and she ran because she was frightened." Witherspoon pursed his lips and frowned. "We've no evidence she even knew Jake Randall. So why would she want to shoot him?"

"Well, we do have Mrs. Cubberly's statement that she caught the girl makin' eyes at Randall once when he was round there," Barnes said thoughtfully. "But I don't put much store by that. Jake Randall sounds like the kind of man who'd flirt with any pretty lass who crossed his path. And the girl bein' a thief is just a tad too convenient, if you get my meanin', sir."

"Hmmm, I'm afraid I do." Witherspoon's stomach roared. Embarrassed, he shuffled his feet on the bottom of the cab to try to cover the noise.

"'Course, we don't know it was Cubberly's gun that was used to kill Randall," Barnes continued.

"I've a feeling it was," Witherspoon said. He firmly quashed his earlier doubts. "How many weapons of that sort are there in London? There can't be all that many." He rubbed the bridge of his nose and tried to think. "It all fits, Constable," he announced.

"What does, sir?"

"Whoever took the gun must be the killer." The inspector was suddenly sure of it.

They had independent confirmation that the weapon hadn't been in John Cubberly's possession when he left the house that day. Therefore, Witherspoon reasoned, someone else could have taken it *or* Cubberly could have come back and gotten the Colt himself.

"If we believe their story, sir," Barnes pointed out. "We've only the Cubberlys' word that the gun was left lying in the drawing room."

"The housekeeper confirmed it. Said she'd poked her nose into the room after the maid had gone running out of the kitchen."

"Yes, but I'm wonderin' about that. Seems to me Zita Brown is the type to say anything the Cubberlys want her to. She don't want to lose her position."

Witherspoon thought Barnes had a point. The Cubberlys were hardly the most benevolent of employers. But then again, from the looks of the housekeeper, she wasn't the most competent of servants either.

Grrr . . . He grimaced as another embarrassing sound erupted into the confines of the quiet cab. Unfortunately, they were stopped in traffic, and the horrid noises from his stomach were perfectly audible.

"Sounds like you're hungry, Inspector," Barnes said cheerfully. He glanced out the window. "We're right close to your house, sir. Why don't I drop you off for a bite of lunch? I'll nip on down to the station and get the lads off to the East End. I'll also get them started on checkin' Cubberly's whereabouts on the afternoon of the murder. Not that I think we'll have much luck there, but you never know."

"Oh no, that won't be necessary," the inspector protested. He thought longingly of the police canteen. Visions of pork pies, steak-and-kidney pudding, and sausage and chips floated into his head. He licked his lips. "The canteen will do for me."

"Come now, sir," the constable said. "You don't want to be eatin' that greasy muck when you can have a nice hot meal in your own home."

Witherspoon shuddered at the thought of the meals he'd had at home lately. But he didn't wish to appear ungracious. "That's quite all right, Constable. Dropping me off is too much trouble. I don't want to delay your inquiries."

"Not a bit of it, sir," Barnes assured him. He rapped sharply on the roof and stuck his head out again. "Turn up the next street," he ordered the driver, "and cut on over to Upper Edmonton Gardens."

Mrs. Goodge grinned from ear to ear when Mrs. Jeffries hurried into the kitchen after lunch. "Did the inspector enjoy his meal, then?"

"He didn't eat much of it," Mrs. Jeffries said innocently. "When he left here, he was muttering something about the police canteen."

"Good. A few more days of this and maybe we can get back to our usual way of doing things." Her smile faded and she flushed guiltily. "Did he eat anything at all?"

"He had a few bites of mutton and some mint sauce."

"I don't like feedin' the poor man such wretched meals, Mrs. Jeffries. My conscience is startin' to bother me over it."

"Don't worry, Mrs. Goodge," the housekeeper assured her. "The inspector isn't really suffering. Besides, I do believe this is the only way we can make our point. The inspector isn't in any real financial danger. Some of his investments aren't doing as well as they used to, but that's no reason to stop enjoying life entirely." She glanced around the empty kitchen. "When are the others coming? I've so much to tell them."

"Smythe and Wiggins are upstairs washin' up, and Betsy's not back yet. Should we wait for her?"

"No, we don't have time," Mrs. Jeffries was aware of a vague sense of unease with this case. Despite everything she'd learned from the inspector at lunch, they were still no closer to a solution. She hoped that the others had something to report. Something that made sense, something that would give her the one piece of the puzzle that would make the rest of it fall into place.

She turned at the sound of heavy footsteps coming down the kitchen stairs. Smythe appeared first, with Wiggins right on his heels.

The coachman took his customary place at the table. "Isn't Betsy back yet?"

"Not yet," Mrs. Goodge replied. "And Mrs. Jeffries said we can't wait. If she comes back this afternoon, I'll catch her up on everythin'."

"What do you mean 'if.' Of course she'll be back," Smythe interjected.

"Don't snap my head off, man." The cook shot him an impatient frown. "I didn't say she wouldn't. I'm only sayin' I'll tell her everything, so there's no reason we can't get on with it now. I've found out a few things," the cook said proudly. "And seein' as we're behind on this case, we'd best get crackin'."

Smythe looked like he was going to protest, so Mrs. Jeffries intervened. "Mrs. Goodge is right," she said firmly. She smiled confidently at the coachman. "We had best get on with it. Wiggins, would you like to sit down?"

The footman had wandered over to the sideboard. "What's 'appened to Fred's bone?" he asked as he moved to the table.

"I gave it to the inspector," Mrs. Goodge said, her voice defensive. "And it weren't a bone. It was a decent piece of mutton."

"But you were savin' that for Fred," Wiggins protested. "You told me so this mornin'." Fred, who'd followed him over to the table, raised his head at the mention of his name.

"I know what I told you, but I changed my mind. I've got some nice stew bones for Fred," the cook snapped. "Now, please, let's stop ditherin' about and let me have my say."

Everyone stared at her.

Mrs. Goodge took a deep breath. "Well, I don't know if it has anything to do with Randall's murder, but I've found out that Mr. and Mrs. Cubberly weren't exactly a match made in heaven. And both Hinkle and Dillingham had money trouble."

"Goodness, you have been busy."

"We've got to catch up," the cook said seriously. "I got up at half past four this mornin' to do my bakin'. I've had half of London through this kitchen today and fed 'em good, too. Like I told you, if you feed people, they talk."

Smythe sighed impatiently, but kept his mouth shut.

"Tell me about Cubberly first," Mrs. Jeffries commanded. So far, he was the most likely suspect.

"I couldn't find out much about his past, so I don't know, if he had any connection with Jake Randall before he invested in his silver mine, but I did hear that he married Hilda Cubberly for her money."

Smythe smiled cynically. "Half of London marries for money."

Mrs. Jeffries hid her disappointment well. If Hilda Cubberly had been found with a bullet in her chest, then the information would have been useful.

"Yes, but the reason Mrs. Cubberly married Mr. Cubberly is what's interestin'," Mrs. Goodge continued. "She did it to keep her father from leavin' all his wealth to charity. The butcher's boy has a sister who used to work for Eammon Enright—that's Hilda's father. He said there was a right old dust-up when John Cubberly was courtin' Hilda. Hilda didn't want to marry him. Didn't want to marry anybody, from what I heard. But Mr. Enright, who was in poor health and gettin' older, wanted to see her married and settled. He told her if she didn't accept John Cubberly's proposal, she wouldn't get nothing. As it is, he left John control of all of Hilda's money."

"That was rather unfortunate," Mrs. Jeffries said dryly. "John Cubberly doesn't seem to be doing all that well with his wife's inheritance."

"Oh yes, he is," Mrs. Goodge countered. "Not that you can tell it by the way the Cubberlys live. He's a right miser. Now Hinkle's not a miser, but he's not much of a businessman either. He's lost more money the last two years than any of us'll see in a lifetime. His creditors are pressin' him, too."

"And Dillingham," Mrs. Jeffries prompted. "What kind of trouble was he having?" This information was indeed very useful. If two out of the three suspects were desperate for money, that would explain Randall's murder. Providing, of course, that Jake Randall had the money with him when whoever killed him caught up with him.

Mrs. Goodge laughed. "Oh, Dillingham don't have the kind of money trouble that Hinkle's got. There's no real creditors on him, least not the respectable kind. But he does have a straitlaced old Methodist as a father."

"What's that got to do with money trouble?" Wiggins asked.

"Edward Dillingham likes to gamble." The cook winked slyly. He needs the money he invested in Randall's silver mine to pay off his gaming debts. His creditors may not be respectable, but they're pressin' him for payment. Losing money in business is one thing. The old man probably wouldn't get too angry about that, but he isn't going to want to pay off his boy's gamblin' debts."

Mrs. Jeffries looked thoughtful. "I wonder why Dillingham invested his money in a silver mine if he owed money elsewhere?"

"He didn't owe no one at that time. He'd been doin' pretty good at his gamin' until he hit a run of bad luck a few months ago," Mrs. Goodge explained. "He's twenty thousand pounds in debt. His father thinks gamblin's a sin. If he finds out about his son, he'll toss him out on his ear. And you'll never guess who it was that introduced Dillingham to his first card game neither."

Smythe gave her an exasperated glance. "Well, who was it, then?"

"Rushton Benfield." Mrs. Goodge smiled triumphantly.

"Does Dillingham owe Benfield money?" Mrs. Jeffries asked quickly.

The cook's smile faded. "I don't know. But I'll keep on diggin'. It may take a day or two to find out."

"What else did you learn about Benfield?" Smythe asked.

"Not much more than what you told us before," Mrs. Goodge admitted. "But like I said, I'm still workin' on it. Give me a day or two."

Mrs. Jeffries nodded in satisfaction. The cook's information did provide a motive for at least two of the three men who'd been looking for Jake Randall that afternoon. Unfortunately, it didn't provide a motive for John Cubberly. If Hilda Cubberly had brought money into their marriage, then he was the only one of the three that wasn't desperate to get his investment back, from the murdered man. "You've done an excellent job, Mrs. Goodge." She turned to the men. "Do either of you have anything to report?"

Smythe yawned. "Not much. No luck gettin' anythin' more out of the cabbies and no one near the bridge heard or saw anythin'."

"Oh dear." Mrs. Jeffries smiled sympathetically. "Perhaps you ought to try a different approach."

"Let me keep workin' on them hansom drivers," Smythe said. "Whoever shot Randall didn't walk to Waterloo Bridge that night." He snorted. "Toffs never walk anywhere, so someone had to take 'im."

"'E could 'ave taken the train," Wiggins suggested. "The station's right close."

"I don't think whoever did it took the bloomin' train." Smythe clamped his mouth shut and glared down at the tabletop. A moment later he looked up and smiled sheepishly. "Sorry, but I hate to give up."

Mrs. Jeffries stared at him closely. Something was bothering the coachman. Something about this case. "Well," she said cheerfully, "I don't blame you. I, too, hate giving up. Furthermore, I may have some information that can help you."

She went on to tell them everything she'd learned from the inspector over lunch. "So you see," she finished, "Cubberly admitted the three of them left the house at around half past two and shared a hansom cab to their various destinations."

"Where did they get out at?" Smythe asked sharply.

"Unfortunately, Cubberly got out first. He wasn't sure where the others were going. Either that or he was too drunk to remember. All he knows is his assignment was to go to the Strand. It seems Mr. Randall was fond of the theatre. He used to hang about in the district. Cubberly was going to have a look around that area, check the pubs and the hotels and talk to a few of Randall's associates. He'd been known to be well acquainted with several young women from the district. Actresses, I believe."

"Maybe I'd better have a run over there," the coachman mused.

"I think that would be a very good idea. We want to confirm Mr. Cubberly's movements, if we can. And remember, he was quite drunk," Mrs. Jeffries emphasized. "I'm sure someone will remember him."

"Too bad he wasn't able to tell us where the other two went," Mrs. Goodge said.

"We should have that information by tonight," Mrs. Jeffries replied. "The inspector is interviewing Dillingham and Hinkle this afternoon. But there's something else we must do as well. I think it's imperative that we find Lottie Grainger."

"The maid that run off?" Wiggins said. "But why? She heard the old boy wavin' a gun around, got scared and left. What's she got to do with Randall's murder?"

"Probably nothing," Mrs. Jeffries agreed. "But remember, if she saw Cubberly waving that gun around, as you put it, then she was close enough

to the drawing room to hear and perhaps even see everything that happened during the meeting. I want to know exactly what went on that day.
We've only Cubberly's word to the inspector about what was said and
done. There could be a great deal more."

Smythe propped his chin on his hand. "Did the inspector talk to the
Cubberly housekeeper?"

"He spoke with her, but I'm not sure he asked the right questions,"
Mrs. Jeffries said bluntly. "But don't worry. He left his spectacles at the
Cubberly house."

"And you're goin' back this afternoon to get 'em." The coachman
grinned. "Good. Maybe you can get the woman to tell us somethin' really
useful."

"Should I get over to the East End, then?" Wiggins asked. "I could
take Fred with me. I bet if I could find somethin' that belonged to this
Lottie Grainger, Fred could track her. Just like he did that Benfield feller."

Mrs. Goodge moaned, Smythe rolled his eyes heavenward, and even
Mrs. Jeffries felt a rush of impatience. "No, Wiggins," she said firmly. "I
think it best if you leave Fred here this afternoon. By the way, you haven't
told us what you've learned today."

Wiggins blushed. "That's because it weren't all that much. I hung
about Davies Street and talked to a few people. But no one said anythin'
useful. Exceptin', I don't think that Mrs. Cubberly is as mean a miser as
Mr. Cubberly."

"And why not?"

"'Cause she's a woman," Smythe interrupted. "Wiggins never likes to
think ill of a female."

"That's not true," the footman protested. "It's just that Agnes told me
that she saw Mrs. Cubberly giving some money to a beggar boy once. So
if she was givin' away money, she can't be as mean as her husband."

"Who is Agnes?" Mrs. Jeffries asked gently. She didn't want Wiggins
feeling that his contribution was worth less than the others'. But really,
there were times when she wished that Wiggins wasn't so easily distracted
by a pretty face.

"She's a housemaid at the Brompton place," Wiggins said. "Across the
street from the Cubberlys. She's a right nice girl, told me lots about the
Cubberlys. Said they had a 'ard time keepin' servants."

"We already know that, boy," Mrs. Goodge snapped. She pushed
away from the table and stood up. "Now, if it's all the same to the rest of

you, you'd best be gettin' on. I've got a coal delivery comin' in a few minutes, and I want to see what he can tell me."

They all stood up. Wiggins and Fred wandered off, and Mrs. Goodge disappeared down the hall toward the pantry. Mrs. Jeffries turned to Smythe. "Is something bothering you?"

His heavy dark brows drew together. "I guess you could say that," he muttered. "It's probably nothing, not the sort of thing I want to talk about in front of the others."

"Will you tell me?"

"'Course I will." He gave her a smile that didn't reach his eyes. "But you've got to promise you won't think I'm goin' daft or gettin' fanciful."

CHAPTER 7

Mrs. Jeffries stared at Smythe in surprise. He was the most practical of men. Despite his rough appearance and his heavily accented speech, he was very intelligent. She smiled kindly. "I don't think there is anything you could tell me that I would't take seriously. Regardless of how far-fetched your ideas about this case may seem, I want to hear them."

He relaxed visibly, "Fair enough, Mrs. J. But I warn ya, I don't have any real reason for what I'm thinkin'. It's just a feelin' I've got." He broke off and gave her a sheepish grin. "Cor, I sound like one of them daft old women who sit around stirrin' up 'erbs and potions and claimin' they've got the sight."

"You have excellent instincts, Smythe," Mrs. Jeffries assured him. "You should learn to trust them. Now tell me what's on your mind."

"It's the case, Mrs. J." He brushed a lock of hair off his forehead. "I've got a feelin' we're goin' about it all wrong. Do you know what I mean?"

She knew exactly what he meant. She had the same feeling herself. In all honesty, she had to admit that so far they'd learned practically nothing of any real value. Or at least if they had, she couldn't make sense of it yet. And time was running out.

"Yes, I do," she admitted. "And I'm not sure what to do to remedy the situation. What do you think we're doing wrong? And please, be honest. Don't worry about my feelings. I realize I'm the one that tends to send everyone off in certain directions, but that doesn't mean I'm infallible." She gave him that speech because she knew perfectly well that he'd tiptoe around the truth for hours if he thought she'd be hurt by his words.

Smythe stared at her for a long moment before speaking. Finally, he said, "I don't think it's anythin' we've done. More like it's what we 'aven't done."

"But what haven't we done that we should be doing?" she asked earnestly. "That's what I want to know. Why aren't any of our usual methods working in this case?"

"Because I think it's the case itself that's throwin' us off the scent," he replied. "It's not like most of the others. We've got no real scene of the crime, no witnesses, and we've convinced ourselves that Randall was done in because of that bloomin' silver mine. But what if that ain't the way it 'appened? What if the bloke were murdered for an entirely different reason? We don't know nothin' about this Jake Randall. It's like we're trying to find a straw man."

Mrs. Jeffries suspected he might be correct. There was something decidedly peculiar about this murder and the victim. Maybe they were approaching it all wrong. But she couldn't for the life of her see any other way to go about finding the killer.

"I agree with everything you've said," Mrs. Jeffries replied. "But I don't know what else we can do. Jake Randall is turning out to be the most elusive of victims. The police still haven't found out where Randall was staying between the first of the month and the time he was killed. Furthermore, neither the porter nor any of the other tenants at his former residence knew anything about the man. For that matter, no one seems to know much about him either."

"Benfield probably knows a fair bit."

"Quite possibly," she agreed. "But we haven't heard from Luty or Hatchet yet, and they were the ones trying to find out what they could about Benfield. Perhaps they'll come up with something useful soon." Mrs. Jeffries tried to make her voice hopeful, but could tell by the expression on the coachman's face that she hadn't succeeded. He didn't think Luty and Hatchet would have any better luck than the rest of them had. For all any of them knew, after Benfield had spoken to the inspector, he'd disappeared off the face of the earth. She made a mental note to ask the inspector if the police had verified his movements on the day of the murder.

"Let's look at what we do know about the bloke," Smythe suggested. "He was an American. He liked women and he had Rushton Benfield frontin' for 'im."

"No," Mrs. Jeffries interrupted, "we're only assuming Benfield was, er, fronting for him, as you put it. It could well be that Benfield is entirely innocent."

He looked skeptical. "I don't believe that, and I'm not sure I believe that tale 'e told the inspector that 'e were 'idin' out from the other investors."

"Why not?" she asked curiously.

Smythe smiled faintly. "Remember that conversation we 'ad a few days back? The one where Betsy tried to tell us that rich people don't settle their problems by killin'?"

"I remember."

"Much as I hate to say it, the lass was right. Now, maybe Benfield is the kind to settle a score with a gun or a knife, but you can bet your last farthin' that none of the others are." Smythe shook his head. "Can you really imagine Cubberly or Hinkle or that twit Dillingham beatin' Benfield to a pulp?"

"But Benfield claimed that Cubberly did get violent," Mrs. Jeffries pointed out. "He said he was pushed against the wall."

"But Cubberly was soaked!" Smythe exclaimed. "They'd been drinkin' whiskey. Bloomin' Ada! Benfield knew that the other three weren't goin' to stay snozzled forever. He knew that once they sobered up, the first thing they'd all do was get their solicitors. They weren't gonna come after 'im. Yet *he stayed in hidin' for days*! Why?"

Stunned, Mrs. Jeffries stared at the coachman. He was absolutely right. Why hadn't she thought of it herself? And more importantly, what else had she overlooked? "That's a very good question."

"And another thing," he continued, warming to his subject. "We've got to learn more about the victim. For all we know, Randall might 'ave been a nasty piece of work that 'ad 'alf of London lookin' for 'im with murder on in their 'earts."

"But we've already tried to do that," Mrs. Jeffries reminded him. "Luty and Hatchet are still attempting to learn what they can about both Benfield and Randall. But so far, we haven't had much success."

"No disrespect meant to either of 'em," Smythe said earnestly. "But they may not have the right sources to do it. Luty knows a lot of people, but I'd wager that she don't know many of the sort that'd be able to deliver the goods on Randall and Benfield. They're crooks, Mrs. J. I know. I can feel it."

Surprised by his certainty, she was taken aback for a moment. She stared at the determined expression in his brown eyes and her stomach tightened. "And what do you suggest we do to rectify the situation?"

Smythe regarded her evenly. He hesitated briefly before he spoke. "Let me start workin' on it. There's no point in me hotfootin' over to the Strand today. The inspector'll have the lads in blue confirmin' Cubberly's statement."

"That's true," she agreed. "All right, but what are you proposing to do this afternoon? Continue with the hansom drivers?"

"Nah, I'll do that later. I want to take a crack at findin' out more about Benfield and Randall. But it would mean lookin' up some blokes I 'aven't 'ad much to do with for a long time."

"I see," Mrs. Jeffries said slowly. She had a horrible feeling that Smythe was trying to tell her something. "I take it the people you're referring to aren't particularly respectable?"

He nodded, but continued to meet her gaze. "Right."

For a moment she didn't know what to say, so she just stared at him. She'd trust Smythe with her life, yet suddenly she realized how little she knew of his past.

All she knew for certain was that he'd worked for the inspector's late aunt, loved horses, and was a very good man.

But except for Wiggins, she knew little more about any of the servants of Upper Edmonton Gardens. Chance had brought them together. Or perhaps it was something else, something other than pure chance. In the months they'd lived with the inspector, they'd forged a strong bond. A true bond of respect and friendship for one another, a bond strengthened when they'd all begun working together on Witherspoon's cases.

But despite their closeness, their sense of family, there was something else as well. An unspoken and tacit agreement between them not to ask one another questions. Not to nose about in each other's past. She knew little of Mrs. Goodge save that she'd cooked for some of the finest families in London. There were many gaps in her life, gaps that she didn't share with anyone. Betsy was the same. She'd shown up half-starved and ill on Witherspoon's doorstep soon after Mrs. Jeffries came to work for him. And she never spoke of her past either. Wiggins was the only one they really knew much about. He'd come to work for the inspector's late aunt Euphemia when he was a lad of twelve. He had no family.

And now Smythe was revealing something about himself. About his past. Mrs. Jeffries realized he was watching her carefully, waiting to see her reaction. She smiled calmly and forced her speculations to the back of her mind. "Are you trying to tell me that some of the people you may need to question have criminal associations?"

Smythe smiled sadly. "I'm afraid I am," he admitted honestly, "But I swear, Mrs. J, I'll be careful. I can take care of myself. I won't do anything that's against the law and I won't put our inspector in an embarrassin' situation. But if I could get a few feelers out, I know I could find out the goods on both Randall and Benfield."

"But what if your, er, former associates don't know anything about either of them?" Mrs. Jeffries asked anxiously.

"They'll know about 'em," he replied confidently. "Take my word for it."

Lester Hinkle was just finishing luncheon when the inspector and Constable Barnes were ushered into the dining room.

"Sorry to bring you in here," Hinkle mumbled as he shoved a dessert plate with half a treacle pudding on it to one side, "but my wife has guests. They're in the drawing room, and I don't want them to be disturbed."

"This will do fine, sir," Witherspoon said. His mouth was watering. The air was filled with the lingering scent of roast beef. On the buffet next to the huge cherrywood dining table, the rest of the pudding sat in solitary splendour.

"As long as you don't mind," Hinkle said. He waved his hand towards the empty chairs. "Sit down."

The policemen pulled out chairs and took a seat. Witherspoon watched Lester Hinkle closely. The man looked small and defeated. He was hunched forward over the dining table, his elbows resting on the white damask tablecloth, his gaze locked morosely on the far wall as though he were looking for the meaning of life in the pattern of pink climbing roses on the wallpaper.

The inspector felt a surge of sympathy for him. But he ruthlessly squashed the feeling. This man might very well be a murderer. "Mr. Hinkle," Witherspoon began. Hinkle continued to stare at the wall.

"Mr. Hinkle," he tried again, and this time Hinkle turned vacant, uncaring eyes in his direction. "I should like to know exactly where you went on the afternoon of March seventh."

"So you know," Hinkle replied. "I suppose it was Cubberly who talked, not that it matters. I would have told you the truth eventually."

The inspector wasn't sure he believed him.

"I suppose Cubberly also told you we'd been drinking," Hinkle said. He tossed his linen napkin onto the table. "That's why we acted so stupidly." He laughed harshly. "When Randall didn't show up, we thought we could find the bounder."

"Did you locate Mr. Randall?" the inspector asked softly.

Hinkle slowly shook his head. "No. I was so drunk I couldn't have found my way home, let alone Jake Randall."

"You're not trying to tell us, sir, that you were so drunk you don't remember what you did or where you went?" Witherspoon asked in alarm.

"It's a bit hazy," Hinkle replied. "But not so much that I don't recall my movements." He paused and took a deep breath. "The three of us left Cubberly's house sometime after two. I don't know when exactly. I didn't look at my watch. We sent a beggar boy who was hanging about the front of the house to get us a hansom. Cubberly got off at the Strand. I can't exactly remember why, but I suppose he had a reason."

"He was looking for Randall in the theatre district," the inspector said, hoping the information would help the man remember.

Hinkle nodded. "That's right. It's starting to come back to me."

The inspector silently congratulated himself. "Can you recall what you talked about in the hansom?" It would certainly be helpful if one of them had pulled out the gun and shown it to the others. Perhaps even talked of shooting the man! Then the inspector remembered that both Mrs. Cubberly and the housekeeper had claimed the gun was still in the study after the men had left. Drat.

"What did we talk about?" Hinkle laughed harshly. "Why, we talked about what a scoundrel Randall was. How we couldn't wait to get our hands on him and make him give us our money back. I believe Cubberly was muttering about prosecuting him for fraud. I'm not sure, but I do recall him going on and on about some high-priced solicitor he used."

"And where did you get off, sir?" Barnes asked.

Hinkle seemed to shrink into his chair. "Waterloo Station," he whispered.

Witherspoon went still. Hinkle was admitting that he was less than two hundred yards from where Randall's body was found. "Why were you going to the station?"

"I thought I might find Jake there," he admitted ruefully. "Stupid thing to do, really. But I knew that Randall had spent some time in South America. I had the notion that if I hung around the station and watched the trains leaving for Southampton, I might spot him."

"You were thinking he'd get a ship from Southampton, were you?" Barnes asked. He didn't look up from his notebook.

"Why Southampton?" the inspector asked. He was getting confused. "Why not Liverpool or the London docks? Ships leave from all those places."

"Randall had talked about how he'd taken the Royal Mail Steam Packet to Brazil once. That line leaves from Southampton. I don't know why I thought Jake might show up there, but I did. Whiskey will do that to you. Makes any silly idea you come up with seem reasonable."

"Was that your only reason for going to Waterloo?" Witherspoon pressed.

Hinkle took his spectacles off and rubbed the bridge of his nose. The inspector was sure he was trying to give himself time to think.

"What other reason would there be?" Hinkle shrugged. "I realize how absurd my actions seem in the cold light of day, but remember, Inspector, I wasn't my usual rational self."

"Did anyone see you at the station?" the inspector asked.

"Lots of people saw me," Hinkle replied wearily. "But they were all strangers. I didn't run into anyone I know, if that's what you're getting at."

That was precisely what Witherspoon wanted to know. By his own admission, Hinkle was in close proximity to the scene of the crime. "How long did you stay at the station?"

"Several hours. It was getting dark when I left."

Witherspoon remained silent. He tried to get his thoughts in order. He had more questions to ask and he wanted to make sure he didn't forget any of them.

Barnes asked, "What did you do then, sir?"

Hinkle sighed. "I walked. By late that afternoon, the whiskey had worn off, and I was sober enough to realize how ridiculous it was to be hanging about the railway station on the off chance that I might spot Jake

Randall. But it was too early to go back to the Cubberly house. We planned on meeting there at half past nine that night."

"Did you stop anywhere and have a meal?" the constable asked.

"I wasn't hungry, and I didn't fancy going to my own home, so I just walked the streets."

"So you claim you spent the afternoon at the station and then walked aimlessly until it was time for all of you to meet again at the Cubberly house. Is that correct?" Witherspoon thought Hinkle's explanation was quite weak. But weak or not, it might stand up in a court of law. A good barrister would see to that. Drat. Hinkle had one of those wretched alibis that couldn't be proved or disproved.

"That's correct." Hinkle looked at him with beseeching eyes. "I don't suppose you believe me, Inspector, but I swear it's true. I didn't see Jake Randall that day. And I didn't murder him."

"What happened after you returned to the Cubberly house?" The inspector wanted to see if Hinkle's version matched the one Cubberly had given him.

"Nothing really," Hinkle replied. His shoulders slumped and his mouth turned down in a pathetic frown. "Of course we'd all sobered up by then. Neither Dillingham nor Cubberly would admit to finding Jake, and I certainly hadn't had any luck. So we met back at the house, said a quick good night, and I left."

"You were the first to leave?" Witherspoon asked carefully. Cubberly had claimed that Dillingham left first.

"No, Dillingham went off right before I did. He was in a state. He wanted us to keep looking for Randall. Poor blighter, he kept insisting he had to find the man and get his money back."

Witherspoon looked at Barnes. "Are you saying, Mr. Hinkle, that Dillingham went off to continue the search?" Cubberly hadn't mentioned that.

"I can't say for certain. But that's definitely the impression I got."

The inspector felt certain he was learning something important. He decided to plunge boldly forward. Sometimes, as his housekeeper had once said, a surprise question will yield unexpected results.

"Did you see Mr. Cubberly's gun when you arrived back that evening?"

Hinkle wasn't in the least surprised. He shook his head. "No, the gun wasn't anywhere to be seen. I assumed that John had put it away."

• • •

Mrs. Jeffries tapped softly at the backdoor of the Cubberly house. She held her breath. There were so few servants in the household, she prayed that Mrs. Cubberly wouldn't be answering the door.

The door cracked open, and a pair of suspicious, red-rimmed eyes glared out at her.

She smiled warmly. "Mrs. Brown?" she queried.

"Who wants to know?" The door opened an inch wider.

"My name is Hepzibah Jeffries. I'm Inspector Witherspoon's housekeeper." Her smile softened. "I do so hate to trouble you, but the inspector's left his spectacles here, and I've come to fetch them."

"Might as well come in, then." The woman turned and trudged down a darkened hallway. "Mind you slam the door behind you," she called over her shoulder.

"Yes, of course," Mrs. Jeffries said brightly. "I do so hate to put you to any trouble. It's so very good of you to help me."

She heard a grunt in reply. Oh dear, this woman is not going to be easy to talk with, Mrs. Jeffries thought as she followed her into the kitchen.

The room was dark, the light streaming in through the two windows over the open scullery dulled by the dirt on the panes. The gray stone floor was streaked with dust and grease, several of the wooden slats on the standing pallet next to the sink were broken, and there was a thick line of rust on the edges of the kitchen range.

"Wait here," Mrs. Brown instructed her. She jerked her head toward one of the rickety chairs by the fireplace. "You can have a seat if you like. It might take me a few minutes to find them spectacles. Do you know where he left 'em?"

"I'm not really sure," Mrs. Jeffries replied. "Perhaps Mrs. Cubberly knows where they are."

"Not bloody likely," the housekeeper replied as she left.

As soon as she disappeared, Mrs. Jeffries tiptoed back into the hall. There were two doors along the corridor leading to the backdoor. She hurried to the nearest door, cocked her head towards the kitchen stairs and heard the housekeeper's slow footsteps as she mounted the stairs. Mrs. Jeffries could tell by the woman's progress that she wouldn't be back in a hurry. She turned the knob and stuck her head inside the room.

A meat larder. The walls were lined with slate shelves and the floor was glazed tile. There were hooks for hanging joints dangling from a cross beam, a table, and a chopping block. But the only meat stored was a small, brown-wrapped parcel, which she thought was probably a joint of some kind.

Mrs. Jeffries backed out, closed the door, and dashed to the next one. Opening it, she peeked inside and saw that it was a dry larder. But the shelves that should have been bulging with bread, flour, and other staples were surprisingly bare. There were a few tins of vegetables, a jar of preserves, and half a loaf of brown bread. There was very little food in this household, she thought. As she turned to close the door she noticed a housemaid's box, almost identical to the one Betsy and she used at Upper Edmonton Gardens to carry their cleaning supplies, stuck in the far corner. Mrs. Jeffries went back to the kitchen. She thought about having a quick search through the house when she heard Zita Brown's heavy footsteps on the stairs.

"It took me a bit o' time to find 'em," the woman announced sourly as she plonked the inspector's spectacles on the table.

"Thank you so very much for looking," Mrs. Jeffries replied. "I must say, I'm so sorry to have put you to any trouble."

The only reply was a grunt.

Mrs. Jeffries tried to think of what to do to get the woman talking. Normally, she had no difficulty engaging people in conversation, but this woman was a horse of a different color. "Excuse me for asking," she began, "but might I trouble you for a cup of tea? It's a long way home, and once I get back there, I won't have time to do anything but work, work, work. The inspector is quite a nice man, but he is demanding."

It was precisely the right thing to say.

"Demanding!" Zita Brown shuffled towards the stove. "I can tell you all about that. Do this, do that, cook the meals, do the bleedin' laundry." She snorted as she put the kettle on to boil. "House this big and I'm the only one here. You'd think that old bastard would hire more staff, but no, not him. He's too bleedin' tightfisted to pay fer any more help."

Mrs. Jeffries jumped right in. "Gracious! You don't mean to say you're expected to do everything? But that's absurd. Why, it's positively criminal."

"'Course it is." Zita shuffled back to the table and plopped in her chair. "But he don't care how hard I work, and she don't notice what the bloomin' house looks like. All she cares about is shuttin' herself up in her bleedin' room and readin' them ruddy books of hers."

Mrs. Jeffries assumed the housekeeper was referring to the Cubberlys. But she didn't dare ask. The woman needed a few more moments to vent her rage. "Have you always had to do it all?"

"Sometimes they have a housemaid," Zita admitted grudgingly. "But they never stay."

"Really? How very dreadful? Why do they leave? Is Mr. Cubberly a . . . well, you know. One who takes liberties?"

Zita threw her head back and laughed. "Him! Not likely. The only thing he uses his pole for is takin' a piss. He don't even take liberties with his missus, much less anyone else. But the girls don't stay 'cause the old fart won't pay a decent wage." She suddenly leaned forward. "You wouldn't believe how much they give me. Full housekeeper, I am, and the bastard won't pay more then twenty quid a quarter."

"That's shocking." Mrs. Jeffries was horrified. That was less than half what a proper wage was. "But doesn't the mistress of the house object? Surely, she'd need a ladies' maid. Why, who does her hair? Who helps her undress?"

"No one. She does it herself." Zita broke off and cackled with glee. "Last maid we had run off in the middle of the day. Mind you, I don't much blame her, what with that lot upstairs drinking like there was no tomorrow and wavin' a gun about."

"A gun!" Mrs. Jeffries wished she'd offered to take the woman out for a drink. At this rate, she was going to be here all day. "How dreadful."

The kettle whistled and the housekeeper went to the stove. "It weren't that bad," Zita replied. She poured boiling water into the pot. "It were just Mr. Cubberly and some of his friends playin' about. But Lottie weren't used to that kind of nonsense, and she took it into her head to run off. Mrs. Cubberly was mad as a wet cat over it. Silly cow. Do the mistress good to turn her hand to something once in a while."

"Does Mrs. Cubberly help you?" Mrs. Jeffries asked as Zita placed a cup of tea on the table. There was a piece of dried food on the bottom saucer.

"Her? Not bloody likely. Screamed like a banshee 'cause she had to answer the door herself the day Lottie run off. But I didn't pay her no mind." Zita settled herself into her chair. "These old legs can't take climbin' all them stairs every time someone comes to the ruddy door. There's too much to do down here. Cookin' and cleanin' and polishin'. When she started screaming about it, I told her I only climbs them stairs once a day when I do the sweeping and dustin' upstairs."

"Who takes care of the upper floors?" Mrs. Jeffries asked.

"I do." She picked up her teacup and slurped greedily. "I do everything around here."

Mrs. Jeffries realized she wasn't going to get anything worthwhile out of the housekeeper. "How very awful for you," she murmured sympathetically.

Zita slurped her tea. "Ah, I'm used to it."

"It's unfortunate that Mrs. Cubberly is an invalid," Mrs. Jeffries said. She wanted to get the housekeeper talking about the Cubberlys again.

"She's no invalid," Zita exclaimed.

"I'm sorry. Perhaps I misunderstood, but I thought you said she spends all of her time in her room."

"That's 'cause she's always got her nose stuck in one of them silly books of hers."

"Ah well, I suppose she isn't all that different from most women of her station," Mrs. Jeffries said casually. "Many of them spend so much time sitting, it's surprising their limbs still function."

Zita threw back her head and howled with laughter. "Right enough," she agreed. "Last time her nibs got off her backside was the day Lottie run off. Made Mrs. Cubberly so bleedin' mad she grabbed her cloak and announced she was goin' for a walk."

"I'll bet she didn't walk far." Mrs. Jeffries smiled cynically, hoping to keep the woman talking.

"Don't know how far she walked, but she didn't come back till almost a quarter to seven that night."

"Gracious, you've a good memory."

"Not too hard to remember," Zita said dryly. "As she were leavin' she yelled at me to have her dinner ready by seven o'clock. Put me in a right old pickle, that did. What with Lottie takin' off, and me havin' to do it all that day. But I did like she wanted. Her bleedin' dinner was waitin' fer her when she come down to the dining room. Seven o'clock right on the nose. But did she thank me? Not bloody likely. Just tucked in without a word, stuffin' her face and givin' me orders to leave a cold supper fer Mr. Cubberly."

• • •

"Still no word from the uniformed lads?" Witherspoon asked as he and Barnes waited in the library of the Dillingham home.

"About what?" Barnes dug out his notebook.

"Oh, confirming Benfield's story or locating Randall's lodgings, er . . ." The inspector paused and shifted on the stiff horsehair settee, trying to find a comfortable position. But it was impossible. The seat was as hard as a wooden plank. The other furniture in the large, sparsely furnished room looked equally miserable, too. The only color was a white-fringed shawl draped across a tabletop. A thick Bible sat smack in the center of it. Witherspoon thought it an odd spot to keep a Bible. There were oak bookcases along one wall and all the shelves were empty, save for a few books on one of them. Witherspoon would hardly have called this room a library, but that's what the butler had called it, so he supposed it must be one.

"They've found out Benfield was where he claimed to be, hidin' out at that woman's empty flat. The porter confirmed he'd seen him come in on the Monday afternoon around three. Benfield didn't leave the flat until the night he come to the station. The porter's certain of it 'cause Benfield paid him to fetch him food and drink." Barnes shrugged. "Mind you, that don't mean that Benfield was there the whole time. The porter's an old man. Benfield could have slipped in and out without him seein' him."

"Hmmm . . ." the inspector muttered. That alibi was really no better than Lester Hinkle's or John Cubberly's. "And Randall's lodgings?"

"They haven't found Randall's lodgings yet, sir. Nor the murder weapon." Barnes glanced at the closed double oak doors. "What did you think of Hinkle's statement? Do you think he was tellin' the truth?"

"One hates to think that citizens lie to the police on a regular basis," Witherspoon replied, "but honestly, I've almost reached that conclusion. Hinkle's information about Dillingham became much more damaging after he'd learned we knew about the gun. I think perhaps he was trying to throw suspicion on Mr. Dillingham because his own position is so precarious. But frankly, Constable, I don't know what to make of it yet." He stopped, realizing that he sounded as unsure of himself as he felt. And that would never do. He cleared his throat and straightened his spine. "But like I always say, jumping to conclusions without the facts is useless."

"True, sir," Barnes agreed. He kept his eyes on the door. "But we don't have any facts in this case. All we've got is Hinkle claimin' he was wan-derin' around Waterloo Station or walkin' the streets and practically ac-cusin' Dillingham of killin' Randall."

"Not to worry, Constable," Witherspoon replied firmly. "The truth will out." He thought that sounded rather good.

"Specially if we send a few men over to the station to verify his story," the constable said grimly. "If he was wandering around drunk as a lord, someone's going to remember him."

That wasn't what the inspector meant, but he didn't bother correcting Barnes.

The double doors opened and Edward Dillingham rushed inside the room. Closing them quickly, he turned and dashed across the room to-wards the two policeman. He skidded to a stop right in front of them.

"What on earth are you doing here?" he hissed softly. He glanced to-wards the closed doors.

"We'd like to ask you a few more questions," Barnes replied. He stood up and Dillingham stepped back a few feet.

"But I've already answered all your questions."

There were footsteps outside in the hallway. Dillingham jerked his head around, a panicked look in his eyes.

"Not all of them, sir," Barnes said.

Dillingham didn't appear to hear. His gaze was locked on the door and his ear was cocked that way too.

"Mr. Dillingham," the inspector prompted.

He turned at the sound of the inspector's voice, "You really must go," he beseeched them softly. "I'll be happy to come down to the police sta-tion, but you must leave."

The footsteps stopped outside the door. The knob began to turn, Dill-ingham made a strangled noise of pain just as the door opened.

"Oh God," he muttered frantically. "Now I'm done for."

Luty tossed her cloak over the back of her chair and sat down. "Hatchet'll be here soon," she said. "But he said fer us not to wait."

"In that case," Mrs. Jeffries said, "we won't. We've much to report."

"We only met a few hours ago," Wiggins muttered. "I ain't 'ad time to get out and 'ear nuthin'." He stopped and frowned at the lone plate of bread and butter sitting in the center of the table. "Is this all there is?" he asked, his tone outraged. "What 'appened to them scones you were bakin' this mornin'?" he asked the cook.

"I'm savin' them for tomorrow," Mrs. Goodge said firmly. "This is the third time we've met today, and I'm not wastin' any more sweets on you lot. Got to save 'em for my sources. Besides, this is plenty. Nothing wrong with a good bread-and-butter tea."

"It'll be enough fer me," Luty announced. "And we don't need to bother savin' Hatchet any. He eats too much anyway. Come on, let's git started."

Smythe glanced at the empty chair next to the cook. "Cor, blimey, isn't Betsy back yet? The lass has been gone all day. Where'd she go anyway?"

"I'm not certain," Mrs. Jeffries said. "But I'm sure she'll be along any minute. In the meantime, we've much to discuss." She was eager to tell them what she'd learned from Zita Brown, and she also wanted to talk about Smythe's ideas on the case. "Now, does anyone have anything to report?"

"Hatchet and I found out that Benfield's been disinherited," Luty volunteered. "But I don't think it means much. It happened seven years ago." She turned accusingly to the housekeeper. "And I'm still waitin' fer you to tell me what part of Colorado this here mine is in."

"I'm sorry, Luty," Mrs. Jeffries said apologetically. "I keep meaning to tell you. The inspector told me the mine is located in a town called Pardee. It's near a place called Leadville."

"Well, well," Luty muttered thoughtfully. "That's interestin'."

"Yes, I'm sure it is," Mrs. Jeffries said quickly. "But I don't think it has much bearing on Jake Randall's murder." She was interrupted by the slamming of the backdoor.

Betsy, breathless and with her cheeks flushed, ran into the kitchen. "Thank goodness you're all 'ere," she exclaimed. "I've not got much time."

"Why are you in such a bloomin' 'urry?" Smythe asked.

"I've learned all sorts of things today," she announced proudly. She stripped off her gloves and reached around the coachman for the teapot. "But the most important thing I learned was where Lottie Grainger might be."

"Betsy, do sit down and have a rest," Mrs. Jeffries ordered. She wondered how in the world Betsy had found out about the missing maid. She hadn't been here for either of the two other meetings they'd had today.

"A quick cuppa and then I've got to run," Betsy replied. She looked at the housekeeper, her expression serious. "You see, Lottie Grainger is very important and we've got to find her."

"Why's she important?" Luty demanded.

Betsy smiled triumphantly. "Because she was carryin' on with Jake Randall."

CHAPTER 8

Inspector Witherspoon hoped Edward Dillingham wasn't going to faint or go into fits or something awkward like that. But really, he thought, the man was breathing so hard he sounded like a steam engine, and he'd gone a funny color. "Er, are you all right?" he asked.

Dillingham gave a strange, high-pitched squeak as the library doors opened. A strangled giggle slipped from his throat as the butler stepped into the room.

"Excuse me for interrupting, sir," the servant said, addressing Dillingham, "but your father has gone out. He asked me to give you a message."

Witherspoon could hear Dillingham trying to catch his breath.

"Thank you, Livingstone." Dillingham's voice trembled. "What is it?"

"Mr. Dillingham would like you to join him tonight for dinner, sir. Eight o'clock."

"That'll be fine, Livingstone."

Witherspoon and Barnes looked at each other as the butler left, quietly closing the door behind him. The inspector decided to wait until Dillingham's color returned and his breathing slowed before he would start asking questions. Gracious. He didn't want the fellow to peg out on him.

"I say, I'm dreadfully sorry about that." Dillingham laughed awkwardly.

"Who were you expectin' to come through that door, sir?" Barnes asked softly.

The inspector threw the constable a grateful look. Trust Barnes to get right to the heart of the problem. Edward Dillingham had clearly been frightened of someone seeing him being interviewed by the police. Not just apprehensive or nervous. Scared. Of course, it might be difficult to get the man to admit to such a thing. What could one say? "Excuse me sir, but were you terrified your mother was going to catch you talking to the police?" Thank goodness for constables. So much less inhibited about some things.

Dillingham contrived to look offended. "I've no idea what you mean," he blustered.

"Come now, sir," Barnes persisted. "When you saw that door openin', you looked like you were gettin' ready to lose your stomach. Turned white as a sheet, you did."

"I've had a spot of indigestion," Dillingham said doggedly. Then he suddenly threw his hands into the air. "Oh, what's the use? I was scared. Terrified, if you must know."

"Would you mind telling us why?" Witherspoon asked. It might have nothing to do with the case, but then again . . . For all he knew, Dillingham might have been afraid it was the murderer. In which case, it meant that he knew more than he'd led them to believe.

"I was afraid it was my father."

Witherspoon could understand that. Most young men wouldn't want their parent to know they were a suspect in a murder. But that hardly explained Dillingham's state. Surely there was more to it than that. "I take it you wish to spare your father any needless worry."

"Worry! Believe me, he won't be worried. Livid, aghast, horrified. The very idea of my being involved in a murder will make him furious," Dillingham cried. "He knows nothing about this . . . this wretched murder. And I want to keep it that way. I won't have my father bothered with your questions."

"We'd no intention of asking your father anything," Witherspoon said. "Unless, of course, we find out that he had something to do with Jake Randall."

"He's never even met the man."

"Does he own any shares in the Randall and Watson Mine?" Barnes asked.

"Of course not," Dillingham snapped. He'd recovered completely from his fright. "Now, why don't you say what you've come to say and leave. I'm a busy man, I've no time to stand about chatting."

"Could you tell us where you were on the afternoon of Monday, March seventh?" the inspector asked.

"March seventh?" Dillingham murmured. "You mean" the day we had the meeting?"

"Yes, sir," Witherspoon said patiently.

"But I've already told you what I did that afternoon," Dillingham exclaimed.

"Would you tell us again?" Barnes prodded.

"Oh, all right," he said impatiently. "After I left the Cubberly house, I had a late lunch at the Crown Hotel, then I walked down Oxford Street to Marble Arch. I went into the park and took a walk. Then I went to a pub."

"And what time did you leave the park, sir?" the inspector asked. He sighed silently. Why did people persist in lying to the police?

"Inspector," Dillingham said, "I don't know what you're getting at. But as I told you yesterday, I've no idea what time I left the park. It was getting toward evening. That's all I can remember."

"Have you remembered the name of the pub you went into when you left the park?" Witherspoon prodded. "You weren't able to recall it when you gave your statement yesterday."

"It was a common public house, Inspector, somewhere near Notting-hill Gate. There's no reason why I should remember what the place was called." He pulled a pocket watch out of his waistcoat. "Now I really must ask you to leave—"

"Too bad your memory hasn't improved none, sir," Barnes interrupted. "But then again, not many people have good memories. Take for instance the waiters at the Crown Hotel. None of them can recall you coming in at all."

"That's hardly my fault," Dillingham snapped.

Witherspoon was tired. It was late, he was hungry, and he wasn't going to waste any more time giving this chap the opportunity to tell the truth on his own. "That's most unfortunate," he said. "Because a confirmation of your story from another person would have been most helpful. As it is, we'll have to assume you did not tell us the truth yesterday."

"Now, see here. . . ."

"Come now, Mr. Dillingham, Let's not waste any more time. Both Mr. Hinkle and Mr. Cubberly have admitted that the three of you did not simply go your own separate ways after the meeting. You went looking for Jake Randall. We also know you were all three drunk and that instead of going home the night of the seventh, you returned to the Cubberly house." He paused to take a breath. Dillingham was staring at him with wide, frightened eyes. "We'd like to know exactly where you went that afternoon, and more importantly, did you find Mr. Randall?"

"They told you everything?" Dillingham whispered.

Witherspoon nodded.

"Oh God," he moaned. He stumbled to the settee and sat down. "I know what you're thinking," he murmured. "But I swear, I didn't kill Randall. I didn't even see him. The hansom dropped me on the Pall Mall. My task was to go to the clubs round there. I've a membership at the Carlton, and I've friends at most of the other ones."

"Was Randall a member of the Carlton or any other club?" Barnes asked, scribbling busily in his notebook.

"No, but he had friends and acquaintances who were."

"Did anyone you know see you that afternoon?" the inspector asked.

"Not that I recall," Dillingham said hesitantly. "Oh no, wait. Richard Sedwick saw me at the Carlton. He invited me for a game of cards. I declined, naturally."

Barnes glanced up from his writing. "What time was that, sir?"

"I think around four o'clock."

Teatime, Witherspoon thought. He wished Mr. Dillingham would offer them a cup of tea. But he didn't think that was very likely. "Who else, other than this Mr. Sedwick, saw you? We'll need some additional confirmation of your whereabouts."

Dillingham's mouth gaped open. "But I don't know who saw me. There must have been dozens of people milling about the Carlton, but I can't remember who—"

"What about the other clubs?" Witherspoon asked. "Where else did you go besides the Carlton?"

"Nowhere," Dillingham admitted.

"Then it should be easy to check your story," the inspector said softly. "If you were at the Carlton all afternoon, someone on the staff is bound to remember you."

Dillingham covered his face with his hands. "No, they won't," he groaned.

Egads, the inspector thought as he stared at the distraught man, was he still lying? "Why ever not?"

"Because no one saw me." He looked up. "I wasn't feeling very well. Right after I ran into Sedwick, I went into a back room and curled up in an armchair. It's a room that's not used much. I don't think anyone goes in there. I slept for several hours."

"When did you wake up?" Barnes asked patiently.

Dillingham began to wring his hands. "It was almost nine o'clock."

"Did anyone see you leaving the Carlton?" Witherspoon prodded. "The porter, perhaps, or the doorman?"

Dillingham smiled bitterly. "No, I crept out a side door. I didn't want to risk running into anyone I knew. To be perfectly honest, I was a bit of a mess."

"That's most unfortunate." Witherspoon also thought it very odd. Surely, if one were searching for someone, one made oneself known to the staff and asked questions. But Dillingham claimed all he did was crawl off into an overstuffed chair and fall asleep. Really, he thought, his story doesn't make any sense. "Tell me, sir, did you go back to the Cubberly house anytime during the day?"

Dillingham looked genuinely surprised by the question. "Why should I do that?"

Witherspoon tilted his head to one side and watched the man closely. "To get John Cubberly's gun."

"Who told you that?" Dillingham demanded. "I never went near the house until that night. Until everyone came back."

The inspector noticed he hadn't denied knowledge of the weapon. "No one's accusing you of anything, Mr. Dillingham." He paused. "Did you know Mr. Cubberly's gun is missing? We believe it's the weapon that killed Randall."

"I don't know anything about a gun," Dillingham cried.

Witherspoon held up his hand for silence. "Please, sir, we know quite well that you do. John Cubberly got the gun out earlier—he was waving it about and threatening to kill Randall. We also know that you and Mr. Hinkle were angry as well, so angry, in fact, that Rushton Benfield felt his life was in danger." He paused and looked Dillingham straight in the eye. "Benfield, in fact, has told us everything. We know that the three of you knew that the money was gone and that Randall had taken it."

"Benfield's a liar." Dillingham leapt up from the settee and began to pace the room. "I didn't threaten him. John Cubberly did. Hinkle and I had to pull him off the fellow. He was trying to choke him."

Witherspoon recalled that Benfield had merely said that Cubberly had shoved him up against the wall.

"We were drunk, Inspector," Dillingham persisted. "We didn't know what we were doing. But I assure you, Cubberly may have gotten his gun out, but it was still sitting there when the three of us left. Right on the table. I noticed as I left the room. You can't seriously believe that men of our position would go out and murder someone over a stock swindle."

"But someone did." Witherspoon smiled sadly. "It's been my experience that desperate people commit desperate acts."

"Have you asked Rushton Benfield what he was doing that afternoon?" Dillingham charged.

"Yes, sir. We have," Witherspoon replied. "And we're quite satisfied with his statement." Actually, they still needed additional confirmation of Mr. Benfield's statement. "Let's get back to you, sir. By your own admission, you've no witnesses as to where you really were that afternoon."

"You could easily have gone to the Cubberly house and gotten the gun," Barnes added.

"That's absurd," Dillingham yelled. "Mrs. Cubberly and the servants were there. Ask them if I came back."

"Mrs. Cubberly was in her room and there aren't many servants. It would be an easy matter to have slipped back to Davies Street, nipped into the house, and picked up the weapon," Witherspoon said.

"But why would I do that?" Dillingham's voice took on a whining tone. "I'm not a murderer."

"Mr. Hinkle claims you were still terribly angry when you came back that night," the inspector persisted.

"Hinkle said that?" Dillingham's eyes flashed angrily. "He's just trying to save his own skin. How do you know *he* didn't go back and get the gun?"

"We don't," the inspector replied. "But someone did. According to Mr. Hinkle, even after the three of you had sobered up, you were the only one who wanted to continue looking for Randall. Cubberly and Hinkle were ready to give up. But you, on the other hand, kept insisting you'd continue the search."

Dillingham flushed angrily. "That's a damned lie. I'll admit I wanted my money back, but no more than the other two did. What else did that fool Hinkle tell you? Whatever he says is a pack of lies. He's trying to make it look like I'm the only one with a reason for killing Jake Randall. But that's ridiculous. They wanted their money back as much as I did."

"Really?" Witherspoon smiled coolly. "Mr. Hinkle claims that Cubberly talked of hiring a solicitor to retrieve his funds and Hinkle himself said he can weather the loss."

"Hinkle can no more take the loss than I can," Dillingham said with a sneer. "He's in debt up to his ears, and John Cubberly's too tightfisted to hire a solicitor. Good Lord, the man's so cheap he won't even offer you a cup of tea. I almost died of shock when he opened that bottle of whiskey before the meeting. You've seen that household of his. And if anyone's got something to hide, it's Cubberly."

"What do you mean by that?" Witherspoon asked.

Dillingham's sneer turned into a mirthless smile. "If I were you, Inspector, I'd go back to the Cubberly house and ask John about the overcoat he had on that night. Ask him why it was wet and covered with mud."

Witherspoon blinked in surprise. "His overcoat, sir?"

Dillingham nodded. "I noticed it hanging on the coatrack when I went in that night. You see, Inspector, I'm quite observant. It was damp, dripping in spots, actually, and covered with mud."

"Carryin' on with Jake Randall," Mrs. Goodge repeated. "Are you sure?" She looked offended, as though she were annoyed that she hadn't heard this bit of gossip.

Betsy nodded. "I'm sure."

Smythe got up and yanked out Betsy's chair. "Sit down, girl. You'll not be goin' out again tonight. It's gettin' dark."

Betsy glared at him. "Fat lot you know. I've got to go out again." But she sat down.

"Do have some tea and bread, Betsy," Mrs. Jeffries offered. "I daresay Smythe is right. It is getting far too late to go out."

"But Mrs. Jeffries," Betsy protested. "I've got to find Lottie Grainger. I think she might know more about Randall's murder than anyone."

"What did you find out today?" Mrs. Jeffries asked.

"Let me start at the begginin'," Betsy said, taking a quick sip of tea. "This mornin' I decided to go back over to Chester Square and do a bit of snoopin' about on my own. Didn't have much luck findin' out anythin' useful at first. There weren't no activity around the Cubberly house, and I saw the inspector goin' into Mr. Hinkle's house when I nipped over that way." She paused and took another quick sip of tea.

"Get on with it, Betsy," Mrs. Goodge said irritably.

Wiggins suddenly started to sniff the air. "What's that smell?"

"Stock," the cook replied. She glanced at a huge copper pot on the stove. "I'm boilin' up some bones for stock. Now come on, Betsy, don't keep us in suspense."

"Give the lass a chance to drink her tea," Smythe said.

Mrs. Jeffries cast an anxious glance toward the clock. Time was getting on. It was well past the tea hour.

"Ah." Betsy put down her cup. "That was good. Anyways, like I was sayin', I didn't want to 'ang about the Hinkle house in case the inspector or Constable Barnes come out, so I dashed up the road and went into a tea shop." She leaned forward on her elbows, her blue eyes sparkling with excitement. "Had the best bit of luck. I was sittin' there when the waiter brought me my tea. Well, we started chattin', I was askin' him about the Cubberlys just on the off chance he might have seen or heard something, when all of a sudden, the woman sittin' at the table next to mine happened to say she didn't know much about the Cubberlys, exceptin' that they was tightfisted, but she used to be good friends with Lottie Grainger, the maid."

"Very good, Betsy," Mrs. Jeffries said.

"Sometimes ya git lucky," Luty added, "and sometimes ya don't. Looks like you hit it good."

Betsy smiled. "I did. Wait'll you hear. Anyways, I changed tables and sat down with the woman. Her name was Dolores Singleton. Her uncle owns the grocer's 'round the corner from Davies Street. That's how she met Lottie. They become friends 'cause Lottie did the shoppin' for the household. Dolores told me that Lottie Grainger and Jake Randall were sweethearts. Claimed that Randall was mad over the girl. Said he give 'er money, bought her nice clothes, and even took her to the theatre. That's where Lottie and Jake met, you see. Lottie was workin' for some actress, and Jake took a fancy to her."

Mrs. Jeffries thought that a very interesting piece of information. "You don't, by any chance, happen to know if Randall got her the position with the Cubberlys?" she asked.

"That's just what I asked Dolores. She said Lottie had once mentioned that it were Jake who told her about the job." Betsy shrugged. "But she didn't know if he 'ad anything to do with her gettin' the post."

"But Cubberly's a miser," Wiggins protested. "Everybody knew that. Why would Randall want his sweetheart workin' at such a horrible place?"

Mrs. Jeffries looked at the footman. Sometimes Wiggins surprised her. "That's an excellent observation, Wiggins," she said approvingly.

"If Randall were givin' her money and clothes and takin' care of the girl," Smythe said, "maybe he didn't care if she worked for a miser. It looks like he wasn't plannin' on hangin' about London forever, so maybe he saw Lottie workin' at the Cubberlys' as just a temporary position. Besides, Randall may have had other reasons for wantin' her inside the Cubberly house."

"What reasons?" Mrs. Goodge asked.

"The girl could have warned him if the investors started gettin' suspicious about their money," the coachman replied. "That would explain why Randall disappeared from his lodgings at the first of this month and didn't tell anyone where he was stayin'. Lottie probably got wind of what was goin' on and warned 'im."

"But we don't know that," Betsy cried. "And I don't think we're going to find Randall's killer until we talk to Lottie."

"I quite agree," Mrs. Jeffries said cautiously. "But I don't think it's urgent that you find her tonight."

"But what if the killer finds 'er first?" Betsy cried.

"Don't be so dramatic, lass," Smythe retorted. "You don't know that the killer 'as any interest in findin' Lottie Grainger. For all you know, Lottie might have shot 'im."

Betsy shook her head. "She couldn't. Dolores told me she was as mad about Jake as he was about her. He treated her like a queen. Jake was always doin' special little things for Lottie. Buyin' her sweets and flowers and callin' her by her middle name 'cause the initial matched 'is." She shook her head vehemently. "He took her to the theatre and the music hall and dozens of other places. Why, he once took her to the Criterion Restaurant. Dolores said it made Lottie laugh 'cause Jake had to give the snooty feller that run the place an extra guinea to get a table. Lottie wouldn't've killed him. She loved 'im too much."

"Then she's our most likely suspect," Luty said tartly. "Hell hath no fury like a woman scorned. Seems to me, if Lottie Grainger was so in love with this rascal and she found out he were fixin' to steal a trunk load of money and run off somewhere, she'd be mad enough to kill him."

"How would she get hold of a gun?" Betsy asked.

"She could easily have slipped back to the house and stole Mr. Cubberly's," Mrs. Jeffries said. "But all of this is sheer speculation. Though I agree with Luty that it's possible Jake's murder could have been a crime of passion and not of greed, as we've all assumed. We've no evidence whatsoever that Lottie Grainger had a motive or an opportunity to murder Randall. Furthermore, Betsy, before you go dashing off to look for Miss Grainger, we'd better bring you up to date on everything we've found out today."

By the time she'd finished telling Betsy what they'd learned and reporting the results of her visit to the Cubberly housekeeper to the rest of them, it was quite late.

Hatchet had come in halfway through the recital. He was the first one to speak. "I do beg your pardon for asking, madam," he said to Mrs. Jeffries. "But are you sure this Zita Brown was telling you the truth?"

"Why in tarnation would she lie to Hepzibah?" Luty demanded, giving her butler a puzzled frown.

"Because, madam," he replied, looking down at his employer, "we know for a fact that Mrs. Brown drinks to excess. It's been my experience that people who inbibe to the extent that she obviously does frequently get confused."

Wiggins scratched his chin, Smythe's brows drew together, and even Mrs. Jeffries wondered what Hatchet was trying to tell them.

"Oh, for land's sake, man," Luty exclaimed impatiently. "What are you tryin' to say? Was the woman lyin' or are you tryin' to tell us she's just plain loco."

"Let me put it in very short, simple sentences, madam," Hatchet said pompously. "Mrs. Brown may not have been lying. From the circumstances that Mrs. Jeffries described, the housekeeper would have no reason to fabricate falsehoods—"

"I thought you claimed you was goin' to keep this short," Luty interrupted.

Hatchet ignored her. "However, the woman is a drunkard. For all we know, her account of Mrs. Cubberly going out for a walk on the day of the murder could have happened another time."

"Huh?" Wiggins looked really confused now.

Exasperated, Hatchet leaned forward. "Look," he said impatiently. "I once worked for a drunkard. Someone very much like Mrs. Brown. He was so far gone with drink that he couldn't tell you what day it was, let alone what he'd done that morning. He was always getting his activities confused. Sometimes, on a Monday evening, he'd insist he'd been to church that morning. Do you understand what I'm saying? Mrs. Cubberly may have indeed taken a walk. But she could well have taken that walk on the day before the murder or the day after or even two weeks earlier! You can't take the word of a drunkard," Hatchet said earnestly. "They simply cannot be trusted."

Mrs. Jeffries was the first to speak. "Your point is well taken," she said. But she wasn't sure that he was right. Zita Brown had been very definite.

Betsy pushed her teacup to one side. "I really think I ought to get over to the East End."

Smythe frowned. "Don't be daft. Only a fool would go out that way at this time of day. It's almost dark now."

"But it's important. . . ." Betsy protested.

"Of course it's important," Mrs. Jeffries said gently. "But, that's a very huge area of the city, my dear. How will you ever begin to find the girl?"

"It'll be like lookin' for a needle in a 'aystack," Smythe snapped.

"But we've got to find 'er," Betsy insisted.

"And we will," Smythe promised. "First thing tomorrow mornin', I'll 'ave a go at it myself. It's too dangerous for you."

"You'll have a go at it," Betsy said indignantly. "That's not fair." She turned to Mrs. Jeffries. "Listen, Mrs. J, I know you're thinkin' I shouldn't be goin' over that way, but take my word for it, I'm a lot more likely to find Lottie than anyone else. I know that area. I grew up there and I can take care of myself and . . . and . . ."

The coachman snorted. Mrs. Jeffries held up her hand, her gaze fixed on Betsy's face. "Go on," she ordered. "And what?"

"And there's somethin' else I've got to do. Somethin' I've been puttin' off for a long time." Betsy paused and took a deep breath. "Please don't ask me about it, it's something private."

Mrs. Jeffries studied the pretty housemaid carefully. She was again assailed by the same speculations she'd had earlier. Only this time it wasn't the coachman who was revealing his past. It was their own sweet Betsy. She may not have wanted to reveal why she wanted to go to the poorest part of London, but the very fact that she was so insistent about going told Mrs. Jeffries much.

"Besides," Betsy continued doggedly, "I've got a pretty good idea where to look for Lottie."

Mrs. Jeffries came to a decision. "Where?"

"Dolores told me that Lottie's mum is at the Limehouse Work House. I know that place." She broke off and hastily looked down at her lap. "I know it real well," she said softly.

"All right, Betsy," Mrs. Jeffries said calmly. "Why don't you leave first thing tomorrow morning."

"Cor blimey, Mrs. J," Smythe protested. "That place is filled with pickpockets and cutthroats. The kind o' people that'd kill ya for your shoes. You can't let Betsy go, not by 'erself, anyways. I'll go with 'er. Least with me along, I can make sure she don't get 'er throat sliced."

"I don't know, Hepzibah," Luty added. "I ain't one for thinkin' that just 'cause you're female, you can't take care of yerself, but that's a right nasty part of town. I ain't sure that a pretty girl like Betsy should be over there on her own. I reckon Smythe's right. He should go, too."

Wiggins looked utterly horrified. "You can't do it, Betsy," he said incredulously. "You go over there, and we'll never see you again."

"Don't be foolish, girl," Mrs. Goodge said brusquely. "Let Smythe go lookin' for this girl. Why take them kind of risks when you don't have to?"

"Smythe can't go," Mrs. Jeffries replied calmly. "He's got other matters to attend to. Besides, I think Betsy is right."

"You can't mean that," the coachman protested. "And I can put off gettin' the goods on Benfield and Randall until after we find Lottie."

"What do you mean, 'gettin' the goods on Benfield and Randall'?" Luty interjected angrily. "That's me and Hatchet's job."

"Don't worry, Luty," Mrs. Jeffries said quickly. "Smythe is referring to a different avenue of inquiry." She glanced at the coachman and added, "A very important avenue of inquiry." She turned and smiled cheerfully at Luty. "We'll still need you and Hatchet to continue with your own avenues of investigation."

"Well, I should hope so," Hatchet muttered.

"All right," Luty said grudgingly.

"Listen," Betsy said earnestly. "I appreciate all your concern, I truly do, but I'll be fine."

"At least take Fred with ya," Wiggins pleaded.

Mrs. Jeffries noticed that Betsy carefully avoided looking in Smythe's direction. That was probably just as well, she thought, the coachman looked like he was ready to spit nails. His brows were drawn together ominously, his jaw was rigid, and his hands were clenched into fists.

"Thanks, Wiggins," Betsy said gratefully. "But I really won't need 'im."

"Hmmph," Mrs. Goodge snorted. "I don't like it," she mumbled. "I don't like it at all."

"Me neither," Luty echoed.

"Pardon me." Hatchet tapped the top of the table for everyone's attention. "I do not wish to intrude upon a subject which is clearly not my concern, but—"

"You've never let that stop ya before," Luty mumbled.

Hatchet took no notice of her. "But, as I was saying, I may have a solution that will ensure Miss Betsy's safety without interfering with her investigation or delaying Mr. Smythe with his."

Witherspoon was so glad to be home that he didn't even mind the wretched taste of the sherry. He settled back in his chair and gave his housekeeper a wan smile. "I say, today was rather remarkable."

"How so, Inspector?" Mrs. Jeffries asked. She knew she had to keep him talking as long as possible. They'd spent so much time arguing about Betsy and the case that Mrs. Goodge had been very late in getting dinner started.

"Well, if I do say so myself, we made rather good progress."

"That's wonderful, sir." Mrs. Jeffries smiled in approval. "But I'm not at all surprised. You are, of course, a remarkable detective. Come now, I'm all ears. Do tell me what you've found out."

Witherspoon swelled with pride. Talking to his housekeeper always made him feel so much better. "We found out that none of the principals in this case have particularly good alibis. You know, of course, that Cubberly, Hinkle, and Dillingham went looking for Randall after the meeting on Monday." He couldn't remember whether he'd told her this earlier.

"Yes, sir. You mentioned that at lunch."

"Speaking of lunch," the inspector asked hopefully. "Er, do you happen to know what Mrs. Goodge is serving for dinner?"

"I'm afraid it's a simple supper tonight," Mrs. Jeffries replied. "The household management scheme, you know. Mrs. Goodge is doing her very best to follow your instructions and trim back a bit."

"Simple supper?" Witherspoon repeated. Perhaps it would be eggs and chips or a nice piece of sausage.

"Barley soup. Now, sir, about those alibis?"

Witherspoon pushed the thought of food from his mind. What was the point in looking forward to barley soup? "To begin with, all of the alibis are rather weak." He leaned forward eagerly. "You know what I mean." He began to tell her about his afternoon.

Mrs. Jeffries listened attentively. She wanted to make sure she didn't miss the details. Details that might later prove to be important.

"So you see, Mrs. Jeffries"—the inspector relaxed and absently picked up his sherry—"not one of the principals in the case, not even Rushton Benfield, can be eliminated as suspects."

"Oh dear, sir," she murmured. "That is worrying, isn't it? And I'm afraid you may have to expand your list to include Mrs. Cubberly."

Surprised, the inspector stared at her, his glass halfway to his mouth. "Whatever do you mean?"

"Well, sir. You did leave your spectacles at the Cubberly house," she began, "so naturally I went to fetch them. When I got there, I spoke with Zita Brown, the housekeeper. She told me the most extraordinary thing. She claimed that Mrs. Cubberly went out for a walk after the men left to search for Randall."

"But I questioned Mrs. Brown," the inspector said defensively. "She said nothing like that to me."

"What exactly did she tell you, sir?"

"She told me that Mrs. Cubberly spent most of her time in her room," Witherspoon replied. He frowned. Drat. Had he even asked Mrs. Brown about Mrs. Cubberly's movements that day? He wasn't sure. He'd been so busy getting the taciturn woman to admit to seeing the gun that he may have overlooked the most obvious question of all. "Oh dear, I think I've made a mistake."

Mrs. Jeffries feigned surprise. "You, sir? I'm sure that's not true."

Dejected, he sagged in his chair. "But it is," he insisted. "I've been so stupid. Mrs. Brown didn't tell me about Mrs. Cubberly's walk because I failed to ask her. Frankly, it took so much bother to get the woman to even confirm seeing Cubberly's gun in the house after the men had left that it completely slipped my mind. Stupid, really."

"Don't be too hard on yourself, sir," Mrs. Jeffries murmured sympathetically. "How did Mrs. Cubberly claim she'd spent the afternoon?"

"She said that all the commotion had given her a headache," Witherspoon replied morosely, "And that she'd spent the rest of the day having a rest." He paused off and frowned, "I can't believe I made such a mistake. I really should have asked the housekeeper the right questions!"

Mrs. Jeffries stared at him in some alarm. Inspector Witherspoon had very little confidence in his own abilities. She didn't want him doubting himself now.

"I think, sir," she said slowly, "that you asked just the right questions."

"That's very kind of you, Mrs. Jeffries—" he began.

"I'm not being kind, sir." She had no compunction about interrupting him. "Remember how we've always said that your abilities as a detective are rather unique. Why, everyone talks about your methods and how very unusual they are."

Witherspoon nodded. He was watching her with a wary, hopeful expression. The kind that a child wore when you walked into the nursery with a bag of sweets.

"Well, sir . . ." Mrs. Jeffries paused to give herself time to think. She was making this up as she went along. "I think that one part of your mind deliberately made you leave your spectacles at the Cubberly house. You know what I mean, sir. Sometimes we all do things that we didn't think we meant to do, but we really did."

"Er, yes," he replied. He looked thoroughly confused now. "I think I know what you mean."

"And in leaving the spectacles at the house, you set up the situation so that you'd have a good excuse to go back and have a private chat with the housekeeper. Well, sir, it wouldn't be the first time you've done something like that. You've often told me that servants especially will speak more freely to you a second or third time." She smiled apologetically. "But unfortunately, I ruined things by fetching the spectacles myself. I am sorry, sir."

"Think nothing of it, Mrs. Jeffries," Witherspoon replied.

"So you see, sir," she continued, "you've no reason to feel like you've made a mistake. Your actions were most correct. You probably didn't even realize it at the time, either. But that one part of your mind, that very clever part that makes you so very good a policeman, was guiding you all along."

"Do you really think so?" he asked. Witherspoon couldn't remember any part of his mind acting as a guiding force. But really, there was so much about the mind that one didn't know. And he was a jolly good detective. He'd solved far more than his share of crimes. Perhaps there was something to what his housekeeper claimed.

"Absolutely, sir," Mrs. Jeffries said confidently.

CHAPTER 9

Bright sunshine streamed through the dining-room windows as Mrs. Jeffries entered. She set the silver-covered tray down on the sideboard and yanked open a drawer. Taking out silverware and a white linen serviette, she hastily laid the table for the inspector's breakfast.

Betsy usually did this task, but as the girl wasn't here, it fell to Mrs. Jeffries. She paused and stared into space, thinking. Had she done the right thing? Betsy had looked so small and fragile this morning when she'd left.

Hatchet and Luty had arrived well before dawn, but all of them had been up to see Betsy off. As they'd hustled the girl into the waiting carriage, Mrs. Goodge had mumbled a dark warning of pickpockets and white slavers, Wiggins had kept pressing Betsy to take Fred with her as a guard dog, Luty had volunteered to loan her a six-shooter, and even she had found herself calling out unnecessary warnings. The only one who hadn't put his tuppence worth in, was Smythe. He'd stood by the carriage door, scowling at everyone and looking as though he'd like to wring all their necks.

"Good morning, Mrs. Jeffries," the inspector said cheerfully. He took his seat and poured himself a cup of tea. "What do we have for breakfast this morning?"

"Good morning, sir," she replied. She lifted the cover off the tray and smiled faintly. "It's a lovely breakfast, sir. A fried egg and some toast." She set the plate in front of him.

Mrs. Goodge had outdone herself. The egg was the smallest one Mrs. Jeffries had ever seen.

"Thank you, Mrs. Jeffries." He frowned faintly as he stared at his breakfast. "You know," he mused, "I'm beginning to have second thoughts about my household management scheme."

Mrs. Jeffries smiled innocently. "Really, sir?"

"Hmmm, yes." He picked up his fork. "I'm not sure saving a few pounds each month is worth all this effort. I mean, poor Mrs. Goodge must be at her wit's end."

"It has been difficult for Mrs. Goodge, but she's managing." It wouldn't do to be too enthusiastic about the end of the household management scheme. Not yet, at any rate. She poured herself a cup of tea and sat down next to him. "Inspector," she began, "I'm afraid I've done something you may not approve of, but I really felt I had no choice."

Witherspoon smiled around a mouthful of egg. "I can't imagine you doing anything I'd disapprove of," he said gallantly. "But why don't you tell?"

"It's Betsy, sir," she said. "Last night after you'd gone to bed, a message arrived for the girl. It was from an old friend, a Mrs. Delia Poplar. Unfortunately, Mrs. Poplar is very ill. She may be dying."

"How dreadful."

"It was indeed. Betsy was most upset. She begged me to let her go to see Mrs. Poplar. The woman is quite elderly. I gather she helped raise our Betsy. Well, as you've been working so very hard on this case, I didn't want to disturb you, so I gave her permission to go. She left early this morning. I do hope you don't mind."

"Not to worry, Mrs. Jeffries," Witherspoon said. "You did exactly as I would have done. How long will she be gone?"

"A day or two, sir." She sincerely hoped that was true. None of them could stand the strain of worrying about Betsy's safety for more than that.

"Let us hope that Betsy's friend recovers." He reached for the one piece of toast in the rack. "Er, I say, is there any marmalade?"

Mrs. Jeffries got a fresh jar out of the bottom of the sideboard. "Here you are, sir. You'd best eat every crumb, you'll need your strength today."

"Yes, indeed I will," he agreed.

"What are you planning to do this morning?"

"Today?" He laughed. "Oh, the usual. Poke about here and there and see what I can find. I say, though, Edward Dillingham made an odd statement yesterday. He claimed that when they all returned to the Cubberly home that night, he noticed John Cubberly's overcoat was wet and covered with mud."

"Was Dillingham implying that Cubberly had been near water?" she asked. "Someplace like the river or more specifically the river under Waterloo Bridge."

"I believe so, Mrs. Jeffries." He clucked his tongue. "But it's no good Dillingham telling us about the coat now. I mean, if he'd told the truth at the start, it might have been useful information. We could have asked Cubberly about the coat, or questioned Mrs. Cubberly or Mrs. Brown. But as it is, the garment's probably been cleaned."

"I doubt that, sir," Mrs. Jeffries replied casually. "Unless, of course, Mr. Cubberly cleaned the coat himself. Which, if he is your murderer, he would have done."

"But surely Mrs. Cubberly would have taken care of the coat," the inspector insisted. "From what I understand, wives are very insistent about that sort of thing. I daresay most women wouldn't want their husbands going about in a dirty overcoat."

"Mrs. Brown told me that Mrs. Cubberly did very little around the house," Mrs. Jeffries countered. "And after seeing the state of the Cubberly kitchen, I don't think cleanliness is one of Mrs. Brown's greater virtues."

"So you think I ought to take Dillingham's statement seriously? Perhaps pop around to the Cubberly house and have a look at it?"

She smiled confidently. "Why, thank you, sir, for inquiring after my opinion. I'm most flattered. But we both know you've already made up your mind. Of course you're going to ask Mr. Cubberly to show you his overcoat, and if I know you, you'll ask him to turn out his pockets as well."

Wiggins suddenly stuck his head in. "Sorry to interrupt your breakfast, sir," he said to the inspector. "But Inspector Nivens is here to see you. Shall I bring 'im in?"

"That's very good of you, Wiggins," Witherspoon said. "Please show the gentleman in." He turned to Mrs. Jeffries. "I say, it's jolly decent of the rest of the household to help out in Betsy's absence."

"Yes, it is," Mrs. Jeffries agreed as she got up and shoved her chair under the table. She quickly picked up her teacup and placed it behind the covered tray. Composing her features, she turned and smiled politely as Wiggins ushered the odious Inspector Nivens into the dining room.

"Sorry to bother you, Witherspoon," Nivens said. He nodded at Mrs. Jeffries. "But I wanted to drop 'round and see how you were getting on with this Randall murder."

"Why, you're not bothering me at all," the inspector insisted. "Do sit down and have a cup of tea with me. Have you had breakfast?"

"I've eaten, thank you." Nivens pulled out the chair Mrs. Jeffries had just vacated. "But I could do with some tea."

"I'll get a cup," Mrs. Jeffries volunteered. She moved as slowly as she dared over to the sideboard. Inspector Nivens was about to be served the slowest cup of tea he'd ever had. She wasn't leaving this room until she had some idea what he was doing here.

"Now," Witherspoon said cheerfully, "what would you like to know?"

Mrs. Jeffries opened the glass-fronted cupboard and got the cup. Closing that cupboard, she inched to her left and slowly opened the one containing the saucers.

"I'd like to know how close to an arrest you are," Nivens answered the inspector.

Mrs. Jeffries could feel his gaze on her back. But that didn't make her hurry.

"Oh, I'm not sure how close we are," Witherspoon said. "We've an awful lot of suspects. At least four of them."

"Have you found the murder weapon yet?" Nivens asked. "Forgive me for being so blunt, Witherspoon. But it's rather important to me that we find Randall's killer."

"It's important to all of us," Witherspoon replied.

"Yes, but I've a special interest," Nivens said coldly. "I invested a substantial amount of money in that silver mine. The only way I'm ever going to get it back is if we find the killer."

Mrs. Jeffries inched open the silver drawer and took her time finding a teaspoon.

"I say," the inspector replied, "I'd quite forgotten that. Of course you're concerned about the progress of the case, and well you should be. If you've got a few minutes, why don't I give you a full report—" He broke off as a loud, cracking noise filled the room. "Egads, what was that?"

"I believe your housekeeper just slammed the drawer," Nivens replied.

"I'm so sorry, sir," Mrs. Jeffries apologized. "The drawer slipped. I didn't mean to close it so hard. It used to stick, you see. I'd forgotten that

I'd asked Smythe to fix it last week. Well, as you can hear, he did a superb job."

Barnes and Witherspoon took a hansom to the Cubberly house. John
Cubberly answered the door himself. "Oh, it's you. I suppose you want to
come in?"

"That is why we've come, sir," Witherspoon said politely.

"Hmmph," Cubberly snorted. But he opened the door. "I'll thank you
to keep your voice down. Hilda's not feeling at all well."

"I'm sorry Mrs. Cubberly is ill," the inspector said. He shot a quick
glance at Barnes. "Is she well enough to answer a few questions?"

Cubberly led them down the hall and to the drawing room. "No," he
replied quickly. "She's got one of her headaches and she's lying down.
Unless it's absolutely necessary, I won't disturb her."

"It may be necessary," Barnes said softly.

They'd decided on the way over that it would be wise for the constable
to ask both Mrs. Cubberly and Zita Brown about the condition of her
husband's overcoat on the night of the murder.

"You'll have to convince me that it's necessary. What is it you want?"
Cubberly snapped. His tone was brusque to the point of rudeness, but the
inspector could see the fear in the man's eyes.

"We'd like to have a look at your overcoat," Witherspoon said. He
watched Cubberly's face for a reaction. A flash of guilt in those small eyes
or a dark flush of shame creeping over that muttonchop beard.

But Cubberly only stared at him. "My overcoat?"

"Yes, sir," Witherspoon said patiently. From the corner of his eye, he
saw Mrs. Cubberly hovering near the door. "Oh, I'm so sorry," he apologized, turning to look in her direction. "I do hope we didn't disturb you.
Your husband said you weren't feeling well."

"Do go back upstairs, Hilda," her husband ordered softly.

Hilda smiled weakly. "What is it they want this time? More questions?"

"No, dear," Cubberly answered. "They only want to have a look at my
coat. Heaven only knows why. I certainly don't."

"What coat?"

"My overcoat. It'll only take a moment, and then they'll be gone," he
assured her. "You go upstairs and lie down."

"I don't want to lie down," she retorted. There were lines of strain around her eyes and mouth. She stared contemptuously at the two police-men. "I've no idea why you want to look at an overcoat, but if you'll wait here, I'll get it."

Cubberly moved toward the hall. "Don't trouble yourself, Hilda, I'll get it."

"You won't find it on the coatrack," she told her husband, turning her back on him and walking into the hall. "I took it upstairs to be brushed."

Witherspoon's spirits sank. Drat. If the coat had been brushed, it was no doubt useless as evidence. Not that he'd had any serious hopes that it could be evidence.

Mrs. Cubberly returned a few moments later, a heavy black overcoat in her arms. Constable Barnes took the coat from her and held it up for the inspector to examine.

Witherspoon couldn't believe his eyes. The coat was covered with dried brown mud. There was mud on the pockets, on the lapels, and there was one particularly nasty streak of it running down the back.

"I thought you said you were going to have it brushed, Hilda," her husband complained. "For goodness' sakes, it's a ruddy mess."

"Mrs. Brown has been busy, and we don't have a maid anymore," she replied sullenly.

Witherspoon pointed to the stains. "Mr. Cubberly," he asked, "will you please tell me how this mud came to be on your coat?"

"I got splashed by a carriage," Cubberly replied. He stared at the inspector for a moment. "What's this all about? Why do you care if there are mud stains on my overcoat. They've been there for days."

"Would you please empty the pockets, sir," the inspector asked. He'd suddenly remembered what Mrs. Jeffries had told him this morning.

"Empty the pockets?" Cubberly appeared stunned by the suggestion. "Now, see here—"

"Would you rather empty them down at the station?" Barnes inquired softly.

Sputtering with rage, Cubberly snatched the overcoat away from the inspector. He shoved his hand in the front pocket and turned it inside out. Empty.

"Now the other pocket," Witherspoon prompted.

"Oh really, this is an outrage." But Cubberly did as he was told. He yanked the pocket inside out. Three pennies and a farthing dropped onto the carpet, as did a small piece of folded white notepaper.

Witherspoon reached for the notepaper. He opened it, read the contents, and handed it to Barnes. "Would you read it aloud, please, Constable."

Barnes cleared his throat. "It's dated March seventh and addressed to 'J.' It says: 'Meet me tonight on the footpath by Waterloo Bridge at eight o'clock.' It's signed 'Jake.'"

Hilda Cubberly gasped and stared at her husband with wide, horrified eyes.

"I've never seen that note in my life," Cubberly whispered.

"Then how did it get into your pocket, sir?" the inspector asked. He thought that if Cubberly were faking his reaction, he should be on the stage. The man looked utterly stunned.

"Oh, John," Hilda cried. "How could you?"

"But I've done nothing, Hilda," he beseeched her. "I swear it. I've never seen that before, ever. I've no idea how it got into my pocket."

Barnes stepped closer to the inspector. "Should I get some lads 'round to search the house?"

"You'll do no such thing," Mrs. Cubberly yelped. "Not without a warrant."

Witherspoon dithered for a moment. He had no doubt that with this new evidence, they could obtain a warrant, but that would take time. And there was one part of him that wasn't sure it was the right course of action. Perhaps, he thought, the "guiding force" that Mrs. Jeffries had mentioned this morning was trying to tell him something.

"Not yet, Barnes," he told the constable. He ignored Mrs. Cubberly. "But we will station a man outside the front and back doors of this house. Mr. Cubberly, please don't try to leave town."

"And what about me?" Mrs. Cubberly asked. "Am I a prisoner, too?"

The inspector could think of no reason for asking Mrs. Cubberly to remain available for further questioning. "No, Mrs. Cubberly," he said politely. "And your husband isn't a prisoner either. That's not the way we do things in this country. We're merely asking him to make himself available for further questioning. As for you, you may come and go as you please."

Betsy wished she'd never agreed to meet Hatchet at regular intervals. With his thick, white hair, straight erect carriage, and elegant black coat, he stood out in this district like a sore thumb. Holding her hand over her nose to keep out the smell, she darted around a stopped rubbish cart sitting smack in the middle of the Whitechapel High Street and hurried toward the tall man craning his neck in an effort to locate her.

"I'm right 'ere, Mr. Hatchet," she called. She giggled as she saw Hatchet step pointedly around a frowsy, middle-aged woman blocking his path and talkin' at him a mile a minute. Betsy was fairly certain what the woman was offerin' as well.

"Thank goodness you're all right, Miss Betsy," Hatchet said. He glanced over his shoulder, saw the woman in hot pursuit and grabbed Betsy's arm. "Let's walk," he suggested quickly.

"What's yer hurry, ducks?" the woman called. "We can talk about me price, you know."

Hatchet pretended not to hear. "I'm so glad to see you're safe," he told Betsy. She practically had to run to keep up with his long strides.

"Of course I'm safe," she panted as he steered her around the corner. "This area used to be home to me. I know my way around."

"Nevertheless"—he glanced over his shoulder again, saw that his pursuer had give up, and sighed in relief—"I've been quite concerned. How are your inquiries going?"

"Lottie's mum is dead," Betsy said bluntly. "But one of the women at the lodgin' house where she used to live saw Lottie a couple of days ago. She thought the girl had gone over to her aunt's on Wentworth Street. That's where I'm 'eaded now."

"Would you like me to accompany you?" Hatchet asked.

Betsy didn't have the heart to tell him that he'd just slow her down. "No thanks, I'll be fine on my own."

"As you wish," Hatchet said formally. "As per our arrangement, I'll be back here for you at five o'clock."

Inspector Witherspoon pushed his empty plate to one side and burped delicately. Ah, sausage and chips, he thought, a repast fit for a king. He decided he'd seriously underestimated the pleasure of a good meal. Perhaps he'd have a word with Mrs. Jeffries this evening when he got home. Enforcing thrift in a household was certainly wise, but really, he'd come to dread some of the ghastly concoctions Mrs. Goodge had foisted upon him in the name of economy. He gazed around the busy police canteen for a moment, then leisurely reached for the mug of strong, sweet tea.

"Did you enjoy your food, sir?" Barnes asked. He sat down opposite the inspector. "Mind you, I don't know why you want to eat this greasy muck when you can nip home and have a proper meal."

Witherspoon smiled. This had been the best meal he'd had in days. "Actually, Constable, I quite enjoyed my lunch. Have you eaten?"

"Yes, sir, I had a couple of sausage rolls while I was talkin' to the lads. If you don't mind my askin', sir, why didn't we search Cubberly's house?"

The inspector sighed. "I didn't think the time was right, Constable. Something about finding that note in Cubberly's pocket struck me as very odd. Before we violate a man's privacy and search his home, I want to be very sure that he's guilty."

"And you think Cubberly isn't?" Barnes asked incredulously. "But he was the only one that knew where Randall was going to be that evenin'. He had a message from the victim tellin' him the time and place to meet him."

"Yes, but why did Randall want to meet Cubberly?" The inspector frowned thoughtfully. "That's what I want to know."

"Well, if you want my opinion, sir, I think Cubberly and Randall was in it together. I think they both planned to steal the investment money, split it and then go their separate ways. But Cubberly got greedy. He wanted it all. So he sent the other two out on wild-goose chases to make sure they was out of the way. Then he met Randall, shot him and stole the money. It's probably hidden somewhere in his house right now."

"Yes, but doesn't it strike you as strange that he would be foolish enough to keep the evidence? Why didn't he burn the note?" Witherspoon asked. That detail bothered him greatly.

Barnes pursed his lips. "I don't see that it's all that odd, sir," he mused. "We know Cubberly's a miser. He probably stuck that paper in his pocket out of habit. You know what I mean, sir. He's the kind that uses both sides on a piece of paper, keeps writing on the bloomin' thing till it's completely covered in scribbles. My aunt Gemma used to do that. Used to send us letters that people had written to her, only she'd cross out their bit and cram her own news onto the top and sides. Horrible to read, they were."

"I suppose it's possible Cubberly could have done so. Gracious, we're all creatures of habit," the inspector said thoughtfully. Yet still, there was something wrong with casting Cubberly in the role of murderer. Something that didn't fit. But he couldn't put his finger on what it was.

"I think that's exactly what he did, sir," Barnes insisted. "And our list of suspects is gettin' smaller. We know that the murder was done at around eight o'clock, so that means Mrs. Cubberly couldn't have done it. Zita Brown says she was back at the house by seven forty-five. And Hinkle couldn't have done it either. While you was eatin' lunch he showed up 'ere with Lady Augusta Waddington." He paused and took a breath. "Lady Waddington claims she saw Hinkle walking near Holland Park on Monday the seventh. She called out to him from her carriage, but he didn't hear the lady."

"What time did she see him?" Witherspoon asked.

Barnes smiled. "A quarter to eight. She remembers because she was late gettin' to a dinner engagement over on Mortimer Street that was due to start at eight. So Hinkle couldn't have done the murder. I can't see someone like Lady Waddington providin' an alibi for Lester Hinkle just because she likes him."

"Yes, but there's still Benfield and Dillingham," the inspector insisted. "Either of them could have done the murder."

"We're still workin' on that," Barnes admitted. "If Dillingham were asleep and Benfield were in hidin', it might be hard comin' up with anyone who can confirm their story. But neither of them knew where Randall was goin' to be that night. Cubberly did."

Witherspoon was sitting with his back to the room so he could look out the window at the pigeons in the police yard. Barnes was standing beside him. Neither of them had noticed Inspector Nivens coming up and standing behind Witherspoon's chair. "I quite agree with the constable," Nivens said softly.

Startled, the inspector swiveled around in his chair and stared at Nivens. "I say, I didn't hear you. Gracious, you are a quiet fellow."

"Treading softly is a most useful characteristic in a policeman," Nivens replied. He walked around the table and pulled out a chair. "I didn't mean to eavesdrop, but I couldn't help but overhear your conversation. You really ought to search the Cubberly house."

The inspector drummed his fingers on the tabletop. Perhaps the constable had a point. Perhaps he was paying too much attention to his "guiding force" and not enough to proper police methods. Yet still, he wasn't sure. He did so hate violating a man's privacy without absolute, positive proof that it was necessary.

"Even with two men watchin' the house," Barnes continued doggedly, "if he wants to make a run for it, we might not be able to stop him. Cubberly made a mistake, but I don't think he's stupid. He might be able to give our lads the slip if he takes it into his head to leave while the gettin's good. We'd have egg on our faces, then, sir. I don't fancy explainin' to the chief how we let our prime suspect get away."

"The chief isn't known for his tolerance of mistakes," Nivens added.

Witherspoon capitulated. He didn't relish the thought of explaining it to the chief either. "All right, Constable. Get some uniformed lads. We'll search the Cubberly house."

Tea was a dismal affair at Upper Edmonton Gardens. Everyone, including Mrs. Jeffries, was thoroughly depressed.

Mrs. Goodge slammed a plate of digestive biscuits on the table and shoved them toward the center. They missed crashing into the teapot by a hairsbreath. "Uh, sorry," she mumbled. "But I've had a miserable day. Didn't learn anythin' worth repeatin'."

"I'm sure that's not true," Mrs. Jeffries said soothingly. "But let's have our tea before we begin our discussion." She wasn't in any hurry to start talking about the case either. She'd achieved absolutely nothing today herself. She'd spent the whole day reviewing every possible aspect of this case and she was no closer to the solution.

Smythe picked up his mug. "If you don't mind, Mrs. J, I'd like to get started. I want to get back out."

Mrs. Jeffries brightened. "Does that mean you have something interesting to report?"

"Nah, at least nothing that seems to 'ave anythin' directly to do with Randall's murder," he replied. "But I'm meetin' someone tonight who might be able to 'elp some. All I found out today was that Jake Randall and Rushton Benfield go back a long way. They was involved in some kind of property fiddle about seven or eight years ago."

"That's better than what I heard," Mrs. Goodge muttered darkly. "But it weren't my fault. I couldn't keep my mind where it should be, what for worryin' about the girl."

"I'm sure Betsy will be just fine," Mrs. Jeffries said firmly. She wished she could believe it herself. "After all, Hatchet is keeping a close eye on her."

"Fat lot of good that's goin' to do," Smythe snapped. "No disrespect meant, Mrs. J. But Hatchet's not exactly a spring chicken. The toughs over in that area could eat someone like 'im for breakfast."

"Don't you be too danged sure of that," Luty said tartly. She was standing in the kitchen door. "I let myself in," she explained as she hurried over to the table. "And don't you be thinkin' that Hatchet can't hold his own with anybody. Take my word fer it, he can. He'll bring Betsy back safe and sound. Now, what was you sayin' about Benfield and Rushton pullin' some property fiddle?" she asked the coachman.

He shrugged. "I weren't able to get the details. But I know that they didn't get away with any money. Randall ended up hightailin' it back to America, and Benfield got disinherited. There was talk of prison, but Benfield's father managed to pay off the victims and get everythin' hushed up."

"That figures," Luty mumbled. "Goes along with what I found out, too."

"Excellent, Luty." Mrs. Jeffries smiled brightly. Perhaps their luck was changing. "Do tell us."

"I heard the same story Smythe did," she replied. "And I couldn't get many details neither. But I think I figured out the reason Benfield took off and holed up after that meetin' broke up on the day Randall was murdered, and it weren't because he was scared of the other investors, neither."

"Then who was he hiding from?" Mrs. Jeffries asked curiously.

"No one. I think Benfield was tryin' to lay low, stay out of sight, so to speak. I think he was tryin' to distance himself from any scandal that might break because Randall was swindlin' the silver-mine investors."

"Why would he do that?" Mrs. Goodge asked. "Surely he weren't daft enough to think the others would forget they'd been swindled out of fifty thousand pounds. There was bound to be a fuss."

"Yeah, but I think he was hopin' to stay out of sight till the worst of it was past. Benfield's pa took sick a few months back and has had a change of heart about his boy," Luty explained. "Accordin' to Letitia Knowles—she's that neighbor of mine who knows everything that goes on in this town—Sir Thaddeus Benfield has put his baby boy back in the will. I reckon that Benfield panicked when he found out Randall was up to his old tricks. He probably wanted to stay out of sight till everything blew over. He sure as shootin' didn't want his pa to find out about the swindle. And the old man's dyin'. By the time the scandal becomes public knowledge, Sir Thaddeus may be six feet under. 'Course, Benfield hadn't counted on Randall bein' murdered. Unless he's the killer."

"This is ridiculous," Hilda Cubberly snapped. "What on earth do you hope to find? I tell you, you've no right to be here without a warrant."

Inspector Witherspoon sighed inwardly. "Mrs. Cubberly, I realize this is a most uncomfortable situation for you, but we're well within our rights. If you like, you may send for your solicitor."

Witherspoon had taken the precaution of rereading the Judge's Rules and the Police Code before beginning the search of the Cubberly home.

"That won't be necessary," John Cubberly said wearily. He looked at his wife, who was pacing angrily in front of the fireplace. "Do sit down, Hilda," he begged. "You'll wear yourself out."

She didn't answer him.

From upstairs, they could hear the sound of footsteps and the opening and closing of doors as the upper rooms were searched. The downstairs had already been done.

Mrs. Cubberly stopped pacing and glared at the ceiling. "Your men had better put everything back as they found it," she cried angrily. "And there'd better not be anything missing."

"I assure, you, madam," the inspector said, "our police are not thieves."

"Inspector." Barnes's voice came from the top of the staircase. "You'd better get up here, sir. We've found something."

Witherspoon, with Hilda and John Cubberly on his heels, hurried toward the stairs.

"You couldn't have found anything," Cubberly charged. "There's nothing to find, for God's sake."

"Shut up, John," Mrs. Cubberly said in a low, quiet voice. "Don't say another word until we get a solicitor here."

Barnes stood at the top of the staircase. He jerked his head to his left. "Down here, sir. It's in Mr. Cubberly's dressing room."

They trooped down the hallway and into a large, monkish bedroom. The walls were a plain white and bare of ornamentation or pictures, the windows covered with cheap brown cotton curtains and the furniture scratched and old.

On the far side of the room was another door. A young uniformed police constable was standing beside it.

"In the dressing room, sir," Barnes said. He led them into the small room and pointed down at a pair of boots covered with a polishing cloth. "Have a look in there, Inspector."

"Wiggins." Mrs. Jeffries smiled kindly at the footman. He looked dreadfully depressed. "Have you had any success today?"

He shook his head. "No. The whole bloomin' mornin' was a waste of time."

"Exactly where did you go today?" she persisted.

Wiggins blushed. "Over to Davies Street. I wanted to try and talk to Agnes again. Spent half the day 'angin' about the area, and the only person I talked to was that little street arab that 'angs about lookin' for errands to run."

"At least you didn't have to spend yer mornin' 'round a bunch of thieves and scoundrels," Smythe said.

Mrs. Jeffries gave the coachman a sharp look. Obviously, seeing his former associates and friends hadn't been a particularly happy experience for him. She wondered if Betsy would come back equally morose.

From outside, they heard the sound of a carriage. Smythe leapt from his chair and flew down the back hall to the backdoor. "It's Betsy and Hatchet," he yelled. "And they've got someone with 'em. It's a woman. Bloomin' Ada, I bet it's Lottie Grainger."

Witherspoon knelt down and pushed the cloth to one side. The handle of a gun protruded out of the boot. He swallowed and carefully reached for the weapon. Guns made him dreadfully nervous. Cautiously, he grasped the handle and pulled it out of the boot.

Barnes shook his head gravely. "That's a Colt forty-five, sir." He reached for the weapon. "If you don't mind, sir, I'll have a look at it."

"Er, do you know much about firearms, Constable?" He handed the gun over.

"A bit, sir," Barnes replied. Holding the gun with the barrel pointed toward the floor, he cocked it open and peered into the chamber. "Looks like we've found the murder weapon, sir," he stated softly. "One bullet's been fired."

CHAPTER 10

Lottie Grainger, lovely, green-eyed, dark-haired and very nervous, twisted her hands together in her lap. She stared anxiously at the seven people gathered 'round the table.

"Betsy told me you was all 'elpin' to find out who killed my Jake," she said softly. "Is it true?"

"Yes, it is," Mrs. Jeffries said firmly. "But we're going to need your help."

"I don't know," Lottie replied. "I don't much like gettin' mixed up with the police and all that."

"Do you want Jake's killer to go unpunished?" Mrs. Jeffries prodded. The girl was as skittish as a kitten in a room full of bulldogs. One false move and she would probably bolt for the door.

"Of course I don't," Lottie said. "But Jake . . . Jake was doin' some things that weren't proper. I didn't really know all that much about 'em, but the police may not believe me."

"If you are innocent of any wrongdoing," Mrs. Jeffries told her, "then you needn't worry about being arrested. You have my word."

Lottie stared at her for a few moments. "All right. I don't want whoever killed Jake to get away with it. I'll do what I can to 'elp you."

"Good. Now, we think the best way of going about our task is for you to tell us all you know about Jake."

Lottie's eyes filled with tears. "Jake were wonderful," she murmured, brushing at her cheeks. "'E treated me like a queen." She held her hand out. "'Ere, look it this, Jake give it to me less than a fortnight ago. It was our engagement ring."

On her finger was a ruby set in an ornate gold setting. Mrs. Jeffries was fairly certain the gem was real. Jake Randall had obviously thought enough of his sweetheart to give her an engagement ring of real value.

"It's lovely," Luty said softly. She tilted her head to one side and gazed at the grief-stricken young woman. "He musta loved you a lot."

"'E did," Lottie whispered.

"Then if you want to see his murderer brought to justice, you gotta trust us. You gotta tell us the truth, even if it makes Jake look bad. Even if it makes you look bad, ya understand. You can't hold nothin' back. Tell us everything you know and answer all our questions," Luty said earnestly. "We'll make sure the no-'count varmit that put a bullet through yer man's heart swings from the gallows. You've got my word on it."

Lottie wiped her eyes and straightened her spine. "Ask me anything you want."

"If it's all right with everyone," Mrs. Jeffries said, "I'll ask the questions. If I miss anything, the rest of you be sure and speak up." She glanced around the table, and one by one they nodded.

"Right, then." Mrs. Jeffries paused and took a breath. She really must get her thoughts in order. She must ask the right question. "Where did you go after you left the Cubberly house?"

"I went to Jake's lodgin' house," Lottie replied. "I wanted to warn him."

"Warn him about what?"

"About the gun. I'd already warned him they was gettin' suspicious about the mine, but this was different. They was out for blood. Mr. Cubberly was wavin' that gun around and threatenin' to kill Jake. So I left as quick as I could and went to warn 'im. But Jake wasn't there. I waited all day. All day and 'e never come." Her eyes filled with a fresh batch of tears, but she quickly wiped them away. "'E was already dead. Cubberly had found 'im."

"Why do you think John Cubberly's the killer?"

"'E were the one with the gun," Lottie said earnestly. "Who else coulda done it?"

Mrs. Jeffries knew this wasn't the time to tell Lottie there were a host of suspects. She didn't want the girl to stop talking. "When did you find out Jake was dead?" she asked softly.

"Same as everyone else," Lottie said wearily. "I saw it in the newspaper on Thursday morning."

"How long did you stay at Jake's lodging house?" Mrs. Jeffries thought this a most pertinent question. She wanted to understand the girl's movements on the day of the murder.

"Until late Monday night. I waited as long as I could, you see. But then I got scared."

"Scared of what?" Mrs. Goodge interjected.

"Jake and me was supposed to go off together, and when 'e didn't show," Lottie explained, "I thought . . . I thought . . . Oh God, I'm ashamed to admit it now. But I thought 'e'd gone off without me." She started crying again.

Smythe looked away from the weeping woman, Betsy reached over and patted the girl's arm, Luty rolled her eyes impatiently, and Wiggins fidgeted in embarrassment. Mrs. Goodge had the good sense to refill the teapot.

Mrs. Jeffries waited until the emotional storm had passed. But this was taking far too long, she thought. If they weren't careful, the inspector would come home and find them questioning the girl. She decided to try a different method. "Lottie, I know this is most distressing for you, but I think it would be more efficient if you told us about Jake in your own words."

"Where should I start?" Lottie sniffed. "I mean, do you want to know 'ow I met 'im, or what?"

"Just start talking," Mrs. Jeffries suggested. "And we'll see where that leads us." She was an excellent listener. It had often been her experience that if one listened carefully, people opened up like a sieve.

"All right." Lottie tilted her head to one side and her eyes took on a faraway look. "I met Jake about six months ago when I was workin' as a ladies' maid for this actress. But I wasn't happy there, didn't much like the sort that 'angs about the stage, if you get my meanin'. Jake didn't like me being there either. Jake told me he'd 'eard of a position as a housemaid for the Cubberlys. He warned me right off the wages was poor, but he thought it'd be best if I went there anyway. I weren't that worried about the wages. Jake give me plenty of money." She shrugged. "Besides, it weren't goin' to be for very long. He'd asked me to marry 'im and we were plannin' to go to the United States together."

"Did Jake ask you to do anything for him while you worked at the Cubberlys'?" Mrs. Jeffries asked gently.

Lottie hung her head. "'E asked me to keep me ears open and to tell

him if they ever started gettin' suspicious about Jake's business dealin's."
She lifted her chin. "I know I shouldn'a done it for him. But I loved Jake.
I didn't want anyone to hurt him. And I didn't know he was plannin' on
stealin' the investment money, I really didn't. I found out about the money
bein' gone from the bank when I was listenin' at the door when they was
havin' their meetin'. That's the first I knew of it, I swear. I know Jake did
some things that was wrong," she said defensively. "But 'e didn't deserve
to be murdered."

"No one does," Hatchet murmured.

"Go on," Mrs. Jeffries prompted. "Tell us the rest. What prompted
you to be listening outside the door that day?"

"Because I knew somethin' was wrong. A few days before they had
this meetin', Mr. Hinkle come over to the Cubberly house. Now, I weren't
listenin' at the door that time, but I did hear what Hinkle was tellin' Mr.
Cubberly. Blimey, I'm surprised the whole neighborhood didn't hear
Hinkle. He were shoutin' at the top of his lungs. He told Mr. Cubberly
he'd had a cable from some cousin of his about Jake's mine. Said the mine
wasn't bein' worked. Said there might be trouble with their investment
money, but he wouldn't find out for sure until he received his cousin's
letter."

"Did you tell Jake this?"

Lottie nodded. "Oh yes, I 'ad to wait until Mrs. Cubberly had gone up
to her room for the day and Mr. Cubberly had gone to the city, but as
soon as they left, I nipped out to the front gate and waited till Harry
showed up."

"Who's 'Arry?" Smythe asked.

"'E's the little street beggar that 'angs about Davies Street and Chester
Square," Wiggins answered. He smiled at Lottie. "I'm right, aren't I?"

Lottie laughed. "Yes, but 'ow do you know Harry?"

"Let's just say I've met 'im in the course of our inquiries," Wiggins
said proudly. "'E's a nice little nipper. 'E misses you, you know. Told me
the other lady at the Cubberly house weren't near as nice as you."

"What did you have this Harry do?" Mrs. Jeffries asked. She was getting rather impatient.

"I sent the boy off with a note for Jake. Warnin' 'im," Lottie replied.
"That's 'ow Jake and I used to stay in contact with each other. 'Arry was
always bringin' me notes, tellin' me where to meet Jake or bringin' me
some money from 'im."

Mrs. Jeffries pressed on. "And then what happened?"

"Jake come around that night and I told 'im what I'd overheard. He wanted me to leave with him then. But I couldn't. So he moved out of 'is hotel and into a lodgin' house over near Westminster. Jake made sure none of the investors knew where 'e was stayin'."

"So that explains why Jake Randall moved," Mrs. Jeffries said thoughtfully. "But why couldn't you leave with him when he asked you to?" she asked Lottie.

"'Cause of me sister. She were gettin' ready to 'ave her baby and I didn't want to leave the country while she were expectin'. America's a long way off and I knew it'd be years before I could see her and the baby. I wanted to stay until it was born. Her time was close, so Jake said it would be all right. Said he could stay out of their way." Lottie sighed deeply. "Jake didn't want to 'ang about, but 'e knew how much I wanted to be here for the baby's birth, so 'e stayed. He stayed because of me and he got murdered . . ."

"There, there," Betsy murmured softly. "You mustn't blame yourself. You didn't know he'd be murdered. 'Ere now, what did your sister have? A boy or a girl?"

"She had a baby boy. She named him Jake."

Inspector Witherspoon's ears were still ringing when he arrived home that evening. Gracious, what a day! Handing his bowler hat and coat to Mrs. Jeffries, he sighed in relief at the blessed peace and quiet of his home.

"I've had a dreadful day," he told her as they walked into the drawing room. "Positively dreadful."

"Oh dear," Mrs. Jeffries murmured. "I'm so sorry to hear that. I thought you were making progress on this case."

"We are," he replied, settling himself in his favorite chair. "I'll probably be making an arrest in a day or two."

Mrs. Jeffries's hand stilled as she reached for the sherry bottle. "Really?"

"Yes, indeed. As soon as I get confirmation of one or two details, I'll be arresting John Cubberly for Randall's murder."

Mrs. Jeffries forced her fingers to close around the sherry bottle. Her first thought was that her carefully laid plan to bring Lottie Grainger here tomorrow morning might not be a wise idea, after all. "Cubberly? So he's the murderer."

"Oh yes, yes indeed . . ." His voice trailed off. "Actually, I'm not absolutely certain that it's him. But honestly, there doesn't seem to be anyone else who could have done it."

"You found mud stains on his overcoat, then?" she asked. If that were all the evidence the inspector had, his case was as weak as rainwater.

"Indeed we did. You were absolutely right about Mrs. Brown. She hadn't bothered to clean the coat. Mrs. Cubberly had taken it upstairs, but she hadn't gotten 'round to giving it a brush-up either. But that's not the only evidence we have." He told Mrs. Jeffries about finding the note in Cubberly's pocket and the gun in Cubberly's boot.

"So you see," he continued, "the evidence is mounting against the fellow. He, of course, protests that he's innocent."

"Do you believe him, sir?" she asked. She was thinking frantically, trying to fit all the details the inspector had just revealed into the overall pattern. Lottie had claimed that there was no money with Jake's possessions at the lodging house. Therefore, one could assume that Jake had the money with him when he was killed. But did he? And could Cubberly possibly have known that?

"Not really." The inspector sighed. "But then again, he seems so sincere. I tell you, Mrs. Jeffries, if the man is lying, then he missed his true calling. He should have been an actor. Cubberly seemed genuinely stunned when we found both the note and the gun."

"May I see the note, sir?" She smiled uncertainly. "I know it's probably against police regulations, but really, you know how terribly interested I am."

"Of course you may see it," he replied. "Mind you, I should have given it to Barnes to take back to the station, but I'm afraid I forgot and put it in my pocket instead." He rummaged around in his waistcoat and drew out a folded piece of paper. "Ah, here it is." He handed it to Mrs. Jeffries.

She scanned it quickly. "I take it you're now certain that Cubberly met Randall at eight o'clock and killed him. Presumably, he stole the money as well."

"That's our theory."

"Then why, sir," she asked, handing the note back to him, "did you say you'd had such a dreadful day? It sounds to me like you're making excellent strides towards solving this murder."

"Oh, Cubberly was blubbering like a baby, Mrs. Cubberly was screeching at the top of her lungs, and Constable Barnes was pressing me to arrest Cubberly on the spot." He shuddered. "It was terrible, I tell you. Absolutely terrible."

"Why didn't you arrest Cubberly?" she asked curiously.

He toyed with his sherry glass. "I'm not sure. But somehow I couldn't bring myself to do it. I've left two police constables at the Cubberly house. We don't want Mr. Cubberly makin' a run for it, so to speak. But there's something about the whole situation I don't really like." He paused and gave her a sheepish smile. "Perhaps it's that 'guiding force' you mentioned yesterday. Perhaps it's telling me to dig a bit deeper in this case. In any event, I didn't think it would do any harm to sleep on the decision. I'll arrest Cubberly tomorrow. Though, mind you, the way Hilda Cubberly was ranting and raving, it will be a wonder if we get the man out of the house without losing our hearing. That woman has a very strong voice."

"I expect it's normal for a woman to want to protect her husband," Mrs. Jeffries said. "Though it certainly doesn't help Mr. Cubberly's position to have his wife screeching at the police like an enraged fishwife."

"Oh, she wasn't screeching at us," Witherspoon said.

"She was angry at her husband?" Mrs. Jeffries thought that most odd. According to what the inspector had told her earlier about Mrs. Cubberly, she would have expected the woman to be protecting her husband. Not screaming at him.

"That's putting it mildly. She was furious at him. Honestly, Mrs. Jeffries, if I hadn't seen her obvious devotion to her husband when we were questioning him yesterday, I'd have thought she hated the fellow."

While the inspector ate his meal Mrs. Jeffries told the others about John Cubberly's impending arrest.

"Well, that's it, then," Smythe said sullenly. "Looks like 'e solved this one without much 'elp from us."

"Don't be too sure about that," Mrs. Jeffries said. "The inspector isn't certain that Cubberly is guilty. For that matter, neither am I."

"Who else coulda done it, then?" Wiggins mumbled. "Even Lottie said there weren't no money at Jake's lodgin' 'ouse. That means 'e 'ad it with 'im. Cubberly's known to be a greedy miser—'e killed the bloke and stole the money."

"But how did Cubberly know where to meet Randall?" Mrs. Jeffries persisted.

"From the note," Mrs. Goodge said firmly. "It's quite clear what happened. John Cubberly was in cahoots with Jake. You said the note was addressed to 'J'—and Cubberly's the only one at the house with that initial."

"Perhaps," Mrs. Jeffries mused. She turned to Wiggins. "I want you to get over to Davies Street early tomorrow morning."

"Tomorrow mornin'? What 'ave I got to go all the way over there for? I wanted to be here when Miss Lottie come to see the inspector."

Luty had taken Lottie home with her. Everyone had agreed the girl needed some hot food and a good night's rest before she told the inspector her story.

"That's the point, Wiggins," Mrs. Jeffries told him patiently. "We need you to find out exactly who Harry gave that note to—assuming, of course, the note isn't a forgery."

"Lottie should be able to say whether it's a forgery or not," Mrs. Goodge put in. "She ought to be familiar with Jake Randall's handwriting. But I can't believe that note from Randall was meant for her. Why would he put the wrong initial on it? Besides, if Lottie had gotten the note, she woulda met him at eight o'clock that night. Instead, she spent the evenin' waitin' for him at his lodgin' house."

"We only have her word that she did wait for him," Mrs. Jeffries said tartly. "That's why talking to Harry is important."

"Do you think Lottie's lyin', then?" Betsy asked.

Mrs. Jeffries stared at her sharply. The girl's voice was flat, her expression downcast, and her shoulders were sagging. She'd been this way ever since she'd come back from the East End. "I think it's possible she could have done the murder."

"Oh, Mrs. Jeffries, that couldn't be true," Wiggins cried. He looked horrified by the idea. "Lottie's innocent, I tell ya. She couldn'a shot Jake. She loved 'im. Why, just talkin' about Randall made 'er cry 'er eyes out."

Mrs. Jeffries slept poorly that night. At half past twelve, she got up, wrapped herself in her warm, woolly shawl and stared out the window into the darkness.

There was something about this case that bothered her. Something someone had said. A clue of some kind. A piece of the puzzle that made everything else fall into place. But for the life of her, she couldn't put her finger on it.

She took a long, calming breath to clear her mind. Then she made herself start at the beginning. Jake Randall was shot on the evening of March 7, possibly around eight o'clock.

The only suspects who had alibis for that time were Lester Hinkle and Hilda Cubberly . . . She paused. Perhaps she'd better eliminate Rushton Benfield as well. According to the inspector, the porter at the block of flats where Benfield had been hiding was adamant that the man hadn't gone out that evening.

That left John Cubberly, Edward Dillingham, or Lottie Grainger. Mrs. Jeffries smiled slightly. Unlike Wiggins, she had no illusions about what the female of the species was capable of doing. Lottie Grainger had to be considered a possibility for the role of murderess. Luty might well have been right the other day when she was speculating that Lottie could have had the most common motive of all for killing her fiancé. She was going to be abandoned. Seduced and abandoned. It had happened often enough before.

Furthermore, Mrs. Jeffries thought, Lottie was the only one who knew where Jake lived. Despite the ready tears and the face like an angel, Lottie could well have been lying through her teeth today. She'd admitted she knew that Jake had stolen the investment money before she ran out of the Cubberly house. Lottie could just as easily have found out Jake was planning on leaving the country without her. The girl also knew the Cubberly household. By her own admission, she'd seen John Cubberly's gun. She could have pretended to leave that day, knowing that she could slip back inside, grab the gun, and meet Jake.

But was that what happened? Mrs. Jeffries wondered. And if Jake Randall was planning on abandoning Lottie, why would he send a note to the Cubberly house? Surely, there would have been other, less risky ways for him to meet John Cubberly.

And what motive did Cubberly really have for murdering Randall? True, Cubberly was a miser. But there was no evidence he was having financial difficulties. On the contrary, he was the only one of the investors who genuinely could have weathered the loss. So why would he stoop to stealing and murder? Why risk losing everything he had? Miserliness wasn't a particularly noble character trait, yet it didn't necessarily follow that because one was a miser one was also a murderer.

She closed her eyes and tried to let her mind wander. After a few moments she sighed. This was doing no good whatsoever. Perhaps tomorrow it would come to her. Perhaps a good night's rest would jog her memory.

"Has Wiggins returned yet?" Mrs. Jeffries asked Mrs. Goodge.

"Not yet, but it may take him a bit o' time to find Harry," the cook replied. "How'd the inspector like his breakfast?"

"He enjoyed it very much," Mrs. Jeffries said. "He'll be in the right frame of mind to listen to Lottie when she arrives. I only hope that Wiggins is able to find the boy. We need to know who Harry gave that note to."

They'd made their plan most carefully. Mrs. Goodge had relented and fixed the inspector a superbly filling breakfast of bacon and eggs. Wiggins had nipped off at the crack of dawn to find the street boy, and Lottie Grainger was due to arrive any moment.

Betsy, who was standing at the kitchen sink, rose on her tiptoes and peeked out the window to the street. "A hansom's just pulled up in front," she announced. "It's probably Lottie, so I best get upstairs."

Smythe watched her as she left the room. He waited until he heard her footsteps on the stairs before saying, "What's wrong with the lass, Mrs. Jeffries? She ain't acted 'appy since she come back from the East End yesterday."

"I don't know, Smythe," Mrs. Jeffries replied. She was worried about Betsy, too. "Perhaps it was going back to her old haunts. Perhaps it brought back unhappy memories. I don't think she was very happy when she lived in that district." She shook her head and pushed the matter to another part of her mind. She'd have a quiet word with Betsy later. Right now, she had to keep her wits about her. "I'd better get upstairs. You know what to do?"

"Don't worry," Smythe said. "We know exactly what to do."

"Oh, Mrs. Jeffries," the inspector called. "Could you come in here a moment?"

She walked calmly into the room, not giving a hint that she'd been hanging about the hall waiting for his summons. "Yes, sir," she said politely. "Is there something I can do for you or your guest?" She smiled at Lottie, who was sitting demurely on the settee.

Witherspoon cleared his throat. "I'd appreciate it if you'd sit down.

Miss Grainger would like to make a statement." He paused and shot a fast, wary glance at Lottie. "She'd prefer to have another . . . woman present, if you don't mind."

The inspector was most perplexed and just a bit offended. Really, he thought, did this young woman think he wasn't to be trusted? But being a gentleman, he did as she requested.

"I don't mind in the least, Inspector." Mrs. Jeffries sat down next to Lottie.

She was delighted that her plan was working. She'd told Lottie to insist on having a woman in the room while she spoke to the inspector. Lottie, of course, believed Mrs. Jeffries was there to give her moral support, and to some extent that was true. But Mrs. Jeffries was also there for another reason. She wanted to make sure Lottie told the inspector the same story she'd told them.

"Now," Witherspoon said briskly. "Could you please tell me where you've been since leaving the Cubberly residence?"

Lottie smiled shyly. "I've been at me aunt's house over at Wentworth Street. My sister lives with 'er, you see, and she's just had a baby."

Witherspoon's cheeks turned pink. "Er, uh, congratulations to your sister, then."

"Thank you, sir. She had a lovely little baby boy. If you don't mind, sir, I'd like to make me statement in me own words. Is that all right?"

Taken aback, Witherspoon blinked. This was a most odd development. For a moment he seriously considered asking the young lady to wait until Constable Barnes arrived before she began her statement, but that would be so rude. Furthermore, the girl had come here of her own accord. But really, this was most unusual. "Er, if that's what you would prefer," he said cautiously. "Then I suppose it's all right." He knew he could always ask her additional questions later.

"Thank you, sir." She gave him a dazzling smile. The inspector blushed again.

"I'll begin with a few days before I left the Cubberly house," Lottie began. She told the inspector everything she'd told Mrs. Jeffries and the others the day before.

Mrs. Jeffries watched Lottie carefully while she talked.

Today, she had her emotions well under control. Her words were strong and confident. They were also non-incriminating. They'd spent some time last night coaching Lottie on how to phrase her statements. It wouldn't do if the inspector thought she'd had anything to do with swindling the money out of the stockholders of the Randall and Watson Mine.

"Now, let me see," Witherspoon queried when she'd finished. "You're saying you left the Cubberly house because you were afraid there was going to be trouble and you wanted to warn Jake. Is that correct?"

"Yes, sir."

"Hmmm. And Randall was in the habit of sending you notes. Is that right?"

"Yes," Lottie replied. "'E used to send Harry 'round with one every afternoon. Jake liked to make sure I was all right. And sometimes he'd tell me where and what time to meet 'im."

"Excellent," Witherspoon said. "In that case, you should be able to help." He reached into his waistcoat and pulled out the folded note. "Can you look at this, please, and confirm that it's Jake Randall's handwriting."

Perplexed, Lottie took the note and opened it. She studied it for several moments. "This is Jake's writin', but I've never seen this one before in my life."

"But of course you haven't," the inspector replied with a smile. "There's a 'J' at the top. We think it was meant for John Cubberly."

Lottie stared at him for a moment. "Oh no, sir. You're mistaken. This was meant for me."

Mrs. Jeffries sat bolt upright.

"But Miss Grainger," Witherspoon said patiently. "Your name starts with an 'L,' not a 'J.'"

"I know that Inspector." She laughed. "But Jake always called me by my middle name—Jane. You know, 'e thought it was sweet that way. Jane and Jake. 'E was quite a romantic, my Jake was."

Witherspoon's eyes widened. "So this note was meant for you," he exclaimed. "Then how did it end up in Mr. Cubberly's overcoat? That's what I want to know?"

Mrs. Jeffries quietly got up and went to the mahogany table by the window. She pulled open the drawer and took out the heavy oak-rimmed magnifying glass her husband had given her.

"Excuse me, Inspector," she said politely. "But if you'll allow me to make a suggestion. Perhaps you might learn something more about the note if you examine it with this."

Mrs. Jeffries was beginning to put the puzzle together. One or two of the pieces were starting to fall into place.

"Er, a magnifying glass?" he murmured.

"Of course, sir." She smiled. "You are the one who always said one should never take anything at face value."

He looked confused for a brief instant. "Indeed I do, Mrs. Jeffries," he said, reaching for the glass. Holding the glass over the note, he examined it carefully.

After a few moments he said, "Mrs. Jeffries, would you have a look at this for me? I'm not sure, but it does look as though someone has added a top stroke to the number eight. There's a slight difference in the color of the ink as well."

Mrs. Jeffries stared at the magnified figure. The inspector was right: not only was there a difference in ink color between the top and the bottom of the "8," but if you looked carefully, you could see the side stroke of the figure had originally been one long, continuous motion. Someone had added the top "O" to the number. "You're right, sir. I believe this eight was originally a six."

"Then that would mean"—the inspector paused, his forehead wrinkling as he concentrated—"that the note originally said, 'Meet me at six,' not eight. Gracious, Mrs. Jeffries."

"There's somethin' else you should know," Lottie said. She pointed to the top of the paper. "This 'ere's got a date on it. See, seven/three. But Jake never dated 'is notes to me. Why should 'e? He sent one every day."

There was a pounding on the front door. Mrs. Jeffries, who was thinking furiously, glanced up and saw Wiggins rushing down the hall towards the front door. A moment later she heard voices and then a pounding of feet.

Constable Barnes burst into the room. "Sorry for interruptin' like this, sir," he cried. "But somethin' awful's happened."

"Egads, Barnes," the inspector replied. He stared at him in alarm. "You're in a frightful state. What on earth is the matter?"

"It's that bloomin' Inspector Nivens," the constable yelled. "The silly fool's just gone and arrested John Cubberly."

"Mr. Cubberly's been arrested," Lottie repeated. She seemed most confused.

Witherspoon rose to his feet. "Nivens has arrested Cubberly? But that's unheard of. Why would Nivens do such a thing? Surely you're mistaken. This is my case."

"I'm not mistaken, sir," Barnes cried. "I seen it with my own eyes. He did it because the smarmy bastard wants the collar for himself. I tried to stop him, but he claimed he'd got the go-ahead from the chief. Said you was takin' too long and that they was afraid Cubberly would make a run for it. Nivens arrested him and took him down to the station."

"Gracious, Barnes." Witherspoon was shocked by Nivens's behavior. "I'm afraid I really will have to protest. This is an outrage."

Mrs. Jeffries saw Wiggins waving to her from the hall. She backed out of the room.

"What did you find out?" she whispered.

Wiggins checked to make sure the inspector and Barnes hadn't noticed him. "Sorry it took me so long to get back," he hissed, "but I saw Nivens and his boys goin' into the Cubberly 'ouse and I wanted to 'ang about a bit and see what was goin' on."

"Good work, Wiggins," she replied quickly. The inspector was starting to pace up and down the room. He was truly angry. "Now, what did Harry tell you?"

Wiggins smiled. "You'll never believe this, Mrs. J. He took the note there that day, all right. But 'e didn't give it to Lottie nor to Mr. Cubberly. I told ya Lottie couldn't 'ave done it, I told ya she were too in love with Randall to kill 'im."

The pieces were falling rapidly into place now. Mrs. Jeffries knew that whoever had gotten their hands on that note was the person who'd killed Jake Randall. She was fairly certain she knew who the person was, too.

"Yes, Wiggins, I know you did," she hissed impatiently. "And you were absolutely right. Who did Harry give the note to?"

"Hilda Cubberly."

CHAPTER 11

———⊰•⊱———

The last piece fell into place. "Excellent, Wiggins, You've done a superb job."

"You shoulda been there, Mrs. J.," Wiggins continued excitedly. "Nivens hustled Cubberly out of the house fast as you please."

"Yes, I'm sure it was very interesting." Mrs. Jeffries was trying to think of the best way to approach the inspector. She gazed at him through the doorway. He was still pacing angrily up and down the room. She'd have to handle this most carefully, she thought, she'd never seen the inspector in such a state.

"It were better than just interestin'," he countered. "It was like watchin' one of them puppet shows at the fair. Five minutes after Mr. Cubberly got taken off, Mrs. Cubberly comes 'urryin' out with the housekeeper 'ot on 'er 'eels."

Mrs. Jeffries turned to stare at him. "What?"

Wiggins laughed. "You shoulda seen it, Zita Brown was 'angin' onto Mrs. Cubberly's skirts and askin' for her wages. Mrs. Cubberly was strugglin' with her carpetbag and tryin' to push the housekeeper off at the same time that she were tryin' to get into a hansom. Constable Barnes was shoutin' at her that she shouldn't be leavin' and she were shoutin' right back that she couldn't be compelled to give evidence against her husband and that she'd go anywhere she damned well pleased. It were a right old dust-up, I tell you."

"Oh my goodness. Do you know where Mrs. Cubberly was going? Think, Wiggins. Think. It's vitally important."

"'Course I know where she were goin'. She had to shout to the driver over Mrs. Brown and Barnes. She told 'im to take her to Waterloo Station."

"Quick! We've no time to lose. Run down to the kitchen and tell Smythe to bring the carriage here."

"You mean now?"

"Yes, now. Run. Tell Smythe to hurry as well."

Wiggins ran down the hall. Mrs. Jeffries took a deep breath and calmly walked back into the drawing room.

"Mrs. Jeffries." The inspector stopped his pacing and turned to look at her. "I'm going right to the chief superintendent. I've never been so offended in my life. This is an outrage. Have you ever heard of such a thing! Inspector Nivens arresting John Cubberly right out from under my nose."

She smiled serenely. "I can see that you're upset, sir. But really, you are planning to have a good laugh at Inspector Nivens's expense when you walk into the station with the real murderer."

Witherspoon's jaw gaped open.

"I beg your pardon, ma'am," Barnes said. "But what are you talkin' about? John Cubberly is the killer."

"Oh, 'course he isn't. That's why the inspector didn't arrest him," Mrs. Jeffries said confidently. She sent up a silent prayer that she was completely correct in her deduction. "Come now, Inspector, it isn't fair to keep the good constable in suspense. You know very well you've deduced the identity of the real murderer."

"I have?"

"Naturally you have." She smiled at Lottie. "Miss Grainger has just told you that she never received the note that day. Tell me, Miss Grainger," she asked the confused-looking young woman, "would your friend Harry have given the note to Mr. Cubberly or the housekeeper, Zita Brown."

"Oh no," Lottie replied quickly. "'E was scared of both of them. Mind you, he might've given it to Mrs. Cubberly. She'd once paid 'im for runnin' an errand for 'er."

"Mrs. Cubberly?" the inspector repeated. He looked confused, too.

"Why yes, sir," Mrs. Jeffries said hastily. "Why, you've even been giving me little hints about the real identity of the killer. Hilda Cubberly is the only one who could have done it. She was the one who brought you her husband's overcoat that had the note in it. She wanted you to believe that the murder took place at eight o'clock. A time when she had an alibi. Furthermore, she'd made sure the overcoat was still mud stained by taking it upstairs so the housekeeper wouldn't brush it off. Who else but Mrs. Cubberly could have slipped the note in Cubberly's pocket? Who else but she knew where Jake Randall was going to be that night? And who else but she had the best motive of all for murder? Money." She wagged her finger at the inspector. "Oh, sir, admit it, you've been dropping little clues all along to see if I could figure it out Jake Randall knew that the investors were after him. Why on earth would he have allowed one of them to walk up and shoot him in the chest? If Randall had been killed by any of the other suspects, I'll wager that he'd have been shot in the back. He'd have turned and tried to run if he'd seen a man approaching him on a dark footpath by the river. But he was expecting to meet a woman. He'd think it was Lottie coming towards him. Until, of course, it was too late."

"Er . . . yes, yes, of course," the inspector cried. "Gracious, I'd better get over to the Cubberly house right away."

"That won't do us any good, sir," Barnes cried. "Mrs. Cubberly's gone. Packed a carpetbag and left for the train station. I heard her telling Nivens she wasn't going to stay in London and be humiliated by her husband's arrest."

"Oh dear," the inspector mumbled. "I suppose if we miss her at the train station, we can wire the police somewhere further down the line."

"But, sir," Mrs. Jeffries interjected, "do you really think that is wise? You don't want to give her an opportunity to hide that carpetbag full of money, do you?"

Witherspoon's brows drew together. "Er . . . why do you think the money is in the carpetbag?" he asked.

"Well, of course it is, sir. Hilda Cubberly's a lady. If she were really leaving her husband because she couldn't face being humiliated, she'd have spent the day packing her trunks. She wouldn't have run off carrying a carpetbag. Ladies do not carry their own luggage." It was weak, but it was the best she could come up with on the spur of the moment. And it was imperative that the inspector arrest Mrs. Cubberly with the money in her possession.

"But she's got such a head start on us," Witherspoon said anxiously.

"Not to worry, sir," Mrs. Jeffries assured him. "As it happens, Smythe is bringing the carriage 'round this morning. He was going to take me to Elstree to buy some fruit. He should be here any minute."

"Do hurry, Smythe," the inspector shouted through the carriage window. "We mustn't let her get away."

"'Ang on, sir," the coachman yelled back, "I know a shortcut." He whistled sharply and the horses broke into a gallop. They took the corner on two wheels.

"Gracious," the inspector said as he was bounced back onto his seat, "I do hope Smythe knows what he's doing."

The ride got faster and wilder. They careened through tiny streets at breakneck speed and cut through mews with barely inches to spare on each side of the carriage.

Finally, they pulled up in front of Waterloo Station. Barnes leapt out of the carriage and Smythe tossed the reins to a porter. The inspector jumped out and frantically tried to think of which platform to search.

"Why don't we try the boat train," Barnes suggested eagerly. He took off at a run through the doors with Smythe and Witherspoon right behind him.

Oblivious to the stares of the passengers milling around the entrance hall, they ran toward the gates leading to the trains. They stopped on the other side of the barrier and searched the platforms.

The platforms were crowded with passengers, porters, freight, and handcarts filled with luggage. On the far side of the station, a train was pulling in, while on the platform nearest them, one was pulling out.

"Oh no," Witherspoon moaned. "I think we're too late. She was probably on that one that's just leaving."

"There she is, sir," Barnes cried. He pointed to the far side of the station. Halfway down the platform, Hilda Cubberly stood waiting to board the train, the carpetbag dangling in her right hand.

They ran across the cavernous room, dodging passengers and getting shouted at by porters and ticket takers. Reaching the end of the platform, they charged towards Hilda Cubberly.

Smythe ran ahead of the inspector. Witherspoon and Barnes were almost upon her as the last of the disembarking passengers got off and Hilda stepped toward the open door. A conductor shouted, "All aboard."

"Halt," the inspector yelled.

Startled, she looked towards them. She recognized him instantly and turned to flee, the carpetbag clutched to her chest. As she spun around she ran smack into Smythe's massive chest.

"I believe, ma'am," he said politely, "the two gentlemen behind you would like to have a word with you."

"Get out of my way, you great fool," she hissed.

"Mrs. Cubberly." The inspector skidded to a halt and tried to catch his breath. "We'd like to have a few words with you," he panted.

"I've nothing to say to the police," she snapped. "Now get out of my way, I'm going to catch this train."

"Are you in a hurry to go somewhere?" Constable Barnes asked.

"That's none of your business."

"Mrs. Cubberly," Witherspoon said politely. "Could you please open your carpetbag? I assure you, I'm well within the law by requesting that you do so."

"And if I don't?" she challenged. "What are you going to do? Arrest me?"

Witherspoon stood his ground. He looked her directly in the eyes. "If I have to." He held out his hand for the bag.

She stared at him for a moment as though she didn't believe him. Then she handed him the carpetbag.

Witherspoon was surprised at how very heavy it was. He gave it to Constable Barnes, who knelt down, flipped the clasp and yanked it open. "It's filled with pound notes, sir," the constable said quietly. "Hundreds of them."

Witherspoon nodded. He turned to face her. "Mrs. Cubberly, I'm arresting you for the murder of Jake Randall."

In disbelief, she gazed at him. Then she laughed. "Do you think they'll hang me, then?" she asked merrily. Her eyes were wild, her laugh hysterical and frightening. "It doesn't matter if they do, you see," she continued conversationally. "I'd rather hang than live one more minute with that bastard I'm married to."

"Please, Mrs. Cubberly." The inspector was aware of a growing crowd gathering. "I really don't think you ought to say anything more till we're at the police station. Perhaps you'd best be quiet until we notify your husband—"

"Husband!" She threw back her head and laughed louder. "He's not a husband. He's a demon. A miserly devil from the pits of hell. Nothing you could do to me would be worse than what he's done. . . ."

She kept on laughing all the way to the police station.

"You shoulda seen her," Smythe said. "She were even worse once we got her down to the station."

"Sounds like she were bad enough at Waterloo," Mrs. Goodge said. "Poor Inspector Witherspoon. Imagine havin' to arrest a woman makin' a right old spectacle of herself."

Wiggins reached for a piece of seedcake. "Go on," he urged the coachman, "tell us everythin'. What did Mrs. Cubberly do?"

"Well, once we got her down there, she confessed to killin' Randall. She couldn't get it out fast enough." Smythe shook his head. "She admitted that she was the one that got the note that day. After hearin' her husband and the other investors talkin' at the meetin', she was fairly certain Randall would have the money on him. So she waited till they left, grabbed 'er 'usband's gun and took off for Waterloo Bridge." He paused and his face grew serious. "'Earin' Mrs. Cubberly talk so calmly about 'ow she just walked right up to Jake Randall and shot 'im made me half-sick. Poor blighter didn't stand a chance."

"Of course not," Mrs. Jeffries said. "He was expecting Lottie Grainger. In the darkness of the footpath, he wouldn't be the least suspicious of a woman coming towards him."

"You know what I don't understand," Luty said. "Where'd she hide the money? The police searched the Cubberly house and they didn't find hide nor hair of it."

"Mrs. Cubberly was clever," Smythe said. "She didn't hide the money in the house, least not when she knew it was goin' to be searched. When she first come back that night, she hid it under her bed. But as soon as the police found the note in Cubberly's pocket, she knew it wouldn't be long before they searched the house. So she grabbed the money and hid it next door in the neighbors' garden shed. She put it under some old tarps."

"That's a bit risky," Betsy said. "What if the neighbors had found it?"

"They was gone," Smythe explained. "Mrs. Cubberly wasn't takin' any risk at all."

"So that explains why she was so adamant about the inspector not searching the house when he found the note in her husband's pocket. The inspector mentioned she told them they would have to get a warrant." Mrs. Jeffries mused. "Now we know why. She needed time to hide the money."

"Why didn't she just leave then?" Betsy asked. "I mean, she had the money. Why hang about waitin' to get caught?"

"I don't think her goal was simply to murder and steal," Mrs. Jeffries replied. "I think she wanted her husband to hang for Jake Randall's murder. It was a way to get rid of him and eventually gain control of her own money."

"All right now," Mrs. Goodge said to the housekeeper. "Tell us how you figured out it was her?"

"I didn't figure it out until it was almost too late," Mrs. Jeffries replied with a modest shrug. "But what really made it all come together in my mind was Wiggins getting confirmation that Harry had given the note to Mrs. Cubberly. According to Zita Brown, Hilda Cubberly ordered her to have her dinner ready at seven o'clock that evening. Now, that was odd. The household was extremely lax. Being ordered to serve dinner promptly at seven o'clock was unusual enough that Mrs. Brown remembered the occasion. As she was meant to remember it. Mrs. Cubberly insisted on having dinner served at that specific time to give herself an alibi. She had the note. She knew that she'd meet Randall at six, shoot him and then be back to her home by a quarter to seven. And she knew all of this before she left the house that day. She was the only one of the suspects to make sure she had an alibi for eight o'clock. That was simply a bit too convenient."

"Is that the only clue you had?" Hatchet asked as he gazed at her in admiration.

"No, there were several others. But I didn't understand them at the time," Mrs. Jeffries admitted. "Looking back, though, you can see what should have been obvious. First of all, there was the overcoat. Hilda knew her husband was a suspect in a murder that had been committed by the river. Yet instead of cleaning the mud off that coat, she took it upstairs. Why? Because she wanted to make sure that Mrs. Brown wouldn't accidentally clean it herself. Also, when the inspector asked to see the coat, it was Hilda who went and got it. I think she slipped the altered note in the pocket at that time, putting it there so the inspector would be sure to find it."

"Two clues," Luty murmured. "That's still pretty danged good thinkin' on your part."

"Now, now, it wasn't all my doing," Mrs. Jeffries replied. "I couldn't have done it without all of you. You and Hatchet found out about the gun, Luty. Smythe alerted us to the fact that the investors had gone looking for Randall in the first place, Wiggins located young Harry, Betsy found Lottie Grainger, and Mrs. Goodge gave us the information that clearly explained Hilda Cubberly's motive."

"I did?" Mrs. Goodge looked puzzled and pleased at the same time.

"Of course you did," Mrs. Jeffries said warmly. "If it hadn't been for you finding out that Hilda had been forced to marry John Cubberly, none of this would have made sense. Hilda hated her husband. Yet, like many women, she was trapped. Jake Randall stealing that fifty thousand pounds must have seemed a godsend to her. Not only would she have enough money to live on while her husband was tried and convicted, but she had enough to get completely out of the country."

"Right," Smythe agreed. "That train was headin' for Southampton. We found a ticket for a steam packet in the carpetbag, too. She were headin' for South America."

"Do you think she deliberately tried to fix it so Mr. Cubberly would be arrested?" Betsy asked.

"No, I think originally she just wanted the money." Mrs. Jeffries reached for her teacup. "She was probably just going to disappear. But then when Randall's body was discovered, I think she cleverly found she could manipulate the police and implicate John Cubberly. She did hide the gun in her husband's boot. And she did it only after she'd made such a fuss about a warrant that the police were sure to be suspicious and search the house."

Mrs. Jeffries was glad to see Betsy taking an active interest in the discussion. The maid had brightened somewhat, but Mrs. Jeffries could tell she was still a bit melancholy about something.

"It's kinda sad, isn't it?" Betsy sighed. "Poor Lottie's lost her fiancé, Mr. Cubberly's ruined and grieved, and Mrs. Cubberly's goin' to 'ang."

"Don't be too sure o' that, lass," Smythe said gently. "The way she were rantin' and ravin', they may lock her up in a madhouse."

"Whether she hangs or they lock her up don't seem to make much difference," Betsy said sadly. "Nothin'll bring Jake back. What's Lottie goin' to do? Where's she gonna go?"

"Please don't worry about Miss Grainger." Hatchet reached over and patted Betsy's arm. "Madam has kindly invited her to stay with us for a while." He glanced at Luty. "Haven't you, madam?"

Luty snorted. "Didn't have much choice, did I? Couldn't toss the girl out on the streets. Her sister and her aunt don't have a hill a' beans. Wouldn't be fair to expect 'em to take in another mouth to feed."

Mrs. Jeffries noticed that Hatchet had been watching Betsy anxiously since he'd arrived. For that matter, they'd all been concerned about the girl. Smythe would barely let her out of his sight, Wiggins had hovered over her like a mother hen, and Mrs. Goodge was continually offering her tea. She made up her mind to get to the bottom of what was bothering the maid. They were all going to worry themselves to death if she didn't.

Luty shoved her chair back. "Come on, Hatchet," she commanded. "It's gettin' late. We'd best be goin'. I've got to go to that danged theatre tonight."

"But you've been looking forward to going, madam," Hatchet told her as he got to his feet.

"Yeah, but tonight I'm tired. I'd much rather stay here until after the inspector comes home so we can get the rest of the details."

"Don't worry about the details, Luty," Mrs. Jeffries said as she got up and followed them down the hall. "We'll have another gathering soon. A proper tea party. We'll go over the whole case then."

"Good, I'd hate to miss anythin'."

"Good night, Mrs. Jeffries," Hatchet said. He reached for the door handle.

"Hatchet," she said. He stopped and looked at her. "I'd like to have a word with you. It's about Betsy."

"Girl's been mopin' about with a long face ever since she come back with Lottie Grainger," Luty said to her butler. "Do you know anything about it?"

Hatchet didn't say anything for a moment. Then he sighed softly. "I'm afraid I do. But it's a rather private . . . oh heavens. You see, I saw something and I'm not sure it's right to tell anyone."

"Land sakes, man," Luty sputtered. "We're only concerned for the girl's welfare. You kin trust us not to go blabbing to everyone else about Betsy."

Hatchet hesitated. "All right, but please, don't say anything to her. This is the sort of thing that Miss Betsy must work out for herself."

"What in tarnation is it?" Luty hissed.

"Grief," Hatchet said quietly, "Miss Betsy is grieving. On the way back here with Lottie, she asked me to stop the carriage. We were by a small church. I did as she requested. But after she got out, I became rather concerned. The church was in a dreadful part of the city. So I bade Miss Grainger to stay put and, well, I followed her. She'd gone into the churchyard. She was kneeling in front of a grave. I believe she was crying." He looked down at the floor. "It was a pauper's grave. There was no headstone marking the spot, just a large rock. I didn't want to intrude. But Betsy happened to look up and she saw me. She told me the grave belonged to her mother."

The inspector was utterly exhausted when he came home. Mrs. Jeffries hustled him into the drawing room and into his favorite chair.

"I thought tonight you might like a brandy, sir," she said.

His face was drawn and pale, his eyes sad. "Thank you, Mrs. Jeffries," he said, taking the glass and putting it on the table beside him. "That's most thoughtful of you. I suppose I should be happy, but I'm not."

"I know, sir," she said gently. "How did it go?"

"We arrested Mrs. Cubberly," he said, "but it was rather monstrous. The woman's consumed with hatred. Quite mad, in my opinion. You should have heard the awful things she said to her husband. She actually looked that man in the face and told him she'd rather swing from a gallows than spend one more minute living with him."

"She confessed, then."

"Oh yes." Witherspoon took a sip of his drink. "Nivens looked a right fool. Yet still, it was a rather depressing day."

"You're a very kindhearted man, sir," she told him truthfully. "It's no wonder the day's events have saddened you. Yet you must take comfort in the fact that justice was done. Jake Randall may have been a thief and a swindler, but he didn't deserve to be shot and shoved in the river. It was your brilliant investigating that solved this heinous crime."

"You do make me feel better, Mrs. Jeffries," he said. "But as for me being a brilliant investigator . . ." He paused and shrugged modestly. "I'm still not certain exactly how I did it. I think perhaps it was my 'guiding force,' as you call it. I couldn't quite bring myself to arrest John Cubberly.

I expect I wouldn't have determined that the killer was Mrs. Cubberly if Miss Grainger hadn't come forward when she did."

Mrs. Jeffries relaxed. The inspector had now convinced himself he'd solved the murder. "What about Miss Grainger?"

"Oh, we're not pressing any charges against her," Witherspoon replied. "She may have been planning on marrying Jake Randall, but she had nothing to do with the theft of the investment money."

Mrs. Jeffries nodded. Poor man, he was still a bit down in the dumps. She decided he needed to talk it all out. Once he got it off his chest, he'd feel much better. "Are the investors going to get their money back?" she asked.

"Oh yes. With Mrs. Cubberly's confession, there won't be a full trial of course, only a sentencing. So the money needn't be held for evidence." He smiled faintly. "Dillingham and Hinkle's solicitors were already at the station when I left. I think they were bending the chief's ear to get the process speeded up a bit. Not that it'll do them much good—it's the judicial system which has authority now."

He continued to talk about the case for the next half hour. Mrs. Jeffries listened carefully, occasionally asking a question or shaking her head sympathetically.

"I say," Witherspoon finally said. "I'm famished. Er, a, what's Mrs. Goodge cooked for us tonight?"

"A nice roast beef and Yorkshire pudding." Mrs. Jeffries pulled a sheet of paper out of her pocket "I know it's not within keeping of the household management scheme," she said apologetically. "But we decided that you'd been working so hard, you needed a good meal." She handed him the paper. "However, after you eat, sir, we do need to go over the scheme. Mrs. Goodge has come up with some wonderful ideas to save money."

The inspector took the paper, got to his feet, and walked to the fire. He tossed the paper into the flames.

"Why, sir," Mrs. Jeffries exclaimed. "Whatever are you doing? That's our household management scheme."

"I know, Mrs. Jeffries." He gave her a wide smile. "But I've decided we don't need the wretched thing anymore. Life is short. For many, life is short and cruel. We are very lucky here at Upper Edmonton Gardens. My investments may not be doing as well as I'd like, but that's no reason to turn into a miser. Gracious, look at poor John Cubberly. No more pennypinching. In the future, we shall eat, drink, and be merry."

• • •

They had their gathering a week later. To celebrate the event, Mrs. Goodge had outdone herself. There were sausage rolls, cock-a-leekie soup, mutton ham, Dundee cake, jellies, currant buns, and plenty of good, strong tea.

"Now, that's what I call a proper feed." Wiggins patted his stomach and looked down at the floor. "Even Fred's too full to move." The dog was sound asleep on his side, his stomach bulging with all the treats he'd been slipped.

"Mrs. Goodge," Mrs. Jeffries said, "this tea was superb."

"Excellent repast, madam." Hatchet bowed formally at the cook.

"Danged good grub," Luty agreed.

Betsy laughed. "We've all made pigs of ourselves," she said gaily.

Smythe grinned. "That's all right lass, we've earned it."

Mrs. Jeffries was delighted that everything was back to normal. Betsy had gotten over her grief, Smythe and Wiggins were out and about and up to their usual activities, and Mrs. Goodge had been cooking up a storm.

"Well, I've got an announcement to make," Luty said. She grinned. "Lottie's goin' to Colorado."

"Colorado?" Mrs. Goodge repeated.

"In America?" Wiggins said incredulously.

"Whatever for?" Mrs. Jeffries asked.

Luty laughed. "She's goin' to Colorado as the new owner of half of the Randall and Watson Silver Mine. She was Jake's heir. He left her everythin' he owned. He'd done a will."

"But the mine's worthless," Smythe said.

Luty shook her head. She reached for her muff and pulled out a piece of paper. "No, it ain't. It's loaded with silver. I got this telegram from my people today." She turned to Mrs. Jeffries. "Remember when I asked you to find out exactly where the mine was located?"

Mrs. Jeffries nodded. "Yes, but—"

"No buts about it," Luty snorted. "Soon as you mentioned the word 'Leadville,' I sent off a cable. I knew there might be silver in that mine. There's tons of silver in that part of Colorado. And I was right."

"Do you think Jake knew there was silver there?" Wiggins asked.

"Probably not. But it don't matter now." Luty cackled. "The investors was so happy to get their money back, they give all the shares they bought back to Randall's solicitor. None of them made a profit! Now it all belongs to Lottie. Just goes to show you, don't it?"

"Exactly what does it show us?" Mrs. Jeffries asked cautiously.

"That takin' stock would have been a lot smarter than takin' the money," Luty replied tartly. "But that's all right. I reckon Lottie'll do a lot more good with a mine full of silver than any of the investors. They were a pretty sorry lot, if you ask me."

"I think, Luty," Mrs. Jeffries replied with a smile, "you're absolutely right about that."

MRS. JEFFRIES ON THE BALL

This book is lovingly dedicated
to the memory of Doris Annie Arguile

CHAPTER 1

⟐

The woman was no better than a common streetwalker!

Hannah Greenwood glared at the tall blonde following the butler through the double doors. Her lip curled in disgust as she watched the odious creature make her way toward the center of activity, Rowena Stanwick. The cow. With her head held high and her long, slender back ramrod straight, she entered the Marlow drawing room as though she were the queen herself.

Hannah snorted derisively, ignoring the startled expression on the face of Mrs. Putnam, who was sitting in the chair next to her, as she glared at the Stanwick woman. The tart might have the rest of them fooled, she thought, but she doesn't pull the wool over my eyes. All of her pretentious airs and fancy clothes won't protect her one whit, not when I'm through with her. I'll make her pay for what she's done. Really pay.

"I'm so dreadfully sorry to be late," Rowena apologized to the group at large. Dressed in a dark red afternoon gown that contrasted beautifully with her coloring, she moved gracefully to the velvet settee in the middle of a semicircle of chairs placed in front of the marble fireplace. "Exciting as Her Majesty's Jubilee celebration might be, it does make for an extraordinary amount of traffic. It took us ages to get down Regent Street. The streets were mobbed, absolutely mobbed."

"That's quite all right," Dr. Oxton Sloan assured her. "We've only just started. Do sit down and catch your breath."

Sloan, the president of the Hyde Park Literary Circle, waited until the latecomer settled next to Shelby Locke. He cleared his throat and called for attention. "The Hyde Park Literary Circle will now come to order," he announced. Wiping his high, balding forehead, he asked Mr. Warburton, the secretary, to call the roll.

Sloan sat down behind the table, turning his back slightly so he had a good view of the membership. As the first names were called, his eyes narrowed assessingly.

"Mr. and Mrs. Horace Putnam."

Sloan glanced at the middle-aged couple seated to his left. Mrs. Putnam, gray-haired and round as a barrel, was listening intently to the roll call. Her husband, on the other hand, appeared to be asleep. He immediately discounted them. They weren't serious about literature. They were only here for social reasons. Neither of them would know a decent verse from doggerel.

"Miss Lucinda Marlow."

He studied her with more interest. She certainly was a fetching creature with all that lovely dark brown hair and those big hazel eyes. Sloan frowned. He was forgetting himself, Lucinda Marlow could be a danger to him, and he'd best remember that. She was the one who'd started the group. Unlike many females of his acquaintance, she actually read books. Worse, the poem she had written and read to the circle at their last meeting hadn't been half-bad. Not up to his standards, of course, but acceptable, nonetheless.

"Mr. Shelby Locke."

Sloan gritted his teeth as he stared at the tall, auburn-haired man sitting beside Rowena Stanwick. Blast. Now, there was real trouble. Locke actually had brains. Even worse, he was well read. The man could spout Shakespeare at the drop of a hat. He watched as Locke turned to gaze adoringly at Mrs. Stanwick. A slow, crafty smile crossed Sloan's thin face. Perhaps Mr. Locke wouldn't be much of a competitor after all, he told himself. The fool was so besotted with the fair Rowena, he probably couldn't write a decent verse if his life depended on it. No doubt they'd all be treated to some ridiculous maudlin romantic drivel about the Queen and Prince Albert's courtship. If the fool managed to turn in anything at all.

"Mrs. Hannah Greenwood."

He glanced at the widow Greenwood, and his heart almost stopped. She was looking straight at him. Sloan shifted uneasily. The expression on her face was strange. He didn't like it one whit. Her thin mouth curved upward in a sly, mirthless smile, and her eyes gleamed with cold malevolence. He suddenly remembered her cryptic comments from their last meeting, and panic, like bile, rose in his throat. Surely she didn't know. She couldn't know. It was impossible. He'd been far too careful. Sloan immediately pushed the troublesome Mrs. Greenwood from his mind.

"Mrs. Lester Hiatt, Miss Cecilia Mansfield, and Lady Cannonberry." Warburton's voice droned on as he called the rest of the roll.

Sloan didn't even bother to glance at these people as their names were called. None of them were important. But he did watch the secretary carefully. Edgar Warburton was an unknown. He'd been a member of their group for only a little over a month. The man was such a dreadful snob it had been difficult for Sloan to ascertain precisely how much he actually knew about literature. Warburton seemed to deem it a favor even to speak to you. He'd bear watching as well. Sloan didn't like surprises.

"As you know," Sloan began when the roll call was finished, "we agreed at our last meeting to honor our sovereign's Jubilee in our own unique fashion. I am, of course, referring to our poetry contest. I trust that you are all working diligently."

Lucinda Marlow knew what was coming next, so she ignored their esteemed president and turned her attention toward the center of the circle where Rowena Stanwick was sitting far closer than propriety dictated to Shelby Locke.

Lucinda's fingers curled into fists beneath the fold of her simple yellow day dress. She wished she'd worn her lavender gown. Leave it to Rowena to overdress for the occasion, she thought hastily, as she saw Shelby flash a warm smile in the widow's direction. Men are such fools, they didn't have the intelligence to see a sow's ear dressed like a silk purse even when it was sitting right beside them.

"I take it all of you have, by now, allowed the muse free rein of your creative endeavors," Sloan said. "As I promised at our last meeting, I did, indeed, arrange for the esteemed poet, Mr. Richard Venerable, to act as the judge in our own modest but most exciting contest. Mr. Venerable will announce the winner of the poetry contest at a ball to be given here, at Miss Marlow's residence, in two weeks' time."

Edgar Warburton, who was sitting next to Miss Cecilia Mansfield at the end of the circle of chairs, slanted the widow Stanwick a hate-filled glance. The bitch. Who did she think she was? With one long, skinny finger Warburton stroked the rim of his muttonchop whiskers and then smoothed a lock of mousy brown hair off his high forehead. He kept his gaze on her for several minutes, willing her to look in his direction so he could have the pleasure of snubbing her. But Rowena Stanwick only had eyes for Shelby Locke. She kept giving him coy, secretive smiles and little pats on the hand.

Warburton forced his attention away from the couple. He glanced around the overly furnished drawing room, and his lips curled in a faint sneer. The walls were covered with a ghastly emerald-green embossed wallpaper. Every table was cluttered with china figurines and ugly vases of flowers sitting on cream-colored silk table coverings. The settees and chairs, though of good quality mahogany and done in fine fabric, were the same hideous green as the wall, and the most awful gold and brown Brussels carpet covered the floor. The house and its contents were opulent, expensive and in horribly bad taste. But that was only to be expected. The Marlow wealth, extensive as it was, came from trade. He looked at the owner of the house, Lucinda Marlow, and felt a tinge of shame. Poor woman, of course her home was furnished with no regard to art or beauty. How could it be any different? Tradespeople, really! Regardless of how much money they spent or how many paintings they purchased, they were hopelessly lost.

Warburton wished he could be attracted to Lucinda. God knows, though he was by no means poor, a fortune of that size could always come in handy. But there was something decidedly odd about her. Despite the Marlow family wealth, he'd heard she'd never had a proper Season. And of course, the way she lived here all alone, with only her servants to look after her. Scandalous, really. You'd think she'd have the decency to find some old relative to hang about and act as chaperon.

He saw Lucinda turn her head and frown at Locke and Rowena, and he immediately forgot what he'd been thinking about as another shaft of anger flooded his thin body.

Dr. Oxton Sloan droned on about the silly poetry contest and Warburton continued to ignore him while he fed his rage about Rowena Stanwick.

Damn the woman. She'd brought him low. He'd only joined this ridiculous group to be near her, and she treated him like dirt. That upstart of an adventuress. That nobody. His mouth flattened into a cruel, thin line as he glared at her. She'd taken one look at Locke and tossed him aside like an old pair of gloves. But he wouldn't stand for it. Not anymore.

We'll just see who has the last laugh here, he thought bitterly. He'd make the bitch sorry she ever laid eyes on Shelby Locke.

"Of course, the form of the poem is entirely up to you," Sloan said enthusiastically, "and as you know, the topic of the poem can celebrate any aspect of Her Majesty's life, reign, or achievements." As he spoke, Sloan felt his confidence return. Even with those few who might actually know how to write a poem, he didn't think there was much reason for worry. Not a lot of competition here, he thought. Most of them wouldn't know good poetry if it walked up and bit them on the arse.

They were such fools. Richard Venerable, their judge, hadn't written anything worthwhile in years. He'd hardly read anything more than labels on a whiskey bottle! Sloan hoped the man wouldn't be so drunk he couldn't give out the prize medallion at the ball. He was looking forward to that particular ceremony. He intended to win.

Shelby Locke tried to concentrate on Dr. Sloan's instructions for the contest, but really, how was one expected to concentrate when the love of one's life breezed into the room and sat down next to one? He stole another quick look at Rowena and his heart fluttered. She was so beautiful. So sweet. And she was in love with him. His fingers tightened around the bound leather notebook in his lap.

"Are there any questions?" Sloan asked.

Locke looked down at the notebook. He'd dozens of poems written, of course. But he couldn't conjure up a whit of enthusiasm for the contest. Who cared about the Queen's silly Jubilee? His poems were about life. About love and feelings and that exquisite torment of two souls overcoming obstacles so they could come together.

Shelby Locke only wrote about those things which had meaning to him. He poured his heart and his spirit into his words. Why, only this morning he'd written the most eloquent poem about Rowena. About their wonderful night together. Shelby smiled secretly. Perhaps the poem was too bold? Perhaps she would be offended when he presented it to her tonight at dinner. But surely, she'd understand what he was trying to express. Physical love was to be celebrated as much as spiritual love. It wasn't as if anyone else would ever see the poem. No, he thought, glancing again at his beloved, Rowena wouldn't be in the least offended.

An hour later the meeting concluded and Miss Marlow led the way into the dining room for refreshments. The group milled around the buffet table.

Lucinda Marlow circled the room, making sure her guests had food and drink, Mrs. Stanwick and Mr. Locke stood close together in one of the far corners, talking in low voices. Mrs. Greenwood had cornered Dr. Sloan and was speaking to him with a set, earnest expression on her face. Mr. Warburton picked up a glass of sherry and walked over to the window to stare morosely out into the summer night.

Lady Cannonberry smiled politely as Mrs. Putnam prattled on, but she wasn't really listening. Her mind was fully occupied thinking about the ball. She would so like an escort. Yet there were so few gentlemen that a genteel, middle-aged woman could prevail upon. Of course, there was her neighbor, that nice Inspector Witherspoon. But he was so dreadfully shy. Lady Cannonberry sighed softly.

"Are you all right?" Mrs. Putnam asked briskly. "Oh, I know, you're probably anxious about your poem. But you mustn't worry so, I'm sure you'll do fine. Why, Horace and I have already done ours. It's really quite easy. But you must make sure you end each line with a simple word. A nice word, one that has many other words that rhyme with it. You know, like *moon* and *June* or *two* and *who* or *queen* and *mean*. There are any number of good words to choose from, just be sure not to use a difficult one like . . . oh, *pianoforte*. There aren't many words that rhyme with *pianoforte*. I know—Horace ended one of his lines with that word. Took him ages to think up another one. I tell you, Lady Cannonberry, if you keep it simple, writing good poetry is as easy as writing a supper menu."

"I'll keep that in mind," she replied quickly. She wasn't in the least worried about her poem. She was worried about being the only woman at the ball without an escort.

If only Inspector Witherspoon weren't so very reticent. The few times they'd spoken, while they were walking their dogs in the park, she'd found him a most congenial man. Perhaps she could have a word with his housekeeper, Mrs. Jeffries. Mrs. Jeffries was the most understanding of women. One could really talk to her. Yes, Lady Cannonberry thought, that's precisely what she would do. She'd have a word with Mrs. Jeffries and see if there wasn't, some very delicate way to best let the inspector know she was in dire need of an escort.

Across the room Cecilia Mansfield stared enviously at Rowena Stanwick's slim figure. The opulent gown stood out like a bright crimson poppy in a field of weeds. The pleated overskirt and the curve of the bustle emphasized Mrs. Stanwick's tiny waist. The touch of lace on the cuffs showed off her remarkably slim wrists and hands to perfection, and the dainty buttons around the high neck of the dress lent a graceful air to her already perfect carriage. Cecilia sighed. She'd spent a fortune at the dressmakers and still never managed to look as wonderful as Mrs. Stanwick. It wasn't fair. Mrs. Stanwick had already had a husband, she didn't need to find another one. "I wonder what she'll be wearing to the ball," she murmured to Mrs. Hiatt.

"Who?"

"Rowena Stanwick," Cecilia replied. "I wonder what she'll wear to the ball. I hear she's got her dressmaker copying princess Beatrice's gowns."

"Half the women in London are copying the princess's gowns," Mrs. Hiatt replied as she studied the table in search of a tidbit she hadn't tasted yet. "More important, I wonder what they'll serve for supper?" She put an apple turnover on her plate and picked up her fork. "Do you think it'll be hot or cold?"

"What?"

"The supper at the ball," Mrs. Hiatt said impatiently.

"Miss Marlow always does things correctly," Cecilia replied, turning to stare at their hostess. "I expect she'll have both a hot and cold buffet. Goodness, look at that. She's squinting again, the poor thing. I say, I do think she ought to wear her spectacles. Everyone knows she doesn't see all that well without them."

Mrs. Hiatt smiled cynically. "I do believe Miss Marlow is more concerned with her appearance than she is with seeing clearly," she stated. "You can't blame her for wanting to took her best, especially with Mr. Locke here. With all the mourning she's done, she hasn't had much chance for young men to pay court to her."

Cecilia frowned. She hadn't had all that many men paying court to her, either, and she hadn't noticed any sympathy for her from Mrs. Hiatt. But it would be uncharitable to say such a thing. "That's true, I suppose," she said grudgingly.

Mrs. Hiatt looked up from her plate. "Indeed it is."

Thinking she might be considered less than kind, Cecilia forced herself to smile benevolently. "Poor Lucinda. She has had a rather bad time of it. But I've had it on good authority that she and Mr. Locke will be announcing their engagement at the ball."

Mrs. Hiatt, who was not a romantic, having seen enough of human nature to disabuse her of foolish notions, shook her head. Her gaze shifted to Rowena Stanwick, who was standing indecently close to Shelby Locke and talking to him with an earnest, entreating expression on her face. "Really?"

Cecilia gave her a puzzled stare. "Yes, really. You're the one who implied Mr. Locke was paying court to Miss Marlow."

"You're quite mistaken, Miss Mansfield," Mrs. Hiatt said slowly, her gaze still on the couple across the room. "I implied that Miss Marlow was interested in Mr. Locke. And at one time he was certainly interested in her, but I do believe things have changed."

Cecilia snorted. She was getting rather annoyed with Mrs. Hiatt. Honestly, the woman thought she knew everything. "Well, I know for a fact that Miss Marlow has ordered a whole new wardrobe. We have the same dressmaker, you know. Madam Deloffre told me specifically, and, of course, in the strictest confidence, that it's her trousseau."

Mrs. Hiatt merely smiled. "She may have ordered a trousseau, my dear. But that doesn't mean she's getting married."

Bright June sunshine poured through the windows of the kitchen in Upper Edmonton Gardens, home of Inspector Gerald Witherspoon. The shafts of light danced against the copper utensils lining the walls, the air filled with the scent of peppermint and lemon. On the long oak table a pink-flowered teapot sat next to a tray of mouthwatering gooseberry tarts.

Five people were sitting in a semicircle at the far end of the table. They were Inspector Witherspoon's loyal servants.

Mrs. Goodge, the cook, banged her fist against the tabletop. "When's that horrible woman goin' to leave so we can have a bit of peace!" she cried. Her considerable bulk shook with fury, and a lock of gray hair dislodged itself from her bun and dangled across her ear. From behind a pair of spectacles her eyes narrowed in anger.

Mrs. Jeffries, the housekeeper, sighed inwardly. She was a kind, motherly looking woman who always listened to the servants' grievances. She was good at listening. It was one of her foremost abilities. Her hair was a dark auburn, liberally sprinkled with white at the temples, her eyes a deep, understanding brown. Though small of stature and rather plump, she had the air of one used to the rigorous demands of leadership.

She wasn't in the least surprised by the cook's outburst. Edwina Livingston-Graves, the inspector's cousin and houseguest, had a rather unfortunate effect on the staff. Truth to tell, Mrs. Livingston-Graves had a rather unfortunate effect on everyone. She wasn't a particularly nice person. "I'm afraid Mrs. Livingston-Graves will be here until after the Jubilee," Mrs. Jeffries said cautiously.

"After the Jubilee!" the cook yelped. "But that's not for another two weeks! I swear, Mrs. Jeffries, if I have to put up with her for a fortnight, I'll not be responsible for my actions. Do you know what she had the effrontery to say to me today after lunch? She claimed the rabbit was *tough*. She actually had the nerve to ask if we had any Cockle's Antibilious Pills! Claimed she had indigestion. Did you ever hear the like? My stewed rabbit and onions . . . one of my best dishes . . ."

"At least she didn't stand over your shoulder and natter in your ear while you was cooking it," Betsy interrupted. The pretty blonde maid was as furious as the cook. Her ivory complexion was rosy with anger and her slender frame stiff with indignation. "That's what I had to put up with this mornin' while I was polishin' the furniture in the drawin' room. Half an hour, it was, too," she continued, her blue eyes widening. "And on and on she went about how I was goin' to ruin the shine if I didn't stop usin' the wrong polish. And it was Adam's Furniture Polish I was usin' as well, the kind we've used for years. It's bad enough we haven't had a decent murder in weeks. . . ."

"Well, if I catch that woman kickin' Fred again," Wiggins, the footman, chimed in, "we will 'ave us a murder right 'ere."

Mrs. Jeffries didn't take the footman's threats all that seriously. Wiggins was only just past his twentieth birthday, a slightly pudgy brown-haired lad with apple cheeks and a generally affable nature. He didn't look very affable at the moment, though.

"Kicking Fred?" Smythe's heavy brows drew together. "You didn't tell me the old girl 'ad a go at Fred."

Fred, a shaggy mixture of black, brown, and white fur, raised his pointed nose in the air as he heard the coachman mention his name. Wagging his tail, he rose to his feet from his spot in the sunlight by the door and wandered toward the table. He looked hopefully toward the tray of tarts.

Wiggins shook his head. "I saw it with me own eyes. She give 'im a right 'ard kick in his ribs, she did. And all because poor Fred were just defendin' 'imself against that wretched cat of hers." He paused and took a breath.

"Maybe I should take the dog down to the stables until she's gone,"

Smythe mused. Tall and strong, with a headful of thick black hair, olive complexion, and full mouth, he would have been a brutal-looking sort to be sitting in a cozy kitchen save for a pair of twinkling, kind brown eyes.

"I'm afraid that won't do at all," Mrs. Jeffries said quickly. "You know how devoted the inspector is to Fred, he'd miss him terribly."

"Then what are we goin' to do?" Smythe asked. "Mrs. Livingston-Graves and her ruddy cat show up on our doorstep just a few days ago and already she's actin' like she owns the place. Her and that silly animal is enough to drive a man bonkers. Cor, it's a good thing we ain't investigatin' one of the inspector's murders! Be hard to keep things to ourselves with that old harridan snoopin' around."

"At least you can escape to the pubs of the evening," Betsy said, making it sound like an accusation. "We've got to put up with her twenty-four hours a day. She's always sneakin' about and eavesdroppin'! I caught her listenin' at the door this morning when Mrs. Goodge was havin' a word with the man from the gas works."

"She were eavesdroppin' on me and Albert?" Mrs. Goodge was truly outraged. Her relations with the various people who trouped through her kitchen were her own private domain. In all their investigations for the inspector, she'd used her sources to provide many important facts and clues. How dare that woman snoop!

Mrs. Jeffries held up her hand. "Please," she began, "I know you're all upset. Mrs. Livingston-Graves is a trial, but we all have our crosses in life to bear."

"And she's a mighty heavy one," the coachman muttered. He crossed his arms over his massively muscled chest.

"But she won't be here forever," the housekeeper continued. She fervently hoped that was true. But she wasn't certain. Of late, Mrs. Jeffries was beginning to suspect that Cousin Edwina was angling to be invited to stay on a permanent basis. However, she wasn't going to mention her suspicions to the rest of the staff. They were upset enough. "And the Jubilee Thanksgiving procession isn't that far away. So why don't we all go about our business and try to ignore the lady."

"But what if we gets us a murder?" Wiggins asked. "What'll we do then?"

Mrs. Jeffries looked thoughtful. The lad had a point. If their inspector did get involved in another murder, of course they'd have to step in. The dear man had no idea his devoted staff actually investigated his cases, of course. That would never do. They were most careful to keep their inquiries discreet. None of them would ever want the inspector to feel that he couldn't solve a murder on his own. That, of course, wasn't quite true. But they would have a problem if the inspector were to get another case. Thanks to their prodigious efforts, the inspector now had a reputation to uphold. His superiors at the Yard were amazed at the "unsolvable" cases the man solved. She shook herself slightly. It was pointless to fret over something that hadn't happened yet. She had other matters involving the inspector on her mind. "We'll cross that bridge when we come to it," she said firmly. "As it is, we don't have a murder to investigate at the present, and if we're very lucky Mrs. Livingston-Graves will be gone by the time we do. Right now our only concern is to get through the next two weeks with a minimum of disruption to our normal routines."

From the stairwell they heard the sound of rapidly descending footsteps. Knowing who it was, Smythe pushed back his chair and leapt to his feet, but he wasn't quick enough.

Mrs. Livingston-Graves sailed into the kitchen. Thin, medium height and possessed of a raw-boned face and mousy brown hair that she wore pulled back in a severe bun, she frowned at them. "I say, Mrs. Jeffries," she said in a nasal whine, "how many tea breaks do the servants take in this household? Every time I come into the kitchen someone's sitting here sipping tea. That's not what my cousin pays your wages for, surely."

Mrs. Jeffries forced a polite smile to her lips. "Was there something you wanted?"

The woman's lips flattened to a disapproving line as she realized the housekeeper was not going to answer her question. "I'm looking for Alphonse."

Fred scurried under the table.

"I'd best get down to Howard's," Smythe announced as he edged toward the back door. "The carriage needs a good clean."

Wiggins got up. "I'll finish up oiling them hinges on the back gate, Mrs. Jeffries," the footman muttered as he, too, hurried from the room.

"Better finish dustin' the landing," Betsy said as she leapt to her feet.

Mrs. Goodge fixed Mrs. Livingston-Graves with a cold stare. "I'd better see to them berries," she said slowly as she heaved her bulk out of her chair and made her way down the hall toward the wet larder.

From outside the kitchen window there was the sound of a hansom drawing up. Mrs. Jeffries cocked her head to one side and listened intently.

"I asked if you'd seen my cat," Mrs. Livingston-Graves said loudly.

The footsteps crossing the pavement were as familiar to Mrs. Jeffries as her own. She glanced at Mrs. Livingston-Graves. "I do believe that Alphonse is out in the garden," she said calmly.

"Out in the garden!" Mrs. Livingston-Graves screeched. She turned on her heel and flew down the hall. "Oh, my gracious. The poor baby's probably terrified. He's not allowed outside without me!" she cried.

Mrs. Jeffries nodded in satisfaction as the woman disappeared. She needed to speak privately to the inspector.

Inspector Gerald Witherspoon peered around the corner of the drawing room door. "I say," he said to Mrs. Jeffries, "where is Mrs. Livingston-Graves? Up in her room?"

Tall and robust, with a fine-boned angular face, a neatly trimmed mustache, a sharp, pointed nose, clear blue gray eyes, and thinning brown hair, the inspector crept quietly into the room and headed for his favorite armchair.

"Your cousin is out in the gardens, looking for her cat."

He sighed in relief. "Excellent. The fresh air will do her good. Where's Fred?"

"Hiding under the kitchen table," she replied as she poured out two glasses of fine sherry. She gave one to her employer and sat down opposite him.

"Whyever is he hiding?"

"I'm afraid that poor Fred has been rather cowed by Mrs. Livingston-Graves and her cat. Presumably he feels that discretion is the better part of valor."

"Oh, dear." Witherspoon frowned. "That is awkward. I mean, she is, after all, my relation. I don't like the idea that she's been less than kind to the poor dog, but then again, what can one say?"

"I shouldn't worry about it if I were you," Mrs. Jeffries said firmly. "You can always take Fred for a nice long walk yourself this evening. That'll make him feel better. How was your day, sir?"

"The usual," he replied, sipping his sherry. "There's an enormous amount of planning, what with the Jubilee celebrations and all. Thank goodness, I've no other pressing cases or murders to investigate. Most of my time is tied up in planning traffic routes."

"Oh, yes, the Jubilee." She sighed dramatically.

Concerned, Witherspoon leaned forward. "Why, Mrs. Jeffries, is something wrong?"

"Nothing's really wrong, sir," she said carefully. "It's just that I feel so very sorry for our neighbor, Lady Cannonberry. She's been invited to a Jubilee ball and she hasn't an escort. It's a rather embarrassing situation for the poor lady. You see, the ball is being given by a young woman who is a member of the same literary circle as Lady Cannonberry. It's really for the members of the circle. They're having a contest to see who can write the best poem celebrating Her Majesty's Jubilee. So it's not as if Lady Cannonberry can in good conscience decline the invitation. She is a very supportive member of the circle."

Witherspoon gulped his sherry. "Oh, dear."

"You can see her difficulty, sir," Mrs. Jeffries said. "You know sir, I was wondering . . ."

"Now, Mrs. Jeffries," the inspector protested, "surely you're not going to suggest that I offer to escort Lady Cannonberry? That would never do. She's a member of the nobility and I'm merely a humble policeman."

"That's not true, sir. You are a fine, honorable gentleman. You have a beautiful home, excellent employment and your prospects are superb."

As the inspector had inherited his fine home and most of his servants from his late aunt Euphemia, he didn't really feel he could take all that much credit. "Yes, but—"

"There's no *buts* about it, sir," his housekeeper continued doggedly. "You've not only persevered in a very difficult and important occupation, you've become famous for your brilliance at solving the most heinous of crimes. Why, just look at all the cases you've had—those horrible Kensington High Street murders, that terribly difficult one involving that fake medium, that dreadful one where that poor girl was brutally stabbed and buried in the bottom of an abandoned house. If it hadn't been for you, none of those murders would have been solved. You've every right to be proud of yourself, sir. You're much too modest."

Witherspoon smiled shyly. "Well, yes, I suppose I have been fortunate when it comes to homicide," he began modestly. "But escorting Lady Cannonberry would be an entirely different matter." Panic fluttered in his stomach. Solving murders was one thing; spending an entire evening in the company of a woman was something else entirely.

"Furthermore," Mrs. Jeffries said firmly, "Lady Cannonberry was a simple country doctor's daughter before she married her late husband. And he wouldn't have inherited his title if his two elder brothers hadn't taken it into their heads to sail to South America and both been lost at sea."

The sharp, clicking heels of Mrs. Livingston-Graves pounded down the hallway. The inspector visibly cringed. Mrs. Jeffries hid a smile behind her glass of sherry.

"Good evening, Gerald," Mrs. Livingston-Graves barked as she charged into the room. She held a rather dirty and bedraggled Siamese cat in her arms. "Will you just look at this," she complained, shoving the animal under the inspector's nose. "Alphonse is absolutely filthy. I found the poor dear outside, cowering under a bush, trembling; with fear."

Alphonse snarled and swiped at Witherspoon's nose with his paw.

"Er, is something wrong?" The inspector shrank back from the hissing cat.

"Of course something's wrong," Mrs. Livingston-Graves snapped. She pushed the cat's paw down and dumped the animal directly in Witherspoon's lap. "Dear Alphonse has been attacked. Go on, have a look at him."

Witherspoon forced himself to examine the animal closely. All he saw was dirt and mud, no sign of injury. "I don't see any blood," he murmured finally.

Alphonse stared up at him from a pair of cold blue eyes and hissed.

"Don't be absurd, Gerald. Of course he's injured. You just can't see it. His poor nerves will probably never be the same. He's very delicate, you know." Mrs. Livingston-Graves snatched her precious darling to her bosom and began stroking the animal's back.

"How do you know Alphonse has been attacked? Did you see it?" Witherspoon asked, wanting to placate his angry cousin.

"No, I didn't see it, but it's obvious." She glared pointedly at the housekeeper. "Someone deliberately left the back door open so poor Alphonse could wander off. Your entire staff hates my cat. By the time I found him, he was dreadfully upset. And I saw that wretched spaniel again. I know the horrid creature attacked my darling."

"Spaniel?" the inspector mumbled. "I'm sure you must be mistaken. The only spaniel that I know of out in the gardens belongs to Lady Cannonberry. She's a very nice little dog, quite a harmless animal. Why, she and Fred often go tumbling about together having a jolly good time."

"Speaking of Fred"—Mrs. Jeffries glanced at the carriage clock on the mantelpiece—"I do believe you'll have time to take him for a walk, Inspector. He does so love a brisk perambulation in Holland Park. Dinner won't be served for another hour, so you've plenty of time."

"But what about my poor Alphonse?" Mrs. Livingston-Graves sputtered. "Something really must be done. I won't have him being mistreated."

"Why don't you take Alphonse upstairs and give him a saucer of milk," Mrs. Jeffries suggested.

Witherspoon, knowing a good escape when he saw one, leapt from his chair and hurried toward the door. "I'm sure Alphonse will be fine as soon as he's had his milk," he called.

"But, Gerald . . ." Mrs. Livingston-Graves protested. She scurried after him, her dark skirts swishing angrily.

Mrs. Jeffries leaned back in her chair and smiled. If everything went as she planned, her dear employer should be running into Lady Cannonberry in less than ten minutes.

CHAPTER 2

On the night of the Hyde Park Literary Circle's Jubilee Ball, the weather was perfect: warm, dry, and with a light wind from the north that blew the worst of London's noxious odors well away from the Marlow home. The front of the tall redbrick house blazed with welcoming light. Hansom cabs *clip-clopped* up and down the length of Redcliffe Square, dropping off guests. Inside the house, ladies in opulent gowns and gentlemen in formal black evening wear danced, drank, and ate with great enthusiasm.

The festivities spilled out into the garden. Enclosed by high brick walls, the guests at the ball were assured of privacy as they enjoyed themselves. Couples strolled through the open French doors, the music spilling onto the terrace. Giant torches flamed from the first-floor balcony, casting dancing shadows on the people milling about below. Above the first floor only an occasional light could be seen, leaving most of the rear of the imposing structure in darkness, a stark contrast to the brilliance illuminating the garden.

Lucinda Marlow had spared no expense for her guests' enjoyment. Japanese lanterns, limelights, and additional torches had been strategically placed around the huge garden. The scent of summer roses filled the air. A maze of paths meandered through the heavy shrubbery and leafy trees, beckoning those young people who were of a mind to slip away from the eagle eyes of their chaperons.

Cecilia Mansfield shook her head and glanced at the clusters of people scattered across the terrace. "Everyone's acting most peculiar this evening," she commented to Mrs. Hiatt, who was sitting on a bench holding a plate of pastries.

"Really? How so?"

"No one from our circle seems to be having a good time at all," Cecila said slowly. She smoothed a wrinkle out of the overskirt of her pink tulle dress. "I saw Dr. Sloan and Mrs. Greenwood a few minutes ago. I think they were exchanging words."

Mrs. Hiatt shot her companion a sharp glance. "Did you actually hear them quarreling?" she asked. "Or are you only guessing?" She was annoyed that Miss Mansfield always seemed to know everything.

"Well," Cecilia replied, "I didn't actually hear what they were saying, but you could tell by their expressions they were arguing. Dr. Sloan's face was as red as a radish and Mrs. Greenwood looked positively livid."

"I shouldn't take any notice, if I were you." Mrs. Hiatt shrugged. She eyed her plate carefully, trying to decide whether to eat the lemon tart or the napoleon next. "Mrs. Greenwood's never in good spirits. I don't know why she even bothered to come tonight. It's not as if she likes our company overly much. Besides, she's been in a snit all evening: She took one look at Rowena Stanwick's dress and flounced off in a rage. Not that it was Mrs. Stanwick's fault, of course. Half the women here are wearing blue gowns. It's become a very popular color this Season. Princess Beatrice favors it."

Cecilia giggled. "Mrs. Greenwood's not the only one who's in a tizzy. I was standing by the door when Mrs. Stanwick arrived. You should have seen Miss Marlow's face, and Miss Gordon didn't look all that pleased, either. Half the women in the room were shooting daggers at poor Mrs. Stanwick. Of course, her gown is a bit grander than the others. I must say, I think the bustle is just a tad overdone."

"Her bustle isn't any larger than Mrs. Greenwood's," Mrs. Hiatt said. "But I daresay I think you're right about our circle. I've seen more than one long face this evening. None of them seem to be enjoying themselves very much."

Cecilia was visibly startled. "You've noticed it as well, have you?"

"Naturally, when one gets to be my age, one doesn't have much else to do but eat and observe. Mr. Warburton's been walking around with a dog-in-the-manger expression all night," Mrs. Hiatt continued, taking satisfaction in seeing the look of surprise on her companion's face. She pressed her advantage. "He's spent most of his time glaring at Mrs. Stanwick's back. Miss Marlow looks as though her smile is beginning to crack, and Mr. Locke is still moaning about his notebook."

"He hasn't found it?"

Mrs. Hiatt shook her head. "I actually overheard him implying to Dr. Sloan that his notebook had been stolen. He claimed he had it here at our last meeting, and when he went to leave, it was gone."

Cecilia snorted delicately. "That's ridiculous. Who'd steal it?"

Mrs. Hiatt chuckled. "He didn't exactly come right out and say so, but from what I heard, I think he suspects Miss Marlow."

"But that's absurd. Why should she care about his silly poems?"

"I think it's this contest. Everyone's nerves are on edge. Gracious, the way Mr. Locke was haranguing poor Miss Marlow, you'd think the prize for winning the ruddy contest was a chest of gold and not just a silly medallion."

Cecilia's eyes widened. "You overheard him speaking to Miss Marlow?"

"Oh, yes, didn't I mention that?" Mrs. Hiatt smiled smugly. From the corner of her eye she saw Lady Cannonberry and her escort come out of the French doors and onto the terrace. "I wonder who that gentleman escorting Lady Cannonberry is?"

Now it was Cecilia's turn to look smug. "That's Inspector Gerald Witherspoon. He's with the police."

"Lady Cannonberry's with a policeman?"

"He's not just any policeman," Cecilia said quickly. She liked Lady Cannonberry very much and she'd rather liked the shy gentleman she'd met earlier in the evening. "He's actually quite famous. He's the one who solved those horrible Kensington High Street murders last year and the murder of that American man they found in the Thames a few months ago. They say he's quite brilliant."

Inspector Witherspoon wasn't feeling in the least brilliant. Dressed in the most uncomfortable set of formal black clothes and a pair of tight shoes, he hoped the evening would progress quickly so he could go home. He still hadn't a clue how he happened to be here. One moment he was walking Fred in Holland Park and the next he was walking with Lady Cannonberry. Before he could snap his fingers, he'd found himself asking if he might escort her to the Jubilee Ball.

"I do so hope you're enjoying yourself, Inspector," Lady Cannonberry said politely. She lifted the hem of her heavy sapphire-blue gown as they approached the stairs leading to the garden.

"Very much," Witherspoon replied. He tried desperately to think of what to say next. Drat. Talking with ladies was such a chore. Gracious, how on earth did some men manage it? "Er, did you get your poem finished in time for the contest?" he asked.

"Yes." Lady Cannonberry frowned slightly. "But I wasn't very pleased with the verse. I don't think I've a chance at winning. But then again, winning isn't all that important to me. Everyone expects that Dr. Sloan will take the prize. He's the only one in the group who's actually published, you see."

"What did you write about, if I may ask." Witherspoon began to relax. Perhaps the trick to talking to ladies was to ask them questions about those topics which interested them.

"Oh, nothing terribly exciting, I'm afraid. I . . . uh, well . . ." She hesitated and took a breath. "I wrote about trains."

Witherspoon stopped and turned to stare at her. "Trains?"

"Yes," Lady Cannonberry replied enthusiastically, "I'm quite fond of them, you see. The rules of the contest said we could write about any aspect of Her Majesty's reign. The railroads have expanded enormously and Her Majesty is such a supporter . . . well, I do so love steam engines. . . ." Her voice faltered.

"How wonderful!" the inspector cried. He took her arm and continued down the terrace steps. "I quite like steam engines and trains as well. Tell me, Lady Cannonberry, have you seen the new engine on the Great Northern?"

"But of course," she replied, smiling radiantly. "It's wonderful. However, I still believe it's not really all that much of an improvement on the classic British four-four-oh. I saw the North British Railway's number two-twenty-four on her first trip out. She was magnificent. Four coupled wheels, inside cylinders, and a leading bogie."

Witherspoon laughed. His nervousness was somehow completely gone. "I'm familiar with the four-four-ohs. You're right, they are wonderful trains." He paused. "Number two-twenty-four? I'm sure I know that train. I know most of them, you see. Train spotting is rather a hobby of mine. I say, isn't she the one that had to be fished out of the Firth of Tay?"

"Well, yes, but it wasn't the train's fault the bridge collapsed. Besides, she was rebuilt."

• • •

Mrs. Horace Putnam was frantic. She sighed in relief as she spotted two members of the Hyde Park Literary Circle and rushed across the terrace toward them. "Have you seen anyone?" she cried.

"We've seen quite a few people," Mrs. Hiatt replied. "The house is full of them."

"I'm not looking for people," Mrs. Putnam retorted. "I'm looking for members of our group. It's almost time to make the announcement and I can't find, anyone."

"Lady Cannonberry's just over there," Cecilia said helpfully as she pointed in the direction of the couple hovering near the steps.

"Oh, good. But where is Dr. Sloan or Mrs. Stanwick or Mr. Locke? Merciful heavens! Everyone's disappeared. Miss Marlow and Mr. Warburton are nowhere about, and Mrs. Greenwood seems to have vanished into thin air as well."

"I saw Mrs. Greenwood about fifteen minutes ago," Cecilia said. "She was in the drawing room, talking with Dr. Sloan."

"They aren't in the drawing room now," Mrs. Putnam snapped "They aren't anywhere that I can find, and neither is anyone else. I've looked everywhere. It's almost ten thirty. We're supposed to announce the winner of the contest."

"Do calm yourself, Mrs. Putnam," Mrs. Hiatt said briskly. "I don't think it will matter if the announcement's a few moments late."

"But of course it will matter. It must be done as soon as possible or it won't be done at all. Our judge, Mr. Venerable, seems well on his way to being incapacitated. One doesn't like to tell tales, but I think he's in his cups."

"You mean he's drunk," said Mrs. Hiatt bluntly. She loathed euphemisms.

Suddenly there was a loud scream. Everyone on the terrace froze.

A body plummeted through the air and landed with a sickening thud on the stone pavement two feet away from where the ladies stood.

Cecilia screamed, Mrs. Putnam gasped, and Mrs. Hiatt leapt to her feet. She hurried over to the unmoving form and knelt down. "Oh, my God, there's a knife sticking out of the back!" she cried. Her face grim, she gently reached down and brushed a stray lock of blonde hair off the side of the woman's face. Mrs. Hiatt looked up at Mrs. Putnam. "I do believe we've found Mrs. Greenwood."

• • •

Witherspoon, who'd been engrossed in discussing steam engines with Lady Cannonberry, broke off in midsentence as he heard the scream. Not believing his eyes, he blinked as the body landed on the terrace. For a moment he was so surprised he couldn't move. Then, remembering his duty, he hurried over to where Mrs. Hiatt was kneeling beside the body.

"Excuse me, madam," he said politely, "I'm a police officer. Perhaps I'd better just have a look here."

Having a look was the last thing the inspector wanted to do. He was quite squeamish.

He knelt down beside the woman and took a deep breath. The body lay on its side. Witherspoon shuddered as he saw the knife protruding obscenely from the poor lady's back. The first thing he had to do was establish if she was dead or merely injured.

Witherspoon swallowed and felt for a pulse. There was none. He continued looking for signs of life, finally giving up when he realized that not only had the victim been stabbed, the side of her skull was crushed from the fall.

The inspector stood up. "I'm afraid I'll have to ask all of you to please go into the ballroom."

"What's happened?" Lucinda Marlow's frantic voice cut through the crowd that had gathered. "Has there been an accident?" She broke through the ring of people and stopped dead, her eyes widening as she saw the figure lying on her terrace. "Oh, my—"

"Miss Marlow," the inspector said softly, "please send someone for the police. One of your guests has been murdered."

An hour later the inspector and the uniformed branch had things well under control. The police surgeon had examined the body and taken it away. The murder weapon, or at least the knife taken out of Mrs. Greenwood's back which Witherspoon would assume was the murder weapon until the autopsy was completed, was identified as belonging to the Marlow house. More precisely, the butler had verified it had last been seen slicing roast beef at the cold buffet table.

Witherspoon had allowed those guests who could verify they were in the ballroom or in the garden at the time of the murder to leave. The rest were waiting for him in the drawing room.

Smythe had driven Lady Cannonberry home. Witherspoon sighed as he entered the now almost deserted ballroom. He spotted Constable Barnes, a robust gray-haired man with a craggy face and hazel-green eyes, coming toward him from the other end of the room.

"Evening, sir," Barnes said. "I got here as soon as I could. The report is there's been a murder."

"Unfortunately, yes. The victim was one of the guests, Mrs. Hannah Greenwood. Someone stabbed her and pushed her off the third-floor balcony."

Barnes clucked his tongue. "That's horrible, sir. Sounds like the killer wanted to make doubly sure she were dead. Good thing you were here, isn't it, sir?"

"It certainly seems that way," Witherspoon replied. Actually, he thought it rather appalling that he'd been "on the scene," so to speak. Oddly, he felt guilty, as though he should have stopped the murder. Of course, he knew that was nonsense. One doesn't go to a Jubilee Ball and expect a fellow guest to be stabbed and tossed off a balcony. It just wasn't done.

Cecilia Mansfield rushed across the floor and hurried toward the inspector. "Excuse me," she said firmly. She was a bit annoyed. Every time she tried to speak to any of the policemen, they ignored her. "But I must speak with you, Inspector."

Witherspoon stared at the plump young woman with the light blue eyes and pale skin. "Yes, Miss Mansfield. What can I do for you?"

"I've got some rather important information, and none of your policemen seems in the least interested in listening to me."

"We'll be happy to take your statement, Miss," Barnes said politely. "Now, what have you got to tell us?"

"To begin with, I don't think you ought to bother questioning anyone who isn't a member of the Hyde Park Literary Circle. None of the other ball guests had anything to do with Mrs. Greenwood," Miss Mansfield stated.

"How do you know that?" the inspector asked curiously.

She gave him a superior smile. "Because Mrs. Greenwood herself mentioned it to me when she first arrived tonight. She wasn't an overly sociable person, you know. She took one look at the mob hanging about the punch bowl and told me that except for the members of our group, she didn't know a soul here and didn't want to, either."

"Thank you, Miss Mansfield," Witherspoon said. "I'm sure that information will be very useful to us." He wasn't merely being polite to her, either. Knowing that the victim had no connection to any of the other ball guests could drastically reduce the amount of time it would take to solve this murder.

"But that's not all I've got to say," Cecilia protested. "I saw Mrs. Greenwood having an argument with Dr. Sloan earlier this evening. Don't you think that's important?"

"Yes, of course it is," Barnes said smoothly. "We'll speak with Dr. Sloan about it right away."

Cecilia shook her head. "But you can't. He's left and so have most of the others."

"Left?" The inspector frowned. "Oh, dear. I specifically wanted to question the members of your group."

"Then you knew that Mrs. Greenwood wasn't acquainted with anyone outside the group, sir?" Barnes asked. He gazed in admiration at his superior. The inspector felt his confidence increase just a tad.

"I can't say that I actually knew, Constable," he admitted honestly. "But I suspected that might be the case."

"I do hope you catch the murderer soon," Cecilia said earnestly. "I daresay, we probably won't find out who won the poetry contest until this matter is cleared up."

The inspector didn't know how to respond to this outrageous statement. Really, people amazed him. Here a perfectly innocent woman had been murdered, and all Miss Mansfield was concerned about was who won the contest. "Er, yes, I suppose that might be true," he murmured. "Is there anything else?"

Cecilia cocked her head to one side, her plain face creased in thought. "I don't think so. Now, if you don't mind, I must get home. Mama and Papa will be dreadfully put out when they find out what's happened."

She flounced away, her bright pink skirts swishing with every step she took.

Barnes turned to the inspector. "What do you think, sir?"

"I think, Constable," Witherspoon replied glumly, "that this case is going to be very nasty. Very nasty, indeed."

"Not to worry, sir," Barnes replied cheerfully. "You're good with the nasty ones. Brings out the best in you, so to speak."

The inspector suppressed a shudder. He knew he was going to get stuck with this murder. He just knew it. And Inspector Nigel Nivens would no doubt raise a terrible fuss. Nivens seemed to think that Witherspoon was "hogging all the homicides," when really, it was hardly his fault that he got them. And certainly being here tonight wasn't his fault, either. He hadn't even wanted to come.

"Thank you, Constable," he replied. "Let's have a word with Miss Marlow, the owner of the house. Then let's get up to the balcony and have a look round. Perhaps we'll get lucky and find that our killer has made a mistake and left some valuable evidence lying about."

"Right, sir. Was the victim a good-size woman?"

"A bit taller than average, I'd say. She wasn't fat, but she wasn't slender, either, if you understand what I mean."

Barnes nodded. "Then even with a knife in her, I'll warrant she didn't go over the edge without puttin' up a bit of a struggle."

They made their way to the drawing room. Lucinda Marlow, looking pale and frightened, sat huddled on the settee. The inspector cleared his throat. "Miss Marlow," he said softly.

"Inspector Witherspoon," she said, her voice shaky. "I expect you want to ask me a few questions."

"Only a few, Miss Marlow, I assure you," he said kindly. "I realize this must be most upsetting for you."

"It's awful." Her lovely hazel eyes filled with tears. "But please, ask me whatever you like."

The inspector's mind went blank.

They stood there for a moment and the silence grew. Finally Barnes cleared his throat. The inspector blurted out the first thought that sprang into his head. "Er, how well did you know Mrs. Greenwood?"

"Not very well at all," Miss Marlow replied. "She joined our circle a few months ago, but she's not very friendly. Frankly, I was surprised when she came tonight. I quite expected her to stay away."

"But I thought the winner of your poetry contest was going to be announced tonight. Surely, Mrs. Greenwood would have been interested in that," Witherspoon said.

Miss Marlow gave a dainty shrug. "Perhaps she was."

"Did you see anything unusual tonight, Miss Marlow?" Barnes asked.

"Anyone following Mrs. Greenwood, anyone acting in a strange manner toward the lady?"

"No, I can't say that I did."

The inspector stifled a sigh. This was going to be a complicated case. He could feel it in his bones. It was going to be one of those terrible murders where no one saw or heard a ruddy thing of any use at all to the police. Drat. And he did so want justice to be done. Even if the victim hadn't been a very friendly person, she certainly hadn't deserved to be murdered. "Do you know if she had any enemies?"

Lucinda Marlow looked down at the carpet. "Actually, Inspector, I can't say that she had any enemies, but I do know that she didn't like Mrs. Stanwick. She's also one of the members of our group. There were several occasions that I can remember when Mrs. Greenwood went out of her way to be rude to Mrs. Stanwick."

"How about Dr. Sloan?" Barnes asked. "Did she dislike him as well?"

Miss Marlow glanced up in surprise. "Dr. Sloan? No. As far as I know Mrs. Greenwood had no feelings about Dr. Sloan one way or the other. I certainly wasn't aware of any animosity between them."

"Miss Marlow, is Mrs. Stanwick still here?" Witherspoon asked hopefully.

She bit her lip and blushed. "No, I told everyone they could leave," she stammered. "I'm sorry, I hope that was all right. But that young policeman took down everyone's name and address, and well, surely you don't think one of my guests or one of our circle actually murdered Mrs. Greenwood."

"Don't distress yourself, Miss Marlow," he replied, feeling terribly sorry for the poor woman. "We've formed no opinion as to the identity of the murderer whatsoever. We'll speak with the other members of your circle tomorrow. What we really need now is someone to show us the way to the third-floor balcony." Though she really shouldn't have taken it upon herself to let everyone leave, he couldn't be annoyed with her. The dear lady looked so terribly distraught.

"That's most kind of you, Inspector," she said, giving him a brilliant smile. "I'll have the butler take you upstairs."

The balcony opened off a large, wood-floored passageway that bisected the top floor of the house. But the killer hadn't made any mistakes and left any evidence lying about, at least not as far as the inspector could tell.

He sighed and stared at the French doors, their panes grim and coated with dust, that opened out onto the balcony. "The butler said that Miss Marlow had this door opened to keep the air circulating. He said she always did it when the house was full of people."

"That sounds right, sir." Barnes scratched his chin. "With all that crowd milling about downstairs, it probably would get pretty warm, especially on a night like tonight. Mind you, I don't expect the poor woman thought one of her guests would wander all the way up here and get herself murdered."

The balcony was small, round, and made of stone and mortar. Witherspoon and Barnes stepped outside.

"Blimey, sir," the constable said as he squeezed into the tiny space behind the inspector, "there's hardly room for a body to move. I wonder why Mrs. Greenwood took it into her head to come up here."

"Perhaps she wanted some fresh air," the inspector suggested. "Though I must say, that's a jolly good walk up all those stairs, and if she only wanted air, she could just as easily have gone outside."

"Maybe she just wanted to look at the view."

From where he stood, Witherspoon could see the garden in great detail. The illumination, so thoughtfully provided by Miss Marlow for her guests, brightened even the darkest paths and deepest shadows.

"The rail is a good height," Barnes said thoughtfully. He slipped past the inspector and peered over the edge. "Even with a knife in her back, it must have took some doing to get her over the top here."

The inspector looked up sharply. The constable was a tall man, close to six feet. The side of the balcony came up to his waist. "You're right, Barnes. I think we can conclude our killer is probably a man. I don't think a woman would have the strength to have lifted Mrs. Greenwood over the edge."

"Course, she could've fallen forward," Barnes suggested. "And then whoever was standin' behind her could have just given her a good shove."

"Possible," the inspector said thoughtfully, "but not likely. It's been my experience that stabbing victims usually fall backwards, not forwards." Actually, he wasn't really sure of that fact. But it did sound quite clever.

• • •

Smythe knocked softly on Mrs. Jeffries's door. He cocked his ear to the wood and heard a faint rustling sound. "Mrs. Jeffries," he hissed, "it's me. Smythe. Get up, I've got to talk to you."

The door flew open and the housekeeper, wrapped in a heavy burgundy wool dressing gown, peered out at him. "Gracious, Smythe, it's the middle of the night. What's wrong?"

"Nothing's wrong, Mrs. J. But I think we might 'ave ourselves another murder. One of the guests at that fancy ball the inspector went to tonight took a tumble off the third-floor balcony. She's dead. And as she 'ad a knife stickin' out of her back, it weren't no accident."

Mrs. Jeffries brightened immediately. "Get Wiggins and then get down to the kitchen. I'll wake Betsy and Mrs. Goodge. But be very quiet; we don't want Mrs. Livingston-Graves to hear us."

He turned and tiptoed quickly toward the stairs leading to the fourth floor.

"Smythe," she called out softly. "When's the inspector returning?"

"He told me to come back for 'im in a couple of 'ours," the coachman replied. "So we've got a bit of time."

Mrs. Jeffries turned and crept down the hallway to rouse the maid and the cook.

Unlike most households, the female servants all had their own rooms. They were located on the third floor of the huge house. The housekeeper's rooms consisted of a small sitting room and a bedroom. Mrs. Jeffries made certain the rest of the staff had full use of her sitting room if they wanted. Betsy's room was located nearest the stairwell, and Mrs. Goodge, as befitting her station as the cook, had the larger, sunnier room next door. Up the staircase onto the fourth floor there was an attic on one side and a largish "box" room on the other. Smythe, Wiggins, and Fred, when he wasn't sneaking down to the inspector's room, shared those quarters.

Within a few minutes they were gathered round the large table in the kitchen. Even Fred, looking sleepy and grumpy, had come down.

"What's all this, then?" Mrs. Goodge mumbled. "Should I put the kettle on?"

Betsy, her long blond hair tumbling over her shoulders, yawned. "Have we got us a murder?"

Wiggins, who didn't look like he was quite awake yet, mumbled something under his breath.

Smythe, who was staring at the maid, didn't say anything.

"Please, Mrs. Goodge," Mrs. Jeffries said. "I think a cup of tea would be wonderful. Now, Smythe." She turned toward the coachman, but he didn't seem to hear her. "Uh, Smythe," she repeated, poking him lightly on the arm.

"'Ave I got a wart on my nose?" Betsy asked grumpily.

Smythe flushed and drew his gaze away from the maid. "Well, let's see now. As I told Mrs. J., a woman took a tumble off the balcony at that fancy ball tonight. She had a knife in her back. Her name was Hannah Greenwood, she was one of the guests."

"Doesn't sound like it was an accident, then," Mrs. Goodge muttered. She moved slowly toward the stove, teakettle in hand.

"As soon as I found out what were goin' on," Smythe continued, "I 'ad a word with this Mrs. Greenwood's coachman. Nice bloke, works out of Piper's Livery. . . . Well, this feller does a lot of drivin' for Mrs. Greenwood. Said tonight she weren't upset or unhappy about anythin'. He claimed if anythin', she were right pleased about somethin'. Besides, he says this Mrs. Greenwood's a right old tartar. He didn't seem in the least surprised she'd got herself done in."

Mrs. Jeffries digested this piece of information. Mr. Jeffries, the housekeeper's late husband, had been a policeman in Yorkshire for over twenty years. She'd learned a great deal about murder investigations from him. Unlike many of his colleagues, he hadn't assumed that because one was a servant, one was an idiot. On the contrary, when Constable Jeffries was working on a case, he took servants' observations very seriously. Mrs. Jeffries made it a point to follow his lead. She'd found that servants were not all that different from their masters. True, some were stupid, lying, and lazy. But many were intelligent, observant, and perceptive. By respecting people and not status, she and the other members of the household at Upper Edmonton Gardens had solved several murders.

Not, of course, that they ever let on to the inspector. He thought he did it all himself. And they were all dedicated to keeping him thinking that way as well.

She glanced around the table, smiling slightly as she took in their sleepy but earnest expressions; Smythe and Wiggins had originally worked for the inspector's late aunt Euphemia. When she'd passed away, leaving her fortune and her home to Inspector Witherspoon, he'd kept both men on out of the goodness of his heart. He no more needed a coachman than he needed a hole in his head. And as for Wiggins—he was no more a trained footman than he was a dancing bear. But Gerald Witherspoon never considered tossing them out. He'd hired Mrs. Goodge, a superb cook, but getting on in years, for the same reason—his kind heart. Betsy had shown up sick and penniless on his doorstep, and he'd given her employment as a maid, after hiring Mrs. Jeffries to run his household and nurse the girl back to health. Was it any wonder they were all so loyal to the man?

But Mrs. Jeffries didn't fool herself that their devotion to detection was totally altruistic. As Betsy once told her, dashing about following suspects and digging for clues was decidedly more interesting than scrubbing floors and ironing linens.

"So her own driver wasn't surprised she'd been murdered. That's a very interesting observation," she said softly.

"And that's not all."

The kettle whistled. Betsy got down the cups and Wiggins went to the cooling larder for a jug of milk. They waited until Mrs. Goodge had poured the tea.

Again, Mrs. Jeffries marveled at how easily they all ignored the stringent codes most households followed. There was no hierarchy of false status here. No one needed to have their sense of worth bolstered by giving in to the foolish practices of most other households. They worked together as a team. Mrs. Goodge didn't expect a maid or a footman to wait on her just because of her position as the cook, and Smythe didn't balk at doing anything asked of him.

The inspector's household was unique. Mrs. Jeffries took some small pride in feeling that she'd helped make it that way. After all, she had been the first innovator. She remembered their shocked expressions the day she'd called them all to her sitting room shortly after the inspector had hired her. She'd told them precisely what their duties were, and then she'd told them she didn't give a fig when they did their chores as long as they got done properly. Once their work was finished, their time was their own. The only one who'd balked had been Mrs. Goodge. But even she'd softened after Mrs. Jeffries had announced she was getting rid of the odious practice of morning prayers. As far as the housekeeper was concerned, how one dealt with the Almighty was one's own business. And no one wanted to get up at the crack of dawn and gather in the drawing room for a Bible reading anyway. Least of all the inspector.

When they were all settled, they sipped their tea and waited for Smythe to tell them the rest.

"Well, go on," Mrs. Goodge urged. "We've not got all night."

"I found out a few other things about this Mrs. Greenwood, too," he said. "But I'm not sure it 'as anythin' to do with her death."

"Tell us anyway," Mrs. Jeffries suggested. "As we've learned many times in the past, the most innocuous information can help us greatly."

"This Mrs. Greenwood, she weren't all that good a friend of the 'ostess, the lady who was havin' the ball."

"And who is that?" Mrs. Jeffries inquired. She wanted to get as many facts as possible.

"Lucinda Marlow." Smythe's heavy brows drew together in thought. "I overheard the footman sayin' that Miss Marlow was havin' a go at a woman in a dark blue dress, and that's the color that Mrs. Greenwood were wearin'. So I'm wonderin' if this Miss Marlow and the victim 'ad been 'avin' words so to speak."

Mrs. Jeffries reached for her mug of tea. "Did the footman actually identify the woman in the blue dress?"

He shook his head. "'E didn't know who Miss Marlow were talkin' to, 'e just 'eard the voices and saw a bit of blue stickin' out from behind the drawin' room door. They was standin' in a corner."

From above, they heard the thump of heavy footsteps. "Hello, hello," Mrs. Livingston-Graves voice could be heard from three flights up. "Is anyone down there."

"Oh, blast," Betsy muttered. "We finally gets us a decent murder, and we've got *her* hangin' about."

Disgusted voices started babbling. Mrs. Jeffries quickly shushed everyone. She got up and hurried to the foot of the stairs. "It's all right, Mrs. Livingston-Graves," she called. "Do go back to bed."

"What are you doing up?" the woman screeched. They could hear her thumping down the second-floor stairs now.

"I couldn't sleep and I'm fixing myself a cup of hot milk. There's no need for you to trouble yourself."

"You sure you're alone down there?"

Mrs. Jeffries rolled her eyes. "Quite sure. Please, do go back to bed. You'll catch a chill."

"All right, then. But mind you, I'll have a word with Gerald tomorrow. It's a bit of liberty, the housekeeper roaming about in the middle of the night and waking decent people."

Smythe swore under his breath. Betsy's eyes narrowed in fury and Mrs. Goodge snorted. Even Wiggins looked stunned by the woman's audacity.

"What are we going to do?" Mrs. Goodge said. "Tryin' to find out anything about this case is going to be bloomin' difficult with that old witch in the house."

"You can say that again," the coachman muttered darkly. "Maybe it's time we figured out a way to send 'er nibs packin'."

Everyone had a suggestion as to how to get rid of Mrs. Livingston-Graves. When the ideas became too outrageous and involved shanghaiing and white slavery, Mrs. Jeffries hid a smile behind her mug and raised her hand for silence. "Don't worry about Mrs. Livingston-Graves," she said softly. "She won't be interfering in our investigation. I'll see to that."

CHAPTER 3

It was past two in the morning when the inspector arrived home. Rubbing his eyes, he crept to the coatrack and hung up his hat and coat. Every bone in his body was tired, his head ached, and he desperately wanted a nice hot drink.

As he turned for the stairs, he saw Mrs. Jeffries coming down the hallway carrying a tray. "Good gracious, Mrs. Jeffries," he whispered, "it's very late. You didn't need to wait up for me."

"It's quite all right, sir," she replied. "I've made a pot of tea. I thought you might need something to warm you up. Smythe said there had been a murder. How very dreadful for you. Shall we go into the drawing room?"

"This is most kind," he said, following her. He watched her set the tray down on a table and pour two cups. "It's been a very strange evening." Settling down in his favorite chair, Witherspoon prepared to unburden himself. "And I was having a jolly good time, as well. Did you know that Lady Cannonberry and I share a common interest? She's quite a railway enthusiast. Isn't that amazing?"

"Very," Mrs. Jeffries replied. She handed him his tea and picked up her own cup. As delighted as she was to hear that he'd enjoyed Lady Cannonberry's company, she didn't really want to talk about it now. She wanted to talk about murder.

"Now, sir, about your murder," she prodded. "Who was the victim?" Unfortunately, she didn't want the inspector to know she'd received any information from Smythe, so she was forced to waste time asking questions to which she already knew the answers. But it was a small price to pay to keep the dear man in the dark about the activities of his household.

"A lady named Hannah Greenwood." He paused and took a quick sip. "Older woman, possibly in her late fifties, and widowed. She's a member of the Hyde Park Literary Circle, so she was one of the guests this evening. The poor woman was stabbed in the back and shoved off an attic balcony. Horrible. I can't imagine why people do such diabolical things, can you?"

"No, sir." But, of course, she could. Evil, greed, lust, revenge, and hatred had been part of the human condition since Adam. Mrs. Jeffries thought it a true mark of the inspector's sterling character that after all his years with the police, he was still genuinely shocked by the dark side of human nature. Most men in the inspector's position would have become extremely cynical.

"But for once, we seem to have had a bit of luck. I mean, there were dozens and dozens of guests at the ball, but it appears that Mrs. Greenwood wasn't acquainted with anyone other than the members of the literary circle."

"How very clever of you to have found that out so quickly."

He smiled modestly. "Not so very clever, I'm afraid. One of the guests, Miss Mansfield, made a point of giving me that information." He shook his head. "Yet even with that bit of luck, I've a feeling this investigation is going to be very difficult. Very difficult indeed."

"Of course it will be, sir," Mrs. Jeffries said briskly. "They always are. But you must admit, you're at your very best when the case is complicated." She gave him an encouraging smile.

"Thank you, Mrs. Jeffries," he murmured. "Well, as I was saying, Lady Cannonberry and I were having this extremely interesting conversation out in the garden, when all of a sudden, Mrs. Greenwood comes hurtling off the balcony and lands on the terrace."

"You actually saw it happen?"

He shook his head. "Not really. I mean, we were outside, but my back was to the terrace. I didn't realize anything was wrong until I heard the screams."

Mrs. Jeffries clucked her tongue. There were dozens of questions she wanted to ask, but she'd learned from past experience that she was apt to get far more information out of the inspector by letting him talk at his own pace.

"Naturally, I took charge. Had to, really, I am the police." He frowned. "At first I assumed Mrs. Greenwood's death was an accident. One doesn't expect to go to a fancy Jubilee Ball and find oneself dealing with murder, does one?"

"Of course not, sir," she agreed, watching him closely. He looked very anxious, very unsure of himself.

"I mean, I realized it was murder as soon as Mrs. Putnam screamed out that there was a knife in the victim's back."

"Who is Mrs. Putnam?"

"One of the other members of the circle. Unfortunately, the, er . . . body landed only a few feet away from Mrs. Putnam and two other ladies."

"How very unpleasant."

"Yes." He sighed. "I'm sure it was. Though I must say, the ladies took it surprisingly well. No one fainted. Odd, isn't it? We're so used to think-ing of women as the weaker sex, yet it was Mrs. Hiatt who got to Mrs. Greenwood first. She didn't hesitate in the least. She leapt to her feet and dashed right over to see if she could be of assistance. You know, Mrs. Jef-fries, sometimes I have a very strong feeling that there is much we don't understand about the capabilities of females."

Mrs. Jeffries could spend the rest of the night lecturing him on ex-actly how capable women were, but she didn't really want to waste any more time. There was a murder to solve. "I'm sure you're quite right," she replied.

"Uhmmm . . . women. Sometimes they're not what they appear to be, are they? Then again, who of us is? Now, where was I?"

"You were describing the murder."

"Oh, yes. Well, after I saw that Mrs. Greenwood was dead, I asked Miss Marlow to send for the police and I told everyone to go into the drawing room. But I'm afraid that I may have made a mistake at this point," he said. "Silly of me, I suppose. But, one assumes people will hang about after a murder."

"Didn't the constables take statements from the guests and the ser-vants?" Mrs. Jeffries asked.

"Of course. But I really should have questioned the members of the literary circle tonight. I intended to, you see. Especially after I spoke with Miss Mansfield. Unfortunately, I must not have made my instructions clear. Miss Marlow, that's the lady who was our hostess, seemed to be under the impression that everyone could go home as long as they gave the constable their name and address. She told everyone to leave. So tomorrow I've got to start from the beginning. You know what that means—the trail will have started to go cold."

"Now, now, sir. Don't be too hard on yourself. No one, not even the chief inspector, expects you to be omniscient. Furthermore, you were in a rather awkward position. You might be a policeman, but you were also a guest at the Marlow home." She knew the inspector needed his self-confidence boosted a tad.

"Thank you, Mrs. Jeffries. One doesn't like to think one is a complete incompetent."

"Nonsense, sir. You're brilliant at solving murders and catching killers. I've no doubt whatsoever that you'll solve this one as well." She smiled. "You know how much I love hearing about your detection methods, so do tell me everything."

Some of the anxiety vanished from his eyes. "To begin with, it was dashedly hard keeping people straight tonight. Half the women there were in blue gowns. They all looked alike from the back. Most confusing. Every time I turned around I was losing track of Lady Cannonberry. But that's neither here nor there. As to the investigation, I did learn a few interesting facts. Mrs. Putnam confirmed that Mrs. Greenwood was only at the ball because she was a member of the circle. Which is most helpful. That fact will certainly narrow down the field of suspects, so to speak."

"Really, sir?"

"Certainly. As the victim wasn't acquainted with the other guests, it's likely that she was murdered by someone from the circle. Why would a stranger lure her up to a dark balcony, stick a carving knife in her back, and then shove her over?"

Mrs. Jeffries wasn't so sure the inspector's assumption was correct. So far, they knew very little about Hannah Greenwood. Despite what Cecilia Mansfield might have said about her not knowing anyone at the ball except for her own circle, she may well have had an enemy she didn't know about. Still, Mrs. Jeffries did understand the inspector's reasoning. Unless the motive was robbery or the killer a madman, one was most likely to be murdered by someone one knew. "Have you discovered if anyone in the circle had a motive?"

"Not yet. But Miss Mansfield, she was one of the ladies with Mrs. Hiatt, did tell me that earlier in the evening, she'd seen Mrs. Greenwood having an argument with Dr. Sloan. He's the president of the group and, I might add, the one in charge of the poetry contest. Miss Marlow also mentioned that Mrs. Greenwood wasn't very well liked. She was surprised Mrs. Greenwood had shown up for the ball. I rather got the impression from both Miss Marlow and Miss Mansfield, that Mrs. Greenwood wasn't a very sociable person. As a matter of fact, Miss Marlow mentioned that the victim had gone out of her way on several occasions to be rude to one of the other members, a Mrs. Stanwick."

"I take it you weren't able to speak with either Dr. Sloan or Mrs. Stanwick?"

"They'd both already left. But I'll remedy that tomorrow." He shrugged. "We were able to account for several of the members' exact location when the murder occurred. Lady Cannonberry was with me, of course. Mrs. Putnam was speaking with Miss Mansfield and Mrs. Hiatt, so the three of them all have alibis, and Mr. Putnam was standing over to one side of the terrace, sneaking a cigar. I remember seeing him myself."

"So who hasn't been accounted for?"

Witherspoon frowned. "Dr. Sloan, of course, and Mrs. Stanwick. Our hostess, Miss Lucinda Marlow . . ." He paused, trying to recall the other names in the circle. Drat, he should have written them down. But Barnes always took down those details in his notebook, and he didn't have the constable here to refresh his memory. He sighed and rubbed his eyes wearily. "There's several other names, but honestly, I'm simply too tired to remember them right now. I'll start afresh tomorrow."

"So the case is definitely yours?" Mrs. Jeffries held her breath. On the inspector's last few cases, one of the other police inspectors, an odious man named Nigel Nivens, had made such a fuss that she'd feared her dear employer would get the next murder snatched right out from under his nose. Inspector Nivens was foaming at the mouth to investigate a homicide. But as Mrs. Jeffries didn't think Nigel Nivens had the intelligence to find a potato in a greengrocer's, she sincerely hoped he would keep his paws off the inspector's case.

"I expect so," he replied glumly. "As I was 'on the scene,' so to speak, I'm sure the chief will insist I continue the investigation. That's not going to make Inspector Nivens very happy. He's always hinting that I'm hogging all the homicides."

"Don't worry about Inspector Nivens," Mrs. Jeffries said firmly. "You've far more experience in these matters than he does. Were you able to get any useful information out of the servants? Had anyone seen any-thing suspicious?"

"We haven't finished questioning them yet," he admitted. "They were all most upset. Two of the maids were weeping hysterically. Mrs. Cray-croft, the housekeeper, was attending to Miss Marlow, and the butler had been totally occupied with the ball. We'll try again tomorrow. Once ev-eryone calms down we should be able to learn something useful." He sighed again. "I tell you, Mrs. Jeffries. Unless we can find an eyewitness or someone comes forward to confess, this might very well be the case I don't solve. We've practically no physical evidence."

"What about the murder weapon?"

"That won't do us much good, I'm afraid. The killer used a carving knife from the cold buffet table. Anyone in the house could have picked it up."

Despite yawns and sleepy expressions, there was an air of suppressed excitement a few hours later. Mrs. Jeffries told the other servants what she'd learned from the inspector in the wee hours. She gave them every single bit of information she'd wormed out of her employer, leaving out nothing, no matter how insignificant the detail.

"So you see," she said, "I think our first task is to learn everything we can about Mrs. Greenwood and the Hyde Park Literary Circle."

Smythe frowned thoughtfully. "What are them names again?"

"Dr. Sloan, Mrs. Stanwick, Miss Lucinda Marlow . . ." She paused. "There are others, but the inspector had already determined that Mr. and Mrs. Putnam couldn't have done it, as they were on the terrace. Nor could Miss Mansfield or Mrs. Hiatt. As he was with Lady Cannonberry when the crime occurred, she's not involved, either."

"What about Edgar Warburton and Shelby Locke?" the coachman asked.

"Who are they?" Betsy demanded, annoyed that Smythe always seemed to get the jump on her.

"Two members of the circle," he replied smugly, giving her a cocky grin. "I overheard Lady Cannonberry mention them when I brung her home last night."

"Thank you, Smythe," Mrs. Jeffries said quickly. She wanted to nip any incipient rivalry in the bud. Devoted as they all were to the inspector, they weren't above trying to outdo one another when it came to digging up clues. "That's most helpful. But I think I'd better have a word with Lady Cannonberry today in order to get a complete list of names. There may be one or two more who were at the ball."

"Cor," muttered Wiggins, rubbing the sleep out of his eyes. "That's a right lot of suspects we've got. What if this woman got herself stabbed by someone else? You know, one of them lunatics."

"Now, how would a lunatic get himself invited to a fancy ball?" Mrs. Goodge said impatiently.

"It don't have to be a 'im," Wiggins argued. "It could be a 'er. And 'ow do we know there ain't lunatics running about loose? Sometimes they look as right as you or me. My old gran told me about a woman who used to live in her village. She were a right respectable lady, too. No one thought there was anythin' wrong with 'er. But one day she locked 'erself in the church and started painting all the walls blue. She even painted over all the pretty stained-glass windows. Claimed that God had told her to do it 'cause he were gettin' right sick of seein' the same old buildin' Sunday after Sunday."

"Don't be daft, boy," the cook snorted. "That's the silliest story I ever heard. If there's anyone who's not right in their head's around here, it's you."

"I'm not so sure about that," Betsy muttered. "I'm beginnin' to think I'm losing my mind."

Surprised, they all stared at her.

"Whatever do you mean?" Mrs. Jeffries asked.

Betsy sighed. "It's the silliest thing, really. I shouldn't have mentioned it. I guess I'm just tired and it popped out."

"Go on, girl, tell us the rest," Smythe urged.

"It's my shoes," Betsy said. She stared at the top of the table. "There was a big hole in the bottom of one of my good black leather walking shoes. I kept meanin' to take it down to Mr. Conner's and get it fixed. But I never got around to it. Well, a couple of days ago, I got the shoes out to make sure they was clean and the hole was gone. There was a brand-new sole on it."

Smythe laughed. "Is that what was worryin' you? Someone just did ya a favor, that's all."

"But why would someone do that for me and not say anything about it?" Betsy shook her head. "I think that's right strange."

"I think Smythe's right," Wiggins said. "Someone's just doin' somethin' nice for ya, but don't want to say nuthin'. It's probably the same person who brought me that new packet of paper."

"Someone's bought you paper?" Mrs. Jeffries asked. She suspected she knew who'd fixed Betsy's shoes, but she didn't think that person would bother buying the footman more writing paper.

Wiggins nodded. "Last week it was. I come in and found the paper in me drawer. Come in right handy as well."

"Are you sure you didn't buy the paper yourself?" Smythe asked. "Admit it, lad, sometimes you're a bit on the forgetful side."

"Sometimes I might forget to clean the back steps or polish the door-knocker," Wiggins protested. "But I've never once in me life forgot spendin' me money. And this 'ere was good quality paper. Whoever bought it paid a pretty penny for it."

"Can we get on with the business at hand?" Mrs. Goodge asked tartly. "We've got a murder to solve. Time's gettin' on. If we don't get crackin', Mrs. Nosy Parker will be down here screaming that we're takin' too many tea breaks."

Mrs. Jeffries stifled her own curiosity. They could learn the identity of this mysterious gift-giver later. "Mrs. Goodge is right. We must get busy."

"So what do we do first?" Wiggins reached down and scratched Fred behind the ears.

"As we have several names already, I think it would be best if we learned what we could about the other members of the literary circle." Mrs. Jeffries drummed her fingers on the tabletop. "Smythe, why don't you see what you can find out about this Shelby Locke and Edgar Warburton. Betsy, I think you ought to get over to the Marlow home and see if you can find out anything about what went on last night at the ball. Try talking to the maids. Wiggins, why don't you nip around to Mrs. Greenwood's house and see what you can learn about the victim herself." She turned to the cook.

Mrs. Goodge grinned. "Don't worry. I've got half of London troopin' through this kitchen today. I'll learn what I can about the members of that literary circle. . . ." Her smile faded. "But what am I going to do about her nibs? Mrs. Livingston-Graves is always poking her nose down here. I can't get much out of anyone if she's hanging about all day, watching how much tea I serve and how many buns I let the delivery boy eat."

"Nonsense, Mrs. Goodge!" Mrs. Jeffries exclaimed. "You're being far too modest about your own abilities. If anyone can hold Mrs. Livingston-Graves at bay, it's you." The housekeeper wasn't exaggerating. She did think Mrs. Goodge was remarkable. Without leaving her kitchen, the cook was able to learn the most intimate details about the suspects in their cases. She ruthlessly pumped information out of a veritable army of delivery boys, rag and bone merchants, chimney sweeps, and men from the gasworks. Additionally, because she'd cooked in so many grand households herself, she had sources of information from a huge network of other servants spread all over the city. There wasn't a morsel of gossip about anyone of importance in London that didn't pass through her kitchen.

"Mrs. Goodge can probably 'andle the old girl, all right," Smythe muttered. "But what about the rest of us? Every time she lays eyes on me, she starts rantin' and ravin' about me cleanin' them attic windows."

"What are we going to do?" Betsy moaned. "We can hardly come and go as we please with her here! She's been after me for two days to air out them bloomin' linen cupboards upstairs. I don't want to air out cupboards, I want to get out and about and find out who killed Mrs. Greenwood."

"Don't worry." Mrs. Jeffries grinned mischievously. "As I told you last night, *I'll* take care of Mrs. Livingston-Graves. I do believe she'll be getting a special invitation today. An invitation she can't refuse."

By ten o'clock Witherspoon and Constable Barnes were back at the Marlow home. His superiors, after learning that the inspector had been a guest at the ball, had instructed him to investigate the matter. Inspector Nivens hadn't been pleased. Witherspoon wasn't sure he was all that pleased about it, either. He'd rather hoped to sit this one out.

"I do hope Miss Marlow is feeling better this morning," the inspector said to Constable Barnes as they waited in the drawing room for the lady of the house. He squinted at the portraits on the far wall. A stern-faced, elderly gentleman with deep-set eyes and white hair, and a grim-looking woman with a thin, flat line of a mouth seemed to glare back at him disapprovingly.

"Thank you, Inspector," a soft voice said from the doorway. He whirled around to see Lucinda Marlow standing just inside, a faint smile on her lips.

"I'm feeling quite well today." She continued as she advanced into the the room. "I noticed you staring at my parents' portraits. Lovely, aren't they."

That was hardly the adjective the inspector would have used, but he was far too much a gentleman to say so. "Yes, Miss Marlow, they most certainly are."

"They were done by Creighton, you know," she said, smiling softly in the direction of the portraits.

As the inspector hadn't a clue who Creighton was, he wasn't sure what to say. Actually, he didn't really have to say anything. Miss Marlow whirled around, her dark green skirts swishing noisily, and said, "But you're not here to look at paintings, are you? I presume you want to ask me more questions about last night's unfortunate incident."

"I'm afraid I must."

"I don't think there's all that much I can tell you, Inspector," Lucinda replied with a shrug. "I can't think of any reason why Mrs. Greenwood would go up to the third floor, let alone why someone would want to kill her."

"When was the last time you saw Mrs. Greenwood?" Witherspoon asked. He saw Barnes whip out his notebook.

She frowned slightly. "Let me think. It must have been close to ten-fifteen. Yes, that's right. I distinctly remember seeing Mrs. Greenwood talking with Mrs. Stanwick."

"Did they see you?"

She shook her head. "I don't think so. They were rather involved in their own conversation. . . ." She paused. "Both ladies had their backs to me, so I don't think they knew I was there."

"Did you happen to hear what the ladies were discussing?" Witherspoon smiled slightly. "One does occasionally overhear a conversation. Not, of course, that I'm implying you were deliberately trying to listen, but in a crowded room, sometimes one can't help but hear what's being said."

Lucinda Marlow arched one eyebrow. "How very diplomatic you are, Inspector. But as it happens, I was too far away to hear what they were discussing."

"Did you happen to notice, Miss," Barnes asked, "if anyone else was standing close enough to hear the two women?"

"Not that I recall." She cocked her chin to one side. "Are you implying that Mrs. Stanwick murdered Mrs. Greenwood?"

"We're not implying anything of the kind," Witherspoon said. "We're trying to establish the facts. Any information about Mrs. Greenwood's movements may be very helpful to us in catching her killer."

"But you are assuming she was killed by one of the other guests, aren't you?"

"As I said, Miss Marlow," the inspector replied patiently, "at this point in the investigation, we're only interested in facts. We're not making any assumptions at all."

"Good." She smiled. "I wouldn't like to think one of my guests had been murdered by one of my other guests or a member of the household. There were dozens of people coming and going during the ball. Extra serving staff, tradesmen making last-minute deliveries and, of course, dozens of coach drivers. I see no reason why some completely unknown person couldn't have slipped inside and done the foul deed."

Witherspoon nodded politely. Miss Marlow could well be correct. However, he thought it most unlikely. People were generally murdered by those nearest and dearest to them, and from what he'd heard of the victim, he suspected she wasn't the sort of woman to be overly close to her coach driver or her maid. "Did you see Mrs. Greenwood after she'd finished conversing with Mrs. Stanwick?"

"No, I was too busy with my other guests."

"Can you give us a list of names of everyone who was in your house last night, please."

"I gave a copy of my guest list to one of the constables last night. Surely you haven't lost it."

"I'm sorry, Miss Marlow," the inspector said. "I didn't make myself clear. We haven't lost the guest list, but we would also like to know who else was in the house. As you just mentioned, there were dozens of outside servants and tradesmen coming and going. I'd like their names, please."

"I'll need to consult with the butler and my housekeeper, Inspector," she said. "It may take me several hours to compose the list. Will that be satisfactory?"

"I'm sorry to put you to any extra trouble, Miss Marlow," the inspector apologized. "However, one never knows what one will find out unless one takes the trouble to look."

"All right, you'll have your list by this afternoon. Is that all your questions? I don't really think there's anything more I can tell you."

"I've only a few more. Where were you at ten thirty last night?" he asked.

"Me!" Lucinda Marlow yelped. She was clearly outraged. "What an impertinent question. I don't think I've got to answer that."

"Please, Miss Marlow, we're only trying to find out what really happened." Witherspoon had no idea why some people were so offended by the least little inquiry.

"I was in the ballroom," she said coldly, "seeing to the welfare of my guests. Where else would I be? After all, I was the hostess."

Mrs. Jeffries timed herself to arrive at the corner at precisely the right moment. She smiled in satisfaction as she spotted Lady Cannonberry coming out of her house, her cocker spaniel at her heels.

Shifting her basket to the other hand, the housekeeper crossed the street. "Good afternoon, Lady Cannonberry," she called cheerfully.

Lady Cannonberry, a woman of medium height with light brown hair, smiled broadly, her placid features and blue eyes expressing delight. She wore a mother-of-pearl gray gown trimmed with cherry-red silk stripes and a standing collar of matching crimson. The color did wonders for her ivory skin. At forty-five, she was well past the first flush of youth, yet remained a very attractive woman. She was also a very nice woman, completely unaffected by her status as the wife of a late peer.

"Hello, Mrs. Jeffries." The cocker began to strain on its leash and bounce up and down. "Boadicea, don't jump up on the lady."

Boadicea, a caramel-colored dog, immediately stopped leaping and flopped down onto her back. She wagged her tail in frantic delight at the sight of the housekeeper.

"Oh, do get up, you silly girl," Lady Cannonberry continued. "I'm so sorry. She doesn't act at all like her namesake, does she?"

Mrs. Jeffries laughed and knelt down to rub the cocker's belly. "No, but I expect she's a great deal more satisfying to have about than some horridly aggressive warrior queen."

"She loves everybody." Lady Cannonberry sighed. "And she certainly gives me a great deal of company. So I mustn't complain."

Mrs. Jeffries stood up. "I'm so dreadfully sorry your evening was spoiled last night."

Lady Cannonberry shook her head in agreement. "It was perfectly awful. The inspector and I were having such an interesting conversation, too. Do you know, he likes trains!" She made this announcement as though it were the most wonderful thing in the world. "Then all of a sudden, poor Mrs. Greenwood, came tumbling down off that balcony. I must say, it quite put a damper on the evening."

"Yes, I rather expect it did."

She nodded emphatically. "But Gerald was wonderful. He took charge immediately. Kept everyone from going into a panic."

Mrs. Jeffries waited patiently while Lady Cannonberry extolled the inspector's many virtues. She nodded sympathetically, tut-tutted in the appropriate spots, and clucked her tongue in agreement when her companion expected it.

"The whole thing must have been dreadfully shocking," Mrs. Jeffries said, "and not just for you. I'm sure your entire group was utterly appalled by what happened. And on the night of your poetry contest, too." She wanted to get Lady Cannonberry gossiping about the other members of the Hyde Park Literary Circle.

"Oh, they were. Miss Marlow almost went into shock—she was as pale as a ghost. I don't blame her. It's not as if the poor woman has much social life at all. Her first party in ages and look what happens—one of her guests is murdered. And Mrs. Stanwick. Goodness, she was so upset she had to lean on Mr. Locke's arm when he escorted her to her carriage."

"How awful," Mrs. Jeffries agreed.

"Oh, it was," Lady Cannonberry said earnestly. "The ball wasn't all that much of a success even before Mrs. Greenwood's fall."

"Really?"

"Personally, I was having a wonderful time." She smiled and ten years seemed to melt off her age. "Gerald is such an interesting companion. But I noticed that practically everyone else in our group was nervous. I expect it was the contest."

"Competitions do sometimes bring out the worst in people, don't they?"

"They most certainly do," Lady Cannonberry agreed. "Mr. Richard Venerable, you know, the poet, was to be our judge. Naturally, I hadn't a hope of winning, but I enjoyed writing the piece in any case. But several others seemed very anxious. Our president, Dr. Sloan—he's had poems published before—I think he thought he stood the best chance. And of course, Mr. Locke was most annoyed . . . he claimed his best poems were lost. He didn't exactly come right out and accuse anyone, but supposedly he'd left his notebook at Miss Marlow's home at our last meeting. But no one had seen it. He virtually implied someone stole the notebook, and of course what he was really implying was that someone stole his poems. But, I can't believe anyone in our group would stoop to such a thing. Another thing for Miss Marlow to worry about."

Mrs. Jeffries nodded sympathetically. She quite liked Lady Cannonberry and she was delighted that the lady seemed so enamored of the inspector. She was even more delighted to find her so very informative. "Poor Miss Marlow, first a theft and then a murder," she murmured.

"Honestly, Mrs. Jeffries, it was a very peculiar evening. Mr. Warburton—he's one of our newer members—was in a rage over something. He didn't even say hello when he arrived, and Mrs. Greenwood—" She broke off. "Oh, dear, one shouldn't speak ill of the dead."

"Please, Lady Cannonberry, do get it off your chest," Mrs. Jeffries said soothingly. "If you saw something amiss with the deceased, you really ought to talk about it. Perhaps what you noticed might have something to do with her murder."

"Well, Mrs. Greenwood had words with Mrs. Stanwick." Lady Cannonberry looked guiltily over her shoulder, as though she expected the ghost of the dead woman to come sneaking up on her. "And I think it was over this silly contest. You know, the next time anyone suggests a literary contest, I shall put my foot down. It brings out the worst in everyone. Even Mrs. Putnam, and she's a very good soul, was muttering about how unfair it was that those of us who were amateurs should be judged in the same category as Dr. Sloan."

"I believe this Mrs. Putnam may have a point," Mrs. Jeffries said quickly. She wanted to get back to Mrs. Greenwood's argument with Mrs. Stanwick. "Why do you think the two ladies were arguing over the contest?"

"I'm not certain they were. But I happened to come up behind them when I went to fetch my handkerchief, and I distinctly overheard Mrs. Greenwood say to Mrs. Stanwick that she'd never set foot in one of our meetings again."

Fifteen minutes later Mrs. Jeffries waved to Lady Cannonberry and turned to go home. Deep in thought, she walked slowly, putting all the small pieces of information that Lady Cannonberry had just given her into some semblance of order. She shook her head as she climbed the stairs. It was no good. The information that she had, while interesting, was far too sketchy to form any conclusion. The best that could be said was now she had a complete list of the members of the literary circle. And from what Lady Cannonberry had said, the inspector was correct earlier when he'd said no one else at the ball had any connection to Mrs. Greenwood. She was a guest solely because she'd been a member of the literary circle. Mrs. Jeffries wasn't discouraged, though. Once she heard what Betsy, Mrs. Goodge, Smythe, and Wiggins had found out today, the pieces would all start coming together.

Mrs. Livingston-Graves met her at the door. "It's about time you got back," she snapped. "There isn't a soul in this house except for that tight-lipped cook. The housemaid's disappeared, I haven't seen hide nor hair of that lazy footman, and even you had the audacity to desert me."

"I had some household matters to see to," Mrs. Jeffries replied. She smiled slightly as she saw the white linen envelope in Mrs. Livingston-Graves's hand. "Is there something I can do for you?"

"Yes, I need someone to help me bring my trunk down." Her narrow eyes gleamed with excitement. "I've been invited to a house party. In Southampton. It seems a mutual friend happened to mention to someone of great importance that I was here in London. So I've been invited."

"How very nice. Does the inspector know you're leaving us?"

She dismissed that with a wave of her hand. "Not yet. But Gerald won't mind. It isn't every day one gets an invitation like this. He wouldn't want me to miss it."

"I'm sure he wouldn't." Considering that the inspector had taken to tiptoeing around the house to avoid his cousin, Mrs. Jeffries was certain he wouldn't mind her going in the least. "He'd want you to go."

"If you can find that lazy good-for-nothing footman, have him bring my trunk down and then make sure the coachman brings the coach round. I want to catch the evening train."

"You're taking your trunk?" Mrs. Jeffries forced herself to keep her expression blank. "Does that mean it will be a long visit?"

"Of course not." Mrs. Livingston-Graves stamped off toward the stairs. "It means I'm taking all my clothes. One doesn't go visit an earl without proper attire."

CHAPTER 4

"I questioned the servants again, sir," Barnes told the inspector as they left the Marlow house. "The footman claimed the carving knife was still on the table at ten-fifteen. He specifically remembers because he overheard one of the guests askin' the time."

"Ten fifteen, hmmm." Witherspoon frowned slightly. "The murder occurred at ten thirty. Did the footman happen to notice when the knife went missing?"

Barnes shook his head. "No, he were too busy servin' people. He didn't know it was gone until he saw it stickin' out of Mrs. Greenwood's back."

"Drat. Well, did he notice who in particular was hanging about the buffet table?"

"That end of the table was right beside the door. The lad says there were more traffic by that spot than hansoms at a railway station. What with guests trompin' up and down the stairs and goin' to and fro down that hallway, he didn't see a bloomin' thing."

"What about the other servants? Did any of them see anything suspicious, anything out of the ordinary?"

Barnes pulled open the front door and stepped back to let the inspector pass. "None of the house servants can remember seein' or hearin' anything unusual. The uniformed lads are interviewing the rest of them, the ones that were brought in to help with the ball."

Witherspoon nodded and started down the steps. "We'll just have to keep digging, Barnes."

"This isn't goin' to be an easy one, is it?" Barnes said gloomily. "What with half of London inside the Marlow house, we're goin' to have a devil of a time finding us a witness."

The inspector cringed. He rather suspected the constable was right.

"Where to now, sir?" Barnes asked.

Witherspoon came to a full stop. Goodness, he thought, where should they go next? There was no point in going back to the station. They didn't really need to know the details of the autopsy report to investigate this murder. Witherspoon knew exactly how and when the victim had died. Besides, he really didn't want to risk running into Inspector Nivens.

"We'll go see the president of the Hyde Park Literary Circle," he announced confidently as he stepped off the bottom step. "Dr. Oxton Sloan."

He stopped again as he suddenly remembered something his housekeeper had once told him when they were sipping a companionable glass of sherry before dinner. *"Sometimes,"* she'd said, *"the best place to start an investigation isn't with the suspects, it's with the victim."*

"Shall we take a hansom to Dr. Sloan's?" Barnes asked hopefully. He looked down at his feet. His shoes, new enough so that the shine hadn't rubbed off, pinched his toes.

"What? Oh, no, Constable," Witherspoon replied airily. "We've no need of a hansom. I've changed my mind. We'll see Sloan later. Right now we must get over to Bolton Gardens. That's not far from here. I daresay the walk will do us both good. I want to interview Mrs. Greenwood's household."

"How come you've been hanging about all mornin'?" The impudent boy stared suspiciously at Wiggins and Fred.

Wiggins stepped out from the tree trunk he and Fred had been lurking behind. The dog woofed softly at the intruder. "Quiet, boy," Wiggins hissed as he stared across the small clearing between the two rows of houses and studied his adversary.

The lad stared right back at him. With pale skin, blue eyes, and unkempt red hair sticking out of a grimy porkpie hat, the skinny child dressed in oversize clothes couldn't be more than twelve.

"What's it to you?" Wiggins shot back. "This is a public street. My dog and I can 'ang about 'ere as long as we like."

"Yeah," the boy sneered and wiped one dirty hand under his nose.

"But you ain't been stayin' on the street, you've been goin' in and out of them gardens there." He broke off and gestured to his left in the direction of Bolton Gardens.

Fred growled low in his throat and the boy stepped back a pace. Wiggins laid a reassuring hand on the animal's head. "That's none of yer business," he replied, then decided to try and see what information he could get out of the youngster. He'd been hanging about the Greenwood house for hours now and hadn't seen hide nor hair of a servant or even a tradesman.

Wiggins was getting desperate. He couldn't go back to Upper Edmonton Gardens with nothing to report. "But if you must know"—he jerked his thumb at the Greenwood residence—"I'm tryin' to talk to someone from that 'ouse."

"That's Mrs. Greenwood's," he said, looking warily at the dog, but by this time Fred had reverted to his natural good-natured self. He wagged his tail. The boy smiled and tentatively reached out a hand.

"Go ahead," Wiggins urged, "you can pet 'im, 'e's a good dog, Fred is. He were only growlin' 'cause you startled 'im. Did you know Mrs. Greenwood?"

"'Course I knew 'er, I worked for 'er, didn't I? 'Course now that the silly old cow's gone and got 'erself done in, all of us is out of a job." He knelt down and petted Fred, his small face creased with worry. "I can't see that pie-faced sister of 'ers keepin' us on. She'll 'ave the 'ouse sold and all of us out in the streets before you can say Bob's Your Uncle."

"What's your name?" Wiggins asked softly. He could see that beneath the boy's bravado was fear. A wave of sympathy washed over him; he knew exactly what it felt like to be afraid you weren't going to have a roof over your head or food to fill your belly.

"Me name's Jon."

"What did you do for Mrs. Greenwood?"

Jon lifted his chin, suspicion clouding his eyes. "What'cha want to know for and why you askin' all these questions? You ain't a copper."

Wiggins knelt down beside him. Fred immediately licked his cheek. "Get off, you silly dog," he murmured. He smiled at Jon as he pushed Fred's snout out of his face. "'Ow do you know I'm not a copper?"

Jon grinned. "Fer starters, you're too young to be anythin' but a peeler, and you couldn't be one of them, cause you ain't dressed like one."

They were kneeling on a small strip of grass and sheltered from view by a low hedge. From the other side of the hedge Wiggins could hear the sounds of the busy street. He wondered how many other people might have spotted him hanging about the neighborhood. "Clever boy. You're right. I'm not a copper, but I do want to ask you some questions about Mrs. Greenwood. I'm sorry you're goin' to be out of work, but ifn' you help me some, maybe I can help you?"

Jon stared at him, his expression a mixture of hope and suspicion. "Why should you do anythin' to 'elp me?"

Wiggins shrugged. "Let's just say I've been out of work a time or two myself," he admitted casually, careful to keep his sympathy for the lad from showing.

"I'm not trained," Jon warned. "Mrs. Greenwood only kept me on because me dad used to work for her son. But there's lots I can do and I'm willin' to work like the devil. There's lots I can tell you about 'er, too. It weren't no surprise to me that she got 'erself murdered. She's been actin' peculiar for months now. Ever since . . ."

From the other side of the hedge, Wiggins heard a familiar voice. Fred did, too. The dog broke away from them and leapt in the direction of the road, barking at the top of his lungs.

Hoping to avoid disaster, Wiggins rushed after him, but he was too late. Fred dashed around the corner of the hedge straight into the inspector.

"Gracious," yelped Witherspoon as Fred bounced happily up and down on the inspector. "What on earth are you doing here, boy?" He glanced up as Wiggins came flying into view. "Wiggins? Goodness, whatever are you and Fred doing round here? We're miles from Upper Edmonton Gardens."

"Good afternoon, sir," Wiggins stammered, his mind racing furiously. "And you, too, Constable Barnes. Come on, Fred, get down, you'll get the inspector's trousers muddy."

"Oh, that's all right," Witherspoon said kindly. He reached down and scratched the animal behind the ears. "Fred's just happy to see me and I'm quite pleased to see him, as well." He broke off and cooed at the dog for a few moments. Wiggins used the time to try and come up with a reasonable excuse for being at Bolton Gardens.

"Now, young man . . ." With one last pat on Fred's head, the inspector straightened and stared curiously at his footman. "What are you doing all the way over here?"

"Uh, uh, I was runnin' an errand for Mrs. Goodge," he sputtered frantically. "She wanted me to pick up that fish you like so much, sir. You know, that special cod from that expensive fishmonger's over on the Brompton Road. Well, me and Fred spotted you a ways back, sir. We was tryin' to find a shortcut like. And, uh, well, you know how fond of you Fred is, so we darted up this way. You know, to surprise you like."

Witherspoon beamed. He was quite touched. In the past Wiggins had always seemed a tad jealous of his close relationship with the animal. "How very thoughtful of you, my boy. Isn't that nice, Constable?"

"It certainly is, sir," Barnes replied, his eyes gleaming with amusement.

"And how very thoughtful of Mrs. Goodge to remember how much I liked that cod," the inspector finished, not wanting to leave anyone out.

"Well, ifn' that'll be all, sir, me and Fred best be on our way." He whistled softly and Fred, after bumping the inspector's knees one last time, trotted over to him. "See you at 'ome, sir," he called.

"Righty ho, Wiggins. You and Fred be careful now."

Wiggins nodded and then scurried off as fast as he reasonably could in the opposite direction. "You almost give us away there, Fred," he chided the dog, who trotted unconcernedly along at his heels. "Next time I might not be able to come up with somethin' so fast."

Wiggins cocked his head slightly, listening for the inspector's footsteps going the other way. After a few moments he turned and spotted the inspector and Barnes rounding the corner. He swiveled around and dashed back to where he'd left the boy.

"Blast and damn!" he muttered as he skidded to a stop behind the hedge. The clearing was empty. Jon was gone.

Inspector Witherspoon and Constable Barnes waited in the gloomy drawing room for the maid to fetch Hannah Greenwood's sister, Amelia Hackshaw. Witherspoon frowned uneasily. "I say, Constable," he whispered. "This place does look a bit . . ." He stopped, not wanting to be rude. "Morbid."

"Well, sir," Barnes replied as he turned to stare at the black-draped windows, "there has been a death in the family."

"Of course. I know that, but Mrs. Greenwood was only murdered last night. How did they get all this up so fast?" Witherspoon exclaimed. He gaped at the mourning cloth draped on every available surface. "And really, this is a bit much. Why, I've seen families lose half their numbers and not put this much black in the house."

Black crocheted antimacassars were draped on the back of the elegant brown settee and the matching chairs. The tables were covered with black fringed cloth, and on the carved mantel, black ribbons were tied around the brass candlesticks. On the wall over the mantel stood a row of portraits, their frames edged in black mourning cloth.

"Did you notice the foyer, sir?" Barnes asked. "The mirrors were covered as well. I think they take death right seriously in this house, sir."

Shaking his head, the inspector said, "Apparently so. You know, I, too, believe in respecting the dead, but really . . ."

"You wanted to see me."

At the sound of the voice, Witherspoon whirled around. His jaw dropped open with shock. Standing in the doorway was a middle-aged, blond-haired woman with thin hawk-like features and cool blue eyes. Ye Gods. It was Hannah Greenwood.

She smiled mockingly when she saw his expression. "Don't be alarmed, inspector," she said calmly as she advanced into the room. "I'm Mrs. Greenwood's sister. We were twins."

"Blimey, sir," Barnes muttered in the inspector's ear. "That give me a right turn."

"Do sit down," she invited, gesturing toward the settee.

Grateful for something to do so he could get his bearings, the inspector and Barnes plopped themselves down. "Er, first of all, Mrs. Hackshaw, please accept my condolences for your loss."

Amelia Hackshaw gave them a tight smile. "Thank you." She smoothed out the skirt of her elegant emerald-green gown and then gazed directly at the inspector. "I appreciate your condolences, but we've no need to waste any more time. Why don't we dispense with the preliminaries, Inspector? Presumably, this isn't a social call. You're here to question me concerning Hannah's murder. I'm not squeamish nor easily upset. So please, do let's get this over with."

Again Witherspoon was taken aback. The house was edged in black, for goodness' sakes. Yet the victim's own sister, who he presumed must have been up half the night digging mourning cloth out of the attic, was as cool as a dish of lime sorbet. "Er, yes, of course." He cleared his throat. "Did your sister have any enemies?"

"Enemies?" She arched one pale eyebrow. "That's a rather silly question, Inspector. Obviously she had an enemy. Someone murdered her, didn't they? Hardly the act of a friend."

"Yes, yes, of course," he replied. "What I meant to say was, do you know of anyone specifically who wished your sister harm?"

"If you meant to say that, then why didn't you?" she said impatiently. "My sister wasn't an easy woman to get along with. She was much like me—she didn't suffer fools gladly." She gave the inspector a withering look. "But I don't know of anyone who actually had a reason to murder her."

"Er, did she have any particular animosity toward anyone in the Hyde Park Literary Circle?"

"Not that I know of." Amelia Hackshaw smiled. "She hated all of them. Thought they were a pack of idiots."

"Then why did she join the group?"

"She had her reasons." Mrs. Hackshaw shrugged. "She didn't share those reasons with me."

The inspector realized this line of questioning was getting him nowhere. "How was your sister's mood yesterday?"

"The same as it always was, bad."

"So she wasn't excited about the Jubilee Ball or the poetry contest?"

"Excited? No, I don't think so." She paused and frowned thoughtfully. "But I could be wrong about that. I think perhaps Hannah had actually gotten interested in poetry. Last week I found her reading one of those dreadfully pompous little literary publications. Some sort of poetry collection from the United States. Nonsense it was, too. I can't imagine why Hannah was interested in it."

"Miss Hackshaw," the inspector began.

"Mrs. Hackshaw," she corrected. "Like my late sister, I am a widow."

Somehow, that didn't surprise him. "Did your sister have many friends or other outside activities?" He decided he might as well get as much information about the victim as possible. One never knew what one might stumble across unless one asked.

She snorted in derision. "Hannah didn't have any friends at all. Her only activity outside this house was the circle. She hasn't been interested in much of anything since Douglas died."

"Douglas?" The inspector straightened. Someone else was dead? Drat. "May I ask who this Douglas person is and how he died?" He sincerely hoped he was an old man who'd died from natural causes.

"Douglas Beecher, Hannah's son. He died in a train accident this past spring. Hannah was devastated."

"I'm sorry to hear that," the inspector mumbled. "Er, Mrs. Hackshaw, do you know of anyone who benefits from Mrs. Greenwood's death?"

"I do," she said bluntly. "Since Douglas is dead, I'll get it all. It's a considerable amount, Inspector. My sister outlived two husbands. She did well by both of them."

"Thank you for your candor, Mrs. Hackshaw," Witherspoon said. He hoped he didn't look as shocked as he felt. "Can you tell me what Mrs. Greenwood did yesterday? Knowing her movements might be helpful in finding her killer."

"No, I can't." She smiled smugly. "I wasn't here. I was visiting a friend in Croydon and I didn't get home until after Hannah had left for the ball."

By the time they left the Greenwood home, the inspector's head pounded and his stomach growled. He knew very little about the victim and even less about her activities on the fateful day of her death. Mrs. Hackshaw was a peculiar woman, to say the least, and the rest of the household seemed too frightened of their new mistress to answer more than the most perfunctory of inquiries. None of them seemed to know much about Mrs. Greenwood's activities, either.

"I'd like to talk to the boy, Jon," Barnes muttered as they trudged down the stairs. "According to the maid, he's the only one who does know what Mrs. Greenwood did yesterday. He were with her."

"Yes, well, we'll come back and speak to him later. If he was with Mrs. Greenwood, perhaps he can enlighten us as to her movements. I daresay, so far we've no evidence she did anything except go to the dressmaker's or whatever it is that women do before going to a ball."

"We do know she were gone most of the afternoon, sir. That's something." Barnes winced. His shoes were killing him now. "Where to now, sir?"

"Let's go have a bit of lunch, Barnes. After that, we'll pay a call on Dr. Oxton Sloan."

Dr. Sloan occupied rooms on the second floor of a house on a small square off the Marylebone High Street.

A smiling and talkative landlady, Mrs. Nellie Tepler, escorted them up the stairs to Sloan's quarters.

"We don't get the police around here very often," she chirped. "Actually, we've never had them here before. Truth is, we don't get too many visitors. Pity really. Some of my gentlemen lodgers are so lonely." She stopped in front of the first door on the second floor. Raising her fist, she pounded against the wood. "Dr. Sloan, you've got some visitors!" she screeched. "It's the police. They want to talk to you."

Witherspoon's ears tingled. Barnes rolled his eyes.

There was no answer. Mrs. Tepler pounded again. "Yoo-hoo, are you in there, Doctor?" She kept right on screeching and pounding until the door flew open.

"I heard you the first time, Mrs. Tepler," Sloan said irritably.

"Oh, sorry." She laughed. "You've some gentlemen to see you."

"Thank you, Mrs. Tepler," he replied. The landlady, with one last curious glance, turned and strolled slowly down the stairs.

Sloan looked at the two policemen standing in his doorway. "I suppose you've come about that awful business last night," he said. He opened the door wider and motioned them inside,

"Yes, sir, we have," the inspector replied. He introduced himself and Barnes.

They entered a nicely furnished sitting room. In one corner stood a rolltop desk and a glass-fronted bookcase. Next to that was a small fireplace with a mustard-colored settee and two matching chairs grouped in a tidy semicircle.

"Well, have a seat, then," Sloan offered, gesturing toward the settee. He went behind his desk and sat down. "And let's get on with it. I've not much time today."

"Are you a medical doctor, sir?" Witherspoon asked.

Sloan looked surprised. "I'm licensed. But I don't practice."

"I see." The inspector wondered why, but he couldn't think of a pertinent reason to ask. It didn't take a physician to stab someone in the back and toss them over a balcony. "Could you tell me, how long have you known Mrs. Greenwood?"

"I didn't really know Mrs. Greenwood," he replied. "Except in the sense that she's a member of our literary group."

"How long has she been a member of the group, then?" the inspector asked patiently.

Sloan frowned. "Let me see, I believe she joined us in February. Yes, that's right. She came about a month later than Mrs. Stanwick, and she joined the group in January."

"So you've known the victim since February," Witherspoon stated. "Do you know if she had any enemies?"

"How would I know that?" Sloan said irritably. He drummed his fingertips on the desktop. "I've already told you, I didn't know the woman personally. She wasn't overly popular in the group, but I don't think anyone hated her enough to kill her."

"Someone did," the inspector reminded him.

"Yes, I suppose someone did at that." Sloan shrugged, as though the matter was of no concern to him. "But I don't see what it's got to do with me or our circle. There were dozens of people in the house. The killer could have just as easily been someone completely unconnected with our group. Probably some madman."

Witherspoon ignored that statement. Really, this case was most difficult. No one seemed to be in the least forthcoming. He decided to charge full ahead. "Where were you at ten thirty last night?"

Sloan eyed him warily. "I was in the drawing room."

"Really, sir? Are you sure? Mrs. Putnam has already told us she looked in the drawing room and didn't see you."

"Of course, how stupid of me." Sloan smiled briefly. "I'd forgotten. I'd been in the drawing room . . . oh, it must have been about ten twenty-five, when I suddenly realized I had to speak to Mr. Venerable. So I went looking for him. At ten thirty I was probably out in the garden."

"If you were out in the garden, sir," Witherspoon asked, "then why did Mrs. Putnam not find you? She searched there, too. She specifically said she was concerned because it was almost time to announce the winner of the poetry contest, and she was alarmed because you'd disappeared."

"I most certainly did not disappear. It's not my fault that confounded woman didn't find me," Sloan snapped, an angry flush spreading over his cheeks. "Now see here, Inspector, are you implying I had anything to do with Mrs. Greenwood's death?"

"Not at all, sir." He sighed inwardly. "We're merely trying to establish where everyone was at the time of the murder."

"I've told you where I was. The garden."

"Where specifically were you in the garden?" Barnes asked quietly.

Sloan closed his eyes for a brief moment. "For God's sake, I was all over the place. I've told you, I was looking for Mr. Venerable. That garden is huge. I searched every path and practically shook the bushes looking for the man."

"Did you see anyone?" the inspector asked.

"I saw dozens of people."

"Could you name them, please?" As Witherspoon himself had been on the terrace with Lady Cannonberry, he wanted to see if the man would remember seeing him.

"I recall seeing Mrs. Hiatt and Miss Mansfield. They were on the terrace. Mrs. Hiatt was sitting on a bench."

Witherspoon nodded. He wasn't certain he accepted Sloan's words. Miss Mansfield and Mrs. Hiatt had been on the terrace for a good half hour. He and Lady Cannonberry had seen them out there talking since ten o'clock. The inspector straightened his spine, rather proud of himself for remembering this particular detail. "Did anyone see you?"

"Lots of people saw me. I expect some of them will remember. I am, after all, the president of the literary circle."

"Did you find Mr. Venerable, sir?"

"No."

"When was the last time you spoke to Mrs. Greenwood?" Witherspoon asked.

"Let me see," Sloan murmured, his forehead creased in thought. "I suppose it was at our last meeting. Yes, that's it. I spoke to her then."

"Dr. Sloan, you were seen having an argument with Mrs. Greenwood only minutes before she was killed."

"That's a lie!" he cried. "We weren't having an argument. We were having a discussion."

"Then you admit you did speak to her last night. What was the discussion about?"

"The contest. Mrs. Greenwood asked me to clarify one of the rules. It was such a minor incident, I'd forgotten all about it until you mentioned it."

"You're absolutely certain you weren't arguing with her?" the inspector pressed.

"Of course I'm certain." He suddenly smiled. "But if I were you, Inspector, I'd have a word with Mrs. Stanwick."

"We intend to speak to all the members of the literary circle."

"Yes, but you should be especially interested in talking to Mrs. Stanwick. She was quarreling with Mrs. Greenwood. To be blunt, Inspector"—Sloan picked a piece of lint off his tweed coat—"they looked like a couple of hissing cats."

"She gone, then?" Mrs. Goodge asked. She darted a quick glance toward the stairs.

"We can speak freely, Mrs. Livingston-Graves is on her way to a tea party," Mrs. Jeffries announced. She took her usual seat at the head of the table. "I don't expect she'll be back for quite a while."

"But a tea party only lasts a few hours," Betsy said.

"Not when it's in Southampton," the housekeeper replied calmly.

Betsy laughed. "Cor, that's rich. Getting rid of her that way."

"I don't know how you managed it, Mrs. Jeffries." Mrs. Goodge shook her head in admiration. "I can't imagine anyone inviting that old biddy out, but my hat's off to you."

"I didn't do it alone," she admitted. "I had some help from Hatchet."

"I thought he was in America with Luty Belle!" Betsy exclaimed in surprise.

"He's back. Luty'll be back next week." Mrs. Jeffries reached for the teapot and began to pour.

"Poor Luty," Betsy said as Mrs. Jeffries passed her a steaming mug. "She'll be ever so annoyed she missed this murder."

"If we've got it solved by then," the cook muttered darkly. "And if my mornin' is anything to go by, we've got a long road ahead of us. I didn't get nothing out of anyone."

Mrs. Jeffries smiled sympathetically. "Don't despair, Mrs. Goodge. The investigation's just started. The murder only happened last night."

Betsy leaned forward. "If it's any comfort to you, I didn't find out all that much, either. Right miserable mornin', it's been."

"Nor have I," Mrs. Jeffries said firmly. "But I've no doubt we will. Now, Betsy, tell us about your inquiries. Were you able to make contact with anyone from the Marlow household?"

"I didn't have any luck findin' someone from the house, so I popped into a couple of shops out on the Richmond Road, that's the nearest place to Redcliffe Gardens where I thought anyone might have had some gossip about the Marlow family. One of the girls knew a bit about Miss Marlow, but it isn't very interestin'.'"

Mrs. Goodge clucked her tongue. "Nonsense, Betsy, all gossip's interestin'."

Betsy smiled. "Well, it seems Miss Marlow's had more than her share of tragedy. Her only brother died of pneumonia the winter before last, and six months later her parents were killed in a carriage accident." She shrugged. "Not much, is it? Do you want me to keep trying?"

"Yes," Mrs. Jeffries replied, "I think so. Mrs. Greenwood's killer was at the ball. He or she had to have taken the carving knife and followed the victim up the stairs and out onto that balcony. Somebody must have seen something. So do keep at it."

"Maybe Wiggins or Smythe will have learned something useful," Mrs. Goodge mused.

"Perhaps the inspector will have found out something as well," Mrs. Jeffries said brightly. "In any case, we mustn't give up and we mustn't feel defeated. As I've said before, the most inconsequential piece of information can lead us in the right direction."

They heard the back door opening, and a moment later Smythe appeared. "'Ello, 'ello me lovelies. Beautiful day, isn't it?"

"He's found out something." Betsy sighed. She hated it when the coachman got the jump on her. "You can tell by the big, cocky grin on his face."

"That I 'ave." He pulled out a chair and sat down. "Not that my news is all that interestin', but considerin' I only started diggin', so to speak, I'm right proud of myself."

"Excellent, Smythe." Mrs. Jeffries smiled. She was rather glad that someone had some information. "We're all ears."

"It's about Shelby Locke. Accordin' to the housemaid—"

"Housemaid!" Betsy yelped. "Why was you talkin' to a housemaid? You usually talk to hansom drivers and footmen."

Smythe grinned. "Well, sometimes, my girl, one's got to be resourceful. But, as I was sayin', Rosie told me that two weeks ago Locke left his case at the literary circle meetin' at the Marlow 'ouse. In that case was all of 'is poems and papers. Rosie claims Locke's been goin' out of 'is mind, tryin' to get the case back. Now Miss Marlow claimed she never saw the thing, and no one else in the circle will own up to seein' it, either."

"Maybe one of the Marlow servants picked it up," Mrs. Jeffries said thoughtfully.

"A case full of worthless poems?" Smythe gave her a pitying look. "The only reason a servant would take it would be to try and sell the case itself, but it weren't valuable. At least not enough to risk losin' a position."

"But why would anyone want a bunch of papers?" Betsy asked.

"That's the point, isn't it?" Smythe poured himself a mug of tea. "Rosie reckons someone pinched the notebook to keep Locke from winnin' the poetry contest."

"That's daft." Mrs. Goodge sniffed. "Even if someone stole his ruddy old poems, if it happened two weeks ago, there's no reason Mr. Locke couldn't have done another one."

"Rosie claims Locke were so rattled by the theft, 'e couldn't concentrate." He shook his head. "And not only that, but 'e's got woman trouble, too."

"Now, that's a piece of important news!" the cook exclaimed. "What kind of woman trouble?"

"The worst kind a man can 'ave; 'E's in love with one, but courtin' another." Smythe grinned. "Seems 'e and Miss Marlow 'ad some kind of understandin', and all of a sudden Mrs. Stanwick appears out of nowhere and steals 'is 'eart. Rosie thinks 'e was goin' to propose to Mrs. Stanwick last night."

"What a cad!" Betsy cried. "Poor Miss Marlow, she puts her trust in the bloomin' feller, and what does he do, he betrays her. Men!"

"Easy, lass." Smythe's grin evaporated. "Don't tar us all with the same brush. Not all blokes is like that."

"Humph," she sniffed.

"I wonder if Mr. Locke told Miss Marlow of his intentions," Mrs. Jeffries murmured.

"I don't see that it matters all that much," Mrs. Goodge replied. "It weren't Miss Marlow that was murdered."

"True," the housekeeper shook her head slightly. "And it probably doesn't have anything to do with Mrs. Greenwood." She looked at Smythe. "Did Mr. Locke know Mrs. Greenwood well?"

"I don't think so," the coachman answered. "When I asked Rosie about 'er, she weren't familiar with the name. But I'm going back to that neighborhood tonight. I thought I might ask about at the pubs, see if anyone knew anything else about Shelby Locke. I figured I'd start askin' about Mr. Warburton tomorrow mornin', if that's all right with you?"

"That's fine, Smythe," Mrs. Jeffries replied. She turned to Betsy. "Would you mind having another go at the Marlow house?"

"I don't mind," she said, her expression uncertain. "But it seems quite a strange place. There's not much comin' or goin' for such a large house. It may take me some time to find someone."

"I realize that, Betsy. But it's imperative that we find someone who can verify people's exact whereabouts at the time of the murder." She drummed her fingers on the tabletop. "Someone had to have seen the killer leaving the room, even if he doesn't realize what he saw."

CHAPTER 5

Barnes moaned softly and tried not to limp. Hoping his superior hadn't heard him, he glanced at Witherspoon's back as they followed a maid into Rowena Stanwick's drawing room. His ruddy feet were killin' him. As soon as he got home tonight he'd take a hammer to these wretched shoes.

"Inspector Witherspoon." A lovely blonde came forward to greet them. "I'm Rowena Stanwick. My maid says you wish to speak to me about poor Mrs. Greenwood's unfortunate . . ." She paused, her blue eyes mirroring her confusion.

"Death," the inspector supplied helpfully. "Yes, indeed, we do have a few questions for you." He gazed around the room, momentarily captivated by its utter charm.

Late afternoon sunlight streamed in through gauzy white curtains. Tables covered in rich, cream-colored fringed shawls were dotted between overstuffed blue velvet chairs and settees. Fresh flowers adorned the top of the mantelpiece. Delicate figurines and crystal trinkets were elegantly displayed in china closets and on tabletops. The inspector had never been in such a completely feminine room in his life. Charmed as he was, he was also just a tad uneasy. He was afraid to move.

A tall auburn-haired man came through the archway. "I expect you'll have a few questions for me as well," he said without preamble. "I'm Shelby Locke."

Witherspoon was momentarily flustered. "Er, yes, Mr. Locke, we will have some questions. However"—he cleared his throat—"we'd planned on calling round to see you later this afternoon."

Locke smiled. "Then I've saved you a trip." He gestured toward the chairs near the settee, "Do please sit down. Rowena, dear, will you ring for tea?"

Barnes scrambled into the nearest chair. Witherspoon gave his constable a puzzled glance and then sat down himself. He was at a loss—he didn't really wish to interview Mr. Locke and Mrs. Stanwick at the same time. It wasn't good police procedure. Yet, he didn't want to appear rude. Drat. Why was he always finding himself in these awkward situations?

He waited until Mrs. Stanwick had instructed the maid to bring them tea before he started speaking.

"Mrs. Stanwick," Witherspoon began. "Perhaps it would be best if we spoke to you alone."

"Alone?" Her eyes widened in alarm. "But why?"

"It's rather standard procedure," he said softly, not wishing to distress the lady unduly.

"What nonsense," Locke interrupted. "This whole episode has been most upsetting for Mrs. Stanwick. I don't care what your silly procedures are, I'm staying here. I'll not have the police browbeating her."

"Mr. Locke," Witherspoon said patiently. "We're not in the habit of browbeating anyone. We'd merely like to ask Mrs. Stanwick a few questions."

"Oh, please," she pleaded. "Can't Mr. Locke stay? This has been so terribly distressing." Her eyes filled with tears.

"Yes, of course he can stay," Witherspoon said quickly, terrified she was going to cry. "We're not here to upset you any further, Mrs. Stanwick." He paused. "How long have you been acquainted with Mrs. Greenwood?"

She sighed and fidgeted with the lace edging on the sleeve of her lavender day dress. "Not very long at all. I first met her at the literary circle. I believe that was in February or March."

"And how long have you been a member of the circle?" Witherspoon asked. He wanted to see if her answer jibed with what Dr. Sloan had told them. Then he realized that was a rather silly idea. What difference did it make how long the women had been involved in a poetry circle?

"Since January. I joined right after I came to London." She glanced down at her hands.

"And where did you come from?" Barnes asked softly. He wanted to make this interview last as long as possible. Sitting in a nice overstuffed chair was much better than battering his poor feet any more than he had to.

"I'm sorry," she replied, her expression puzzled. "But what's that got to do with Mrs. Greenwood?"

Witherspoon wondered the same thing. But he wasn't going to let his constable down. He frequently encouraged Barnes to ask questions during interviews. The fact that this question didn't appear to have any bearing on this case was irrelevant. Or perhaps it wasn't. "Actually, Mrs. Stanwick, the constable's question is quite routine."

She shrugged. "I'm from Littlehampton, that's near Worthing."

"Thank you, Mrs. Stanwick." Witherspoon cleared his throat. "Now, can you tell me if you saw anything out of the ordinary at the ball last night?"

"Nothing, Inspector. Up until Mrs. Greenwood's death, it was like any other ball I've attended. The guests seemed to be enjoying themselves. Everyone was dancing and having a good time."

"Had you seen Mrs. Greenwood earlier in the evening?"

"Oh, yes," she replied. "Several times."

Witherspoon smiled. "Did you speak with her?"

"Only to say hello when she first arrived." She glanced at Shelby Locke and blushed prettily. "I was with Mr. Locke for most of the time. Shelby's a wonderful dancer."

"Thank you, my dear," Locke replied, patting her hand. He turned to the inspector. "I escorted Rowena to the ball. Once we arrived, I didn't leave her side."

Witherspoon gazed at them curiously. It sounded awfully like these two were trying to give themselves an alibi. "That's most odd, Mrs. Stanwick," he said, "for Dr. Sloan has told us he saw you and Mrs. Greenwood having an argument only a few minutes before Mrs. Greenwood was killed."

"That's a lie." Locke jumped to his feet. "Sloan couldn't have seen any such thing. Rowena was with me."

"Shelby, please," Rowena implored. "Do sit down."

With an effort, Locke brought himself under control. He sat back down next to Mrs. Stanwick. "I'm sorry. It's most ungentlemanly of me to call Dr. Sloan a liar. What I meant to say is that he must have been mistaken."

"He seemed most certain of his facts," the inspector persisted. "Furthermore, he isn't the only person to report seeing Mrs. Stanwick speaking with Mrs. Greenwood. Miss Marlow also saw the two ladies together. Her impression was also that they were having a rather heated exchange."

"I don't care who claims to have seen Rowena with that woman," Locke began. "She had nothing to do with . . ."

Witherspoon held up his hand. "Mr. Locke," he said, "I do understand you're wanting to protect Mrs. Stanwick. But this is a murder investigation. We must have the truth. Two separate witnesses saw Mrs. Stanwick arguing with the victim."

"Forgive me, Inspector," Rowena interrupted smoothly. "You're quite right, I did speak to Mrs. Greenwood."

All three of them stared at her.

She sighed audibly and bit her lip. "It's so silly of me, really. I didn't mean to mislead you, Inspector. But considering the later events of the evening, the incident quite slipped my mind."

"Rowena," Locke said sharply.

"It's all right, Shelby," she said. "The inspector is correct. I did speak to her."

"Were you and Mrs. Stanwick arguing?" Witherspoon asked.

Rowena gave a shaky laugh. "Gracious, no. Admittedly, to someone observing us, it may have looked as if we were having a difference of opinion. But the truth is, Mrs. Greenwood and I were discussing the poetry contest. She was so excited when she was telling me about her poem, she got carried away. Her voice got a bit too loud, she was waving her hands about, her face became very expressive, but honestly, that's all it was."

Witherspoon pursed his lips. He supposed Mrs. Stanwick could be telling the truth. Drat. If there were only some way of knowing for sure. "So Mrs. Greenwood wasn't angry at you."

"Heavens, no. Why should she be angry at me? We barely knew each other." Rowena gave Witherspoon a dazzling smile.

His next question went right out of his head.

Barnes coughed lightly. "Excuse me, Mrs. Stanwick," he said, "but would you mind tellin' us exactly what time it was that you was speakin' with Mrs. Stanwick."

"I'm not really sure, but I think it was . . ." She turned and gazed at Locke. "It must have been when you went to speak to Miss Marlow, Shelby. Do you recall what time that was?"

Locke thought for a moment. "I think it was around ten o'clock. Yes, I know it was. Lucinda and I went into the library. Just as we got inside, the clock finished chiming the hour, I remember that. We were only there a few minutes, though. Then I went back to Rowena."

"How long did you and Miss Marlow stay in the library?" Witherspoon asked.

"I wasn't watching the time, Inspector," Locke said impatiently. "But as I just said, it was only a few minutes. I don't really think that a brief conversation with Miss Marlow a good half hour before the murder was committed has any bearing on it."

"Exactly what were you and Miss Marlow discussing?" the inspector asked.

"That's not really any business of the police."

"During a murder investigation," Witherspoon said calmly, "everything is the business of the police. Please answer my question."

Locke's eyes narrowed in anger. "We discussed a private matter."

Witherspoon decided to change tactics. He'd learned it sometimes startled people when you asked them questions they weren't expecting. "Were you speaking with Miss Marlow about your missing notebook?"

Locke started in surprise. He and Rowena exchanged glances. "How on earth did you hear about that?"

Witherspoon gave him what he hoped, was a mysterious smile. "We have our ways, Mr. Locke."

"Apparently so," he murmured. "And, of course, you're correct. We were discussing my missing notebook. It's a trivial matter, I'm sure, and of absolutely no interest to the police."

"And had Miss Marlow found it?" The inspector had no idea why he was asking these questions, but he couldn't quite think of anything else to ask just yet.

"No, she hadn't."

The maid entered and served tea. The inspector used the time to gather his thoughts. As Mrs. Stanwick handed him his cup, he looked at Locke and asked, "How long have you known Mrs. Greenwood?"

"I met her at the same time Rowena did, when she joined the literary circle."

"And how long have you been a member of the circle?" Witherspoon asked. He knew it was another silly question, but this case really didn't make any sense at all.

Locke shifted uncomfortably. "Actually, I joined the group last year. That's when it started." He glanced uneasily at Rowena. "I'd heard about it through Miss Marlow. We were . . . friends. We shared a mutual interest in literature. Once Miss Marlow knew of my interest, she invited me to join."

"Where were you at ten thirty last night?" the inspector asked bluntly.

Locke jerked in surprise. "What do you mean? I was with Rowena. I've already told you that."

"Yes, but where? In the gardens? The ballroom?"

"We were in the ballroom," Locke said firmly. "I was just getting ready to ask Mrs. Stanwick to dance."

Witherspoon stared at the two people on the settee. He reached for his tea. "Do you know of anyone who hated Mrs. Greenwood?"

It was Rowena Stanwick who answered. "*Hate* is a rather strong word," she said slowly. "But she wasn't very well liked. I don't think she and Dr. Sloan got on all that well. I do know that she mentioned she'd had words with him earlier that day."

Witherspoon's cup halted halfway to his mouth, "Excuse me, Mrs. Stanwick, but did Mrs. Greenwood actually tell you that? Did she say she'd seen Dr. Sloan before the ball?"

"Oh, yes," Rowena smiled prettily. "She said she'd gone to his rooms and talked to him. It had something to do with the contest."

"You know, Constable," Witherspoon said thoughtfully as they left the Stanwick home, "I've the strongest feeling that everyone is lying to us."

"Hmmm." Barnes groaned as he stepped carefully down the stairs. His toes were on fire, and he could feel a blister bubbling on the side of his heel.

"So you agree with me," the inspector continued. "Yes, I thought you would. Well, I'm not having it. I know all of them couldn't have killed Mrs. Greenwood, and I suppose they've their own reasons for not telling me the truth, but I'm determined to get to the bottom of this. In the ballroom, indeed. Mrs. Putnam has already told us she searched the ballroom high and low. She certainly has no reason to lie to us. We know she didn't commit the murder. None of them could have been where they claimed to be. Mrs. Putnam isn't blind. She didn't see hide nor hair of any of them, not Dr. Sloan, Mr. Locke, Mrs. Stanwick, or Miss Marlow." He snorted indelicately. "We must find someone who can tell us where everyone was at the time of the murder. Someone observant. Someone interested in the activities of the other guests."

"A busybody?" Barnes suggested helpfully. To ease the pressure off his toe, he bowed his legs as he hobbled down the stairs.

"Precisely! What we need is a good busybody. Someone who sat there and did nothing but watch the other guests. Any suggestions?"

Barnes sighed. It was bloomin' hard to think with his feet throbbin' the way they was. But he didn't want his inspector to know that. He, weren't a complainer, he had his pride. "Well, Mrs. Putnam was dartin' about like a bluebottle fly; maybe she saw more than she realized. Maybe we should talk to her again. Miss Mansfield and Mrs. Hiatt was outside. They struck me as the kind that'd keep a close eye on what everyone else was up to. Maybe they saw more than they think."

"But we've already spoken to them," Witherspoon said doubtfully.

"Maybe we ought to do it again, sir," Barnes suggested. "Remember, they'd just seen a body come flyin' through the air and practically land on top of 'em. Could be they'll recall things a bit better now that they've had some time to get over the shock."

"You might be right about that, Constable," the inspector replied. "But it's getting late and we really must interview Mr. Edgar Warburton today. He's the only one we haven't talked to yet."

"He didn't give a statement last night, either," Barnes groused. "By the time we had the complete list of names for the literary circle, he'd gone."

Witherspoon came to a decision and immediately felt better. Any decision, even a bad one, was better than dithering. "We'll interview Mr. Warburton now. If we've time, we'll speak with the others again."

"Uh, where does this Mr. Warburton live?" Barnes fervently hoped he lived far enough away for them to have to take a hansom cab.

Witherspoon pulled the list of names and addresses out of his pocket. "Oh, not far at all. It's a street just near Regent's Park. It's only a short walk."

Barnes moaned.

Concerned, the inspector stopped and peered anxiously at his constable. "I say, is something the matter?"

"It's nothing, sir."

"Now, now, don't be so reticent, Constable." Witherspoon studied him closely. Barnes didn't look right. "It's not like you to make such odd noises. Are you ill?"

"It's my shoes, sir," Barnes admitted. "They're new and pinchin' me ruddy toes like the very devil."

"Well, why didn't you say so? We can't have you in pain, man! Let's go find a hansom cab."

Edgar Warburton wasn't in the least happy to see the police. "I suppose I've no choice but to talk to you," he muttered when his butler had escorted the men into Warburton's study. "But do make it quick." He gestured for them to take a seat.

"As you're in a hurry," the inspector said, "we'll do our best to get this over with. Mr. Warburton, were you well acquainted with Mrs. Greenwood?"

"No."

"How long have you known her?"

"A little over two months. I met the woman when I joined the Hyde Park Literary Circle."

"And that was two months ago?" Witherspoon asked.

"I've just said that." Warburton frowned. "Perhaps I should just make a statement and you gentlemen"—he sneered slightly as he said the last word—"can be on your way."

"As you wish, sir."

"Fine. I didn't know Mrs. Greenwood well at all except in my capacity as secretary for the group."

"You only joined two months ago and already you're the secretary?" Barnes interrupted.

Warburton gave him an irritated glance. "Correct. Frankly, it's not often a group such as that one attracts a member of my caliber."

"You're well versed in literature, then?" the inspector interjected.

"Really, sir, are you going to let me make a statement or keep interrupting me with questions?" Warburton snapped. "But you miss my point, Inspector. I'm not particularly well versed in literature, though I do, of course, have a degree from Oxford."

"Then what did you mean?"

"Well, if you'd stop interrupting, I'd tell you. What I meant was that for a group like that to actually attract someone of my social standing to become a member was in itself unusual. They were very fortunate I joined."

"So that's why they made you the secretary?" Barnes put in. "Because of your social standing?"

Warburton sighed angrily. "That and the fact their previous secretary had just left, so I volunteered to take on the task. Now, as I was saying—"

"Why'd the last one leave?" the inspector asked.

"How should I know? Perhaps he was a flighty fellow."

Witherspoon made a mental note to ask the name of this person the next time they spoke to Dr. Sloan.

Warburton folded his arms over his chest. "As I was saying, Inspector. I joined the group and made the acquaintance of the members. That was the sum total of my relationship with Mrs. Greenwood."

"How did you find out about the circle?" Barnes asked.

Warburton paced over to stand in front of the window. For a moment he didn't say anything, merely stared out at the garden. Finally he said, "From Mrs. Stanwick."

Witherspoon sensed that he was on to something here. Warburton was still standing with his back to them, so the inspector couldn't see his face. But there was something decidedly different about his tone of voice, and he was standing so rigidly one would think someone had shoved a poker up his spine. "You were acquainted with Mrs. Stanwick before you became a member of the circle?"

"Yes." He turned and faced them. "We've known each other for some time. I've property in Littlehampton. I knew her there. We happened to run into each other after she moved to London. She mentioned this group she belonged to, and though it isn't my usual sort of activity, I thought it sounded interesting."

"Did you see anything unusual last night?" the inspector asked softly. Drat. The man looked completely normal now.

"Nothing at all," Warburton stated.

"Did you see Mrs. Greenwood go up the stairs to the balcony?" Witherspoon asked. He might as well take the bull by the horns. If Mr. Warburton didn't know the woman, he probably hadn't murdered her.

"No, there were dozens of people milling about. It was a warm evening, people were coming and going up the stairs to the second floor all night."

Witherspoon decided to hurry this interview along. "Where were you at ten thirty?"

"At ten thirty?" He shrugged. "I can't recall."

Barnes and the inspector looked at each other curiously.

"I mean," Warburton corrected hastily, "I don't know exactly where I was standing. I'd just gone into the ballroom from the drawing room when I heard the screams."

"Did you see or speak to any members of the circle during the course of the evening? Did anyone say or do anything unusual?"

Warburton hesitated, "I spoke to everyone. There was a good deal of excitement over the contest. The only unusual occurrence was Locke worrying about his wretched notebook. I overheard him asking Miss Marlow if it had turned up yet. Has anyone told you about that?"

Witherspoon nodded. "We understand it had been missing for some time."

"It drove Locke mad," Warburton said with relish. "I don't wonder, either. The man was always going on about how he refused to put anything on paper unless he felt it deeply. Quite pretentious about the whole thing, if you ask me. My personal feeling is that he was making such a fuss, he must have written something quite . . . well, let's just say personal."

The inspector frowned slightly. He wasn't sure what the fellow was getting at, and furthermore, he didn't see that a bunch of silly poems written a considerable amount of time before Mrs. Greenwood's murder could have any relevance to the case. "Did you see anything else?"

"Not really." Warburton shrugged. "The only other thing of interest was my conversation with Mrs. Stanwick. But I don't see what relevance it could have to Mrs. Greenwood's murder."

"Perhaps you should tell us anyway," Witherspoon said politely.

"I spoke to Rowena, Mrs. Stanwick, fairly early on in the evening." Warburton smiled coldly. "We had quite an interesting conversation. She told me she and Mr. Locke were going to be married."

Witherspoon was stunned. Neither Mrs. Stanwick nor Mr. Locke had mentioned this to him. "Did you speak to Mrs. Stanwick alone, or was Mr. Locke present?"

"Alone."

"And where did this conversation take place?"

"In the library."

"What time?" From the corner of his eye, Witherspoon saw that Barnes was scribbling furiously in his notebook.

"I'm not sure. I think it might have been close to ten o'clock, or perhaps a little after. I really couldn't say. Mrs. Stanwick also mentioned that Mr. Locke would be telling Miss Marlow the news as well. I expect they were going to announce it to everyone after the poetry prize had been given."

"Do you know if Mr. Locke *did* mention his impending marriage to Miss Marlow?" The inspector couldn't see that Mr. Locke's nuptial plans had anything to do with Mrs. Greenwood's death, but one never knew. But he did know that if Warburton was telling the truth, then both Mrs. Stanwick and Locke had lied. This was twice that the couple had been separated during the course of the evening. But why tell such a stupid lie? What purpose did it serve? Witherspoon stifled a sigh.

"Undoubtedly. I saw Mr. Locke and Miss Marlow going upstairs toward the second-floor reception room when Mrs. Stanwick and I were coming out of the library." He suddenly began pacing back and forth in front of his desk. "I don't think Miss Marlow was going to like hearing Mr. Locke's news. He'd been courting her, you see."

"Mr. Locke was courting Miss Marlow while he got engaged to Mrs. Stanwick?" The inspector was deeply shocked. Even with his limited experience of the opposite sex, he'd realized Shelby Locke was more than casually interested in Rowena Stanwick. But this was the first he'd heard that Locke had been involved with Miss Marlow as well.

"Oh, yes," Warburton sneered. "But I don't suppose he let that worry him. Men of his class have very little character. Locke took one look at Rowena, and poor Lucinda was left at the post. Women, such stupid, fickle creatures! A silly, romantic fop like Shelby Locke comes along, and any ounce of good sense they have completely disappears." He laughed harshly. "Rowena's like all the rest. A handsome face and a few silly poems, and she thinks she's in love. I suppose it isn't surprising that she'd be taken in by the man. Her late husband was a great deal older than she. Since his death, well, one doesn't like to be ungallant. But there have been a succession of men. Some of them quite young."

"Really?" Witherspoon muttered.

"That's one of the reasons she left Littlehampton," Warburton continued bluntly. "Her reputation was becoming scandalous."

"How very unfortunate for the lady." The inspector began to think that Edgar Warburton, despite his pretentions and obvious wealth, was no gentleman.

"I say, Inspector, I don't think this really has anything to do with Mrs. Greenwood's death," Warburton said, his expression indicating just the opposite. "But I did see the two of them in a rather intense conversation last night. Perhaps you ought to ask Mrs. Stanwick what she and Mrs. Greenwood were talking about. You might find her answer very interesting."

Witherspoon stared at the man. "We already have."

"Where to now, sir?" Barnes asked as they left Warburton's house.

The inspector sighed. "Oh, dash it all. Let's call it a day, Constable. I've much to think about and your feet are hurting."

"They're feelin' a mite better, sir," Barnes replied. But he winced as he walked.

"My good man, it's obvious you're in pain. Go on home and soak your feet. We'll start again early tomorrow morning."

"But it's Sunday, sir. I thought you told me you were going to escort your cousin to see some of the Jubilee preparations."

Witherspoon cringed at the mention of Mrs. Livingston-Graves. "That was before we had a murder to solve, Constable. But if you've promised to take Mrs. Barnes out and about, I think I can manage on my own."

"Wouldn't hear of it, sir. I'll be round your house at eight sharp, if that's convenient for you."

The inspector's mood brightened when he arrived home to find his cousin gone. "You say she's gone to Southampton for tea?" he asked incredulously, a wide smile creeping across his face. He handed Mrs. Jeffries his hat.

"Indeed, sir. She received an invitation early on today and immediately packed up and dashed off for the train. I expect she'll spend the night there."

"I've never heard of anyone going to Southampton for tea," he murmured. "It's a bit of a long way."

Mrs. Jeffries pushed the shaft of guilt that pierced her to one side. "I do believe the invitation was from an earl."

"An earl?" Witherspoon gaped at his housekeeper. "Why would an earl invite my cousin to tea?"

"I've no idea, sir. I believe she mentioned something about a mutual friend. But you look absolutely exhausted. Do come in and have a rest before dinner. Mrs. Goodge has made a lovely steak and kidney pudding."

"Steak and kidney?" He stared at her in surprise. "But I thought we'd be having cod."

"Cod?" she repeated.

"Why, yes. I was quite looking forward to it, too. I ran into Wiggins today, and he said Mrs. Goodge had sent him to the fishmongers over on the Brompton Road."

"Oh, she did, sir," Mrs. Jeffries said quickly. "But they were out of cod."

He nodded. "I see. Oh well, it can't be helped, I suppose. And Mrs. Goodge does make a superb steak and kidney pie. I'm sure I'll enjoy it very much."

They went into the drawing room, and Mrs. Jeffries poured them both a glass of sherry. "Now, sir, do tell me all about your day."

The inspector was glad to. He sighed in pleasure, sipped his drink, and told her every detail.

By the time he was finished talking, Mrs. Jeffries was shaking her head. "It does sound like Mr. Warburton was hinting about something, doesn't it?"

"Yes, I thought so, too," Witherspoon replied, delighted that Mrs. Jeffries was so very perceptive. But then, that was one of the reasons he did so like talking to her. She was perceptive and intelligent.

Why, there were times in his previous cases when it was almost uncanny how she could say one little thing and the whole solution to a murder would fall right into place. "But I can't see that Mrs. Stanwick and Mr. Locke's engagement had anything to do with Mrs. Greenwood's death. The only thing the three of them had in common was that they were all widowed."

"All of them?" Mrs. Jeffries thought that an odd coincidence.

Witherspoon shook his head. "Shelby Locke's wife died of consumption two years ago, Mrs. Greenwood's husband passed away from a heart attack a long time back, and Mrs. Stanwick's husband died of a stroke."

Perhaps it wasn't so odd, Mrs. Jeffries amended silently. Many people were left alone at a fairly young age. Furthermore, it was generally lonely men and women who joined organizations like the Hyde Park Literary Circle.

"But what I found peculiar about Mr. Warburton's statement was his hinting that Mrs. Stanwick had something to hide. He virtually claimed that the woman had to leave Littlehampton because she'd acquired a less than admirable reputation."

"Why did you find that strange?"

"Not so much strange as . . ." He stopped speaking, trying to find the right word to describe the feeling he'd had when he was interviewing Warburton. "It was as if the fellow was trying to make us think a certain way."

"You mean you thought he was trying to manipulate you?"

"Yes, that's it exactly. It seems to me, if the man had something to say, he should have come right out with it. Instead, he dropped sly little hints and damned the poor woman through innuendo. Most unfair." He sniffed the air. "I say, do you think dinner is ready yet?"

Betsy cleared the dessert dishes and Mrs. Jeffries reached for the teapot. Suddenly there was a pounding on the front door. "Do you want me to get that?" the maid asked.

"No," Mrs. Jeffries said as she headed toward the hall. "You take those dishes downstairs. I'll see to the door."

She pulled the door open and saw Lady Cannonberry standing there, a hesitant and slightly embarrassed smile on her face. "Good evening," Mrs. Jeffries said politely.

"Good evening. I do hope I'm not disturbing your dinner. But I'd like to speak to the inspector."

"Please come in." Mrs. Jeffries opened the door wider. "If you'll go through to the drawing room, I'll get him."

She hurried back to the dining room. Witherspoon looked up from his teacup. "Who was at the door?"

"Lady Cannonberry."

Witherspoon's cup rattled against the saucer. "What does she want?"

"She wants to talk to you," Mrs. Jeffries said calmly. She pulled a silver tray out of the top shelf of the sideboard and placed the teapot on it. "I expect it's important. She's been our neighbor for a long time, and this is the first time she's called around unexpectedly."

Witherspoon swallowed nervously and rose to his feet. "Yes, of course, I mustn't keep the lady waiting."

He dashed toward the drawing room. Mrs. Jeffries was hot on his heels.

"Lady Cannonberry." His voice squeaked slightly as he said her name. "How very nice to see you."

"Thank you, Inspector," she murmured. "I'm so sorry to disturb you, but it's really quite important."

"Please have a seat," he invited, gesturing toward the two wing chairs by the fireplace. "Let's do be comfortable."

As soon as they were seated, he said, "Now, what's all this about?"

"It's about Mrs. Greenwood's murder." Lady Cannonberry demurely folded her hands in her lap.

"The murder."

"Oh, yes, well, I heard today that you're interviewing all the members of the circle." She smiled. "I understand we're all suspects."

"Suspects!" Witherspoon gaped at her. "Oh, no, Lady Cannonberry. Nothing could be further from the truth. Of course you're not a suspect. I know you couldn't have had anything to do with Mrs. Greenwood's death. You were with me when it happened."

"Does that mean you don't intend to question me?"

"Well, I might have a few questions for you," he said doubtfully. "But you've already told me what you know of Mrs. Greenwood, so I don't really see much point in it."

"I still think you ought to interview me."

"Yes, well . . ."

"I don't think it's fair to leave me out," she persisted.

"Leave you out!" Witherspoon exclaimed. "Lady Cannonberry, I really don't understand."

"I could have hired someone to do it," she insisted.

Witherspoon's jaw dropped. "I beg your pardon?"

She gave him a bright smile. "I said, I could have hired someone to kill Mrs. Greenwood."

CHAPTER 6

Wiggins took a deep breath and knocked at the back door of the Green-wood house. He'd just ask to speak to Jon. No harm in that. He glanced up the small passageway in which he stood. Fred was still sitting obediently at the end, his attention riveted to a dripping drainpipe.

The door opened a crack and a dark-haired kitchen maid, her cap slipping to one side and her eyes suspicious, stuck her nose out. "What do you want, boy?" she asked sharply.

"Good evenin', miss," he replied, giving her his best smile. "If you don't mind, I'd like to see Jon."

"I do mind. What you wantin' with Jon?" The door wedged open another inch.

"Uh, I need to tell him something," Wiggins said, taking care not drop his *h*'s. "I've got a message for him."

"From who?" the maid asked sarcastically. "Who'd want to give that boy a message? Well, you can't see 'im. 'E ain't here." She started to close the door, but he stuck the toe of his boot out.

"Do you know where 'e is?" he asked, not bothering to mind his speech. "It's right important I talk to 'im."

"Get yer bleedin' foot out of me door," she yelped. "I've told you, Jon's not here. He took himself off early this afternoon, and we ain't seen him since. The mistress is furious."

Wiggins hastily complied and the door slammed in his face.

"Blimey," he muttered as he walked back towards the street, "she weren't very nice." Fred trotted along at his heels as they rounded the house and came out onto the street.

He glanced up at the sky; the day was fading fast. But he didn't want to give up, not yet. Not until he'd found the lad. Jon had tried to tell him something. Something important about Mrs. Greenwood's movements yesterday. Wiggins was determined to find out what it was.

Fred woofed softly and wagged his tail. Wiggins turned and saw a group of boys playing at the corner. They ran to and fro, screaming and tagging one another. He hesitated a moment; maybe these boys knew where Jon had gone. No harm in askin', he thought. "Come on, boy," he said to the dog, "let's see what these nippers can tell us."

The four boys stopped and stared as he and Fred approached. "Any of you know where Jon is?" he asked casually.

A blond-haired child of about ten wiped a grubby hand under his running nose. "Jon's gone."

"Gone where?"

"Don't know." He reached down and scooped up the ball, his pale face sober. "He's just gone. Not that we got to play with him all that much. The lady he works for kept him plenty busy, that's for sure. Wouldn't hardly let him out."

Wiggins tried another line of questioning. "How do you know 'e's gone? Did you see 'im leave?"

"What'cha want to know fer?" a second boy asked warily.

Wiggins saw the child's eyes weren't straight. He felt a momentary rush of pity. He knew all about these boys. They weren't the sons of the families from some of the fine houses around here. They were the children of housemaids and clerks, washerwomen and hansom drivers. He tilted his chin so that he could see that just beyond the corner was a narrow cobblestone alley fronted with small, grimy brick houses.

He smiled kindly at the cross-eyed boy. "I'm a friend of 'is," he explained. "It's real important that I find 'im."

The boy appeared not to have heard him. He was too busy watching Fred. All the boys were watching Fred, and Fred, who loved being the center of attention, was eating it up. He wagged his tail, bounced at their feet, and generally slobbered all over their shoes.

"It's all right to pet 'im," Wiggins said, thinking that if he could get them petting the animal, he might keep them talking longer. He had a bad feeling about Jon's disappearance. If, of course, it was a disappearance.

"Does 'e bite?" the blond boy asked, but he was already stepping closer and reaching out his dirty hand. Fred sniffed the boy's fingers and wagged his tail harder. The urchin laughed in delight, dropped to his knees, and stroked the dog's smooth fur.

"Course 'e don't bite," Wiggins replied.

They all crowded in a tight circle around Fred, who continued lapping up the attention as if he were the Prince of Wales.

"So where's Jon gone now?" Wiggins tried again.

"Don't know," the blond boy said, shrugging his shoulders. He didn't take his eyes off the dog. "But 'e might 'ave gone over to 'is cousin's place in Clapham. 'E were carryin' a bundle of clothes with 'im when 'e left, so I don't reckon 'e's comin' back. Not with Mrs. Greenwood dead."

Curiously, Wiggins stared at the boy. "What does Mrs. Greenwood's death have to do with 'im comin' 'ome? 'E works in the 'ouse, don't 'e?"

The boy lifted his chin, his eyes hard and cynical. "That don't mean nuthin' when one mistress dies and another takes her place. Mark my words, now that old Mrs. Greenwood's gone, that sister of hers will sell off everything, toss the servants out into the street, and be off before you can snap yer fingers. I know, 'cause me mum's the washerwoman there. I heard her tellin' me dad that they're all scairt of losin' their positions. Me mum weren't too happy, either."

Wiggins frowned. "What makes your mum so sure everyone's going to be sacked?"

"She overheard Mrs. Hackshaw talkin' to some bloke who come to the 'ouse with some papers for her to sign."

"A solicitor?"

The boy shrugged. "I dunno, I guess that could be it."

Wiggins was shocked. Hannah Greenwood had been killed only last night and already her sister was making plans. Cor blimey, the woman weren't even decently buried yet. He pushed the thought out of his mind and concentrated on his present problem. "So you think Jon may have gone to 'is cousin's?"

"He might. Couldn't much blame him if he did, what with Mrs. Greenwood gettin' murdered right under his nose."

Aghast, the inspector's jaw dropped even farther. He couldn't believe this. "Lady Cannonberry, have you any idea what you're saying?"

"I know precisely what I'm saying," she retorted brightly. "I'm pointing out possibilities you appear to have overlooked."

"I beg your pardon?"

"What I'm trying to tell you, Inspector," Lady Cannonberry said patiently, "is that you haven't questioned me. I might have seen or heard something about poor Mrs. Greenwood's murder."

"But how could you have?" Witherspoon was truly mystified. "We were together the entire evening."

"That's not true," she corrected. "You left me alone twice. Once while you got us some punch and once while you went back for another slice of cake."

"But I was only gone for a few minutes. . . ."

"Nevertheless," she persisted, "you still must question me. It's not fair that you've spoken to everyone else in the literary circle."

"I assure you, Lady Cannonberry," Witherspoon sputtered, "fairness has nothing to do with how and when I speak to witnesses. We are talking about a murder here."

"I take it you won't be confessing to Mrs. Greenwood's murder?" Mrs. Jeffries queried from the doorway where she'd been standing. She was certain Lady Cannonberry was perfectly innocent and she was equally curious to hear what she had to say.

"Of course not," she admitted. "I only made that outrageous statement to get the inspector's attention. I felt so very ignored."

Witherspoon blushed, coughed, and cleared his throat. "I'm truly sorry," he stammered. "I . . . er . . . I would have got round to you sooner or later, you see. But there were other, more important inquiries . . ." He stopped speaking and turned an even brighter red. "Goodness, I didn't mean that the way it sounded. Of course your evidence is important . . . it's just that as you were with me when the crime occurred, I didn't see how you could possibly know anything . . . Oh dear, this isn't coming out right at all."

"That's quite all right, Gerald." Lady Cannonberry smiled kindly and patted his arm. "I understand what you meant to say."

Mrs. Jeffries rolled her eyes. Really, she had the urge to box her employer's ears. Poor Lady Cannonberry was so keen to see him she'd come running over here on the silliest of pretexts. She sighed silently. Young love was painful enough to observe, poor Wiggins was proof of that. But middle-aged infatuation was positively excruciating. Whatever hopes she had of hearing anything useful about the murder began to diminish as she watched the rapt expression on Lady Cannonberry's face as she gazed at the inspector. Mrs. Jeffries coughed delicately.

Lady Cannonberry blinked. "I expect you want to know what I saw."

"Er, yes," the inspector replied. He sounded very relieved.

"Do you remember when you went to get me a glass of punch?" she asked. At Witherspoon's nod, she continued. "While I was waiting for you, you remember, I was sitting on the settee in the drawing room? The settee that faces the door into the library? Well, as I was sitting there, I saw Dr. Sloan coming out of the library. He was carrying a satchel."

Witherspoon's brows drew together. "What's odd about that?"

"It wasn't his satchel," she stated.

"How do you know it wasn't his?" Mrs. Jeffries asked curiously.

"Because when the inspector and I arrived at the Marlow house, Dr. Sloan and Mr. Venerable were getting out of the hansom in front of us. I noticed them because Mr. Venerable seemed to be leaning to one side. He was holding the satchel, and I remember thinking it must be jolly heavy to cause him to lean so far to his left."

"Perhaps Mr. Venerable was carrying Dr. Sloan's satchel for him?" Witherspoon suggested.

Lady Cannonberry shook her head. "No. As they were going up the stairs, I saw Mr. Venerable stumble. Dr. Sloan helped him and then tried to take the satchel from Mr. Venerable. He wouldn't let it go. He snatched it right back."

"Perhaps Dr. Sloan was getting the satchel from the library to take to Mr. Venerable," Mrs. Jeffries said thoughtfully.

"Why would he do that? I saw Dr. Sloan coming out of the library close to ten o'clock. By then, Mr. Venerable was so drunk, he was asleep."

"Then you've solved your mystery," Mrs. Jeffries said cheerfully.

Both of them stared at her.

"Don't you see," she explained, "it's precisely because Mr. Venerable was drunk that Dr. Sloan had the satchel. He is the president of the circle; therefore, if Mr. Venerable was incapacitated and unable to give out the prize to the winner of the poetry contest, Sloan would naturally have to take his place."

Lady Cannonberry shook her head, her expression stubborn. "He was up to something, I know it. Otherwise, why would he have tried to hide the satchel under his jacket when he went up the stairs?"

• • •

"As you instructed, Mr. Smythe," the banker said timidly as he handed over the small pouch, "it's all in shillings and half-crowns."

"Thank you, Mr. Babbit," the coachman replied. He was the only customer left in the bank, and that was precisely the way he wanted it. The less people there were, the less chance that anyone would see him.

"Er, a . . ." Mr. Babbit cleared his throat. "Do you mind if I make a suggestion, sir?"

"I'm in a bit of a 'urry," Smythe replied, picking up the pouch and dropping it into his pocket. Blimey, if he didn't get a move on, he was goin' to be late.

"This won't take long, Mr. Smythe," the banker said quickly. "It's about your investments in those American cattle ranches. I really don't think this is a good time to sell."

"Good time or not, sell 'em anyway."

"And what shall we do with the money from the sale? At the current market value, there will be a goodly profit."

"Put it in my account. I'll be back in a couple of weeks . . ."

"Weeks!" Mr. Babbit exclaimed. "Really, Mr. Smythe, I would like to see you again as soon as possible. There are decisions you must make. Money doesn't look after itself, you know. And you've quite a lot of it."

Smythe sighed. Money. Bloomin' pain in the neck it was, too. Just look at the grief it was causin' him now. Mr. Babbit complainin' that he 'ad to make decisions, havin' to sneak around just to walk in the bank, and worse, the worst of all, havin' to hide the fact that he had more money than he'd ever spend from the people he cared about most in the world.

"All right, all right." Smythe's brows drew together as he tried to think of when he could get back here. "I'll try and get in next Tuesday even—"

"We'll be closed then," Babbit interrupted. "It's the Queen's Jubilee Day. The parade."

"Oh, yeah, all right, I'll be 'ere Thursday evenin' just before closin'." He hoped they'd have the case solved by then. He wasn't going to give up huntin' a murderer just to keep this ruddy old bank manager happy.

"Fine." Mr. Babbit beamed his approval and stood up from behind his desk. "I'll look forward to seeing you, then, Mr. Smythe. There will be a number of papers for you to sign."

"There always are," Smythe muttered. He quickly left the bank, pausing only long enough before he stepped out into the street to make sure there was no one who might recognize him. He hurried off, wanting to make it back to Upper Edmonton Gardens in time for supper.

He leapt over a pile of rubbish as he crossed the road, the coins jingling in his pocket. The sound made him wince. Guilt pierced his conscience. He hated keeping this part of his life secret. Living a lie didn't sit well with him. But there was nothing he could do about it now. Smythe shook his head. Damnation. How the ruddy hell did he end up in this fix? He should have told them right from the start, but the time were never right. Once Euphemia knew she were dyin', she'd made him promise to stay on and keep an eye on the inspector and Wiggins. After she were gone, the only way he could hang about was to go on bein' a coachman.

Then Mrs. Jeffries and Mrs. Goodge and Betsy had come and settled in. Before you could slap a fly off a horse's bum, they was investigatin' murders and growin' to like each other. By then it was too late. Everyone at Upper Edmonton Gardens had come to mean too much to him. He didn't want to go back to livin' on his own again, it were too bloody lonely.

And, of course, the thought of never seein' Betsy again was too awful to think about.

Smythe scowled and a street arab quickly dodged out of his way. He reached into his pocket and pulled out a shilling. "'Ere, lad," he called, tossing it in the boy's direction. "I didn't mean to scare you." He knew his frown was frightenin' enough to scare the fleas off a dog. But there weren't much he could do about that.

The urchin easily caught the coin. "Thanks, guv!" he yelled, his eyes gleaming in delight at the unexpected bounty.

Smythe sighed. He wished he could remedy the situation at Upper Edmonton Gardens as easily as he'd soothed the child. But he couldn't and that was a fact. Telling them the truth would change everything. They'd feel differently towards him. Treat him differently. And he didn't want that. For the first time in his adult life, he felt like he had a home, a family. And he wouldn't risk losin' that for all the world.

Smythe stopped at the corner and stared at a line of hansoms waiting for fares. He fingered the heavy pouch in his pocket. At least his money was goin' to be put to good use, he told himself as he headed for the beginning of the line. This case wasn't goin' to be an easy one, he could feel it in his bones. It might take a good bit of lolly and a lot of greasin' palms before he could get anyone to give him any useful information at all.

Decision made, Smythe waved at the driver of the first cab and then glanced at the sky. If he hurried, he might be able to have a word or two with someone from the Warburton household before he had to get back to Upper Edmonton Gardens.

Supper was late that night. Mrs. Goodge muttered darkly under her breath as she and Betsy finished dishing up the food.

"What are you on about?" Betsy asked as she took a platter of beef and placed it in the center of the table.

"It's nothing really," the cook mumbled. She averted her gaze and reached for the pot of potatoes, but not before Betsy saw the genuine worry in her eyes.

"Something's botherin' you, Mrs. Goodge. It's written all over your face," she persisted. "What is it? Are you ill?"

"It's not that." Mrs. Goodge sighed. She and the maid were alone in the kitchen. "It's that." She jerked her head toward the kitchen sink.

"Something's wrong with the sink? Well, have Smythe in to have a look at it—"

"It's not the ruddy sink," the cook cried. "It's my medicine."

Suddenly Betsy understood. "Is that what's worryin' you? For goodness' sakes, Mrs. Goodge. I know how expensive it is. If you're a bit short, I can loan you a few shillings—"

"That's just it. The bottle's full and it shouldn't be." She plopped down in a chair.

Betsy frowned in confusion. "What?"

"This is the third time it's happened," Mrs. Goodge said wearily. "And I'm beginnin' to think I'm losin' my mind. I use that liniment every day, so I know how much I've got. Well, for the past few months or so, every time it gets low, I remind myself I need to get more. I write myself a little note and leave it on the counter with me provisions list. But before I can even get to the chemists, another bottle appears. A full bottle."

"I should think that'd make you happy," Betsy said slowly. She wondered if perhaps the cook wasn't getting forgetful. Mrs. Goodge was no spring chicken.

"The first time, it did," she said. "I thought maybe Mrs. Jeffries or the inspector had got it for me. But I asked them, and neither of them knew a thing about it. Then it kept happening. I'm beginning to wonder if maybe I bought the bottles and . . ."

"And forgot about it?" Betsy finished bluntly.

Mrs. Goodge nodded slowly, her shoulders slumped, dejected. "That'd mean I'm gettin' like me old granny," she said softly. "She went right off her head before she died. Kept thinkin' she were ten instead of ninety. Couldn't remember where she'd put things or what she'd eaten for breakfast."

"Don't be silly," Betsy said firmly. "You're not goin' off your head. It's just like my shoes or Wiggins's writin' paper, that's all. Someone in the 'ouse is doin' us favors. But they don't want to own up to it."

"But writin' paper and gettin' soles mended is a bloomin' sight cheaper than buyin' that medicine," Mrs. Goodge replied. "And who around here has that kind of money?"

"There's an explanation for what's happened," Betsy persisted, determined to make the cook feel better. "Maybe the inspector's been gettin' it for you but don't want to say anything about it. You know what a kind man he is."

"You won't say anything to anyone, will you?" Mrs. Goodge asked, "It wouldn't do for any of 'em to think . . ." She stopped speaking as she heard Mrs. Jeffries's footsteps coming down the stairs.

"I won't say a word," Betsy promised quickly.

Mrs. Jeffries hurried into the room. "Where's Smythe and Wiggins?" she asked as she took her seat. "We've much to talk about this evening."

"They'll be here shortly," Mrs. Goodge replied. She placed a bowl of steaming vegetables next to the roast beef. "They may be late sometimes, but they hardly ever miss a meal."

Mrs. Goodge was half right. Smythe arrived a few moments after they started eating, but Wiggins didn't show up at all. By the time they'd cleared the table and sat back down to discuss the case, all of them were throwing anxious glances at the passage leading to the back door.

When a loud knock sounded, they all jumped.

"I'll get it." Betsy leapt to her feet. She hurried down the hallway and threw open the door. "Why, goodness!" she exclaimed. "It's you."

Hatchet smiled politely and took off his shiny top hat, revealing a full head of white hair. "Good evening, Miss Betsy. May I come in?"

"Course you can." She led him back to the others.

Everyone greeted him effusively. Hatchet worked for their friend, Luty Belle Crookshank. He was allegedly her butler, but in reality, his relationship with his eccentric and elderly employer was far more complex than that of butler and mistress. Tall, ramrod straight, and excruciatingly proper, he was still a popular and much beloved friend to the staff of Upper Edmonton Gardens.

"Do sit down, Hatchet," Mrs. Jeffries invited. "Would you care for a cup of tea?"

"Thank you, but no." He smiled slightly, amusement apparent in his clear blue eyes. "I've come to help you."

"Help us?" Betsy gave him a puzzled frown. "With what?"

"With this murder," Hatchet replied evenly. "You certainly didn't think that just because madam is out of town I had no interest in furthering the cause of justice?"

"Bored are you, Hatchet?" Smythe challenged with a cocky grin.

"Extremely. Now," he said, his expression serious, "I am here to place myself completely at your disposal."

"You've already done a great deal for us," Mrs. Jeffries said. "Thank you again for arranging that invitation for Mrs. Livingston-Graves."

"No thanks are necessary," Hatchet replied. "Using my contacts to rid your good selves of that odious personage was almost as amusing as it's going to be when the madam gets back and finds out she's missed a murder." He grinned slowly. "I can't wait. She'll be fit to be tied, as she would say. It serves her right as well. I told her not to go galavanting off to America. But would she listen to me? Oh, no, claimed she couldn't stomach the Jubilee."

"She left because of the Jubilee?" Betsy yelped. "But why? All London'll be celebratin'."

"Madam considers herself a Jeffersonian democrat," Hatchet explained. "She's morally opposed to the idea of a monarchy. And, of course, she did it to annoy me."

"Women'll do that," Smythe muttered.

Betsy threw him a glare and then turned her attention to the butler. "How would her goin' off to America annoy you?"

"I do not approve of the madam traveling without me."

"Then why didn't you go with her?" Mrs. Goodge asked.

Hatchet's eyes narrowed. "I couldn't. She cleverly arranged her trip to coincide with my annual trip to Scotland. I go there once a year to visit my brother. By the time I arrived home, she'd left."

"You've got a brother?" Betsy said, looking interested.

Mrs. Jeffries quickly interrupted. "He's just told us he has, dear," she said gently. "But we really must get on with our discussion. It's getting late and we've much to talk about. Hatchet is more than welcome to stay and help. No doubt his services will come in very handy."

"If you would be so good as to enlighten me as to the progress you've made thus far?" Hatchet said. "I'll endeavour to offer what assistance I can."

Mrs. Jeffries quickly told Hatchet everything they knew about the murder and their circle of suspects. She then went on to share what she'd learned from the inspector and Lady Cannonberry.

"So Dr. Sloan were hidin' the satchel under his coat," Smythe mused. "I wonder why?"

Mrs. Jeffries sighed. "I shouldn't put too much credence in that evidence. Lady Cannonberry . . ." She hesitated, searching for the right words. "Well, she wanted the inspector's attention, and she could easily have misconstrued what she saw."

"You mean she might have just seen him pickin' up the satchel and walkin' off?" Mrs. Goodge asked. "Only she didn't want to be left out, so she made more of it than it really was?"

"That's it precisely."

"Silly woman," the cook murmured. "Anyways, can I go next? I've found out some interestin' bits. Or should we wait for Wiggins?"

"Go right ahead," Mrs. Jeffries replied. "We'll just have to fill Wiggins in later."

"Daft boy," Mrs. Goodge muttered. "Bloomin' inconsiderate of him to be late and worry a body so. But as I was sayin', I've learned quite a bit today. Mrs. Jeffries has already told us that Mr. Warburton was acquainted with Rowena Stanwick before she come to London. But I've found out he weren't just acquainted with the woman, he were in love with her." She paused dramatically. "And he's been in love with Mrs. Stanwick since afore her husband died. He didn't just happen to run into her after she moved here, he followed her to London."

"That's why he joined the literary group," Smythe added. "He's no more interested in poetry and books than Bow and Arrow," he mused, referring to the inspector's horses. "But once he found out Mrs. Stanwick were in the group, he couldn't join fast enough."

"Am I tellin' this or are you?" Mrs. Goodge yelped. She glared at the coachman.

"Sorry." He grinned, not looking in the least bit contrite. "Didn't mean to step on yer toes."

"Humph. Anyways, that's not all I learned. Warburton's got plenty of money. He were fixin' to ask Mrs. Stanwick to marry him, and he'd almost wore her down to the point where she was goin' to say yes. But then she met Mr. Locke and dropped Warburton like a hot potato," Mrs. Goodge finished with relish.

"Did Mr. Warburton take his rejection like a gentleman?" Mrs. Jeffries asked. She'd frequently observed that when it came to matters of the heart, one's social class had no bearing at all on how one acted.

"He didn't take it well at all," Mrs. Goodge answered. "He went over to her house and had a right old set-to with her about it. He accused Mrs. Stanwick of leadin' him on and triflin' with his feelings. The whole neighborhood heard him shoutin' at her."

"When was this?" Hatchet asked.

"Less than a fortnight ago. I couldn't find out the exact date. Do you think it's important?" Mrs. Goodge asked, looking anxiously at the housekeeper.

"I'm not sure," Mrs. Jeffries said slowly. "I don't see how it could have anything to do with Mrs. Greenwood's murder."

"Exceptin' that Mrs. Greenwood had a row with Mrs. Stanwick right before she was killed," Betsy chimed in. "Could be they was arguin' about Mr. Warburton. Maybe Mrs. Greenwood liked Mr. Warburton herself."

"Warburton barely knew Mrs. Greenwood," Smythe said. "Besides, he liked 'em young—" He broke off as he realized what he'd said. "Uh, I mean, uh . . ."

"Are you, perhaps, referring to the fact that Edgar Warburton has a penchant for young females?" Hatchet asked helpfully.

"Mrs. Stanwick isn't all that young," Betsy protested. "She's at least thirty."

"She's twenty-eight," Smythe countered, recovering quickly. "But she looks much younger."

"Smythe," Mrs. Jeffries interrupted before the discussion got out of hand. "You've obviously learned something about Mr. Warburton. Would you like to share it with us?"

Smythe glanced at Betsy and shook his head. "It don't have anythin' to do with the murder."

"How do you know?" the maid demanded. She turned to Mrs. Jeffries. "Aren't you always tellin' us that we don't know what's important and what's not? Shouldn't Smythe 'ave to tell us everythin' 'e's learned?"

In her anger she was dropping her *h*'s again. Mrs. Jeffries drummed her fingers on the tabletop. Betsy was right. "I think you ought to tell us, Smythe," she said gently. She never ordered them about. Their participation in these investigations was totally voluntary.

Smythe shifted uncomfortably. "It's not very nice and it don't have a ruddy thing to do with Mrs. Greenwood gettin' murdered."

"Nevertheless," she said softly, "Betsy is right. We don't know at this point what is or isn't important. If you've learned anything about Mr. Warburton you really must tell us all."

He took a long, deep breath. "Warburton likes women. Young ones, some of 'em barely old enough to be considered women, ifn' you get my meanin'. He pays 'em to go with 'im."

"You mean he pays prostitutes," Mrs. Jeffries clarified. From the corner of her eye she saw Betsy blush.

Smythe nodded. "There's some pretty nasty places in this city. Houses where a man can flash a bit of money about and get whatever he likes. Warburton's a regular customer."

"Sounds as though the man frequents some of the most notorious brothels in the city," Hatchet said calmly. "How very disgusting."

Smythe nodded but didn't volunteer anything else. He'd learned about a few of Mr. Warburton's other habits, too, but nothing short of torture would get that information out of him.

"Had he gone to a brothel the night of the murder?" Mrs. Jeffries persisted. "The inspector told us he admitted he'd just learned Mrs. Stanwick was going to marry Shelby Locke. Perhaps he left the ball and, well, sought solace in the arms of another woman."

"But that would mean he couldn't of done the murder," Mrs. Goodge said.

"Unless there's something about him and his relationship with Mrs.

Greenwood that we don't know," Mrs. Jeffries replied. "She might very well have found out about his, well, extracurricular activities and threatened to expose him. That's not the sort of gossip one wants spread about, you know. Furthermore, Warburton has no alibi for the time of the murder. As you'll recall, he claimed he was in the ballroom when Mrs. Greenwood was killed. But no one can remember seeing him there."

"I don't know if he went to a brothel or not," Smythe replied. "But I can find out."

"I think you ought to," Mrs. Jeffries said.

"What difference does it make where he went *after* the murder was committed?" Betsy asked curiously. "Shouldn't we try and find out where he was durin' it?"

"The victim was stabbed, Betsy," Mrs. Jeffries explained. "Whoever committed the murder may have gotten some blood on his clothes. And no one recalls seeing Warburton after the killing. I know, because I specifically asked the inspector. Mr. Warburton was gone by the time the inspector began questioning the guests."

"But why would Warburton want to kill Mrs. Greenwood?" she persisted. "The worst she could do was spread some nasty gossip 'bout him. That don't seem like much of a motive for murder."

"It's not much of a motive," Mrs. Jeffries admitted, "but it should be looked into."

"Seems to me if 'is feelin's was hurtin' over Mrs. Stanwick givin' him the boot," Betsy continued, "he'd murder her or Mr. Locke."

"We don't know that he'd want to murder anybody," Mrs. Jeffries explained. "We're merely trying to establish where he was both during and after the murder, and, more important, why did he lie to the police. Mrs. Putnam claimed she searched the ballroom and Warburton wasn't there."

They heard the back door open, and a second later Fred bounced in followed by a breathless Wiggins.

"It's about time you got here," Mrs. Goodge said, giving him a good frown.

"I'm ever so sorry to be late," Wiggins explained breathlessly. "But I couldn't come back until I found out what's 'appened to the boy."

"What boy?" Mrs. Goodge snapped. Her concern about Wiggins's absence had transformed to anger now that she knew he was all right.

"And where have you been? Your food's gone stone cold, and I'm not get-tin' up and reheatin' it for you."

"The boy's name is Jon!" he cried. "We've got to find 'im. 'E's in dan-ger, I know 'e is. 'E were with Mrs. Greenwood at the ball. She's dead and now 'e's gone."

CHAPTER 7

"Do sit down, Wiggins," Mrs. Jeffries suggested. "Surely, whatever it is you have to report can wait until you've caught your breath." The lad was prone to exaggerating, so she was quite certain no one was in imminent danger.

"But that's just it, Mrs. Jeffries," he protested, "I'm not sure it can. I think maybe that Jon knows who the murderer is and that's why he's disappeared."

"Who's this Jon, then?" Smythe asked.

"And why do you think he's disappeared?" Betsy added.

"Do you suspect foul play?" Hatchet said doubtfully.

"I best get Fred his supper." Mrs. Goodge reached down and patted the animal on the head. The dog licked his lips and bounced up and down.

"Fred?" Wiggins yelped, outraged. "What about me? I've not 'ad a bite to eat all day."

"Really, Wiggins," Mrs. Jeffries said. "I thought you were concerned about this Jon person."

"I am. But that don't mean I'm not hungry." He blushed. "I mean, I don't think Jon's really in any danger. But I do think he might 'ave gone to ground, so to speak."

Mrs. Goodge chuckled as she got to her feet. "Thought hearing me offer to feed the dog first would snap you back into shape, boy. Now just hang on a minute and I'll have you both tucking into a right tasty meal, not that you deserve it, mind you. I've half a mind to carry through on my threat and serve you your dinner cold."

Smythe glanced at Wiggins and snorted in disgust. "You had us worried there a minute, lad."

"The way you come runnin' in here, you'd have thought this Jon person was bein' tortured," Betsy chided.

"Ah, youth," Hatchet said, "so impetuous. So noble. So concerned with the satisfaction of their stomachs."

As soon as Mrs. Goodge had fed Fred and put a plate of hot food in front of the footman, Betsy cleared her throat. "Well, I found out what happened to Shelby Locke's notebook." She smiled triumphantly. "Lucinda Marlow stole it."

"So she did want to use one of Mr. Locke's poems in the contest," Mrs. Goodge said.

"Oh, no," Betsy said quickly. "She didn't give a fig for the contest. Rupert told me she didn't even bother writin' a poem. She stole Mr. Locke's poems so she could find out what he was up to."

"Rupert?" Smythe asked softly. "Who's 'e?"

"He's the Marlow butler," Betsy admitted proudly. "And he does like to talk. He hasn't worked at the house very long, but he's a right nosy parker, knows what's goin' on. Anyway, he thought it strange that Miss Marlow kept tellin' Mr. Locke she hadn't seen his notebook, when she'd had it ever since their last meeting. Rupert saw her carryin' it out of the drawing room after the others had left. He didn't think much of it until the next day, when Mr. Locke came round looking for it and Miss Marlow stood right there and lied to the man, bold as brass."

"So 'ow does this Rupert reckon Miss Marlow was usin' the notebook to find out what Mr. Locke was up to? It were a bunch of ruddy poems she had, not his diary," Smythe challenged.

Betsy was ready for that question. "One of Rupert's duties is to stand outside the door when the meetings are breaking up. You know, to see people out and hand them their coats and such. Well, he once heard Mr. Locke telling Miss Marlow that his whole life is a poem. He writes about everything that's important to him and puts the poems in the notebook. That's why he was so upset at it bein' gone."

"Do you think this Rupert knows what he's talkin' about?" Smythe asked.

"Of course he does," Betsy replied irritably. "He'd have no reason to lie to me."

"If you was askin' questions, he might 'ave been tryin' to impress you.

Act like 'e knew what was goin' on, tryin' to make 'imself look important." Smythe crossed his arms over his chest "It wouldn't be the first time a man made up a few tales to impress a pretty girl."

Betsy tried to look annoyed but couldn't. She was too flattered by his words. She'd never thought the coachman even noticed she was a female, let alone a pretty one.

"I think we must assume he was telling the truth," Mrs. Jeffries interjected. "Do please go on, Betsy."

"Rupert told me that after Lucinda Marlow found the notebook, she startin' acting right peculiar."

"That's hardly surprisin', now, is it? The poor woman thought she had an understandin' with Mr. Locke, and then she reads some ruddy poem and finds out she's been jilted." Mrs. Goodge made a face. "Nasty, that is. Right nasty."

"Did Rupert explain what he meant by 'peculiar'?" Mrs. Jeffries asked. She really didn't see where all this was leading, but that didn't bother her. It was one more piece of the puzzle.

"She got all quiet like, moody. Wouldn't smile, wouldn't eat much, and she took to going for long walks." Betsy shrugged. "She even took to wearin' her spectacles in public, that's how miserable she was."

"Humph!" Mrs. Goodge exclaimed. "Doesn't seem to me that Lucinda Marlow acted any differently than any other young woman would behave if they'd just read a love poem about someone else."

"But we don't know for certain that Lucinda Marlow did read such a poem," Mrs. Jeffries said.

"What else could it be?" Betsy argued. "Rupert claims she were as right as rain until she found that notebook. She was makin' plans for her ball, sendin' out invitations and doin' up the menu, dashin' out to the dressmaker's, and orderin' a new gown. Then she finds that notebook and starts actin' like her best friend's up and died. She got so melancholy, she even sent her new gown back."

Smythe said, "Isn't Lucinda Marlow the one who's supposedly had such a tragic life? Blimey, there's so many people mixed up in this case it's hard to keep it all straight."

"Her brother is dead and then she lost her parents, so she has had a tragic life," Betsy said defensively. "She's a nice woman, too. Her servants like her. It's right sad, her thinkin' she had an understandin' with Mr. Locke and then findin' out he was just triflin' with her. No wonder she got all weepy and maudlin and had to work out her grief by goin' for long walks."

"I bet I know where she were goin', too," the coachman interrupted. "I'd lay even money that she were snoopin' about Mr. Locke's. Typical female trick."

"What an evil thing to say," Betsy snapped, incensed.

"For goodness' sakes!" Mrs. Jeffries exclaimed. "We don't know that she did anything except read Mr. Locke's poems. We don't even know for sure that those poems had anything to do with Mr. Locke's romantic interests."

"That reminds me!" the cook cried suddenly. "All this talk of bein' maudlin. I've forgotten to tell you what else I found out." She shook her head in disgust. "I must be getting old. Can't keep a thing straight these days."

"It's all right, Mrs. Goodge," Betsy said quickly, then reached over and patted her hand. "Everyone forgets things every now and again. You're not gettin' old."

"How true," Mrs. Jeffries murmured and smiled kindly at the cook. "Do go on."

"I found out that Mrs. Greenwood's been in mourning—that's why the house were done up in black. Remember," she continued eagerly, "you told us the inspector said they had mourning cloth draped everywhere. Well, it weren't put there by Amelia Hackshaw for her murdered sister. It were put there months ago by Mrs. Greenwood herself for her son, Douglas. He died over a year ago, supposedly got hit by a train. But the gossip is, he got drunk and killed himself over a woman."

Mrs. Jeffries tried to keep it all straight in her head, but it was impossible. Dr. Sloan hiding a satchel, a missing boy, Lucinda Marlow stealing notebooks, Mrs. Greenwood visiting Dr. Sloan, and now a suspected suicide. She took a short, sharp breath and promised herself that as soon as she gained the quiet of her room, she'd try to make sense of everything. "That explains the mourning cloth being up so quickly. Mrs. Greenwood did it for her dead son."

"Supposedly, but if she were still in mournin', why'd she join the literary circle in the first place?" Mrs. Goodge frowned. "Don't make a lot of sense, does it? Especially as her sister told the inspector she didn't think Mrs. Greenwood cared a toss for poetry and books and the like."

"None of this makes sense," Mrs. Jeffries muttered. However, she felt a tiny tug at the back of her mind. Something that she couldn't quite put her finger on was falling into place.

"You can say that again," Betsy said. "And the inspector also said that Mrs. Greenwood went to see Dr. Sloan the day of the ball. Why? What reason could she have to go to his rooms?"

"Ah, but that's the mystery, isn't it? Why did she visit Dr. Sloan, and more important, why did she join a group she had absolutely no interest in?"

"Perhaps she was lonely?" Hatchet ventured.

"Lonely?" Betsy repeated. "That doesn't sound like Mrs. Greenwood."

"I don't know," Smythe put in, his expression thoughtful. "Loneliness can drive a body to do lots of strange things."

Mrs. Jeffries detected an odd undertone in the coachman's words. But she didn't have time to think about it now. She had an idea. "Mrs. Goodge, can you find out where this train accident took place?" she asked. "And see if you can learn the name of the woman involved as well."

"I've already got my sources workin' on it," she replied smugly. "But it may take a day or two to get an answer."

"Can I tell you about Jon now?" Wiggins asked.

"Of course."

Wiggins told them about his meeting with Jon and his unfortunate run-in with the inspector. "You'd best buy some cod, Mrs. Jeffries," he said, turning to the housekeeper. "I had to tell the inspector somethin' when he caught me."

"You're lucky he didn't ask where it was tonight," the cook said sternly.

"He did ask," Mrs. Jeffries said. "I told him the fishmongers had run out. But we mustn't digress. Do get on with your account."

"After the inspector left," Wiggins continued, "I tried to find Jon, but 'e were gone. So I asked about and found out that 'e'd been seen leavin' the Greenwood 'ouse carryin' a bundle of clothes. One of Jon's friends said 'e'd probably gone to 'is cousin's in Clapham, but this same lad also said 'e weren't in the least surprised that the boy had gone, seein' as 'ow Mrs. Greenwood got murdered right under 'is nose."

Smythe leaned forward. "Jon had spoken to this lad you were talkin' to?"

"Right. The lad's name is Timmy Reston. His mum's the washerwoman for the Greenwood 'ouse. This morning Jon were jumpier than one of Fred's fleas—remember how bad 'is fleas were this summer?" He glanced fondly at the dog, who wagged his tail.

"Yes, yes, get on with it," Mrs. Goodge snapped irritably. "We haven't got all night."

"Anyways," Wiggins continued, "as 'e were leavin', Jon told Timmy 'e wouldn't spend a minute more in that 'ouse, not with Mrs. Greenwood gettin' herself done in. He said he were scared the killer 'ad seen him in the Marlow 'ouse and 'e weren't 'anging about waitin' for the murderer to come after 'im."

"Let me see if I understand you," Mrs. Jeffries clarified. "Are you saying that Jon was with Mrs. Greenwood in the Marlow house during the ball?"

Wiggins frowned impatiently. "Didn't I tell you that at the beginnin'?"

There was a collective moan.

"No, you most certainly didn't. Or if you did, you didn't make it clear this young man was actually in the house with the victim."

"Oh." Wiggins looked embarrassed. "I must o' left that bit out."

"How the blue blazes did this lad get 'imself in the 'ouse?" Smythe asked. "Or are you tryin' to tell us 'e were Mrs. Greenwood's escort for the evenin'?"

"Jon got in like 'e always did. 'E nipped round the back and slipped in through the kitchen. Timmy told me that Jon boasted about 'ow he got the kitchenmaids and serving girls to feed 'im every time 'e went somewheres with Mrs. Greenwood. Jon even did it a time or two when Mrs. Greenwood went to 'er literary circle meetin's. Accordin' to what Jon told Timmy, the Greenwood 'ousehold was a bit on the stingy side with food. The boy 'ad learned a few tricks to get 'im a bit on the sly, so to speak."

"Are you sure this Timmy was telling the truth?" Mrs. Goodge asked, her expression suspicious. "It's not unknown for young boys to stretch the truth a bit, either."

Mrs. Jeffries wasn't sure it was a good idea for everyone to start questioning one another's sources. "I think," she stated firmly, "that it would be in all our interests if we assumed that people were telling us the truth. Otherwise, we'll never make any headway on any of the inspector's cases."

"You're right, Mrs. J.," Smythe said, glancing apologetically at Betsy. "Sorry, lass, I didn't mean anything earlier. You're a smart one—you'd be able to tell if this Rupert person were 'avin' you on."

"Me, too," Mrs. Goodge admitted. "I'm sure that Wiggins would know if this lad were tellin' tales."

Wiggins nodded. "Timmy was tellin' the truth. Mrs. Greenwood took Jon with her everywhere. I know 'e were with 'er at the ball. Timmy saw 'im gettin' in the carriage."

"She took a carriage to the Jubilee Ball, not a hansom?" Smythe asked.

"It were a hired one," Wiggins replied. "But it was a carriage."

Smythe's expression grew thoughtful. "Did this Timmy 'appen to know which livery Mrs. Greenwood used?"

Wiggins shook his head. "Timmy didn't say and I didn't think to ask, but Berry's Livery is just round the corner from the 'ouse."

"I'll pop round there tomorrow," the coachman muttered.

"Isn't that a bit odd, a young servant boy goin' with her to a fancy Jubilee Ball?" Betsy murmured.

"I suppose it is," Mrs. Jeffries said. "But there are many odd people involved in this case and in that particular literary circle."

"For one thing, none of them seems overly much interested in literature," Hatchet said. "Except, perhaps, for Shelby Locke and Dr. Sloan."

"I expect for most of the members the circle was merely a good excuse for a social occasion," Mrs. Jeffries said. "However, that reminds me. We really must find out more from the other members of the circle."

"But what about Jon?" Wiggins cried.

"I thought you said 'e'd gone to 'is cousin's 'ouse," Smythe said impatiently.

"No, I didn't. I said Timmy thought Jon went there, but 'e didn't. That's why I'm so late. Fred and me went all the way to Clapham and we couldn't find 'ide nor 'air of the boy."

"Did you actually go to the cousin's house?" Hatchet asked calmly.

"Course I did," he protested. "But no one answered the door."

"Then I think we really ought to go back, don't you?" The butler smiled and turned to the housekeeper. "You don't mind if I accompany young Wiggins on his search for the missing boy, do you? I may have some resources which can help should the relatives of the young man not be forthcoming concerning his whereabouts."

Mrs. Jeffries heaved a sigh of relief. In truth, she didn't like the idea of Wiggins searching for what could well be an eyewitness to murder on his own. Hatchet, she had found, was a good man to have about if trouble started.

"I don't mind in the least," she replied warmly. "We'll be very grateful for any assistance you can give us."

"It will be my pleasure, Mrs. Jeffries," he assured her. He reached into his coat pocket and withdrew a cream-colored envelope. "Before I forget," he said, handing it to her, "I must give you this. Should Mrs. Livingston-Graves return earlier than expected, this will no doubt keep her busy for a while."

Mrs. Jeffries grinned. "What is it this time?"

"An invitation to Lord Willoughby's Jubilee Picnic. There will be several hundred guests, and even better, it's in Richmond."

"Thank you, Hatchet." Mrs. Jeffries glanced at the others around the table. She supposed she really ought to give them an explanation. But before she could speak, there was a bloodcurdling howl from outside.

Fred cringed and slithered under the table.

"What in blazes is that?" Mrs. Goodge exclaimed, heaving herself to her feet.

"Sounds like a bunch of tomcats sniffin' after a—" Smythe broke off as another howl sliced through the air.

"Oh, no," Betsy said, "it's that wretched Alphonse. He sounds like he's being clawed to death."

"What's Alphonse doing out?" Mrs. Jeffries asked. She noticed that no one made a move to go and rescue the unfortunate feline.

"He pushed himself out through the kitchen window," Mrs. Goodge said calmly as she sat back down. "Wouldn't have thought the blighter could do it. The window was only open a crack and his backside is bigger than a side of beef."

"Well, isn't someone going to rescue the poor thing?" Mrs. Jeffries demanded. "I know none of us are fond of Mrs. Livingston-Graves or her cat, but honestly, Alphonse is hardly able to defend himself."

Meowww . . . another howl shook the air.

No one moved for a moment, then Smythe sighed and climbed to his feet. "I'll do it. Mind you, if the bloomin' creature digs his claws in me, I'll let 'im spend the night outside. Do that foppy cat a world of good."

The house was very quiet the next morning, but that was to be expected. Sundays were always quiet. Since Mrs. Jeffries had taken over the management of the household, she'd made it clear that the day of rest wasn't just to apply to the master of the house, but to the servants as well. The inspector, naturally, hadn't seen anything wrong with this arrangement and had even offered to boil his own eggs for breakfast.

Mrs. Jeffries wouldn't hear of that; she was quite adept at boiling eggs herself.

Everyone was out sleuthing; Hatchet had shown up several hours ago to pick up Wiggins and Fred, Betsy had decided to see what she could learn by concentrating on the other members of the literary circle, and Smythe had gone off on some mysterious errand he refused to tell anyone about. Mrs. Goodge had taken to her room, claiming she needed to think but leaving the back door open in case any of her "sources" showed up with information.

For all intents and purposes, Mrs. Jeffries and the inspector were alone. As she brought his breakfast tray up from the kitchen, she went over the various pieces of information they'd gathered thus far.

She sighed as she nudged open the dining room door with her foot. So far, she had absolutely nothing. The beginning of the pattern she was starting to discern yesterday evening had completely unraveled. This crime simply had no motive.

Hannah Greenwood was not well liked, but they could find nothing that would make anyone want to actually kill the woman.

Lucinda Marlow was a lovesick girl, but gracious, Mrs. Jeffries thought as she put the inspector's eggs on the table, half of London was filled with lovesick girls. Nor was she the first young woman to rifle through a young man's belongings in hopes of learning his true intentions.

Shelby Locke was in love with Rowena Stanwick, but that gave him no reason to murder Hannah Greenwood. The victim hadn't been standing in the way of Locke's desire for Mrs. Stanwick.

Dr. Sloan's actions were suspicious and his story about being out in the gardens during the murder was probably a lie. But then again, he could be telling the truth. Mrs. Putnam might have missed seeing him.

Mrs. Jeffries paused, her hand hovering over the rack of toast. But Mrs. Greenwood had visited Sloan on the day she died, and Sloan had not seen fit to mention this to the police. Perhaps Mrs. Greenwood did know something about Sloan? Something he'd kill to keep secret.

And then there was Rowena Stanwick. Mrs. Jeffries frowned. Both Warburton and Locke were in love with her. Warburton followed her to London from the country. When she spurned his affections, he was bitter enough to cast aspersions on her reputation. Was he bitter enough to kill? She shook her head. Perhaps he was, except that Mrs. Stanwick wasn't the victim.

And what about Edgar Warburton? Where did he fit in? He certainly hadn't cared about the Hyde Park Literary Circle. So why didn't he leave once Mrs. Stanwick had made it clear her affections were engaged elsewhere? According to what she'd learned, Mrs. Stanwick and Mr. Locke's association had been going on for several months.

The inspector bounced into the room. "Good morning, Mrs. Jeffries." He spotted the delicate china coddlers. "I say, coddled eggs this morning, that is most good of you."

"Not at all, sir. You need a hot breakfast." She poured herself a cup of tea and sat down beside him. Despite spending half the night thinking about this case, the best course of action she'd come up with was to get the inspector to double-check where everyone was at ten thirty. Furthermore, it was becoming increasingly apparent that everyone's story must be verified in some fashion. And, of course, she had to find a discreet method of letting the inspector know about Lucinda Marlow's theft of Locke's notebook. "Will you be continuing your investigation today?"

"It may be the day of rest for the rest of the world, but the pursuit of justice never stops." He reached for his teacup. "Barnes should be here soon and we'll be off."

Mrs. Jeffries clucked her tongue sympathetically. "Are you going back to the Marlow house, sir?"

As the inspector had no idea where he was going this morning, he shrugged. "Er, well, I'm not sure."

"The only reason I mention it is because of what you told me on your last case, sir." She calmly sipped her tea and waited for him to take the bait.

"My last case?"

"Why, yes, sir. Don't you remember? You told me that whenever you got stuck in the middle of an investigation, you always went right back to the source, the scene of the crime, the circle of suspects." She smiled.

"I said that?" Witherspoon gave her a puzzled frown.

"So, naturally, I assumed that you'd be going back to the Marlow house and questioning the servants again." She sighed. "It's so very easy for one to forget the most important things when one is rattled. Being present in a house where a murder is committed would naturally upset the staff. But once one gets over the shock of the event, then one can quite clearly remember details that had completely slipped one's mind."

As understanding dawned, his confused expression cleared. "I say, that's a jolly good idea. I was considering going back to Dr. Sloan's this morning. I mean to ask him about Mrs. Greenwood's visit to him the day of the ball. I want a look at those contest poems, as well. Lady Cannon-berry's statement got me to thinking. If Dr. Sloan was hiding that satchel, then I'd better find out why. But that can wait until after I've questioned the Marlow servants again."

"You know, sir," Mrs. Jeffries said cautiously, "I've been thinking about that missing notebook."

"What notebook?"

"Mr. Locke's."

"Oh." Witherspoon dug into his eggs. "That one. What about it? I'm not certain it's all that important. It probably doesn't have anything to do with Mrs. Greenwood's murder."

"I'm sure you're right, sir," she continued. "But I've been thinking about it anyway." She laughed airily. "It seems to me that there's really only one place it could be. The Marlow house."

Before she could explain, they were interrupted by a loud pounding on the front door. Mrs. Jeffries started. "Gracious, Constable Barnes is mak-ing a racket." She got to her feet and hurried toward the hall. Throwing open the door, her eyes widened in surprise.

"Well, don't just stand there gaping," Mrs. Livingston-Graves snarled, "help me in."

Her elegant pink dress was muddy and torn at the sleeve and her plumed hat leaned to one side, its once white feather broken and hanging askew. Tendrils of lank brown hair straggled around her neck, and as Mrs. Jeffries helped her into the house, the woman hobbled precariously.

"Goodness, Mrs. Livingston-Graves, what happened?"

"I say, Mrs. Jeffries, is that Constable Barnes?" Witherspoon asked as he came out of the dining room. He stopped dead in his tracks at the sight of his cousin. "Goodness, Edwina, what on earth happened to you? Are you all right?"

"Of course I'm not all right!" she yelled. "I've spent half the night in the most wretched inn, and then I had to get up at the crack of dawn to get a seat on the train. But that horrid little toad of an innkeeper kept me haggling over the bill so long, I missed the train. Then I had to hire a carriage."

"Oh, dear," he murmured. "You had to hire a carriage? But why didn't you just wait and take the next train?"

"Because I wasn't going to stay in that awful place another minute!" she cried. "It was bad enough being stuck there as long as I was, but that's not the worst of it. As we were coming back to London, the carriage lost a wheel . . . I suspect the driver was drinking. Then I slipped and fell in the mud. To top it off, once that imbecile of a driver had repaired the wheel and we were on our way again, the blasted door flew open every time we rounded a curve. It was awful, positively awful. And I mean to do something about it!"

"Oh, dear." The inspector started forward.

"Hello, hello," the cheerful voice of Constable Barnes called from the doorway.

Witherspoon took one frantic look at his disheveled and enraged relation and then leapt for his hat and coat.

"I'll leave you in Mrs. Jeffries's capable hands," he sputtered and hurried toward the door. "We'll talk this evening when I return. I'm sure we can get everything sorted out then."

"But you can't leave now, Gerald," she protested. "That carriage driver was drunk! Surely that's against the law. And that conveyance was certainly unsafe. There must be a law against that. You can't go now. You're the police. I want to press charges."

Smythe pulled out a shiny new florin and waved it under the housemaid's nose. "Does this 'elp your memory any?"

The girl smiled, revealing a half-broken front tooth. She snatched at the coin and dropped it into the pocket of her apron. "By rights, I shouldn't be talkin' to ye," she said, "but seein' as how yer a feller that pays 'is way, I expect I can remember a bit more than I told them coppers."

Smythe nodded. He wasn't surprised that the maid hadn't shared everything she knew with the police. Why should she risk, her living for the sake of a murdered woman she didn't even know? "So what can you tell us now, luv?"

"It weren't much." The girl shrugged. "I usually works down in the

kitchen. I'm the second scullery maid. But because of all the people comin'
for the ball, the 'ousekeeper sent me upstairs to work. I was supposed to
keep the punch bowls filled." She laughed softly. "And it were a hard task,
too, the way them toffs was drinkin'. Anyways, I 'ad to run back and forth
between the second pantry and the dinin' room. Well, just as I was comin'
out of the dinin' room, I saw that Mrs. Stanwick havin' a right old row
with Mrs. Greenwood. The woman what was murdered."

"Were you able to hear what they was arguin' about?"

"You'd a 'ad to be deaf as a post not to 'ear 'em," she replied. "Me
name's Lena, by the way." She gave him a coy smile.

Smythe, who was male enough to be flattered by her sudden interest,
was also smart enough to realize that it was probably the coins from his
pocket and not his person that piqued her attention. "Lena's a nice name,"
he replied, giving her a slow smile. "Real pretty, like you. But you were
tellin' me about the argument."

"Oh, yeah. Like I was sayin', they was goin' at it somethin' fierce. Not
screamin' or nuthin' but kinda hissin' at each other. I didn't reckon they'd
appreciate me trottin' back and forth under their noses, so to speak. So I
ducked behind the curtain and waited for 'em to finish."

Right, he thought, *and I'm the King of Spain. The girl'd been deliber-*
ately eavesdropping.

"And what was they on about?" he prodded. He schooled himself to
be patient.

"Mrs. Greenwood was tellin' the other woman, Mrs. Stanwick 'er
name is, that she'd see to it that she wouldn't be able to show her face at
one of their meetin's ever agin."

"Mrs. Greenwood was threatenin' Mrs. Stanwick then?"

Lena frowned impatiently. "That's what I said, in't it? Then Mrs. Stanwick claimed she didn't give a tinker's damn about their group. That
didn't sit well with the old lady. She got all red in the face and said she'd
see to it that some feller, I didn't quite catch 'is name, wouldn't be wantin'
to come sniffin' after Mrs. Stanwick no more. Not when 'e heard about
'er Douglas."

"You're sure the name was Douglas?"

She nodded. "There's nuthin' wrong with me hearin'. The name was
Douglas, all right. Anyway, as soon as this Mrs. Greenwood said it, Mrs.
Stanwick got all quiet. Didn't say nuthin'. Then Mrs. Greenwood started
laughing, a right 'orrible laugh it was, too. She told 'er she was goin' to

pay for what she'd done. She'd see to it that no one ever spoke to Mrs. Stanwick again, and as soon as this feller 'eard about Douglas, 'e'd be finished with 'er, too."

"And then what 'appened?" Smythe asked.

"Then Mrs. Stanwick turned and run off." Lena shrugged. "I think she were cryin'. She were in such a state she ran smack into the buffet table."

"Then what did she do?"

"She righted herself, took off down the 'all, and went up the stairs."

"What time was this?"

"It must of been close to ten thirty."

"What did Mrs. Greenwood do?" Smythe asked slowly.

"She went after 'er."

"Are you sure this is the correct house?" Hatchet asked.

"I'm sure," Wiggins replied.

They were standing in front of a small gray brick row house off Victoria Road in Clapham. The paint was peeling around the windows, the door stoop was dusty, and the street was littered with trash. They'd knocked several times to no avail.

Hatchet knocked again, this time pounding hard enough to make the windows vibrate.

"They's no one home," a disgruntled female voice rang out from above.

They both looked up to see a frizzy blond-haired woman glaring at them from the top window of the house next door.

Hatchet took off his top hat. "Excuse me, madam. I'm so sorry my knocking disturbed you. But do you have any idea when the family will return?"

"It's Sunday," she replied irritably. "They've gone to visit their gran. They'll not be back till tonight. Now quit that poundin' and let a body get some sleep."

"We can't hang about till tonight," Wiggins moaned.

The woman started to close the window. Hatchet yelled. "Excuse me, madam, I'm so terribly sorry to be a nuisance. But did they have a young boy with them?"

"A young boy?" She stared at them suspiciously. "Who are you and why you askin' all these questions about the Hickmans?"

Hatchet gave her his most engaging smile. "The young man we're inquiring about is called Jon. He's cousin to the Hickman family. I'd like to offer him employment with my mistress, Mrs. Crookshank. But she needs him to start working for her right away. She's leaving for Scotland early tomorrow morning and wants someone with her to look after her trunks. Jon was recommended to us as an honest lad in need of a position."

The woman hesitated. She spent several seconds staring at Hatchet and then raked Wiggins with a hard glance. Finally she sighed. "You'd best be tellin' the truth, because I'll remember what you looked like. If you're up to no good, I'll know about it. But I don't want to take the chance on Jon missin' out on gettin' work. Lord knows they"—she jerked her thumb at the Hickman house—"can't afford another mouth to feed."

"Thank you, madam," Hatchet said solemnly. "I assure you, we've only the boy's best interests at heart. If you would be so good as to tell us where the Hickmans went, we'll trouble you no further."

"You'll be wantin' to find the Purty house, then. Their granny's name is Hazel Purty." She started to shut the window.

"Could you be more precise, madam," Hatchet called.

"She lives at Haggar's Lane in Clacton-on-Sea!" she yelled. With that, she slammed the window shut.

"Clacton-on-Sea," Wiggins whispered. "Blimey, that's miles from 'ere."

Hatchet popped his elegant top hat on and leapt spryly off the door stoop. "It's hardly the end of the earth."

"We'd better just nip back and try to have a word with Jon tonight."

"Don't be ridiculous," Hatchet said as he hurried up the stone path toward the street. "We're not going to waste a whole day."

"Where are we goin', then?" Wiggins asked. He practically had to run to keep up with the stiff-backed butler.

"To Clacton-on-Sea."

CHAPTER 8

Inspector Witherspoon wished the young man would sit still. He gave the footman a kindly smile, hoping the poor soul would relax. Gracious, he was only asking a few questions. He tried again. "Now, Ronald, you say you were too busy to notice anyone picking up the knife from the serving table, is that correct?"

Ronald's left shoulder twitched. "That's right, sir. There was so many people milling around the cold buffet, I could barely keep up."

"And how did the knife come to be lying beside the plate?" Witherspoon asked. "I mean, if you were serving such a great number of people, shouldn't the knife have been in your hand so that you could carve?" That sounded like a good question.

"Oh, no, sir, we couldn't do it that way, we'd have people lined up all the way to Hyde Park." He entwined his fingers and began to rotate his thumbs around each other, "We'd carved off part of the beef down in the kitchen. I was heaping it on plates as fast as I could, you know, as the guests come up. Every time I had me a bit of a lull, I'd hack off a bit more. I'd just run out of the last of the meat and I was reachin' over to pick up the knife. But just then I heard all the commotion outside." Ronald stopped twirling his thumbs and began to pump his knee up and down. "Naturally, I run out to see what was goin' on. And there was me carvin' knife, stickin' straight out of that poor lady's back. Blow me for a game of tin soldiers, I thought. I'll never use that ruddy knife again."

Witherspoon sighed silently. Questioning the servants was turning out to be only minimally better than staying home and facing his cousin.

Ronald drummed his fingers against the table. The inspector concentrated fiercely, trying to think of some questions that would get the foot-man past his nervousness. Prime the pump, so to speak. But he'd been talking to the servants now for several hours, and he'd learned nothing new, nothing that seemed to have any bearing whatsoever on Mrs. Green-wood's murder. No one, including Miss Marlow, had seen or heard any-thing amiss until the victim had come tumbling off the balcony with a knife in her back.

Miss Marlow had not been pleased to see them again, but he could hardly blame her for that. Having a murder take place at one's ball did tend to make one less hospitable than usual.

"Do you know which guests are members of the Hyde Park Literary Circle?" the inspector asked.

Ronald nodded. "They meet here all the time, so I know most of them by sight."

"Did you see any of them anywhere near your serving table from the time you put the knife down until the time you heard the commotion outside?" The inspector tried another smile. "Take your time before you answer. Take a deep breath and try to remember."

"Let me see," he murmured, a look of intense concentration spreading across his thin, pale face. "Miss Marlow come up to check that we had plenty of food. But she'd done that all evening."

"Isn't that the butler or the housekeeper's responsibility?" Barnes asked softly.

"Usually, yes," Ronald explained. "Miss Marlow ain't one for inter-ferin' most of the time. But she was very anxious about this ball. Wanted it to go right and all. She watched over the preparations herself, even down to checkin' the linens and lookin' for spots on the crystal. But as for seein' any other members of the circle, well, I don't think . . ." He stopped. "Wait a minute, I did see Dr. Sloan scarpering up the stairs."

They'd already established that Ronald had a full view of the stairs from his position behind the buffet table. Unfortunately, Ronald was not the most observant of witnesses.

Witherspoon and Barnes glanced at each other. Finally the inspector asked, "Was he carrying anything?"

"Yes, he had some sort of satchel or case in his hand."

"Now, Ronald," the inspector said gently, "think carefully before you answer this question. Prior to your seeing Dr. Sloan go up the stairs, had he come anywhere near the buffet table?"

"Now that you mention it"—Ronald chewed his lower lip—"he did." A proud smile spread across his face. "Of course, that's why I remember seein' him go up the stairs. He'd been standing by my table only a minute before. He knocked into the leg with his foot when he scarpered off. That's right, I were a bit nervous, seein' as how Miss Marlow had just come by to make sure everything was runnin' smoothly."

Witherspoon nodded encouragingly. "So both Miss Marlow and Dr. Sloan had been by the table? Do you know what time this was?"

"Near as I could tell, it were probably about ten-fifteen, maybe ten-twenty." He shrugged. "But I wouldn't want to swear to it."

They continued questioning Ronald for a few more minutes, but were unable to get any additional information out of the young man.

For the next hour the inspector spoke to servant after servant. But it was the same as on the night of the murder. No one had seen or heard anything.

"How many more do we have to talk with?" Witherspoon asked Barnes.

The constable squinted at his notebook. "Only two, a scullery maid named Lena Crammer and Rupert Malloy—that's the butler."

A young woman appeared at the doorway. "Mrs. Craycroft says you want to ask me some questions."

"Yes, please come in and sit down." Witherspoon hoped this young woman could be of help. "You're Miss Lena Crammer?"

She nodded, her dark head bobbing as she took the seat that Ronald had just vacated. Her face was narrow and sharp with a beaked nose, hazel eyes, and a slightly protruding mouth. "Right. I'm a scullery maid. I've worked here for the best part of a year now."

"And you were on duty the night of the Jubilee Ball, is that correct?"

"That's right." Lena slipped her hands in her pockets and fingered the coins the big man had given her. She smiled, remembering how he'd told her to tell this copper everything she'd told him. Claimed this one was a good copper, not that there really was such a thing, but blimey, he'd paid good money for her to tell the truth, so she supposed she might as well, Lena thought. Strange feller, he was. Tall and raw lookin' with shoulders as broad as a bridge and muscles stretchin' from here to Sunday. She hoped she'd see him again. It weren't often a girl run into a feller that didn't mind splashin' his money about. "Me job was to nip back and forth between the pantries and the buffet table. I was keepin' the punch bowl filled and makin' sure we had plenty of china and the like."

"On the night of the ball," the inspector began, "did you see anything unusual?"

Lena smiled smugly. "I reckon I did."

"Really?"

"Course I didn't remember it when you was talkin' to us before," Lena said quickly, thinking good copper or not, peelers didn't much like it when you lied to 'em. "I was so rattled by the murder, I barely remembered me own name. We was all in an awful state."

Witherspoon felt his pulse leap. Finally they were getting somewhere. Perhaps he would be able to solve this murder after all. "I quite understand, Miss. Now, what was it you saw?"

"It were a few minutes afore that Mrs. Greenwood come tumblin' off the balcony—her having a row with Mrs. Stanwick," Lena explained.

"You saw Mrs. Greenwood and Mrs. Stanwick arguing?" Witherspoon clarified.

"They was hissin' at each other like a couple of she-cats," she replied, her eyes glittering with excitement. "Course, as they was standing in the hallway, blockin' me way to the pantry, I had to nip behind a curtain till they was finished." She went on and told them everything she'd told Smythe earlier.

When she'd finished, Witherspoon pursed his lips. "Are you absolutely sure about the time?"

"Course I am," Lena replied promptly. "I remember because I was supposed to have the rest of the champagne glasses upstairs to the ballroom by half past. That's why I was on me way to the pantry in the first place. As soon as they was gone, I nipped on down to the pantry. If them glasses was late and the guests had to wait to drink their ruddy toast, Miss Marlow would have me guts for garters. That's when I noticed the other funny thing."

"Other funny thing?" Witherspoon prodded.

"Why, Mr. Locke actin' so peculiar. Mind you, at the time I didn't think nuthin' of it, but later I got to thinkin' and it seemed to me he were actin' a mite funny."

"You'd seen Mr. Locke do what?" Barnes asked patiently.

"I'd seen him come down the hall and slip out the side door."

The inspector frowned. "What time was this?"

"About ten-twenty," Lena replied. "Now, there weren't much odd about that—guests slip in and out all the time. But we keep that side door bolted. Mr. Locke threw the bolt and stepped outside. I thought he were after a breath of fresh air. So you see, what was odd was the door was unlocked. But a few minutes later, when I went to get them glasses, I noticed someone had bolted it again. Then I got to thinkin', if Mr. Locke were after a bit of air, why didn't he go out to the terrace?"

"I see," Witherspoon murmured. Actually, he didn't see a thing. "I suppose one of the other servants could have bolted the door."

She shook her head. "Not likely. I was the only one going back and forth down that hall—the only place it goes is to the china pantry. The other servants was usin' the back stairs."

The inspector wasn't sure what to make of the girl's story. If she was telling the truth, and he couldn't really think of a reason for her to lie, then it appeared as though they'd better have another talk with Mrs. Stanwick. And with Mr. Locke.

Lena cocked her head to one side. "I reckon that's about it."

Witherspoon suddenly thought of something. "You appear to be a most observant young woman," he said. "Do you remember seeing Mr. Warburton during the evening?"

A sly look crossed her face. "I saw him earlier in the evenin'," she said slowly. "But after that, I'd say you'd best speak to Dulcie if you want to know what he was up to."

"Dulcie who?"

"Dulcie Willard, she's the upstairs maid." Lena shrugged. "She's out today. She won't be back until this evenin'. But if I wanted to know about Mr. Warburton, I'd talk to her."

"Did you get her nibs settled, then?" Mrs. Goodge asked.

Mrs. Jeffries nodded. "Yes, finally. Gracious, I feel rather awful. I sent the woman off to get her out of our way, but I didn't expect she'd have such a wretchedly miserable experience."

"Don't fret yourself over it," the cook muttered. "Probably do her good. Give her a bit of excitement in her life."

"True, but I wasn't trying to get her killed."

"She's exaggerating. Don't worry, give her a few hours' sleep and she'll be right as rain. Did she take the bait?"

"That's why she's taking a nap," Mrs. Jeffries answered. "She wants to be fresh for the Jubilee Picnic."

"Cor, she isn't very bright, now, is she?" Mrs. Goodge shook her head in disbelief. "You'd think after what happened she'd be suspicious of any more invitations."

"People believe what they want to believe, Mrs. Goodge," Mrs. Jeffries replied thoughtfully. "And Mrs. Livingston-Graves desperately needs to believe that she's important enough to procure invitations merely on the strength of her connections."

"What connections? Just because her late husband was related to some minor viscount! Nonsense." Mrs. Goodge put the teapot on the table. "If you ask me, the woman's a half-wit." She poured them both a cup of tea. "Anyways, enough about her nibs, I've got a bit of news. A couple of my sources come through for me this morning while you and the inspector was havin' breakfast."

"Excellent, Mrs. Goodge. What have you found out?"

"To begin with, Miss Marlow's had a few problems in her life. Seems she's been sent off a time or two to one of them fancy places out in the country. She suffers from a nervous condition."

"Are you talking about an asylum?"

"Nothing that horrible," Mrs. Goodge replied. "More like a nursing home, I reckon. Mind you, there's good medical treatment there, it's one of them establishments the rich sends their relations when they're not quite right. I don't mean she were actin' crazy or anythin' like that. But she used to get real melancholy sometimes. She'd quit speakin' and wouldn't eat much. It used to be so bad her parents would pack her off to this place out in the country, make sure she got plenty of fresh air and rest. But she hasn't had one of her spells in a long time."

"How awful for the poor woman," Mrs. Jeffries replied sympathetically.

"As for this Mrs. Stanwick, she isn't quite the lady she makes out," Mrs. Goodge said with relish. "It looks like Mr. Warburton's nasty little comments might have more than a grain of truth to them. It seems Mrs. Stanwick didn't leave her country house just to get away from her husband's memory. Seems there was a scandal hangin' over her head. Accordin' to what I heard, she were involved with some young man. Flirtin' with him and God knows what else. And this weren't the first time she'd done it, neither."

"What's so scandalous about that?" Mrs. Jeffries queried. "Mrs. Stanwick wouldn't be the first widow to have a few flirtations."

"It were more than a few, but that's not what got tongues waggin'. With this last young man, Mrs. Stanwick weren't in the least serious about him, but he was dead set to have her. He proposed and she refused. The next day he were dead. It were supposedly an accident. But there was some that whispered it was suicide."

"Hmmm, I can see why people talked and why Mrs. Stanwick felt it necessary to leave her home. Being the cause of a suspected suicide would harm any woman's reputation."

"And that's not all. You'll never guess who the man was. . . ." Mrs. Goodge paused dramatically.

Mrs. Jeffries knew better than to rush her; she enjoyed her small triumphs far too much to be hurried along. Of course, she'd already guessed who the unfortunate young man was, but she wouldn't let on for the world. It would spoil the cook's whole day. "Who?"

"Douglas Beecher. Hannah Greenwood's son."

"Have you finished with your questions, Inspector?" Lucinda Marlow inquired politely. Sitting on the settee in the drawing room, she made a lovely picture of feminine beauty. On her lap was an embroidery hoop, and at her feet a fluffy white cat slept curled on the rug.

"Yes, Miss Marlow. We've finished for the present."

"For the present?" She arched one eyebrow delicately. "Do I take that to mean you'll be returning?"

Witherspoon didn't know. But he wasn't going to give up until he had this case solved. "We may. Naturally, we'll try not to disrupt your household routine any more than necessary."

"My household has already been interrupted," she said with a faint smile. "A murder taking place at one's ball virtually assures one's routine is disrupted."

"I'm very sorry, Miss Marlow." He wasn't sure why he was apologizing, but nevertheless, it seemed the thing to do. "Now, I do have one question I'd like to ask you."

She sighed delicately and picked up the embroidery hoop. "Of course I'll answer any question you like, but I don't see what good it will do."

"Your footman says you went to the cold buffet table a few minutes prior to the murder, is that correct?"

"I don't quite recall the time," she replied. "But I did check the table several times that evening. Why? Is it important?"

"Do you recall seeing the carving knife?"

She glanced up from her embroidery, her expression thoughtful. "Now that you mention it, I don't recall seeing the knife. I think it must have been gone."

Witherspoon stifled a spurt of irritation. Really, she should have mentioned this the first time she was questioned. Then he realized the poor lady was probably so distressed by having murder committed in her own home, it was a wonder she could recall anything. Women were such delicate creatures. "Do you have any idea what time it was that you checked the buffet the last time?"

"I can't say for certain," she said. She stuck her needle into the cloth and gave him her full attention. "The nearest I could estimate is that it was quite close to ten thirty. Perhaps ten twenty-five or so. Oh, yes, that's right. It must have been close to half past because I was getting concerned about Mrs. Stanwick. I was afraid she'd miss the presentation."

Witherspoon's pulse leapt. "Why were you afraid she'd miss the presentation?"

"Well, you see, I'd forgotten until you mentioned me going to the table." She laughed self-consciously. "But that's why I went to the buffet. I'd seen Mrs. Stanwick there only moments before and I was trying to catch up with her. Of course, once I was there, I did check the food supply. Then, when I turned around to try and find her again, she'd disappeared."

"Cor," Barnes muttered. "If this case isn't right muddled, then I'm not a gray-haired copper with sore feet."

"Are your feet still bothering you?" Witherspoon asked.

"I was speakin' figuratively, sir. Actually, I'm wearin' me old boots today. Mrs. Barnes has got the new ones stuffed with coal." Barnes led the way up the stairs to Dr. Sloan's rooms.

"Coal?"

"Yes, sir. If your shoes are too tight, you slip some goodly sized lumps in an old sock, stuff the sock in the boot or shoe, and give the leather a good stretch." He raised his hand and knocked on the door. "Works every time."

They waited for a few moments, but the door didn't open. "That's odd." Witherspoon muttered. "His landlady said Dr. Sloan hadn't gone out today. Try again, Constable."

Barnes pounded harder.

From behind the door they heard a faint moan.

They looked at each other, and before Witherspoon could even get the words out, Barnes was racing down the stairs shouting for the landlady to come and bring her keys.

"Dr. Sloan!" the inspector shouted through the keyhole. "Are you all right?"

No answer.

"Do hang on, sir," Witherspoon tried again. "We're getting your landlady."

A moment later a breathless Barnes and a red-faced Mrs. Tepler, a ring of keys in her hand, pounded up the stairs.

"I do hope the gentleman's not gone off his head," she said, putting the key in the lock and giving it a turn. "They do that sometimes, you know." Barnes pulled her back and pushed the door open. He and the inspector hurried inside.

Dr. Oxton Sloan lay on the settee. His hair stood on end, his shirt was pulled out of his trousers, and an empty whiskey bottle lay on the carpet. He blinked several times, his red-rimmed eyes focusing on the trio standing by the doorway.

"Gracious me," Mrs. Tepler said irritably. "He's as drunk as a lord."

"Ah, I've been expecting you," Sloan said, his voice slurred. He struggled to a sitting position. "Forces of law and order and all that. Wondered when you'd get back round to me. Wasn't my fault, though. Never touched the old bitch. Someone else got her first."

"Well, I never!" the landlady sputtered. "What's got into the man? He never used to drink."

"Thank you for your assistance, Mrs. Tepler," the inspector said. "Perhaps you'd be so good as to bring us up a pot of coffee." He ushered her out of the room.

"Blimey, looks like he's as tight as a newt." Barnes shook his head. "Do you want me to try and sober him up, sir?"

Sloan laughed. "Sober me up? I'm not that drunk. I can hear you perfectly well. Who was it, then? That silly little housemaid? Or was it her nibs herself. Stupid really, should never have trusted her. God, I thought my luck had changed. Once she was gone, I thought I was safe."

The inspector was totally confused, but he certainly didn't want it to show. "I take it you're referring to . . ." He hesitated, wondering who Dr. Sloan was babbling about, and afraid if he guessed wrong, it would shut the man up completely. Not that he was making much sense in the first place.

"I'm referring to that silly cow, Cecilia Mansfield." Sloan hung his head. "She saw me, didn't she?"

"Yes," the inspector said slowly. "I'm afraid she did."

Sloan covered his face with his hands. "I heard her coming up the stairs behind me. I knew I was taking a risk, but God, I had no choice."

Witherspoon wondered if he ought to caution Dr. Sloan.

"She was going to ruin me, you know," Sloan continued. "Absolutely ruin me. Then she was dead and I thought I was safe, but I'm not. There is no safety when you've done what I've done."

"Dr. Sloan, I must warn you that anything you say can be used against you in a court of law," the inspector said quickly. "Do you understand that?"

Sloan raised red eyes and stared at the two policeman. "Caution me? What for?"

Confused, Witherspoon said, "Well, you are confessing to murder, aren't you?"

"Murder?" Sloan laughed. "Ye Gods, Inspector. I'm not a murderer, I'm a plagiarist."

"'Ow much farther do you reckon?" Wiggins asked Hatchet. He took a deep breath, enjoying the crisp sea air of Clacton. Gulls screeched overhead, the sun shone brightly between huge, puffy white clouds, and the wind blew in off the water just enough to keep them from being too hot. They walked down a row of neat houses, each of them with their own front gardens filled with bright red, yellow, and pink summer roses.

"Haggar's Lane should be just at the end of the road," Hatchet replied. He walked faster. "Once we get there, Wiggins, I do believe it might be best if you allowed me to conduct the conversation. Is that agreeable to you?"

"You want me to keep me mouth shut, then?"

"Of course not, my good fellow. Your insights and questions are, I'm sure, most invaluable. It's just that I have noticed people do tend to speak rather more freely to me. Perhaps it's because I'm older."

They stopped at the first house, a small terraced building of brown brick, and asked where Hazel Purty lived. They were directed to the second-to-last house at the end of the road.

Hatchet boldly knocked at the door. It was opened by a pale, middle-aged woman. "Excuse me, Madam," he began, "but I'm wondering if you could be of assistance to me. We're looking for a young man named Jon. I believe he is your cousin."

"What do you want Jon for?" she asked, wiping her hands on the front of her apron. "Has he done somethin? Well, if he has, that's hard luck for you, 'cause he isn't here."

Hatchet smiled. "Of course he hasn't done anything. I'm trying to locate him so that I can offer him employment."

"Doin' what? Jon's not trained. He can't read nor write, neither."

"Nevertheless, we do wish to offer him a position."

"Are you daft?"

"Madam," Hatchet said earnestly, "I assure you, we're quite serious. Young Jon has been highly recommended to us, and I'd like to offer him a position."

She stared at him. "Like I said, he ain't here."

Wiggins glanced down the row of houses. He saw a movement in the bushes in the front garden of the last house. He turned and stared, his eyes narrowing as he saw the top of the shrubs moving in a steady rhythmical motion that couldn't be the wind.

"We'd be most grateful if you could tell us where the young man has gone," Hatchet continued. "The offer of a position is most genuine, I assure you."

The gate at the end of the garden creaked. From where Wiggins stood, his view was blocked by the bushes, but by standing on tiptoes and craning his neck, he did catch a glimpse of porkpie hat and tuft of red hair. "There 'e is!" Wiggins cried.

Jon must have heard him, because a second later they heard the sound of footsteps pounding off down the road. Wiggins took off after him.

"Here now!" the woman shouted. "You leave the lad alone or I'll have the police on you."

Hatchet doffed his top hat as he joined the pursuit. "Thank you for your assistance, madam," he called as he charged after Wiggins. "I think we can find the young man on our own."

They raced after the boy. Jon's hat flew off, but he paid no attention, just continued hurtling toward the end of the road.

"Just a minute, now!" Wiggins shouted at the rapidly retreating figure. "We ain't gonna hurt you. We just want to talk."

Jon ignored them and kept running.

"Thank you, Mrs. Tepler. I'm sure Dr. Sloan will be fine in just a little while. The coffee smells delicious. It was so very good of you to bring it up," Witherspoon said.

"Well, all I can say is this better not become a habit." She sniffed and glared at her hapless tenant. "Otherwise Dr. Sloan can find himself another set of rooms. This is a decent house."

As soon as she'd left, Witherspoon poured a cup of black coffee and handed it to Sloan. The doctor's fingers trembled as he took the cup.

"I suppose I should have told you everything before," he muttered.

"Why don't you tell us now?" the inspector suggested. He wasn't terribly interested in recriminations, he just wanted to get some facts about this case.

"Oh, where to begin." Sloan laughed harshly. "You see, it's important that you understand."

"We can't understand anything if you don't explain yourself," Witherspoon said kindly. "But we're not here to accuse anyone of anything. We're here to learn the truth."

"Truth? What is truth?"

Witherspoon sighed silently. He did so hope Dr. Sloan wasn't going to embark on a rambling philosophical discourse. That sort of thing gave him such a frightful headache. Really, even if he was supposedly brilliant at solving murders, it was moments like this when he longed for his old position back in the records room at the Yard.

A wave of nostalgia washed over him as he thought of his neat rows of ledgers and file after file of tidy police reports. But he mustn't waste any more time woolgathering, he thought, staring at Sloan's haggard face. No matter how distasteful, he really must get this over with. Truth was truth and it was his duty to find it.

"Dr. Sloan," he said patiently, "the only truth we're interested in is what you saw or heard on the night of the murder. Please, this is no time to digress."

Sloan nodded. "Yes, you're right. And I'm not digressing, I'm delaying. Admitting one's weaknesses isn't very pleasant." He closed his eyes briefly. "It all began the day of the ball. I was up here in my rooms, working, when Mrs. Greenwood arrived. She was in a state. Very excitable, almost giddy. I asked her what she wanted and she . . . she told me that if I didn't do as she asked, she'd make sure that everyone at the circle knew I was a plagiarist."

"Does that mean you copied some other person's work and claimed it as your own?" Barnes asked curiously.

"Precisely." Sloan laughed again, a terrible barking sound that didn't have a smidgen of humor in it. "That's exactly what I'd done, and Hannah Greenwood had found out about it. She had a copy of an American publication with her. A small, rather obscure one, at that. God knows where she got hold of it. Unfortunately, it contained a poem I'd read as my own work less than a month ago at one of our meetings. I was amazed. I'd gotten the poem by corresponding with the author. He's a young fellow, very talented. Lives in Colorado. Naturally, I had no idea he'd submitted the poem for publication. If I had, I'd never have claimed his poem as my own."

"What did Mrs. Greenwood want you to do?" the inspector asked. He wanted to get on with it. Gracious, being a plagiarist wasn't very nice, but it was hardly in the same league as murder. He didn't really see why Dr. Sloan was making such a terrible fuss.

"She threatened to expose me," Sloan murmured. "I couldn't let that happen, I just couldn't. I'd have nothing then. Absolutely nothing. I've little money and no position. They haven't let me practice medicine for years. All I have in my life is the circle. Being a published poet. And I didn't steal all of my poems. The first ones that were published were mine. All mine."

"Yes, I'm sure you're a wonderful poet," Witherspoon began.

"Don't you see? I know it was wrong. I know I shouldn't have done it, but I had no choice. No choice at all . . . but she wouldn't listen."

"Dr. Sloan, you're getting off the point . . ." the inspector interrupted.

"But you don't understand. She was going to tell them. She was going to announce it that night at the ball."

"Dr. Sloan!" Barnes yelled. "You haven't answered our question."

"Question?" He blinked groggily. "But I'm answering it now. For God's sake, I'm baring my soul to you."

"What did Mrs. Greenwood want you to do?" Witherspoon persisted. "You haven't told us that yet?"

"What did she want me to do? But I just told you."

"No, you haven't. You've told us what she planned to do to you if you didn't cooperate with her." The inspector took a deep breath and strove for patience. Really, back in the records room he never had to talk to maudlin men who'd had too much to drink.

"Oh? I'm sorry, I thought I had." He took another sip from his cup.

"Well?" Barnes prodded.

Sloan put his cup down on the table. "Hannah Greenwood wanted me to help her ruin Rowena Stanwick."

CHAPTER 9

Wiggins raced after the boy. Holding on to his top hat, Hatchet threw dignity to the winds and doubled his efforts to keep up the pace.

As they turned the corner onto a busy road, Wiggins saw Jon dodge behind a fruit vendor's cart and disappear between two buildings. "There 'e is!"

They ran, oblivious to the stares of startled pedestrians as they rushed by. Wiggins reached the spot where the boy had disappeared and plunged after him with Hatchet hot on his heels. They ran down a narrow passageway lined with dustbins and mounds of refuse. Their feet pounded against the dry dirt, raising clouds of dust.

At the end of the passage Jon turned sharply to the right. Wiggins, breathing hard, blinked as he shot out into the bright sunlight and found himself in a paved courtyard surrounded by buildings. "Blast," he muttered, unable to see any spot where the boy could have escaped.

"There he goes!" Hatchet yelled. He pointed to a narrow wooden gate which was just now slamming shut and dashed toward it, Wiggins right behind him.

They emerged from the courtyard into the center of the business district. Luckily, as it was Sunday, the streets were relatively empty. A few pedestrians wandered about, city folk up from London to take advantage of the sea air. A carriage rolled leisurely up the street and a group of men taking the sun in front of the hotel stared at them curiously as they burst out into view. But Jon paid them no heed. He simply ran as if the devil himself were on his heels.

Twice, Wiggins was almost in grabbing distance, but both times Jon managed to elude his grasp. The third time he was close to the fleeing boy, he shouted, "I only want to talk to you!" He lunged for Jon's coat.

"Leave me be, you ruddy bastards!" Jon yelled. He jumped over a low wall. Wiggins hurdled the wall, his foot snagged on the top, and he landed flat on his belly, gasping as the air was knocked out of him.

Hatchet ignored him and hurried after the retreating figure. "Get up!" he shouted to the footman. "He's headed for the train station."

Wiggins grimaced, pulled himself to his feet and loped off after the butler.

They rushed up one street and down another, past shuttered shops and pubs and hotels. But no matter how fast they ran, the boy stayed well ahead of them.

As he rounded a corner, Wiggins saw Jon slip through the iron gate surrounding the station. Hatchet, red-faced and holding his side, pointed to the spot where he'd gone inside. "Hurry, there's a train leaving. If that boy gets on it, we'll never get our hands on him."

Wiggins charged toward the station, but he wasn't fast enough. Just as he reached the platform, he saw the boy nimbly leap onto the still-open baggage car.

"Well, hell's bells," Wiggins said in disgust. His legs were on fire, he could barely breathe, there was a god-awful stitch in his side, and the ruddy train was on its way to bleedin' London.

And Jon was on it. Bloomin' Ada, as Smythe would say. They'd let the lad slip right through their fingers.

Shoulders slumped in defeat, he went back to where Hatchet stood by the gate. "I didn't make it," he admitted morosely. "The little nipper got to the baggage car just as the train pulled out. He's gone. What'll we do now?"

Hatchet wiped his face with a pristine white handkerchief as he considered the matter. "I think," he said slowly, "we'd better get back to London on the next train."

"What good will that do us?" Wiggins protested. "We've already lost 'im. Who knows where 'e'll go next."

"Well, he certainly won't be coming back here," Hatchet said. He took off his top hat and smoothed a lock of white hair off his forehead. "I had the distinct impression he was not a welcome addition to his cousin's household."

• • •

Mrs. Jeffries set the inspector's dinner in front of him. "I'm afraid it's just cold beef and salad," she said.

"This will be fine," he replied. "I say, I think I'm finally beginning to make progress on this case."

"But of course you are, sir," Mrs. Jeffries poured herself a cup of tea and took the seat next to him. "You always do." It never hurt to bolster the inspector's confidence.

She wondered how she was going to slip him the information regarding Hannah Greenwood's son. She'd already decided to say nothing of the boy, Jon, accompanying Mrs. Greenwood to the ball—they had acquired that information third-hand, so to speak, and before she involved a child in a murder investigation, she wanted to make doubly sure her facts were correct. But she really must tell the inspector about Douglas Beecher. At this point it was all she had. Wiggins and Hatchet still weren't back, Betsy was snooping around the Hiatt and Putnam households, and God knows where Smythe had got to.

"Thank you, Mrs. Jeffries, I do my very best." He sighed. "I daresay, though, sometimes what one learns in the course of a murder investigation is enough to make one, well, a tad cynical."

"Whatever do you mean, sir?"

"I mean, Mrs. Jeffries, that appearances can be deceiving. People are rarely what they seem," he said somberly. "Take this Hyde Park Literary Circle, for instance. One would naturally assume that all of the members came together for a common love of literature. You know, to discuss the great works of writers like Shakespeare or Mr. Dickens or even that American fellow, Mr. Edgar Allan Poe. But I don't believe that's at all true about this particular group. It seems to me that half of them joined just so they'd have somewhere to go and gossip, and the other half joined so they could avail themselves of romantic liaisons or to avenge themselves on one of the members."

Mrs. Jeffries regarded him curiously. "Gracious, sir. That is a rather dark view."

"Take our victim, Hannah Greenwood." He waved his fork for emphasis. "She wasn't in the least interested in books or poems."

"I take it she was one of those more interested in the social aspects of the circle rather than the intellectual ones?"

"Worse than that!" Witherspoon exclaimed. "She joined for the sole purpose of ruining Rowena Stanwick. According to what Dr. Sloan told us today, Mrs. Greenwood holds Mrs. Stanwick responsible for her son's death. Seems the Stanwick woman was leading him on, and when she refused him, he walked in front of a train. The chap's name was Douglas Beecher. He was Mrs. Greenwood's son from her first marriage and her only child."

"How dreadful."

"And on top of that," the inspector continued, "Mrs. Greenwood threatened to expose Dr. Sloan as a plagiarist if he didn't help her ruin Mrs. Stanwick socially."

"I say, sir, you have been very busy today." She gave him her most encouraging smile. "You've learned an enormous amount of information. Why, now you've two members of the circle who had a motive to murder Mrs. Greenwood. Now, sir, do tell me what else you found out."

For the next half hour Mrs. Jeffries listened closely. She was delighted she wouldn't have to bring up the subject of Douglas Beecher herself.

"So you see, at least now we've one suspect with a reasonable motive," the inspector finished.

"Rowena Stanwick?" Mrs. Jeffries guessed. She wondered why the inspector had discarded Dr. Sloan.

"Correct." Witherspoon sighed. "We know from the maid's evidence that Mrs. Stanwick knew that Hannah Greenwood was going to ruin her. And we know from Miss Marlow and the maid that Mrs. Stanwick came close enough to the table to get the knife."

"But didn't the maid say that she saw Mrs. Greenwood follow Mrs. Stanwick up the stairs?" Mrs. Jeffries queried. Something about the sequence of events bothered her. "If that's true, how could she have gotten the knife?"

Witherspoon frowned. "I suppose she could have snatched it off the table when she bumped into it. The knife was sitting right on the end." His expression brightened. "Yes, I'm sure that's what happened. She pretended to stumble into the table so that she could get her hands on the murder weapon. That's probably when Miss Marlow saw her. Then she hurried up the stairs and waited for her victim."

"Did she know that Mrs. Greenwood was following her?"

"I'm sure she did," Witherspoon replied. "She'd just had a very ugly row with Mrs. Greenwood—I expect she knew quite well that the woman would come after her. Mind you, I'm not sure she planned the murder, but I do think that she took advantage of the opportunity when it arose. Bumping into that table and seeing that knife lying so close to her hand was simply too much of a temptation to resist."

"But according to the maid, Mrs. Stanwick was crying by this point. Wouldn't that indicate she was more upset than enraged?" Mrs. Jeffries had no idea where her train of thought was going, but she was determined to follow it through. Logic, rational thinking, and deduction were all very well, but sometimes, she'd learned, it paid to trust one's instincts.

Witherspoon drummed his fingers against the lace tablecloth. "Mrs. Jeffries," he said, "you may find this difficult to believe. I mean, you're such an honest person yourself I do think you find it hard to credit dishonorable behaviour in others. However, it has come to my notice there are some people who are very good at conveying one emotion while feeling another."

Mrs. Jeffries stared at him incredulously. Where the inspector had come by this amazing insight, she couldn't deign to guess. What startled her the most was that he'd had it at all. He was such a delightfully naive fellow. "So you think that Mrs. Stanwick was, shall we say, faking her response to Mrs. Greenwood and hoping the woman would follow her upstairs so she could murder her?"

"I'm afraid I do," Witherspoon replied. "Several other people have told us that Mrs. Stanwick's character is less than"—he paused and blushed—"admirable."

"Are you referring to Mr. Warburton's statements?" she asked, mainly because it annoyed her that a female who had gentlemen admirers was always credited with the worst of character, while a man was considered masculine because of his conquests.

"Not just Warburton's," Witherspoon protested. "Several others have made comments regarding Mrs. Stanwick's reputation. But that's not why I think she may be the murderer. We know she went upstairs and we know that Mrs. Greenwood followed her. We also know she had access to the murder weapon. Besides, she's the only one with a genuine motive."

"What about Dr. Sloan?" she argued. "It seems to me he might have just as compelling a motive. You told me yourself, sir, that Sloan was convinced that if the others learned of his plagiarism, he'd be ruined."

"True." The inspector smiled. "But the man was quite drunk when he made those statements. I'm sure he was being overly dramatic."

"But if he really believed she could ruin him, sir, perhaps he was driven to do something desperate? And what about Lady Cannonberry's evidence? She saw Dr. Sloan hiding Mr. Venerable's satchel under his coat. The footman stated that he saw Dr. Sloan going upstairs, and he also said that he'd been near the table as well. He could just as easily picked up the carving knife as Mrs. Stanwick."

Witherspoon, his mouth full of salad, nodded. "Sloan explained all that," he finally said as soon as he'd swallowed his food. "He admits to taking the satchel upstairs. That's why Mrs. Putnam couldn't find him. He'd taken it to try and get his poem back before the contest. You see, he'd realized that Mrs. Greenwood had only heard him recite the poem he'd stolen from the American chap at one of their earlier meetings. She didn't actually have any proof in hand, so to speak, except for the American magazine."

"I'm afraid I don't understand."

"She didn't have a copy of the poem he'd read aloud," Witherspoon explained. "But Dr. Sloan had plagiarized another poem from this American fellow and it was in the publication Mrs. Greenwood had. Sloan had changed a few words of the poem and submitted it as his Jubilee contest poem. He wanted to get the poem out of Venerable's briefcase before the winner was announced. You see, he had no intention of helping Mrs. Greenwood. He'd already decided he wouldn't say a word about Mrs. Stanwick's past."

"Are you saying that Dr. Sloan thought that if he got the poem back before anyone saw it, Mrs. Greenwood couldn't harm him?"

"Of course." Witherspoon smiled. "Mrs. Greenwood confronted Sloan based on her remembering a poem she'd heard him recite. The only written evidence of Sloan's plagiarism was his contest poem. Once he retrieved that and destroyed it, he could easily say that Mrs. Greenwood was mistaken and that the poem she heard wasn't at all like the one in the magazine. So he pinched Venerable's satchel and nipped up to an empty bedroom on the second floor so that he could search it in private."

"Did Dr. Sloan find his poem?" she asked.

"Oh, yes. Of course by then he'd heard the screams and Mrs. Greenwood was dead."

"I see," she said slowly. "Do you believe Dr. Sloan is telling you the truth?" To her way of thinking, confessing to a bit of plagiarism would be far less dangerous than being arrested for murder.

Witherspoon hesitated before answering. "I think so. But naturally, I'm going to try and verify his story. He claims he left the satchel in the bedroom. He kicked it under the bed when he heard all the commotion outside."

"So if the satchel's still there or one of the servants found it, you'll assume his story is true?"

"Yes."

"Are you going to arrest Rowena Stanwick?"

"Perhaps," the inspector hedged. "But I'm not sure we've really enough evidence at this point."

"Of course not, sir," she said quickly. "Forget I even asked that silly question. I know your methods, you would never arrest anyone on the minuscule amount of evidence you have now."

"I don't believe it's all that minuscule," he said quickly. "Naturally, we'll keep digging to obtain more."

"But what about Mr. Warburton?" Mrs. Jeffries continued relentlessly. "We don't know where he was when the murder took place. He may have had a motive as well." As soon as she said the words, she knew she was stumbling in the dark. So far they had absolutely no indication that Edgar Warburton had any reason to murder Mrs. Greenwood. He barely knew the woman. Or did he? "Have you established in fact that the two weren't better acquainted than appearances would indicate?" she asked. "Perhaps Mr. Warburton had something to do with Mrs. Greenwood's son?"

She knew she was grasping at straws, but she desperately wanted the inspector to keep looking. He was a very good policeman, but unless some other suspect or evidence turned up, he'd eventually have to act on what he had now. Rowena Stanwick would be arrested for the murder of Hannah Greenwood. Perhaps she'd actually been the killer, but there was something tickling the back of Mrs. Jeffries's mind, something that made her want to keep at it.

"I suppose we could follow up that course of inquiry," he murmured softly. "It certainly couldn't hurt. And, of course, one doesn't want to risk arresting the wrong person.

"I'm sure you'd never do that, sir."

"I say," the inspector mumbled as he reached for his water glass and took a sip. "The house is awfully quiet. Isn't it a bit late for everyone to be out? I do worry about Betsy when it starts to get dark. She is a rather innocent young woman, and the streets aren't all that safe, you know, despite our best efforts."

"Don't worry, sir. Betsy is doing some household errands, but she knows to take a hansom home once the sun goes down. And Wiggins is off with Luty Belle's butler, Hatchet. I do believe he's a tad lonely since Luty's been in America."

"Good, good, I know I worry too much. But you must admit, Mrs. Jeffries, policemen do see too much of the dark side of life." He sighed dramatically.

They heard the front door open and then a moment later a high-pitched giggle.

"I daresay that sounds like Betsy now," Witherspoon said.

Mrs. Jeffries didn't think so. For one thing, Betsy didn't use the front door, and for another, she certainly wouldn't come in laughing her head off. From the hallway they heard a feminine voice burst into the first stanza of "God Save the Queen."

"Gracious. That doesn't sound like Betsy, sir," she declared, getting to her feet and heading for the door.

Before the housekeeper reached her goal, Mrs. Livingston-Graves, a silly grin on her face and her bonnet askew, lurched into the room. She propped herself against the doorway. "Good evening, Mrs. Jeffries, Gerald." Her voice was slurred. "I've had the loveliest time."

Mrs. Jeffries stopped dead. From behind her she heard the inspector gasp. "Mrs. Livingston-Graves," she said cautiously. "Are you all right?"

"Edwina?" the inspector said, rising from his chair.

Edwina burped. "Oops!" She giggled and shoved away from the door. "Guess that one slipped out." Weaving slightly, she walked toward the dining table.

Mrs. Jeffries looked at Witherspoon. His jaw gaped open as he stared at his disheveled cousin.

"Edwina," he said, "perhaps you'd better sit down."

She stumbled on the hem of her dress, and Mrs. Jeffries, who was right behind her, grabbed her arm to steady her.

"Thank you," Mrs. Livingston-Graves said, giving the housekeeper a big smile. "I tripped." She burped again. "Oops, there goes another one. Mustn't do this on Tuesday," she rambled. "Mr. Freeley's coming, you know."

As Mrs. Jeffries helped her into the chair, she caught the scent of liquor. The moment the woman's backside made contact with the chair, she sighed, placed her arms on the table, flopped forward, put her head down, and closed her eyes.

"Egads, Mrs. Jeffries." Witherspoon stared at his cousin with alarm. "Do you think we ought to call the doctor? She seems quite ill."

"She's not in the least ill," Mrs. Jeffries replied dryly. "She's passed out. Drunk."

"Are you sure it was Warburton?" Smythe asked. He gave the fat, greasy publican his most intimidating stare. He wanted to let him know he wasn't to be trifled with. It wasn't often he used his size to intimidate people, but he wasn't sure he trusted this bloke. Feller's eyes were shifty.

The barman pocketed the half crown Smythe had placed by his beer mug. "It were Warburton all right," he said. "And that weren't the first time it'd 'appened, either. The man's got a bit of a reputation with some of the girls round 'ere now. Some of 'em won't go with 'im at all."

Smythe hissed softly. This miserable, squalid pub was in one of the worst areas of the East End. Hard. Dangerous. And the girls who plied their trade round here were just as hard and frequently just as dangerous. If they'd put the word out about Edgar Warburton, a rich mark if there ever was one, then the bastard had to be worse than he'd thought. "What was the girl's name?"

"Don't know her proper name." The barman shrugged and slapped a dirty teatowel at a fly that had landed on the counter. "But she used to be known 'round these parts as Dolly Jane."

"Used to be known?" Smythe didn't much like the sound of that.

"She's dead. Died right after it 'appened."

"What'd she die of, Warburton's beatin'?"

"Nah, she were used to the beatin's," he replied casually. "Besides, he paid her well for her trouble. She died of the consumption." He leaned forward, his small blue eyes glittering with greed. "Look, if you're lookin' for somethin' like Dolly Jane, I can fix you right up. 'Alf the girls that come in 'ere'll—"

"No, thanks." Smythe couldn't keep the contempt out of his voice. "I ain't interested. I just want to be sure you're tellin' me the truth about Edgar Warburton."

"Course I am, mate," he replied. "It's just like I said. He comes in here once a week or so. The girls start comin' in 'round six in the evenin'. Warburton flashes a bit of coin, they go off together, and the next time I see the girl, she's usually got a few bruises showin'." He gave a short, ugly bark of a laugh. "And Warburton's a real odd duck. Dolly Jane told me somethin' funny about 'im, right afore she took sick."

"And what was that?" He wasn't sure he really wanted to know.

"She said the last time she were with 'im, he kept callin' her by another woman's name."

"What name would that be?"

Wrinkles creased his fat, greasy face, as though he were concentrating and it really hurt. "Don't know that I can remember," he finally mumbled. "It's been awhile, you know. A body can't recall every little thing."

Smythe couldn't decide if he was angling for more money or if he was genuinely stupid. To be on the safe side, he reached into his pocket and pulled out another half crown. "This help you remember?" he asked, slapping it on the counter next to the beer.

"Reckon it does, mate," he said, snatching the coin. "He kept callin' her Rowena. Nice name, in'n it," He chuckled. "One thing I'll say about Warburton, he's a right 'ard man to please. Only went with the pretty ones. Liked 'em young, too. Dolly Jane couldn'a been more than fifteen."

By the time Mrs. Jeffries got Mrs. Livingston-Graves upstairs to bed, the inspector had retired and the servants were gathered in the kitchen.

"Was she really drunk, then?" Mrs. Goodge asked.

"As a lord," Mrs. Jeffries replied. "I must say, I was quite surprised. Mrs. Livingston-Graves is the last person I would ever guess was a secret drinker. However, I do believe her overindulgence may work to our advantage. I don't think she'll be bothering us tomorrow. From the look of her, she'll probably stay in bed all day."

"Cor," Smythe said, "if we'd known that was all it took to keep the old girl out of our way, we could've been slippin' 'er gin all along." He grinned to show he was jesting and Mrs. Jeffries relaxed.

She'd been concerned about the coachman. He'd arrived back at Upper Edmonton Gardens looking like he was carrying the weight of the world on his shoulders. It was good to see him smile, even if it was at Mrs. Livingston-Graves's expense.

As soon as they were all settled, Mrs. Jeffries told them everything she'd learned from the inspector. "So you see," she concluded, "unless one of you has come up with anything else, it appears as though Rowena Stanwick is our leading suspect."

"Sounds to me like she probably did it," Mrs. Goodge said. "Like the inspector said, she had a bloomin' good motive. For a woman like her to be ruined socially would be the end."

"But she weren't the only one with a motive," Smythe protested. "What about this Locke fellow? Seems to me, if 'e was really in love with Mrs. Stanwick, 'e'd want to protect 'er. And no one knows where 'e was during the murder."

"Wasn't Mr. Locke outside?" Hatchet ventured.

"That's what 'e says," Smythe replied, "but 'e could've come back in, seen the women 'aving a go at each other, and nipped up the back steps when 'e saw 'em going up the main staircase. Lena, the maid, admitted she were deliberately keepin' out of sight. Maybe Locke slipped in when she weren't lookin'."

"But how would he have obtained the knife?" Mrs. Jeffries asked. "The footman didn't report seeing him anywhere near the buffet table."

"But 'e couldn't say Mr. Locke *'adn't* been there, either," Smythe argued. "For all we know, Locke could've gotten the knife before 'e let 'imself out that side door."

"But what about the maid?" Wiggins said. "She claimed she saw Locke slip outside, and then a few minutes later the door were bolted, so how could 'e 'ave gotten back inside?"

Smythe shrugged. "That's my point. Locke could've nipped back in and bolted the door 'imself."

"Why did he go outside in the first place?" Mrs. Goodge asked. "That's what I want to know."

"Could be," Smythe mused, "that 'e saw Lena comin' and goin' from the pantry. Maybe he went out deliberately when he knew the maid would see him leave."

"You think he was deliberately arranging an alibi?" Mrs. Jeffries thought the coachman might be on to something. Shelby Locke did have an interest in Rowena Stanwick's reputation. He was planning on marrying the woman.

"It's possible, ain't it?" He leaned forward, crossing his elbows on the table. "If Lena overheard Mrs. Greenwood and Rowena Stanwick goin' at each other, isn't it possible that Locke 'eard 'em, too?"

"I suppose," she replied doubtfully. "But I'm not sure the timing is right. According to the maid, she was quite certain of the time. If she's correct, then Shelby Locke would have already been outside when the argument occurred. However, the inspector is going to be talking to Mr. Locke again tomorrow." She turned to Smythe and said, "And I think it might be wise for us to try to find out exactly who is telling the truth here. If Mr. Locke was outside, someone might have seen him."

"I'll ask some of the drivers," Smythe said. "See if they saw 'im skulkin' about and, more important, exactly what time it was."

"Were you able to learn anything today?" Mrs. Jeffries asked. She was wildly curious as to what he'd been up to.

He hesitated and a slow blush crept up his cheeks. "Not much," he mumbled, looking down and studying the tabletop. "Just a bit about Warburton. But I didn't hear anythin' that 'as any bearin' on what went on the night of the murder."

"Well, I found out plenty about Edgar Warburton," Betsy added. "And it's not very nice, either."

Smythe shot her a quick, sharp look.

Betsy ignored him and went right on. "I had a little chat with Dulcie Willard, you remember the other maid at the Marlow house."

"And what did she tell you about Warburton?" Smythe demanded.

"Like I said, it's not nice, but I think she were tellin' the truth." Betsy sighed. "It seems he does have an alibi for the time of the murder. He were with Dulcie." Her voice faltered and a rosy blush crept over her cheeks. "They was in a bedroom up on the third floor. . . ."

"I think we all understand what you're saying, Betsy," Mrs. Jeffries said hastily. Hearing about Warburton and, the maid's amorous activities didn't particularly embarrass her, but she wasn't so certain about the rest of them. Mrs. Goodge was listening with wide-eyed amazement, Wiggins's mouth was hanging open, Hatchet was staring straight ahead at a nonexistent spot on the wall, and Betsy and Smythe were both blushing furiously. "Was Dulcie sure she was with Warburton at the time the murder actually took place? Not before or after?"

"She were sure," Betsy replied. She glanced at Smythe. "Unless Smythe heard differently, she'd have no reason to lie to me."

"No, lass," he said softly, "I heard nothin' about that night."

"Just a minute, now," Mrs. Goodge said before anyone else could protest. "I thought we were all agreed that we'd share everything we learned. Seems to me Smythe isn't tellin' us all he knows."

"I would if I'd learned anythin' worth repeatin'," he snapped. "But what I 'eard today don't have nuthin' to do with the murder. It were just the same nasty old gossip I told you earlier, and I ain't repeatin' it in front of decent folk." He clamped his mouth shut and sat back, his expression utterly determined.

"In that case," Mrs. Jeffries said soothingly, "why don't we hear what the others have to say. Hatchet"—she smiled at the butler—"you and Wiggins seem bursting with news."

"Actually, Mrs. Jeffries," Hatchet began, "we do have news of sorts." He told them how he and the footman had successfully followed Jon's trail to Clacton. "I believe," he concluded, "that Wiggins's earlier information is correct. Jon did see something the night Mrs. Greenwood was murdered."

"Did he tell you that?" Mrs. Jeffries asked.

"No. Unfortunately, as soon as we arrived at the Hickman home, he ran off."

"Wouldn't a thought the little blighter could run so fast," Wiggins muttered. "I've still got a bit of stitch in me side from chasin' 'im all over Clacton."

Mrs. Jeffries ignored Wiggins's grumbling and looked at the butler. "Then what makes you think Jon knows something?"

Hatchet smiled. "He ran, madam. That means he was scared. The moment we appeared, he took off like a bat out of hell, if you'll pardon the expression. I believe he was genuinely afraid of us. Unfortunately, he managed to leap onto the London train before we could allay his fears."

"Bloomin' boy slipped right through our fingers," Wiggins muttered.

"However," the butler continued, "though we have momentarily lost the lad and his whereabouts are still unknown, we do have a plan."

Wiggins snorted. "Fat lot of good that's gonna do us."

"Now, Wiggins," Hatchet chided. "Don't be such a naysayer."

"I'm not," he protested. "But I don't see what good it's goin' to do 'angin' about the Greenwood 'ouse."

"I take it that's your plan?" Mrs. Jeffries interrupted.

Hatchet nodded. "Precisely. My theory is that the boy will go back to someplace with which he's familiar."

"Why not back to his cousins?" Betsy asked. "Wouldn't he be more likely to go to his kin?"

Hatchet shook his head. "I don't think so. I think he'd be afraid that would be the first place we'd look. My guess is that he'll go back to the Greenwood house. I suspect he might make contact with Timmy Reston or one of the other children in the neighborhood." He paused. "Actually, Wiggins and I went there before we came here. We spoke to Timmy."

"Had he seen Jon?" Mrs. Jeffries asked.

"No. But Timmy did tell us something else," Hatchet said gravely, "something which leads me to believe that Jon could well have seen the murderer that night."

"'E could've been lyin' 'is 'ead off, too," Wiggins protested.

"I don't think so," Hatchet replied, shaking his head. He looked at Mrs. Jeffries. "Timmy Reston is Jon's friend. He wouldn't deliberately give us information that might land the lad in big trouble."

"What kind of trouble?" Mrs. Goodge asked.

"Well," Hatchet said thoughtfully, "from the start, I've wondered why Jon was so frightened. Then I realized it might be because he'd seen the murderer. But from what we know, the only way Jon could have seen the killer was if he was on the second or third floor of the house. But how could he possibly be there? He'd admitted going to the kitchens and talking a few cooks and scullery maids out of a bite to eat, but the kitchen in the Marlow house is two floors below the place he'd have to have been to see anything useful. So I asked Timmy about it. After a good bit of hemming and hawing and trying to evade the question, Timmy admitted that Jon probably had been on the second or third floor that night. He occasionally did a bit of petty pilfering."

"You mean the lad's a thief!" Smythe exclaimed.

"I'm afraid so," Hatchet replied. "According to Timmy, Mrs. Greenwood was so stingy with food, the lad was often hungry. Jon pilfered a bit here and there, sold the goods, and used the money for food."

"That's disgusting," Mrs. Goodge snorted.

Hatchet held up his hand. "Don't judge the boy too harshly," he said. "Jon didn't just feed himself. He bought food for Timmy and some of the other children. Once, he even bought a bottle of cough medicine when one of younger Restons had the croup."

"That's no excuse," the cook protested. "Thieving is thieving."

"It bleedin' well isn't!" Betsy cried. "Not when you're starvin' to death."

Shocked, they all looked at her.

"Sorry," she mumbled, "I shouldn't have yelled. But I don't think it's right to condemn the boy because he lifted a few trinkets to buy a bit of food. If that nasty old Mrs. Greenwood had paid 'im a decent wage and fed 'im proper, he wouldn'a done it."

"How do you know he wouldn't a done it?" Mrs. Goodge asked. "Maybe he just likes stealing."

"Have you ever been hungry?" Betsy demanded, staring at the cook. "Have you ever had to walk the streets with your belly touching your backbone and wonderin' if you was ever goin' to have a hot meal and roof over your 'ead again? Have you ever been so hungry and so scared that you didn't give a fig for what anyone else thought was right? You'd do whatever you had to to stay alive."

Smythe reached over and laid his hand on Betsy's arm. "Easy, lass," he said softly. "No one's condemnin' the boy. We'll not be 'andin' 'im over to the police when we find 'im."

Betsy sank back in her seat and stared at her lap. She was deeply embarrassed. Her outburst was so obviously personal that you'd have to be deaf, dumb, and blind not to realize she'd been talking about herself. About her own past.

Mrs. Goodge patted the maid's shoulder. "I didn't mean to upset you, Betsy," she apologized softly. "Sometimes my tongue runs away with me. I know what you're sayin', though. Before the inspector give me a position, I was scared, too."

Betsy lifted her chin and gave the cook a shaky smile. "I'm sorry, too, I shouldn't have said anything—not to you, anyway. You feed half of London in this kitchen."

Mrs. Jeffries cleared her throat. "Well, now that we've cleared the air, so to speak, perhaps Hatchet can continue."

"There isn't really much else to tell you," he said. "Except to say that Timmy claims Jon was quite familiar with the Marlow house. He'd accompanied Mrs. Greenwood there many times."

"Lifted a few trinkets, too," Wiggins murmured.

"Tomorrow I'll go back to the Greenwood house and Wiggins will keep an eye on the Hickman house, just in case Jon does show up there. We'll take care to conceal ourselves. When the lad shows up, we'll do whatever we can to earn his trust." Hatchet looked at Betsy. "I promise you, we won't scare him or threaten him, and we certainly won't be handing him over to the police."

CHAPTER 10

"Has Mrs. Livingston-Graves come down?" Witherspoon asked Mrs. Jeffries. He pushed his empty breakfast plate to one side.

"Not yet, sir," she replied, turning her head slightly to hide a smile. When she'd walked past their houseguest's bedroom on her way downstairs, she'd heard the woman snoring loud enough to shake the walls. "I expect she'll sleep quite late this morning."

"Yes, well, that doesn't surprise me. But I do hope she's well enough to attend the festivities tomorrow."

"Festivities?"

Witherspoon dabbed at his lips with a white linen napkin. "The Jubilee," he reminded her. "Tomorrow's the Royal Procession. Surely you haven't forgotten? Why, the West End is ablaze with color. There are flags in Trafalgar Square, all the clubs along the Pall-mall have put up box seats, and the houses along the procession route are decorated with crimson banners and festoons. Gracious, they're even going to have a gigantic mound of fresh flowers in the middle of Piccadilly Circus. It will be a magnificent spectacle. I want the entire staff to have the day off. Everyone must get out and enjoy themselves."

"Why, thank you, sir," Mrs. Jeffries replied honestly. "How very kind of you. I'm sure it will be delightful." Actually, in light of the fact that they were investigating a murder, she'd quite forgotten about the Jubilee celebration. "Will you be continuing your investigation today?"

Witherspoon made a face. "I'm afraid I must. Duty before pleasure. I thought I'd pop around and have another chat with Shelby Locke."

"Are you going to tell him you have witnesses that saw him going outside?" she asked.

"If I must. Naturally, I'd prefer the fellow tell me the truth straight out." He sighed. "But I've not much hope of that. He seems very much in love with Mrs. Stanwick. I suspect he'll try and give her an alibi until the bitter end."

"From what you've told me, Mr. Locke does appear to be quite enamoured of the lady." Mrs. Jeffries reached for her teacup.

"I suppose being in love makes some men forget their principles," he muttered. "Understandable, really. But still, we can't have people dashing about and committing murder, can we?" The inspector cleared his throat. "Er, Mrs. Jeffries, I've a favor to ask."

She looked up sharply. "Of course, sir. What is it?"

"Well, you see, uh . . . I'm thinking about inviting Lady Cannonberry round for tea next Sunday afternoon."

"What a splendid idea, sir." She hoped they'd have this case solved by then.

"It seemed the least I could do," he mumbled, his cheeks turning pink. "After all, our evening at Miss Marlow's Jubilee Ball certainly didn't end very well. I was hoping you might write the invitation for me," he said, giving his housekeeper a pleading look. "I'm not very good at that sort of thing. And, if you'd be so kind as to plan the menu, I'd be ever so grateful."

"I'd be delighted, sir." She smiled broadly. "Mrs. Goodge and I will plan a splendid tea party for you and Lady Cannonberry. Just leave everything to me."

As soon as the inspector and Constable Barnes had left, Mrs. Jeffries hurried down to the kitchen.

Mrs. Goodge looked up from the pan of bread she'd just pulled out of the oven. "Is the inspector gone, then?"

"He and Constable Barnes are going to interview Shelby Locke this morning. Where is everyone else?"

"Wiggins and Hatchet took off right after breakfast to try and lay their hands on that boy." She carefully eased the loaves onto a cooling rack. "Betsy went upstairs to air out the linen cupboard, and Smythe's round back getting a bucket of coal."

From the staircase, they heard the heavy thump of slow footsteps. Then a low moan.

"That'll be her nibs." Mrs. Goodge smiled diabolically. "Too bad she's missed breakfast. I'll have to do up something special for her, won't I?"

"Mrs. Goodge," Mrs. Jeffries whispered sharply. "What are you up to?"

"Keepin' her nibs out of our hair," she hissed back just as Mrs. Livingston-Graves shuffled slowly into the room.

"I want a pot of tea," she croaked, glaring at them. Pale face a chalky white, thin hair straggling around her ears, and eyes bloodshot and ringed with purple, the woman looked like death warmed over. "What are you two staring at?" she snapped. Then she groaned and leaned against the cabinet. "I'm not well this morning."

"Morning, Mrs. Livingston-Graves," the cook said cheerfully.

She winced and her hand flew to her temple. "Morning," she muttered.

"How are you feeling?" Mrs. Jeffries asked softly.

"Would you like some fried bread for breakfast?" Mrs. Goodge said loudly. "I've just baked a fresh loaf, and I've got some really good bacon grease. Fresh, too. Cooked half a pound just this morning. You just sit yourself down and I'll fry you up a few slices in no time."

"Oh, God." Mrs. Livingston-Graves put her hand to her mouth and fled the kitchen. "I'll spend the rest of the day in my room," she choked out as she hurried down the hall.

"Good one, Mrs. Goodge," Smythe said, strolling in from the back hall, a bucket of coal dangling from each hand. He chuckled as he walked over to the stove and put the buckets down. "With the way 'er stomach's probably rumblin', just the thought of fried bread ought to keep Mrs. Livingston-Graves 'anging over a chamber pot for the rest of the day."

"Really, Mrs. Goodge"—Mrs. Jeffries tried hard to be stern, but her eyes twinkled—"that was most cruel."

"No, it wasn't." The cook grinned from ear to ear. "We've got a lot to do today. I didn't want her nibs hanging about stickin' her nose in our business."

"What did you do to Mrs. Livingston-Graves?" Betsy asked as she dashed into the room. "I just saw her on the stairs and she was positively green."

"She's not well," Mrs. Jeffries replied. "But that at least will serve to keep her out of our way today. Now, what are we all going to do?"

"Since I've aired them bloomin' linen cupboards," Betsy said, picking up a teatowel and starting to dry the plates, "I thought I'd slip back over to the Marlow house and see if I can find out anything else."

"What are you going to do, Mrs. Jeffries?" Smythe asked. He leaned against the doorway.

"Actually, I'm going to do some thinking," she replied, "There's something about this case that's been niggling me from the start. But I can't quite think what it is. Perhaps I should dust the drawing room. Mindless, repetitive activity frequently helps me to think better. Are you still planning on going to see what you can find out about Shelby Locke?"

The coachman shrugged. "Might as well. I'm still not convinced he's innocent. Protectin' a woman you're in love with is a powerful motive for a man. And he's definitely crazy about Mrs. Stanwick."

Smythe fiddled with filling the coal bins until Mrs. Jeffries, the feather duster neatly tucked under her arm, went upstairs. A moment later Mrs. Goodge trotted off toward the cooling pantry, mumbling something about gooseberries.

He and Betsy were alone. He looked at her. She stood with her back to him, stacking dishes in the cupboard. Smythe silently took a long, deep breath and gathered his courage. He couldn't stand the way she'd been avoiding him since her outburst yesterday. It was as though she were shamed that he and the others had had a glimpse of her life, her past. At breakfast this morning she'd kept her head down, staring at her lap like it was a newspaper, and then bolted from the table the minute she'd finished one bloomin' cup of tea. She hadn't even tried to eat Mrs. Goodge's homemade sausages. He wasn't havin' any of that.

What they shared together, all of 'em, was too precious. Betsy had no call to be embarrassed because she'd let something about herself slip out. And she should know them well enough to understand that there was nothin' in her past that would change the way he, or any of the others, felt about her. He was bloomin' tired of seein' her walk around with her eyes down and her shoulders hunched.

"Betsy," he said softly. "I'd like to talk to you, lass."

"What about?" she asked, without turning around.

"About what 'appened last night." He faltered, unsure of exactly what was the best way to say what he thought needed saying.

"I've already said I'm sorry for losin' my temper," she said defensively.

He sighed. This wasn't going to be easy. "Betsy, no one's lookin' for any apologies. I'm tryin' to tell ya we understand. I can tell you're still smartin' over it, and you've no need to. It's not like any of us 'asn't been . . . well, hard up a time or two in our lives."

Slowly she turned and stared at him. "It's nice of you to try and make me feel better, but I still feel a right fool. It were bloody obvious I was talkin' about myself." She gave him a shaky smile. "And it's embarrassing."

"There's no shame in 'aving been poor," he protested. "You did the best you could. You 'ad to survive."

She looked down at the floor. Blast and damn, he thought, I'm goin' about this all wrong. Maybe I shoulda kept my big mouth shut.

"So you don't think any less of me," she murmured so quietly he almost didn't hear her.

He took a step closer. "Not at all, lass. I'm just glad you're 'ere with us now." He reached out a hand, intending to touch her shoulder, but he snatched it back quickly as they heard the pantry door crash against the hallway wall.

"I'm going to skin that boy alive when I get my hands on him!" Mrs. Goodge cried as she charged into the kitchen. She stopped in surprise when she saw them. "You two still here, then?"

"Who are you goin' to skin alive, Mrs. Goodge?" Smythe asked, giving her a cocky grin.

"Wiggins, that's who! And when I'm finished with him, I might skin that ruddy Fred. They've been into them gooseberries again!"

"Mr. Locke," the inspector said politely. "We'd like you to tell us again about your movements on the night of the ball."

Locke arched an eyebrow. "I've already told you. Rowena and I were together the whole time except for those few moments when I was in the library with Miss Marlow. For goodness' sake, do you want me to give you a blow-by-blow account of every step we took?"

"That would be most helpful, sir," Barnes said politely.

"Don't be absurd!" Locke got up and began pacing the room. "Is this inquisition necessary? Rowena's waiting for me in the drawing room. We're going out."

The inspector sighed. He did so wish that people wouldn't persist in lying. It was so very demeaning. "Mr. Locke, we've had statements from several people who saw you leave the ballroom and go outside. Alone."

Locke stopped in front of a balloon-back chair. "Who told you that?"

"That isn't important. What is pertinent is that you weren't with Mrs. Stanwick at the time of the murder and we can prove it." Witherspoon stared him directly in the eye. "Not only were you outside, but Mrs. Stanwick was seen going upstairs after she'd had a rather heated argument with the murder victim. An argument, by the way, that was overheard by a witness."

The color drained out of Locke's face. For a moment he didn't say a word. "Rowena didn't do it," he finally said. "I don't care what anyone says they saw or heard. She didn't like Hannah Greenwood, but for God's sake, she didn't kill her."

"Mr. Locke, why don't you sit down and tell us the truth," the inspector suggested kindly. The man had gone so pale, Witherspoon was afraid he might faint. "I'm sure we can clear this matter up very quickly once we have all the facts."

"Facts?" He laughed harshly. "What have facts to do with hatred?" Sighing wearily, he dropped into the chair. "I'm not sure where to begin," he said. "I suppose everything began to go wrong when I asked Lucinda to come into the library with me. But you already know about that. What you don't know is that I wasn't discussing my missing notebook with Lucinda, I was telling her that I'd proposed to Rowena." Locke closed his eyes briefly. "I shouldn't have done it, you know. None of this would have happened if I hadn't left Rowena alone. That old witch couldn't have threatened her if she'd been with me."

"By 'old witch,' I take it you're referring to Mrs. Greenwood?" Witherspoon wanted everything crystal clear. Gracious, with these people, one never knew to whom they were referring unless one asked.

"Absolutely. And I don't care if she's dead," Locke said angrily. "She was an old witch. She couldn't wait to ruin Rowena's life." He paused and brought himself under control. "But that's not important now. I left Rowena alone in the ballroom, and I asked Miss Marlow to come into the library."

"So you were in the library longer than you originally led us to believe?" Witherspoon asked.

"I'm afraid so," he replied. "You see, I didn't want to admit that I'd been away from Rowena for such a long period of time. I was actually talking to Miss Marlow for a good ten, perhaps fifteen minutes."

"I take it Miss Marlow didn't take the news of your impending marriage very well," the inspector suggested.

"No." He shook his head. "She was actually very kind about it. Wished me well and all that. But, dash it all, I was concerned about her, you see. I mean, she was saying all the right words, yet her expression was so very odd that I kept right on talking to her. I suppose it was guilt on my part—I did, at one time, have an understanding with Miss Marlow. Anyway, she finally insisted she had to get back to her guests, and we left the room."

"So how did you come to be outside, sir?" Barnes asked.

"I went outside to get some fresh air." Locke rose to his feet. "Look at it from my point of view. I'd just behaved abominably to a lovely young woman, and she'd taken it with the best of grace. I was ashamed of myself. I wanted to get away where no one could see me and pull myself together." He began pacing the room again. "So I went down the hall, unbolted a side door and slipped outside."

"How long were you out there?" Witherspoon asked.

"I didn't come back inside until after Mrs. Greenwood was killed," he said softly. "After I'd been outside a few minutes, I tried to get back in, but someone had bolted the door on me. That side of the house leads off onto an alley, and the only way back in is to walk round to the front. It's a long walk, Inspector."

"Where was Mrs. Stanwick when you arrived back?"

"She was coming down the stairs."

"And Mrs. Greenwood was already dead."

Locke nodded. "But Rowena didn't kill her."

"Did you see anyone else come down the stairs?" Witherspoon prodded.

"A number of people." He flung his hands wide. "They were all coming down to see what the commotion outside was about."

Rowena Stanwick clutched Shelby Locke's hand. Her face was pale and her lovely eyes wide with fear. "Shelby's telling the truth, Inspector. I saw him coming in the front door as I came down the stairs."

"Do you admit you had an argument with Mrs. Greenwood?" Witherspoon asked. "And that she followed you upstairs?"

"Don't admit anything," Locke told her. "Don't say another word until we've talked to your solicitor."

She shook her head. "It's all right, Shelby. We don't need to send for Mr. Borland yet." She straightened her spine and looked at the two policemen sitting in front of her fireplace. "We did have an argument. A vicious one. She was going to ruin me. She was going to tell everyone that her son, Douglas, had committed suicide because I'd refused to marry him."

"Rowena, don't," Locke pleaded.

"It's all right, darling," she said, giving him a sad smile. "I must tell the truth. I'm not afraid anymore. Douglas Beecher didn't kill himself because of me. He had a terrible problem with alcohol. That's why I refused him. I'm not all that certain he committed suicide at all. When he was drunk, he did the most appalling things. Stepping in front of that train was most likely an accident. I'm sure of it."

"But Mrs. Greenwood was sure you were responsible," Witherspoon said. "And she threatened to tell the rest of the world—a scandal like that would have ruined you socially."

"Yes," she agreed, "it would have. But I knew it wouldn't cost me the one thing that really mattered to me. Shelby's love." She looked at him again.

"It hasn't," he promised softly.

"So after the argument, you went upstairs," the inspector prodded.

"Yes, I wanted to get away from her." Rowena crossed her arms over her chest. "She was half out of her mind that night. The things she said to me, it was unbelievable and very upsetting. When I realized I was losing control, I knew I had to get away from her. I went upstairs to the second floor."

"Did you hear her behind you on the stairs?" Barnes asked.

"No. I'd no idea she was following me. All I wanted to do was to find a quiet place to calm down," she explained. "I was in tears and I didn't want Shelby to see me like that. So I hurried upstairs and popped into an empty bedroom. A few minutes later I splashed some cold water from the washbasin on my face and started down. By that time someone had murdered Mrs. Greenwood. People were running about and shouting. I hurried downstairs to see what the commotion was, and that's when I saw Shelby coming in the front door."

"Are you certain you went no further than the second floor?" Witherspoon asked. He wasn't sure what to make of her story. Dash it all, unless the lady was a superb actress, it sounded as though she were telling the truth.

"I'm certain."

"Did anyone see you go into or come out of the bedroom?"

"No." She smiled bitterly. "Unfortunately. No one can verify my story. I was alone when I reached the top of the stairs. There was no one about. I didn't like Hannah Greenwood," she said earnestly. "But you've got to believe me, Inspector, I didn't kill the woman."

Wiggins poked Hatchet in the side and pointed toward the row of tiny houses. "Over there," he whispered. "There's someone movin' about in that passageway."

Stealthily they scurried out from behind their hiding place behind a heavy wagon loaded with rubbish and dashed across the road. They heard the sound of feet again, in the narrow space between the last two houses. "Go round the end," Hatchet hissed, pointing toward the end of the road. "Double back to the passageway. We can trap whoever's in there."

"But what if it's not Jon? What'll we say?"

"Get on with it, Wiggins," Hatchet snapped. Really, the lad was very good-hearted and all that, but sometimes he was a bit of a trial. "If it's not Jon, then it's probably a cat and we won't have to say anything."

Wiggins nodded and took off. Hatchet gave him what he hoped was enough time to complete the circuit before he moved to his end of the opening. The tiny space, barely wide enough for a broad-shouldered man to get through, was shrouded in deep shadows despite the afternoon sunlight.

Hatchet stepped inside. He heard a scrape, like a foot dragging against the ground. "Jon," he called out. "If you're there, don't be afraid. We only want to talk to you. I promise you, no one's going to hurt you."

There was no answer.

At the far end, he heard, rather than saw, Wiggins move into position. But the overhanging roof made the passage so dark he couldn't quite see. That, and the fact that his eyesight wasn't what it used to be. Squinting, he plunged farther inside.

Suddenly, he heard the hammering of footsteps as whoever it was made a run for it. Hatchet took off after them.

"Got you then, you little blighter!" Wiggins cried as a bundle of terrified boy exploded out of the passage and rammed into him hard enough to knock the wind out of him, but not hard enough to make him let go of the lad's arm.

Mrs. Jeffries had dusted the furniture, polished the brass candlesticks on the mantel, and buffed the banister until it gleamed in the late afternoon sun, but she was no closer to a solution. This case was simply baffling. She had the horrible feeling that she was missing something, but for the life of her, she couldn't figure out what it was.

Placing her tin of Adam's furniture polish on the table, she sat down and stared blankly at the rows of copper pots hanging below the window.

Mrs. Goodge had retired to her room to have a nap before dinner, and the rest of the staff was still out. She hoped they were having a better day than she was. She sighed and forced herself to go over everything one last time.

Hannah Greenwood had been viciously murdered by one of the other guests at the ball. There was no reason to believe a servant or an outsider had done the killing, because the victim was an isolated, lonely woman who didn't much care for people. She'd joined the circle only to have an opportunity to avenge her son's death.

Most of the members of the circle could account for their whereabouts at the time of the murder, so that let them out. Of the members that were left, the only ones that could have a reason to murder the victim were Dr. Sloan and Rowena Stanwick. Unless, she reminded herself, you included Shelby Locke. But his motive would only be reasonable if he'd known that Mrs. Greenwood planned on ruining Rowena Stanwick's reputation. And they had no evidence that he'd known anything of the kind. She made a mental note to talk to the inspector as soon as he came home.

Dr. Sloan's motive was fairly weak. Or was it? He'd confessed to being a plagiarist. Far less dangerous than confessing to murder. And, perhaps, far more clever.

Edgar Warburton. She made a face of distaste. Smythe had quietly told her the rest of the information he'd picked up about Warburton before breakfast this morning. She didn't much blame the coachman for not wanting to repeat what he'd heard in front of the rest of the household. Wiggins would have blushed to the roots of his hair. Warburton was obsessed with Rowena, enough so that he called other women by her name.

But if they believed Dulcie Willard, he did have an alibi for the time of the murder.

"Mrs. Jeffries."

Startled, she jerked her head around. "Yes, Mrs. Livingston-Graves. Is there something I can do for you?"

"Do you happen to have a stomach powder?" she asked, clutching her midsection. She staggered over to stand at the far end of the table. "I'm a bit under the weather today."

"I'm sorry you're not feeling better." Trying to keep a straight face, Mrs. Jeffries got up and went to the cupboard underneath the window. Rummaging around inside, she found a tin of Dinneford's Fluid Magnesia. "I'm afraid this is the best I can do," she said, holding it up.

Making a face, Mrs. Livingston-Graves reached for the medicine. She suddenly looked up at the window and gasped. "Oh, no, it's Mr. Freeley. He's not supposed to be here until tomorrow. Oh, dear, I can't receive him now!"

Mrs. Jeffries peeked around Mrs. Livingston-Graves and saw the back of a man paying off a hansom driver. "Would you like me to tell him you're indisposed?" she asked.

The man turned around.

"Thank God." Mrs. Livingston-Graves breathed a heartfelt sigh of relief. "It's not Mr. Freeley. But from the back, it certainly looked like him. I must get back to bed—I don't want to be ill tomorrow. Mr. Freeley is escorting me to the Royal Procession." Clutching the tin to her scrawny bosom, she hurried from the kitchen, muttering to herself with every step.

Mrs. Jeffries shook her head. Considering the state their houseguest was in yesterday, it was a wonder the woman had any notion of what this Mr. Freeley looked like.

At dinner that night the inspector told Mrs. Jeffries about his meeting with Shelby Locke and Rowena Stanwick. "So you see," he finished, "Mrs. Stanwick does not have an alibi at all."

"Neither does Mr. Locke," Mrs. Jeffries pointed out.

"I'm afraid he does," the inspector replied. "After we talked to both of them, Barnes and I checked with the carriage and hansom drivers who were outside the Marlow house that night. One of the drivers remembers seeing him."

"The driver is sure it was Shelby Locke?"

"Oh, yes, he knew Mr. Locke on sight, you see. He'd driven Mr. Locke and Mrs. Stanwick to the ball earlier." Witherspoon crumbled his napkin and tossed it next to his plate. "He also drove them home that night. He said Mrs. Stanwick was in an awful state."

"Are you going to arrest her?" Mrs. Jeffries asked. She held her breath.

"I'm afraid I may have to," he replied softly. "Though, I must admit, I tend to believe she's telling the truth. At the very least I'll have to bring her in tomorrow to answer some more questions."

"But tomorrow's the Jubilee and the Royal Procession."

"That makes no difference." He smiled sadly. "Nothing, not even a celebration of Her Majesty's ascension to the throne, is more important than justice."

His words would have sounded pompous, but Mrs. Jeffries knew he sincerely meant them. She sat back in her chair and tried to think. She could quite understand the inspector's reasoning, but something was bothering her. Something that was probably right in front of her but she couldn't see it. She glanced up and saw Betsy standing in the doorway of the dining room, waving frantically. "Excuse me, sir," she said, getting to her feet.

Betsy jerked her head toward the hall. "Hatchet and Wiggins is back," she hissed as soon as they were out of earshot. "They've got Jon with them, and they want to speak to the inspector."

"Goodness." Mrs. Jeffries frowned. "That could cause all sorts of problems."

"Hatchet's got it all figured out. He's goin' to send Jon round to the front door. Jon's goin' to claim he come to see the inspector 'cause he heard he was an honest copper. The boy won't let on he's talked to any of us," she said quickly. "Is that all right with you?"

"Fine," Mrs. Jeffries replied. "Send the boy around. I'll get the inspector into the drawing room."

Jon stared suspiciously at Witherspoon. He hoped them toffs wasn't havin' him on. If he ended up in Coldbath Fields or Newgate, he'd be right narked. Mind you, they'd done all right by him so far. Filled his belly with a hot meal before they begun askin' all their questions and that white-haired gent 'ad promised him work.

"Now, young man," Witherspoon began. "My housekeeper says you're here to see me about the murder of Mrs. Greenwood. Is that correct?"

"That's right," Jon replied. He'd been well coached on exactly what to say. "I come here instead of goin' down to the station 'cause I heard you was a good copper. Not like some of them others. I don't like havin' anythin' to do with the police, not if I can 'elp it. But I've heard about you, and I reckoned this might be important."

The inspector smiled at the boy. He was really quite flattered. Gracious, perhaps he was becoming a tad famous. "Finding Mrs. Greenwood's murderer is important," he said. "And you did right to come to me. But really, my boy, you've no reason to fear the police. We're here for your protection."

Jon grinned. The bloke looked like he actually believed what he said.

"Now"—Witherspoon waved at the settee—"do sit down." He waited until the boy had seated himself. "What is it you want to tell me?"

"It's about Mrs. Greenwood," he began. "About her gettin' herself done in. I were there that night."

"There," the inspector echoed, looking confused. "Where?"

"At the Marlow house," Jon explained. He hoped he didn't muck this up. This was goin' to be the tricky part. Tellin' the copper what he'd seen without tellin' him why he was hidin' up them stairs. "You see, I worked for Mrs. Greenwood. She always took me with her when she went out anywhere."

"Why did she do that?" he asked curiously.

Jon shrugged. "Who the bloody hell knows? I think she were half crazy. But I'm tellin' the truth. If'n you don't believe me, you can ask Mrs. Hackshaw, that's her sister. She'll tell you."

"I didn't say I didn't believe you," the inspector said hastily. "It's just that's a very odd thing to do."

"I think she wanted company," Jon said. "Not that she ever talked that much. Anyways, like I was sayin', she took me with her all the time when she went out."

"Did you accompany her to Dr. Sloan's rooms on the day of the ball?" he asked.

"Yeah, I did." Jon scratched his nose. "Even for her, she were in a strange way that day. Kept mumblin' to herself about vengeance and justice and how she'd have 'em both. By the time she come out of the old gent's rooms, her eyes were all bright and shiny like, and she were laughin' her bloomin' head off. Scared me some, I can tell you."

"Yes, I'm sure it did."

"Like I said, she took me with her, even to that ruddy ball," Jon continued. "She got out of the carriage, then she told me to stay close 'cause she wouldn't be stayin' too long. Give me strict instructions to be in front of the house at half past ten."

"Half past ten," the inspector murmured.

"Right. Now it get's a bit borin', hangin' about on the streets, so I nipped round and slipped in the kitchen door." He flushed in embarrassment and stared down at the carpet. "Sometimes the cooks or one of the maids will slip me a bit of food, and well . . . I was hungry."

"Of course you were, my boy," Witherspoon said kindly. "No one can fault you for wanting a bite to eat. Why, I've done that sort of thing myself when I was a lad of your age."

Jon looked up sharply. He couldn't imagine this gentleman ever bein' cold or hungry. But maybe he was wrong. Maybe the bloke did understand. "They was all busy in the kitchen; no one even noticed I were there." He didn't add that he'd deliberately ducked behind a table and hotfooted it up the back stairs.

Jon cleared his throat to give himself a moment to think. He had to say this part just right. Nice bloke or not, this gent was still a copper. "Anyways, like I said, I was right hungry. Mrs. Greenwood were on the stingy side, there were never enough food round there, and all I'd had for me dinner was a bit of hard beef and bread."

Witherspoon clucked his tongue. Really, the way some people treated their servants. It was an absolute disgrace! "I'm sure you were dreadfully hungry," he said sympathetically.

He nodded. "They was so busy in the kitchen, I didn't think they'd take kindly to me botherin' them for something to eat, so I nipped up the back stairs . . . I'd been there before, you see, and I was hopin' there might be some food in the pantry."

"Yes, yes, I quite understand."

"There was." Jon grinned. "And there was no one in there, either, so I helped meself to a couple of rolls and some ham, slapped 'em together like. Then I heard footsteps comin' and, well, I didn't want anyone to see me helpin' meself to the food, so I left and scampered up the back stairs to the second story. There's a nice little nook up there that's covered by a long curtain. I hid myself away and ate."

"How long were you up there?"

Jon knew he was on thin ice here. He'd spent a good two hours upstairs. But he could hardly explain his activities to the police. "Well," he said hesitantly: "I don't rightly know. There was lots of people comin' and goin'. And then a couple walked by, they was gigglin' and. . . . well, I think they was kissin'. They come right up to where I was hid. I was afraid they was going to open the curtain and see me. But at the last second someone called out to 'em and they left. But I knew I'd better not hang about where I was. So I waited till there was no one about and I nipped up to the next floor."

"So now you're on the third floor," Witherspoon stated, trying to keep everything straight in his mind.

"Right," Jon said. "I was tired by this time, so I tucked meself away in a corner behind the stairs and kept my eyes and ears open. It got tirin' after a while, even though I could see the floor below if I peeked over the side. I was there for a long time. Finally, when I thought it might be gettin' close to half past, I figured I'd better scarper. Mrs. Greenwood would be madder than a skinned cat if I was late. I was just gettin' out of me hiding place when all of a sudden, here she comes up the stairs. For a minute I thought I'd been found out and she was up there to tear a strip off me. But she didn't even look at me, kept right on goin', a funny look on her face."

"She continued up the stairs?" Witherspoon clarified. "Is that correct?"

"That's right. I wondered where she were goin'. Wasn't nothing up there but the attic and a box room, but that's where she went all right. A minute or two later I heard more footsteps. By this time I'd come out from behind the staircase, and I didn't reckon I could make it back before whoever was comin' up those stairs saw me, so I flattened myself behind a set of curtains over the window at the end of the hall and prayed that whoever it was wouldn't see me feet."

"And who did you see coming up the stairs?" the inspector asked quietly.

"A pretty lady in a blue dress. She were carrying a knife."

CHAPTER 11

The day of the Jubilee dawned clear and beautiful. Mrs. Jeffries smiled as she pulled open the drawing room curtains and let the sunshine fill the room. She still wasn't certain about this case; that tiny niggle at the back of her mind refused to go away.

And she didn't understand why. Jon's statement had made it quite clear that Rowena Stanwick was the killer. Why, even the inspector had remembered Mrs. Stanwick's spectacular blue gown. She shook herself. Really, she must be getting old and fanciful. A smidgen of doubt hovering in the corner of one's mind was no substitute for facts.

And besides, she told herself, as she started for the kitchen, once Jon got a good look at Mrs. Stanwick today, all her concerns would be laid to rest. The boy had no reason to lie.

She smiled again as she recalled the adroit maneuvers of last night. Her staff had done her proud. Just as the inspector was wondering where to put Jon for the night, Hatchet, as planned, had shown up. Upon hearing of the inspector's dilemma, he'd immediately volunteered to take the lad home with him. As he'd said to Inspector Witherspoon, "It wouldn't do for the defense counsel to find out the Crown's only eyewitness was living with the policeman who solved the case."

Actually, Mrs. Jeffries thought as she marched down the back stairs to the kitchen, she didn't see what difference it made where the boy stayed. But the inspector had seemed to think Hatchet was correct, and Jon had gone off quite happily.

In the kitchen Betsy and Mrs. Goodge were sitting at the table, drinking tea.

"Is Smythe back yet?" Mrs. Jeffries asked.

"Not yet," Betsy replied. "It might take him longer than usual. The streets are packed with people. You can barely move out there. All the main roads are closed because of the Royal Procession." She frowned. "I hope he doesn't have any trouble gettin' back. I won't really be able to enjoy myself today unless this case is solved."

"Don't worry about Smythe," Mrs. Goodge said. "He'll not have any problem gettin' through the mob. He knows this city like the back of his hand. He'll not need the main roads. The man knows every back street and mews from here to Liverpool Street."

"I hope you're right, Mrs. Goodge." Mrs. Jeffries cast a worried glance at the kitchen clock. "Hatchet and Jon are due here in a few minutes."

As it would be impossible for the inspector to find a hansom today, considering the number of people clogging the streets of the West End, Smythe had volunteered to bring round the inspector's carriage and drive him and Jon to Rowena Stanwick's home. Naturally, the inspector had protested, not wanting his coachman to have to work on a day the rest of London was celebrating. But Smythe had assured him he didn't mind in the least.

"Are they goin' to take Jon straight to Mrs. Stanwick's house, then?" Betsy asked. "To see if he can identify her?"

"That's the plan."

"Mrs. Jeffries!" Mrs. Livingston-Graves's voice screeched down the stairs. "Could you come up here, please?"

"Right away, Mrs. Livingston-Graves." Rolling her eyes, she got to her feet.

"She's got no call to be orderin' you about like that," Betsy mumbled resentfully.

"At least she said please," Mrs. Goodge put in mildly.

"Not to worry," the housekeeper replied cheerfully as she hurried toward the door. "Her Mr. Freeley should be here soon, and she'll be out of our way for the rest of the day." She paused in the doorway. "Let's hope that today she can recognize the man."

Betsy and Mrs. Goodge laughed.

"What took you so long?" Mrs. Livingston-Graves whined as soon as Mrs. Jeffries appeared at the top of the steps. "Mr. Freeley will be here any minute, and I can't get these silly buttons done up." She lifted her arms, revealing the unbuttoned sleeves.

"Let me help you," Mrs. Jeffries said. Deftly she pushed the tiny black buttons through the gray fabric. "There," she said, "you're all done. And I believe I hear footsteps coming up the front stairs now."

"Answer the door, then," Mrs. Livingston-Graves ordered. She stepped back and smoothed her skirts.

There was a timid knock. Mrs. Jeffries threw open the front door. Before her eyes stood a short, rabbitty-faced man in spectacles wearing a brown bowler hat, brown suit, and carrying an umbrella. "Good morning, I'd like to see Mrs. Livingston-Graves." He smiled hesitantly.

"Please come in," Mrs. Jeffries said politely. "And I'll announce you."

As Mrs. Livingston-Graves had dashed into the drawing room, Mrs. Jeffries had to go get her. "Your escort is here," she said formally.

Nose held high, Edwina Livingston-Graves waltzed into the hall. She stopped dead, her small eyes blinking in surprise. "Mr. Freeley?"

He smiled broadly. "Edwina," he said, "how delightful to see you again. But I did ask you to call me Harold. My, don't you look lovely today."

Mrs. Jeffries wondered if he needed new spectacles. She also wondered exactly how much Mrs. Livingston-Graves had had to drink before she made Mr. Freeley's acquaintance.

Hatchet and Jon arrived a few minutes later. Mrs. Jeffries had started up the stairs to get the inspector when Smythe burst into the room.

"Somethin' funny is goin' on at the Stanwick house," he said without preamble. "And I think the inspector ought to hear about it."

"Hear about what?" Witherspoon asked as he strolled into the kitchen.

Smythe shot Mrs. Jeffries a quick, hard look. "Well, sir. I were on my way back from the livery with the coach, and I had to pass by the Stanwick place. I saw the oddest thing—that Mr. Locke were at her front door, arguin' with the maid."

"You saw all this from the coach?" Witherspoon asked in confusion.

"No, sir," he admitted, shooting another uncertain glance at the housekeeper. "I, uh . . . uh. . . ."

"Oh, it's all right, Smythe." The inspector smiled. "I know how you and the rest of the staff are always looking after my interests. It's quite all right for you to admit you stopped the coach and did a bit of snooping."

Mrs. Jeffries held her breath. Gracious, had the inspector cottoned on to what they'd been doing?

"That's right, sir," Smythe replied. "That's exactly what I did. A bit of snoopin', as you call it." He took a deep breath and plunged ahead. "I overheard the maid tellin' Mr. Locke that Mrs. Stanwick weren't at home. The maid said Mrs. Stanwick had just left, she'd gotten a message sayin' there was an emergency meetin' of the Hyde Park Literary Circle."

"Gracious!"

"Mr. Locke got right angry. Said 'e was a member of the circle and 'e 'adn't 'ad any message."

"Where was this meeting to take place?" Mrs. Jeffries asked.

"At the Marlow house."

Mrs. Jeffries saw Betsy start in surprise.

"Oh, dear," the inspector murmured. "This does complicate matters."

"What are they talkin' about, guv?" Jon said to Hatchet. "I thought I was goin' to identify the woman that come up them stairs,"

"That's right, boy," Hatchet replied, throwing Mrs. Jeffries a rather puzzled look. "And so you will. But I do believe we may have to postpone that for an hour or two. At least until the inspector decides what he wants to do."

"I say"—Witherspoon shook his head—"this is getting muddled." Dash it all, what should he do now? He couldn't go haring all over London looking for Rowena Stanwick. Goodness knows where the woman had gone. There was no point in sending a message to the Yard, either. With the mobs of people in town for the Jubilee, it would be pointless for the uniformed lads to even try spotting her at the train stations or the coach houses. Drat.

"All right," Jon muttered. "I don't mind waitin'."

Betsy rose and went into the hall. Mrs. Jeffries went after her. "Mrs. Jeffries," the maid whispered. "Something's wrong. Very wrong."

"What do you mean?" Mrs. Jeffries had great respect for the maid's intelligence and even greater respect for her instincts.

"There can't be any emergency meetin' at the Marlow house," Betsy said earnestly. "Rupert told me yesterday that Miss Marlow was givin' them all the day off. A woman like her don't have guests round unless there's a house full of servants to wait on 'em."

"But why would Rowena Stanwick . . ." Mrs. Jeffries suddenly stopped. A vision of Mrs. Livingston-Graves standing in front of the kitchen window flashed into her mind. The last puzzle piece fell into place, "Oh, Lord," she exclaimed. "We've got it all wrong."

Turning, she dashed back into the kitchen. They all looked at her in surprise. "Jon," she said, "what color hair did the lady have, the one coming up the stairs with the knife?"

Jon, who was reaching for one of Mrs. Goodge's currant buns, snatched his hand back when he heard his name. "Huh?"

"I asked what color the lady's hair was?"

"Brown," he said promptly. "She had brown hair."

"But that can't be right," Witherspoon exclaimed. "Mrs. Stanwick has fair hair." He stared at Jon. "Are you absolutely certain?"

Jon nodded and snatched up a bun. "Course I am. I'd a told you last night, but no one asked."

Smythe cracked the whip in the air and urged the horses down the narrow mews. Blast, they'd never make it to the Marlow house in time, and he had a bad feelin' about this one. Real bad.

"Do hurry, Smythe," Witherspoon called from below.

"We're almost there!" he yelled back. He pulled the reins hard, guiding the animals round a sharp corner and onto the small road that connected with the mews behind the Marlow house.

Smythe set the brake and jumped down. "This is as close as we can get," he said, jerking open the door. "There's too much traffic out front to get through, so we'll have to go round."

Witherspoon, Hatchet, and Wiggins, accompanied by Fred, jumped out of the carriage. They raced down the road.

When they arrived at the front of the Marlow house, Witherspoon was breathless, Hatchet was red in the face, and Fred was barking his head off.

"Stay outside with Fred," the inspector told the footman. "Hatchet, you and Smythe come with me."

Wiggins nodded and quieted the dog while the inspector banged the brass knocker hard against the wood. From inside they heard a scream.

"Egads!" Frantically Witherspoon tried the doorknob. It was locked.

Smythe shoved the inspector out of the way. "Let me 'ave a go at it," he said, bashing his shoulder against the door. He winced in pain, but the door didn't budge.

"This way," Hatchet called. "You'll never get through that door. It's solid mahogany."

They whirled around and saw Hatchet shove a booted foot through the front window. From inside the screams started again, Fred started barking again.

Within seconds they'd kicked the glass out of the way and climbed inside. The screams were louder now, frantic.

Running, fearing the worst, the three men charged for the drawing room. Smythe had no trouble shouldering that door open as he hurtled himself into the room, the others right behind him.

He came to a screeching halt at what he saw. Behind him, Witherspoon and Hatchet froze.

Lucinda Marlow had a knife to Rowena Stanwick's throat.

"Don't come any closer," she warned.

"Now, now, Miss Marlow," the inspector said gently. "We don't want anyone to get hurt, do we?"

Lucinda laughed and jerked her captive's head back farther. "Of course we do, you stupid fool. That's why I've got a knife."

Smythe looked helplessly at Hatchet. The inspector didn't dare take his eyes off that awful knife. He tried again, "Miss Marlow—"

"Shut up," she ordered, pushing the blade harder against her victim's throat. "Just shut up and let me think."

Rowena whimpered and, without moving, pleaded with her eyes for the inspector to save her. "Please," she moaned. "Let me go."

"I told you to be quiet," Lucinda snapped. "This is all your fault. You should have already been dead." She yanked Rowena's head back farther and dug the blade in deeper against the woman's throat.

Rowena screamed.

Witherspoon didn't know what to do. He couldn't stand and watch a helpless woman be murdered before his eyes.

Suddenly Fred burst into the room, barking his head off.

Lucinda Marlow yelped in surprise and tightened her grip on Rowena's hair. Rowena screamed again. The confused dog, sensing that something was terribly wrong and not knowing what it was, lunged at the two women.

The knife went flying in the air as they fell backwards. Hatchet slammed his foot down on the blade seconds after it clattered on the floor. Smythe leapt across the settee and made a grab for Rowena Stanwick. The inspector, who'd never mishandled a female in his life, wished he were anywhere else but here, did his duty, and pounced on Lucinda Marlow. He didn't really have to do much, though. Fred had already taken care of her.

Sitting on her chest, he wagged his tail as he licked her face.

"Cor blimey," Wiggins said from the doorway. "I'm sorry about Fred, but he heard the screams and I couldn't hold him back. He thought somethin' was happenin' to the inspector."

"How did you know it were Lucinda Marlow?" Mrs. Goodge asked as soon as everyone but Witherspoon had returned. Poor Witherspoon had arrested Lucinda Marlow. He was going to spend the rest of Jubilee Day taking statements and filling out forms.

"I didn't know until Betsy mentioned that Miss Marlow had given her servants the day off." Mrs. Jeffries pushed the plate of cakes down the table to Jon.

"How did that make you realize what was goin' on?" Betsy asked. "The inspector give us the day off."

"Yes, but the inspector is a very rare sort of human being." She picked up her teacup. "As I said from the start, something about this case bothered me. Yesterday, when Mrs. Livingston-Graves saw that man get out of the hansom cab, she thought it was Mr. Freeley. As soon as he turned around, she realized her mistake." She looked at Betsy. "When you told me that Lucinda Marlow had given everyone the day off, everything fell into place."

"I still don't get it," Wiggins mumbled.

"It's very simple," Mrs. Jeffries explained. "So simple that none of us understood until it was too late. Hannah Greenwood was never the intended victim. She was murdered by mistake."

"Mistake?" Smythe mumbled.

"Lucinda Marlow murdered the wrong woman. Rowena Stanwick told the inspector the truth," Mrs. Jeffries continued. "She hadn't gone up that second flight of stairs. But Lucinda Marlow didn't know that— remember, she'd seen Rowena go upstairs, and that gave her the perfect opportunity. She followed her, went all the way to the balcony at the very top, shoved the knife in her back and toppled her over."

"But she didn't kill Mrs. Stanwick," Smythe said.

"But she didn't know that until it was too late." Mrs. Jeffries smiled.

"All she saw was a slender blond woman in a blue dress going upstairs. Miss Marlow has very poor eyesight."

"That's right!" Betsy exclaimed. "Rupert told me she wears spectacles when there's no one about."

"It's a wonder we figured it out at all." Annoyed with herself for being so dense, Mrs. Jeffries shook her head in disgust. "It was so obvious from the start. From the moment we learned that Shelby Locke's poems had been stolen, we should have known."

"Huh?" This from Mrs. Goodge.

"Don't you see?" Mrs. Jeffries explained. "We've been looking at it backwards from the beginning. Mrs. Greenwood was never the intended victim. All along, it was Rowena Stanwick. I think Miss Marlow started planning to murder Mrs. Stanwick from the moment she realized she'd lost Shelby Locke forever."

"But the murder weren't planned," Smythe pointed out. "Or if it were, it were right messy."

"The actual crime itself wasn't planned," Mrs. Jeffries said, "but I think from the moment Miss Marlow realized Locke was genuinely in love with Rowena Stanwick, she'd planned to kill her. Look at it this way. Locke told Miss Marlow of his intentions that night in the library. According to what Locke said, she took it very well—she should have, she'd had plenty of time to prepare herself. They leave the library, and she watches Shelby let himself out the door at the end of the hallway. Then, from her vantage point somewhere in the dining room, she sees Rowena stumble into the buffet table and go upstairs."

"But wouldn't she have seen Mrs. Greenwood following Mrs. Stanwick?" Hatchet asked.

"No, you see, she wanted to make sure she had some time alone with Mrs. Stanwick, and the one person liable to disturb them was Shelby Locke. So she hurried down the hall and rebolted the door. It was at this point that Mrs. Greenwood started up the stairs. But Miss Marlow couldn't have seen that. She hurries back and starts up—but she doesn't realize that Mrs. Stanwick has ducked into a bedroom on the second floor. All she sees is a blond-haired woman in a blue dress going up to the third floor." She paused. "Of course, you know the rest."

"But how did she get downstairs so quick after she done the murder?" Wiggins asked.

"The back stairs," Mrs. Jeffries replied. "Once the commotion started, all the servants had run outside to see what was going on. Miss Marlow had a clear run at it. She dashed down, rushed out onto the terrace, and it was at this point that she realized she killed the wrong woman."

The inspector didn't get home until late that night. Betsy, Smythe, Wiggins, and Jon had gone out with Hatchet to see the lights and decorations. After that the butler was treating them all to a late supper. No one had seen hide nor hair of Mrs. Livingston-Graves, but Mrs. Jeffries refused to worry about the woman or to say anything to the inspector. From the look of him, he'd had a very trying day.

Mrs. Jeffries placed a cup of cocoa in front of him as he sat glumly at the kitchen table. "There, sir. This ought to help revive your spirits."

"Thank you, Mrs. Jeffries, but I'm not sure anything can revive me." He took a sip and closed his eyes briefly. "She's quite mad, you know. She kept telling us over and over that she had to kill her."

"Was it jealousy, sir?"

"No," he replied. "Some may call it that: But it was really madness." He toyed with the handle of his mug. "Do you know, I couldn't quite get her to understand that she'd killed the wrong person. That her first victim had been Mrs. Greenwood and not Mrs. Stanwick. But she wouldn't believe it, she kept insisting that Mrs. Stanwick, Rowena, as she called her, wouldn't stay dead."

"She sounds quite mad."

"She is." The inspector sighed. "But I doubt she'll stand trial. Her solicitors are already working on her case. The family stepped in immediately, of course. They don't want any scandal. I finally asked her, I said, 'Miss Marlow, surely you didn't think you'd get away with murder? You were bound to get caught.' Do you know what she replied? She gave me this very bizarre smile, it was as though she could see right through me, and said, 'Why should I think they'd catch me? They never did before.'"

It was several days before the household settled back into its normal routine. Mrs. Livingston-Graves had crept back to Upper Edmonton Gardens in the wee hours of Jubilee Day. She and Alphonse left for home the next morning. No one was sorry to see either of them go.

Mrs. Jeffries and Mrs. Goodge were in the kitchen making a provisions list when Betsy burst into the room. "Look at this!" she cried, putting a bright gold coin on the table. "Someone's left it on my pillow."

"I got one, too," the cook said.

"As did I," Mrs. Jeffries added. She picked up the coin. "It's a Jubilee sovereign," she explained, "newly minted. See, here's the date, 1887. Someone wanted us to have a souvenir."

"Did everyone get one?" Betsy asked.

"One what?" Wiggins asked as he and Smythe entered the room. Fred trotted along behind them.

"One of these." Betsy showed him the coin.

"Found it on me pillow this mornin'," Wiggins answered.

"Me, too." The coachman sat down next to Mrs. Jeffries.

The teakettle began to whistle, and Betsy and Mrs. Goodge made tea.

"I wonder who give these to us?" Betsy said. "Do you think it was Mrs. Livingston-Graves?"

"Not bloomin' likely," Smythe replied.

Mrs. Jeffries looked doubtful. "I shouldn't think so, Betsy. Mrs. Livingston-Graves didn't strike me as a particularly generous soul."

"Maybe it was Hatchet," the cook guessed. "He's a right kind-hearted man. Look at the way he took Jon in and give him a position."

"Wonder what Luty Belle will think of that." Smythe grinned.

"We can ask her herself in a few moments," Mrs. Jeffries said, nodding her head toward the back door. "That sounds like her coach pulling up now."

A few moments later Luty Belle, loaded down with gaily wrapped packages and followed by a grinning Hatchet, charged into the kitchen of Upper Edmonton Gardens. "I'm downright mad at the bunch of you!" she exclaimed, dumping the packages on the table. "But seein' as I brung this stuff thousands of miles, I'll give it to you anyways."

"Why, Luty, whatever is the matter?" Mrs. Jeffries asked.

"Madam is rather annoyed that in her absence we investigated a murder," Hatchet explained with a smirk.

"The minute my back's turned," Luty grumbled, giving Betsy a quick hug, "someone gets themselves murdered and I miss it!"

She cuffed a grinning Wiggins on the ear and patted Mrs. Goodge on the hand. Smythe laughed and scooped the elderly American woman up in a bear hug. Luty snickered, caught herself having fun and sobered instantly. "Put me down, you sneakin' varmint. I knows you all did it a purpose. Couldn't wait till I was gone so you could start havin' a good time."

She glared at the smug smile on her butler's face. "And you can wipe that gloat off yer face, Hatchet," she called as Smythe released her and she swung into a chair next to Mrs. Jeffries.

"I'm not gloating, Madam," Hatchet replied.

Luty snorted. "Stop lying, man, you'll grow warts on yer tongue. But enough of this. Now you all open them presents I brung you, and then you tell me every single thing. Just 'cause I weren't here don't mean I don't want to know everything."

Laughing and chatting, they did as she ordered.

Mrs. Jeffries opened her box first. "Why, Luty, this is magnificent," she said. "How very kind of you." She drew a pair of binoculars out of the box and held them up. "And they'll be so very useful."

"That's why I brung 'em for ya." Luty chuckled. "They's the best kind made, not like them piddly little opera glasses. Considerin' all the snoopin' you do on the inspector's cases, I figured they might come in handy. Bought myself a pair, too."

Mrs. Jeffries appeared stunned. "I don't know what to say. These must have been dreadfully expensive. . . ."

"Pish-posh," Luty snapped. "Just say thank you and leave it at that. Betsy, girl, you open yours now."

Betsy tore the paper off the rather large box, popped open the lid and gasped. "It's a traveling bag!" she cried, pulling the brown leather case out.

"Well, open it up," Luty ordered.

Betsy sprung the catches. "Look at this, it's got everythin' in it." Carefully she drew out the removable center. "Ivory brushes, soap box, toothbrush box, glove stretchers—goodness Luty, it's got bloomin' everything in it. Oh, thank you, thank you so much."

Luty acknowledged her thanks with a wave. "Your turn, Mrs. Goodge."

The cook opened her package and let out a squeal. She held up a watch and shiny gold chain. "It's a lady's watch and a Victoria chain. Oh, really, Luty, I shouldn't accept this. . . ."

"Pish-posh," Luty said again. "What's the good of havin' money if I can't spend it on my friends? I bought that watch in New York, and you're danged well gonna enjoy it."

"Can I open mine now?" Wiggins asked, clutching his package.

At Luty's nod he ripped open the box. "Cor blimey!" he cried, drawing out a pair of shiny black boots. There was elaborate engraving on the leather.

"Those are cowboy boots," Luty told him. "And I had to guess about the size, so you'd best try 'em on."

Smythe opened his last. He tossed the lid to one side and his eyes widened.

"Well, show us," Betsy ordered as he continued to stare at the contents of the box.

Slowly, holding his breath, he drew out the gun and held it up.

"Don't worry," Luty said, "it's not loaded."

"Blimey, Luty Belle," he muttered with a wide smile, "you sure know how to surprise a bloke."

"It's a Colt .45," Luty said chattily. "I picked it up in Colorado. Thought you might like it. Hatchet said he'd be glad to teach you how to use it."

"I know how to use it," Smythe replied as he studied the weapon. "But thanks for the offer." He glanced up and faltered as he saw all of them staring at him.

"You know how to use that weapon?" Mrs. Jeffries queried softly.

"Well," he sputtered. "Not very well. But I did use one a time or two when I was in Australia."

"I didn't know you was ever in Australia," Betsy said hastily. "How come you never said anything?"

Smythe was quite sure he'd already said way too much. Mrs. Jeffries had been giving him funny looks all morning. Maybe buyin' them sovereigns hadn't been such a good idea. But blast, he'd wanted them all to have a remembrance. And them sovereigns was worth a pretty penny, enough so that Betsy wouldn't ever have to feel destitute again. She'd have a little somethin' to hang on to if he weren't around to look after her.

"All right, now that you've had your presents," Luty ordered, settling back in her chair, "tell me all about this latest murder."

Mrs. Jeffries, after giving Smythe one last puzzled glance, did just that.

When she'd finished, Luty shook her head. "Sounds like you all did a right fine job. Did the inspector ever find out what Lucinda Marlow meant, you know what I mean, when she claimed the police hadn't ever caught her before?"

Mrs. Jeffries shook her head. "No. Right after she made those statements, she . . . well, she stopped talking."

"Faking bein' crazy?" Luty suggested.

"I don't think she's fakin'," Smythe put in. "The woman's as mad as a march hare."

"The inspector did tell me that they suspect Lucinda Marlow may have murdered her brother," Mrs. Jeffries explained. "She was nursing him when he died. He spoke to the Marlow physician. The doctor admits he was surprised when the Marlow son died, because he'd been on the mend. Right before he'd become ill, he and Lucinda had had a terrible row over some young man. He'd ordered her not to see him again. Then he died. Lucinda did as she pleased. But whether she murdered her brother or not, no one will ever know."

Luty shrugged. "I reckon we won't. Still, I'm sorry I missed it."

"You don't mind about Jon?" Betsy asked quickly. "I mean, this is twice now you've had to take on more staff because of one of our cases."

Once before, Luty had taken on a young girl and given her a position because of her involvement in one of the inspector's murder investigations.

"Essie Tuttle's worked out real well," Luty replied.

Hatchet snorted.

"Course she drives Hatchet crazy," the American cackled with glee. "She does love talkin' about books and politics."

"It was your idea that I teach Essie to read," he complained. "So you've only yourself to blame if the girl becomes an anarchist."

"Fiddlesticks, she ain't no anarchist, Essie just likes a good argument." She grinned wickedly. "And Hatchet's her favorite target. He bein' such a fan of the established order and the monarchy. But as long as this Jon don't get a case of sticky fingers, we'll get by just fine. He seems a smart boy."

"That's very good of you, Luty," Mrs. Jeffries said.

"Well, like I said, I'm right sorry to have missed everything," Luty said. "Course none of you are to blame. It's all *her* fault."

"Whose? Hannah Greenwood, the victim?" Mrs. Jeffries asked. "But she didn't plan on getting murdered."

"Who said anything about Hannah Greenwood!" Luty exclaimed. "I'm talking about Queen Victoria. It was her danged Jubilee that sent me running for the hills. Well, never again. This is the last time I'm going to miss me a murder."

MRS. JEFFRIES ON THE TRAIL

To Bob and Virginia Woods. Two wonderful people who never minded opening their hearts or their home to a horde of nieces and nephews. With love and thanks for golden afternoons of summers past and for letting a daydreaming little girl spend hours on your front-porch swing.

CHAPTER 1

"It's deader than a ruddy rat's arse tonight, ducks. You might as well pack it in and give yer feet a rest," Millie Groggins yelled to her friend on the other side of the Strand. She tossed the end of her thin, tatty scarf over her shoulder and sauntered towards the flower seller.

Annie Shields smiled wearily and glanced around the deserted street. Millie was right. It'd been over fifteen minutes since the last person had passed and that had been a copper. Suddenly she heard footsteps. She tensed and stared hard in the direction of the sound.

"'Bout bleedin' time we 'ad some trade," Millie muttered, cocking her head to one side and plastering a warm smile on her bony face.

From out of the fog, a man dressed in a caped greatcoat and carrying an umbrella came towards them. Annie stared at him hopefully. He brushed past her without so much as a glance.

"'Ello, love," Millie called. But the man ignored her, too.

Disappointed, Annie sighed. There wasn't any point in hanging about any longer. They weren't coming. No one was coming. She gave the street one last, long look, but she couldn't see much of anything now. Even the bright lights of the theatres just ahead had been dimmed by the thick fog drifting in off the Thames. She shivered and shuffled her feet. It was bloody cold, too.

The whole area was empty. Almost frightening. Annie shook herself and was glad that Millie hadn't left yet. She'd been stupid to come out tonight.

"I reckon you're right, Millie," she said as she reached for a basket of chrysanthemums and stacked it on her cart. "We both might as well pack it in. Neither of us'll 'ave any business tonight."

"You can say that again," Millie agreed, her tone disgusted. She gazed thoughtfully at the flower seller. "What you doin' out this late?"

Annie hesitated. "Just tryin' to pick up some extra business," she finally said. No sense in telling Millie everything.

"You picked a bad night for it," Millie muttered angrily. "Bleedin' riots." She glared in the direction of the theatres.

"What's the riots got to do with it?" Annie asked. She didn't really care all that much. But she was starting to feel fidgety and the sound of a familiar voice helped keep her nerves steady.

"They've got everything to do with it. Them riots today is what's kept our customers away. Everyone's afraid to go out what with them damned nationalists takin' to the streets. Bloody Irish! Always screamin' and fightin' about somethin'. And who pays fer it? We do! That's who." She snorted angrily. "'Ow's a body to make a livin' when the bloomin' streets are empty? And 'ow am I gonna make me rent tonight? That's what I'd like to know?"

Annie gave her one quick, sympathetic glance and then looked away. Millie stood huddled under the gas lamp, blowing on her fingers to keep them warm. "Ruddy 'ell, it's cold tonight," she said in between puffs.

Annie knew desperation when she heard it, but she didn't look up. Millie Groggins wasn't her problem. It didn't do to go sticking your nose in other people's troubles. But then she heard the familiar clicking sound of chattering teeth. She couldn't stand it. She patted her coat pocket and bit her lip. Despite the lack of customers, she had money. Swallowing hard, she forced herself to look towards the dim circle of light where the other woman was vainly trying to keep warm.

Annie's heart sank. From the look of things, Millie was flat-out skint. With her threadbare coat, a scarf that was nothing more than a scrappy bit of thin yarn, and a tatty hat with droopy plumes, even in the poor light, Millie looked pathetic. Her expression was stark and fearful, her body thin from not having enough food, and her clothes were no protection at all against the damp cold of night.

Annie shivered. At least she had a roof over her head tonight, she thought. Poor Millie would be sleepin' in a doorway if she didn't help her. Besides, she reasoned, tomorrow *he'd* come and he was always good for a fiver. But what if he didn't come?

Millie suddenly ran her hands up and down her arms in another futile attempt to get warm. Annie made up her mind. Millie was her friend, and if she had to kip out tonight, she might get sick. It was too bloody cold.

Never mind that any coins she slipped to Millie would probably never be repaid. She'd had a bit of good fortune lately and it wouldn't hurt to share it with someone who was down on her luck.

Annie finished putting her few remaining flower baskets onto the cart. When she loaded the last one, she glanced at her friend again. Millie was still muttering curses on the heads of the Irish, the anarchists, the police, and the cowardly toffs who were locked up safely in their houses. Her colorful curses made Annie smile.

Most of the other flower sellers wouldn't even speak to someone like Millie, but Annie liked her. She was good company and she felt sorry for her too. No one liked havin' to walk the streets at night and sell their bodies just to keep a bit of food in their bellies. Horrible, that was. But she could understand why some had to do it. She'd come close to having to do it herself.

Even if *he* didn't come, she had a bit tucked away for a rainy day. Annie reached into her coat pocket. Her gloved fingers were stiff with cold, so it took her a moment to get the coins in her hand. She strolled over to stand next to her friend. "'Ere, take this," she ordered.

Millie stared at Annie's outstretched palm, her eyes widening at the sight of the florins and shillings. "What's all this, then?"

"What's it look like? It's money. A loan. It's too bleedin' cold out tonight to have to spend it on the streets. You can pay me back when business picks up."

"I don't like takin' it off you," Millie muttered, but she reached for it anyway. "I'll pay ya back tomorrow, just see if I don't." She laughed. "Trade'll be good, you'll see. There's lots of men that can't go more than a day or so without it. They'll be 'ere tomorrow night."

"Pay me back when ya can," Annie said. "I'd best be gettin' these flowers back to the market, then."

"Thanks, luv—fer the money, I mean," Millie called as she turned and darted towards the river.

Annie watched her disappear into the fog. The heavy, yellowish gray mist had thickened and now it covered the street like a cotton-woolly blanket. She could barely see her cart.

She stood for one more minute before moving, her head cocked and her ears straining for the sound of approaching footsteps. But she heard nothing. Grasping the handle, she turned and began to push the cart slowly forward.

The wheels squeaked and groaned as she crossed the road and eased the old contraption around the corner and up Southampton Street. It seemed as though the fog thickened with every step she took. The farther she got from the gas lamps of the Strand, the darker and colder it got too. She was suddenly jerked forward as the front wheels of the cart crashed off the curb. Blast, Annie thought, squinting down into the heavy mist. It's worse than walkin' through a cold bowl of soup, it were so bleedin' thick. She'd better slow down or this old contraption wouldn't make it back to the garden. Annie grimaced as she pushed the heavy cart across the road.

The wheels didn't squeak so loud now, but that was somehow worse. Made her realize how quiet the street was. Goose bumps rushed up her arms and she didn't know if it was from cold or fear. Because suddenly she was scared. Like someone had just walked over her grave. Nights like this wasn't natural, she thought, looking over her shoulder and seeing nothing but the gray fingers of fog. Too empty by half.

Sundays weren't usually real busy, but this was the first time she'd ever had to go back to the market without sellin' something. She frowned. Mr. Cobbins weren't goin' to be pleased, that was for sure. But it weren't her bloomin' fault there weren't no one out and about.

From behind her, she heard footsteps. Annie stopped. The footsteps stopped as well.

She opened her mouth to call out who she was, then just as quickly clamped it shut again. Every instinct she had was screaming at her to be quiet. To run. Annie glanced down at the heavy cart. Run? She couldn't do that. She was bein' silly, actin' like one of them fancy ladies she saw goin' in and out of those elegant shops on Regent Street where she had her regular flower stand. The cart might be old and rusty, but Mr. Cobbins would have her head and she'd be out of a job if she come back without it.

After a moment Annie took a deep breath and told herself the foot-steps probably belonged to another flower seller or streetwalker. She grasped the handles tightly and moved forward.

So did the footsteps.

She stopped and whirled around. Staring into the fog, she tried to see if the person behind her was male or female. But the mist was too thick to see anything. She turned and started forward again. So did the footsteps.

Her heart slammed against her chest, her throat went dry, and the hair on the back of her neck stood up. "Who's there?" she called frantically, hoping against hope that it was a copper.

The only reply was the sound of the steps coming closer. They seemed to be moving faster as well.

"Bloody 'ell." Annie took a deep breath and tightened her fingers around the wicker handle of the cart. The sense of danger she'd had a few moments ago was back, and this time she wasn't going to ignore the warning.

With all her might, she shoved the cart hard and charged up the street. The wheels screamed in protest, but Annie didn't care.

The footsteps started to run.

Annie ran, too, pushing the cart with all her might and flying towards the end of the street and the safety of Covent Garden. Flowers flew off the cart in every direction, but she didn't care. A bundle of chrysanthemums bounced to the ground, a nosegay of violets flew past her arm, and a bunch of expensive roses landed in a pool of mud, but she didn't slow. The footsteps were gaining on her. She could hear them closing the gap behind her.

Suddenly a wheel popped off and the cart careened wildly, pulling out of Annie's hands and tumbling onto its side. Annie tripped, tried to regain her balance, and fell over the end of it. The fall knocked the wind out of her. Gasping, she struggled to sit up. Her instincts, honed by working the city streets for the past year now, were screaming for her to run. She was in trouble. Bad trouble.

She opened her mouth to scream just as a cloaked figure burst through the fog.

But the scream abruptly ended as the first blow landed on the back of her head.

"It was appalling, Mrs. Jeffries," Inspector Gerald Witherspoon said. "Utterly appalling." He took off his regulation uniform hat and sat it down on the table next to him. His clear, blue-gray eyes were troubled, his thinning brown hair mussed, and even his mustache drooped.

"The whole experience must have been dreadful for you, sir," Mrs. Jeffries agreed. As housekeeper to the inspector, she knew him very well. The poor man was upset. Unlike most policemen, until she'd come to work for him, Inspector Witherspoon had spent most of his career working in the records room. Today he, along with practically every other policeman in the whole city, had been called out for a show of force against a mass procession in Trafalgar Square. Handling unruly mobs was as foreign to the man as eating buffalo steaks for breakfast. Mrs. Jeffries gazed at him sympathetically. "Civil unrest is a terrible circumstance."

"I'm not so sure there would have been any civil unrest if Sir Charles had let them have their silly procession." Witherspoon shook his head and reached for his sherry.

Mrs. Jeffries couldn't believe her ears. Perhaps some of her "freethinking" ideas were actually making an impact on the inspector. "Whatever do you mean, sir?"

He brushed her question aside with a wave of his hand. "Forgive me, Mrs. Jeffries, I'm talking nonsense."

"You never talk nonsense, sir." She was curious about what he'd been thinking, though now she suspected he wasn't going to share it with her. Surprising really, the inspector generally shared everything with her, including the details of each and every one of his murder cases. Sometimes he startled her by hinting or almost revealing something quite extraordinary about how his mind worked. "Did you mean that you thought the police commissioner caused the riots by issuing the edict against the procession?"

"No, no," he said hastily. "Really, it's not for me to question the wisdom of my superiors . . . yet I can't help but think that it might have been the police regulation posted on every lamppost in the city that got so many people there in the first place. After all, how many people are really interested in the Metropolitan Radical Federation?"

"The Metropolitan Radical Federation?" Mrs. Jeffries queried. "I thought the whole thing was about Mr. O'Brien. You know, that Irish MP that was arrested."

"Oh, it was," the inspector said. "But you know how these things happen. Some of the people there were no doubt truly disturbed by the problems in Ireland, but many of them were there to protest all kinds of what they call 'social ills.' Frankly, Mrs. Jeffries, if the police commission had just ignored the whole thing, most people wouldn't have bothered to turn up at all." He set his glass down. "I mean really, who wants to listen to the rantings of a bunch of politicians, socialists, and anarchists?"

"There are many who seem to feel that people with such ideas are dangerous," she remarked. "Sir Charles Warren is obviously one of them."

"I mean no disrespect to the commissioner of the police," Witherspoon said, "but I do feel that the entire incident should have been handled differently. An unruly mob is certainly an impediment to public safety, but we don't know that they'd have been an unruly mob if they'd been allowed to have their march. Perhaps there would only have been a few speeches, a couple of banners waving about, a slogan or two painted on a wall. In which case, the only danger they'd pose is boring their audience to death."

Mrs. Jeffries laughed.

"Still," the inspector continued thoughtfully, "whether allowing them to have their march was right or wrong isn't really for me to say. But I do know I was quite shocked by the way some of my fellow policemen behaved. There was some dreadfully uncalled-for roughness." He looked troubled. "Some of the constables were quite brutal."

Mrs. Jeffries gazed at his face. She knew the inspector was no coward. So his distress wasn't merely the result of fearing for his own safety. Since she'd come to work for him, he'd gone from being a records-room clerk to an outstanding Scotland Yard detective. Naturally, no one could understand this metamorphosis. No one, of course, except the household of Upper Edmonton Gardens.

If the inspector was upset by the brutality of what he'd seen at Trafalgar Square this afternoon, it must, indeed, have been a frightening spectacle. "Were any of the marchers equally brutal?" she asked gently.

"Oh yes." He sighed. "There was the requisite number of rocks and missiles thrown."

"Then perhaps the police were merely defending themselves," she ventured. She did hate seeing the inspector so despondent. Gracious, from the way he acted, you'd think he felt personally responsible for everything that had happened today. But she really ought not to be surprised. Inspector Gerald Witherspoon was one of nature's gentlemen. Save for his salary, he'd never had any money until the death several years ago of his aunt Euphemia. He'd inherited a modest fortune and this beautiful home. Yet he was still as kind and compassionate as he'd ever been.

"For the most part, you're right." He sighed again. "But there were one or two—" He broke off and shook his head.

"Well, sir," Mrs. Jeffries said briskly, "it's over and done with. Mrs. Goodge has fixed a lovely dinner for you."

Witherspoon got to his feet. "I'm sorry, Mrs. Jeffries. But I think I'll go right on up to bed. I don't have much of an appetite this evening."

Mrs. Jeffries watched him leave. Beneath his uniform jacket, which he'd had to wear today for the first time in a long while, his shoulders drooped as he trudged towards the door. Poor man, he hadn't liked having to do what he'd done today, and even worse, he certainly hadn't liked watching what some of his fellow police officers had gotten up to.

She turned and hurried down to the kitchen. There was no point in delaying the staff's evening meal. The inspector would bounce back in his own good time.

Half an hour later Mrs. Jeffries and the other servants sat down to their dinner.

"It's not like the inspector to be off his food," Betsy, the maid, said. Blonde, blue-eyed, and very pretty, she was also intelligent and perceptive beyond her twenty years. "Is he not feeling well?"

"He's a bit depressed, that's all," Mrs. Jeffries replied. "The riots in Trafalgar Square today upset him. I don't think he approved of the way some of his fellow officers dealt with the crowd."

"Too kindhearted, he is," Mrs. Goodge, the plump gray-haired cook, said bluntly. "They ought to have arrested the whole lot of them. That's what I say."

"Why should them people have been arrested?" Wiggins, the footman, asked. With his dark brown hair, pale skin, and round apple cheeks, he looked much younger than his nineteen years. His youth, however, didn't stop him from having an opinion on most subjects. He wasn't particularly bothered about whether or not it was an informed opinion. "This is a free country. They've got as much right to 'ave a march and a meetin' as anyone else."

"They don't have a right to throw rocks and go about breakin' windows and upsettin' decent folk," the cook shot back. Behind her spectacles, her eyes narrowed angrily. "What do they want anyways? Some Irish MP gets arrested and every Tom, Dick, and Harry's got to take to the street. Let the courts do it, that's what I say."

"Sometimes," Smythe, the coachman, interjected, "you've got to take matters into yer own hands." He leaned back and crossed his muscular arms over his broad chest. Dark-haired, tall, and with heavy, almost brutal features, he wasn't anyone's idea of male beauty. But his warm brown eyes and cocky grin made more than one pretty maid turn her head when he passed by. "We do it often enough."

Mrs. Jeffries smiled at the coachman. Everyone knew he was referring to the fact that all of them frequently nosed about in their employer's murder cases. As a matter of fact, they did it every time Inspector Witherspoon had a homicide. And, of course, that was one of the reasons they were all being so argumentative this evening. They were bored.

Here it was November and they hadn't had a good murder to work on since last June. If she were truly honest, Mrs. Jeffries thought, she'd have to admit she was as bored as the rest of them. Not that she condoned murder, of course. However, human nature being what it was, she didn't think the foul deed would stop just because she personally found taking a human life abhorrent. If murders were going to happen, then wasn't it lucky that she and the rest of the staff were available to help bring the miscreants to justice?

Fred, their brown-and-black mongrel dog, who wasn't supposed to hang about the kitchen but did anyway, especially at mealtimes, suddenly jumped up from his spot beside Wiggins. Barking excitedly, he raced out and down the darkened hallway to the back door.

"What's Fred on about?" Mrs. Goodge complained as loud pounding sounded on the back door.

Wiggins started to get up, but Smythe put a restraining hand on his shoulder. "It's dark, lad, best let me see to this."

They waited curiously to see who'd come visiting on a cold, foggy evening. There was the sound of the door opening and then muffled cries of greeting. "It's Luty Belle and Hatchet," Smythe called.

Luty Belle Crookshank, resplendent in a bright orange evening dress, matching feathers in her thin white hair and hanging on to a magnificent black walking stick, hobbled quickly into the kitchen. Hatchet, her tall, dignified, white-haired butler, was right behind her.

"Luty Belle and Hatchet," Mrs. Jeffries said, rising from her chair. "How very nice to see you."

"Evenin' everyone," Luty called gaily as she headed for an empty chair. "Hope you don't mind me and Hatchet droppin' by, but it's as quiet as a grave out tonight." Fred bounced joyously around the hem of Luty's skirt. She bent down and patted him on the head. "Howdy, nice feller. My, my, you're happy to see your friend Luty, ain't ya, boy?" Fred licked her hands, butted her knees with his head, and generally made a fool of himself.

"If you and Fred have finished greeting one another," Hatchet said, "perhaps we can sit down."

"So where have you two been tonight?" Smythe asked, slipping into the chair next to Betsy.

Hatchet sniffed delicately.

Luty grinned. "Don't mind him," she said, an impish twinkle in her black eyes. "His nose is out of joint 'cause of my women's meetin'. Me and a few other ladies get together every once in a while and try to come up with ideas fer gettin' females the vote."

"Getting women the vote," Wiggins repeated in a puzzled voice. Suddenly his eyes widened. "You mean you want *women* to be able to vote?" He sounded absolutely flabbergasted at such an outrageous idea.

"That's what I said," Luty shot back. "What's wrong with women votin'? Or doin' anything else a man can do?"

Smythe laughed. "Get on with you," he said. "Gettin' the right to vote is one thing, but thinkin' they can do anythin' a man can is daft. Why, the next thing ya know, you'll be sayin' they can drive trains or carriages or sit in Parliament. I tell ya, it's daft."

"Daft, is it?" Betsy interrupted. "Hmmph. Seems to me that exceptin' for heavy labor, a woman could do anything a man could. Why shouldn't a woman have a few chances at life?"

"But a woman is supposed to get married, take care of her 'usband and her little ones," Wiggins said quickly. "If all the women was out workin' and votin' and drivin' trains and doin' typewritin', who'd take care of the children? That's what I want to know."

"What about women who don't have husbands?" Mrs. Jeffries said, warming to the subject. She'd long thought the division of labor in society utterly ridiculous. "What are they supposed to do? Live off their relatives? And what about the police? Do you honestly think a woman couldn't be as good at solving crimes as a man?"

That shut everyone up. Every one of them knew that it was Mrs. Jeffries who'd been responsible for solving virtually every one of the inspector's murders. The only person who wasn't privy to this knowledge was the inspector himself. They'd all agreed to keep him in the dark about their various investigations on his behalf.

Luty cackled. "That's tellin' 'em, Hepzibah."

"Really, madam." Hatchet gave her a quelling glance, which she completely ignored. "I hardly think that comparing Mrs. Jeffries's undoubted superior detection skills to the average woman outperforming a male is a true test."

"You don't, huh?" Luty said smugly. "Well, I danged well think it is."

"Obviously," Hatchet continued, "Mrs. Jeffries has a special gift. But that was one of nature's . . . well, shall we say, errors. In the true scheme of things, it should have been the inspector who was blessed with such a talent. However, nature does occasionally make a mistake. But that's hardly evidence for your contention that females are as capable as males. Let us be truly honest here, everyone knows how women are."

"And precisely how is that?" Mrs. Jeffries asked softly.

Hatchet, who didn't notice the gleam in the women's eyes, went blithely on. "Women are, of course, delightful creatures. But they are also weak willed and emotional. They need the firm guidance of a man."

"Hatchet's right," Wiggins said smugly.

"Hatchet needs his head examined," Mrs. Goodge said tartly. "It'll be a cold day in the pits of hell before I'd let some man 'guide' me."

"Really Mrs. Goodge," Hatchet said defensively. "You misunderstand my meaning. All I'm saying is that if women begin trying to take over everything and forget their true place in the scheme of things, the entire fabric of society will come unraveled."

"Maybe it should be unraveled." Betsy snorted. "It's not like it's all that wonderful for everybody. There's only a few that have much of a decent life. For most people, life's hard. There's more that's poor than there is them that's rich. There's plenty of sufferin' and plenty of starvin' in lots of places in this city. So maybe it wouldn't be so bad if there was some changes made, some unravelin' done."

"You tell 'em, Betsy," Luty said encouragingly. "That's what I've been tryin' to get through his thick head, but like most men, he ain't got the brains to listen to a different point of view."

Hatchet swelled with outrage. "I'll have you know I'm exceedingly open-minded and liberal in my thinking."

"Cow patties," Luty shouted. "You're about as liberal as the kaiser and just as much of a stuffed shirt, too!"

The argument raged in earnest then. For once, Mrs. Jeffries didn't try to intervene. She agreed with everything Luty and Betsy had said. Even Mrs. Goodge had surprised her.

"It's not enough for you to actually correspond with those females," Hatchet said heatedly to Luty. "But you're giving them money!"

"What females?" Wiggins asked curiously.

"The American Woman Sufferage Association," Luty said. "I've been writin' to 'em for over a year now." She turned to glare at Hatchet. "And you're doggone right I'm sendin' them money. I'd give the women on this side of the ocean some cash, too, if they wasn't such a bunch of twittering gits!"

"Why don't we have a contest?" Betsy yelled to make herself heard.

The room fell silent. They all turned to stare at her.

"What kind of contest did you 'ave in mind?" Smythe asked, giving the maid a cheeky grin. "Drinkin'? Sawin' logs? One of them bicycle races?"

"You can wipe that smirk off yer face, Smythe." Betsy crossed her arms over her chest. "I'm not talkin' about anything that would give you men a physical advantage over us. I'm talkin' about our brains. You know, that little thing that rattles around up in yer head when you try and think."

The women laughed. Smythe narrowed his eyes but managed to keep silent.

"Are you thinking what I think you're thinking?" Mrs. Jeffries asked. She couldn't quite hide a smile. The men *were* awfully arrogant.

"That's right," Betsy said. "I'm thinking that the next time we 'as us a murder to investigate, let's just see who's the smartest."

Witherspoon was far more cheerful the next morning. Mrs. Jeffries was glad to see him tuck into his breakfast with his usual gusto.

There was a hard knock on the front door. "Were you expecting someone this morning, Inspector?" she asked as she hurried out to the front hall.

"No, not that I remember," he called.

Mrs. Jeffries threw open the door to see Constable Barnes standing on the stoop. "Good morning, Constable. Dreadful day, isn't it?"

Behind him, she could see the thick yellow fog lying like a blanket of wool over the whole street.

"Not fit for man nor beast," Barnes agreed cheerfully. "I'd like to see the inspector, if you don't mind. It's urgent, or I wouldn't be disturbin' his breakfast."

She ushered him into the dining room. "Would you like a cup of tea, Constable?"

"That'd be lovely, Mrs. Jeffries."

"Gracious, Barnes." Witherspoon frowned. "I thought I was meeting you at the station."

"You were, sir." He smiled gratefully at Mrs. Jeffries as he accepted a cup of hot, steaming tea. "But there's been a murder. Inspector Nivens is right upset, too, because he was due to get the next homicide and he got called out on an important jewel robbery late last night at the Duke of Hampton's residence. So you're gettin' this one."

"Oh dear." Witherspoon sighed. "Nivens always takes it so personally. I do hope he doesn't raise a fuss."

"Don't matter if he does," Barnes said. "Heard some gossip that you're gettin' this one because someone very important wants to make sure the investigation's handled right. Wants to see justice done."

Mrs. Jeffries tried to make herself invisible while she took in every word. She prayed that Barnes would keep talking. Anything, even a name and address, would be enough to get them started.

"Who's the victim?" Witherspoon reached for his teacup.

"A flower seller name of Annie Shields. Young woman. They found her late last night. A hansom driver on his way out come across her in the fog. It were so bloody thick over near the Strand that he practically run the body over. She'd been coshed on the head."

"Poor woman," Witherspoon murmured. "How old was she?"

"I haven't seen the body," Barnes replied. "They've taken it to the mortuary. Potter's going to have a look at it this morning."

Witherspoon groaned. Dr. Potter was his least favorite surgeon. The man kept threatening to retire and go off to Bournemouth and grow roses, but he never did.

Barnes reached inside his pocket and whipped out a small brown notebook. "According to the uniformed lad that made the first report, Annie Shields was well-known in the area. The body was discovered on Southampton Street. The victim lodges over in Barston Street and worked for Harper's out of Covent Garden."

"You're certain she was a flower seller and not a, er . . ."—the inspector reassured himself that Mrs. Jeffries was still busy with the tea things—"prostitute?"

"She were layin' over a cart of flowers when she were found," Barnes replied.

"I suppose we'd better get to the mortuary." Witherspoon's lip curled. He really did hate this part of being a policeman. Corpses were not very pleasant. Especially when he had just had breakfast. But he knew his duty. "Er, Barnes, did you say the woman had been hit over the head?"

"Right, sir. And she were a bit mangled by the hansom cab." Barnes gulped the rest of his tea. "But it were just her limbs that was mangled, sir, or so the street copper said."

Witherspoon gulped but gamely forced himself to stand up. Head injuries were so nasty. Not quite as bad as bullet wounds or an ugly slashing, but not very nice nonetheless.

Mrs. Jeffries tried to contain her impatience as she fetched the inspector's hat and coat and generally got him out of the house. The moment the door closed behind him and Barnes, she flew down the hall to the backstairs. Pausing at the top, she listened for voices.

From below, she could hear Betsy and Mrs. Goodge chatting quietly. Satisfied, she hurried down the stairs and into the kitchen, taking care not to say a word until she made sure the men were gone.

"Are we alone, ladies?" she asked. Mrs. Goodge glanced up from the dough she was kneading. "Just us women, unless you count Fred. And like most males, he's sound asleep." The cook was still very irritated by the battle of the sexes they'd had last night. So were Mrs. Jeffries and Betsy.

"Smythe is over at Howard's and Wiggins is picking up the meat order from the butchers," Betsy added. "Why?"

Mrs. Jeffries, who would have sworn she didn't have a childish bone in her body, grinned. She certainly wasn't going to exclude the men of the household from the investigation. Oh no, that would never do. But the discussion they'd had last night had been most enlightening. She'd honestly been surprised to find that Smythe and Wiggins had such ridiculous notions about women.

"Because, ladies, we've much to discuss. Betsy, do you think you could pop over and get Luty here?"

Betsy wiped her hands on a towel. "Of course I could."

"Good, make sure you speak to Luty alone. I don't want Hatchet overhearing anything."

"What's this all about, then?" the cook asked curiously.

"We've got a murder," Mrs. Jeffries announced. "Isn't it a pity the men are all out and won't be able to start their own investigations until later?"

CHAPTER 2

———◦◦◦◦◦———

"Oh dear," the inspector murmured as he stared down at the body on the table, "she's hardly more than a child. Who could do such a vile thing?"

Witherspoon didn't want to look directly at the hideous wounds on her temple. But he knew he should. Fighting nausea, he forced himself to gaze at her for several moments. Disturbing as the sight might be, he knew his duty. As his housekeeper had once pointed out, knowing precisely where the fatal wounds had been inflicted might come in handy during the questioning of a suspect. It was amazing what people gave away when they started talking.

"Sad, isn't it?" Barnes clucked his tongue. "She was a pretty young woman, too." He cleared his throat. "As far as we can tell, the victim was killed sometime before eleven last night."

"That was when the hansom driver found her, I take it." He looked at Barnes. "Does Dr. Potter have any idea of the actual time of death? Had she been dead long before she was found?"

"Really, Inspector," a petulant voice said from behind them, "you know very well I don't like guessing games." Dr. Potter, portly and pompous as ever, came towards them. He was wearing a heavy apron and carrying a satchel. On his heels were two young porters pushing a gurney.

"I was merely hoping you'd be able to tell us something," Witherspoon said. He leapt out of the way as the porters pushed the gurney level with the table.

"Well, I can't give you any information yet," Potter snapped. "But as the victim was found on a public street, I suspect she couldn't have been there very long. Really, Inspector, I'd have thought even you'd have reasoned that out. You there, boy," he shouted at one of the porters, and pointed to the victim's head. "Mind you don't leave any skull fragments on that table when you shift the body. Take her down to number three. I'll be along in a minute or two to open her up."

Witherspoon's stomach turned over. If he hadn't suddenly felt like he was going to faint, he would have pointed out to Potter that though the victim was on the street, the streets had been so deserted the poor woman could have been lying dead for hours before that hansom came across her. "Er, we'll just get out of the way," he murmured, turning his head to avoid the sight of the porters starting to move the corpse. He decided to try one more time. Even Potter must have some notion of how long she'd been dead. "But surely you've some idea as to when the victim was killed? It's frightfully important that we have something to go on."

"Blast it, Inspector. I've only given the woman a cursory examination. The best I can say is that death probably didn't occur until fairly latish in the evening. But that is just a guess and you won't hear me saying it at the coroner's inquest." Potter glared at the two policemen. "At least that's my estimate from the temperature of the body. But don't go taking that as the gospel. You'll have to wait till a proper postmortem's been done before I'll say another word, and even then, you know as well as I do that estimating time of death is risky. There are far too many factors to ascertain with any degree of accuracy when someone actually died."

Witherspoon knew that was the best he was likely to get out of the doctor. He started to edge towards the door. "Thank you, Dr. Potter."

Barnes was gazing at the victim. "Was she interfered with?"

"Do you mean raped?"

One of the porters snickered.

The inspector glared at the man and his grin faded.

"That's what I'm askin', sir," Barnes clarified. "Was she raped?"

Potter sighed. "I've already told you, I've *not* done a proper examination yet. Besides"—his lips curled in a sneer—"with these street girls it's almost impossible to determine if they've been forcibly raped."

"She was a flower seller," Witherspoon snapped, suddenly incensed. He didn't like Dr. Potter's attitude. The victim, whatever her life had been, deserved to be treated with respect. "Not a prostitute."

Potter's eyes widened at Witherspoon's tone. He actually took a step

back. "I'll let you know when I've finished the postmortem," he said frostily. "Until then, kindly leave me in peace to do my job."

"The local PC's outside," Barnes muttered in Witherspoon's ear. "We
can talk to him while we're waiting for the victim's clothes and personal
effects."

The inspector nodded.

The uniformed officer who'd been called to the scene waited outside
in the reception hall. He was a tall, red-haired chap with a pale complexion and weary, bloodshot eyes. He sprang up to attention when he saw
Barnes and Witherspoon coming towards him. "Good morning, sir," he
said. "I'm PC Popper."

Witherspoon nodded. "Good morning. You look as though you're
tired."

Popper smiled wearily. "Up all night, sir. As soon as we got this victim brought in, I had to go right back out on another call. Robbery down
at the docks, sir."

"Well, then, I'll not waste any time. I expect you'd like to get home and
get some sleep." Witherspoon glanced at Barnes and saw that the constable had whipped out his notebook. He turned back to Popper and
asked, "What time were you called to the scene of the crime?"

"Just past eleven last night, sir. I was walking the Strand when I heard
someone screaming for help," Popper explained. "It took a while for me
to figure out where all the shoutin' was coming from, though; that fog was
so thick you couldn't see two feet in front of your hand. Finally I figures
it was comin' from a ways up Southampton Street. When I got there, I saw
this hansom cabbie hanging on to his horses and screamin' his head off."

"Where, precisely, on Southampton Street?" Witherspoon was fairly
certain this was a pertinent question. Sometimes he had the feeling that
none of the questions he asked were appropriate.

Popper thought for a moment. "About halfway between the Strand
and the flower market. I reckon she were on her way back to the market
when she was killed."

"Is it possible the hansom ran her down?" the inspector asked.

"No, sir," Popper replied. "Even if he'd hit her, he wouldn't have done
much damage to the poor woman. He was movin' too slow because of the
fog. Besides, the horses make enough noise that if she'd been alive when
he come near her, she'd have heard him comin' and gotten out of the way."

"Had the cab run completely over her?" Barnes asked.

Popper shook his head. "No. Matter of fact, I don't think the horses or the cab even touched the body. It was the cart they hit first."

"What did the hansom driver tell you?" Witherspoon asked.

"He said he were goin' down the street on his way in for the night when all of a sudden one of the horses stumbled and reared back. He pulled up then and jumped down to see what the problem was. Then he saw her. She was lying to one side of the cart, her head bashed in."

"Do you think he's telling the truth?" Witherspoon didn't think it impossible that the driver might be lying. If he'd accidentally run the flower seller down, he might not want to admit it. Then again, the story did make sense. It was dreadfully foggy last night. And the constable was probably correct. Unless the victim was as deaf as a post, she would have heard the approach of a cab. He made a mental note to ask Potter to check for deafness.

"Yes, sir," the police constable replied. "He's got no reason to lie. If he'd run her down and not want to be admittin' it, he wouldn't have been screamin' blue blazes for help. He'd have just left. There weren't no one on the streets last night to be seein' what he'd done."

Witherspoon nodded. "Were there any witnesses?"

"Not really, sir. But one of the other constables had passed by the corner where Annie Shields was sellin' flowers at around nine forty-five. She was alive then, of course. There was another woman there as well. A prostitute."

Witherspoon knew that was important information. It meant that Annie Shields had been alive at a quarter to ten. Her body had been discovered a little after eleven. "What's this constable's name?"

Popper told him. "Blackman, sir. Ronald Blackman."

Barnes scribbled the information in his notebook and then asked, "Any sign of a weapon?"

Popper shook his head. "None that we could find. Had a good look about the area, but couldn't find anything with blood on it. Of course, the fog's not helping any. But I did ask around about the victim early this morning when we was finished up at the dock."

"Excellent, Constable." Witherspoon beamed. This young man would go far. Showed initiative. "What did you find out?"

Popper smiled proudly. "Well, sir. She's quite well-known in the district. Annie Shields has worked as a flower seller for Harper's for about a year. Decent woman, worked the theatre area a couple of nights a week and the rest of the time she took her cart over to Regent Street. She's widowed and she has lodgings on Barston Road."

"Widowed," Witherspoon repeated. "Did she have any known enemies? Anyone who might have a reason for wanting her dead?"

Popper looked surprised by the question. "Well, sir, I didn't think to ask."

"Why not?" Witherspoon asked curiously. Surely that would be one of the first things one should ask.

"Because, sir, the victim was robbed," Popper said hesitantly. "I mean, sir. She didn't have any money on her when we found her."

Witherspoon smiled patiently. "That means nothing, Constable. The lack of money on her person could mean she hadn't sold any flowers. It doesn't necessarily mean she'd been robbed."

"I hadn't thought of that." Popper smiled sheepishly. "After that riot yesterday the streets was pretty empty last night. But that wasn't the only reason I thought she might 'ave been robbed. Her glove was off, you see."

"I'm sorry." The inspector frowned. "I don't quite understand."

"Well, sir," Popper explained, "it were a cold night. The cart had fallen over because it had lost a wheel. I reckon she were runnin' from whoever coshed her. But she had her gloves on—at least there was still a glove on her left hand when she was found. But the right hand glove was laying on the street, like someone had ripped it off to get at her rings."

"Rings?" Witherspoon mumbled. "What would a flower girl be doing wearing rings? Was her wedding ring gone?"

"No, sir, it were still on her finger."

"Exactly my point, Constable," Witherspoon said. "Why steal a ring from her right hand and then leave a perfectly good wedding ring on her left?"

Luty clapped her hands together. "Hatchet'll be madder than a wet hen when he finds out."

"Smythe and Wiggins'll have their noses out of joint, too." Betsy giggled.

"Serves 'em right," said Mrs. Goodge.

"Now, ladies," Mrs. Jeffries cautioned, "we're not going to exclude them entirely. That wouldn't be fair. However, given their attitudes about our fair sex, I don't feel in the least guilty about getting the jump on them."

"So tell us what all you know," Luty ordered. "I'm rarin' to go."

"Uh . . ." Mrs. Jeffries hesitated. There really wasn't any polite way to mention this, and really, if she hadn't been so annoyed with those arrogant males, she'd have thought of it before she brought Luty over here. "Luty, uh . . ."

"Come on, Hepzibah," Luty said irritably. "Quit tryin' to think of a polite way to say it and just spit it out."

"How did you know that was what I was doing?"

"'Cause yer cheeks always get pink when you're tryin' to come up with a nice way to ask me somethin' you don't want to ask."

"Yes, I suppose they do." She took a deep breath and plunged ahead. "Well, if we're not going to inform Hatchet about the murder, how on earth are you going to—"

"Get around without him?" Luty cackled and held up a beaded handbag. "Got me a purse full of coins here, Hepzibah. I reckon there's enough hansom drivers in this town to get me where I want to go." She patted the fur muff in her lap. "And don't worry none about someone botherin' me. I may be an old woman, but I've got my protection right in here."

Alarmed, Mrs. Jeffries stared at her. "Oh no, you don't have that horrible gun, do you?" On several of their other investigations Luty Belle had brought along her gun, a wicked-looking weapon popular in her native America, a Colt .45.

"'Course I've got it." Luty looked at her incredulously. "Don't get yourself all het up, me and my Peacemaker won't have no trouble if'n people stay out of my way. You've got to admit, it's come in handy a time or two."

Unfortunately for Mrs. Jeffries's arguments, Luty was absolutely correct. Her gun had come in very handy indeed a time or two. "For goodness' sakes then, be careful with it."

"Is it loaded?" Betsy asked, staring wide-eyed at the muff.

"Yup." Luty patted the muff again. "Loaded and rarin' to go, just like I am. Now"—she grinned at Mrs. Jeffries—"what should we do first?"

Mrs. Jeffries drummed her fingers on the tabletop. "We don't have all that much to go on. The victim is a young flower seller named Annie Shields. From what I heard, she was probably killed sometime last night."

"A flower seller," Mrs. Goodge muttered. She frowned. "I won't have much luck learnin' anything about a common flower seller."

Mrs. Jeffries gazed thoughtfully at the cook. Mrs. Goodge looked very troubled. "Now, Mrs. Goodge, just because our victim isn't well-known in society doesn't mean you won't be able to learn as much as you always do."

When they were investigating one of the inspector's cases, Mrs. Goodge never left her kitchen. But she certainly did her fair share. She knew every morsel of gossip in London. A veritable army of people trooped through her kitchen and she pumped them ruthlessly. From the gasworks man to the rag-and-bone man to the chimney sweep, Mrs. Goodge plied them with buns and tea and wrung them dry. But as most of their other cases had involved members of society, the poor woman was worried no one would know anything about a mere flower girl. Well, Mrs. Jeffries would have to convince her otherwise. It was easier than trying to get her out of this kitchen!

"But who'll know tuppence about a flower seller?" Mrs. Goodge wailed.

"Very few, probably," Mrs. Jeffries said crisply. "But once they've heard she was murdered, they'll all be learning every scrap they can about the poor girl." She smiled. "You, of course, will find out exactly what they know. Besides, with your chain of connections I'm sure you must know someone who works at Covent Garden."

Mrs. Goodge cocked her head to one side. "Come to think of it, my cousin Ada's second boy delivers for Pearson's. Maybe I'll have him round to see what he knows. If this girl's been sellin' flowers from over there, Augustine should know her."

"Augustine," Betsy repeated. "Your cousin named her son Augustine?"

"Horrid, isn't it?" the cook agreed. "But Ada never did have much sense. That and she was right fond of saints."

"What should I do?" Luty asked.

"Constable Barnes said the victim was known in the area where her body was found. She was found on Southampton Street up from the Strand. A hansom driver practically ran over her. Perhaps you can ask about and see what you can find out from the people in the area. For all we know, someone might have seen something last night."

"Maybe you should let me do that," Betsy suggested.

"You think I'm afraid to ask a few questions?" Luty charged.

Betsy smiled and shook her head. "You're not afraid of anything! I only meant that if I ask about, I might run into someone I know." She looked helplessly at Mrs. Jeffries. "Oh, you know what I mean. . . ."

"Of course I do, Betsy," Mrs. Jeffries agreed. "And you're absolutely right." She turned to Luty. "Betsy has a number of acquaintances. Any one of them might be useful if she should run into them. They'd be more apt to answer her questions than yours."

"Then what in the blazes am I gonna do?" Luty snorted. "If'n you think I'm gonna sit around and do nothin', you've got another think comin'. This is the first chance I've had to show that stiff-necked old fool that works fer me that females is as smart as men and I ain't gonna miss it."

"Of course you're not going to miss your chance," Mrs. Jeffries said calmly. "I quite agree that Hatchet as well as the other men need to be shown up a bit. But I've got something entirely different in mind for you."

Luty leaned closer. "Now yer talkin'."

"Annie Shields had lodgings in Barston Road," Mrs. Jeffries explained. "I don't know the address, but if you go over there and ask about, you might be able to find where she lives. Talk to her landlady and anyone else who might have known the woman. Find out anything you can."

"Mrs. Jeffries," Betsy said slowly, "what if Annie Shields was killed by someone who didn't even know her? You know, like a robbery or even a . . . a . . . ."

"Rape?"

Betsy blushed and nodded.

"I've thought of that. It could well be the case." Mrs. Jeffries pursed her lips. "But remember, the streets were deserted last night. Luty mentioned that when she dropped by. The riot in Trafalgar Square had sent everyone inside. Therefore, you have to ask yourself, if there was no one on the streets, why would a young woman bother going out and trying to sell flowers when there wasn't any foot traffic? Furthermore, why would a robber wait until the one night of the year when his victim hadn't made any money before he committed murder, a hanging offense? If I was going to take a risk like that, I'd at least wait until my victim had something worth stealing."

"You mean, the streets was empty, so the girl probably hadn't sold any flowers, so she couldn't have had any money?" Mrs. Goodge said. "That makes sense . . . I think. But what if she were just raped?"

"Then why kill her?" Mrs. Jeffries sighed. "Look, it could well be an incredibly stupid killer who hadn't even the intelligence to realize his victim didn't have anything worth taking. Or it could have been a rape by some maniac. We don't know. We won't know until the inspector gets home this evening. But do we want to miss this opportunity to learn what we can?"

"'Course not," Luty declared.

"Reckon we can get a bit of a head start," Mrs. Goodge muttered. "If it turns out to be one of them stupid, senseless killin's that never get solved, well, it won't be because we sat on our backsides and didn't even try."

"Uh, Mrs. Jeffries," Betsy asked, "we are going to tell the men about the murder, aren't we?"

"Let 'em read about it in the papers," Mrs. Goodge said.

"Do the whole uppity bunch a world of good to be left out of this one," Luty agreed. "Teach 'em not to be so dang-blasted arrogant all the time. Especially that old fussbudget Hatchet."

"Now, really, ladies," Mrs. Jeffries said quickly. "We mustn't let our competitive instincts completely overrule our consciences." Though if she were to be honest, she was sorely tempted. "Of course we must tell them."

"All right," Mrs. Goodge said grudgingly.

"Do ya have to do it tonight?" Luty asked hopefully. "Couldn't you delay fer another day or two?"

"Delayin' tellin' them won't do us any good," Betsy said. "They're bound to hear somethin' from the inspector."

"Not necessarily," Mrs. Jeffries mused. She caught herself. Surely, she wasn't seriously considering Luty's suggestion. Surely, she wasn't that small and petty-minded. Oh, but she was. Last night her blood had boiled with some of the asinine statements Hatchet, Smythe, and Wiggins had thrown about the table as if they were the gospel truth. "Actually, Smythe said he wouldn't be in until late tonight. He's taking the carriage out for a run."

"What's he doin' that for?" Betsy demanded.

"He claims the horses need the exercise. Come to think of it, Bow and Arrow did look a bit pudgy the last time Smythe brought the carriage round."

"I can send Wiggins out this evenin'," Mrs. Goodge announced. "I've been meanin' to get that ruddy sausage-makin' contraption fixed. I'll send the lad over to the ironmonger, as slow as old man Craxter is, Wiggins'll be there half the night."

"And Hatchet's way behind in Jon's lessons," Luty mused. "Maybe it's time fer me to remind the two of them about our agreement."

"How's the boy doin'?" Betsy asked. "It's hard to imagine Hatchet havin' much patience with a mouthy little beggar like Jon."

On their last case, which Luty had missed because she'd gone to America to avoid the Queen's Jubilee, Hatchet had ended up bringing a homeless lad, one of the principals in their investigation, into Luty's household.

"Jon's doin' just fine," Luty replied. "Squawks about doin' his lessons, but he's a sharp one. Hatchet and I are already squabblin' on where we're goin' to send him to college." She rose to her feet. "Much as I've enjoyed chattin', ladies, I expect I'd best be off. Do you want me to pop back round here this evenin'?"

Mrs. Jeffries nodded. "Come after eight. The inspector should have finished his dinner by then. He always retires early when he's on a case."

Betsy got up, too. "Hang on a minute, Luty, while I get my coat. I'll walk out with you."

"I'd best get crackin', too," Mrs. Goodge said, glancing at the clock as the two women made their way to the back door. She heaved herself to her feet and walked over to the china cupboard. Opening the glass door, she took out a brown glass bottle with a cork stopper.

"Is your rheumatism bothering you?" Mrs. Jeffries asked sympathetically.

"Just a bit," she replied, unstopping the bottle and rubbing some of the strong-smelling, clear liquid into her hands. "But this here liniment helps." She smiled wryly. "I used to only put it on when my fingers got really achy. You know what I mean. It's bloomin' expensive, this stuff. But since some good soul around here's taken it into their heads to make sure there's always a full bottle, I use it whenever I need it. Got to keep me fingers limber. The grocer's boy comes round about four and I want to have a bit of bakin' done. As well as I remember, Albert's right fond of my currant scones."

"Odd, isn't it?" Mrs. Jeffries said thoughtfully, her gaze on the brown bottle. "We've all become so adept at solving mysteries, but we can't solve the one that affects us every day of our lives."

She referred to the fact that objects kept appearing out of nowhere. Not only did some mysterious benefactor ensure that Mrs. Goodge always had a full bottle of her expensive medicine, but this same person also kept Wiggins supplied with notepaper so he could write his poems and love letters, bought Betsy several useful and expensive items of clothes, and slipped the latest edition of Mr. Walt Whitman's poems into Mrs. Jeffries's bookcase.

"Reckon we're not tryin' to solve that one all that hard," the cook said dryly. Mrs. Jeffries knew just what she meant. Whoever their benefactor was, he or she was a member of the household and that person obviously wished to keep their identity secret. Of course, Mrs. Jeffries knew perfectly well who this person was. But naturally, she wouldn't say a word.

Inspector Witherspoon looked around the shabby but clean room which had belonged to Annie Shields. He and Barnes stood just inside the door of what was a combination bedroom and sitting room. On one wall, a lumpy bed with a faded dark green covering stood next to a small cot covered with heavy layers of gray blankets and quilts. A rickety table with two chairs, one of which had a spool missing at the top, stood near the only window. Pale gray light pierced the limp rose-and-green curtains, bathing the room in a depressing light. On the other side of that was a small nook containing a wooden cupboard with crockery stacked on top. A wardrobe, one of its knobs missing and its mirror cracked, stood next to a dented trunk.

"Who's goin' to pay the rent, that's what I want to know," the querulous voice of Mrs. Basset, the landlady, sliced through the chill air.

"Was Annie Shields behind in her rent?" the inspector asked. He turned to face the landlady.

She stared at him through angry, slitted hazel eyes as a dull red flush crept slowly up her fleshy cheeks. "Not yet," Mrs. Basset replied, lifting her three chins just a fraction. "She were paid up to the first of next week. But she's had this room fer a long time. It's downright inconvenient tryin' to find a new tenant without proper notice."

"I don't expect she thought she'd be murdered," Barnes said softly. "How long had she lived here?"

"Four years," Mrs. Basset said. "Moved in right after her and David got married."

"And when did Mr. Shields die?" Witherspoon felt that knowing as much as possible about the victim was a very good thing. One never knew. It certainly wasn't unheard of for someone from the past to pop up with a motive for murder.

"A bit over a year ago." Mrs. Basset pursed her lips. "He were killed in an accident down at the brewery. Annie had to go out and work then, what with David not havin' anythin' to leave her."

"How very dreadful," the inspector murmured. Poor girl. Life hadn't been very kind to her.

"Did Annie Shields always go out to work at night?" Barnes put in.

Mrs. Basset shrugged. "Not really. Sometimes when she were a bit short she'd go out. Never more than a couple of nights a week, though. Mostly she worked days. Had a patch over near Regent Street that did right well."

"What time did she leave last night?" Witherspoon asked.

"Right after it got dark," she replied. "Annie liked to get the supper trade if she was goin' to bother workin'."

"Do you know of any particular reason Mrs. Shields needed money last night?"

"Everyone needs money." Mrs. Basset stared at him incredulously.

"But last night wasn't a very good night to be going out to work, was it? There were riots yesterday afternoon and the streets were deserted." Really, Witherspoon thought, did he have to explain every little thing?

"Oh, I see what ya mean. Well, I guess she must have been in a bad way if she went out, mustn't she?"

"Was she ever late paying her rent?" Barnes asked.

"No. Always paid right on time. First of every week—" She broke off and frowned thoughtfully. "Come to think of it, it were odd her goin' out last night."

The inspector's spirits lifted. Now they were getting somewhere. He noticed Barnes staring uneasily around the small room. "Why?"

"'Cause she ain't been short of money lately," Mrs. Basset said bluntly.

Witherspoon was surprised. Before he could ask another question, though, they heard the front door slam.

"That's that bleedin' Maples feller." The landlady spun around and ran toward the hall. "He owes me a week's rent."

"But, Mrs. Basset," the inspector called, "we've more questions for you."

"You'll have to ask 'em later," she yelled as she charged down the stairs. "Maples," she screamed. "It's no good hidin' in yer rooms. I want me bloomin' rent."

"Honestly," Witherspoon murmured. "One would think her precious rent money was more important than finding a murderer."

"Should we search the room now, sir?" Barnes asked. He scratched his chin.

"As we're already here, we might as well." He noticed that Barnes was shaking his head and looking puzzled. "I say, Constable, is something wrong?"

"Well, sir, since you ask, there is something that's botherin' me." He gestured around the shabby room. "This place, sir, it's much too grand for a flower seller."

"Really?" Witherspoon was genuinely surprised.

"Yes, sir," Barnes continued. "You don't know how poor most of the people over in this end o' town is. . . ."

"Come now, Constable. I realize the East End isn't by any means affluent. But this isn't the East End, is it?"

"No, sir, it ain't and that's one of the things I'm wonderin' about." Barnes shook his head vigorously. "Annie Shields was a flower seller. How could she afford to live here? She'd be lucky to make a farthin' or a couple a tuppence on any bunches she sold. And a room like this, in a clean house and with this much furnishin', would cost a good deal more than she could bring in."

Witherspoon thought about it. Dash it all, Barnes was right. There was something decidedly odd about Annie Shields living in a room all on her own. Most poor people lived crowded in horrid tenements or doss houses. Yet this room, for all its shabbiness, was clean and warm. "Good observation, Barnes. Where did she earn the money for this room?" He thought of something. "Perhaps she did more for her customers than just sell them flowers."

Barnes laughed. "Even if she were a prostitute, sir, she'd still not be able to afford this place. Most girls earn just enough to pay for a bed in a doss house and buy a pint of gin and a bit of tea. There's too much competition for any of 'em to make much money at the game. According to last month's report, there's over twelve hundred prostitutes in Whitechapel alone."

The inspector felt a flush creep up his cheeks. He knew he was a bit naive about some things. "Er, then, if she wasn't supplementing her income, how on earth did she earn enough money to pay her rent? Perhaps her husband left her something her landlady didn't know about."

"Maybe." Barnes shrugged. "I don't know, sir. But knowin' you, I expect we'll find out. Expect we should get crackin' on the search. Are we lookin' for anythin' in particular?"

"Not really." Witherspoon wished they were looking for something specific. He suddenly remembered that Barnes had told him someone important was pressing for an investigation into this poor woman's murder.

For the first time he wondered who that person could be and, more to the point, what their interest was in a young flower seller. A flower seller who apparently lived beyond her means.

He glanced around the room, again noting the limp curtains, the threadbare carpet. How sad, he thought, a room this shabby was all the woman had to call home, and he, by virtue of being a policeman, thought it more than someone of her station could ever hope to aspire to. Witherspoon wasn't sure what it was he felt. Yet he was decidedly uncomfortable. There was something very wrong with a system which kept people like himself in the lap of luxury while others lived in such abject poverty.

"Barnes," he said quietly, "do you know the name of the person who pressed for an investigation in this case?"

The constable hesitated. "Well, sir, officially, the chief inspector isn't admittin' anyone pressured him to put you on the case."

"But unofficially." Witherspoon laughed. "Come now, Constable. You know you've more sources at Scotland Yard than the East End has pickpockets. Who is it?"

"It was a solicitor, sir. Important one, too. Man named Harlan Bladestone." Barnes raised his finger and pointed. "Should I start with that wardrobe?"

"Right, I'll take the trunk."

They searched the victim's room. Under the bed, the inspector found a wooden box. Opening the lid, he found a small, empty drawstring pouch, a lock of blond hair, some buttons and a slim bundle of papers. The papers were empty envelopes. David Shields's old pay packets with the name of the brewery written on the front and some plain white envelopes as well. "It appears Mrs. Shields was frugal. She saved old envelopes to be reused."

In the wardrobe, Barnes found a few dresses, a set of woolen underwear, a worn shawl, and a pair of scuffed shoes. Oddly enough, he also found a bundle of baby clothes. On the floor of the wardrobe, he found a wooden rattle.

Further examination turned up nothing interesting, certainly nothing that indicated where Annie Shields had obtained her rent money. "We might as well go," the inspector said when they'd finished. "We've found precious little here."

"Where are we going next, sir?" Barnes brushed the dust off his hands.

"Let's pay a call on her employer," Witherspoon said. "Perhaps he can be of some help. First, though, I'd like to have another word with the landlady."

Mrs. Basset was standing in the front hall, her arms folded across her chest. "Bleedin' Maples, if'n he don't have my rent by tomorrow, out he goes," she declared as the two policemen came down the stairs.

"Did Mrs. Shields have a family?" the inspector asked quickly. Really, he thought, he should have asked that question straightaway. If there were relatives, they had to be notified.

"Annie were an orphan," Mrs. Basset snapped, glaring at the closed door of the impoverished Maples. Her tone implied that it was Annie's fault she had no parents. "David never mentioned his family. Certainly none of them turned up 'ere offerin' to take Annie and the girl in."

"Girl?" Witherspoon's eyebrows shot up. "What girl?"

"Emma. Annie's daughter."

CHAPTER 3

"Well, dang and blast," Luty Belle muttered to herself as she spotted Inspector Witherspoon and Barnes coming down the steps of a shabby house at the end of the street. Quickly, she looked around for a place to hide. Spotting a cart pulled up waiting to unload barrels, she scurried behind it just as the two policemen turned and headed her way. Luckily, they were on the other side of the road, but Luty wasn't going to take any chances.

"You lookin' fer somethin'?" a voice asked.

Luty glanced up. A young man with dark curly hair and the brightest blue eyes she'd ever seen grinned down at her. "No," she replied tartly. "If I was looking for something, I'da said so."

"Really, now." His smile widened. "Then whatcha hidin' behind me cart for?"

Luty rolled her eyes. "Why do ya think? I'm tryin' to not be seen."

He lifted his chin and gazed across the road. "Ah, I see. You're not wantin' them coppers to spot you, eh?"

"That's right." Luty saw Witherspoon glance towards the cart. She ducked her head.

"You an American?" he asked, looking down at her.

"Yup." Luty was completely crouched behind the row of barrels right behind him. If the silly fool kept turnin' his head and blatherin' at her, the inspector might see him. Luty didn't relish the thought of trying to explain why she was hiding behind a cartful of barrels. "Listen, if'n you don't mind, would you kinda look the other way, least until they gets past?"

He chuckled but turned towards his horses. "Now, ain't this some-thing? Here I finally meets me a Yank and she's hidin' from the law. You'll be fine in just a second, luv. They're almost gone," He paused. "There. They've rounded the corner. You can get up now."

She groaned as she rose from her crouch. Her knees creaked and her ankles felt like they were on fire. Gettin' old was hell, she thought. Maybe she should have brought her cane along, "Thanks fer not givin' me away," she told him.

He stared at her, his expression frankly curious as he took in her fancy peacock-blue dress, elegant feathered hat, and fur muff. Not to mention her white hair. "If you don't mind me askin', what'd you do to have the coppers lookin' fer ya?"

Luty was tempted to make up some wild tale involving shoot-outs, radical politics, and six-guns, but as she actually had a Colt .45 in her possession, she thought better of it. The young man appeared to be sym-pathetic, but you never knew. "They ain't actually looking for me," she admitted. "But I thought it best if they didn't see me, that's all."

"Last I heard it was a free country," he retorted. "You've a right to go where you like. You've made me right curious. What's a woman like you doin' hidin' from the law?"

Dang, Luty thought, a feller with nose trouble. He was goin' to keep at her until she told him something. She could tell by the way his chin jutted. Stubborn cuss. 'Course she really couldn't fault him for being curi-ous. She was of a curious nature herself. "Let's just say I'm doin' a bit of private inquiring round here. I don't think the police would take kindly to my activities."

"So they know who you are, then?"

"What makes you say that?" Dang, Luty thought, a smart feller with nose trouble.

"Because if at least one of them coppers didn't know who you was, you wouldn'ta bothered to be hidin' behind my barrels, would you? Even coppers don't go about aggravatin' well-dressed ladies unless they've got a reason. So I figures, they know ya."

"All right, so they know me." She started to walk away.

"Hey, just a minute, luv," he called. Luty stopped and turned to face him.

"Whatcha inquiring about?" he asked seriously. "I live around these parts, maybe I could help ya some."

Luty thought about it for a moment. "Young woman who lived over there"—she pointed to the house at the end of the row—"got murdered last night. I aim to find the one that did it."

He gaped at her. "You mean Annie Shields?"

"You knew her?" Dang, Luty thought, she should have been spending her time askin' him questions, not wittering on about why she was hiding.

His face tightened and all the amusement vanished from his eyes. "Everyone round here knew her. Liked her, too. Poor Annie, I hope they hang the one that did it."

"Sounds like you feel pretty bad about what happened to her."

"She were real nice. Loaned me a bob or two when I was short." His expression became wary. "Why is Annie your business? What was she to you?"

"I can't really tell ya," Luty said honestly. "But like I said, I'm tryin' to help find who killed her, if that's any comfort to ya. What's yer name?"

"Harry Grafton. What's yours?" He still looked a bit frosty, but Luty could tell he was starting to thaw.

"Luty Belle Crookshank." She walked back to the wagon and stuck up her hand. He gazed at her for a brief moment and then reached down and grasped her fingers in a firm handshake. "I reckon you knew Annie pretty well, didn't ya?" she continued.

He nodded. "Her and her husband. Me and David worked together. He was a driver, too. We both worked for the brewery. It were right sad when he got killed. Poor sod was crushed by a load of barrels." He shook his head in disgust. "And now Annie gettin' coshed on the head by some bloody thief so's they could steal the only decent thing the woman owned. It makes me sick, it does, right sick to my stomach."

Luty stared at him sharply. "You sure know a lot."

Harry shrugged. "News travels fast round these parts."

"What makes you so sure it was a robbery?"

"Why else would anyone kill her? She didn't have any enemies. Worked hard, minded her own business, and tried to do right by others, too, when she could. It's bloody obvious, is'n it? Someone murdered Annie for a bleedin' ring. Kitty—that's me wife—was always sayin' that opals was unlucky. Looks like she were right. Annie had that damned ring on last night and some bloody bastard saw her wearin' it and killed her for it."

"How do you know she had the ring on?"

Harry pulled off his flat workingman's cap and scratched his head.

"I saw it, didn't I? Annie come over to see the wife last night. We was all down at the Cock o' the Walk havin' a bit of a drink. She had the ring on when she come in. Kitty told her she shouldn't be wearin' it. But Annie said she had to. Said she needed to show it to someone. Daft it was, wearin' that bloody ring just so she could show off a bit."

"The Cock o' the Walk?" Luty repeated. "Where's that?"

"Just round the corner there," he said, pointing up the street.

"Did Annie often go in there for a drink?" Luty was trying to decide if she should go there next or to Annie's house. She wanted to get as much information as fast as possible.

He laughed. "Nah, Annie didn't hardly drink. She come in lookin' for Florrie Maxwell. Needed Florrie to look after her girl 'cause she were goin' out that night."

"Girl? What girl?" Luty asked.

"Her daughter, Emma. Sweet little mite, she is. Smart as a button, too. Well, Annie don't like leavin' Emma at night, unless'n she can leave her with Florrie. 'Course I can understand her feelin's. Emma's hardly more than a baby. She's only three."

"How on earth can that woman be so callous," Witherspoon exclaimed. Barnes grunted in assent. "She as good as admitted Emma Shields had lived in her house since the day she was born, yet she's no idea of her whereabouts!"

Barnes cleared his throat. "Now, sir, all Mrs. Basset said was she didn't know who took care of the lass while Annie worked."

"That doesn't do us any good," the inspector moaned. "Somewhere out there"—he gestured expansively with his hand as they hurried down the road—"is a poor orphan and no one seems to care in the least about her. Certainly not that landlady!"

"I expect we can find out by askin' about the neighborhood," Barnes said soothingly. "Do you want me to get onto it?"

Witherspoon hesitated. He hated the thought of that poor child being all alone out in the world, but if he personally took time to look for her, he'd delay finding her mother's murderer. "No." He sighed. "We'll have some of the uniformed lads start inquiring. The local coppers can probably find the girl faster than you and I. We still need to get over to Covent

Garden and speak with her employer and we also must interview this Harlan Bladestone."

"That shouldn't be difficult, sir," Barnes said, whipping out his notebook. "I looked up his address before I left the Yard this morning."

"Constable." Witherspoon came to a full stop. "This won't create difficulties for you?"

"You mean because I wasn't supposed to know who'd been on the chief?" Barnes laughed. "Don't worry about it, sir. I may have me sources at the Yard, but Bladestone's comin' in and raisin' a ruckus weren't no secret. It was all over the canteen by eight o'clock this morning."

"Excellent." Witherspoon stopped again and looked around. "Now, let's see. Where are we exactly? Ah, yes." He waved towards the busy crossroads just ahead. "There's a constable just past the hotel. We'll have him nip round to the local police station and find some lads to start inquiring about Emma Shields."

It took only a few minutes to give the constable his instructions. Witherspoon hailed a passing hansom and he and Barnes were on their way to see Mr. Harlan Bladestone.

"What are your ideas, Barnes?" Witherspoon asked.

"Reckon she was killed durin' a robbery," the constable replied thoughtfully. "Least that's what it looks like. I don't know, though, sir. After seein' her room, somethin' don't seem right."

Witherspoon frowned. Much as he hated to admit it, the constable had a valid point. There was something decidedly odd about the victim living in such circumstances. Furthermore, he didn't altogether trust that landlady. He couldn't put his finger on what it was that bothered him, but he'd learned to trust his feelings. Why, just a few months ago, Mrs. Jeffries had told him he was gifted with a strong, "inner force." The inspector wasn't precisely sure what she meant, but he no longer worried about that either. Whatever this force was, it had helped him solve a number of homicides. It was going to help him solve this one, too. "Apparently, there's more to Annie Shields than meets the eye. For one, she was living in quarters far more extravagant than an average flower seller could afford."

"She might have had a settlement or some kind of income from her husband's people," Barnes replied.

"That's possible."

"But you think it's doubtful?"

"I do," Witherspoon explained. "From what Mrs. Basset said, it certainly didn't sound like the husband's family was all that keen to help the woman. And there was something about that landlady I didn't quite trust."

"What do you mean, sir?" Barnes asked curiously.

Witherspoon hesitated. It was difficult to put his feelings into words. "She didn't seem to know enough," he explained. "Oh, I can't quite say what I mean, but Annie Shields had lived at that house for four years, and in all that time, the landlady didn't know how she got the money to pay her rent, who took care of the child while she went out to work, or if either Annie or her husband had any relations." He shook his head. "I'm sorry. But my experience has been that landladies as a whole make it their business to learn as much as they can about their tenants. Mrs. Basset didn't seem to know anything."

"Or she wasn't tellin'," Barnes muttered darkly.

"That's a possibility, too," the inspector agreed. "It's amazing how many people there are in this city who have no sense of duty. But there's something that bothers me a great deal more than what Mrs. Basset does or doesn't know."

"What's that, sir?"

"Why is a prominent solicitor putting pressure on Scotland Yard to solve this murder? More importantly, how did Harlan Bladestone know about the murder?"

"Couldn't have read about it in the papers," Barnes said. "For me to hear about it in the canteen, he must have been onto the chief before the mornin' papers come out. Well, sir, however he found out, we shall soon know."

The offices of Harlan Bladestone were located in chambers near the Temple Bar. An unsmiling clerk dressed in a stiff collar and black frock coat led them down a dark hallway and into a quiet room where two other clerks were hunched over their desks busily scribbling.

"Please wait here, Inspector," the clerk said, pointing to a single high-backed chair. "I'll tell Mr. Bladestone you're here."

A few moments later a tall, smiling man with dark brown hair, an enormous mustache, and a florid complexion barreled into the room. "Inspector Witherspoon." He extended his hand. "I'm so glad you've come. I'm Harlan Bladestone. I've been waiting to talk to you. I told your chief

I particularly wanted you to investigate this dreadful business." He smiled at Barnes.

"How do you do, sir," Witherspoon said, getting up and taking the proffered hand. He was surprised by the warmth of the man's greeting. "This is Constable Barnes."

"Good, good, please"—Bladestone turned abruptly and started back the way he'd come—"do come into my chambers."

They followed him down another dark hallway and into a room with floor-to-ceiling shelves of books on all the walls. Pale light from the overcast day filtered in through two narrow windows behind a massive desk.

Bladestone gestured at two well-worn leather chairs and the constable and Witherspoon sat down.

"I expect you're here to find out why I'm so interested in Annie Shields's murder," he said bluntly.

"Yes, sir." Witherspoon was rather taken aback. Gracious, another surprise. Not only did the man greet him like he was a long-lost friend, but he was actually going to get to the point. How very peculiar. It had been his experience that most legal men wittered on for hours without saying anything. Especially as this was a murder investigation. Why, most people became positively tongue-tied when you tried getting any useful information out of them. "We've several questions to ask you, Mr. Bladestone. The first one, of course, is what your interest in this poor unfortunate woman was."

"Don't you want to know how I found out about the murder so quickly?" Bladestone asked.

"Er, yes, of course we do. How did you know?"

"Actually, I sent my footman along to Covent Garden this morning with a message for Annie. Well, of course, by the time he arrived at the flower market, the news had already spread that she'd been murdered. As soon as I heard that, I went straight to your chief." He smiled wryly. "He's an old friend."

"And your interest in Annie Shields?" Witherspoon was getting more curious by the minute.

"Ah." Bladestone sat back in his chair and steepled his fingers. "This may take a while in the telling, sir."

"We've plenty of time, Mr. Bladestone."

"I suppose I must begin at the beginning." The solicitor's eyes took on a wistful, faraway expression as he stared over the inspector's shoulder at a spot on the far wall. "You see, I've known Annie for over a year now. Ever since her husband died. But my meeting Annie isn't where it all began."

"Where what all began?" Witherspoon asked, getting more confused by the moment.

"The murder, or at least the circumstances leading up to it." The lawyer smiled apologetically. "Do forgive me, sir. But this is most difficult. You see, I may be completely wrong. It could well be that Annie was murdered by some vicious animal who wanted to steal what little she had. The events of twenty years ago may have had absolutely nothing to do with her death."

Betsy glared at the young, dirty ruffian blocking her way. Keeping her gaze locked to his, she lifted her hand and shoved hard against his shoulder. "Get out of my bleedin' way," she ordered in a harsh voice.

"'Ere now, I was only tryin' to be friendly like." The oafish lad stumbled backwards, his filthy porkpie hat sliding off his greasy blond hair in the process. "No call fer you to be so pushy." His small, piglike eyes narrowed as he stared at her.

Betsy knew he was taking in every detail of her neat, oxford-cloth blue dress, her shiny black shoes and the fact that the cape she wore wasn't patched with holes. Her fingers tightened on her purse. He was either a pickpocket or an out-and-out thief. He'd been following her for ten minutes now and she was fairly certain it wasn't because he'd fallen in love with her face. Whatever he wanted, she knew how to deal with the likes of him. She glanced to her left and saw that the constable was still there, walking his patrol. She'd picked her time carefully, waiting until she was in full view of the policeman and on a busy public street. This stupid lout hadn't even noticed the copper. "I'll be plenty pushy if'n you don't stay out of me way," she said, deliberately roughening her tone of voice even further and reverting back to the speech patterns of her childhood. "I'm not some doxy streetwoman you can manhandle any way ya like." She jerked her chin towards the constable. "So keep yer bloody distance or I'll call that copper."

Surprised, he gaped at her as she stepped past him. Betsy forced herself not to look over her shoulder as she hurried towards the flower market.

A sigh of relief escaped her when she didn't hear any footsteps coming from behind her. Besides having to put up with that stupid oaf, she'd had a miserable day. She'd learned nothing on Southampton Street, so rather than go back empty handed, she'd decided to try her luck here. After all, Covent Garden was where Annie Shields got her flowers. But so far, everyone she'd talked to hadn't told her a blooming thing. The best she'd gotten was that Annie Shields had usually set up her cart over near the arcade on Regent Street.

Maybe I'll go there next if I don't have any luck here, she thought. Betsy slowed as she came near a flower seller humping a load of flowers into a wheeled cart. "Excuse me," she said politely, "but I'm wonderin' if you could help me."

"You wantin' to buy somethin'?" the girl asked. She was short, thin to the point of emaciation, dark-eyed, and pale-skinned, with reddish hair bundled under a cotton head scarf.

Betsy hesitated. She had plenty of coins. Thanks to their unknown benefactor back at Upper Edmonton Gardens, she hadn't had to spend any of her wages to buy the new shoes she was wearing. Truth was, she hadn't had to spend any of her own money on anything lately. Their benefactor kept her well supplied.

"I'll take a nosegay, please," she said, digging out her coin purse.

The girl handed her the flowers. "That'll be sixpence, please," she said. "They's a bit more than usual 'cause during the fall and winter they's grown in the greenhouse."

Betsy wondered if the girl told all her customers this. She handed her a shilling. "Keep the change." She smiled warmly. "I'm wonderin' if you could help me with some information? I'm lookin' for a woman named Annie Shields."

"What you want with Annie?" She eyed Betsy warily.

Betsy decided to try a bit of subterfuge. Honesty hadn't gotten her any information today. "Oh, we used to live on the same street back when I was a girl. I heard she was workin' round these parts as a flower seller and I thought I'd look her up."

"You're a bit late." The girl's smile was both cynical and sad. She picked up another bundle of flowers and put them on the cart. "Annie got herself done in last night. She were murdered."

Betsy tried to look suitably shocked. "Oh no. Poor Annie. What happened?"

"They say she got coshed over the head and robbed. But I don't believe a word of it." She dusted off her hands and grasped the handle of the cart.

"Why don't ya believe it?" Betsy said quickly, lest the girl get away. "I mean, from what I remember of Annie, no one would want to hurt her. She weren't the kind to be makin' enemies." She fervently prayed this was true. As she'd found out very little about the victim, she could only hope that Annie Shields hadn't been a right old harridan from hell.

The girl studied her for a moment. "'Cause like you said, Annie weren't the kind to make enemies. She weren't no fool either. She knew 'ow to take care of 'erself when she was workin' nights. There's only one person I know of that'd want to 'urt her. That bloody Bill Calloway."

"Who's he?" Betsy stepped directly in front of the cart. She didn't want her source leaving before she was through asking her questions.

"He's a mean bastard, that's who 'e is. 'E's been sniffin' around Annie since the day she buried her Davey. And if'n 'e's the one that killed 'er, I hope they catch 'im and hang him." Her eyes narrowed in anger. "You sure you were a friend of Annie's? You don't talk much like she did."

Betsy was ready for that question. "Oh, I went into service over near Holland Park. The housekeeper's been 'elpin' me to learn to talk proper. About this Calloway feller, why do you think he killed 'er?"

She laughed harshly. "'Cause she told 'im to sod off. Billy didn't take kindly to that. No, sir, not the way Annie did it. Stood right where you are and told 'im to leave her the 'ell alone." She stopped abruptly, her gaze growing even more suspicious. "You're asking an awful lot of questions. You sure you're not a friend of Bill's? Be just like 'im to send out one of his fancy pieces to find out the lay of the land."

"I don't know this Bill Calloway," Betsy retorted, stung by the words *fancy piece*, "and I'm askin' questions 'cause I'm curious."

"Don't pay to be curious around these parts."

Betsy ignored this. "Listen, did Annie have any special friends round 'ere? Someone I could talk to? I'd some nice things to give her, and if'n she's dead, I might as well try and find someone else to give 'em to. By the way, what's yer name?"

"Me name's Muriel. Muriel Goodall." She licked her lips. "Uh, what kind of things you got? Come to that, I was as good a friend to Annie as anyone round 'ere."

"I've got a cloak and a pair of good boots—oh, and a nice woolen sweater and a pair of gloves." Betsy smiled widely. "Why don't we go have a cup of tea somewhere and you can tell me all about Annie. I would so like to hear what my friend's been up to these last few years."

Muriel glanced over her shoulder towards the flower market. A big, burly fellow with a fierce frown and a stained apron over his fat belly glared in their direction. "That's Mr. Cobbins. I work for 'im. So did Annie. Tell you what, I'm supposed to do Annie's shift over at the arcade on Regent Street. Why don't you meet me there in an hour or so?"

Luty cocked her head and plastered what she hoped was a grandmotherly smile on her face. She lifted a gloved hand and knocked on the door of the small row house. A moment later the door opened and a short, heavy woman wearing an old-fashioned mobcap and a huge apron over her starched brown dress opened the door.

"Yes?" the woman said cautiously.

"Good day, ma'am," Luty began in her politest voice. "Are you Florrie Maxwell?"

"I am. Who might you be?"

"My name is Luty Belle Crookshank." She smiled, pulling a pristine white, elegantly printed calling card from her muff. "My card. I'm wonderin' if you'd be so kind as to spare me a few moments of your time."

Impressed by the calling card, Florrie Maxwell held the door open and motioned her inside. "Uh, please, come in."

A few moments later Luty was sitting smack in the parlour. From upstairs, she could hear the sounds of children playing. "I'm sure you're very curious as to why I'm here," Luty began. "Actually, it's, well . . ." Ye Gods, what if this poor woman didn't know Annie Shields was dead?

"Is it about Annie?" Florrie asked quietly.

Luty nodded. Florrie's eyes filled with tears. She swiped at one that rolled down her plump cheeks. "I don't know who I expected to come claim Emma, but you look like a kind lady. Are you a relative of David's? He had some family that went to America."

For the first time in many years Luty was stumped. But that only lasted a second or two. "Does Emma know her mama's gone?" she asked softly.

Florrie nodded. "But she doesn't really understand what it means. She's just a baby. I'm so glad you've come. Much as I hated the idea, I was goin' to have to take the child to the orphanage. Not that I wouldn't love to keep her myself, but I can't afford another mouth to feed around here, not with my Arnold down sick and Edgar bein' out of work. Fact is, we're goin' to be goin' to Leicester today. Edgar's mother says one of the shoe factories is hirin'. We might not be back."

"I'm sure you'da been right good to the girl," Luty said sympathetically, "but it's best she be with her relations. Uh, where is she?"

"She's upstairs taking a nap."

Luty's mind raced frantically. Was taking an orphan child the same as kidnapping? Oh hell, what did she care anyway? She had a big empty house, dozens of staff, and an army of lawyers. Surely, one of them ought to be smart enough to keep her out of jail. Taking the girl in for a few days would be better than lettin' the poor little thing go to one of them orphanages or, even worse, a workhouse. "Good, then we'll let her sleep. Why don't you and I talk a spell while we wait for Emma to wake up. Tell me, do you have any idea why anyone would want to hurt Annie?"

Florrie swiped at another tear. "Gracious, no. Annie worked hard and minded her own business. She was a good mother, too. She always brought Emma round here when she was workin', not like some that just leaves 'em on the streets all day."

"I know it was right hard for Annie to get by," Luty said cautiously. "I reckon she had to work day and night sellin' flowers to afford to keep a roof over her head and food on the table. I'm real sorry Annie didn't let me know how bad things was. I'da liked to help her."

"Oh, but aren't you the one that's been sendin' her—" Florrie broke off in confusion.

"Sendin' her what?"

"Money," Florrie replied. "Haven't you been sendin' Annie money every week? Or is it someone else in the family that's been doin' it? She couldn't have afforded her own room or to pay me if someone hadn't been helpin' her. I just thought it were someone from David's family. The money started right after he were killed."

Luty shrugged nonchalantly. "It was probably my cousin Herbert," she lied. "Tell me, how'd Annie get the money? Did she get a paper she had to take to the bank every week?"

"You mean a bank draft or a check?" Florrie's tone grew a mite frosty.

"Sorry, didn't mean no offense." Luty grinned. "Just back where I come from half the folks wouldn't know what a check or a bank draft was, that's all."

"It's all right." Florrie smiled. "Half the people round here wouldn't know either. The money come in cash. First of every week. That's usually how Annie paid me. As soon as the boy brought the envelope, she'd come round here and pay me in advance for watchin' over Emma. Then she'd pay her landlady."

"A boy brought her the money?" Luty frowned. "Huh, musta been one of the other relatives," she muttered, getting into the spirit of her fib. "That don't sound like Herbert. He'da brought the money himself and made Annie sign a receipt. I expect it was Eugene that was sendin' the cash. He's a right trustin' sort. When did the boy come? I mean, what day of the week was it?"

"Every Monday morning. Annie'd be round here by ten to pay me."

"So he come to her rooms?"

Florrie nodded. "Annie didn't tell me anything else about him. Why? Does it matter?"

"Not really, exceptin' that if it was Eugene sendin' the money, I'd like to know." She leaned forward. "There's been a bit of bad feelin' between Eugene and Herbert ever since David died. You know what I mean, family trouble."

"I know just what you mean," Florrie said, bobbing her head again. "My aunt Geraldine went twenty years not speakin' to her sister, Lydia."

Satisfied that the mythical Herbert and Eugene and their alleged feud had quenched Florrie's curiosity, Luty tried to think of another plausible reason to keep asking questions. Florrie was sympathetic but not stupid. "I expect it was good that Annie found you to take care of Emma. Especially as she was workin' evenin's."

"I was pleased to do it. But Annie didn't work all that often. Only a couple of times a week." Florrie chewed on her lip. "Fact of the matter is, she hadn't planned on workin' last night at all. It come up sudden like." Florrie glanced down at her hands. "She still owes me for last night."

Luty reached for her muff and drew out a wad of notes. She peeled two off the top. "I'll settle up fer her. After all," she lied, "she was family."

"Gracious." Florrie stared at the notes like they were fixing to bite her. "This is way too much!"

"Seein' as how you've been so good to Annie and Emma, why don't you just keep it?"

Flustered, Florrie hesitated.

"Go on now," Luty urged.

A towheaded lad about eight came running into the parlour. "Here now," Florrie scolded. "You're not to run in the house. Haven't you got eyes in your head, boy. We've a lady visitin'."

"Sorry, Mama," the boy said. He stared at Luty.

"This here is Mrs. Crookshank," Florrie said.

"Pleased to meet you." Luty smiled.

The boy's eyes widened at her accent. "You sure do talk funny."

"Hush, Harvey." Florrie turned to Luty. "I'm so sorry."

Luty laughed. "That's all right. I don't mind the boy's honesty."

There was a loud thump and then a distinct wail from the room over their head. Florrie got to her feet. "That's probably Emma. I'll go up and get her."

Harvey continued to stare at her. "You one of Emma's relations?"

"Yup," Luty lied. "You one of Emma's friends?"

"Nah, she's just a baby."

"So you don't play with her, none."

"What can a baby do?" Harvey shrugged. "But I do keep me eye on her when we goes outside. Sometimes Mam makes me take her out to get the fresh air."

"I bet you take good care of her, too," Luty said.

"Sure do. I kept that woman from botherin' her, didn't I?" Harvey's thin chest swelled with pride. "She were probably one of them baby stealers or one of them god-awful heathens. But I run her off good, didn't I?"

"What woman?"

"That veiled lady. The one who was hangin' about and watchin' the house every time Annie brung Emma over here."

"Now be real quiet, Wiggins," Smythe commanded as he eased open the back door. "Slip up the hallway, make sure the kitchen's clear, and then nip up the back steps right to the top."

Wiggins gripped the three bunches of flowers closer to his chest. "Who gets what?" he hissed.

"Roses go to Mrs. Jeffries, carnations to Mrs. Goodge, and the mixed bunch are fer Betsy." He glanced back at the carriage. "Now hurry up, before someone spots us."

"I still don't see why we've got to give 'em flowers," Wiggins whispered. "Besides, I'm supposed to be gettin' the meat order. What if Mrs. Goodge asks where it is?"

"Tell her the butcher's deliverin' it later today," the coachman replied impatiently. "You know Mrs. Goodge, she loves havin' goods delivered. And we don't *have* to give them flowers. But seein' as how we probably offended all three of 'em last night, I'm thinkin if we ever want a decent meal or kind word from any of 'em again, we'd best mend some fences."

"These musta cost a bloomin' fortune. Where'd you get that kinda money?" Wiggins eyed the coachman suspiciously.

"I hit a winner at the races last week," Smythe lied smoothly. "A long shot and I got these on the cheap, so they didn't cost us 'ardly anythin'. Now go on, get movin'."

"Do we have to take Luty Belle flowers, too?" Wiggins asked. "We was just as rude to 'er."

"We wasn't rude, boy." Smythe resisted the impulse to grab the ruddy flowers and take them upstairs himself. He would have, but he didn't want to leave the footman in charge of his beloved horses. "And Luty Belle is Hatchet's problem, not ours. Now 'urry up. I don't want Mrs. Goodge gettin a spot of nose trouble and comin' out to see what we're up to. These flowers is supposed to be a surprise."

"Still don't see why we're givin' them flowers," Wiggins muttered as he started down the hall. As he neared the kitchen he heard voices, so he quieted his steps.

"So you don't know Annie Shields?" he heard Mrs. Goodge say.

"Never heard of the girl until this morning," a squeaky but decidedly male voice replied. "'Course, once we heard she'd been murdered, everyone was talkin' about her. Poor woman. Mind you, Henrietta Tavers said she wasn't in the least surprised that Annie had been killed. And she didn't think it were no robbery neither."

Murder? Wiggins's mouth gaped open. He sidled up to the edge of the door so he could hear more.

"Really," Mrs. Goodge said, "why's that? Do have another bun, Augustine. They're awfully nourishing."

"Thank you, I don't mind if I do. It was ever so nice of you to invite me round today. I was ever so surprised to get your message this afternoon. Mum will be right pleased."

Message? This afternoon? Wiggins didn't need to hear more. He knew instantly what those females were up to. They were trying to get the jump on a murder case. Both he and Smythe had come in for lunch. Mrs. Goodge had looked surprised to see them, but she hadn't said one word.

Not a bloomin' word. Now he knew why she'd looked so guilty when he'd asked where Betsy and Mrs. Jeffries were. They was out investigating.

He stared down at the flowers in his arms.

"Hmmph," he snorted as he turned on his heel and marched towards the back door, not caring how much noise he made. "Flowers, indeed!"

Once he told Smythe that those females were investigating a murder without them, the coachman wouldn't want to give them flowers either. And he'd bet his next month's wages that Luty Belle Crookshank was in on it, too!

Just wait until Hatchet found out about that.

CHAPTER 4

"Then again, in good conscience I must tell you everything." Harlan Bladestone sighed dramatically. "Inspector, as I said, there is a real possibility that what happened twenty years ago could have a direct bearing on Annie's murder. It's a rather complex narrative, so please bear with me."

"You have my full attention, Mr. Bladestone," Witherspoon said. Really, he did wish the man would make up his mind.

"Twenty years ago one of my clients, someone who, for the moment, really must remain nameless, fell in love with a charming young woman. Unfortunately, he wasn't able to marry her." Bladestone smiled wryly. "Due to financial circumstances, my client married another woman."

"Financial circumstances?" Witherspoon wondered if Bladestone meant his client had married for money. Well, there was nothing particularly mysterious about *that*. From what he'd observed, more couples came together for gain rather than for love. Though, to be honest, Witherspoon thought it rather sad.

"Financial in the sense that the man was very poor, but very talented at his occupation." Bladestone shifted uncomfortably. "He was, at that time, a carpenter. I suppose it would be more accurate to say he married not for love, but for a, well, a business opportunity."

"Yes, I suppose I understand."

"To make a long story short," Bladestone continued, "my client married the wrong woman. He prospered financially, but at great cost to his personal happiness. As a matter of fact, he's now quite rich. But as is often the case in these matters, 'fate,' as they say, 'is stronger than anything I have known.'" He paused dramatically. "Euripides," he murmured, when the two policemen stared at him.

"Er, yes. I suppose some do think fate is quite strong," the inspector retorted.

Bladestone gave him a world-weary smile, then cleared his throat. "My client"—he jabbed his hands in the air for emphasis—"and I daresay, my friend, was miserable in his marriage despite his prosperity."

Gracious, Witherspoon thought, this man has missed his calling. He should have been an actor. "Yes, sir, you've already mentioned that."

The solicitor blinked, seemed to catch hold of himself and gave them a self-deprecating smile. "So I did, sir. Forgive me. Sometimes I do get carried away. But back to my narrative. As chance would have it, my client's wife died several years ago. Not that that fact has any direct bearing on this matter, of course. However, what does matter is that my client was now a widower. Rich, successful, and suddenly unencumbered. For the first time in his life he had the time and leisure to take stock of his life, and what he found did not please him. More importantly, the young woman my client left behind so many years ago was with child."

Witherspoon drew in a quick breath and Barnes glanced up from his notebook.

Bladestone raised his hand. "Please don't think harshly of the man. In his defense, my friend did not know about the child. He would never have abandoned the woman had he known."

Well, I should hope not, the inspector thought, but he did manage to keep the sentiment to himself. Despite Mr. Bladestone's defense of this man, he didn't much care for him. He sounded like a selfish cad. "I take it this child or this woman you speak of has something to do with Annie Shields's murder?"

Bladestone nodded. "I think it might have everything to do with this foul crime." He smiled sadly. "The sins of the father . . ."

Honestly, Witherspoon thought, a poetic lawyer. He did wish the fellow would get on with it. Beside him, Barnes shifted restlessly.

Suddenly the door burst open. A tall man with dark hair liberally sprinkled with gray at the temples charged inside. On his heels was the stiff-faced clerk.

"Have you heard the horrible news, Harlan," the man cried. "She's dead. Oh God, how can I bear it? She's been foully murdered."

"I tried to stop him, sir," the clerk sputtered, wringing his hands.

Harlan Bladestone paled and leapt to his feet. "Henry, for God's sake, get a hold of yourself." He gestured at Witherspoon and Barnes. "These men are from the police. This is Inspector Witherspoon and Constable Barnes."

"The police? Oh, thank God." He hurried towards them. "You can help me, then. You can find the savage animal that took my darling from me."

"And who would you be, sir?" the constable asked in his soft, calm voice.

"Henry Albritton."

"And are you referring to Mrs. Annie Shields, sir?" Barnes continued.

"Well, of course I am." Henry's eyes filled with tears, but he bravely blinked them back.

"You knew the victim, sir?" the inspector managed to ask. He did so hope the man would get hold of himself. Egads, what if he started to cry?

"Knew her!" Henry swallowed heavily. "How could I not know—"

"Henry," Bladestone interrupted. "Before you say another word, I'd like to speak to you in private."

Henry ignored him. He turned beseeching eyes to the two policemen. "How could I not know her? She was my darling, my angel. My future. Inspector, you must find the fiend that took her from me."

"Were you planning to marry her?" The inspector blurted out the question without thinking.

"Marry her?" Henry repeated, his tone incredulous. He shook himself slightly as though he couldn't quite believe what he'd heard. "Good God, no. Why would you suggest such a vile thing!"

"Excuse me, Inspector," Bladestone interrupted again, "but you don't quite understand. We've reason to believe that Annie Shields was Henry's daughter."

"And then, Mrs. Jeffries, this Henry Albritton practically insisted I come along home with him and arrest all his relations." Witherspoon picked up his glass of sherry and took a gulp. "The poor man was at his wit's end, I tell you. He's got a whole passel of relatives, none of whom he likes, and Albritton, of course, can't decide which one of them actually murdered Annie Shields. At one point during the conversation he seemed to think they'd all done it." He sighed wearily. "I don't see why this couldn't have been a simple case of robbery. Just my luck, isn't it? I get stuck with what looks like a very nice, easy crime, and before you can snap your fingers we're up to our elbows in complications, melodramatic lawyers, greedy relations, and a host of other loose ends."

Mrs. Jeffries smiled sympathetically. Poor Witherspoon, he was in an awful state. For, that matter, so was the rest of the household. "Not to worry, sir. I'm sure all the pieces will soon fall into place. They always do. Now, sir. What else did you learn today?"

She listened carefully as he told her everything, beginning with his arrival at the morgue to his meeting with Harlan Bladestone and Henry Albritton. Mrs. Jeffries occasionally interjected with a question, but for the most part, she listened carefully, filing away every little detail in the back of her mind.

"So Henry Albritton is convinced that Annie Shields was his illegitimate daughter?" she finally said.

"Virtually. Unfortunately, he'd only met the girl a couple of weeks ago." He broke off and glanced at the clock on the mantelpiece, "So he hadn't really established a relationship with her. I say, what time is dinner?"

Mrs. Jeffries curbed her impatience. "In about ten minutes, sir. But from what you just told me, it seems that Harlan Bladestone had suspected that Annie Shields was Mr. Albritton's daughter for over a year. Why did he take so long to tell him?"

"Because Bladestone wasn't sure." Witherspoon took off his spectacles and rubbed his eyes. "You see, he met Mrs. Shields last year when her husband was killed in an accident. Mrs. Shields had come to his office to see if she had a case of negligence against the brewery, but she didn't. The moment she entered the office, Bladestone noticed how much she resembled Dora Borden—that's the young woman Henry Albritton was in love with before he married Frances Strutts. Er, a, she's the one he married for money."

Confused, Mrs. Jeffries said, "But I thought you said that Mr. Albritton's wife had died. If Bladestone thought Annie looked like the woman Henry was once passionately in love with, why didn't he mention it to him?"

"Bladestone didn't want to upset Albritton. Furthermore, he wasn't sure that Annie Shields had had any connection at all with Dora Borden.

He wasn't going to say anything to Albritton until he knew for certain if Annie was Dora's daughter."

"Why didn't he ask Annie when she came to his office?"

"He did," Witherspoon replied. "But Annie had no idea. Her mother died when she was a baby and she had been raised in an orphanage."

"Surely the orphanage kept records," Mrs. Jeffries persisted.

"It burned down five years ago." The inspector took another sip. "And all the records went up in flames as well. The truth was, the only thing Annie had known about her past was that she was illegitimate and that her mother was dead. She'd no idea who her father was."

"So let me see if I have this right," Mrs. Jeffries said slowly. "Bladestone notices the resemblance between Annie Shields and the woman his client had loved and abandoned twenty years ago, is that correct?"

"Yes."

"And he immediately sets about inquiring as to who Annie's parents were, correct?"

"Correct." Witherspoon's stomach growled and he took another quick peek at the clock.

"Then can we assume that Bladestone knew that Dora Borden had been expecting a child? Otherwise why would he begin the inquiries at all? I mean, if you meet someone who looks like someone else, you don't immediately assume there's a family relationship."

"I wondered the very same thing," Witherspoon replied. Actually, it had been Barnes who'd raised this issue with the solicitor. "Bladestone assured me he hadn't known about Dora's condition at the time she was expecting the child. But several years later he'd run into a mutual acquaintance who'd mentioned that Dora Borden had died during childbirth. When he asked *when* she'd died, he'd realized there was a real possibility the child might be Henry Albritton's."

"Did he tell Mr. Albritton?"

"No, at that time Albritton's wife was still alive and he didn't think it would be wise to say anything. However, Bladestone made some inquiries to try to find the child, but he wasn't successful."

"I still don't understand. Bladestone thought Annie Shields was Henry's daughter for over a year. Yet he said nothing. Why? Albritton's wife is now safely dead, so it's not as if she would be hurt by the knowledge."

"I gather Albritton's had a few problems with melancholy and, well, depression the past couple of years. Bladestone didn't want the man to be upset or disappointed in case it turned out Annie's resemblance to Dora Borden was merely a coincidence. So the upshot of it was, Bladestone said nothing until two weeks ago."

"What happened then?"

"It seems Albritton finally told Bladestone he was so miserable with his life, he was going to sell off his boatyards and move away." Witherspoon's eyebrows rose. "Bladestone was rather alarmed. I gather Albritton had gotten involved with radical politics. He thought that if Henry saw the girl and perhaps made some inquiries as to who she was, well, perhaps that would give him a new perspective about his life."

"Oh dear, how sad." Mrs. Jeffries wasn't sure she followed precisely what the inspector was saying, but she was sure she could sort it out later. "So he did actually meet Annie Shields?"

"Oh my, yes." Witherspoon smiled. "He's been buying enormous bunches of flowers from her every day for the past two weeks. And tipping her generously. I think it was his way of giving her money. Thank goodness he *was* tipping the girl; her employer at Covent Garden certainly wasn't wasting any of his time mourning the poor woman. I can't imagine what he must have been like to work for!"

"Did you learn anything useful there?" Mrs. Jeffries asked.

"Not really." The inspector sighed. "Dreadful, how hard some of these poor girls have to work to make a living. Absolutely dreadful. Oh, before I forget, we may be interrupted this evening. I left instructions at the police station that I was to be informed immediately when Emma Shields was located. So don't be alarmed if you hear someone knocking on the door in the middle of the night."

"Thank you for telling me, sir." Mrs. Jeffries got up. "I do hope they find the little girl before too long."

"So do I, Mrs. Jeffries, so do I."

Hatchet was outraged. Eyes blazing and chest puffed up like a bullfrog's, he gazed resolutely at his fellow sufferers. "This is war, you know."

"War! Crimminey, all they did was get the jump on us with this murder," Wiggins protested. He'd calmed down some now that he'd had a few minutes to think about it.

"Don't be naive." The butler began pacing the length of his elegantly appointed rooms. Rooms that now contained three vases of fresh flowers. "Those women deliberately kept us in the dark. They're out to prove a point. They're out to prove they're superior to men." He stopped and straightened his spine. "And they'll stop at nothing to achieve their ends."

"Don't you think you're bein' a bit dramatic, Hatchet," Smythe said. He propped his feet up on a footstool and watched the agitated butler start pacing again. Cor blimey, if he weren't careful, he was goin' to walk a hole in that fine Belgian rug.

"I most certainly am not." Hatchet flung out his arms. "Are you two blind? Don't you understand what this means? If we let them get away with this, before you know it they'll want to run for Parliament, they'll demand to be let on the police force, they'll take over the banks, the schools, the hospitals. Soon no place will be safe for man nor beast."

"What do ya suggest we do?" Smythe rather enjoyed the butler's outrage. Made a change from listenin' to Wiggins's awful poetry.

Hatchet's expression grew thoughtful. Finally he said, "I think we must teach them a lesson."

Smythe snorted and Wiggins giggled.

Hatchet glared at both of them. "I fail to see what's so amusing."

"And how we goin' to be teachin' this lesson?" the coachman asked. "Don't matter much what we say, the truth is, they's a pretty sharp lot."

"Sometimes"—Hatchet smiled slightly—"it takes more than intelligence to achieve one's end. Sometimes, one has to be as sly as a fox and as merciless as a banker."

"'Old on now." Smythe sat up. "What're you suggestin'?"

"If you'll give me a moment to explain. I wasn't suggesting anything untoward or improper. I was merely thinking that with this new murder, we've the perfect opportunity to show those heartless women exactly how much they need us."

"How we goin' to do that?" Wiggins asked.

"It's very simple, my boy." Hatchet gave them a wide smile. "With this case, we'll just have to make sure that we solve it first."

"But Mrs. Jeffries is usually the one that comes up with the answer," Wiggins protested. If the truth were known, Wiggins wasn't all that sure they could solve the case on their own. Mrs. Jeffries had somethin'. Somethin' special.

"Admittedly, that's the way it's been in the past," Hatchet said. "But that's no reason to think we're not as capable as she is of finding a killer."

"Bloomin' Ada," Smythe exclaimed, "we don't even know for sure the women was deliberately tryin' to keep this one to themselves! Wiggins only heard part of a conversation. For all we know, they might have 'eard about the murder after we left the 'ouse today."

"Oh no," Wiggins put in, "that's not so. We was both in at lunch. Besides, I 'eard what that feller said to Mrs. Goodge. He said he'd got her message this afternoon. That means she musta sent it sometime this mornin'. Remember how funny she acted when we asked where everybody was."

"Of course they knew about the murder. Probably fairly early this morning, too. And as I recall, madam slunk out of here like a thief in the night right after breakfast." Hatchet shook his head, his expression stubborn. "She was up to something, all right."

"Look"—the coachman gave up trying to reason with the other two—"you might be right. Maybe the women is tryin' to get the jump on us. We'll know tonight. If they say nuthin' about the murder, then we'll know they's tryin' to keep it to themselves."

"Indeed we will," Hatchet muttered. "If Luty Belle Crookshank thinks she can investigate a murder without me, well, she's got another think coming."

As soon as the inspector had retired for the evening, Mrs. Jeffries hurried down to the kitchen. She was eager to hear what the others had found out.

Betsy and Mrs. Goodge were waiting for her at the kitchen table. "Luty's not back yet," the cook said as Mrs. Jeffries took her usual seat, "and it's gettin' a mite late. I'm afraid the men's going to show up before she gets here."

"The men's already showed up."

They turned and saw Smythe and Wiggins, who had entered the house with unnatural quiet, standing just inside the kitchen near the entrance to the back hallway.

"Good." Mrs. Jeffries gave them a bright smile. "I'm so glad you're back. There's been a murder."

Some of the suspicion left Smythe's eyes and Wiggins visibly relaxed. "Well, looks like we come home just in time, then." Smythe strolled towards the table. "Good thing I cut Bow and Arrow's run short, or I'da missed this." He pulled out a chair and gave them a cocky grin. "Who's been murdered, then?"

Mrs. Jeffries, knowing darned good and well that neither man was surprised to learn of the homicide, decided to plunge straight in. After all, the women were already ahead of them. In good conscience, she couldn't exclude them further. "A young flower seller by the name of Annie Shields. She was bludgeoned late last night."

"Ah . . . Mrs. Jeffries," Wiggins said nervously, darting a quick glance at the coachman. "Maybe you'd better wait a minute to start. I think Hatchet might be on his way over."

"Really? How very convenient," Mrs. Jeffries replied. "We're waiting for Luty Belle, too. Isn't it a remarkable coincidence that all of us should end up here when none of you even knew a murder had taken place?"

Smythe sighed. Irritated as he was with the women, it wasn't in his nature to play coy. "We knew there was a murder, Mrs. J," he said bluntly. "Wiggins overheard Mrs. Goodge pumpin' someone earlier today when he nipped back 'ere."

"Why didn't you come into the kitchen and get that ruddy sausage machine?" Mrs. Goodge asked, frowning at the footman.

"I, uh, didn't 'ave time."

Smythe ignored them and ploughed straight ahead. He wanted to clear the air. "And fer a while today, we was afraid you ladies was tempted to keep this one fer yerselves."

"We'd never do that," Betsy exclaimed.

He raised one eyebrow as he looked at her. "Then why didn't you mention the murder when Wiggins was 'ere earlier? Then we coulda all gotten started."

"How could I tell Wiggins anythin' if he was tiptoeing about eavesdropping," Mrs. Goodge snapped. Of course, it was an out-an-out prevarication. She'd seen the footman several times since learning of the murder and she'd seen both of them at lunch.

"I weren't tiptoein' about tryin' to listen to people," Wiggins shot back. "I come back for that bloomin' contraption and 'eard you goin' off behind our backs investigatin' a murder."

"Why shouldn't we try to get a bit ahead of you," Betsy said angrily. "After all them nasty things you men was sayin' about us. It's only natural we'd look for an advantage. It's not like *I* can go out pub crawlin' at night lookin' for clues." It had long been a sore point for the maid that Smythe's activities weren't restricted to the daylight hours as hers were.

"We wasn't sayin' nasty things," Smythe protested. He was truly astounded that she'd taken such deep offense at what he'd thought was merely a spirited exchange of views. Blimey, maybe he shoulda made Hatchet give 'em back the flowers. He'd known her nose was out of joint, but he hadn't thought she'd still be steamin' over it. On the other hand, perhaps he shouldn't have made that comment about females being weak minded and overly emotional during the full of the moon. Come to think of it, it had been a fairly stupid thing to say.

"Now, now," Mrs. Jeffries interrupted, "please calm down. This is getting us nowhere. We've already discussed our various opinions about the rights of women and I don't think any of us are going to change our views. But in case you've forgotten, we do have a murder to investigate here."

"What about Luty Belle and Hatchet?" Mrs. Goodge asked.

Mrs. Jeffries paused and then flicked a quick look at the clock. "We'll give them another few minutes and then we'll start. In the meantime I think we could all do with a spot of tea."

By the time Betsy was putting the pot on the table, they heard the back door open. Fred, who'd snuck down to the kitchen in hopes of cadging a treat off Wiggins, shot out from under the chair and scampered down the hall, barking joyously.

"Splendid, splendid," Hatchet's strong voice rang out. "Good dog, that's right, always guard your castle." He and the animal, who was now bouncing so hard at his feet that poor Hatchet practically had to skip and hop his way into the kitchen, took their spots at the table.

"Good evening, Hatchet," Mrs. Jeffries said.

He swept off his black top hat and pulled out a chair. "Good evening, everyone," he said, his tone formal and frosty.

Betsy and Mrs. Goodge exchanged a quick grin and even Mrs. Jeffries hid a smile. As Luty Belle would say, Hatchet had a bee in his bonnet about something and Mrs. Jeffries was fairly certain she knew exactly what it was.

"I'm so glad you're here," she said, "we've been waiting for you."

"Waiting for me?" he asked archly. He sniffed delicately. "Whatever for? I only decided to come round to see if madam was here." He gave them a cool smile. "She's been gone all day on some mysterious errand of her own. An errand that she refused to talk about. You ladies wouldn't, by any chance, happen to know where she might be?"

"They knows, Hatchet," Wiggins said. "We've already 'ad a right old to-do about it and they claims they was only tryin' to get a bit of a jump on us, not keep us out completely."

"Really?" Hatchet stared straight at Mrs. Jeffries.

She couldn't stop herself, she laughed. "Really, Hatchet. Did you honestly think we'd try and investigate a murder without the valuable services of the male of the species?"

His features eased, the ghost of a smile softening his stiff mouth. "Well . . ." he said doubtfully. Then he laughed. "Of course not, though I will admit Wiggins and Smythe and I had rather a good time today imagining the worst and doing some plotting of our own."

Mrs. Jeffries sagged in relief as she saw the tight faces around the table relax. Like the steam off the teapot, the tension seemed to evaporate into thin air. No doubt they'd all enjoyed their dramatics, but none of them really wanted to damage the sense of camaraderie working on a case always gave each and every one of them. Well, not too much, she thought, noticing the determined lift of Betsy's chin and the sheer brightness of Smythe's brown eyes. "Good. I'm so glad you enjoyed yourselves. Now, should we wait for Luty or should I go ahead and start?"

"Why don't you go ahead and start," Hatchet said smoothly. "I can always tell madam everything she's missed on the drive home."

Several other voices murmured agreement, so Mrs. Jeffries cleared her throat and started. She told them everything the inspector had told her earlier.

"Did the inspector give you the names of these relations this Mr. Albritton wanted arrested?" Smythe asked.

"I got them from him over dinner," she replied. She whipped a piece of paper out of the pocket of her stiff brown skirt. "There were so many of them, I wrote them down . . . let me see, well, first of all, there's Henry Albritton himself. He could have had his own reasons for murdering Annie Shields."

"Why would he do that and then raise such a fuss with the police?" Wiggins asked.

She shrugged. "I don't know, I'm merely saying that we mustn't take him or anyone else connected with this case at face value."

Betsy asked, "How many relations has he got? I mean, how many suspects have we got?"

"Several." Mrs. Jeffries frowned at her handwriting. She'd scribbled the names in such haste, she could barely make them out. "There's Albritton's sister-in-law, Lydia Franklin. She's lived in the household for years. Then there's Gordon Strutts and his wife, Hortense. Strutts is also one of Albritton's late wife's relations . . . let's see. I think that's the only ones actually living in the Albritton house."

"What about the solicitor, this Harlan Bladestone?" Smythe reached for his mug. "Seems to me he might be a suspect, too."

"Why do you think so?" Mrs. Jeffries asked curiously. The coachman was very intelligent and perceptive. She had a lot of respect for his opinion.

He took a long, slow sip before answering. "Well, by 'is own admission, 'e's known Annie Shields for a long time. She come to 'im askin' for legal advice when her husband were killed. From what we've 'eard, Annie might 'ave been a comely lass. A widow. Maybe the victim and the solicitor knew each other a bit better than 'e let on."

"Annie wasn't like that," Betsy protested.

"How do you know?" Hatchet asked.

"'Cause I learned a lot about her today," she replied. "And since David Shields was killed, she's not looked at another man."

"You do seem to have heard quite a bit," Mrs. Jeffries said encouragingly. "Do go on, I've finished with what I had to say."

Betsy smiled smugly. "All right, if you're sure you're finished. I spoke to one of Annie's friends today. A girl named Muriel. She said Annie kept to herself and worked hard. There's been several men who were interested, one more persistent than the others, but she didn't want nuthin' to do with any of 'em."

"Who was the persistent feller?" Smythe asked.

"A man named Bill Calloway." Betsy frowned. "I think we should definitely put him on our suspect list. Accordin' to what Muriel told me, he'd been hangin' about Annie Shields for ages. On the day of the murder, she'd gotten fed up with him and told him to leave her alone. Said, she never wanted to see him again. Did it publicly, too. Muriel said that Calloway looked, angry enough to wring Annie's neck, only there were a police constable on the street, so he didn't quite dare lay a finger on her."

"But if he were in love with Annie," Wiggins said innocently, "surely he wouldn't hurt her."

They all stared at him incredulously.

"Who said he were in love with 'er?" Smythe retorted, "And even if 'e were, that don't mean he didn't do it. More women's been murdered in the name of love than for any other reason. Least that's what the man always says."

"Disgusting," Betsy interjected. "But true. I remember when I was a little girl, the man living in the rooms next to ours almost killed his wife just because he'd seen her talking to another man." Her eyes grew troubled and distant as she recalled the ugly memory. "He half beat the poor woman to death and no one did anything at all about it. It was horrible. All that screamin' and cryin'. My sisters and I were so scared, we clung to each other and hid under the blanket till it stopped. That was even worse. There was just this awful silence."

They all stared at her. She looked down at the table.

"Sisters," Wiggins muttered.

Smythe motioned for him to be quiet. "Betsy, lass," he said softly. His voice seemed to draw her back into the room and she gazed around, blushing as she saw everyone watching her. "That must have been really 'orrible for you."

She nodded slowly. "It was." She laughed nervously. "But that was life in the East End. Always someone screamin' and cryin' and carryin' on about something." She picked up her cup of tea and quickly took a drink.

Wiggins opened his mouth to ask the question they were all thinking, but Mrs. Jeffries quickly said, "What else did you find out about Calloway?"

"He don't seem to have a position, but he's always got coins in his pocket, if you know what I mean." Betsy cleared her throat and men continued, her voice slightly off pitch. "Annie didn't trust him. She told Muriel she thought Calloway might be part of a ring of thieves. Calloway hangs about at a tavern on Pinchin Street down at the docks."

"What's the name of this tavern?" Smythe asked.

"The Sail and Anchor," she replied. "Why? You thinkin' of goin' over there?"

"Don't you think that'd be a good idea? You just said yerself that he might be a suspect."

"Well, yes," she admitted slowly, a suspicious frown creasing her forehead. "But I was kinda hopin' to nip over that way myself tomorrow."

"Don't be daft, girl," Mrs. Goodge exclaimed.

"You can't go into a place like that all on your own," Wiggins said.

"Absolutely out of the question." Hatchet sniffed.

"You'll go over my dead body," Smythe muttered, but he mumbled the words so softly only Betsy heard them.

"Betsy, for once I'm forced to agree with the others," Mrs. Jeffries said.

Betsy shot Smythe a puzzled glance and then turned towards the housekeeper. "But why? I've gone to the East End on me own before."

"You weren't quite alone, Miss Betsy," Hatchet said smoothly. "If you'll recall, I went along as well." He'd gone when they were searching for a missing woman on one of their other cases. Because of Betsy's familiarity with the district, it had only been logical that she should go and find the person they were seeking. But as a precaution, Hatchet had trotted along for protection. Irritated as he was with the ladies about some of their recent radical ideas and featherbrained thinking, he certainly wasn't going to let one of them put herself in danger.

"But you didn't go marchin' in and out of sailors' taverns on the last trip," Smythe shot back. "It's too bloomin' dangerous, you silly woman."

"Silly woman!" Betsy yelped.

"You don't need to be screamin' like a banshee now." He leaned towards her, his face set in a fierce frown. "There's nuthin' wrong with my 'earin.'"

"But there's somethin' wrong with your brain," she argued.

Wiggins, Hatchet, and Mrs. Goodge jumped into the discussion. The conversation became so heated that none of them heard the back door open or the heavy footsteps.

"Where should I put her?" The voice was loud and unfamiliar.

They all turned and looked. A man holding a huge blanket-wrapped bundle cradled against his chest stood in the doorway next to Luty Belle.

"Well, madam," Hatchet said pompously as he rose to his feet. "It's about time you got here."

"Evenin', everybody," Luty said cheerfully. She jabbed her parasol in the direction of the butler. "Give her to that feller there," she ordered. Hatchet pushed back his chair and started across the room.

The driver, for that's what he was, a hansom driver, gave his bundle to the puzzled-looking Hatchet, tipped his hat, pocketed Luty's fare money and generous tip, and took off out the way he'd come.

Hatchet stared at the bundle in his arms. "Madam," he said, "precisely what is it you've thrust upon me?"

From inside the bundle came a loud wail. Startled, Hatchet lifted his hand and threw back the top of the blanket.

A teary-faced child with brown curly hair and big blue eyes stared back at him.

"Well, I never."

The little girl gazed at Hatchet through her tears for a moment and then broke into a huge grin.

"Luty," Mrs. Jeffries said slowly. She couldn't take her eyes off the child and the stiff-necked butler who was now smiling so broadly it was a wonder his cheeks didn't burst. "Is that who I think it is?"

Luty sighed heavily. "Now, before you all go gettin' all het, I brung her here 'cause I didn't have no choice."

The child giggled, poked her hands out of the blanket, and yanked at Hatchet's stiff collar.

"This here's Emma," Luty continued. "Annie's daughter."

CHAPTER 5

There was a moment of stunned silence as they each understood the exact implications of what Luty had done. Even Fred, who'd been sniffing the bottom of the blankets in Hatchet's arms, stopped wagging his tail and stared at the elderly American.

Then they all started talking at once.

"Good heavens, madam," Hatchet exclaimed, "what have you gotten us into now?" Emma squirmed and he obligingly tossed the blankets off and lowered her gently to the floor.

"We're really in the soup now," Mrs. Goodge added.

"Crimminey, the inspector'll 'ear about this for sure," Wiggins moaned.

"Luty, have you lost your mind? Bringin' the girl back here?" Betsy stood up. "That's all we need!"

"Now, before all of you decide I've gone loco," Luty began, "just hear me out. Like I said, I had to bring Emma here; otherwise, she'd have been put in an orphanage."

"Better that than the inspector sussin' out what we've been up to," Wiggins muttered.

"Oh, come now, madam," Hatchet snapped. "Surely there must have been another way."

"What we goin' to tell 'im when he finds out Luty took Emma?" Betsy wrung her hands. "And he's bound to find out. Mrs. Jeffries says he got coppers combin' the area lookin' for the girl. They'll find out she was taken by an American and then, sure as the sun follows the stars, they'll find out you brought her here. The first thing he'll want to know was why you was snoopin' about in one of his cases! And he ain't daft. He'll soon find out we've all been snoopin'."

"I really think everyone ought to watch what they're sayin'," Smythe said softly, his gaze directed at the child. He nodded in Emma's direction and gave her a gentle smile. "We wouldn't want her to think she was unwelcome."

But no one listened to him.

Hatchet continued berating his employer, Betsy and Mrs. Goodge were loudly lamenting the death of their detective days, and Wiggins was adding his tuppence worth as Luty vigorously defended her actions. Mrs. Jeffries said nothing. She was too busy thinking.

Fred, sniffing the discarded blankets, got excited by the raised voices. He woofed in confusion and bounced up and down. Emma, who'd been staring at the adults with a bewildered expression on her little face, whirled around. She saw the prancing dog and started to wail. Turning frantically, she spotted Smythe sitting calmly at the table and smiling at her. Emma took off for him at a dead run.

Fred dashed after her. Emma screamed as she heard his paws pounding on her heels. The big coachman opened his arms, scooped her into his lap, and chucked her under the chin.

"Now, now, lass," he soothed. "There's nothing to be scared of. Fred's just a big friendly dog, that's all." He reached down and calmed the dog with a quiet word. Fred plopped down on his rump and nudged his head against Smythe's knees.

Emma stopped crying and watched as he slowly stroked Fred's head. She stuck out her hand, hesitated for a brief moment, and then reached down and imitated his motions. She giggled as the animal licked her fingers.

Emma's outburst shut them all up.

"You've got a right nice way with younguns," Luty said.

"Cor blimey." Wiggins grinned. "You've sure charmed the little 'un."

"Thank goodness you kept your head," Hatchet agreed. "We really must watch raising our voices. No wonder the poor child was frightened."

"You ought to have a couple of your own," Mrs. Goodge said sagely. "Looks to me like you'd make a good father."

"Indeed," Mrs. Jeffries agreed. "Smythe does seem to have the knack. He did know how best to handle what is a very unusual situation."

The only one who didn't say anything, Smythe noticed, was Betsy. She

simply stared at him and the child on his lap with one of those odd, female expressions where you hadn't a ruddy clue as to what was going on
in her head. He would have given a lot to be able to read minds at that
moment. Especially Betsy's.

Mrs. Goodge stood up. "Let me get the girl a bun to chew on," she
said, hurrying towards the dry larder down the hallway. "Never seen a
little one yet that didn't like sweet buns."

"Is she hungry, then?" Wiggins asked.

Luty shook her head. "No, Florrie fed her right afore we left."

"Who's that?" Betsy asked.

"The woman who was mindin' her for her . . ." Her voice trailed
off. "You know, her *m-o-t-h-e-r.*" She spelled the word out and gazed
anxiously at the child. But Emma was too busy patting Fred to notice
anything going on around her.

"Listen now," Luty continued. "I knows I was takin' a risk bringing
the youngun with me. But I had to do something. Florrie Maxwell and
her family was leavin' tonight and she was fixin' to take the child to the
orphanage or the foundlin' hospital afore she went. She ain't goin' to be
back fer a while, so they's no way the police can find out I took the girl.
Who's gonna tell 'em?"

"I should think a whole host of informants could tell them," Hatchet
said. "The neighbors, local tradespeople, shopkeepers—"

"Don't worry about it, Luty," Mrs. Jeffries interrupted the butler's
morose litany. "What's done is done. I daresay, I, for one, think you
did just the right thing. We'll think of something. Even if the inspector
does discover you were the one who took Emma, he won't necessarily
connect that act with all of us helping him solve his cases. Let's not go
anticipating the worst."

Hatchet snorted in disbelief.

Luty shot him a glare. "You can stop acting so high-and-mighty,
Hatchet. Seems to me this is a bit like the pot calling the kettle black.
Who was it that come draggin' Jon home a few months ago?"

"That's hardly the same thing, madam," he protested. "Jon didn't
have anywhere to go . . ." His voice trailed off as he realized that Luty had
neatly trapped him.

"Just what I said," she said smugly, "and that poor little gal didn't
have no place to go neither."

"Give it up, Hatchet," Smythe said softly. "Sometimes the ladies are right. Lettin' this child go to one of them orphanages would'na been right."

"Here you are, ducks." Mrs. Goodge bustled up to the table and put a plate of buns in front of Emma. The child immediately ceased petting Fred and snatched up her treat. Wiggins reached for one as well, but the cook swatted his hand back.

"Ow," the footman yelped.

"You let that child eat her fill before you start stuffin' in yer mouth," she warned.

"We really must get on," Mrs. Jeffries said. She glanced at Hatchet. "Can you tell Luty everything on the drive home?" He nodded. "Good. Now, Luty, did you learn anything useful other than Emma's whereabouts?"

"Sure did." Luty told them about her meeting with Harry Grafton. "So, you see, Annie was wearin' the ring when she was ki . . ." She faltered and glanced at the child. But Emma, her mouth caked with bread crumbs, had fallen asleep against Smythe's massively broad chest. "You know."

"So it could have been nothin' more than a robbery." Betsy frowned thoughtfully. "If she was showin' that opal off in the pub, there's lots that could of seen her. But that don't sound right either. Accordin' to what Muriel said, Annie Shields knew how to take care of herself and she were careful."

"Perhaps this one time she wasn't careful," Mrs. Jeffries said.

"And she was wearin' that ring to show it off," Luty added. "That's what Harry told me. He and his wife had been onto her about wearin' it out at night. Annie had told him she had to, that she was goin' to show it to someone."

"The truth is, we have no idea whether or not she was killed for the ring or for some other reason," Mrs. Jeffries said firmly. "We don't have enough evidence to make any assumptions. Furthermore, the inspector's information has definitely been interesting. If Harlan Bladestone and Henry Albritton are correct, there are several other suspects with a motive for murder."

"Who's that? What other suspects?" Luty demanded.

Hatchet gave her an evil grin. "I'm afraid you'll have to rely on me to tell you, madam. You mustn't expect everyone to repeat themselves. It's getting too late."

"Hmmph." Luty's eyes narrowed. "Well, then, maybe I won't be so eager to tell ya what else I learned today."

"Oh now, Luty." Mrs. Jeffries determined it was time to intervene. They had enough troubles now with Luty having spirited Emma right into their midst. Whatever rivalries were brewing would just have to wait until the next case. "Please go on. We've really got enough on our plates to worry about at the moment without everyone getting secretive."

"All right," Luty agreed reluctantly. "I found out that someone's been sendin' Annie"—another quick glance towards the coachman to make sure Emma was still sleeping—"money."

"How often?" Smythe asked softly.

"Every week. Come in cash and was delivered to her lodgin' house by a young man."

"Who was sendin' it?" Wiggins asked.

"Florrie didn't know." Luty shrugged. "Annie was real closemouthed when it come to money."

Smythe shifted the sleeping child slightly. "What day did it come on?"

Luty smiled. "Every Monday mornin', like clockwork."

"Interesting," Mrs. Jeffries murmured. "Very interesting." The more she learned about Annie Shields, the more she was convinced that this was no simple robbery gone awry. "When did the payments start?"

"Right after Annie's husband was killed," Luty replied. "That's why Florrie was pretty sure that someone in David's family was the one sendin' the cash. She thought it was just his relations helpin' the widow out some."

"Maybe it was a settlement for her husband's death," Mrs. Goodge suggested.

"Oh no," Mrs. Jeffries assured everyone. "That's not true. Inspector Witherspoon told me specifically that the brewery had no liability in the accident that killed David Shields. Annie Shields had gone to Solicitor Bladestone for that very reason. That was how he'd met her in the first place. Bladestone also told her she had no case."

Luty tossed another disgruntled frown at Hatchet. "I hope you remember who everyone is," she told him. "'Cause I ain't got a clue who you're all talkin' about."

Mrs. Jeffries smiled. "Did you find out anything else?"

"Not really," Luty admitted. "Harvey Maxwell, that's Florrie's boy, told me he'd seen some veiled lady hangin' around Emma. But I don't set much store by it."

"Why not?" Wiggins asked.

"'Cause when I questioned him about it, he couldn't remember when he'd seen this woman, or how many times he'd seen her, or whether she was tall, short, fat, thin, or walked bowlegged." Luty grinned. "Besides, his ma brought Emma in just as Harvey was tellin' me all this and Florrie told me not to pay him any mind. Said Harvey's got a history of tellin' some pretty tall tales."

Emma whimpered in her sleep. Smythe soothed her with a gentle pat on her back. "The little one's tired. She needs to get to bed."

Hatchet started to get up. "I'll take her."

"Before you go," Mrs. Jeffries said quickly, "we really must decide who is going to do what tomorrow."

The butler nodded and sat back down.

"I've got to try and find a woman named Millie Groggins," Betsy said. She shot Smythe a quick, impatient frown. "Seein' as Smythe has decided I'm not fit to set foot in a tavern . . ."

"I told ya," he shot back in a loud whisper, "it's too ruddy dangerous."

The maid ignored him. "I'd best see if Millie can tell me anything. Accordin' to Muriel, Millie was on the Strand that night, the same as Annie." Betsy deliberately didn't tell them that Millie's occupation was decidedly not a flower seller. She really didn't need Smythe or Wiggins, or for that matter even Mrs. Jeffries or the cook, trying to tell her not to be seen talking to a prostitute. She could take care of herself.

"Who's Millie?" Wiggins asked interestedly.

"She, uh, worked with Annie," Betsy replied.

"I'll pop round the Sail and Anchor," Smythe offered. "Even if Calloway's not about, maybe one of 'is mates will know where I can find 'im."

"See what you can learn about Henry Albritton as well," Mrs. Jeffries said.

"Albritton?" Smythe looked puzzled. "Now, why would he be killin' his own flesh and blood?"

"Flesh and blood!" Luty yelped. "Now, this is gettin' plum loco. Who the dickens is this Albritton?"

"I'll tell you later, madam," Hatchet said impatiently. "We can't sit here all night explaining every little detail."

"Annie Shields was probably Henry Albritton's illegitimate daughter," Mrs. Jeffries said quickly, reaching over and patting Luty's hand. "Hatchet will tell you all about it. Do you think you can find out about a woman named Lydia Franklin? She's part of Albritton's household. His sister-in-law, as a matter of fact."

Somewhat mollified, Luty nodded. "Where do they all live?"

"On Linley Close. That's just off the Edgeware Road." Mrs. Jeffries turned to Wiggins. "And could you nip over there tomorrow morning and see what you can find out about Hortense Strutts."

"What about 'er 'usband?" the footman queried.

"Of course," the housekeeper replied, "but I was also going to ask Hatchet to see what he can find out about Mr. Gordon Strutts." She gave the butler an encouraging smile. "You have so many different sources of information, I was rather hoping you'd see what you could learn about all the gentlemen involved in this case."

Hatchet smiled slightly, but he was pleased as punch. "That would be Albritton, Gordon Strutts, and the solicitor Harlan Bladestone."

"Nell's bells," Luty exploded. "I'm a few minutes late and you've got more suspects than there are fleas on a dog."

They all ignored her outburst. Hatchet did have truly remarkable information sources. He easily knew someone in every gentleman's club in London. He also knew butlers, footmen, cabbies, and a host of odd and rather colorful individuals.

"Exactly, Hatchet," Mrs. Jeffries replied. "Learn what you can about all of them. It would be most helpful to see if you can determine their whereabouts last night."

"In other words," Hatchet said cheerfully, "determine if they have alibis."

"I expect you want me to do my usual?" Mrs. Goodge asked.

"Of course," Mrs. Jeffries said. She rose to her feet and they all followed suit.

"Good, now that we've got a name to work with, so to speak," Mrs. Goodge muttered, "we'll see what we can find out." A name to her meant someone who moved in society. "My poor cousin's boy did the best he could," she explained. "But he really didn't know much about the victim. Claimed some around there weren't surprised about the killin' and most seemed to think it weren't robbery. But when I questioned Augustine a bit further, it turned out he was only repeatin' what he'd heard. He didn't know a bloomin' thing and he didn't have the ruddy sense to ask. But not to worry, I sent him back with a flea in his ear, and when he comes round on Thursday, I expect he'll know a few facts. Considerin' where he works, he should have learned somethin' by then."

"Here"—Hatchet reached for the sleeping child—"I'll carry her out to the carriage."

"Leave her ta me," Smythe said softly as he cradled the child tenderly against his chest. "I don't want us jostlin' her and wakin' her up. She might get scared seein' as we're all strangers to 'er."

"All right." Hatchet turned to Luty. "Are you ready to leave, madam?"

"Might as well." Luty rose to her feet. "I expect you'll jaw my ears off once we get home, might as well git it over with."

"Don't worry," Mrs. Jeffries said cheerfully, "we'll think of something to tell Inspector Witherspoon should he find out you took Emma."

"Poor little thing." Mrs. Goodge gazed sympathetically at the bundle in Smythe's arms. Then she looked at Luty. "What *are* you going to do with her?"

Luty shrugged. "Keep her fer a few days, I reckon. Maybe by then we'll know what kinda man this Albritton feller is. If'n he's decent and he turns out to be Emma's flesh and blood, maybe we'll take her round to him. But I sure as shootin' wasn't going to let her git dumped in some orphanage like she was a sack of flour."

As they said their good-nights Mrs. Jeffries noticed that Betsy watched Smythe carrying the sleeping child down the hall. Admiration and respect shone in her eyes. Considering how the maid and the coachman were frequently sparring with one another, Mrs. Jeffries thought Betsy's attitude rather telling. Goodness, she thought with an inward smile, the girl's staring at him like she expects him to sprout a halo and wings.

The Albritton house was located in one of the more fashionable areas off the Edgeware Road. The huge four-story Georgian structure of pale beige brick and white-trimmed windows stood at the end of the street, surrounded by its own garden and backing up against the grounds of St. Phillips Church.

Witherspoon gazed mournfully at his reflection in the ornate hall mirror as he and Barnes waited for the butler to return with his master. "Still no word on little Emma?" he asked.

"PC Popper reported they've located the house where the child was stayin', but it looks like the woman that was takin' care of Emma has gone to visit relations somewhere up in Leicestershire."

"Was the child with her?" Witherspoon asked hopefully.

"The neighbors didn't know," Barnes said. "But from everything Popper heard about Florrie Maxwell, she sounds like a decent woman. Not the kind to just abandon the girl."

"Do we know *where* in Leicestershire this Florrie Maxwell went?"

Barnes shook his head. "Not really, sir. One of the neighbors seemed to think it was some village outside Leicester, but another neighbor insists the Maxwells aren't in Leicestershire but at Nottingham. We're still trying to get it all sorted out, sir."

"Drat."

"Inspector Witherspoon," Henry Albritton exclaimed as he dashed into the hall. "A good morning to you, sir, and to you as well, Constable. Do please come into the drawing room. I'm sure you've an enormous number of questions you need to ask me. I do apologize for being in such a state yesterday. I daresay I was still in a state of shock. Do come this way, please."

Albritton swept them into the drawing room. The walls were covered with emerald-green-and-white-striped wallpaper. Emerald-green velvet curtains tied back with elaborate tassels surrounded three large windows which overlooked a good-sized garden. The floors were highly polished dark wood that gleamed brightly even in the pale autumn light. The other end of the room contained a huge marble fireplace adorned with silver candlesticks, exquisite porcelain pieces and large Oriental vases. Each vase contained an enormous bunch of flowers. A multitude of wing chairs, curved two-seater settees, and tables covered with fringed shawls completed the room. On every surface were small objets d'art and more flowers. Exquisite landscapes and seaside paintings adorned the walls.

"Exactly how many people are there in your household?" the inspector asked.

Albritton motioned them towards a settee by the fireplace. "If you include the servants, almost a dozen. But I expect you're not including the staff, are you?" He smiled cynically. "Servants aren't generally considered people, are they?"

Offended by the comment, Witherspoon stared at him for a long moment. "On the contrary," he replied honestly, "I consider every human being on the face of the earth a person."

Albritton flushed slightly. "Forgive me, Inspector, that remark was uncalled for. As you can understand, I'm rather not myself today. Annie's death has caused me great grief."

Witherspoon's annoyance evaporated in a wave of sympathy. "I quite understand." The inspector gazed at him for a moment and then straightened his spine. Questions had to be asked, even painful ones. This was a murder investigation.

"Mr. Albritton, do you know for certain that Annie was your daughter?" The inspector needed to get this point perfectly clear in his own mind. He wasn't quite sure, but he felt it might be very pertinent to this case. Perhaps, even, the very heart of the motive itself.

"For certain?" He smiled sadly. "Yes. In my own mind, I'm absolutely satisfied that Annie was my daughter. Do I have proof?" He waved his hands dismissively. "Not the sort that would satisfy a court or a policeman. But I took one look at her face and I knew. She was the spitting image of my Dora."

"Excuse me, sir," Barnes said. "But did you ever say anything to Annie about this resemblance?"

Albritton hesitated. "Well, yes. As a matter of fact, I did. Last Friday, as a matter of fact. I asked her if she knew anything about her mother. Naturally, she didn't. After all, she was hardly more than a baby when she was taken to the orphanage."

"So she'd no idea that she had any connection with you," the inspector said.

"I don't think that's quite true," Albritton said hastily. "You see, Annie was very intelligent. I think she was beginning to suspect something. I asked her if she had any keepsakes from her mother. I was hoping she had a trinket or a letter or something which would help to identify the woman."

"And had she anything?" Witherspoon asked curiously.

"The only thing she had from her mother was a ring. An opal." He smiled shyly. "I can't tell you how I felt when Annie told me about the ring. You see, I know where Dora got that ring. I gave it to her over twenty years ago."

"Was it a betrothal ring?" Witherspoon asked.

"Oh yes, I'd given it to Dora when I asked her to marry me. I know they're supposed to be unlucky. But I was very poor and it was all I could afford at the time. Dora was thrilled when she saw it. She hadn't expected it, you see."

"And she didn't give it back when the engagement ended?"

Albritton gazed down at the floor. "She tried to. But I refused to take it. I felt so horrible about not marrying her that I wouldn't let her. You see, it was a few days after I proposed to Dora that the man who became my father-in-law, William Strutts, came to me and offered me the opportunity of a lifetime if I'd marry Francis." He looked up and the cold, empty expression in his eyes sent a chill down Witherspoon's spine. "I was young and greedy, Inspector," Albritton continued bitterly. "And I sold myself for the sake of a business opportunity. By doing so, I ruined the life of one I held dear and condemned my own flesh and blood to a lifetime of poverty and misery."

Witherspoon didn't know what to say. He could hardly agree with Mr. Albritton. The poor man was already dreadfully upset and morose. "Now, now, sir. You mustn't be so hard on yourself. I'm sure you didn't think things would turn out so badly."

Albritton appeared not to have heard him. He stared straight ahead, his gaze unfocused and his face set in misery.

The inspector cleared his throat. "Right, well, we must get on with this. Let me see if I have this straight. Mrs. Shields told you about the ring on Friday, correct?"

"That's right. She was going to bring it on Monday and let me have a look at it. I made it a point to stop at her stall on Regent Street."

"Why didn't she bring it on Saturday?" Barnes asked.

"I had a meeting with my partner, Sherwin August, on Saturday morning."

"But she was murdered on Sunday night," Witherspoon said. He glanced at his constable. Barnes nodded slightly. They were both thinking the same thing. There had been no ring on Annie's finger when her body was found, nor had there been a ring in her room.

"Yes," Albritton murmured. "She was murdered."

"And what would you have done when you saw this ring?" Barnes asked.

"Done?" He stared at them incredulously. "Why, I'd have done what I should have done years ago. Sold everything including my half of the boatyards and packed Annie and myself off to a new life in San Francisco. I'm quite a wealthy man, Inspector. Not that my money has ever brought me any real happiness, but I'd have enough to buy a good life for my only child." He stopped and stared at the painting of a sailing ship over the mantelpiece. "You see, I've known for a long time I ought to leave. Once

I had real proof, proof that I could convince Annie with, I'd have taken her away. Taken her someplace where her lack of education, her lack of social graces wouldn't have made a difference. I'm not a fool. I wouldn't have brought her into this house and expected people to accept her. I know the only way she could have had the kind of life and happiness she deserved was if we went away."

"What do you mean, proof that would have convinced Annie?" Witherspoon thought that a rather odd statement. He'd learned, long ago—well, actually, just since he'd begun investigating homicides—that one ought never to ignore an odd statement.

"Annie didn't know me, Inspector." He took a deep breath. "Because of the great wrong that I did her mother, my own flesh and blood was raised in poverty, ignorance, and misery. To say the least, she was a bit cynical about the motives of a middle-aged man who'd started buying flowers from her every day. Annie was a good girl. She wouldn't have gone off anywhere with me unless she knew for certain I was her father. The ring would have proved it. The opal has a small flaw on one side of it, one that you wouldn't notice unless you knew exactly where to look."

"Was the ring your only evidence?" Barnes asked.

"No." He flushed slightly. "Annie's age was another factor. She was nineteen. Her birthday is in March. Well, let's just say that would put her conception at precisely the right time. And I know Dora wasn't involved with other men all those years ago. She loved me." He broke off and laughed harshly. "She loved me and I deserted her. But as God is my witness, I wouldn't have married Frances if I'd known Dora was carrying my child."

"I'm sure you wouldn't've, sir," Witherspoon replied. Really, what else could one say to such a statement? He could hardly call the man a liar. "Did any of the other members of your family know about Mrs. Shields being your daughter?"

"I think they suspected something had changed in my life"—he glanced at a vase of chrysanthemums on the table—"but I never told any of them. Frankly, it wasn't any of their business."

"Then why, sir, do you think that one of them might have been responsible for Mrs. Shields's murder?" Witherspoon asked.

Albritton's expression grew cold. "Because each and every one of them, is more than capable of murder, and even though I said nothing about Annie's existence, they could easily have found out. I'm not good at hiding my feelings. Meeting Annie made me happy. So happy that I'm afraid I got careless. I'd already started making plans, you see. I left some correspondence on my desk. An inquiry to my bank—I wanted them to contact a bank in San Francisco and begin searching for an adequate house for Annie and me. I suspect that several members of my household saw that correspondence. That alone would be enough to rouse their suspicions."

"Do you know for certain that anyone actually saw it, or are you guessing?"

"Well, I wouldn't bet my life on it," Albritton retorted. "But I could see that someone had gone through those papers. I'm a most meticulous man, Inspector. I can tell when someone's gone through my desk."

The inspector was beginning to think the man wasn't thinking clearly. Really, he'd nothing more than suspicions about his relations. He hadn't actually seen any of his family searching his desk, and he'd admitted he'd told none of them about Annie Shields. But Witherspoon realized that pointing this out would do no good. Henry Albritton needed to focus his pain on someone. Grief could do that to a person. However, he'd be remiss in his duty if he didn't investigate the situation thoroughly. "Yes, sir, I quite understand. Now, we'd like to speak to the various members of your family."

It wasn't the food that attracted anyone to the Sail and Anchor, Smythe mused as he looked at the man next to him hacking at the crust of a pork pie. Unable to stand watching any more of the fellow's futile attempts to saw off a bit of crust, he turned and gazed at his surroundings.

The tavern was crowded with dockworkers, day labourers who'd earned the price of a pint, costermen, whores, and old sailors. A gang of toughs took over one corner of the room, talking in hushed whispers, and glaring at anyone who dared come too close. Several thin, bedraggled women huddled in front of the small, mean fire sputtering in the hearth and vainly tried to warm their hands at the meager heat. The rest of the patrons sat at the rickety benches of the long, scarred oak tables or leaned against the bar. The few pathetic chairs scattered about the room were taken by gaunt, elderly men who looked like they'd been sitting there since the last coronation.

The tavern was an ugly place, not just in appearance but in what it was. A place without much hope. The room was crowded, yet strangely silent. Smythe fought back a wave of melancholy. Bloomin' Ada, this place'd depress a saint. He took a swallow of beer and grimaced. Stuff tasted worse than one of Luty Belle Crookshank's home remedies. 'Course, that was only to be expected. The only reason anyone would walk into this place was the beer. It was bleedin' cheap.

Smythe frowned as one of the toughs in the corner cuffed his companion on the side of the head. No one else even noticed. Blimey, what a miserable place. Thank God everyone had helped him talk Betsy out of trackin' down Calloway to this den of sin. Silly girl. Place like this would eat the lass alive and no one would lift a finger to help her. He squinted as the front door opened and a skinny male frame stood silhouetted against the light.

"That's 'im." The barkeep touched Smythe lightly on the elbow and pointed to the man standing in the doorway. "That's Fairclough. He's a mate of Calloway's."

Smythe slipped the publican a half crown. Information round these parts was expensive, but he didn't mind paying. He'd do anything to keep Betsy from nosing into a pit like this and he wouldn't mind getting ahead of the women on this case. It wasn't like he had much else to spend his money on, he mused as he watched Fairclough make his way towards the group sitting in the corner. Smythe frowned. Money. He'd made a ruddy ton of it, but because of a situation not of his own making, he was stuck living a lie.

Fairclough tugged at the sleeve of a heavyset bearded man. The man stared at him, shook his head negatively, and brushed Fairclough's hand away. Smythe watched him appeal to the other men at the table, but the reaction was always the same. Whatever he wanted, they weren't going to give it to him. Shrugging, Fairclough wandered over to the bar. "Give us a pint," he called to the publican.

"Let me see yer coin first."

"Come on now, I've never cheated ya yet," Fairclough whined.

"Only because I ain't let ya," the barman replied. He swiped at the top of the bar with a greasy gray cloth.

"I'll stand ya a drink, mate," Smythe said amicably.

Fairclough's thin face grew wary, his pale, watery hazel eyes narrowed in suspicion. But his thirst for liquor overcame his mistrust. "That's right nice of ya, thanks." He jerked his chin at the barman. "Give us a pint, then."

Smythe waited till Fairclough had his beer and had taken several long, thirsty swallows. "You skint, then?" he asked.

Fairclough nodded. "Who isn't? Ain't had no work in weeks now. Used to make a bit cartin' coal or lumber, but me back's gone, so I can't do that no more."

Smythe nodded sympathetically. In this part of London, there was fierce competition for even the lowest of employment. "Ruddy 'ard to find a decent job. But maybe I can 'elp you some."

Fairclough put his tankard down. "You 'iring?"

"No, but I've a mind to buy some information."

"Information? What kind?" Fairclough asked slowly. He glanced at the corner, but the men there were intent on their own conversation and ignored him.

"You know a man named Calloway?"

Fairclough wiped his nose with the back of his hand and looked pointedly at his empty tankard. "Maybe."

Smythe got the hint. "Barman," he called, nodding towards Fairclough's empty tankard. "Another round 'ere."

They didn't speak until the tankard was full again and the barman had gone back to swatting the flies off the meat pies at the other end of the bar.

"Yeah, I know 'im," Fairclough said, with a sly smile.

"You know where I can find 'im?"

"'Ow much you payin'?" Fairclough asked. He turned and looked Smythe up and down, taking in the well-fitting but simple clothes, the clean hands and the good boots. "Sometimes it ain't wise to go runnin' off at the mouth about people, if you know what I mean."

"I'm payin' enough. More than you'd be seein' in a day's honest work, that's for sure." Smythe wasn't about to flash his money in this place. He could handle himself as well as the next man—well, better than most if the truth were told. But he wasn't a fool. He didn't want to get his throat slit over a few quid. "Finish up yer beer and let's go for a walk."

Fairclough hesitated.

"I'll make it worth your while," Smythe promised as he lifted his tankard to his mouth. "'Ow does five pounds sound?"

"Five quid?" Fairclough whispered, his eyes bulging. He picked up his drink and drained it in seconds. "Let's go, then, mate. For that kinda money, I'll tell ya everythin' I know about 'im. Believe me, it'll be worth every penny of it, too. 'Cause I know plenty."

CHAPTER 6

Witherspoon took a deep breath. He sat down in a high-backed chair as he waited in the foyer for the butler to announce him to Albritton's nephew and his wife. Constable Barnes was busy looking at the row of paintings lining the wall of the staircase, so the inspector decided to use these free moments to get his thoughts in order.

Albritton was utterly convinced one of his relations was guilty of murder. But so far, he'd certainly not produced any real evidence. Then, of course, there were other aspects he must consider. Now that he knew for certain that Annie Shields was wearing an opal ring, he couldn't ignore the possibility that she'd been the victim of a robbery gone awry. Especially as he knew the ring was a keepsake. Annie might have been accosted, refused to give up the last link she had to her dead mother, and tried to fight her assailant. Or at least tried to outrun him. But if it was a robbery, why did the thief leave Annie's wedding ring?

Witherspoon sighed inwardly. This case was not at all clear. Despite what his dear housekeeper had told him this morning over breakfast, he wasn't in the least confident of his abilities to bring this murderer to justice. His frown deepened. Mrs. Jeffries had also brought up a number of other matters. Now, what had she said? Something about widows? He remembered they'd been talking about his friend Lady Cannonberry, and Mrs. Jeffries had commented that she thought it nice that Lady Cannonberry had the opportunity to go visiting her friends in Devon. Actually, Witherspoon thought wistfully, he rather missed Lady Cannonberry. He did so hope she'd soon come home. But what exactly was it that Mrs. Jeffries had said after that? He wished he could remember. At the time he'd thought it might be a good idea to . . . to . . . Suddenly his eyes widened as he recalled everything his housekeeper had said. "Poor Mrs. Shields," Mrs. Jeffries had murmured sympathetically. "First she loses her husband, then probably has to put up with all sorts of revolting behavior from other men—" At this point he'd interrupted and asked what she'd meant. She'd explained that it was quite common for young widows to be the targets of unwanted attentions after their husbands died. He'd been shocked, of course. What decent man wouldn't be? But then Mrs. Jeffries asked him if he had spoken to any of Annie's female friends at Covent Garden. She'd said that perhaps there had been a man in Annie's life. Someone who perhaps resented her for refusing his attentions. When he reminded his housekeeper that they had indeed questioned Annie's employer, she laughed and said that kind of information wasn't the sort of thing an employer, especially a man, would take any notice of. The inspector smiled slightly. Sometimes it was so good to have a woman to talk with. They had such a different perspective on life. In this case, a perspective which might be wise to pursue.

"Barnes," he said suddenly. "Have someone go back to the flower market and talk to some of the other flower sellers. Have them find the victim's friends, especially the women, and question them."

"Anything in particular you want them to be askin' about?" the constable wanted to know.

"We need to find out if there have been any men bothering the victim. You know, unwanted suitors, that sort of thing."

"Good idea, sir," Barnes said. He looked down the still-empty hall and saw no sign of the returning housemaid. "I'll just nip out to the constable on the corner and give him his new instructions. Anything else you want me to tell him?"

"Yes, have him find out if *anyone*, anyone at all, has been seen hanging around the victim."

Gordon and Hortense Strutts were not amused by the presence of the police. Perched stiffly on a green flowered settee at the end of the room, they stared at Witherspoon and Barnes with almost identical expressions of distaste.

Hortense Strutts, a chubby, brown-haired woman with a pale, moon-shaped face, a short pugnacious nose, and lips that looked frozen in a perpetual pout, was the first to speak. "I've no idea why Uncle Henry chose to involve us in this ridiculously sordid affair," she declared. She smoothed one of the ruffles on the overskirt of her elegant lavender day gown. "He must have taken leave of his senses."

"It's positively absurd," her husband added.

Young Mr. Strutts was a handsome man with dark-brown hair, green eyes, high, rather prominent cheekbones, and lips that were so well shaped, they looked almost feminine. He was dressed just as elegantly as his wife.

"Why on earth would either of us know anything about this person?" He sneered, bringing a pristine white handkerchief to his lips and coughing delicately.

"Mrs. Shields was a flower seller," the inspector said. "That's all she was, you know. A decent, hardworking young woman who happened to sell flowers for a living. As to why your uncle thinks you may know something about her murder, well, you'll have to take that issue up with him."

"You can rest assured that we will," Hortense replied tartly. "Now, I've an appointment with my dressmaker in a few minutes, so please do get on with your business."

"Really, Hortense," her husband soothed. He flicked a speck of lint off the sleeve of his coat. "There's no reason to be so rude. I've an appointment as well, but I can at least be civil."

"Where were you last night?" the inspector asked. He wasn't going to mention Annie's possible relationship with Henry Albritton unless he had to. In domestic matters, he frequently felt that the less said, the better.

"I was here, of course," she replied.

"Really?" Witherspoon said. "Your uncle seems to be under the impression that you were out."

"Uncle Henry was mistaken," Hortense replied. "We'd planned on going to the theatre last night. However, with all those hooligans in Trafalgar Square, we changed our minds and stayed home."

Witherspoon smiled politely. "Are you quite sure, Mrs. Strutts? Mr. Albritton has already told us he heard the carriage pull up in front. He's quite positive you left. He didn't see you and he was here all evening."

"He didn't see us because we went to our rooms," she said. She glanced at her husband. "Gordon and I changed our plans at the last moment, that's why Uncle Henry heard the carriage. We sent it away, though, we didn't go out."

"I thought you'd changed them because of the riots in Trafalgar?"

"That was only one of the reasons we decided to stay home. Actually, after dinner I developed a headache. I went straight up to lie down, and Gordon, of course, stayed with me. Uncle Henry seemed most preoccupied. He shut himself up in his study the minute he finished eating. We didn't wish to disturb him, so when we decided not to go out, we went directly upstairs."

"Is that correct, Mr. Strutts?" the inspector asked.

"Yes."

"Did your maid or any of the other servants see you after dinner?" Barnes asked softly.

"Just the butler." It was Gordon who replied. "And he only saw me when I told him we wouldn't be needing the carriage. As my wife said, she had a headache. We've a suite of rooms upstairs—I helped her up to bed, turned off the lights, and then went into the little sitting room to read. As I didn't see fit to tell the servants my plans had changed, there was no reason for them to come into my rooms. My wife and I aren't in the habit of having the staff wait up for us when we go out in the evening."

"So after dinner," the inspector prodded, "no one saw either of you?"

"That's correct." Gordon smiled and rose to his feet, clearly dismissing them. "Now, if that's all you wanted to know, I've a busy day planned and my wife must get to the dressmaker's."

Witherspoon got up and Barnes followed suit. "What were you reading?"

Gordon blinked in surprise. "Reading? Oh, I was—"

"You were reading Mr. Pryce's novel. I believe it's titled *An Evil Spirit*" Hortense interjected quickly. "You remember, you mentioned it to me the next morning."

"That's right." Gordon smiled at the two policemen. "As you can see, my wife has a much better memory than I do."

"You enjoy novels, do you, sir?" Barnes asked.

"Oh, not all that much," Gordon replied. "Actually, the book belongs to Hortense. Novels of that sort are much more suited to ladies than gentlemen. The book was amusing, but hardly the sort of literature one should take seriously. But I'd nothing else to read and I wasn't tired enough to sleep."

The inspector wondered what to ask next. If neither Mr. nor Mrs. Strutts had gone out, then they couldn't have had anything to do with the murder. He would, of course, check with the butler to make sure the carriage had been sent away and not used by one of the Strutts. "I see. Well, that takes care of that."

In a gesture of dismissal, Hortense rose to her feet. "If that's all you wanted, then I really must be going."

"Thank you, Mrs. Strutts, Mr. Strutts," Witherspoon said politely. He must remember to speak with the servants as well. Mrs. Jeffries was always telling him it was his ability to make people feel at ease and get them to talk to him that gave him his really useful clues. Perhaps it would be best to find someone who could confirm the Struttses' story. Surely someone in a household this size must have known they hadn't gone out. On the other hand, even if no on had seen hide nor hair of them all evening, it wouldn't prove they'd left the house. Drat. Why did everything have to be so dreadfully difficult? "If you would be so good as to ring for your butler, we'll speak with Mrs. Franklin next."

The butler appeared as soon as the Struttses left. The, inspector asked him about the carriage. "They sent it away, sir," the man replied.

"Are you sure, Mister . . . er a . . ."

"Nestor, sir. Simon Nestor. Yes, I'm quite sure they sent it away." The butler sniffed.

"Thank you, Nestor. Would you please fetch Mrs. Franklin for us?"

"Very good, sir."

"So it looks like the Struttses was tellin' the truth," Barnes said as soon as the double doors slid closed behind the servant.

"At least about sending the carriage away," the inspector muttered. "But we'll need to interview the servants. I'd like someone else to confirm their story."

"They claimed no one saw them," Barnes said, raising his eyebrows and grinning. "But I'll warrant in a household this size, the servants knew exactly who was where and what they were doin'."

"My thoughts exactly, Constable."

The doors slid open. A thin, middle-aged woman dressed in a drab but well-cut brown-and-gold-striped dress with a high neckline and long, tight sleeves stepped inside. "I believe you wanted to see me? I'm Lydia Franklin."

Tall and blond, she swept past them and sat down on the settee like a judge taking a seat on the bench. She stared at them out of a plain, angular face, lifting her chin slightly and watching them down her long, sharp nose. The expression in her deep-set hazel eyes was mildly contemptuous and her lips were pursed in distaste. "I'd like to make it perfectly clear that the only reason I'm bothering even to speak to you is because Henry insisted."

"Thank you, Mrs. Franklin," Witherspoon replied. "We do appreciate your cooperation. I'm Inspector Witherspoon and this is Constable Barnes. Did Mr. Albritton explain the nature of our inquiry?"

She smiled coolly. "He said it was something to do with a murder. A flower seller, I believe. Though what that can have to do with me is certainly beyond my comprehension."

Witherspoon wondered if he ought to tell her and then quickly decided he shouldn't. He hadn't mentioned Albritton's relationship to the victim to the Struttses. Perhaps it was best to say nothing for the time being. One could always bring it up later. "May I ask what you were doing on last Sunday evening?"

"The same as I do every Sunday evening. I was at church."

"Evensong service?" Witherspoon suggested.

"That is correct."

"Which church did you attend?"

"St. John's. It's just across the way." She gestured vaguely to her left, fluttering her hand. The inspector noted she wore no rings.

"And what time did you leave St. John's?"

"As soon as the service was finished." She yawned.

"What time would that be, ma'am?" Barnes interjected.

"About eight o'clock," she replied. "No, wait a moment, that's not quite true. I stayed after the service and spoke to the vicar about some church matters."

"How long did you talk to him?" Witherspoon asked. He wished she'd ask him to sit down. Asking questions while standing was getting tiresome. He was beginning to feel like he was visiting a bank.

"I spoke with him for fifteen minutes or so. I don't recall exactly." Again she smiled coolly. "Then Mrs. Spreckles and I left the church. We walked most of the way home together. The Spreckles live just down the street."

"What time was it when you arrived back?" Barnes asked as he glanced up from his notebook.

"I've really no idea."

"What's your best guess?" Witherspoon asked.

"Eight fifteen or eight thirty. But I can't say for certain. I simply wasn't paying any attention to the time. There was no reason to, was there?"

"What did you do when you arrived home?"

"I went straight up to my room."

"Did anyone in the household see you?" Witherspoon prodded.

"No."

"Isn't that odd?" The inspector was beginning to think that everyone living in this house must be invisible. "Surely in a household this large some of the servants must be in attendance when a member of the family comes home?"

She smiled again, but the smile didn't reach her eyes. "One would think so. But Henry, unfortunately, has come under some rather untoward influences recently. Out of the clear blue, he took it into his head to give the entire staff the evening off. He claimed we oughtn't exploit people. He wouldn't even listen to me when I tried to point out that he was already exceedingly generous with the servants. They already had a reasonable amount of time free." Her voice rose slightly. "Now they were to have Sunday evenings as well. It's disgraceful. Utterly disgraceful. But Henry won't even discuss the subject calmly. It's all those books he's been reading. All those awful, radical, disgusting books that shouldn't be allowed to be published."

Witherspoon stared at the woman in alarm. Lydia Franklin's cheeks were flushed with rage and her hands were balled into fists. He really didn't think a discussion of Henry Albritton's changed social views was pertinent to Annie Shields's murder, so he quickly cast about for another, less controversial question to ask.

"Er, did you happen to speak to Mr. or Mrs. Strutts at all on Sunday evening?" He wondered why neither of the Struttses had mentioned Mr. Albritton giving the staff the evening off. For that matter, neither the butler nor Albritton had said anything either.

Lydia got a hold of herself and took a long, deep breath before answering. "No, I didn't. As far as I know, they went to the theatre."

"But they weren't at the theatre," the inspector corrected. "Both of them claim they changed their minds and stayed in."

She gave him another cold, mirthless smile. "If that's what Gordon and Hortense said, then I'm sure it must be true."

• • •

Betsy slipped behind a lamppost and stared at the young woman with the sad eyes and frizzy blond hair. Knowing she had to be careful, she waited until her quarry had wandered into a pub. Betsy took off after her. The best way to get someone like her to talk was to buy her a gin.

The pub was loud, dirty and filled with the kind of people Betsy had grown up with. The working poor. Hungry, cynical, and scared, most of them had such miserable existences they lived only for the moment. Tomorrow was bound to be worse, so you might as well have a few laughs today. Betsy wasn't sure they were all that wrong, either. If she hadn't been lucky enough to end up working at the inspector's, she was fairly certain her fate would have been much like Millie Groggins's.

She waited till Millie sidled up to the bar. Betsy stepped inside the pub. To her left, a fat, beefy man with a bright red face leered at her. "'Ello, me lovely, new girl on the street?"

"Sod off," she snapped at him, and cringed as the fellow next to the fat man belched loudly. Quickly, she hurried up to the bar.

Millie didn't look up from her gin.

Betsy cleared her throat. "Can I buy you a drink?"

"You talkin' to me?" Millie slowly raised red-rimmed puffy eyes. It was impossible to tell if the woman was drunk or weeping.

"I said, can I buy you a gin?" Betsy ignored the interested stares of the men leaning against the bar.

"Bugger off," Millie growled. "I only does men." She turned her head away. The publican snickered.

"I ain't one of your bleedin' customers," Betsy snapped. "I only want to talk to you a bit. And I'll pay for what I need to know."

Millie turned her head and squinted, trying hard to focus her eyes. "You'll pay."

"Yes." Crimminey, Betsy thought, between givin' away some of her things and offerin' money for information, it was a good thing someone at Upper Edmonton Gardens was keepin' her supplied. But she really wasn't concerned. God knows, these people needed them a sight worse than she did. "I'll pay ya. You tell me what you know about Annie Shields and I'll give you five shillin's."

Millie jerked her head towards the back of the pub. "Get me another gin and we'll talk."

The prostitute chased a drunk away from a small table in the shadowed corner. Betsy carefully set the gin in front of Millie and then sat down.

"Ta." Millie picked up the drink and took a long swig. "So what do ya want to know?"

Betsy knew she'd get a load of rubbish if she wasn't careful. Millie might take her money and tell her nothing. She'd have to gain the woman's trust. "First of all," she began, "I used to live round these parts."

"Lucky you." Millie took another swallow.

"Nah, it weren't lucky. It was bloody awful, I got out 'cause a decent man took pity on me when I collapsed on his doorstep. But one of me little sisters weren't so lucky. She died." The memory sent a sharp stab of pain through Betsy. Pain she thought she'd buried years ago. "And me other sister went off with a feller years ago and we never heard from her again." More pain, but she ignored it. "So I'm tellin' ya I'll know if you're havin' me on. You tell me the truth about Annie and I'll be straight about payin' ya."

"Whatcha wanta know about Annie for?" Millie said. She looked curious and amused by Betsy's speech. "She's dead."

"And I aim to help hang the one that killed her," Betsy declared.

Millie eyed her shrewdly for a moment. "All right, ask me whatever you like. Maybe I'll even tell you the truth."

"I understand you and Annie was friends."

"Not really friends," Millie admitted. "Some of them sellers thinks they's too good to even speak to the likes of us, but Annie weren't like that. She were nice to me. Always treated me like I was someone, you know?"

"Did you see her on Sunday night?"

Millie nodded her head. "Yeah, we was both workin' the Strand." She broke off and laughed. "'Course Annie was only tryin' to sell a few flowers. But there weren't no business at all. Streets were deader than a rat's arse and twice as mean."

"What do you mean?"

"It was bloody cold. There was a right horrid fog driftin' in and not a drop of business for either of us." Millie quickly tossed back another swallow. "I was bloody worried. If I didn't make a few bits, I knew I was goin' to end up kippin' on the streets."

Betsy looked down at her own gloved hands. She knew exactly what Millie was talking about. If you couldn't pay, you spent the night out on the streets. She'd done it herself a time or two. She'd die before she ever did it again. "Was Annie worried about money?"

"Annie was always worried about money," Millie replied. "Who isn't? She had the little one to take care of. But she weren't skint, if that's what yer askin'. Her business was off, too, but she still lent me a bit of coin so I wouldn't have to sleep in the street. But somethin' was botherin' her. The whole time we was out, she was always lookin' over her shoulder. Every time we 'eard footsteps she got all quiet and stiff like."

"You mean she knew someone meant to harm her?"

Millie's expression grew thoughtful. "No, more like she was expectin' someone. You know what I mean? We'd hear footsteps, but 'course it was so bloody foggy you couldn't see anyone till they was right on top of you. Every time someone passed by, she'd sort of sag, you know, like she was disappointed."

"Did she actually say she was expecting someone?"

"No. But she must've been, mustn't she?"

"What makes you think that?"

Millie shrugged one shoulder nonchalantly. "'Cause she never worked late. Annie always worked the crowds *before* they went inside theatres, never stayed to work 'em comin' out. Nah, she was waitin' for someone that night."

"Maybe she needed extra money?" Betsy suggested.

Millie shook her head stubbornly. "If she'd been short she wouldn't have lent me any, would she?"

Betsy thought that was probably true. No matter how kindhearted a body was, if your own survival was at stake, you wouldn't be handing out money to Millie Groggins. "What time did you last see her?"

"Ten o'clock," Millie said. "I heard the chimes at St. Matthew's ring the hour just as I was leavin'. Annie was fixin' to leave then, too. She'd already packed her cart."

Wiggins smiled at the homely kitchen maid. "Let me help you," he said, nodding towards the basket of vegetables the girl struggled to hold on to while she futilely tried to relatch the back gate.

The girl gave him a wary glance, almost dropped the basket and finally nodded. "Ta," she said as Wiggins neatly slipped the bolt closed. "This thing's so heavy I'd never have gotten that gate latched."

"Can I carry it for you?" Wiggins asked politely. He concentrated on speaking properly. Sometimes young girls were a bit frightened of men, but if they thought you were a gentleman, they'd be a bit easier in their own minds.

"It's too much bother," the girl said, lifting the heavy basket onto her hip and turning towards the street at the end of the mews. "Really, I can manage."

"Oh please, miss, I'm walkin' the same way you are, I'd be pleased to help. That's an awfully big basket for a dainty little person like yourself."

"Well . . ." She smiled suddenly. "Thanks, awfully." She handed him the basket. "I'm takin' it back to Rutger's, the greengrocers on the Edgeware Road. Cook says half these vegetables is old and not fit to eat."

They started walking and Wiggins chatted amicably. By the time they reached the Edgeware Road, Abigail, for that was the kitchen maid's name, was talking freely.

"Sounds like your mistress has bloomin' high standards," he said casually, looking down at the basket.

"We ain't got no mistress, she died a few years back. We've a master." Abigail shrugged. "But he don't half notice what he eats. It's the rest of 'em that raise a ruckus if the food's not good."

"Hard to work for, are they?"

"Mr. Albritton's a right nice master," she said. "But he's got a pack of his dead wife's relations livin' there and none of them is very nice."

"That's too bad. But if they're his wife's relations, maybe they'll leave one of these days."

Abigail snorted. "It'd take a case of pox to get 'em out of there. They's all living off Mr. Albritton. 'Course I can see why he lets his sister-in-law stay on. I mean, Mrs. Franklin did help take care of his wife when she was so ill. But he's got his wife's nephew and wife there, too."

"Uh, what's their names?"

"The Struttses." Abigail made a face. This was obviously a subject she relished talking about. "Hortense and Gordon. What a pair."

"Does Mr. Strutts, uh, take liberties?"

Abigail laughed. "Nah, he's too scared of his wife to say boo to a goose in a barnyard. Don't know why either. He's a right handsome fellow and she's as plain as a pikestaff. Not that she's built like one. She's gettin' big as a bloomin' house, she is."

"Doesn't sound like she's easy to work for," he murmured. He deliberately slowed his steps as they came closer to a row of shops.

"And the worst part is, poor Mr. Strutts spends every last pence of his allowance on her. He's always buyin' her gowns and jewelry and expensive chocolates." Abigail shook her head in disgust. "God knows why. She's never grateful for anything. Why, he even bought her one of them fancy bicycles last year and all she did with it was ride it once and then toss it in the back shed."

"I've never heard of a woman ridin' a bicycle," Wiggins said seriously. He'd always wanted a bicycle.

"Don't be daft," Abigail said, tossing her head. "Lots of women rides 'em. Even that stiff-necked Mrs. Franklin's done it a time or two. Mrs. Franklin's the sister-in-law." She snorted. "Not that it helps her be the lady of the manor. Mr. Albritton might be grateful to her, but he don't let her put on airs. Least ways not with the servants. Do you know she tried to talk 'im out of givin' us the evenin' off last Sunday. Stupid cow. Wonder how she'd like to spend every wakin' moment peelin' vegetables and scrubbin' pots."

Wiggins wanted to get Abigail back on the subject of the Struttses. "Maybe Mr. Strutts is madly in love with Mrs. Strutts," he suggested. "Maybe that's why he's always buyin' her things. I'd sure want to buy nice things for my wife, if I had one."

"So you're not married, then." Abigail gave him a sly smile.

"No. Guess I've just not found the right girl yet. Not like Mr. Strutts . . . I mean, he must really be in love with his wife."

"Guess he must"—Abigail shrugged—"but you wouldn't know it to watch the two of 'em when they was together. He barely speaks to her and she's always harpin' about him ignorin' her." She laughed. "'Course it's her own fault, you know. Maybe if she'd sleep with 'im every once in a while he'd do more for her than just buy her things."

Wiggins felt his cheeks flame. Really, he thought, some young women were so bold. Luckily, they'd come to the greengrocers and he handed the basket to Abigail. "Would you like me to walk you back?" he asked.

"That'd be nice," she said, giving him a coy smile.

As he waited for her to return he tried to think what to ask next. So far, he'd learned nothing of any real value. Hortense wasn't a nice person and her husband gave her gifts. What did that tell him? Nothing. And he refused to go back to Upper Edmonton Gardens at teatime with only this to report. He just knew that Betsy and Luty and even Mrs. Goodge would have heaps of information by now. It was a matter of pride. He couldn't let the other men down! Not now. Not with Betsy's superior smile still fresh in his mind.

"There, that's all taken care of," Abigail said as she trotted out of the shop with her head held high. "He'll not be sendin' any more old vegetables around, I can tell you that."

They started walking back the way they'd come. Wiggins estimated he had less than ten minutes to pry something interesting out of the kitchen maid. "You was tellin' me about the Struttses," he reminded her.

"Oh them." She gave him a suspicious glance. "You're awfully curious."

He forced a laugh. "Well, if the truth be known, they sound like a couple me mam used to work for." He gave her his best smile, the one that used to make Sarah Trippet bat her eyelashes and blush. Well, not exactly blush, but she did take notice of him. "Besides, talkin' about them is a good excuse to keep walkin' with you."

The wariness in her face vanished. "Oh, so that's the way of it. Well, me half day out is Thursdays. You can take me out then, if you've a mind to. I could fancy goin' out somewhere nice."

Wiggins didn't dare let his dismay show. With great effort, he kept his smile firmly on his features. "That'd be lovely, Abigail."

"Now, where was I? Right. The Struttses. Well, she's not much to look at, so it's a mystery to me why Mr. Strutts puts up with her."

"Was they both at home on Sunday evenin'?"

"Don't know," she replied. "I was out meself. I know they was plannin' on goin' to the theatre, and they musta done. Mr. Strutts's coat was hangin' on the backstair banister when I come in. Even though it's not my job, I did take it upstairs to the cloakroom."

"Maybe he'd left it there earlier," Wiggins suggested. "I mean, that don't mean he went out."

"'Course it does," she insisted. "The bloomin' thing was damp through and through. And he's right particular about his clothes, is Mr. Strutts, has a right fit if there's a spot on 'em."

"Strange couple," Wiggins said slowly. He racked his brain to think of more questions. He had to keep her talking. Blimey, now he was stuck going out with her day after tomorrow.

"In more ways than one," Abigail said. "She's the really odd duck, though."

"In what way?"

"She listens at keyholes. Just two weeks ago I was goin' up to the butler's pantry to get the brewer's yeast for cleanin' the coppers? Well, them jugs was heavy, so I nipped down the front stairs instead of the back like I was supposed to, and there she was, Mrs. Strutts—her ear was pressed to the keyhole of Mr. Albritton's study. Mr. Albritton was in there talkin' to his solicitor, too."

"Of course I know who Henry Albritton is," Miss Myrtle Buxton exclaimed. "Really, Luty, I know everyone in London."

Luty had no doubt this was true. That was precisely why she'd sashayed across the road from her own Knightsbridge home to call on Myrtle. The room alone, with its pale pink walls, matching pink settees and chairs, dozens of draped tables loaded with knicknacks and silver, Oriental carpets, flowery drapes, and footstools so thick on the floor you had to be careful where you stepped, was enough to make her eyes water. The place gave her a headache. But the woman was very useful to know. Besides, Luty sort of felt sorry for her. For all her gadding about, Myrtle didn't really have many friends.

Myrtle Buxton, rich, silver-haired, and still single, devoted every waking moment of her life to socializing. She knew everything about anyone of wealth in the entire city. Luty wasn't sure but that she didn't know about the rest of the country as well. Yet for all this, Luty had noticed that not many people came to call.

"He's not a real gentleman," Myrtle continued. "After all, he did make his money in trade. But he's done very, very well."

"I thought he was a carpenter," Luty said bluntly.

"He was. Started out workin' at his father-in-law's boatyard fifteen—or was it twenty?—years ago." Myrtle paused and her eyes narrowed thoughtfully. "Yes, that's right. Then he married Francis and took over the business when old Mr. Strutts died. The business should have gone to his son, Edmond Strutts, but he was already dead." She reached for a tea cake and popped it into her mouth. Chewing delicately, she cocked her head to one side. "Why are you so interested in Henry Albritton?"

Luty was ready for that question. "I'm thinking about buying into the boat business."

"You can't, the company isn't public." Myrtle reached for another cake. "And it's really a pity, too, as he's done well. He turned that one boatyard into seven."

"Seven!"

"Three in London, two in Liverpool, one in Southampton, and one somewhere up in Scotland." Myrtle eyed the cake in her hand, made a face, and then put it back. "Of course, he didn't do it alone. As soon as old Mr. Strutts was buried, Albritton took in a partner. A man named Sherwin August." Her eyes took on that greedy gleam Luty had seen many time before. It meant she had something really juicy to say. "But there's been some strange talk lately, too. August has told several people he thinks Albritton may be ill." She gently tapped the side of her head. "You know, this kind of illness."

"You mean crazy?"

"I wouldn't put it as strongly as that," Myrtle replied. "But supposedly, Henry Albritton's become"—her voice dropped—"a radical."

"Hmm, well, I guess I won't be puttin' my money there," Luty, mused. She thought this information interesting, but she wanted more. It would be a cold day in hell before she would let that stiff-necked butler of hers beat her to solving this crime. "So when did Mrs. Albritton die?"

"A few years back," Myrtle replied. "What's so odd is that Albritton's a handsome man for his age. Half the widows in London had their eye on him. You'd have thought he'd have married again."

"Some people don't much like bein' hitched," Luty declared bluntly. Her own marriage had been a relatively happy one, but she'd seen enough of life to know the misery of being tied to someone you didn't love. Luty knew half a dozen women who'd happily buried husbands and declared that nothing short of a bullet aimed at their heads would ever induce them to marry again. No reason a man couldn't feel the same way.

"I think he'd have liked to have married again," Myrtle protested. "I mean, it's only natural that he would."

"Nothin' natural about it at all . . ." Luty tried to interrupt.

But Myrtle wasn't listening. She kept right on talking. "But, of course, Lydia made sure no one got close enough to do any real damage to her position. She wasn't going to have anyone take her place as the mistress of the house."

"Lydia?" Luty prodded, pretending ignorance of the name.

"Lydia Franklin. She lives in the Albritton house. Once Frances died, she took over as mistress. Her husband was Warren Franklin. Quite a good family, the Franklins, but Warren was exceedingly unlucky. Lost every cent he ever made. He and Lydia lived in some awful little house south of the river. He left Lydia so destitute she had to move in with her sister when Warren died." Myrtle smiled coyly. "The gossip has it that Lydia set her sights on Henry the day they buried Frances." She giggled. "Gossip also has it that Henry can't stand the woman."

CHAPTER 7

Mrs. Jeffries stared curiously at the woman sitting at the next table. She frowned. The lady had her back turned and was swaddled in a heavy gray coat, a bright red scarf, and an enormous hat. It was impossible to tell who she was. Yet there was something very familiar looking about her. Perhaps, Mrs. Jeffries thought, she really should have taken the time to glance at the woman's face when she'd noticed the lady coming behind her into the tearoom. But she pushed that notion aside. She had more important things to think about than whether or not someone who looked vaguely familiar was an acquaintance or not. Still, she thought, she mustn't get careless. She didn't want to take the chance that one of her neighbors might mention seeing her this morning. That wouldn't do at all. She didn't want the inspector to know who she was meeting for tea. Then again, she told herself, it was highly unlikely that any of the people from Upper Edmonton Gardens or thereabouts would have any idea of the identity of the young man she hoped to meet here.

She glanced up as she felt a cold draft coming from the door. She smiled in delight as she spotted the familiar face. Hanging on to his hat, Dr. Bosworth pushed the door closed against the heavy wind and started towards her, picking his way carefully through the crowded tables.

Her spirits soared. Her quarry had risen to the bait!

"Good day, Dr. Bosworth," she said gaily. "I'm delighted you could come. It's so very kind of you."

Bosworth pulled out a chair, accidentally bumped the elbow of the lady swathed in heavy coats at the next table, muttered an apology, and sat down. "Not at all, Mrs. Jeffries. I was quite thrilled to get your note this morning."

Red-haired, tall, and earnest, the doctor might be able to give Mrs. Jeffries some answers. She wasn't sure how much she should tell him, though. Bosworth was quite an honest young man and she certainly didn't want him to compromise his position by assisting her. Unless, of course, he wanted to.

The waiter appeared and Mrs. Jeffries slipped into her role as hostess. "You will have tea, sir?" she queried. At his nod, she told the young man to bring them a full tea complete with cakes and fancy biscuits. "I do so love these Lyons Tearooms, don't you?"

"I don't get a chance to frequent them all that much," Bosworth said politely. He cocked his head to one side and studied her for a moment, his eyes amused. "Mrs. Jeffries, you'll forgive me for getting right to the point, but I must return to the hospital soon. However, you'll be pleased to learn I did have time to nip in and examine Annie Shields."

"You examined her?" Mrs. Jeffries watched his face carefully. Her note had mentioned the victim's name, but she hadn't dared hope Bosworth would take it upon himself to do precisely what she needed done without more prodding on her part.

He grinned broadly and his pale, serious face was immediately transformed. "I did. I had to do it on the sly, too. Old Potter hung about for a long time."

"Oh dear, I do hope you won't get into any trouble," she said earnestly. "I know my note was rather vague, but you see . . ."

"Your note wasn't just vague, it was deliberately intriguing. You must have known the moment I realized it was one of the inspector's cases, my curiosity would be aroused."

Mrs. Jeffries decided to take the bull by the horns. This young doctor was far too intelligent to swallow the story she'd cooked up to lure him here. "I was counting on it. You see, doctor, you've been so helpful in the past. "On that case last spring, your insights were so useful I was rather hoping you'd lend your expert opinion to this one as well."

"I'm not certain my opinion is all that expert," he said with an embarrassed smile. "All I did was identify the kind of weapon used in the murder." He paused as the waiter brought their tea.

"Don't be so modest, Dr. Bosworth," Mrs. Jeffries said as soon as they were alone. "Your identification of the gun used in that crime helped to solve it."

He picked up his tea and stared at her, his expression thoughtful. "Do you always take such an interest in the inspector's cases?"

"Actually . . ." She hesitated, not sure of exactly how much she should admit. He was, after all, a man. Like many of that sex, he might resent a woman using her mind. On the other hand, he might not. Constantly trying to dream up stories and excuses to pry information out of people without their knowing what she was up to was getting very wearing. Furthermore, an ally like Dr. Bosworth could come in handy on future cases. "Yes. I do," she admitted. "However, I make certain the inspector has no idea of my interest or my involvement."

"Good." He took a sip from his cup. "The world could use more people like you. You care. Even better, you manage to make sure your inspector keeps his pride. A rare quality, in either a man or a woman. How can I help you?"

"Thank you," she said modestly. She was enormously relieved that he was reacting so splendidly. But her instincts had told her she could trust him. "As you have examined the victim, is there anything you can tell me that might be useful?"

"By useful, I take it you want my opinion as to the murder weapon?"

"That and anything else you think important." She didn't wish to interrupt at this point by telling him that her methods of investigation deemed all information useful in some form or another. That could come later. "I realize you probably can't be specific about the weapon, but I would like your opinion nonetheless."

"My examination was very cursory. But I'm inclined to think she was killed with a hammer." He grinned as he saw her start in surprise. "That's right, Mrs. Jeffries. I'm fairly sure that poor woman was bashed on the head with a common hammer."

There was an audible gasp from the woman at the next table. Mrs. Jeffries leaned closer. "Perhaps we ought to keep our voices down," she said in a low voice. "Goodness, doctor, you are full of surprises. I'd no idea you'd be able to tell what it was that actually killed Annie Shields. Why do you think it was a hammer?"

Bosworth leaned forward, too. "Naturally, I'm not one-hundred percent certain. I could be wrong, but I don't think I am. I examined the victim's wounds very carefully. There were three separate blows."

Fascinated, Mrs. Jeffries asked, "Gracious. You can tell how many times she was hit just by looking?"

"Certainly," he said, his voice rising enthusiastically. "Each blow leaves some kind of wound mark. Naturally it would have been better had I been able to examine a bare skull, one without flesh and hair. But I could hardly soak the poor woman's head in acid and see what the skull would tell me. Even old Potter's bright enough to notice I'd been poking about if he saw a skull instead of a head."

There was a strangled, choking sound from next to them. Bosworth glanced at the woman, who was now sitting bolt upright and ramrod straight. He lowered his voice a fraction. "Mind you, I am guessing. But by carefully examining the wounds, I was able to come to some conclusions. You must realize, though, not every physician agrees with these methods. Some claim it's all nonsense."

"I think it's jolly clever of you, doctor." She beamed at him. Her attention was caught again by their neighbor. The woman now appeared to be leaning back, her ear turned towards them. Mrs. Jeffries still couldn't see her face; that wretched scarf was in her way. She couldn't be certain, of course. But it was almost as if the lady were trying to eavesdrop.

"Thank you, Mrs. Jeffries. As I was saying, there were three separate and distinct blows. Two of them left round, blunt-edged wounds. Admittedly, there are many objects that could hit a person and leave such an edge, but the third wound left a jagged edge. A very interesting edge that looked to me like the kind of wound the claw end of a hammer might make."

"So you think the killer struck twice with the blunt end of the hammer," she said slowly, trying to picture the action in her mind, "then turned the hammer around and struck a third blow with the sharp end?"

"That's correct," he said. "Either that, or he used two separate weapons."

"It hardly seems likely he'd have used two weapons." She frowned slightly. "Yet in order to use both ends of the hammer, the killer would either have to turn his hand completely over—"

"Or turn the hammer over," Bosworth finished calmly. "It's not quite as farfetched as it sounds, Mrs. Jeffries, once you think about it. First, imagine the killer. He hits his victim twice using the blunt end, the end most people would think likely to do the most damage. The victim falls. The killer kneels beside her and drops the hammer to check for signs of life. The victim perhaps moans or flutters an eyelid, even people on the doorstep of death can groan or twitch a bit. The killer panics. He grabs the hammer. Remember, he'd dropped it hastily, it could easily have shifted or rolled. For all we know, there might be blood on his hands and he can't get a decent grip on the weapon. But for some reason, the wrong end is up, and when he strikes the third and killing blow, it's the claw end not the blunt end that does the poor woman in."

Mrs. Jeffries was speechless. She gazed at him in admiration. "I'm amazed, doctor. Your analysis makes perfect sense."

The lady next to them leaned farther back. Alarmed, Mrs. Jeffries watched her, certain that any second she was going to topple in Dr. Bosworth's lap. She nodded her head and the doctor quickly looked around. He moved his chair slightly and the woman hastily drew back into her own seat.

"Thank you," Bosworth whispered. "But it's not all that difficult, really. Anyone who sat down and actually thought about it could have come to the same conclusion. Assuming, of course, that I'm correct about the identity of the weapon."

"Dr. Bosworth, you're brilliant." Whether he was right or wrong wasn't really the point, though. Coming up with a sequence of events that was both plausible and possible was what impressed Mrs. Jeffries most.

"Thank you, again." He smiled modestly. "That's the only way I can account for the blows and, more importantly, for the difference in the kinds of wounds they made. I mean, can you think of another instrument that's blunt on one side and claw-edged on the other?"

She couldn't, but that didn't mean such an instrument didn't exist. "Not one which is easily obtainable and available to most people," she replied. "In murder, people generally use the kinds of weapons that are convenient, and let's be blunt, doctor—practically anyone can get their hands on a hammer." She noticed the woman leaning their way again. Really, how very rude.

Bosworth nodded, picked up his teacup and drained it. "Was there anything else you needed to know?"

"I'm not certain. Was there anything else about the body you think worth mentioning?"

"I can't really say," he replied, frowning. "Old Potter was hovering so close I only just got a good look at the wounds. I didn't have a chance to examine the rest of her."

"Oh dear, that's a pity."

He pushed back in his chair. The woman quickly leaned forward over her own table. Bosworth got up. "Yes, it is. Next time I'll try and slip in early of a morning."

"Next time?"

Bosworth grinned. "Our next case, Mrs. Jeffries. Only you'll have to be a bit quicker in contacting me. Here, let me give you this." He reached inside his pocket and drew out a card. "This is my address. Send someone round early the next time, and I should be able to slip into the mortuary before old Potter gets there. He doesn't like doing postmortems on an empty stomach, so he's never in before nine in the morning."

Stunned and grateful, she took the card. He was actually agreeing to help them! "Thank you so much, doctor. You've been so very, very kind. And I promise, on our next case we'll get word to you straightaway."

"Yes, well, let's just hope whatever bodies we have get sent to St. Thomas's. It would be a bit difficult even for me to be snooping around corpses at another mortuary or hospital. In case you haven't noticed, medics are dreadfully territorial about their patch. Now I must be off, but do let me know if there's anything else I can do to help on this one."

"Thank you so much," Mrs. Jeffries said again. "You really must come round for tea soon. I'll send you a note, shall I?"

"That would be lovely." He bowed to her, threw an amused glance at the nosy woman's back and left.

The woman rose as well. She turned slowly and faced the housekeeper.

Shocked, Mrs. Jeffries stared at the slender, blond-haired woman standing in front of her. "Lady Cannonberry," she exclaimed. "You're supposed to be in Devon. What are you doing here?"

"Actually, Mrs. Jeffries"—Lady Cannonberry gave her an innocent smile—"I followed you."

"Hello, hello," the inspector called out as he entered the front hall of Upper Edmonton Gardens. "Mrs. Jeffries, Betsy. I'm home." He waited for a moment, but no one answered his summons. That's most odd, he thought. There's generally one of the staff home at this time of the day. Shaking his head, he started towards the backstairs when suddenly he heard the front door open.

"Why, hello, Inspector," Mrs. Jeffries said. She hurried forward, taking off her hat and coat as she went. "This is certainly a nice surprise."

"I thought I'd pop home for a spot of lunch," he said.

"Lovely." She smiled. "Why don't you just have a seat in the dining room and I'll go get you something to eat."

"If you don't mind, I'll just nip down and get Fred. We could both use a ramble out in the gardens."

"That's a wonderful idea, sir." Mrs. Jeffries fervently hoped Wiggins hadn't taken it into his head to take the dog with him. "Lunch should be ready in just a few minutes."

She watched the inspector disappear down the backstairs, heard the sound of Fred's excited barking, and heaved a sigh of relief. Really, she thought, today has been just full of surprises.

She dashed down the kitchen stairs and found Mrs. Goodge hurrying towards the larder. "It's a good thing the inspector weren't ten minutes earlier," she warned. "Otherwise he'd have caught me talkin' to one of my sources. The rag-and-bone man is a cousin to someone who works at Albritton's boatyard. He give me a right earful, too."

"Excellent, Mrs. Goodge. Now let's hope you have something for the inspector's lunch."

"Not to worry, I'll heat up some soup and there's some sliced cold beef and fresh bread. That'll do him."

"Good." Mrs. Jeffries leaned closer to Mrs. Goodge. "You'll never guess who I ran into this morning. Lady Cannonberry. She's back from the country. She followed me to the tearoom and then managed to eavesdrop on my conversation with Dr. Bosworth."

"Followed you?" Mrs. Goodge frowned. "Why would Lady Cannonberry be following you and eavesdroppin'?"

"It's a long story and quite accidental, I'm sure. I'll tell you all about it when the others get back. They'll be here for tea, won't they?"

"Right. Luty and Hatchet will be round, too."

Mrs. Jeffries went back upstairs and set the dining table. Her mind was working furiously.

The murder weapon was probably a hammer. That may or may not be important. But it was definitely something the inspector should know. But how to get that information to him without revealing her involvement?

Ten minutes later Witherspoon, looking very relaxed, came into the room and took his chair. "I say, this looks jolly good."

Mrs. Jeffries poured herself a cup of tea. "Well, sir, how has your investigation gone so far?" she asked calmly.

"Not as badly as I'd first feared, but not as well as I'd hoped." He shrugged and told her what he'd learned that day.

"I do fear," he said as he finished his narrative, "that I've wasted an awful lot of time at the Albritton house. But really, I could hardly refuse to question the man's relations."

"Then you don't think one of them could have done it?"

"I don't think it's likely." He took a bite of roast beef. "Not only do the rest of the family have alibis of a sort, but there's no evidence that any of them even knew of Albritton's interest in Annie Shields. Albritton, of course, has an idea that people have been rifling through his desk. He claimed he'd started inquiries about finding a house in San Francisco for himself and Annie Shields, and that someone had gone through his correspondence, but he's no proof."

"Had he bought many flowers from the victim?"

The inspector stared at her. "I don't really know . . . why? I mean, what made you ask that?"

She laughed. "Come now, Inspector, that's the sort of question you'd ask yourself. I was merely thinking that if he'd been in the habit of buying flowers from the girl every day, and from what you said yesterday it sounded as though he had, then I'm sure all of his female relations would have noticed. A man bringing in fresh flowers every day soon becomes the talk of the whole household. Unless, of course, it had always been his habit to do so." She fervently hoped she was right. For all she knew, Henry Albritton could have brought flowers from Annie Shields by the basketful and then dumped them in the Thames to avoid his relatives getting suspicious. But she didn't want the inspector to give up so easily.

Witherspoon grew thoughtful. "You're right, you know. By his own admission he bought some from her every day. Of course the women would notice. I'm going back there this afternoon; perhaps I'll have another talk with Mr. Albritton."

"Have you spoken to Mrs. Shields's female friends at Covent Garden?"

"I've got police constables doing that this very afternoon, and I believe I might go round there again myself tomorrow morning." He speared another piece of beef. "Of course, it would be most helpful if we knew what the murder weapon was. Although, I'm not all that sure why it would be useful. The killer probably tossed whatever he used in the Thames."

Mrs. Jeffries sent up a silent prayer of thanks. The inspector had inadvertently given her the opening she needed. "You know, it's quite odd you should mention that. You'll never guess who I ran into this morning. Dr. Bosworth—you remember that bright young man who was so very helpful in the case of that American who was killed during the Jubilee?"

"Oh yes, I remember him. He also helped out in that servant girl's murder last year. Clever chap." Witherspoon's fork was halfway to his mouth. He set it back down on his plate and stared at her incredulously. "You don't mean to say that Bosworth has some ideas about this case?"

Mrs. Jeffries was ready for that question. "To be perfectly honest, yes. As a matter of fact, I suspect young Dr. Bosworth has become something of an admirer of yours."

"An admirer of mine? Gracious. Really." He beamed with pleasure.

"Don't be so modest, sir," she said. "Why shouldn't he admire you? You're brilliant at solving homicides. Why, everyone says so."

"Thank you, Mrs. Jeffries. It's good of you to say so."

"I must say I was rather surprised when I ran into Dr. Bosworth," Mrs. Jeffries continued chattily. "He invited me to have tea with him. I'm not altogether sure that he didn't plan to run into me all along."

"Goodness. Why would he do that?"

"Because, sir, I suspect Dr. Bosworth sneaks over to the mortuary and has a good long look at every one of the victims whenever he learns you're investigating the case." She hoped the good doctor wouldn't object to her stretching the truth this way, but she had to do something. "Naturally, he couldn't come right out and approach you with what he thought. Officially, it was Dr. Potter who had charge of the postmortem. From what I hear, medical men are dreadfully territorial about their domains, so poor Dr. Bosworth had to sneak his peek on the sly, so to speak. Yes, indeed. He's become an admirer. It seems to me that Dr. Bosworth just can't keep away from your corpses."

Witherspoon gulped and pushed his plate away.

"So he approached me with what he'd found out," she continued.

"I take it he had examined Annie Shields?"

"Yes, sir. As I said, I don't think he can keep away. He thinks the murder weapon was probably a hammer."

"How on earth could he determine that?" Witherspoon was enormously flattered to have the doctor's admiration. But of course, he really did have to know how Bosworth had reached his conclusions. The young chap was very bright, but it wouldn't do to accept anything he said at face value.

"That's just what I asked him," she replied. She went on to tell him about Bosworth's examination of the three head wounds, taking care not to be too colorful in her description. Though the inspector gamely fought to hide it, the truth was he had a dreadfully weak stomach.

"Very interesting," Witherspoon said as he reached for his tea. "But even if it's true, it won't be much use to us. Anyone can get their hands on a hammer."

Witherspoon was deep in thought as he waited in front of the Albritton house for Constable Barnes, who was rounding the corner and heading his way at a fast trot. "No need to exert yourself, Constable," he called.

"Thank you, sir," Barnes puffed between breaths. "I just got word from the lads, sir. Still no word on Emma Shields. She's probably with the Maxwells. Should we send a telegram to the local police in Leicester and Nottingham and have them do some checking?"

Witherspoon pondered this as he turned towards the front door. "Yes," he said slowly, reaching up and banging the brass knocker, "I think we must. I don't like the idea of that poor child being unaccounted for."

Nestor let them inside. "Mr. Albritton is in his study," he said. "This way, gentlemen."

Witherspoon and Barnes followed the butler down the hallway. They were still some distance away when they heard raised voices. "I believe we'll wait here until Mr. Albritton is free," the inspector said, waving at two chairs outside the study door.

The butler looked uncertain. Finally he said, "As you wish, sir."

As soon as the man had left, they each took a chair. The voices behind the door rose in volume. Barnes whipped out his notebook and flipped it open. The inspector leaned his ear closer to the oak door.

"You can't keep going on this way," they heard an unfamiliar voice shout. "The business isn't going to run itself. We've got orders on three boats held up because you can't be bothered to decide which supplier to use."

"I've told you," Henry Albritton replied, "we won't use Cantilever's because of the way they treat their workers. Heddleston's no good because of the transport schedules, so that only leaves Bickston's. I gave my clerk instructions to wire them yesterday. So don't tell me I can't run my business. I'm doing my duty."

"You're doing your duty, but nothing else. Don't you see, the delay on this decision is only the tip of the iceberg. You really must put your heart back into work, Henry. You must or we'll all be ruined."

"We'll be ruined," Albritton repeated, his voice rising. "Have you ever stopped to think of how many other people are already ruined? People who through no fault of their own have no decent employment, no decent place to live, no decent chance to educate their children, or provide them with anything but the most meager of existences?"

"Oh, for God's sake," the voice shouted. "Are we back onto that nonsense again? I thought you'd finally come to your senses. We're hardly responsible for the plight of the poor."

"If we're not responsible, then who is?" Albritton yelled. "Besides, why should I care if we're ruined? Who have I got to leave my money to? An idiot nephew with a greedy wife and a mean-spirited sister-in-law on the hunt for a husband? Why should I care if we all go to hell in a hand-basket!"

"Henry!"

There was a heavy thump and the sound of something crashing. Alarmed, Witherspoon and Barnes both leapt to their feet and flung open the door.

Henry Albritton was standing in front of an overturned chair, the other man was flattened against the study window, his eyes wide with alarm and his face pale.

"Er, we didn't mean to interrupt," the inspector began, "but . . ."

"It sounded like there was an altercation takin' place," Barnes supplied helpfully. "Are both you gentlemen all right?"

Henry Albritton flushed slightly. "My apologies. Inspector, Constable, Sherwin." He nodded to all of them in turn. "I quite forgot myself." He picked up the chair and sat it upright. "Clumsy of me. I knocked it over when I jumped to my feet. Poor Sherwin was quite alarmed."

"That's quite all right. You've been under a considerable strain lately." The man peeled himself away from the window. "I shouldn't have pressed you about business. My apologies, Henry." Turning towards the inspector, he extended his hand. "We mustn't let the police believe this sort of behavior is common to us. Despite appearances, Albritton and August Boatbuilders generally have very sedate business discussions. My name's Sherwin August. I'm Henry's business partner."

Witherspoon took the proffered hand and introduced Constable

Barnes. August was portly, of medium height with thick blond hair and muttonchop whiskers. Behind the smile in his bright blue eyes, he regarded the policemen cautiously.

"Why don't we all sit down?" Albritton said, once the amenities were finished. "Perhaps I should ring for tea?"

"I can't stop long, Henry," August replied. "I must get back to the office."

"Where are your offices located?" Witherspoon inquired. He was still rather puzzled over the argument he'd overheard. Gracious, it sounded as though Mr. August thought Henry Albritton had become a radical socialist! But just as the thought entered his mind he pushed it to one side. Annie Shields's murder had nothing to do with Albritton's political ideas.

"We've three yards here in London," August said. "Our offices are at our largest one. On Castle Street, just near St. Paul's Pier."

"Sherwin," Albritton said softly, "I think perhaps you ought to tell these gentlemen where you were Sunday night."

The inspector was rather irritated. He'd have gotten round to asking the man himself, and he didn't much like having someone put their oar in, so to speak. Furthermore, they had no evidence that Sherwin August knew anything at all about Annie Shields.

"Where I was?" August was more puzzled than annoyed. "Why should the police wish to know that?"

"Because someone very dear to me was murdered," Albritton snapped. "And you've got as much motive as anyone for wanting to get rid of her."

Mrs. Goodge had a lovely tea laid when they all returned at five o'clock. Betsy had arrived home first, but instead of saying a word to Mrs. Jeffries or the cook, she'd dashed up to her room. Luty and Hatchet, quarreling with one another, arrived next, followed immediately by Wiggins. By the time Betsy came back to the kitchen carrying two brown paper parcels in her arms, Smythe had strolled in and taken his customary seat.

"What's that?" he asked, nodding at the parcels.

"Some old clothes," Betsy said airily. "I'm giving them to one of Annie's friends. She needs them worse than I do."

"Excuse me," Hatchet said stiffly. He glared at Luty and then quickly looked at Mrs. Jeffries. "But before any of us begin, I do think there's something we must discuss. We must decide what to do about Emma."

"Oh dear." Mrs. Jeffries had hoped they could wait a day or two before dealing with that. "Is the child being troublesome?" she asked.

"Not at all," Hatchet replied. "She's a very sweet little girl. It's just that she misses her mother. She's very confused right now, very frightened. I do feel that we must get her settled somewhere soon—"

"You mean afore you get so attached to her it'll break yer heart to let her go," Luty interrupted.

The butler shot his mistress another fierce glare. "I'm not getting attached to the child. But I could hardly let the poor little thing cry all night, could I? She was frightened. She was in a strange place with unfamiliar people."

"Hatchet's been fussin' over Emma like a mama cat," Luty explained. "He spent most of the night rockin' her in my old rockin' chair."

"Me! What about you? You were in and out of that room so many times last night it's a wonder the poor child got any sleep at all," Hatchet shot back. "Go ahead, admit it, you're getting quite sentimental over Emma yourself. You let her sit on your lap all through breakfast."

"Really, Luty, Hatchet," Mrs. Jeffries interjected. "Do you think we could get back to the point? I quite agree with Hatchet. For the child's own good, we must get her settled somewhere. Now, I do have an idea. But before I tell it to you, I'd like to hear what you've all learned."

"Can I have another slice of cake?" Wiggins asked, pointing to the Madeira cake in front of Mrs. Goodge. Mumbling about people's teeth rotting out of their heads, she cut him a second slice.

"Well, I didn't have much luck today," the cook announced as she slapped Wiggins's plate in front of him. "Albritton's not got any scandal to him, at least not that I've sussed out yet. Me sources told me he's rich as sin, but he made it all in trade. Seems like he's been havin' some trouble with his partner lately, though. Albritton's got some newfangled idea about how the workers ought to be treated, and Sherwin August—that's his business partner—is goin' round tellin' everyone that Albritton's gone off his head."

"You've learned quite a bit, Mrs. Goodge," Mrs. Jeffries said. "Before anyone else goes, why don't I tell you what I've found out." She told them about her meeting with Dr. Bosworth and about everything she'd learned from the inspector at lunchtime.

"The Struttses are lyin'," Wiggins said around a mouthful of cake. "I know 'cause the kitchen maid told me she found Mr. Strutts's coat hangin' on the banister. Said Gordon Strutts is real particular about his clothes and it were damp through and through, like he'd been out."

"Hmm. It was a particularly foggy night on Sunday as well," Hatchet put in. "Did she have any idea when Mr. Strutts was out?"

"She didn't know fer sure. She and the other kitchen maids had been out to church and then taken their sweet time comin' home. She didn't get in till almost eleven."

"A young kitchen maid out till eleven!" Mrs. Goodge was positively scandalized.

Wiggins grinned. "I don't think they was at church either. More likely they was out larkin' about with friends. Anyway, Abigail told me about Mr. Strutts's coat bein' so damp and she'd no reason to lie."

"How'd they get in the house that late at night," the cook asked.

"Seems they'd cooked up a scheme with one of the footmen to leave the back door unlatched. Guess they knew they was goin' to be gettin' in late."

"Shocking," Mrs. Goodge muttered, "Absolutely shocking."

Wiggins ignored her. "Abigail also told me something else. Mr. and Mrs. Strutts coulda known about Annie. Seems Mrs. Strutts listens at keyholes. Abigail saw her doin' it about two weeks ago, and one of the other maids told her that she'd seen Hortense Strutts do it lots of times."

"How does that mean that the Struttses could have known about Annie Shields?" Luty asked.

"What if Mr. Albritton had been talkin' about Annie to this solicitor fellow and Hortense overheard it?" Wiggins suggested.

"Do you think you can find out for certain if Hortense Strutts knew about Annie?" Mrs. Jeffries asked the footman. "It's very important." To establish that anyone in the house had killed Annie Shields, it was urgent to establish that they knew about her in the first place. If one of them had known, there was a good possibility the others had as well. People did tend to talk, especially in matters of self-interest. As far as Mrs. Jeffries could tell, everyone in the household had something to lose if Henry Albritton opened his house and his bank account to an illegitimate daughter.

"But Abigail doesn't know," Wiggins replied, frowning. "I already asked her."

"Then try askin' someone else," Betsy ordered impatiently. "Try askin' Hortense's maid. She'd probably have some idea." She wanted them to get on with it. She was dying to see the look on Smythe's face when she told them what she'd learned.

"I guess I can try," he murmured, looking very dubious. Trying to get more information out of that household would mean that he had to see Abigail again. He didn't feel right leadin' the poor girl on. But blimey, what else could he do? He had to help solve this case. If one of the women come up with the right answer, the men'd never live it down.

"Do the best that you can," Mrs. Jeffries said. "If no one in the household knew of Annie's existence or her importance to Mr. Albritton, then I'm afraid we're all wasting our time on this particular course of inquiry."

"Someone knew of her existence," Smythe said softly. "You can count on it. Fact is, someone knew plenty about the poor lass." He gave them a cocky grin, leaned forward and waited till he had everyone's attention. "Someone had been following Annie Shields for over a week before she was murdered."

CHAPTER 8

"How do you know *that*?" Betsy demanded, glaring at the coachman. He gave her an insolent grin. Honestly, she thought, Smythe looked as smug as a cat that'd just stole the cream. She'd love to wipe that silly smirk off his face. She was itching to tell everyone what she'd found out today. Now she was going to have to sit through another one of his puffed-up, drawn-out speeches. Leave it to a ruddy man!

"The same ways as I get all my information," he replied with a nonchalant shrug. "I use me brains." It would be a cold day in the pits of hell before he'd ever let on he'd paid for everything he learned today. But what else could he do? Fair was fair. Betsy wasn't above battin' her eyelashes at some footman to find out what she needed to know. He'd seen her use her wiles a time or two when they was on the hunt. Besides, this wasn't just another one of the inspector's cases they was investigatin', this was a matter of pride. Male pride. "A man can learn a lot if 'e's clever enough."

Betsy's eyes narrowed, but she clamped her mouth shut. Mrs. Jeffries, watching the pair, was sure the maid was biting her tongue. "Then do tell us," she said calmly. "We've quite a bit more to get through this evening."

"Yeah, stop wastin' time and git on with it," Luty put in. "I've got me own story to tell, you know."

"Give the man a chance," Hatchet said defensively. He smiled at Smythe and Wiggins. "I suppose we must forgive the ladies their impatience. The fairer sex is so much more emotional than we."

"Now you're wastin' time," Luty charged.

The butler lifted his chin. "I'll have you know, madam, neither of us is 'wasting time,' as you persist in saying. If you were a man, you'd understand. One must tell what one has learned in a logical, rational and calm manner if it is to have any true meaning."

"You mean you're all too slow-witted to get out more than five words in a row without havin' to stop and think," Luty muttered darkly. She stroked her fur muff. The other women were just as irritated as she was by Hatchet's pompous speech. Mrs. Goodge snorted, Betsy sighed irritably, and Mrs. Jeffries rolled her eyes.

Smythe, perhaps sensing an outright mutiny from the ladies, quickly said, "All right, all right, I'll get on with it. I know Annie Shields was being followed 'cause I met a man, feller named Fairclough. He's a friend of Bill Calloway's."

"But you didn't find Calloway?" Betsy asked.

"Not yet," Smythe retorted easily. "But I will. As soon as we're finished 'ere."

"Yes, yes," Mrs. Jeffries said, "I'm sure you'll find Calloway very quickly. Now, what did this Fairclough person tell you?"

"First of all, 'e claimed that Calloway ain't been seen since Sunday night."

"It's only Tuesday," Mrs. Goodge muttered.

"I know what day it is, Mrs. Goodge," the coachman said in exasperation, "but that's not the point."

"Then what is the point?" Betsy demanded. "You've been rattlin' on for five minutes now and you haven't said anything interesting."

"Rattlin' on?" Smythe repeated incredulously. "I'll 'ave you know men do not rattle on. We leave that to the ladies."

An all-out argument erupted. Luty, Mrs. Goodge, and Betsy were outraged. Hatchet and Wiggins, feeling, of course, that they must defend their gender, immediately jumped in on Smythe's side. Mrs. Jeffries let them shout at one another for a few moments and then she lifted her hand, balled it into a fist, and banged the table so hard the teapot jumped. "I do believe we'll have to postpone the hot issue of which sex 'rattles' the most until another time," she said forcefully. "In case you've all forgotten, we've got a murder to solve. Time is wasting."

Muttering under her breath, Mrs. Goodge contented herself with giving the men one final good glare. Betsy flattened her mouth into a stubborn line and Luty fingered her muff as she stared at Hatchet's chest.

The men, chastened but not bowed, shut up as well.

Mrs. Jeffries turned to the coachman. "Would you please continue with your narrative."

"As I was sayin'," Smythe continued, giving Betsy one quick anxious glance, "Calloway ain't been seen since Sunday evenin', and that's not normal 'cause the bloke practically lives at the Sail and Anchor. Fairclough told me that Calloway had told 'im he was worried cause 'e'd seen someone sniffin' around Annie Shields."

"You make her sound like a dog," Betsy mumbled.

"I don't mean it like that," he explained. "I mean, Fairclough claimed Calloway saw someone following the girl and then 'e found out this same feller was askin' questions about her."

"When did this happen?" Mrs. Jeffries asked.

"Accordin' to Fairclough, Calloway noticed the man about a week ago. That'd be last Tuesday or Wednesday. Fairclough wasn't sure exactly which day it was. But Calloway were spittin' mad about it. Supposedly, he watched the man follow Annie home on Tuesday night and then again on Wednesday. On Thursday the man started askin' people around the neighborhood questions about 'er."

"Calloway told Fairclough all this?" Mrs. Jeffries frowned. "Why?"

"They was good friends," Smythe explained, his big hands toying with the handle of his mug, "and also, Calloway wanted Fairclough to 'elp 'im. You see, Calloway went after the bloke."

"Went after him," Luty asked. "What fer?"

"To find out why he was so curious about Annie," Smythe replied. "That's why 'e told Fairclough what was goin' on; 'e needed 'im. They waited until Saturday night. Fairclough was to 'elp Calloway if they spotted him anywhere near Annie Shields. Well, they did spot 'im. 'E was followin' 'er 'ome from work. They took off after the bloke, but 'e saw 'em comin' and give 'em the slip. But Fairclough says while the fellow was runnin', he dropped one of them little white cards out of 'is pocket. 'Ad the man's name and address on it."

"What was the name?" Mrs. Jeffries asked excitedly. Finally they were getting somewhere on this case.

"Fairclough didn't know," Smythe admitted." 'E can't read and neither could Calloway. But Calloway was goin' to take the card to another man down the tavern and get 'im to read it. Fairclough saw Calloway come in the tavern on Sunday evenin', but he didn't 'ave no card with 'im. Calloway just 'ad a pint of beer and took off."

"How unfortunate," Mrs. Jeffries said. "Do you know where Callo-way is now?"

Smythe nodded. "I'm goin' there right after we finish up 'ere. I may not be back till late."

"That's not fair," Betsy protested. "I can't go back out tonight and I've got plenty of things I need to find out."

"Betsy, lass," Smythe said soothingly. He thought perhaps he'd pushed her enough for one day. "It's too dangerous for you to go runnin' about at night."

Mrs. Jeffries held up her hand. This was an old argument, one she'd just as soon not get into now. For once, she had to agree with the coach-man. She didn't relish the idea of Betsy or any other pretty young girl being out by herself. "Why don't you tell us what you've learned," she said, smiling sympathetically at the maid.

"All right," Betsy said grudgingly. "I tracked down a woman that was workin' on the Strand with Annie Shields the night she was murdered."

"Another flower seller?" Smythe asked softly.

Betsy turned and stared at him, her gaze meeting his levelly. "A pros-titute. Her name is Millie Groggins. I found her in a pub over near Aldgate Pump."

Smythe's face hardened. He started to speak, but Luty neatly inter-rupted him, "Good fer you, Betsy. What'd she tell ya?"

"Millie told me that Annie was right nervous that night," Betsy began.

"Did Millie say how she knew that?" Hatchet asked. "Had Annie said anything that indicated she was apprehensive?"

Betsy shook her head. "No, but Millie says she could tell by the way Annie was actin' that somethin' was bothering her. Remember how bad the fog was that night? Well, Millie says it were really bad down on the Strand; 'course it would be with them bein' right by the river. You couldn't see more than a few feet in front of you."

"That's true," Mrs. Goodge murmured. "That was a terrible night. My rheumatism was actin' up somethin' awful."

"Anyway, Millie says it was awful quiet. Neither of them had much business," Betsy continued, blushing slightly. "But every once in a while, while they was out there, they'd hear footsteps. Millie says it were never anyone interested in what they was sellin'."

"Flowers and flesh," Luty interjected.

"But by then, Millie had noticed that every time they heard someone comin' close, Annie'd get all stiff like and cranin' her neck to try and see who it was. When they'd walk on, she'd sort of sag, like she was disappointed. Millie's sure she was waitin' for someone."

"Millie might be sure, but I think she's wrong," Smythe commented.

"What makes you so sure *she's* wrong?" Betsy demanded.

"'Cause of what I just told ya," Smythe said patiently. "Calloway spotted someone followin' Annie. She wasn't stupid. She'd probably spotted the man as well. 'Course she'd be nervous, she was probably expectin' to see 'im poppin' out of the fog every time she 'eard someone comin'.'"

"If Annie had seen anyone following her and she was worried about 'im," Betsy said stubbornly, "she'd have said something to Millie. Women out on their own like that look out for each other. As it was, she didn't. Besides, Millie is almost sure Annie was supposed to be meeting someone that night."

"Did Annie tell Millie that?" Hatchet asked.

"No, but Millie claims Annie never worked late," Betsy replied.

"But we know she worked the Strand before," Mrs. Jeffries said doubtfully.

"That she did, but accordin' to Millie, Annie always worked the streets *before* people went into the theatres and restaurants. She claimed the gentlemen were more apt to buy their ladies a nosegay or corsage early in the evening. Millie was right surprised to see her out workin' a half-dead street at almost ten o'clock at night. So I think that considerin' how Annie was actin', she was only workin' late that night because she was going to meet someone."

"Betsy, lass," Smythe cut in, "Annie probably was workin' late 'cause she needed the money."

"That shows how much you know." Betsy smiled triumphantly. "She wasn't short that night. If she had been, she wouldn't have loaned Millie Groggins money."

Luty cackled. "Sounds to me like you've proved yer point."

"I would hardly say she's actually proved anything," Hatchet retorted. "However, there is some rationale to Miss Betsy's deduction. Hardly precise, but rather logical."

"And Harry Grafton did tell Luty that Annie had on the opal ring. A ring she was supposed to show someone," Mrs. Jeffries said thoughtfully.

"It sounded more like Harry thought Annie was wearin' it to show it off," Luty said doubtfully. "I didn't think he meant she was wearin' it 'cause she had to *show* it to somebody."

"But we don't know, do we?" Mrs. Jeffries smiled. "I'm not disputing your interpretation of what Harry told you, Luty. However, isn't it possible that Harry misinterpreted what Annie said that night in the pub?"

"It's possible, I suppose. Reckon we'll never know fer sure, though. Come to think of it, you might be right. From what we've heard of Annie Shields, she weren't no silly git. She don't sound like the type to wear a valuable ring out at night just to be impressin' someone."

"I think we ought to go on the assumption that Annie had that ring on for a specific reason," Mrs. Jeffries said. "The most logical reason, of course, is because she wanted to show it to Henry Albritton."

"But he was supposed to see the ring on Monday," Mrs. Goodge put in.

"True," Mrs. Jeffries agreed. "So that means the person she was going to show the ring to either wasn't Albritton or that Albritton had changed the time."

"Does he have an alibi for Sunday night?" Wiggins asked.

"According to what the inspector told me, his alibi is the same as everyone else's in his household. He was at home."

Mrs. Goodge made a face. "Sounds like a right miserable household, doesn't it? The whole lot of them at home together on a Sunday evenin' and no one saw or talked to anyone else."

"And Albritton had given the servants the evening off," Smythe said. "That makes you think, doesn't it?"

"Yes, indeed." Mrs. Jeffries smiled at Betsy. "You've done very well, dear."

"Any ideas on who done it?" Wiggins asked. He shot a quick look at Hatchet and Smythe.

"Not yet," the housekeeper replied confidently, "but I'm sure we'll continue making progress." She was nowhere near as self-assured as she sounded, but she wasn't about to admit it in front of the men.

Luty leaned forward. "Can I talk now?" As no one said anything, she plunged straight ahead. "I went to see Myrtle Buxton today."

"Who's she?" Wiggins asked.

"She's that friend of mine who lives across the road," Luty explained. "Remember, she was the one that give us all that dirt on that medium and the Hodges murder last fall. I asked her if'n she'd ever heard of Henry Albritton and she give me a real earful."

"Excellent, Luty," Mrs. Jeffries said. She hoped Luty had been discreet with her questions, but she could hardly ask her. Despite her colorful speech and seeming toughness, Luty Belle Crookshank was very sensitive.

"She told me that Albritton married his wife for money," Luty said.

"We already knew that, madam," Hatchet sneered.

"Yeah, but what you didn't know is that ever since his wife died, Albritton's sister-in-law has been eyein' him like he was a prize bull in a field of steers."

"Lydia Franklin," Mrs. Jeffries clarified. "Is she in love with him?"

"Don't know if she's in love with the feller," Luty said bluntly, "but she sure as shootin' does her best to keep anyone else out of the way. Myrtle told me that a year or so after Frances Albritton died, Henry started seein' another woman. Out of the blue, some really ugly gossip started about this woman and she cleared outta town like the devil himself was on her heels. Myrtle's purty sure it was Lydia who started the gossip and that there weren't no truth to it."

"That's very interesting," Mrs. Jeffries said slowly. "Does Myrtle remember the woman's name?"

"Oh, she recalled it just fine, but it ain't gonna help us none. Her name was Clara Hemmings. But she's gone. The woman was so humiliated she went all the way to India. Ain't been back since." Luty snorted. "Now, if'd been *me* someone was jawin' about, I wouldna been the one leavin' town. They would."

"What else did this Myrtle Buxton tell you?" Mrs. Goodge asked. Her tone was slightly petulant. But everyone pretended not to notice. Generally, it was the cook who had the richest sources of gossip in London. Understandably, she was a bit put out to hear that Luty had been tapping another, perhaps equally rich, vein.

"Not all that much. I didn't want to be gone too long," Luty admitted. "I just popped out fer a few minutes while Emma was havin' her nap. The only other thing Myrtle told me was that Lydia's husband left her poorer than a prospector with a empty mine. Franklin Warren sounds like he didn't have any more sense than a bank mule. Left Lydia flat busted broke when he finally died. She had to move in with her sister and rent out her house."

"What did this Mr. Franklin do for a livin'?" Wiggins asked, not because he particularly cared but because he wanted to contribute to the meeting, too.

Luty frowned slightly. "I ain't rightly sure. But from the way Myrtle described him, I think he was a . . . well, what we'd call a traveling sales-man back home. I ain't sure what you'd call it over here. But he traveled some and he sold as he went. You know the kind of stuff I mean, one month he'd be selling safes, the next month it'd be bicycles or ladies trav-elin' bags. Right before he died he was sellin' lawn tents, billiard tables, and gout medicine."

"How very interesting," Hatchet said. "If you're quite finished, madam, I'd like to share what I have learned."

"When did you get out?" Luty asked sharply.

"Early this morning," he replied. "Naturally, I kept my inquiries short and to the point."

Luty snorted. "Yeah, so short you probably didn't learn nuthin'."

"On the contrary, madam." Hatchet gave her a smug smile. "I learned a great deal. To begin with, I can tell you that Mr. and Mrs. Gordon Strutts knew full well that Annie Shields might be Henry Albritton's daughter." He turned and beamed at Wiggins. "You were quite right in your supposition. Mrs. Strutts had overheard Mr. Albritton discussing the situation with Harlan Bladestone."

"Gracious, Hatchet, that is rather remarkable," Mrs. Jeffries com-mented. "How did you find out so very quickly?"

Hatchet's chest swelled with pride. "Like Smythe, I, too, have my sources."

"You got lucky," Luty muttered.

"I assure you, madam," he replied frostily, "luck had nothing to do with it. I got clever. Oh drat, what I meant to say was that in my usual calm, rational fashion, I ascertained the likeliest sources for the most ef-ficient gathering of information and I pursued them. According to what I learned, both the Struttses were well aware of the possibility of Henry Albritton having a child, and more importantly, they were quite alarmed by the prospect."

"Alarmed?" Mrs. Jeffries asked curiously. "In what way?"

"They were alarmed enough to start following Albritton. Gordon Strutts has been keeping a close eye on Albritton's movements. His wife, Hortense, has kept an eye on Annie Shields."

"The veiled lady," Luty yelled. "Maybe Harvey Maxwell wasn't tellin' tales when he told me he'd seen someone hangin' around Emma."

"I fear it's far too early to make that assumption," Hatchet said, annoyed at his employer for trying to steal his thunder. "Hortense Strutts was watching Annie Shields, not Emma."

"Cor blimey, sounds like 'alf of London were watchin' the poor woman," Wiggins interjected. "Pity none of 'em was there to see who murdered her."

"One of 'em was there, all right," Smythe muttered. "Too bad it was the murderer."

Mrs. Jeffries tried to keep it all straight in her mind. Now there were several people who knew of the connection between Annie Shields and Henry Albritton. And at least two people who had been watching the victim on the sly! However, she didn't attempt to reach any conclusions yet. She'd wait till she'd gained the quiet of her own rooms to do her real thinking. And now she had so much to try to sort out!

"Seems to me the men have done their fair share of investigatin'," Smythe said with another one of his cocky grins. "And you ladies 'aven't done 'alf bad neither."

"What about Lady Cannonberry?" Betsy asked Mrs. Jeffries. Like the other women present, she was eager to change the subject. If the men got any more puffed up with pride, they'd have to knock a ruddy hole next to the door so it'd be big enough for 'em to walk through.

Mrs. Jeffries sighed. "I'm afraid we've a bit of a problem."

"Problem?" Mrs. Goodge asked. "With Lady Cannonberry? What's all this about then?"

"Well, it's rather odd, really. Lady Cannonberry came back to London on Saturday evening." Mrs. Jeffries was suddenly determined not to discuss the subject of Lady Cannonberry in front of the men. First of all, she was irritated with the way they were all gloating, except for Wiggins, and that was only because he hadn't learned to gloat yet. Secondly, because she wasn't certain what she had to say was any of their business. It was women's business. Instantly, she made up her mind. "Actually, I ran into her today as I was leaving the tearoom. She sent everyone her regards."

"But I thought you said you 'ad a problem," Smythe protested.

"It's not really a problem," she replied airily. "I merely meant we'll have to stay on our toes. Now that she's back, she does occasionally pop in to say hello to the inspector. We wouldn't want her suspecting we were all out nosing around, would we?"

Smythe gave her a suspicious look but said nothing.

"What should we do next?" Wiggins asked.

"Next!" Luty protested. "Nell's bells, boy, I still ain't finished with doin' my first job."

"Luty's right," Mrs. Jeffries said smoothly. "I think if we all continue digging, we're bound to come up with even more."

"I'm going to pop out for a bit," Betsy said, glancing at the clock. "It's important."

"Where are you goin'?" Smythe demanded.

Betsy ignored him, leapt to her feet and dashed for the coatrack. Slipping on her heavy cloak, she turned to Mrs. Jeffries and said, "I should be back in time to serve the inspector his dinner. There's just one little thing I want to do. It won't take long, I promise."

"Are you goin' to let her go, then?" Smythe asked Mrs. Jeffries. He looked outraged, incredulous.

"Of course I'm going to let her go," Mrs. Jeffries said calmly. "It may be dark, but it's still quite early. The streets should be safe enough. There are plenty of people about." She was leery of letting the girl go out, but really, it was only half-past five. Besides, she was rather annoyed at the way the men had learned so much more than the ladies. It didn't seem fair.

Over dinner, Mrs. Jeffries learned even more about the case from the inspector. "You were absolutely right about the flowers," he said as he leaned back in his chair. "The family and the servants had noticed he was bringing home huge bunches of them every day. Mrs. Franklin especially was most upset about it."

"How very clever of you," Mrs. Jeffries said.

"Really, Mrs. Jeffries," the inspector exclaimed, "you're the one who suggested it."

"Yes, but I'm sure you were the one who was intelligent enough to confirm it by talking to the servants and not the family." Under the table, she crossed her fingers that she was right.

He beamed. "Oh, you know my methods so well. I spoke with the housemaids, actually. Mrs. Franklin noticed the flowers the first day Albritton brought them home. Mrs. Strutts didn't notice for several days."

"Odd that Mrs. Franklin didn't mention them to Mrs. Strutts," Mrs. Jeffries said.

"Not really." The inspector reached for another peach turnover. "The ladies, so I was told by both the housemaid and the butler, don't have all that much to do with one another. As a matter of fact, they rarely ever speak. Mrs. Strutts seemed to feel that she should be the lady of the house, but as Mrs. Franklin had got there first, she was a tad resentful."

"I see." Mrs. Jeffries thought this very interesting. "How sad that they don't get on."

"It is, isn't it?" He eyed the last peach turnover on the plate as if trying to make up his mind. "And I found out that Mr. Albritton's business partner has an alibi for the night of the murder." He lunged for the turnover and slapped it onto his dessert plate. "Honestly, everyone seems to be accounted for. Despite what Mr. Albritton says about his relations and partner, I don't think any of them could have done it."

"Where was Mr. August?"

"He was working, late at his office." The inspector smiled. "Of course, we'll be able to confirm it easily enough as well. Though Mr. August doesn't realize it. Luckily for us, there was a robbery at the warehouse next to the boatyard offices. The police were there taking a report from ten past nine until well after ten o'clock Sunday night."

"They questioned Mr. August?"

"Oh no, no. But Constable Barnes was going to check with them to see if they saw lights on and that sort of thing." He popped a bite into his mouth and chewed thoughtfully. "Gracious, one can't work in the dark. And according to the report, there were a number of police about. As a matter of fact, one of the constables was in the boatyard itself. The whole area was thoroughly searched. Good thing for Mr. August, too. Otherwise, he'd be my prime suspect."

"Really." Mrs. Jeffries was all ears. "Why?"

"Because as far as I can tell, he was the only one who had any idea who Annie Shields was, and furthermore, he was the only one who knew that Henry Albritton was planning on selling up and taking the girl and leaving. He admitted that today."

• • •

"Why the bleedin' 'ell should I tell you anythin' about Annie?" Bill Calloway sneered. He leaned back in the chair and glared at the huge black-haired stranger.

"I reckon talkin' to me would be a mite easier than spendin' the night 'elpin' the police with their inquiries," Smythe answered. He glanced around the small, filthy back room of the restaurant where he'd tracked his quarry. The walls were spotted with damp, the ceiling sagged, the floor beneath his feet felt slimy, as though it were coated with grease, and there was a faint stench of rotting fish in the air. Smythe was glad the only light in the room was from a stubby candle set in the middle of the table. God knew what there was lurkin' in the dark shadows of the corners. Smythe knew he didn't want to find out. Trackin' Calloway had cost him plenty, but that was all right. He had a feeling it was going to be worth it. "So what'll it be? Me or the coppers?"

He wanted to get this over with fast so he could get back to Upper Edmonton Gardens and make sure Betsy had gotten safely home. Ruddy women. Always worryin' a man half to death.

Calloway wiped one dirty hand over his pointed chin. His hazel eyes narrowed suspiciously. On his cheek there was a crooked, two-inch scar. A wispy brown mustache hid the top of his thin lips. If Smythe had met him on the street, he'd have described him as "shifty," not dangerous.

"Don't see no reason to talk to either of ya," Calloway sputtered. But his eyes were frightened.

"Don't waste me time. I'm twice yer size. Either you tell me what I want to know, or I'll drag ya down to that copper that's walkin' the beat on the corner," Smythe said lazily. "And they wants to get their 'ands on you. You'd make a right good suspect. You're the only person who 'ad a reason for killin' that poor woman."

"Look." Calloway's voice was desperate. "What's it got to do with you, then? Huh? Annie and me knew each other a long time. We was friends. Why would I want to kill 'er?"

"I 'eard she give you the boot." Smythe grinned. "The police 'eard it, too. Lots of murders been done for that reason."

"You heard wrong," Calloway exploded. "Annie was stubborn and she sometimes got above herself, but she loved me."

"You're claimin' she didn't tell you to sod off?"

"She did." He obviously realized that lying would be pointless. Too many people had witnessed the incident. "But she didn't mean it."

"When was the last time you saw 'er?"

"Sunday evenin' before she went to work."

"Was she wearin' her opal ring?" Smythe asked, watching Calloway carefully. He was rewarded for his observations. Calloway flushed slightly.

"Yeah, so what? Sometimes she wore it."

"Did you see her that night?"

"I already told ya, the last time I saw her she was as alive as you or me."

"But you were angry at 'er, weren't you? You were mad 'cause she told you to sod off in front of the whole world."

"She might 'ave told me to sod off and maybe I didn't much like 'ow she did it, but I wouldn't hurt her."

"You followed her, didn't you? Followed her, killed her, and stole her ring so it'd look like a robbery."

"No. Damn it, I loved her." Tears sprang into his eyes and Smythe found himself warming a little. "I loved her, I tell ya. I'da been good to her and to the kid. I offered to take her away and start a new life. But she said no. Said she had somethin' better planned than goin' off with me."

He was crying in earnest now. "She stood right in front of me and told me she never wanted to see me again. And after all I'd done for 'er."

"All you'd done fer 'er. You mean like findin' out who the bloke was that was followin' her?"

Calloway swiped his cheeks. "Who you been talkin' to? Did that little sod Fairclough sell me out?"

"You ought to pick yer friends more carefully. Fairclough's already told me you followed the man that was followin' Annie." Smythe leaned in closer, forcing Calloway to lean farther back against the wall. "Who was 'e?"

Calloway stared at him for a long moment and then shrugged. "If Fairclough's been shootin' off his gob, he musta told you I don't know."

"You found the bloke's card." Smythe pulled a handful of coins out of his pocket and tossed them next to the flickering candle. Intimidating and bullying people went against his nature. Even people like Calloway. "Listen, I don't have much time tonight. Tell me what you know about Annie and who it was that were followin' her that week and I'll pay ya."

Calloway looked at the coins and then up at Smythe. He hesitated a moment before he snatched them up. "Fair enough. Annie's dead. I reckon nuthin' I can say will 'urt 'er now."

"All right, talk."

"The bloke followin' Annie was a private inquiry agent. His name is Albert Caulkins."

"Where can I find 'im?" Smythe shoved his chair back and started to rise.

Calloway put his hand on his arm and stopped him. "Now, why do you want to be talkin' to Mr. Caulkins? He can't help ya."

"I want to find out who 'ired 'im." Smythe stared at the hand on his arm and then up at Calloway.

"You don't need to."

"Really." He wondered if he was going to have to pop Calloway one before he got out of here. He didn't much like being touched. Unless, of course, it was by someone like Betsy. Not that that happened all that much. Bloody hell, he was so worried about the girl he was letting his mind wander. "And why is that?"

"Caulkins can't talk right now. Seems he's had an accident. Someone busted his jaw."

Smythe pulled his arm away. He felt dirty. "I hope someone had the brains to ask 'im who 'e was workin' for before they took a swing at 'im."

"Oh, they did," Calloway said. "They did. But that information's gonna cost." His expression was a mixture of fear, greed, and bravado.

Smythe didn't know whether to pity him or pound him.

Calloway obviously wasn't above using his fists to get what he wanted. He'd just admitted to breaking the man's face. On the other hand, Smythe could understand that. If someone had been hanging around Betsy, he wasn't sure he'd be above using his fists, too.

But he hoped he wouldn't take such pleasure in it.

Sighing, Smythe reached into his jacket pocket and pulled out a handful of pound notes. He was tired of playing guessing games. Tossing the bills onto the table, he said, "I want the name."

Calloway grabbed the money, stuffed it into the pocket of his filthy coat and then looked up. "Albert Caulkins was hired two weeks ago. The man who 'ired 'im was a bloke named Sherwin August."

CHAPTER 9

Mrs. Jeffries forced herself to sit down. If she continued pacing, she'd wear a hole in the floor. She cast another anxious glance at the clock, saw that it had gone nine and promised herself she wouldn't get genuinely worried until half past.

Surely Betsy would be back by then.

But what if she wasn't? Mrs. Jeffries would never forgive herself if some harm came to the girl. She should never have let her go out. This is what comes of letting pride dictate action, she thought.

If she'd insisted Betsy stay in this evening, she wouldn't be worrying herself to death now. Mrs. Jeffries sighed. But she'd honestly thought Betsy would be fine and she'd certainly expected to see her safely back home by now. Besides, she'd so wanted to learn more. Oh, be honest, Hepzibah, she told herself. The real reason she'd let Betsy go out this evening was because she'd wanted one of the women to bring in the clue that cracked the case. Childish, really. But sometimes one was childish.

Oh dear. She twisted her hands together and glanced at her cape hanging on the coatrack. Perhaps she should go looking for the girl. Then again, she'd no idea where Betsy had gone. She heard the back door open and she leapt to her feet. But the heavy steps stomping down the passage weren't Betsy's.

Smythe, his brows drawn together in a fearsome frown, charged into the warmth of the kitchen. He took one look at the housekeeper's anxious face and leaned against the doorjamb. "She's not back yet, is she?"

"No," Mrs. Jeffries admitted, "I'm afraid not."

For a moment he didn't say anything. He just stared straight ahead, his mouth grim and his jaw rigid. Finally he said, "Do you have any idea where she were goin' tonight? It's gettin' late, Mrs. Jeffries. Much too late for her to be out on the streets."

"I know, Smythe. She should have been back hours ago. This is all my fault. I shouldn't have let her leave after tea," Mrs. Jeffries said.

Again the back door opened, and this time Betsy's hurried footsteps could be heard running down the hall.

"Bloomin' Ada," Smythe exploded as soon as the girl popped into the kitchen. "Do you know what time it is?"

"It's only a little past nine," Betsy replied haughtily. She grinned at Mrs. Jeffries and started unbuttoning her coat.

"We were getting worried, Betsy," Mrs. Jeffries reprimanded her lightly. "I'd no idea you'd be out so late."

"Sorry, Mrs. Jeffries," Betsy replied, slinging the coat onto the rack. "I didn't mean to worry anyone, but it was worth it. You won't believe what I've found out."

"Why don't ya start with tellin' us where the bleedin' 'ell you've been," the coachman snapped, glaring at her as she sat down.

"Now, Smythe," Mrs. Jeffries soothed, "Betsy's home safe. That's what's important. Let her tell us what she's learned in her own good time. Should I get Mrs. Goodge and Wiggins?"

She wanted them here because she'd sensed today they were both feeling left out. Furthermore, this ridiculous rivalry had gone far enough. While she'd been pacing the floor and worrying about Betsy she'd realized one of the reasons she'd not gotten a clue about this case was because they'd all been so concerned with topping each other's information—and she considered herself equally guilty in this—that she hadn't done any proper thinking about the murder. It had to end. They had to work as a team.

"I'm going to get both of them right now," she announced as she headed for the stairs. "I've something to say that all of us should hear."

Leaving Betsy alone with the still-frowning coachman, she fairly flew up the stairs.

Betsy gave him a cheeky grin. "What are you looking so miserable about? What's wrong? Didn't you have much luck this evening?"

Smythe gave her a long, level stare. She didn't have a clue. Not a ruddy clue. When he'd walked into the kitchen and seen Mrs. Jeffries's anxious face, his heart had almost stopped. He'd been scared to death that something had happened to her. But by heavens, he wasn't going to let her know it.

"Nuthin's wrong," he said, forcing himself to smile. "I found out plenty. As soon as the rest of 'em gets down, I'll tell ya."

Mrs. Jeffries returned with Mrs. Goodge, a yawning Wiggins and Fred in tow. As soon as they'd all sat down and Fred had taken his usual spot beside the footman's chair, she started in on her speech.

For a good fifteen minutes she lectured. She didn't spare herself either, but took as much of the blame for their idiotic behaviour as she heaped on everybody else. By the time she was finished, they were all looking a bit sheepish.

Wiggins was the first to speak. "Thank goodness all this is over with, then," he said, reaching down to pat Fred on the head.

"We have been a bit silly," Mrs. Goodge agreed. "Reckon it's time to get on with getting this murder solved."

"Seems to me it was the men that started it," Betsy murmured softly. "But we did our share of stirrin' it up, too."

"All right, then," Smythe agreed, "we've all been actin' like children. Startin' now, let's try and remember we're in this together. Betsy, why don't you go first?"

Surprised, she replied, "That's right kind of you. Actually, I will."

"Where did you go tonight?" Mrs. Jeffries asked.

"Covent Garden." Betsy put her elbows on the table and leaned closer. "I went to have another chat with Muriel. Once Smythe mentioned that someone had been followin' Annie, I realized there were some important things I needed to ask. First of all, Muriel agreed with what Smythe found out. Someone was following Annie, and Annie knew it."

"For goodness' sakes," Mrs. Goodge exclaimed. "Why didn't the girl tell you that the first time you spoke to her?"

Betsy smiled. "Because I didn't ask. You've got to understand how a lot of those people are."

"What people?" Wiggins asked curiously.

"Poor people. Especially poor people from the East End. They don't much trust anyone. They can't. It takes a while before they'll open up even a little," Betsy gestured with her hands. "Most of them have never even seen a place like this, let alone lived in one. Muriel only answered the questions I asked when I talked to her that first time, and even that was like pulling teeth out of a tiger. Tonight I took some of my old clothes over to her and bought her a hot drink from one of them street costers. We got to chattin', you see, that's why I was gone so long. I knew it would take a while before she'd tell me much."

Wiggins looked puzzled. "You mean she was grateful like?"

"No, no." Betsy shook her head vehemently. "That's not what I mean at all. She weren't grateful. She's got 'er pride. Oh, it's hard to explain . . . it was sorta like, I told 'er a lot about myself, about my past and my family and watchin' my mother and sister die, and about bein' so poor you didn't know where your next bite to eat was coming from. That made Muriel feel she could trust me. That she could tell me things and I wouldn't think less of her or use what she'd told me to take what little she's got away from her. I know it sounds downright peculiar . . . but in a way, I give her hope. I mean, she saw that I'd got out and made a better life for myself and maybe she can, too. Oh . . . I'm not explainin' it very well."

"You're doin' just fine," Smythe said quickly.

"Yeah, I think I know what you mean now," Wiggins agreed. "It's like you convinced her you was a lot like 'er."

Betsy nodded. "Anyways, once she felt she didn't have to watch her back with me, she talked plenty. As I said, she knew Annie Shields was being followed. Annie had told her. But Muriel was pretty sure the person following her was a woman"—she looked at Smythe— "not a man. So I'm thinkin' there musta been two people keepin' their eye on her."

"Was Muriel absolutely certain it was a woman?" Mrs. Jeffries asked.

"Oh yes."

Mrs. Jeffries thought about that. "Perhaps it was Hortense Strutts. Did Muriel ever see this woman?"

Betsy nodded. "Last week. But she couldn't see her all that well, not enough to identify her. The woman was all covered up like, she had on a big hat with a veil and a heavy coat. Annie spotted her when they was loadin' their carts to go out that mornin'. She looked up, went right pale, and said, 'She's back.' When Muriel asked her what she meant, Annie told her that she was bein' followed and she was gettin' right sick of it. Muriel told her she ought to have it out with the woman, but Annie wouldn't hear of it." Betsy paused and took a deep breath. "On Sunday, Muriel spotted the woman again. She pointed her out to Annie, but Annie wasn't in the least upset. Said she'd taken care of it. She was meetin' someone that night that was goin' to take care of it once and for all."

"So Annie Shields had arranged to meet someone the night she died," Mrs. Jeffries said thoughtfully.

"I'm sure of it," Betsy said slowly. "But Muriel told me she had the impression it wasn't somethin' Annie was lookin' forward to."

"What did she mean by that?" Mrs. Goodge asked.

"It was just an impression Muriel had," Betsy admitted. "So I don't much think we can consider it evidence, but Muriel said she had the strongest feelin' that Annie was bein' forced to meet whoever she was goin' to meet."

They fell silent as they digested Betsy's information. After a few moments Mrs. Jeffries glanced at Smythe and nodded for him to begin.

"I found Calloway," he began. He didn't tell them it had cost him an arm and a leg. "And he give me an earful." He told them every little detail of his meeting with Bill Calloway. "So you see," he finished, "Sherwin August had been keepin' an eye on the victim for two weeks. He knew everything about her."

"Including the fact that she was Henry Albritton's illegitimate daughter," Mrs. Goodge mumbled.

"Right."

"So that means that both the Struttses and Sherwin August knew who she was." Mrs. Jeffries frowned. "But only the Struttses knew that Albritton was planning on taking the girl and leaving the country. And we don't know *that* for certain. We're only guessing that Hortense Strutts did overhear Albritton's plans."

"I think it's pretty likely, though," Mrs. Goodge said thoughtfully. "I mean, if they knew who Annie was, then there's a good chance they knew what Albritton was plannin' on doin' right? Albritton had talked freely to his solicitor, and it was that conversation that we think Hortense was listening to. Besides, why would Hortense follow the girl unless she knew what was goin' on?"

"Huh?" Wiggins looked very confused.

"What Mrs. Goodge means," Mrs. Jeffries said smoothly, for she'd only just followed the cook's logic herself, "is that Annie Shields was a pretty young woman. If Henry was merely infatuated with a flower girl, then there would have been no reason for Hortense Strutts to be alarmed. Infatuations with flower girls generally don't last very long, especially between middle-aged men and young widows. But the Struttses were upset enough to follow both Albritton and Annie. That means they must have realized that Henry's relationship with this young woman was not some temporary romantic infatuation. It was serious enough to threaten them into taking action." She reminded them of what the inspector had told her about Albritton's own suspicions concerning his relations.

"What about Lydia Franklin?" Betsy asked. "Wouldn't the Struttses have told her about Annie?"

"The inspector didn't think so," Mrs. Jeffries said. "According to what the Albritton servants told him, Mrs. Franklin and Mrs. Strutts didn't confide in one another. I think it highly unlikely the Struttses would have included Mrs. Franklin in any of their plans. Especially if those plans included getting rid of Annie permanently."

"But we don't know it was the Struttses," Smythe said.

"If it weren't them, then how come they lied to the inspector about their alibi that night?" Wiggins asked. "They claimed they hadn't gone out at all, but that maid told me that Gordon's coat was damp when she got home. Now, if Gordon was gone, seems to me that means Mrs. Strutts coulda been gone, too."

"You're absolutely right, Wiggins," Mrs. Jeffries said hastily. "But so is Smythe. They may have both been out that night, but that doesn't mean they murdered anyone."

"Then 'ow come they lied?" Wiggins persisted.

Mrs. Jeffries shrugged. "Well, it's possible that Gordon Strutts was out doing something else, something he didn't wish the police to know about. He could have been gambling or seeing another woman . . ."

Mrs. Goodge choked on her tea. Wiggins, who was sitting next to her, immediately began pounding her on the back. "Are you all right, Mrs. Goodge?" he asked, thumping her hard between the shoulder blades.

"I'm fine," she sputtered, lunging forward in order to avoid another blow. "Leave off pounding me, boy. The tea just went down the wrong way."

Mrs. Jeffries gazed at her in concern. The cook's cheeks had gone bright red. "Mrs. Goodge, is everything all right?"

"All right . . . well, of course everything's all right. I just choked on my tea. Oh bother." Sighing, she made a face. "Well, if you must know, I've uh . . . learned a few things and well . . ."

"You've kept 'em to yourself 'cause you was afraid one of us men would get the jump on ya?" Smythe supplied helpfully.

Looking thoroughly chastened, she nodded wearily. "It was wrong of me, I know. But crimminey, you men were awfully arrogant. But that wasn't the only reason I didn't say anything." Her cheeks flamed again. "The information is a bit . . . it's not the sort of thing I'd want to talk about in front of Betsy or Wiggins."

Betsy gasped in outrage, Wiggins gaped at the cook, and Smythe laughed.

"I take it the information is of an intimate nature," Mrs. Jeffries guessed as she tried to keep a straight face.

"Gordon Strutts likes boys," Mrs. Goodge blurted. "He only married Hortense to keep up appearances. And she only married him to get away from her father." She dropped her gaze and studied the top of the table. "Truth of the matter is, Gordon and Hortense can't stand each other. It's a marriage of convenience, Gordon was terrified his uncle would find out about his . . . er, habits and Hortense's old father was a real Tartar. She'd have married the devil himself to get away from him."

Betsy giggled. "Oh, Mrs. Goodge. You shoulda said something. Wiggins and I ain't babies. We both know about people like Gordon. And Hortense isn't the first woman to ever get married to get out of the house. Stop tryin' to protect us. Even Wiggins and I know about things like that."

"Well, you oughtn't to," the cook shot back. "You're both too young. You ought to have a better view of life and marriage. It's disgustin', that's what it is. Marriage of convenience, indeed!"

Mrs. Jeffries could see that Mrs. Goodge was quickly getting over her embarrassment. What had started as a delicate subject had soon become a matter for an informed opinion like her own.

"I think it's safe to assume, then," Mrs. Jeffries said, "that given Gordon's . . . uh . . . predilections, it's quite possible he was out on Sunday night visiting his, shall we say, friend." She heard Smythe mutter a word she hadn't ever heard before under his breath. She thought it best to ignore it. "That would explain his damp coat. In other words, he may have been gone from the house, but that doesn't mean he was out murdering anyone."

Mrs. Goodge nodded.

"'Course," Smythe said casually, "even if Gordon was out with one of his 'friends' Sunday night, that still don't let the Struttses out as suspects."

"I know," Mrs. Jeffries said. "If Gordon was gone, then that means that Hortense has no alibi. Besides, there's something else about their story which convinces me he wasn't home reading on Sunday night. Remember, the inspector told me that Gordon had supposedly been reading a novel called *An Evil Spirit* that night."

"What about it?" Betsy asked.

"Gordon Strutts told the inspector it was 'amusing,'" Mrs. Jeffries said thoughtfully. "But the truth is, I've read that novel and there's nothing in the least amusing in it. It's a rather tragic tale. Gordon Strutts never read that book. He lied. And his wife lied, too."

They discussed the case for another fifteen minutes. But nothing seemed to come to any of them regarding a solution. Finally Mrs. Jeffries said, "The inspector is going to speak to all the principals in this case again tomorrow. I've got to find a way to let him know everything we've learned. Perhaps by breakfast, something will have occurred to me."

"Have you come up with any ideas about gettin' Emma Shields out of Luty's house?" Smythe asked.

"Actually, I have." Mrs. Jeffries quickly told them what she'd decided to do. "However, I do think we ought to wait another day or two before taking any action. It could be dangerous for the child to go to the Albritton house until we figure out who the murderer is." They all agreed this was true.

"But Mr. Albritton does know about Emma?" Betsy asked. "He knows he's got a granddaughter?"

Mrs. Jeffries shook her head. "No. The inspector hasn't told him."

"But Albritton's Emma's grandfather," Mrs. Goodge insisted. "He's a right to know about the girl."

"We don't know that for a fact, Mrs. Goodge," Mrs. Jeffries said calmly. "Furthermore, until we find out who the murderer is, I'm not sure it is safe for Mr. Albritton to know of her existence. Annie Shields was probably murdered because someone suspected she was Henry's daughter. I don't think that person would take kindly to knowing there was now a granddaughter in the picture."

"But surely the killer knows about Emma already?" Smythe put in. "Cor blimey, 'alf of bleedin' London was watchin' the woman before she was killed. They was bound to know about Emma. And you can bet your last farthing that that inquiry agent, Caulkins, told Sherwin August."

"Yes," Mrs. Jeffries agreed. "And I find that most interesting."

"Have you got some idea who the killer is, then?" Betsy asked eagerly.

"It's far too early for that," she replied. She refused to speculate further, no matter how hard they pressed. "Come on now, it's getting very late."

"And what about Lady Cannonberry?" Wiggins said grumpily. "You still haven't told us about her."

Mrs. Jeffries hesitated. "It's a rather delicate situation," she began.

"I thought we agreed there'd be no more secrets," Smythe interjected.

She thought about that for a moment. "You're right." She took a deep breath. She wasn't really violating Lady Cannonberry's confidence. The woman had only asked her not to mention anything to the inspector. Furthermore, perhaps a male point of view might be helpful here. "Lady Cannonberry came up from Devon on Saturday. She came home early so she could participate in the march in Trafalgar Square on Sunday."

As one, they all gaped at her. For the first time that Mrs. Jeffries could remember, the entire household was speechless with shock.

Wiggins found his voice first. "Lady Cannonberry come up to riot?"

"No, of course not," Mrs. Jeffries hastily explained. "She came up to what she thought was going to be a peaceful demonstration. Lady Cannonberry is a woman of conscience. Remember her father was a vicar. He helped in the battle to end slavery in those places in the British Empire where that evil institution was established. He was a friend of Wilberforce."

"But what's the Metropolitan Radical Federation got to do with endin' slavery?" Smythe asked incredulously.

"My point is that Lady Cannonberry has followed in her father's footsteps," Mrs. Jeffries clarified. "Mind you, while her husband was alive she did try to avoid doing anything that would embarrass him. But, of course, he's dead now. So she can do what she likes."

"Wilberforce? Slavery? I still don't see what that's got to do with marchin' in Trafalgar Square?" Mrs. Goodge mumbled. "I'm confused. A widow of a peer riotin'?"

"Slavery has nothing to do with why Lady Cannonberry came to London. She came because she's opposed to oppression and injustice." Mrs. Jeffries folded her arms over her chest. "The march in the square wasn't supposed to be a riot," she continued, trying her best to hang on to her patience. "If you'll recall, a number of groups were represented."

"Bunch of Irish, anarchists, and socialists," the cook muttered darkly, "and all of them plottin' to overthrow our way of life."

Mrs. Jeffries would have dearly loved to debate the issue of their way of life, but right now she didn't have time. "Nonsense," she said firmly. "Many of those people were motivated by the noblest of reasons. There is a great deal of injustice and downright misery in our way of life. But that's not the point."

Wiggins yawned. "What is the point, then?"

"The point is, Lady Cannonberry saw the inspector that day. Her conscience is bothering her."

"Why should her conscience be kickin' up a fuss?" Betsy said bluntly. "Seems to me she were only there to try and do something to make this world a better place."

"Her conscience should be kickin' up a fuss," Smythe interjected before Mrs. Jeffries could open her mouth, "because she and the inspector have a . . . a . . . well, they likes each other. So she shouldn't be trottin' off to do things 'e wouldn't approve of."

"Wouldn't approve of!" Betsy yelped. "What's it to him? Lady Cannonberry isn't his dog."

"But he wouldn't be pleased to know she'd been in Trafalgar Square," Wiggins gasped. "Why, the inspector could have actually arrested her! Oh, he wouldn't have liked that at all. It'd be ever so awkward 'aving her round to tea if the inspector 'ad carted 'er off to jail."

"Bother on whether or not the inspector approves," Mrs. Goodge snapped. "Lady Cannonberry can do what she likes. She doesn't have to answer to any man."

Surprised, Mrs. Jeffries stared at Mrs. Goodge. The fact that she'd just neatly turned her back on her own opinion was obviously not going to bother the cook. Female independence was altogether a much more important issue than a mere trifle like overthrowing governments. However, Mrs. Jeffries didn't want any more dissension in the group. At least not until after this case was solved.

"Please, everyone," she commanded. "Calm yourselves. Lady Cannonberry's dilemma will have to wait for a few days. In case you've forgotten, we've a murder to finish."

"Exactly what is her dilemma?" Wiggins asked curiously.

"I've told you. She wants to know whether or not she should tell the inspector." Mrs. Jeffries didn't add that Lady Cannonberry now suspected exactly what she and the household were up to as well. That, too, could wait until after this case was resolved.

Betsy and Mrs. Goodge both snorted.

The next morning Inspector Witherspoon dawdled over his breakfast so long, he was almost late for his appointment with Harlan Bladestone. He hurried down the street, his breath coming in short painful gasps. Constable Barnes was right on his heels.

Of course, Witherspoon thought, it wasn't really his fault. He dashed up the steps and yanked open the door to the building where Bladestone had his office. Mrs. Jeffries and he had had the most interesting conversation over toast and eggs.

Witherspoon nodded to the porter and hurried on past. Gracious, now he had all sorts of useful avenues of inquiry to explore. Sometimes it was so good to talk out one's thoughts. Why, he'd dozens of different things to think about. He hoped the solicitor wouldn't beat about the bush all day. Considering what he needed to do today, he really must get cracking.

"Hurry, Constable," he called over his shoulder to Barnes as he raced down the hall towards Bladestone's office. "We're running a bit late."

A few moments later found them sitting in front of Bladestone's desk. The solicitor was frowning.

"You mean you still haven't found the child?"

Witherspoon shook his head. "No, I'm afraid not. We've sent word to the local police in both Leicester and Nottingham. We're hoping they might be able to help us find Florrie Maxwell."

"Then you're certain Emma is still with her?"

"We think it's likely," the inspector replied. "We've checked the local orphanages and foundling hospitals. No little girls of Emma's age have turned up there, so we're fairly certain she's still with Mrs. Maxwell."

Barnes coughed slightly. "I wouldn't worry about her safety, sir. By all accounts, Mrs. Maxwell was right fond of the girl. Even if she isn't with her, I'm sure she wouldn't have turned Emma out onto the streets or given her to someone she didn't trust."

Bladestone looked worried. "I should never have kept her existence a secret. If I'd acted on my natural instincts instead of searching for proof about Annie's parentage, Annie would still be alive and both she and her daughter would be safely living with Henry."

This was the opening the inspector had been hoping for. "Mr. Bladestone. Why didn't you tell Mr. Albritton about Emma?"

"Because I wasn't sure," Bladestone said in disgust. "It's this damned legal training of mine. I needed proof. For the past year I've known Annie was probably Henry's daughter, but I delayed and did nothing."

"You realize," Witherspoon said softly, "that we must tell Mr. Albritton about Emma. If there is a chance she's his granddaughter, he has a right to know about her."

"Don't we have to find her first?"

"We will," the inspector assured him. "Could you tell me exactly what Mr. Albritton was planning to do once he found his daughter?"

"But I've already told you. He was going to take Annie to America."

"Yes, but what was he going to do about his business interests?"

"Sell everything." Bladestone's eyes narrowed. "Inspector, I do believe I've mentioned that before."

"Yes, of course you have." Witherspoon smiled sheepishly. "What I meant to ask was, did Mr. August know of Albritton's intent?"

Bladestone didn't answer for a moment. "I'm not sure," he finally said. "But I suspect he did. I do know that Henry didn't tell him. For that matter, Henry didn't tell anyone but me."

"Then what leads you to believe that Mr. August was aware of Mr. Albritton's intent?" Witherspoon was very proud of that question.

Bladestone hesitated. "Look, Inspector. You'll forgive me, but well, this is damned difficult. You see, August came to see me a while back. I told him that I couldn't help him, that I was Henry's legal adviser, but that didn't seem to make any difference to the man. Before I could stop him, he was insisting that Henry was losing his mind and for the sake of the company I had to help do something about it." Bladestone waved his hands angrily. "I asked him to leave, of course. Henry may have become interested in peculiar politics, perhaps picked up some ideas that none of us approve of, but that hardly means he's insane."

"I don't see how that means August knew what Mr. Albritton's plans concerning Mrs. Shields were," Witherspoon said slowly.

"It doesn't—not directly, that is," Bladestone agreed. "But naturally, August's attitude was no secret to Henry. Henry told me he thought Sherwin was spying on him. Going through his papers, his desk, that sort of thing."

Witherspoon tried to hide his disappointment. "If there was trouble between the two of them, isn't it possible that Mr. Albritton only imagined this?"

Bladestone smiled. "Absolutely not. Henry's the most methodical man I know. He writes everything down. If so much as an inkwell has been shifted even one inch on his desk, he'd spot it. If he thinks someone was going through his papers, then take my word for it, someone was."

"What would happen to Mr. August's half of the business if Albritton had sold out?"

"Mr. August doesn't own half the business," Bladestone replied. "He's not a full partner."

"Really? But I most definitely had the impression . . ."

"No doubt Sherwin meant for you to get the wrong impression," Bladestone said tartly. "But believe me, he owns less than twenty-five percent of the overall company. He originally owned half, bought in when Henry's father-in-law died. But August is a terrible spender. He and his wife both love money. Over the years he's sold some of his interest in the company back to Henry. In the event of Henry selling to someone else, I suspect August would have lost his position. He'd still own his twenty-five percent, mind you. But Sellinger's would put their own people in to run the boatyards."

"Sellinger's, you mean the shipbuilders?" Witherspoon was most surprised to hear this. Sellinger's was one of the biggest shipbuilders in the world.

"Yes, they've approached Henry several times wanting to buy him out," Bladestone said. "The last approach was a month ago. Henry refused. Then, after he saw Annie, he began to reconsider."

"Did Mr. August know this?" Barnes asked.

"Yes. He knew Henry had refused the offer," Bladestone replied. "But I'm sure he'd heard the gossip that Henry was thinking of changing his mind. It's impossible to keep that sort of thing quiet."

The inspector thought about this. Gracious. This case was getting terribly complicated. He calmed himself and cast his mind back to his breakfast conversation with Mrs. Jeffries.

"Furthermore," the solicitor continued, "I think that there is a good possibility that in addition to Sherwin August, everyone in the Albritton household knew that Henry had decided to make a major change in his circumstances. A change which would affect all their lives."

"Where does Mr. Albritton keep his papers?" Barnes asked.

"In his study at home."

"Not in his office?" The inspector was surprised. "In that case, it could hardly have been Mr. August going through Albritton's desk."

"I beg to differ, Inspector," Bladestone said. "August has very free access to Henry's home."

Witherspoon wondered what that meant. He could hardly imagine Sherwin August sneaking through a window of Albritton's house. "You mean he was in and out frequently. But surely, Mr. Albritton would have been there while Mr. August was there?" Egads, this was getting confusing.

Bladestone leaned forward. "Sherwin's very clever. He could have waited till Henry had stepped out of his study and then had a good snoop. But whether it was August or not, I don't know, I'm merely saying it's possible. Because someone had gone through that desk. Someone had seen that correspondence. And in that correspondence, Henry had made it clear he was looking for a suitable house for himself and his daughter. He'd also written a letter to Sellinger's telling them he was willing to open negotiations."

The inspector suddenly thought of another question. "If Mr. Albritton had moved to San Francisco, what would have happened to his relatives? Would they have stayed on at this home?"

"Hardly. Henry felt he had a duty to all of them, but he fully realized he didn't need to support them in quite the style they're living in now." Bladestone sighed. "You've got to understand, Inspector. Henry's done a great deal of thinking about his life. Why should his relatives live in a grand house with servants to do their bidding when so many others in this world have nothing?"

"Had Mr. Bladestone made provisions for his relations?"

"They were all going to be taken care of," Bladestone said. "The Struttses were to be given the leasehold on one of Henry's properties in Islington. Henry felt it only fair to provide them with a place to live. But he wasn't going to continue giving them an allowance. Gordon has a small income from his father and Henry thought it would do the young man good to get out and make his own way in the world. Mrs. Franklin was going to be given a small allowance and sent back to her own home. They wouldn't have been destitute or left wanting, but they wouldn't be living in luxury either."

"I see," the inspector murmured. "And when did he make these provisions? When did he tell you?"

"A few days after he first met Annie Shields. He asked me to come by and we went into his study. Mrs. Franklin and the Struttses were all there. They didn't come in, of course. But they suspected Henry was up to something. He was terribly excited. Happy. He felt he had something to live for. Someone to care about and love."

"Why didn't you tell him about Emma at that time?" Barnes asked.

Bladestone looked down at his desk. "Because I still wasn't certain Annie was Henry's daughter. The circumstances were right and she did look enough like Dora to be her twin sister, but there was still the chance that she'd no connection to Henry whatsoever."

"Yet you were the one that made sure Henry saw the girl?"

"Yes. I deliberately steered him down Regent Street that morning two weeks ago. I knew Annie would be in front of the arcade." Bladestone smiled wistfully. "I told Henry I wanted to stop and buy some flowers for my wife. You should have seen his face when Annie turned around. He gaped at her. Stared at her like an awestruck boy. For the first time in weeks Henry was happy." He sobered suddenly. "A few days after that Henry asked to come round. That's when he made the provisions for his relations. It's also when he changed his will."

CHAPTER 10

"You're sure that the constable couldn't have made a mistake?" Witherspoon asked Barnes as they waited in Sherwin August's office. "They're absolutely positive there were no lights on here Sunday night?"

Barnes, who was keeping an eye on the door while they waited for August, nodded. "Not only didn't the constable see any lights, but he knows there was no one here 'cause he come up and pounded on the bloomin' door. No one, answered."

Witherspoon took a deep breath. "Right then, we'll see what Mr. August has to say for himself."

"If he ever comes back," Barnes muttered, his expression suspicious. "You don't think he's made a run for it, do you?"

"No, no, Constable," the inspector said, with more confidence than he felt. "I'm certain he's just out in the yard checking on a shipment. The clerk will find him. Besides, he's no idea we know his alibi is false. Have the constables we sent round to the Albritton house reported back yet?"

"I spoke to PC Lund when you was in talking to the chief," Barnes whipped out his notebook and glanced at the open door of Sherwin August's office to make sure they weren't being overheard. "Lund's a good man, knows how to get the servants to feel at ease enough to speak freely, if you know what I mean."

"I certainly do, Constable," Witherspoon agreed. He was so glad he'd thought to send someone round to question the Albritton servants again. After his chat with Mrs. Jeffries this morning, he'd had a whole different perspective on the case. "What was he able to learn?"

"Well, he got a kitchen maid talking and she's fairly certain that Mr.

Gordon Strutts had gone out that night. His coat was damp when the girl come in." Barnes squinted at the paper. "Oh yes, and the girl also admitted the kitchen door had been left unlocked. The maids had arranged with one of the footmen to keep it open so they could come in when they liked."

"That means anyone could have come in and out as they pleased," Witherspoon murmured.

"Yes, sir. It also means they coulda done it without bein' seen." Barnes glanced up, his face full of admiration. "You was right about that, too, sir. Lund says that door opens onto a passageway that leads to the Albrittons' back garden and that connects to the churchyard at the end of the road. Whoever was comin' and goin' that night didn't even have to walk down the street. They coulda nipped in through St. John's."

Witherspoon smiled modestly. Double-checking the physical entries to either a household of suspects or the scene of a crime was one of his prime rules. He was so glad Mrs. Jeffries had reminded him of that this morning. "Routine, Constable. Simply routine. Did Mr. Albritton give permission for us to search his house and grounds?"

"Yes, sir. Lund said they was still lookin' when he left. Mind you, the Struttses put up a fuss and so did that Mrs. Franklin, but Mr. Albritton soon quieted 'em down. But as of midmorning, they hadn't found either a hammer or a set of bloody clothes."

"And they may not, Constable," Witherspoon admitted honestly. "I really have been remiss in my duty. What was I thinking? I should have had that house and the grounds searched immediately."

"Don't be too hard on yourself, sir," Barnes said sympathetically. "We'd no idea how complicated this case was goin' to get, did we?"

"Indeed, not," Witherspoon agreed emphatically. "Did Lund have any luck in confirming Mrs. Franklin's alibi?"

"Oh, he did, sir. Said the vicar were a bit nasty about it, seein' as we'd already asked him about Mrs. Franklin before." Barnes chuckled. "He seems to think highly of the lady, sir. But he confirmed she were at evensong service and that he'd spoken to her afterwards for a few minutes. The earliest she coulda got home was half past eight. So that let's her out, sir. Mrs. Franklin couldn't of gotten from the Albritton house all the way over to the Strand and murdered Annie Shields by ten o'clock." He broke off at the sound of rapidly approaching footsteps coming down the hall.

"I'm so sorry to keep you waiting, Inspector," August said briskly as he came into the office. "Do forgive me. What can I do for you?"

"You can clarify a rather odd problem for us, sir."

"Certainly. I'm always happy to cooperate with the police." He gave them a wary smile. "Though I must say, I've no idea how I can be of help. I'd never even heard of this Annie Shields person until Henry mentioned her."

"Mr. August, you told us you were working late on Sunday night, is that correct?" Witherspoon watched him carefully.

August looked faintly puzzled. "Yes, it is." He sat down behind his desk and clasped his hands together in front of him. "My wife was visiting friends that evening and I thought I'd come in and get some work done rather than stay home alone. We're a bit behind these days. Henry hasn't been himself lately and he's . . . well, neglected a few, rather important matters. I thought I'd come in and clear them up."

"Are you sure you're not mistaken?" Barnes asked softly.

"I'm positive. Sunday night I was right here in this office." He began to drum his fingers on the desktop.

"Mr. August," the inspector said, "I'm afraid that's not true. We know perfectly well you weren't here. There was a robbery right next door. The police were there from nine until half past eleven. A good number of police, I might add." Witherspoon waited for August to realize the importance of his statement. He didn't need to wait long. August's jaw dropped in surprise.

"First of all," the inspector continued, "if you had been here, you'd have mentioned the commotion to us when we first questioned you. There was a good deal of noise and excitement here that night. If you'd been here, you couldn't possibly have missed it. Secondly, the constables investigating that robbery are certain this office was empty. There were no lights on. Unless you were working in the dark, sir, you weren't here."

August went pale. "I don't know what you're talking about," he sputtered. "I tell you I was here. I must have had the shades drawn."

"The constables pounded on the door," Barnes added. "No one answered."

"Then I was out in the boatyard," August said, his voice starting to shake. "That's right, I'd gone out to the yard to check that we'd received a rather large shipment of lumber. The lumber's stored in the back. That's why I didn't see or hear your men."

"The boatyard was searched," Witherspoon said softly. "One of the constables thought one of thieves might be hiding there. Come now, Mr. August. Why don't you tell us the truth? Where were you on Sunday night?"

"Where is everyone this morning?" Mrs. Goodge said irritably.

"They're all out digging for more information," Mrs. Jeffries replied calmly. "Smythe's questioning the hansom drivers over on the Edgeware Road. Betsy's going to have a go at some of the local tradespeople in the area and Wiggins is . . ." She paused. She'd no idea where Wiggins had gone.

"Wiggins is where?"

"I just realized I've no idea," she admitted. "But I'm sure he's doing something useful."

"I reckon." Mrs. Goodge plopped down at the table and stared at Mrs. Jeffries. "I've been doin' some thinkin' about this case. And I think maybe I've figured somethin' out."

"How very clever of you." Mrs. Jeffries wished she'd been able to come up with some reasonable ideas. But so far, she'd drawn a blank.

"I reckon that Calloway fellow is innocent."

"How did you come to that conclusion?" Mrs. Jeffries asked curiously. To her way of thinking, at this point, no one could be eliminated as a suspect.

"'Cause of the way Annie Shields was killed," Mrs. Goodge replied. "Calloway wouldn't of left her lyin' in the middle of the street. Unless he were stupid, of course. Which I don't think he is. He knew that considerin' what had happened between him and Annie, he'd be the prime suspect. Now, maybe it would take the police a bit of time to suss it out, but accordin' to what Betsy found out, half of Covent Garden heard Annie tellin' Calloway to leave her alone. The police would be bound to find out about it sooner or later. If he were goin' to do her in, he'da hidden the body better, at least long enough to buy him some time to get out of town. But she were discovered not long after she was killed, laying flat out on the road for anyone to stumble over."

"That's true," Mrs. Jeffries said thoughtfully. "And I did put a flea in the inspector's ear this morning. I'm sure he's already got men over at Covent Garden questioning people again."

"Besides," Mrs. Goodge said quickly, "if Calloway was goin' to kill her, in the heat of passion, so to speak, he'd a done it the day she told him to leave her alone. He wouldn't have waited till Sunday night. He'da done it while he was still angry, not after he'd had a chance to cool down some. And he seemed to genuinely love the woman. He were angry at her, yet he still cared enough about her to try and protect her. After all, he's the one that chased down that inquiry agent that were watchin' her." She shook her head. "If he cared enough about her to do that, he didn't kill her. It don't seem right, you know what I mean?"

Mrs. Jeffries thought about it for a few minutes. Actually, the cook's theory did make a lot of sense. "All right, let's suppose that Calloway is innocent. That leaves us with the Struttses, Lydia Franklin, Sherwin August, or Henry Albritton."

"I'd knock Albritton out of the runnin', too," Mrs. Goodge said. "As far as we can see, he'd got no reason to kill her,"

"Fair enough. Unless, of course, Albritton's not telling the whole truth about what happened twenty years ago. We've only his word that Annie Shields was his daughter."

"What about the solicitor?" Mrs. Goodge pointed out. "He'd have no reason to lie and he's convinced Annie was Albritton's."

"True." Mrs. Jeffries sighed heavily. She wasn't making head or tails of this case, "I'm not thinking clearly."

"Let's go over it again." Mrs. Goodge gave her an encouraging smile. "We'll take our time and put our heads together and see what we come up with. First of all, let's look at the Strutts. They had plenty of motive. If Albritton took his daughter and left the country, their nice life would be gone. More importantly, they wouldn't be the heirs, would they?"

"That's right," Mrs. Jeffries agreed. "So even if they didn't know what Henry Albritton's plans were concerning Annie Shields, they'd still have a motive."

"And we're pretty sure they did know about Annie— Hortense listens at keyholes."

"What about Lydia Franklin?" Mrs. Jeffries murmured. "What did she have to lose? She probably wouldn't have been Henry Albritton's heir in any case.

"I reckon she's out of the runnin', too," Mrs. Goodge said. "We've no evidence she even knew who Annie was. The Struttses wouldn't tell her. Albritton didn't confide in her and I can't see Harlan Bladestone telling her anything either. In other words, she's the only one who didn't know about Annie Shields."

"But she saw the flowers coming into the house every day," Mrs. Jeffries countered. "Surely she'd realize something had changed in Mr. Albritton's life. A man doesn't start buying bushels of flowers every day for no reason."

Mrs. Goodge dismissed this with a wave of her hand. "She'd probably be more worried that he'd met a woman he was romantically interested in, not a long-lost daughter."

That made sense, too. Mrs. Jeffries wished she knew what the inspector had learned this morning. There were times when she would dearly love to be a fly on the wall.

"All right," August said slowly. "I'll admit I wasn't here that night."

"Where were you, sir?" Witherspoon asked.

"I went for a long walk." August closed his eyes.

"In the fog, sir?" Barnes asked.

"Yes, it was foggy."

"Mr. August, did you walk on Southampton Street?" the inspector suggested. "That's less than a half mile from here."

"What makes you say that?" August had gone completely white now and his hands were shaking. "I uh . . . I'm not sure where I walked. Like you said, it was foggy."

"Mr. August," Barnes said softly, "why don't you just tell us the truth? You were walkin' on Southampton Street, weren't you?" He gave the inspector a quick glance and went on. "And you had a hammer with you, didn't you?"

"No, no," August moaned, his voice shaking with fear.

Witherspoon would have stopped his constable, but he was too surprised to say a word.

"But of course you did, sir. And you came across a nice little flower seller," Barnes continued relentlessly. "A sweet young woman, she was, sir. But her very existence could ruin you, couldn't it?" His voice rose. "So you raised the hammer and you bashed her head in, didn't you, sir?" he shouted. "Didn't you, Mr. August?"

"No, no. That's not the way it happened at all," August screamed. "She was already dead when I got there. I swear, as God is my witness. She was already dead."

Wiggins stared in horror at the bundle Fred deposited at his feet. "Good dog," he said, kneeling down and patting the animal on the head. "Good dog."

Fred wagged his tail and began sniffing the bloodstained white material. Wiggins's stomach turned over, but he forced himself to move. Reaching down, he shoved Fred's nose out of the way and scooped up the tightly rolled garments.

From directly ahead, he could hear the sound of policemen searching the Albritton garden. Trying to avoid touching the bloodstains, he picked up the bundle and crouched lower behind the headstone where he was hiding. Fred wagged his tail again and started to woof softly as they heard the constables stomping around just ahead of them.

"Quiet, boy," Wiggins said sharply. "I've got to think."

He looked around for a way out. He had to get these bloodstained clothes back to Upper Edmonton Gardens. But he couldn't sneak out this way, there were police everywhere. He turned his head towards the church and chewed on his lip. The vicar was still in the sanctuary, so he couldn't nip out that way.

But he had to get back. He and Fred had found the clue that would solve this case. Bloodstained clothes didn't walk all by themselves into a churchyard. They didn't roll themselves under a bush. Whoever had murdered Annie Shields had hidden these clothes, and once he got 'em back to Mrs. Jeffries, they'd have this case solved.

He couldn't help but feel a surge of pride. Mrs. Jeffries had been right when she'd lectured them on actin' like a team. He didn't like all the arguing and fighting that had been going on lately. But he was ever so glad he'd gotten it into his head to nip round here with Fred and see if he couldn't find something. Wasn't he lucky Fred had been sniffing round those bushes and found them.

The back door of the church flew open and Wiggins crouched lower. "Down, boy," he whispered to Fred. He watched the vicar bang the door shut and then hurry off round the other side of the church. He waited till he'd disappeared before he stood up. "Come on, boy. This is our chance. Let's make a run for it."

"Why didn't you arrest him, sir?" Barnes asked. He raised his hand at a passing hansom and waved it to a stop.

"Because he sounded as though he were telling the truth," the inspector replied. He nimbly stepped into the hansom. Barnes gave the address to the driver and they were off.

"But he had Annie Shields's ring," Barnes said, as soon as he'd settled back against the seat. "And he admitted he knew who she was and that Albritton was planning on selling out the company and taking the girl to America. August would have lost everything. He had motive and opportunity."

"He also admitted to hiring that private inquiry agent, Caulkins," Witherspoon said, "and that's precisely why I didn't arrest him." Actually, the inspector wasn't sure why he hadn't arrested Sherwin August. But, as his housekeeper always said, he must listen to his "inner voice" and that voice was telling him that August was not a murderer.

"Furthermore," the inspector continued, "August showed us the money he was going to use that night. He still had the cash in his office. Now, that proves he wasn't going to kill her. He wouldn't have bothered to go to his bank and get that much money if he was going to cosh the girl over the head and steal her ring. It was obvious to me he was going to do exactly as he said. He was going to buy her off."

"Why should she take money from August when she could have it all if she was Albritton's daughter?"

"But she didn't know she was Albritton's daughter," Witherspoon said smugly. "Albritton hadn't told her yet. He was waiting to see the ring."

Barnes shook his head. "I still don't trust him. Any man who'd take a ring off a dead woman's finger is capable of the worst. Uh, Inspector, I hope you don't mind me takin' off after August the way I did . . ."

"Not to worry, Constable," Witherspoon said quickly. "I was a bit surprised, but your method did get results. As to why August took the ring, he explained why he felt he had to."

Barnes snorted derisively. "He didn't want Albritton to know for sure that Annie was his daughter. Even though he saw the poor woman lyin' there dead in the street, he was still worried about his precious position."

"Indeed, it doesn't speak well of his character." The inspector sighed. "Of course, once Albritton saw the ring, he'd know for certain Annie Shields was his own flesh and blood. Which would make Emma Shields his granddaughter, thus starting August's problems up all over again."

"Right. Albritton would just take his granddaughter and leave for America. Leaving Sherwin August with nothin' but twenty-five percent of a company bein' sold to someone else. Disgustin'. He'd get money for his share, but I reckon he didn't think he'd get enough."

"Sherwin August is a rather nasty person," Witherspoon commented. "But that doesn't make him a murderer. Gracious, if everyone who was a nasty person was a murderer as well, there wouldn't be enough prisons in the whole country to hold them all."

"You must put these back exactly where you found them," Mrs. Jeffries told Wiggins.

"Put 'em back," he said, clearly disappointed. "But I only just found 'em. Besides, it's right hard to get in and out of that place. There's police everywhere."

"Wiggins." Mrs. Jeffries gave him a warm smile. "You've done excellent work. You are a born detective. It was very clever of you to think to search the churchyard. However, this is evidence. We really must let the police find it for themselves."

"But what if they don't?" Mrs. Goodge said,

"We'll just have to make sure they do," Mrs. Jeffries replied. She took the bloodstained shirt and trousers and rolled them back into a tight bundle. Handing them to Wiggins, she instructed, "Take these back to the churchyard and leave them lying in plain sight."

"But what if the police still don't see 'em?" he asked worriedly.

"They will. Because you'll draw their attention to their presence. You'd better leave Fred here, though," she said. She thought for a moment. "Once you get there, find a small stone. You've quite a good throwing arm, Wiggins. Do you think you could hit a policeman?"

"You want me to throw a pebble at a copper?" Wiggins yelped in surprise.

"Precisely." Mrs. Jeffries gave him an innocent smile. "That's exactly what I want you to do."

"Mr. Albritton," the inspector said softly. "Do you recognize this ring?" He handed him the opal ring he'd gotten from Sherwin August.

Albritton stared at it for a long moment. His eyes filled with tears and he slowly shook his head. "I gave this to Dora twenty years ago. See, you can see the flaw. Where did you get it?"

"From your partner, Sherwin August. He took it off Annie Shields's finger on Sunday night."

Albritton drew a deep, long breath. He swayed and stumbled, Barnes leapt forward, grabbed his arm, and hustled him towards the settee. "You'd better sit down, sir. You're not lookin' well at all."

"Mr. Albritton," the inspector said quickly, "are you all right?"

Albritton seemed dazed. He shook himself. "Sherwin murdered my daughter?" he mumbled. "But why? Why would he hurt her?"

"He didn't murder her, sir. At least I don't think so." The inspector watched Albritton carefully as he spoke. He didn't want the poor man getting too distraught. Gracious, chap looked like he was getting ready to peg out. White as a sheet, eyes as big as saucers. "You see, Mr. August knew Annie was your daughter. He'd hired a private inquiry agent to look into the matter. He'd arranged to meet her on Sunday night. He was going to try to pay her off; give her money to leave town. But he claims she was already dead when he found her."

"He's lying," Albritton said bitterly. "The bastard is lying."

"I don't think so," Witherspoon replied. "August showed us the cash he'd withdrawn from his bank. Furthermore, his story has the ring of truth to it. He admitted searching your desk and he admitted he knew you were going to sell out your company and leave the country."

"But why did he take the ring?"

The inspector cleared his throat. Oh dear, this was going to be very difficult. Especially as they'd no idea where on earth Emma Shields might be. "Mr. Albritton," he said softly, his voice sympathetic, "Sherwin August took the ring because he wanted no absolute proof that Annie Shields was your daughter. You see, sir, Annie had a child. A daughter."

Albritton went utterly still for a moment. When he looked up, the expression in his eyes filled Witherspoon with pity. Wariness, fear, and hope stared at him out of the face of a ravaged man. A man who couldn't take much more.

"A daughter," he whispered, as though he were afraid to believe it. "My Annie had a child. I've got a granddaughter. For God's sake, why didn't you tell me? Where is she? When can I see her? Oh, dear God, please don't tell me that she's dead, too."

"No, sir, she's fine." The inspector hesitated. Spotting Mrs. Franklin hovering in the open doorway, he said brightly, "Mrs. Franklin, would you mind getting us some tea. Mr. Albritton has had quite a shock."

An hour later the inspector left the new grandfather pacing in his study. "I do hope," he said to Barnes as they followed Nestor up to the Struttses' sitting room, "that we find Emma Shields quickly. That man is going to have a nervous collapse if he doesn't see his grandchild soon."

"We'll find the girl, sir," Barnes said confidently, "The lads haven't turned up anything on the grounds yet, sir. They've searched the shed and the garden, but they found nothing out of the ordinary. Just the usual gardening tools and a bicycle. They're searching the house now."

As before, the Struttses were sitting on the settee, waiting. The inspector didn't waste time with amenities. "Mr. Strutts, we've reason to believe you were not in this house on Sunday evening. Would you like to amend your earlier statement?"

"I don't know what you're talking about," Gordon Strutts said peevishly. But his voice lacked conviction.

"You were out, sir," Barnes said. "Unless'n, of course, someone else was wearin' your coat."

"That's absurd." Hortense Strutts sneered. "Gordon was right here. Reading. We've already told you that and you can't prove otherwise."

"I think we can," the inspector said calmly. "Once we start looking."

"You may look all over London," Hortense snapped. "But it won't do you any good."

"I think it will." Witherspoon steeled himself to be ruthless. Much as he disliked the subject, the gossip he'd gotten Mrs. Jeffries grudgingly to repeat this morning echoed in his mind. "And I'm quite sure that neither of you would want Mr. Albritton to learn about the kind of people we'll be forced to question." He kept his gaze on Gordon Strutts. "Young men."

Gordon gasped.

"Young men who are paid for certain services," Barnes added.

"How dare you?" Hortense whispered furiously. Her eyes narrowed dangerously as she rose to her feet. "How dare you imply such disgusting things about my husband?"

"I assure you, madam," the inspector said, "we're implying nothing. However, if you persist in your original story, we'll be forced to question—"

"No. You'll not question anyone," Gordon said. He grabbed his wife's hand and pulled her back to the settee. "Sit down, Hortense. For once, I'll handle this."

"Don't be ridiculous—"

"Shut up," he snapped. "I'll not let George get dragged into this mess."

"Oh, you'd protect your precious George, would you?" Hortense glared at her husband with loathing. "Well then, I'll leave you to it." She turned to the policemen, her eyes blazing with contempt. "I'd like to amend my earlier statement. Gordon wasn't here that night. He was gone from eight o'clock until almost eleven. I was alone."

Witherspoon, who was trying terribly hard to keep from looking shocked, nodded.

Gordon laughed harshly. "You're a fool," he jeered at his wife. "Why don't you tell them the rest? Why don't you tell them the truth? I'm not the only one who was gone that night," he said maliciously. "And unlike you, I can prove I wasn't over on Southampton Street committing murder. I was with someone."

"Someone who would die before they'd ever publicly admit you'd been with them." Her temper flared. "Do you really think that the son of a peer of the realm is going to tell them the truth to save your sorry skin?"

"Er." Witherspoon looked helplessly at Barnes, who shrugged. "Excuse me," he tried to say. But the Struttses were now going at it like cats and dogs.

"You fat cow." Gordon gave his wife a hard shove. She toppled to the side and slipped off the settee onto the floor.

"Don't touch me, you sickening ponce," she screamed as she bounced onto the carpet.

Appalled, Witherspoon leapt towards the hapless woman, who was now tangled up in her own heavy skirts. "Please, Mr. Strutts," he commanded. "Calm yourself. We can't have this sort of behaviour. I won't stand for it."

He reached down to offer Mrs. Strutts his hand, but she pushed it away. Her round face was red with rage, her eyes filled with loathing as she glared pure hatred at her husband. "He killed her," she said. "No matter what he says, no matter who he claims he was with, he murdered that poor woman. I can always go home to my father. But if Uncle Henry had taken that bastard daughter of his and left the country, Gordon would be out on his ear. He can't work. He's too stupid to do even the simplest thing. He's not got enough money to live on and none of his little friends would lift a finger to help him if he didn't pay them. That's what he does, you know. He pays them."

"Shut up, you stupid fool! How would you like it if I told them what I found in your room when I got home that night," Gordon yelled. "You were still wearing your coat and hat when I walked in. Where the hell had you been? Out taking a lovely walk in the fog? And you were the one that had been following Annie Shields. You were the one who was going out to meet her that night. Not me."

"You bloody liar," Hortense screamed. "You know very well I never saw her. I told you."

"Could you please calm yourselves?" the inspector shouted.

Still glaring at one another, they both shut up. Hortense rose stiffly to her feet and stumbled towards the chair. As soon as she'd sat down, Witherspoon tried again. "Now, why don't we start from the beginning? Apparently, both of you would like to amend your earlier statements."

There was a commotion from downstairs. "Should I go and see what that is, sir?" Barnes asked.

Witherspoon started to nod, took another look at the Struttses and said, "No, why don't we all go downstairs? There's no reason we can't discuss this calmly in the drawing room."

He wanted everything out in the open. This case was getting far too muddled and complex. Suddenly no one had an alibi, half of London seemed to have been on Southampton Street the night Annie was murdered, and he was getting a dreadful headache.

Barnes nodded and motioned for Hortense Strutts to go ahead of him. No doubt the constable felt there might be a good deal less chance of further bloodshed if he placed himself between husband and wife.

Witherspoon came behind Gordon Strutts. They trooped towards the stairs.

Below, two uniformed constables, one of them holding a bundle tucked under one arm, were trying to get Lydia Franklin or Nestor to go and get Inspector Witherspoon.

"You can wait a few moments," Lydia Franklin said sharply. "Nestor doesn't work for the Metropolitan Police. He works for this household and I'll not have him neglecting his duties running up and down the stairs for the police."

"Please, ma'am," the younger of the two policemen pleaded. "It's very important. If you'll just tell us where he is, we'll go find him ourselves."

"I'm not having your muddy feet all over the carpets," she retorted. "You can just wait outside."

"Lydia," Albritton called. "What's going on here?"

She gave him a stiff smile. "Henry, why aren't you resting? There's nothing at all going on. I was merely trying to get these gentlemen—"

"I know what you were trying to do," Albritton said. Witherspoon saw him glance up as he heard the noise from above. Puzzled, he stared at the spectacle of four people, their faces grim as death, marching single file down the stairs.

"Inspector?" Albritton queried. "What on earth—"

"Inspector Witherspoon," the constable with the bundle interrupted. "We think you'd better take a look at this." He thrust the bundle into the inspector's hand.

Witherspoon, recognizing the heavy red stains on the material, felt his stomach tighten. But he knew his duty. He unrolled the top garment and held it up.

"Looks like a man's shirt," Barnes said, stepping forward and examining it closely, "And this is blood, or I'm not an English copper."

"Yes, I'm afraid you're right," Witherspoon muttered. He handed Barnes the shirt and unrolled the dark brown material still in his hand. It was a pair of trousers. Holding them up, he couldn't see any bloodstains, but as the trousers were a dark colour, he realized they'd need to be examined in strong light before they'd reveal much.

"Probably what the killer was wearin' that night," Barnes said.

"Probably," Witherspoon agreed. "Where did you find these?" he asked, turning to the two constables.

"Well . . ." The younger policeman looked at the older one, who nodded encouragingly. "Go on, tell it like it happened," he ordered.

"We found them in St. John's churchyard," the younger one continued.

"On whose authority did you search the churchyard?" Witherspoon suddenly had visions of nasty defense lawyers and equally nasty Judges' Rules.

"We wasn't tryin' to search the churchyard," the young policeman explained. "But you see, I was standing on this side, searching Mr. Albritton's garden, when I felt something sharp sting me neck. Someone had thrown a pebble at me. When I looked up, I saw a lad disappearing through the headstones. Well, you can't have boys throwin' stones at policemen and gettin' away with it, can you?"

"Er, no. I suppose not."

"So I nipped after him. When I got into the churchyard, I practically stumbled over these." He jerked his chin towards the bloodstained clothes.

"I see." Witherspoon frowned. "Well, thank you, Constables, you were absolutely correct in bringing this to my attention, I think it may be very important evidence. These garments could well be what the killer wore that night."

The two constables took their leave.

As soon as they were gone, Albritton said, "Let's go into the drawing room. Maybe one of us will be able to recognize the garments."

"That won't be necessary," Lydia Franklin said bluntly. "I know who those clothes belong to." She smiled maliciously toward the Struttses. "They're Gordon's."

CHAPTER 11

"I almost got caught," Wiggins exclaimed. "Cor, I didn't think that copper could run so fast! Lucky for me, he didn't grab that bicycle he and the other copper'd been larkin' about on and take off on it. He'da caught me for sure."

"What're you complainin' about?" Betsy grumbled. "At least you've had a bit of excitement in your day. I talked to every ruddy shopkeeper on the Edgeware Road, and all I learned was that Hortense Strutts is fond of chocolates and Lydia Franklin's got thin blood. Oh yes, and Gordon Strutts's got asthma."

Wiggins made a face. "Thin blood? Are you 'aving me on? 'Ow'd a shopkeeper know anything about someone's blood."

"Thin blood means you feels the cold," Mrs. Goodge said impatiently.

Betsy giggled. "Lydia Franklin wore her coat in church during the whole service last Sunday evenin'. The butcher's wife was sittin' behind her the whole time. Said she didn't so much as unbutton the collar. Some people. Rich as sin but that don't keep 'em from sufferin' like the rest of us. Even poor old Gordon don't get to enjoy himself much, the least little bit of exertion and he's wheezin' like a teakettle." She glanced at the coachman. "Did you learn anything interestin'?"

"No. Between the riots and the fog, the streets was empty." Smythe grinned. "No one picked up any fares near the Albritton house. I'm goin' out in a few minutes, though. One of the Albritton footman goes into the local pub for his pint as soon as they finish up after lunch. This is their half day. 'E might know somethin'. Seems to me like the only one that's 'ad a brush with excitement 'ere is our Wiggins."

"Now, now," Mrs. Jeffries said soothingly. "You should all be very proud of yourselves. We're finally getting somewhere on this case. Once those clothes are identified, I'm sure an arrest will follow." Even as she said the words something tugged at the back of her mind.

"Who do you think it'll be?" Mrs. Goodge asked eagerly. "My money is on that Hortense Strutts. From what I heard about her old father, she'd do anything to keep from livin' with him again."

"What does Annie Shields's murder have to do with Hortense Strutts livin' with her father?" Wiggins asked curiously. "Ain't married ladies supposed to live with their husbands?"

"Of course they are," the cook said. "But if Mr. Albritton had taken his daughter and gone off to some heathen land to start a new life, the Struttses might not have stayed together."

The footman looked stunned. "You mean they'da"— he lowered his voice—"divorced?"

"I don't think they'd of gone that far," Mrs. Goodge replied. "But from the gossip I heard the last couple of days, they probably wouldn't have bothered to live together. Gordon Strutts probably would have moved into some den of sin in Chelsea with one of his 'friends,' so poor old Hortense wouldn't have had much choice. She'da had to move back in with her family."

"My money's on Gordon," Smythe said. "He's the only one of the lot who we knows was actually out of the house on Sunday night." He shoved his chair back and got up. "I'd best push off, then, and see what this footman knows."

Smythe disappeared down the hall. Mrs. Jeffries said, "I was rather hoping the inspector would pop in for luncheon. But as it's past two, I don't think he will." Her head jerked towards the window over the sink as she heard a hansom pull up outside. She got up, hurried over, and peeked outside. "I told a lie," she called to the others. "The inspector has come home."

They leapt into action. Wiggins called for Fred, Mrs. Goodge dashed towards the larder, and Betsy hurried upstairs to set the dining table. Mrs. Jeffries was right on her heels.

She made it to the front hall, smoothed her hair out of her face, and smiled serenely as the door opened and Inspector Witherspoon stepped inside. "Good afternoon, Mrs. Jeffries."

"Good day, sir. What a delightful surprise. I'm so glad you were able to come home for lunch. Mrs. Goodge has a lovely cheese-and-onion tart ready."

"Thank you, Mrs. Jeffries." The inspector handed her his hat and coat. "But all I really want is a cup of tea and some of those remarkable headache powders of yours. Would that be too much trouble?"

"Of course not, sir," she said. "I'm so sorry you're not feeling well. Is the case going badly?"

"Oh no, it's actually going quite well. We've arrested Gordon Strutts."

"Mr. Strutts?"

"Naturally, he started to deny everything. Then he shut up tighter than a bank vault and refused to say another word until his solicitor arrived. But we've quite good evidence against him."

"I'm sure you do, sir."

"But it's still been a most distressing day. I left Constable Barnes in charge and thought I'd nip home and get something for this headache. You won't believe the way people behave. Why, it's positively shocking. The Struttses at each other's throat. Mrs. Franklin refusing to say anything to anyone, and Mr. Albritton practically having to be locked in his study to keep from murdering his nephew."

"Poor inspector. You have had a most trying time." Mrs. Jeffries gestured towards the drawing room. "Why don't you go and sit down, sir? I'll get you some tea and those headache powders."

Betsy, who'd been hovering by the dining-room door, popped out, nodded at Mrs. Jeffries, and hurried towards the backstairs. Mrs. Jeffries, knowing full well that the maid was already putting a tea tray together, hurried up to her own rooms for the headache powder.

Now that an arrest had been made, it would be safe to get Emma to her grandfather. They didn't have a moment to lose. The plan she'd come up with yesterday had to go into effect. Immediately.

If they were going to get Emma Shields into Henry Albritton's house without anyone finding out where she'd been and what *they'd* been up to, they had to act fast.

A few minutes later Betsy appeared with the tea tray. "I've brought you some sandwiches, sir," she said to the inspector as she set the tray down. "Mrs. Goodge was afraid them headache powders might upset your digestion if you took them on an empty stomach."

"How very thoughtful of her," Witherspoon said. Gracious, he was such a lucky man. "Do tell her I said thank you. I'm sure the sandwiches will be delicious." He reached for a sandwich and eagerly took a bite. "I say, these *are* good."

"You were telling me about your terrible day, sir," Mrs. Jeffries prompted.

"Oh yes." The inspector told her everything. From his interview with Henry Albritton to the discovery of the bloodstained clothes. Before he knew it, he felt much better. His headache was gone, his stomach was full, and he could think far more clearly.

"I say, that was quite nice," he said as he wiped the last of the sandwich crumbs from his mouth. "I hadn't realized I was so hungry." He pulled out his pocket watch. "Egads, look at the time. I must get back. Strutts will have had time to talk to his solicitor by now, and we're still searching for the murder weapon."

"Now, you will make sure she don't get scared," Luty instructed Betsy. "She don't like loud noises and she don't like goin' to bed without a story. You be sure and tell Henry Albritton that." She blinked back tears as she lifted the child into Betsy's waiting arms.

"I'll make sure," Betsy promised. Behind Luty, she could see Hatchet fighting his own tears. She shifted Emma onto her hip and tried to give them both a reassuring smile. Emma giggled, threw her arms around Betsy's neck and hugged her tight.

"Emma will be just fine," Mrs. Jeffries said quickly. "You'll see. Her grandfather will be good to her."

"He'd better," Hatchet said darkly. "Or he'll answer to me."

"And to me," Luty muttered.

That both Hatchet and Luty were miserable was obvious. Mrs. Jeffries was utterly heartsick. These two had grown very attached to the child. Watching Emma cuddle and giggle with Betsy showed what a loving, sweet-natured child she was. Who wouldn't grow to love her? But she had to go. It was only right that she go to her grandfather. And it was best she go quickly. Before they all ended up in tears.

"I'd best get started, then," Betsy said.

"Do you remember what to say?" Mrs. Jeffries asked.

"I'm to tell the inspector that a young police constable brought the girl here, thinkin' he was still here havin' lunch," Betsy said, repeating the plan they'd all agreed upon. "And then I'm to say that the child started fussin' and the constable got flustered. I offered to take her to the inspector myself."

"Excellent. Now, you'd better hurry. I'm not sure how long the inspector is going to be at the Albritton house."

It was another five minutes before Betsy got out the door and into a hansom cab. Luty and Hatchet kept delaying her with last-minute instructions and last-minute hugs for Emma.

"She'll be just fine," Mrs. Jeffries said reassuringly as they all trooped back into the kitchen. "Just fine. Come on now, why don't we all have a cup of tea and cheer up."

Ten minutes later their spirits were a little better. Mrs. Jeffries had filled Luty and Hatchet in on everything she'd learned from Witherspoon at lunch.

"That sure is somethin'." Luty shook her head. "But I ain't so sure it is Gordon Strutts."

"But they were his clothes I found," Wiggins pointed out.

"But money's a pretty powerful motive," Luty pointed out. "And seems to me that the person who really had the most to lose was Sherwin August. He's admitted he was fixin' to meet the girl. How do we know she was dead when he took that ring?"

"Took what ring?" Smythe asked as he came into the kitchen.

"Annie Shields's opal," Mrs. Goodge replied. "There's been an arrest."

"And *I* found the clue that did it." Wiggins jabbed himself in the chest as he spoke.

"Good work, boy." Smythe pulled out his chair and sat down. "Cor, it's gettin' bad outside. Another fog's rollin' in. So they've arrested her, have they?"

There was a stunned silence.

Her? Mrs. Jeffries felt her insides grow cold. "What do you mean, Smythe?"

Smythe stared at their faces. "Lydia Franklin. The footman I spoke to, he saw her Sunday night. He was in the churchyard with a . . . well. . ."

"This is not time for delicacy, Smythe," Mrs. Jeffries said. Dear God, she prayed silently. Please let the inspector still be there when Betsy and Emma arrive at the Albritton household. She knew what Smythe was going to say. That odd note in the back of her mind had turned into a full symphony now.

"He and a girl were takin' advantage of Albritton givin' 'em the evenin' off," Smythe said slowly. "They was bein' intimate, you might say. That's why neither of 'em would tell the police what they'd seen. They didn't want to lose their positions. But about ten thirty, Lydia Franklin come flyin' into that churchyard on a bicycle. She was wearin' men's clothes and a flat cap."

"Is the footman absolutely certain it was Lydia Franklin?" Mrs. Jeffries asked anxiously. "The fog was terrible that night, how could they tell who it was?"

"They're sure. She come right close to where they was hidin'. And they was scared she'd recognize them, too. So when she ducked behind a tree to change, they snuck off."

"Nell's bells," Luty yelled. "Betsy and Emma are on their way to the Albritton house now."

"Don't worry, Luty," Mrs. Jeffries said hastily. "The inspector and Mr. Albritton are both there. But I do think it would be a good idea . . ."

Smythe and Hatchet had already gotten to their feet and were racing towards the back door.

"Hey, wait for me," Wiggins yelled, charging after them.

Betsy stepped down and lifted Emma out of the cab. She paid the driver and turned to the front door. Taking the child's hand, she shivered. The day had changed.

The sun was gone and a mean, yellow-gray fog was settling over the city like a grim, ugly blanket.

Emma whimpered and Betsy bent down and picked her up. The child was dead on her feet. "Tired, lovey," she cooed as she studied the Albritton house. "Well, we'll soon have you cuddled down in a nice warm bed." She laughed and started up the pavement towards the front steps. "If your grandfather lets you out of his sight, that is."

Betsy's footsteps faltered as she came up the steps. She shifted Emma onto her hip so she could free a hand to bang the door knocker. This is odd, she thought, the place looked deserted. Empty.

Inside her, her old instincts, the ones that had kept her alive on the mean streets of the East End, suddenly urged her to take the child and run away. But the door opened and Betsy told herself she was just being silly.

A tall, blond woman stood in front of her. "Yes," she asked coldly, "what do you want?"

"I'd like to see Inspector Witherspoon," Betsy began. "I work for him, you see."

The woman didn't say anything for a moment. "And who is that?" she asked, nodding at Emma.

"This is Mr. Albritton's granddaughter," Betsy replied. "And she's very tired."

"Please come in." The woman opened the door wider. "I'm Lydia Franklin. Henry's sister-in-law."

Betsy stepped inside. Again, she felt the urge to run. Something was wrong. "Uh, is the inspector here?"

The house was utterly silent.

"Wait here," Lydia Franklin ordered, her gaze never leaving the child in Betsy's arms. "I'll get him." She turned and went down the hall.

For some reason, Betsy had the urge to follow. Tightening her grip on the now sleeping child, she tiptoed after her.

Lydia Franklin disappeared inside a room at the far end of the long hallway. Betsy, holding her breath and praying Emma wouldn't wake up, peered through the crack between the door.

She could only see one side of the room, but it was the side that counted. Lydia Franklin was standing by a massive mahogany sideboard. She closed the top drawer and Betsy saw a flash of silver. Then she turned, and what she held in her right hand made Betsy's blood run cold.

Lydia Franklin had a carving knife.

The biggest ruddy knife Betsy had ever seen.

Betsy tightened her grip on Emma, turned and ran, not caring that her pounding footsteps made enough racket to wake the dead. She wanted people to hear her.

From behind her, she heard footsteps.

"I don't want to hurt you," Lydia called. "It's the girl I want. Drop her on the floor and I won't kill you."

"Sod off," Betsy yelled. She dashed past the drawing room and flew round the staircase into the foyer. For a split second she hesitated. Then, spotting the fog through the window, she charged for the front door. Thank God, she'd had a head start. She'd taken the woman by surprise and bought herself a few precious seconds to escape. No doubt the silly bitch had thought she'd drop the child and save her own skin. Well, she had another think coming.

Luck was with Betsy, for Lydia hadn't closed the door properly. She yanked at the handle and jerked it open. She flew out and down the stone steps into the now thick fog. Emma whimpered. Betsy could hear the woman close behind her. Frantically, she looked up and down the street. No one. Nothing but thick fog.

She turned to her left. Towards the churchyard. She had to hide, to lose this lunatic woman in the mist until she could find help.

"Come back, you stupid girl!"

Betsy ran on. Emma woke and started to whimper again. "Hush," Betsy gasped as she kicked open the iron gate and charged through into the churchyard. Her feet pounding over the uneven ground, Betsy rounded the corner and almost slammed into a tree. She skirted it at the last second and then stumbled on a low headstone. She almost went flying, but managed to right herself and retain her grip on Emma at the last moment.

"Just leave me the girl and I won't hurt you," Lydia screamed again.

Betsy stopped. It sounded like she'd put some distance between herself and the lunatic. She didn't know what the ruddy 'ell was wrong with Lydia Franklin, and right now she didn't much care. She had to get help. She had to get that crazy woman as far away from Emma as she could.

"Mmm . . ." Emma struggled to be put down.

"No," Betsy whispered sharply. Quietly, barely daring to breathe, she edged towards the other side of the church building. Fingers of fog moved and shifted, obscuring shapes and sound. One second, Betsy could see clearly ahead; the next, the gray mist descended and she'd have to creep at a snail's pace, picking her way over graves and grass.

Harsh laughter sliced through the eerie silence. Betsy froze. The woman was close. Too close.

She glanced down at the child in her arms and knew she was running out of time. The fog wouldn't hide them long. The mist drifted and Betsy could make out more headstones ahead of her.

"Where are you?" Lydia called out in the singsong voice of a child.

Chills raced down Betsy's spine and fear turned her insides to jelly. The woman was mad as a loon. And she had a knife.

Betsy ran for the headstones. Emma whimpered.

"I can find you . . ."

Suddenly a figure leapt out of the fog, the knife raised high and slashing madly at the air. Betsy skidded to a halt, screamed and jerked the other way.

She ran like a demon was after her. Emma was howling her head off, Betsy was dodging headstones and trying not to fall. She could hear horrible laughter and pounding steps right behind her. She ran straight for a pocket of thick fog, hoping against hope she'd find the gate of the churchyard directly ahead. She slammed into a low stone wall. From far away she heard voices.

"Help," Betsy screamed. Emma howled. Betsy had to act fast. She dumped the child over the wall and turned to face her pursuer. She had no idea where she was. She had no idea what she'd do when that crazy woman burst through the fog.

"Run," she whispered to the terrified child.

Emma stared at her, confusion and fear on her little face.

"Run," Betsy ordered again.

Lydia Franklin came running straight at her, the knife held high. She screamed when she spotted Betsy standing with her back to the wall and charged straight for her.

"Run," Betsy yelled at the child. Emma ran just as Lydia Franklin leapt out.

But Betsy hadn't survived on the London streets without knowing how to take care of herself. As the woman came at her her hand shot up and she grabbed Lydia's wrist. She could hear Emma screaming. But the girl had started to flee; the screams were moving away from the struggling women.

"Run, run, run," Betsy kept yelling as she grappled with the the madwoman intent on killing her. They fell backwards. Betsy's shoulder slammed against the wall and she lost her footing.

Lydia jerked her hand free of Betsy's grip and shoved her hard, forcing her onto the ground. She raised her hand to strike. The knife flashed. Betsy closed her eyes, praying quickly that Emma had made it to safety. Suddenly Lydia screeched in rage as she was yanked back and tossed to the ground.

The knife went flying as Smythe's booted foot kicked it hard to one side.

"Good God, Betsy. Are you all right? Did she hurt you?" Smythe asked, his voice frantic. He dropped beside her and quickly began running his hands over her arms, searching for wounds.

"I'm . . . fine," Betsy panted. She heard Lydia howling like a banshee as she struggled with two police constables who were dragging her away. "Emma, oh God. Where's Emma?"

"Now, now, she's fine. We found her as we come into the churchyard," Smythe said, tenderly helping Betsy to her feet. "She's being taken to her grandfather."

Betsy, who'd never been so glad to see anyone, threw her arms around Smythe's neck, collapsed against his chest, and promptly burst into tears.

Hours later Betsy and the rest of them were gathered round the table at Upper Edmonton Gardens. Smythe, who couldn't seem to move more than a foot away from Betsy, kept shooting her anxious glances. "Are you sure you're all right?" he prodded. "'Adn't you better lay down and 'ave a rest?"

"I'm fine," she retorted. "Thanks to you, Emma and I are both in one piece."

"I don't think I'll ever forgive myself for this fiasco," Mrs. Jeffries said. "It's all my fault."

"Leave off, Mrs. J," Smythe said soothingly. "Stop blamin' yerself. You didn't know it was Lydia Franklin and you didn't know the house was empty when you sent Betsy and the child over there."

"But that's just it," Mrs. Jeffries moaned. "I should have known! All the clues were there. If I'd been thinking clearly, I'd have realized the killer was Lydia and not Gordon."

"Come on now, Hepzibah," Luty said bluntly. "You couldn't have possibly figured that out. There was no way to know until Smythe come in and told us about that footman."

"True, madam," Hatchet agreed. "Your powers of deduction are truly remarkable, but in this case, you didn't have all the facts until after Miss Betsy had left the house."

Mrs. Jeffries knew they were trying to comfort her. But they were wrong. Had she been thinking clearly, none of this would have happened and Betsy wouldn't have had that horrible experience. "We didn't need all the facts," she said firmly. "The whole problem was that I kept looking at the case the wrong way."

"Wrong way?" Wiggins muttered. "What does that mean?"

"It means," Mrs. Jeffries explained, "I fell into the trap of accepting everything at face value, including the reason for the murder itself. We all assumed that Annie Shields was killed because of who she was— namely, Henry Albritton's daughter. But if I'd been thinking clearly, I'd have realized there was another motive in this case. A motive Luty discovered almost immediately."

"I discovered?" Luty said in surprise. "Uh, would you mind refreshin' my memory?"

Mrs. Jeffries laughed. "Remember what Myrtle Buxton told you about Lydia Franklin. According to her, Lydia Franklin was so distraught over the idea that Henry Albritton might be seriously interested in another woman that she started some vicious gossip about that poor lady. The woman was so humiliated, she left the country."

"So you're sayin' Mrs. Franklin was insanely jealous," Wiggins asked curiously.

"In a sense, yes," Mrs. Jeffries replied. "But I don't think she was jealous of him so much as she didn't want to lose what he provided. Lydia Franklin had spent a good part of her life being poor and humiliated. I think she'd determined from the moment she came to live at the Albritton house that she was never going back."

"She killed Annie Shields because she didn't want to be poor again?" Wiggins asked, his tone incredulous.

"Precisely. Let's look at the facts. One, Henry Albritton had had some very real changes in his attitude about wealth and privilege. I'm sure that frightened her. Two, she was living in that great house on sufferance, and three, she was the only one who didn't positively know that Annie was Albritton's daughter."

"Then why would she kill her?" Betsy asked.

"She was afraid Henry was in love with the girl," Mrs. Jeffries said thoughtfully. "Remember, the only information she had to go on was that he was suddenly happy and he was suddenly very interested in flowers. Now it's one thing to live in a house with a niece and nephew. It's quite another to think a new young wife would let you stay on as mistress."

"I wonder how she found out about Annie?" Hatchet mused. "If the Struttses or Sherwin August didn't tell her, how could she know that Annie even existed?"

"I think I've got that sussed out," Smythe said. "I reckon the first time old 'Enry walked in with a big bouquet of roses, she got suspicious he was seein' another woman. She followed 'im."

Luty shook her head. "Well, I still don't see how we coulda known it was her. Not until today. I mean, Nell's bells, the woman had an alibi. Who'da thought she'd hop on a bicycle and run all over town on the foggiest night of the year to murder someone."

"But that's precisely what we should have realized," Mrs. Jeffries said earnestly. "The clues were all there, but I didn't interpret them correctly. Lydia's husband sold bicycles at one point and there was a bicycle available to her. I should have realized that she could easily ride one. It's not so very difficult. Secondly, she kept her coat buttoned in church at evensong service. Betsy told us that today."

"What's that got to do with anythin'?" Mrs. Goodge asked. "Sometimes I don't take off my coat in church."

"True, but I'll bet you unbuttoned the collar. Lydia didn't dare. She couldn't risk anyone seeing that she was dressed in Gordon's clothes."

"Hello, hello," the inspector's voice called from down the kitchen hall.

"What's he doin' using the back entrance?" Mrs. Goodge asked in a shocked whisper.

"Good evening, everyone," he said as he came into the kitchen. "How are you feeling, Betsy?" he asked, hurrying towards the girl. "I must tell you, I was so shocked at what happened to you today. Thank goodness Wiggins had the good sense to get those constables."

"I'm feelin' fine, sir." Betsy gave Smythe a quick, adoring smile. "Smythe saved my life. If he hadn't come and pulled that madwoman off of me, I'da been done for."

"What's going to happen to Lydia Franklin?" Mrs. Jeffries asked quickly.

"Huh? Oh, she'll be charged with murder," Witherspoon replied. "She's admitted killing Annie Shields. Do you know, I think she's quite mad. She stood right there in front of Henry Albritton and accused him of ruining *her* life. Claimed it was all his fault she'd had to kill his daughter. Said if he'd left well enough alone, they could have all continued living happily together." He shuddered. Happy was the last word he would use to describe the Albritton household. "Apparently, she was under the impression that Albritton was romantically interested in Mrs. Shields. She'd been following him, you see. On the night of the murder, Mrs. Franklin admitted she'd followed Hortense Strutts. Mrs. Strutts had sent the girl a note, asking her to meet her. But Hortense Strutts got frightened in the fog, couldn't find Annie's flower stand, and came home. Obviously, Lydia Franklin was made of sterner stuff." He sighed in disgust. "She found poor Annie, used a hammer she'd taken from the garden shed, killed her, and then tossed the hammer in the river. Then she got on a bicycle and went home as though nothing had happened. Horrible."

"Well, at least you've got your murderer safely behind bars," Mrs. Jeffries said cheerfully.

"Yes, indeed." Witherspoon frowned. "But I must say, I can't seem to find any constable who'll admit to bringing Emma over here and leaving her. I'm rather annoyed about that. Poor Betsy was almost murdered because she tried to do a good deed."

"Yes, well, luckily Betsy's just fine," Mrs. Jeffries said. "And all's well that ends well."

"But it could have ended very badly for Betsy," the inspector persisted. "Still, I don't think I'll ever solve the mystery of the missing constable. I'm sure whoever it was that brought the child here must have heard what had happened and realized they'd made a grave mistake."

"True, sir," Mrs. Jeffries prompted. "So perhaps it's best to get on with other things."

Witherspoon yawned. "Oh, dear. Excuse me, but I'm dreadfully tired. I think I'll go right on up to bed."

He said his good-nights to Luty and Hatchet, patted Betsy sympathetically on the shoulder, and told her to spend the next day resting and left.

Mrs. Jeffries let out a long sigh of relief when he was gone.

"You know what I don't understand," Mrs. Goodge said. "Who was sendin' Annie money every week?"

"I think I know," Betsy said quickly. "I think it was Harlan Bladestone."

"I do, too," Mrs. Jeffries agreed. "I think Bladestone knew deep in his heart exactly who Annie was the first time he saw her, but being a solicitor, he needed proof."

"That's how I figure it, too," Betsy added. "He couldn't bring himself to tell Albritton, but he knew Annie's husband had just died and that she'd be needin' money. So he sent 'er some every week. Not enough to make her feel bad or any thin'. Just enough so's she'd be sure and take it without feelin' beholdin' to 'im."

"Reckon no one wants to feel obligated to someone else," Smythe said, his expression enigmatic.

Betsy gave him a soft, very private smile. "Oh, I'm not so sure about that, Smythe. There's some people I don't mind bein' beholdin' to at all."

• • •

A few days later Luty, Hatchet, and the household were having their very own celebration. The case was closed and the murderer brought to justice.

"I wonder how Emma's gettin' on?" Luty said wistfully.

"She's doin' fine," Betsy said. "Mr. Albritton invited me over yesterday so he could thank me for keepin' her safe from Mrs. Franklin. You ought to see them together. He loves her so much. He's fixin' to leave soon, though. He's goin' through with his plan to move to San Francisco. But guess what? He's takin' Hortense Strutts with him to help out. Well, he told me he didn't really have much choice. Gordon Strutts has left and moved in with his 'friend' and he didn't feel right leavin' Hortense on her own."

Mrs. Goodge snorted. "I don't wonder that Hortense is leavin'. Her husband takin' off and livin' with another man! Why, it'll be the talk of London. Poor Hortense wouldn't be able to hold her head up."

"What's goin' to 'appen to Sherwin August?" Smythe asked.

"'E's retirin'," Betsy replied. "Takin' his wife and movin' to the country."

"Well, this case has indeed been an odd one," Mrs. Jeffries said.

Fred woofed softly.

Wiggins turned to the dog. "Be quiet, Fred . . . good gracious, it's Lady Cannonberry."

"I'm so sorry," Lady Cannonberry said softly. "I did knock on the back door but no one answered. The door was open, so I just came in."

"Of course, ma'am," Smythe said quickly, getting to his feet.

"Please." She held up her hand. "Do sit down. I didn't mean to intrude. Actually, I came round because I saw Mrs. Crookshank's carriage." She looked at an empty chair. "Do you mind if I sit down?"

"Where are our manners?" Mrs. Jeffries said hastily. "Please, Lady Cannonberry, do have a seat."

Still shocked, the others watched her sit down.

Lady Cannonberry took a deep breath. "I know my barging in like this must seem odd," she began. "But I had to ask you something."

"If it's about your participating in that march in Trafalgar Square," Mrs. Jeffries said, "I was planning on coming round and talking to you about it this afternoon."

"Oh no, it wasn't that," Lady Cannonberry said quickly. "But your opinion on that issue would be most welcome."

"Lady Cannonberry," Luty began.

"Do please call me Ruth," she interrupted, giving them all a big smile. "I wish all of you would call me Ruth. I've always thought 'Lady Cannonberry' sounded rather silly."

"Uh, Ruth." Luty frowned. She'd forgotten what she was going to say.

"Would you care for some tea?" Mrs. Jeffries asked politely. Mrs. Goodge and Hatchet both looked as though they'd gone into shock, Wiggins and Betsy were staring at the woman with puzzled frowns, and Smythe was trying not to grin.

"I'd love some, thank you." Ruth took another deep breath. "I'm sure you're all wondering why I've come."

"Yes, madam." Hatchet finally found his voice. "We are."

"I . . . oh dear, there's no way to say this except to just say it." She took another breath. "The truth is, I overheard Mrs. Jeffries talking to that young doctor about the inspector's case. Well, that got me to thinking and I well . . . I know you all help him. Don't worry," she said hastily. "I won't say a word. But you see, that got me to thinking."

"Thinking about what?" Mrs. Jeffries prompted.

"You see, I've got this friend and she's in a great deal of trouble. Do you think you could possibly help her?"